MELNITZ

Charles Lewinsky studied German literature and theatre studies in Zurich and Berlin. Among the numerous novels that he has written, he received the Schiller Prize Zürcher Kantonalbank for his novel *St. John's* (2001) and was nominated for the 2011 Swiss Book Prize for *Gerron* (2012). He lives in Zurich and the French Vereux.

MELNITZ

Charles Lewinsky

Translated by Shaun Whiteside

Atlantic Books
LONDON

First published in Switzerland in 2006 by Nagel & Kimche Verlag.

First published in Great Britain in 2015 by Atlantic Books,
an imprint of Atlantic Books Ltd.

This paperback edition published in Great Britain
in 2016 by Atlantic Books.

We acknowledge the support of

swiss arts council
prɔhelvetia

in funding this translation.

10 9 8 7 6 5 4 3 2 1

A CIP catalogue record for this book is available from the British Library.

Paperback ISBN: 978 1 84887 767 2
E-book ISBN: 978 1 78239 405 1

Printed and bound by CPI Group (UK) Ltd, Croydon, CR0 4YY

Atlantic Books
An Imprint of Atlantic Books Ltd
Ormond House
26–27 Boswell Street
London
WC1N 3JZ

www.atlantic-books.co.uk

For my wife
without whom I would not be

1871

1

Every time he died, he came back.

On the last day of the week of mourning, when the loss had dispersed into the everyday, when you had to make a special effort to seek out the pain, a gnat-bite which stung yesterday and which you hardly feel today, his back aching from sitting on the low stools assigned by ancient custom to the bereaved for those seven days, there he was again as if it were the most natural thing in the world, walking inconspicuously into the room with the other visitors, indistinguishable from them in outward appearance. But he brought no food with him, even though that would have been the custom. In the kitchen the pots and covered bowls waited in line, a guard of honour for the deceased; he came empty-handed, took a chair, as one does, said not a word unless addressed by the other mourners, stood up when they prayed, sat down when they sat down. And when the others, murmuring their words of condolence, took their leave, he simply stayed on his chair, he was there again, as he had always been there. His smell of damp dust mingled with the other smells of the house of mourning, sweat, tallow candles, impatience; he was part of it again, he joined in the grieving, took leave of himself, sighed his familiar sigh, which was half a groan and half a snore, fell asleep with his head drooping and his mouth open, and was there again.

Salomon Meijer rose from his stool, lifted his body up like a heavy weight, like a quarter of a cow or a mill-sack of flour, stretched so that the joints in his shoulders cracked, and said, 'So. Let us have something to eat.' He was a tall, broad man, and the only reason he didn't create an impression of strength was that his head was too small for his bulk, the head of a scholar on a peasant's body. He had grown side-whiskers which were in places – far too early, Salomon thought – already turning white. Beneath them, framed by his beard, a network of little burst veins formed two red patches that always made him look tipsy, even though he only drank wine for the festive kiddush, and otherwise one or two beers at most on very hot days. Anything else befogs the head, and the head is the most important part of a cattle dealer's body.

He dressed entirely in black, not out of mourning, but because he couldn't imagine wearing another colour; he wore an old-fashioned frock coat of heavy cloth which, since no more visitors were expected, he now unbuttoned and dropped to the floor behind him without looking round. He assumed that his Golde would pick up the frock coat and lay it over the arm of a chair, and there was nothing tyrannical about it, only the naturalness of spheres clearly assigned. He straightened his silk cap, a superfluous gesture, since it had not slipped for years, for no unruly hair grew on Salomon Meijer's head. Even as a young man his friends had called him Galekh, the monk, because the bald patch on his head reminded them of a tonsure.

On his way to the kitchen he rubbed his hands, as he always did when food was in store; as if he were already washing his hands, even before he had reached any water.

Golde, Frau Salomon Meijer, had to lift her arms over her head to shake out the frock coat. She was short, and had once been delicate, so delicate that in the first year of their marriage a jocular habit had come about, one which no outsider understood or even so much as noticed. When, at the beginning of the Sabbath, Salomon uttered the biblical verse 'Eyshes chayil, mi yimtza' in praise of the housewife, he paused after the first words and peered questingly around, as if he had said not 'Who can find a virtuous woman' but 'Who can find the virtuous woman?'. Long ago, having married young and fallen in love young too, every Friday he had accompanied the words with a pantomime, looking with exaggerated foolishness for his fine little wife, and had then, having found her at last, drew her to him and even kissed her. Now all that remained of that was a pause and a look, and if anyone had asked him why he did it, Salomon Meijer himself would have had to ponder.

Golde had grown fat over the years, she hurried stoutly through life, a hasty peasant sowing seeds, she wore her dress with the black silk ribbons as a pot wears a tea-cosy, and her reddish sheitel, even though it was made by the best wig-maker in Schwäbisch Hall, sat on her head like a bird's nest. She had developed the habit of pulling her lower lip deep into her mouth and chewing on it, which made her look toothless. Sometimes it seemed to Salomon as if at some point – no, not at some point, he had to correct himself – as if, after that lengthy and painful childbed, after those uselessly wailed-through nights, a young woman had left him and a matron had taken her place. But he could not reproach Golde for that, and he who finds a virtuous woman, as the Bible says, has gained riches beyond rubies. He said it every week, paused and looked searchingly around.

The frock coat now hung over the arm of the leather armchair in which Salomon liked to rest after a long day on the country road, but which today he had offered to the rebbe, Rav Bodenheimer. Now the chairs had to be lined up in a row again, order had to be re-established around Uncle Melnitz, whose chin hung on his chest as if he was dead.

'Well? I'm hungry!' cried Salomon from the kitchen.

Usually, or rather whenever the man of the house was not away on business, the Meijer household ate in the front room, which Mimi liked to call the 'drawing-room', while her parents called it the 'parlour' plain and simple. Today the big table in there had been pushed up against the wall, so that the Shabbos lamp hung in the void, they had had to make room for the visitors, a lot of room, because Salomon Meijer was a respected man in Endingen, a leader of the community and administrator of the poor box. Anyone who had raised a glass of kirschwasser 'to life' at his Simchas also came to him at a shiva to pay his respects, not least because one could never know when one might need him. Salomon acknowledged this without reproach.

So for once they ate in the kitchen, where Chanele had already got everything prepared. She was a poor relation, said the people in the community, even though the old women most skilled in Mishpochology were unable to say exactly which branch of the Meijer family tree she might have sprouted from. Salomon had brought her back, more than twenty years ago now, from a business trip to Alsace, a wailing, wriggling bundle, swaddled like a Strasbourg goose. 'Why would he have taken her in if she hadn't been related to him?' asked the old women, and some of them, whose teeth had fallen out and who therefore thought the worst of everyone, suggested with a significant nod of the head that Chanele had exactly the same chin as Salomon, and that one might wonder what had taken him to Alsace so often in those days.

The truth of the matter had been quite different. The goyish doctor had explained to Salomon that the son that they had had to dismember to get him out of his mother had torn Golde so badly that she would not survive another difficult birth; he should be grateful that he had at least *one* child, even if it was only a girl. 'Thank *your* God,' he had said, for all the world as if there were several of them, and as if they had divided their responsibilities among themselves as clearly as the duty physician and the cattle vet.

Now everyone capable of thinking practically knows that one child on its own makes far more work than two, and when on one of his trips the opportunity presented itself – a mother had died in childbed and her husband had lost his mind over it – Salomon intervened with an investment as practical and unsentimental as buying a calf cheap and feeding it up until it paid for itself several times over as a milk cow.

So Chanele was not a daughter of the house, but neither was she a serving-girl; she was treated sometimes as one and sometimes the other, she was in no one's heart and no one's way. She wore clothes which she sewed herself or which Mimi didn't like any more, and her hair was hidden away in a net, as if she were a married woman; she who has no dowry need not stay on the look-out for a husband. When she laughed she was even pretty, except that her eyebrows were too broad, they crossed through her face as one crosses through a calculation that is wrong or has been dealt with.

Chanele had laid the meal out on the kitchen table. There had been nothing to cook, because food is brought to a shiva to spare the mourners the task. Even so, a powerful fire was blazing in the stove, crackling fir logs that quickly gave off their heat. It was still freezing outside at night, although they would already be celebrating Seder in two weeks; Pesach fell early that year, 1871.

'So?'

When Salomon Meijer was hungry, he grew impatient. He sat at the table, hands left and right on the wood, as the mohel lays out his instruments before a circumcision. He had already said HaMotzi, had sprinkled salt over a bit of bread, said the blessing over it and put it in his mouth. But after that he had not gone on to help himself, because he placed value on everyone sitting with him at table when he was, after all, at home. He could eat alone any day of the week. Now he drummed his right hand on the table-top, repeatedly lifting his wrist in rhythm, as musicians do when they wish to demonstrate their skill to the audience. His fingers danced, although it was not a cheerful dance, one that might easily, in a public house, have led to a fight.

Mimi came in at last, with a theatrically tripping step designed to demonstrate how much of a hurry she was really in. Although there was no real need, she had changed her clothes again, and was now wearing a mouse-grey dressing gown, slightly too long, so that the hem dragged along the stone floor. 'Those people,' she said. 'All those people! Isn't it *ennuyant?*'

Mimi loved precious words, as she loved everything elegant, she picked them up in goyish books that she borrowed secretly from Anne-Kathrin, the school-master's daughter, and scattered her everyday conversation with them as if they were gold-dust. Inclined as she was towards refinement, she didn't like the fact that everyone still called her Mimi, a children's name that she had long – 'Really, Mamme, for *ages now*' – outgrown. At fifteen, and nobody could remind her of this for fear of provoking a storm of tears, she had once flirted with Mimolette, and Salomon, never averse to a joke, had actually called her that for a few days, before confessing with a laugh that in France it was the name of a cheese. Since then she had tried to gain acceptance at least for Miriam, which was her actual name, but had been unable to do anything about the old family habit.

Mimi had everything a beauty needs, immaculate white skin, full lips, big brown eyes that always glistened a little mistily, long, softly wavy black hair.

But for some reason – she had spent hours at the mirror and been unable to find an explanation for it – the perfect individual parts didn't really fit together where she was concerned, just as a soup sometimes simply refuses to taste right despite being made of the best ingredients. She gave no sign of this self-doubt, tending on the contrary to behave in an arrogant and even patronising manner, so much so that her mother had asked her more than once if she actually thought she was Esther out of the Bible, waiting for messengers, in search of the most beautiful virgins, to come to Endingen to bring her to their king.

Now the four of them were sitting around the table. There were bigger families in the community, but when Salomon Meijer considered his loved ones like this, he was quite content with what God had given him, a very practical contentment based on the fact – and who knows this better than a cattle dealer, who gets around the place? – that he could have been much worse off.

There was, as there always is after shivas, far too much food on the table. Three bowls alone of chopped boiled eggs, half a salted carp, a plate of herrings, but just a few, meagre herrings, for red-haired Moische was a stingy man, even though he had had a sign painted for his shop that was bigger than the premises itself. It was customary simply to put down the food one had brought, without a name and without a thank-you, but people knew the patters of the plates, knew to whom which crockery belonged – otherwise, how could they have given it back the next day? The pot of sauerkraut, it wouldn't even have taken the broken handle to know, came from Feigele Dreifuss, known to everyone only as Mother Feigele, because she was the oldest in the village. Every autumn she made two big vats of sauerkraut with juniper berries, even though there had been no one in her house to eat it for a long time now, and then gave it away at every opportunity, brought it to women in childbed to strengthen them, and to the bereaved to comfort them.

On the sideboard, wrapped in a newspaper and shoved into the furthest corner like stolen goods, lay a plaited loaf, a beautiful berches scattered with poppy-seeds, which they would inconspicuously remove from the house tomorrow and feed to the ducks and hens. Christian Hauenstein, the village baker, in whose ovens they baked all their Shabbes loaves and warmed their Shabbes kugels, had sent it, of course without coming by himself. He was a modern man, a free-thinker, as he liked to stress, and wanted to prove to his Jewish customers that he valued them and nurtured no prejudices towards them. No one had ever had the heart to tell him that they couldn't eat his well-intentioned loaves because they weren't kosher.

But who needs bread when there's cheesecake on the table? Above all when it's the legendary cheesecake that only Sarah Pomeranz could bake. Naftali

Pomeranz, whose very name revealed him as an incomer, might have been an important man, a slaughterer *and* a synagogue sexton, shochet *and* shammes, he even seemed to want to found a dynasty in these offices, and his son Pinchas, whom he was training up as his successor, was as skilled at delivering a clean slice to the throat as his father, but it was still Sarah who ensured the true reputation of the family with her cake, a masterpiece, everyone agreed, so good 'that Rothschild himself could not eat finer', and that was the highest accolade that the village could supply in matters culinary.

Salomon had asked for a second piece to be put on his plate, and chewed with pleasure as Golde, who was not made for sitting still, wondered, with her lower lip sucked in, what should be transferred to which bowl so that all the alien crockery could be washed clean and returned. Mimi toyed with a little piece of cake that she divided with her fork into ever smaller halves, while making the discreetly disgusted face of a doctor forced by his profession to conduct an unpleasant operation.

'Tomorrow I must leave the house at four,' said Salomon. 'You can wrap up all the leftover cake for my journey.'

'*Almost* all. A piece must be left for me.' Chanele, whose uncertain position in the household had made her a good observer, knew precisely when she could risk such pert little remarks. Now Salomon had eaten well; that meant that he was in a benevolent mood.

'Nu, so be it, part of the leftovers.'

Mimi pushed away her crumbled cake. 'I don't know why you all like it so much. It tastes *ordinaire*.' She spoke the word with lips pursed, to stress the Frenchness of the word.

Golde took the plate, looked at it darkly – 'the waste!' her expression said – and put it with the other crockery that Chanele would later wash up. 'Where are you off to tomorrow?' she asked her husband, not out of genuine interest, but because an eyshes chayil asks the right questions.

'To Degermoos. The young farmer, Stalder, has said he wants to talk to me. I can imagine what it's about. He's running out of hay. He wouldn't believe me when I told him he's putting too many cows out on his poor land. Now he wants me to buy them back. But I'm not buying. Who needs cows when the grass isn't growing yet?'

'And that's why you're going? Not to do a deal?'

'Not this deal. There's someone in Vogelsang with cow-pest in his herd. He has too much hay. I'll tell Stalder, and he can stock up.'

'What do you get out of it?'

'Nothing today. And perhaps nothing tomorrow, either. But the day after tomorrow...' Salomon ran his fingers through his sideburns, because of the cake-crumbs and because he was pleased with himself. 'Sooner or later he'll have a beheimes to sell, and it'll be an animal that I can use. I'll make him an offer, and he'll take it because he'll think to himself: "The Jew with the brolly is a decent fellow." And then I will do my deal.'

The business with the brolly was this: whenever Salomon Meijer travelled across the country he carried with him a fat black umbrella, tied at the top so that the fabric puffed out like a bag. He used the umbrella as a walking stick, pressed it firmly down on to the ground with each step and left an unmistakeable trail on muddy paths or in the snow: the impressions of two hobnailed soles and to the right of them a row of holes as regular as the ones a tidy farmer's wife would make when planting beans. The special thing about the umbrella, the thing people talked about, was that Salomon never opened it, whatever the weather. Even when the rain was cascading down as if the time had come for a new Noah and a new Ark, Salomon just drew his hat lower over his forehead, if it got very bad, pulled the tails of his long coat over his head and walked on, leaning on the umbrella and drilling the tip into the ground with every second step, so that the rain collected in a row of little lakes behind him. He was known because of this around Endingen, and laughed at because of it too, and if, like red-haired Moische, he had had a shop-sign painted, to bring customers to the right place it would have had to say not 'Cattle-trading Sal. Meijer', but 'The Jew with the Brolly'.

Salomon belched pleasurably, as if after the big Shabbos sude, when it is practically a mitzvah, a god-pleasing act, to eat too much. Mimi pulled a face and murmured something to herself that was probably French but certainly contemptuous. Salomon took a pinch from his snuff-box, screwed up his nose and contorted his face into a grimace and finally sneezed, loudly and with a great sense of relief. 'Now there's only one thing I need,' he said, and looked around expectantly. Chanele, since they would probably go on sitting in the kitchen for a while, had gone into the parlour to fetch the second paraffin lamp, and now she drew an earthenware bottle from one apron pocket, a pewter mug from the other, and set them both in front of him. 'She can do magic like the Witch of Endor,' Salomon said contentedly and poured himself a drink.

Then the conversation in the kitchen had fallen asleep, as a child suddenly falls asleep in the middle of a game. Chanele washed the crockery in the big brown wooden bucket; it clattered as if in the distance. Golde put the dried plates back in the cupboard, took the few steps individually for each plate, back and forth, a dance without a partner, to which Salomon, eyes closed, droned a tune, more out of repletion than musicality. Mimi reproachfully brushed invisible crumbs from her dressing gown and wondered whether she shouldn't have chosen a different fabric; she had only taken this one because the shopkeeper had called it 'dove-grey', such a beautiful, soft, gleaming word. Dove-grey.

At the house next door – which was actually the same house yet a different one because the law demanded as much, at the other entrance of the house, then, there was a sudden hammering on the door, impatient and violent, as one knocks at the midwife's door when someone is entering the world, or at the door of the chevra, the funeral fraternity, when someone is leaving it. It was not a time of day when people in Endingen paid a visit, either to Jews or to goyim. In the other half of the house, with its own front door and its own stairs, to meet the requirements of the law according to which Christians and Jews were not allowed to live in the same house, their landlord lived, the tailor Oggenfuss, with his wife and three children, peaceful people if you knew how to take them. They were good neighbours, which meant that they benignly ignored one another. The death of Uncle Melnitz, and all the mourners who had come to the house for seven days, had gone assiduously unnoticed by the Oggenfuss household, with the practised blindness of people who live closer together than they would really like to. And even now, when something unusual was going on, something practically sensational by Endingen standards, in the Meijers' kitchen they merely looked quizzically at one another, and already Salomon shrugged his shoulders and said 'So!' – which in this case meant something like, 'They can break the door down if they want to, it has nothing to do with us.'

Footsteps were heard next door, a restless to-ing and fro-ing, from which, if one had been curious, one might have worked out that someone who had already gone to bed was looking for a candle, a spill, to light it from the embers of the oven fire, a shawl, to cover their night-shirt, then the shutter clattered against the wall, a noise that really belonged to early morning, and Oggenfuss, as unfriendly as fearful people are in unfamiliar situations, asked what was so urgent and what sort of behaviour was that, dragging people out of bed in the middle of the night.

A strange, hoarse voice, interrupted by a bad cough, gave an unintelligible answer. Oggenfuss, switching from Aargau dialect to High German, replied. The stranger repeated his sentence, from which one could now make out the words 'please' and 'visit', but in such an unusual accent that Mimi said with delight, 'It's a Frenchman.'

'Sha!' said Golde. She stood there with an empty bowl in her hand, in the open kitchen door, where the corridor acted as an amplifier, so that even if one

10

wasn't curious, one could hear everything going on in the street. But all that came from outside now was the coughing of the nocturnal visitor. Oggenfuss said something final, and a shutter upstairs was closed. Then Frau Oggenfuss could be heard, her words impossible to make out but her tone urgent. After a pause the stairs creaked next door, although no individual footsteps could be heard, the sound made when someone wears slippers, the front door was opened, and Oggenfuss said in the suffering voice of someone forced to show politeness that he doesn't feel: 'So? Who are you? And what do you want?'

The strange man had stopped coughing, but still said nothing. In the Meijers' kitchen no one moved. When Salomon talked about it later, he said it was as if Joshua had made the moon stand still over the Valley of Ajalon. Chanele had taken a plate from the bowl; the dish-cloth had stopped in mid-air, and water dripped on the stone tiles. Mimi stared at a strand of hair that she had wrapped around her index finger, and Golde simply stood still, which was the most unusual thing of all, because Golde was otherwise always in motion.

And then the stranger had found his voice and said something that everyone in the kitchen understood.

He said a name.

Salomon Meijer.

Chanele, who never did such a thing, dropped the plate.

Salomon leapt to his feet, ran to the front door, opened it so that two men now stood on the same little pedestal, three steps above the frost-glittering street, one in night-shirt and night-cap, a woollen blanket over his shoulders, a candle in his hand, the other, although without a frock coat, very correctly dressed. They stood almost side by side, for the two doors of the house were only an arm's length apart. Oggenfuss made an exaggeratedly polite gesture which made the blanket slip from his shoulders, and said in a formal voice that contrasted strangely with his half-naked state: 'It's you the gentleman wants to see, Herr Meijer.' Then he vanished into his half of the house and slammed the door behind him.

The man in the street began to laugh, coughed and painfully doubled up. In the faint light that came from the house he could only be seen indistinctly, a slim figure apparently wearing a white fur cap.

'Salomon Meijer?' asked the stranger. 'I'm Janki.'

Only now did Salomon see that it was not a fur cap, but a bandage.

2

It was a thick, dirty white lint bandage, inexpertly wrapped around the man's head, with a loose end that hung over the stranger's shoulder like an oriental ribbon. Nebuchadnezzar out of the illustrated Bible stories wore a turban exactly the same shape, in the picture in which Daniel interprets his dream. Except that the Persian king's turban was adorned with diamonds, not with blood. A couple of inches above his right eye a bright red spot had spread on the bandage, but if there was a fresh wound underneath it seemed to have stopped hurting. A few black curls peeped from under the edge of the white fabric. 'A pirate,' thought Mimi, because there had also been sea-robbers in the books that she secretly borrowed.

The stranger's face was narrow, his eyes big and his lashes noticeably long. His skin was tanned, like that of someone who works outside a great deal, which irritated Salomon; the winter had been so long, that now, with spring apparently so reluctant to come, even the peasants were pale. In his dark face, his teeth looked remarkably white.

They had lots of time to look at him, they could study at their leisure his red and black uniform jacket, whose insignias did not match those of any troop known hereabouts, they were able to marvel at the Bohemian-looking double-knotted yellow silk kerchief that contrasted so defiantly with the rough material of the jacket; they were able to look at his narrow hands, the deft, mobile fingers, the nails, clean and neat in an unsoldierly fashion, and try to interpret what they saw as they might have interpreted an obscure verse of the Bible. Everyone seemed to be using a different commentary: Salomon saw the stranger as a scrounger, to be kept at arm's length because he wanted something from you; Golde was reminded of the son who, had God so willed it, would have been the same age right now as this unexpected young guest; Mimi had moved on from pirates and decided he was an explorer, a global traveller who had seen everything and had much more still to see. Chanele was busy at the stove, and didn't seem interested in the solution of this mystery that had dropped in out of nowhere; except the line of her eyebrows was higher on her face than usual.

The visitor didn't wait to be offered a chair, he chose a seat at the table, his back so close to the stove that Golde was worried he would burn himself. But no, he replied, if someone had been as cold as him, nothing could ever be too hot again.

And then he ate. And how he ate!

Even before the water was put on for his tea, he grabbed, without bothering to ask, the goyish berches, he tore fist-sized pieces from it with his unwashed hands, and without a word of blessing, and stuffed it into his mouth. He went on bolting it down even when Salomon told to him why the bread wasn't kosher, he choked in his greed, he coughed and spat half-chewed chunks on the table. Even Mimi's dove-grey housecoat got a spatter, which she rubbed away with her finger before, when everyone else was looking at the strange guest, sticking it quickly in her mouth.

Nothing was left of the chopped eggs, the carp had disappeared, so had the herrings, and even the pot of Mother Feigele's sauerkraut, which could have satisfied a big family for a week, was more than half empty. Eventually Golde looked questioningly at her husband, and he nodded resignedly and said, 'Very well, then.' Golde went into the little room in which the window behind the bars was always slightly open, brought in the package that she'd been keeping cool, then set it down on the table in front of the stranger and pulled open the cloth. And he, even though he had already eaten more than a whole minyan of pious men after a feast day, stared as ecstatically at Sarah's cheesecake as the children of Israel once gazed upon the first manna in the desert.

Then the cake too was devoured to the very last crumb. The man had set aside his cutlery, and instead clutched a steaming glass so firmly that it was easy to tell: he hadn't yet warmed up. Chanele had prepared the special mixture that was known in this family as Techías Hameisim tea, because it was said to be able to raise the dead; candy sugar dissolved in a camomile brew with honey and cloves and a big shot of schnapps from Salomon's private bottle. The stranger drank in great slugs. It was only when he had emptied a second glass that he began to tell his story.

He spoke Yiddish, just as they all spoke Yiddish, not the supple, musical language of the East, but the ponderous, peasant form common in Alsace, the Great Duchy of Baden and of course here in Switzerland, too. The melody was slightly different – more elegant, Mimi thought – but they had no trouble understanding each other.

'So I'm Janki,' said the man, whose coughing seemed to have calmed down. 'You will have heard of me.'

'Perhaps.' A cattle dealer never says 'yes' too quickly, and never too quickly 'no'. Salomon knew lots of Jankis, but not one in particular.

'I come from Paris. That is to say: I actually come from Guebwiller.'

Salomon pushed back his chair, as he always did, without noticing it himself, when he started to become interested in a business deal. Paris was far away, but Guebwiller was a known quantity.

'Did the son of your uncle Jossel marry into Guebwiller?' Golde asked Salomon. 'What was his name again?'

To her surprise it was the strange man who answered her question. 'Schmul,' he said. 'My father's name was Schmul.'

'Was,' he had said, not 'is', so they all murmured their blessing for the Judge of Truth before they all started talking at once.

'You are...?'

'He is...?'

'What uncle Jossel would that be?'

An uncle, according to traditional Jewish practice, is not just the brother of the father or the mother. Even a much more distant relation can be an uncle; the tree is important, not the individual branch. Salomon hadn't really known this uncle Jossel, he just thought he remembered a small, nimble man who had danced for so long at a chassene that the trumpeter's lips had hurt. But at the time Salomon had been fifteen or sixteen, an age when one is interested in all kinds of things, just not strange relatives who come all the way to a wedding and then disappear again.

'What uncle Jossel?' Mimi asked again.

'He was a son of Uncle Chaim, who you don't know either,' Salomon tried to explain, 'and his father and my great-great grandfather were brothers.' And he added after a pause, 'I think. But am I Mother Feigele?' Which was supposed to mean: if you want to know more, ask someone who has nothing more sensible to do than deal with family trees all day.

'Mishpocha, then.' Mimi sounded strangely disappointed.

'But very distant mishpocha,' said Janki and smiled at her.

'He has lovely white teeth,' she thought.

'My father, Schmul Meijer,' explained Janki, 'actually came from Blotzheim—'

'Exactly!' said Salomon.

'—and moved to Guebwiller, because my mother owned an inn there, which the peasants particularly liked to go to. In Guebwiller there's a market every week. That is: the pub belonged to my grandfather, of course, but he wanted to be a scholar, and when his daughter married, he passed everything to the young couple. I only ever saw him in the pub room sitting over a big tome, at his table by the window. He murmured to himself as he studied, and when I was a little boy I thought he could do magic.'

His voice became hoarse again, and Chanele quickly refilled his glass.

'But he couldn't do magic,' said Janki, when he had drunk. 'During the

14

cholera epidemic of 1866 he wrote amulets and hung them above all the doors. Except that the disease probably couldn't read his handwriting.'

'He died,' said Golde, and it wasn't a question.

'They all died.' Janki stirred his finger in his glass and stared into it, as if nothing in the world could be more interesting than a whirlpool of boiled camomile blossoms. 'In three days. Father. Mother. Grandfather. The old man held out the longest. Lay on his bed, his eyes wide open. Not blinking. He probably thought the angel of death could do nothing to him as long as he stared it in the face. But in the end he blinked.' He paused and then added, still without looking up from his glass, 'I can still smell their beds. Cholera doesn't smell of roses.' He shook a drop from his finger, as one does at Seder, when one gives away ten drops of the feast wine so as not to be too happy about the ten plagues of the Egyptians.

'I could have a son his age,' thought Golde. 'And he could be an orphan already. Praised be the Judge of Truth.'

'You have no brothers and sisters?' she asked, and it was the first time anyone in the house had called him Du, not Ihr, as they would have addressed a stranger.

'It isn't easy to be the only one,' Janki replied, and Mimi nodded, without noticing. 'That is: it isn't hard. One is responsible only for oneself, and that is fine.'

Mimi was still nodding.

'Everyone expected me to go on running the pub. I wasn't yet twenty, and I was to spend my whole life pouring schnapps, washing glasses, cleaning tables and laughing at the stories of the drunk peasants. I didn't want that. But on the other hand: that was what my parents had left me. If it was good enough for them – who was I to want something else?'

'So you made up your mind?'

Janki shook his head. 'It was taken away from me. People stopped coming to the inn. Too many people had died in the house, and the suspicious peasants no longer found it quite heimish. I got a decent price for it, not very good, not very bad, and with that I went to Paris.'

'Why Paris?' asked Chanele, who had listened in silence until that moment.

'Do you know a better city?' he asked back, folded his hands behind his head and leaned far back. 'Does anyone know a better city?'

It was a question that no one in this kitchen could answer.

'I wanted to get away from Guebwiller. I wanted to be something that would mean I never had to go back there. Something special, something strange.'

Explorer, thought Mimi. Pirate.

'I wanted to go where the masters are. Just as some people go to Lithuania or Poland because a rabbi that they want to emulate teaches there. Except I wasn't looking for a rabbi.'

'But?'

'A tailor.'

If Janki had said 'a knacker' or 'a gravedigger', the disappointment around the table could not have been greater. A tailor was more or less the most ordinary thing they could think of, there were tailors on every street-corner, a tailor was neighbour Oggenfuss, a lanky, short-sighted man who sat on his table all day and was bossed around by his wife. A tailor? And that was why he had gone to Paris?

Janki laughed when he saw their baffled faces, he laughed so hard that his coughing started up again and his face contorted. He held the end of his bandage in front of his mouth like a handkerchief and gesticulated for more tea with his other hand. When the attack had settled down again, he went on speaking in a very quiet, careful voice, like someone setting a sprained foot hesitantly on the ground.

'I ask your forgiveness. It's the cold. And the hunger. But at least I'm still alive. That is: I've even been living very well since I've been here. What was I going to say?'

'A tailor,' said Mimi, holding the word between pointed fingers.

'Of course. A tailor in Paris, you must know, is not simply someone who stitches a pair of trousers together always using the same cut, or, when making a skirt, considers how much fabric he can have left over. Of course, there are such tailors, and there are many of them. But the ones I mean, the real ones, are something quite different. It's like ... like ...' He looked around the kitchen in search of a suitable comparison. 'Like a sunrise compared with this oil lamp. These men are famous artists, you understand. Great gentlemen. They don't bow to their customers. They never pick up a needle themselves. They have other people to do that.'

'A tailor is a tailor,' said Salomon.

'Perhaps in the village. But in a proper city. Not,' he made his voice higher, as one does in the minyan, when after the naming of the divine names everyone is supposed to reply with a blessing, 'not if one is called François Delormes.'

No one in the house had ever heard of François Delormes.

'I have worked for him. He was the best, a prince among tailors. Someone who could even afford to say no to the emperor.'

'Well,' said Salomon, who was used to being suspicious if someone over-praised a deal to him, 'it can hardly have been the emperor.'

'It was his valet. The personal valet of Napoleon the Third. He came to Monsieur Delormes and ordered a tailcoat. For the emperor. A midnight blue tailcoat with silver embroidery. Says Delormes: "No." "Why not?" inquires the valet. And Delormes replies: "Blue doesn't suit him." Isn't that wonderful?'

'It can't have happened.'

'I was there. I have held in my own hand the swatch of fabric chosen by the valet.'

'Midnight blue,' said Mimi quietly. It sounded even more elegant than 'dove grey'.

'So you're a tailor?' Chanele, who had been standing the whole time, now sat down at the table with the others. 'What sort of tailor?'

'None at all,' said Janki. 'I soon realised that I'm not cut out for it. I may have the skill, but not the patience. I am not a patient man. All day one stitch and another stitch and another stitch, and all exactly the same length − it's not for me. No, I worked in the fabric store. I was there when the customers came. Showed them the patterns. The bolts of material. We had a selection... There was shantung silk in more than thirty different colours.'

'Shantung silk,' Mimi thought, and knew that she would never like another fabric more for the rest of her life.

'I learned a lot,' said Janki. 'About materials. About fashion. Above all about the people who can afford both. And they began to get to know me too. I started to become someone. Somebody advised me to set up on my own. Wanted to lend me money. In the end I rented a little shop with a little flat. And then I made my mistake.'

'Mistake?' asked Golde, startled.

'I came back to Guebwiller to collect the few pieces of furniture that I'd left with a drayman. They were glad when I arrived. They gave me a cordial welcome. Took me in their arms and wouldn't let me go, those swine!' He had been speaking in muted tones, but he shouted those last words so loudly and with such fury that Golde looked fearfully at the wall, behind which the Oggenfuss family must have long been asleep.

'"How nice that you're here," they said.' Janki's voice had become quieter and quieter, but there was something in it that made Mimi think, with a pleasantly creepy shudder: 'If he had to kill somebody, he would poison them.'

'"We've been waiting for you," they said. "You're on the list," they said. They'd had enough time to manipulate them. There'd been nobody there to take my side, to bribe the right man at the right time. I was on the list, and there was nothing to be done about the list. And so, rather than opening a shop in Paris, I was marched to Colmar along with two dozen others, and became a soldier. Twentieth Corps. Second Division. Fourth Battalion of the Régiment du Haut-Rhin.'

There are wines that you have to drink quickly once the barrel has been tapped, otherwise they go sour. As long as the bunghole is firmly closed, they keep for years, but once they've been opened...Janki's story came bubbling out of him, and like a badly kept wine there were some things floating around in them that might have spoiled one's thirst or curiosity.

He talked about his training, 'The same thing a thousand times, as if you were a fool, an idiot, or were to be made into a fool', about the marching that his fine city boots hadn't endured for long, 'If you wrap rags around your feet, you have to soak them in urine first, it's good for the blisters,' about the officers' horses, which were treated better than the young recruits, 'because horses kick'. He talked about what it feels like when you're crammed together with people you have nothing in common with, how you have to smell and taste and put up with them, how you have to listen to their jokes, in which you yourself come up as a caricature again and again, 'Their second favourite subject was food and their third favourite the Jews.'

But even when he was talking about things so revolting that Mimi had to shake herself like someone who's had her throat burned by rough brandy, but who knows already that the next slug will taste better and the one after that better still, even if he was describing experiences that made Golde involuntarily stretch out her hand, as if she had to pull him away and bring him to safety, indeed, even when he suggested experiences that cannot be avoided when young men live in such close proximity – Chanele raised her eyebrows and Salomon uttered a warning 'Now, then!' – even then his story had an undertone of longing, a memory of times that might not have been good but were better than the ones that came after. And they all knew what had come after. Even in Endingen, where the waves of world history lapped only wearily at the shore, they knew about the war, they had heard of the imprisonment and deposition of the Emperor, of the big battle on the first of September in which a hundred thousand Frenchmen had fallen – and Janki had perhaps been there, had experienced the horrors of that day and had now, by some miracle, a real nes min hashamayim, got away.

'No,' said Janki and made a sound that might have been a laugh, a cough or a sob, it was impossible to tell, 'I wasn't in Sedan. We new recruits didn't make it that far. They did make us swear oaths. To the Emperor. Or to the fatherland. To something or other. I don't remember. An ancient colonel spoke the oath for us. One of the ones who have to hollow their backs so that their medals didn't topple them over. With a high, squeaking voice. And then, standing in rank and file, we couldn't make out what he said. So I swore something and have no idea what it was.' This time it was unambiguously a laugh, but not a pleasant one. 'If we were engaged in a cattle-trade,' thought Salomon, 'I wouldn't buy now.'

'I don't know what I would have done in a battle,' said Janki. 'I would probably have tried to run away.'

'No,' thought Mimi. 'You wouldn't have done that.'

'But it didn't come to that. All we did was march. I never found out whether we were marching away from the Germans or towards them. Marching, marching, marching. Once for fifteen hours straight, and in the end we were back in the same village we'd started from. Six hours there and nine hours back. Without food and water. We weren't marching at the end, we were creeping on two legs. But I never saw an enemy soldier. They had no time for us. They were too busy winning the war. When the old colonel with the bird voice, the oberbalmeragges from the oath-swearing, told us it was all over, we lay on the floor like dead flies, too exhausted to get up and listen. And he used such beautiful patriotic words. If we'd believed him, the capitulation was a triumph. Why not? What was the point of being in a war if you can't be a hero afterwards? I'll tell my children I fought like a lion.'

They were all polite and didn't ask the question. But even evasive eyes can pierce like needles. Chanele rubbed a dry plate still drier, Golde sucked her lower lip, and Salomon was earnestly preoccupied with a renegade strand in his sideburns. Only Mimi started to say, 'Where did...?' but stopped mid-phrase and ran her hand over her brow, at the exact position of the bloodstain on Janki's dirty white turban.

'The bandage?' he asked. 'Oh, yes, the bandage.'

He stretched his arm out in an elegantly demanding gesture, a young prince in one of Mimi's novels, inviting a pretty kitchen-maid to dance. 'If you would care to help me, Mademoiselle?' he said to Chanele.

He untied the knot himself, but then she was the one who unrolled the bandage, slowly and carefully, as one unwinds the strips of cloth around the scrolls of the Holy Scripture. It was so quiet in the kitchen that everyone gave a start when the first coin fell to the floor.

Only Janki didn't move. 'Thieving is rife among one's dear comrades,' he said. 'One has to come up with a good hiding place for one's small fortune.'

'He's a pirate,' thought Mimi.

'He's a ganev,' thought Salomon.

There was another clatter on the stone tiles, then Chanele was ready and collected the coins from the bandage as soon a they appeared. What lay neatly aligned on the table at last, in silver and twice even in gold, was a minted picture book of French history, Louis XV, a fat baby, Louis XVI, a fat grown-up, the winged genius of the Revolution, Napoleon as a Greek bust, Louis XVIII with his pigtails, Louis-Philippe with his laurel wreath and Napoleon III with his tufted beard.

'The blood on the bandage was real,' said Janki. 'But luckily it wasn't mine.'

And then, now apparently as wide awake as he had been exhausted when he arrived, he told them how they had marched off again after the armistice, marched, marched, marched, about how no one had known where they were going because none of their superiors had told them anything – 'They keep you stupid, because otherwise no one would stay a soldier' – about how the rumour had gradually spread that their general, who hadn't been able to win the war, now wanted at least to win the defeat, that it was no longer a matter of beating the Germans but just not falling into their hands, how they had finally, completely exhausted, crossed the border and, with ludicrous pride, fallen in step once more on the snow-covered road with the soldiers of the Swiss Confederation – 'Basically they were a pathetic shower, and we were a whole army' – how they had bundled their rifles into clean pyramids, always eight and then eight again, how the officers had been allowed to keep their swords, of course, how the senior gentlemen had behaved correctly and even genially towards one another, regardless of whether they were interning or internees – 'When they aren't actually shooting at each other, they're a big mishpocha. His eyes turned moist as he described what their first soup had tasted like, how it had been ladled from the big pot, boiling hot, but how no one wanted to wait, not for so much as a minute, how they had burned their mouths and been happy none the less, and how a Swiss soldier – 'He wore a uniform, but he spoke like a civilian' – had apologised to them, actually apologised for not having anything better to offer than a pile of straw on the floor of a barn – 'As if we would otherwise have been sleeping on a downy bed, with silk nightcaps' – how they had at last had time to rest in the camp, how they had slept, just slept, for a night and a day and another night. He was talking faster and faster, the way you get faster and faster during the last prayer on the Day of Atonement because the time of fasting is over and food is waiting, he described how the camp had not been a camp at all, just a village, a snowed-in peasant village in the Alb, where the guards were just as bored as those they guarded, and how they started to talk to each other, how useful his Yiddish was to him, how he had befriended a soldier from Muri who wanted to try out his stumbling French on him, and he copied the man, jumping about like a badchen entertaining the guests at a wedding, and he demonstrated how he had copied him word for word without having even the faintest understanding of the meaning – 'Dancing a minuet in wooden clogs' – he made them laugh and yet felt troubled by their laughter, didn't want to be interrupted, just as he hadn't tolerated interruption over dinner, and he uttered his tale like a prayer whose every section had been repeated a thousand times: how the soldier demanded three Louis d'Or from him, but had then been negotiated down to only one, how he even wrote down the journey, from large town to large town, how simple it had been to walk out among the patrols, either because they didn't expect escape attempts or because they didn't care – 'One more, one less, what did it matter?' – and he told them how he had marched, marched, marched, marched, only by night at first, but soon by day as well, how he had slept in haystacks and once in a kennel, pressed up against the farm dog, which shivered just as much as he did, and he told them how he had begged, unsuccessfully, from suspicious farmers who begrudged him so much as a word of greeting, how once, at the market in Solothurn, he had stolen a brown cake filled with almond paste, the best, best, best that he had ever tasted in his life, how 'Endingen' had become a magic word for him, all those endless days, how he had given himself courage, how he had cried, just with happiness, when someone told him, just one more town, then he'd be there, how he'd felt as if the tears were freezing on his face, how he had arrived at last, chilled to the bone and almost starving, and then a goy had opened the door to him and yelled at him, and how he was there now and wanted to stay there, with his relatives, for ever.

'For ever?' Salomon thought.

'For ever,' thought Mimi.

3

Next morning Janki had a high fever.

His cold, only temporarily concealed by the excitements of the previous evening, had returned invigorated, if it was indeed only a cold and not, heaven forfend, bronchitis or worse. Salomon had set off for Degermoos early in the morning, without seeing his guest again, and so it was left to the three women to tend to the patient.

They had set up a bed for him in the attic room, and there he lay now, his whole body boiling hot and still shivering with cold. His vacant eyes were open wide, but if you moved your hand in front of them, the pupils didn't follow the movement. Every now and again a dry cough shook Janki's body, as if an unknown person were hammering his chest from within. His lips trembled, like a premature baby that wanted to cry but didn't yet have the strength, or an old man who had already used up all the tears that life had assigned him.

The room was dark and sticky. Up here, where only a shnorrer would ever have spent the night, there was no real window, just a hatch that could be opened a crack to let in a little light and air. But outside it was icy cold and frozen, one of those jangling late winter days when every breath cuts your throat, and Golde said Janki had – me neshuma! – had enough. So the hatch remained closed, and lest the patient be left entirely in the dark, they had had to light some flickering candles that almost went out every time someone's skirt stirred in the cramped room. Practical Chanele suggested putting the candles in jars, but Mimi emphatically resisted the idea, and when Chanele asked for a sensible reason, Mimi wiped tears from her eyes and refused to answer. The inexpressible reason, and Golde felt this exactly as her daughter did, was of course that such candles would have looked like the commemorative ones set up on the day of a relative's death.

Among the candles on the old bedside table – one leg was missing, and they had had to put a plank of wood underneath it – framed by the flickering wicks, lay Janki's yellow neckerchief, in which Golde had tied his coins, all the kings, emperors and revolutionary spirits. She avoided looking there, because when she held the heavy lump in her hand, a thought of which she was still ashamed had passed through her mind. 'Enough for a levaya,' she had thought, 'enough money for a funeral.'

Trying to do something good for Janki, the three women jostled one another by his bed, elbow to elbow. With a damp cloth Chanele dabbed away the white crust that kept forming on his lips, like a baby bringing up sour milk. Golde tried to pour a slip of lukewarm tea between his lips, but it just ran down his chin to the collar of his shirt. The trail of fluid shimmered for a moment on his hot skin, and had then vanished again. Mimi had fetched a comb, her own comb, and cleared the hair from his damp forehead for the third time.

Then Janki suddenly began to speak.

It was more of a murmur, turned inwards, not outwards, he was saying something to himself to remind himself or to forget. They couldn't make out the words, even though they were always the same few syllables, over and over and over.

'He's praying,' said Golde, and forbade herself from thinking what prayer a man who was seriously ill might utter.

'Perhaps he's hungry,' said Chanele.

'Sha!' said Mimi, and bent so low over the sick man that his smell, unsettlingly clean and slightly sour like bread dough, enveloped her as if she were caught in its embrace. Her ear was close to his mouth, but she didn't feel his breath, just sensed the words, which were French but incomprehensible, and which made her pointlessly jealous, an alien conversation in which she was not involved. 'It doesn't mean anything,' she said more loudly than necessary. 'It doesn't make any sense. He is ill, and he needs peace and quiet, and, generally speaking, us treading on each other's feet here won't help him.' And with those words she ran from the room, they heard her footsteps on the stairs, and the other two women, who had known Mimi for a lifetime, took a look to agree that she would now shut herself away in her room and there would be no sign of her for the next few hours.

'Then I'll go to Pomeranz,' said Golde after a brief silence. Where Techías Hameisim tea did not help, she liked to deploy her most powerful weapon in the battle against illnesses of all kinds: a beef broth cooked so fiercely that a whole pound of meat produced only a single cup. Usually she would have sent Chanele to shochet Pomeranz to fetch the piece of stripped flank, but the short walk through the cold air would do her good, she thought, it would clear her head, foggy from the stuffy air. 'You take care of things in the meantime,' she said to Chanele, and was already outside the door.

Freed equally from Golde's clucky concern and from Mimi's impractical over-eagerness, Chanele first of all opened the hatch in the roof – even with a fever, she said to herself, you can't freeze under a thick eiderdown – blew the candles out, then sat down by the bed with a bowl of vinegar water and methodically changed the cold compresses that were supposed to draw the fever to the feet and from there out of the body. Once, struggling with the stranger in his chest, Janki rolled over so violently that he threw the eiderdown to the floor. The skin on his legs was paler than that of his face, and his penis was long and thin.

The French words that he repeated so often, without being able to remember them later, were two lines from a song: about a drummer drumming the march and the ravens sitting in the trees and waiting.

In a village the night has many eyes and even more ears. Their night-time visit was already bound to have travelled around the community, and Golde knew that everyone she met would ask questions, some of them spoken out loud, but most, even more pressing, silent. So she didn't go straight to the Marktgasse, but took a detour via the Mühleweg, along the Surb and past the mikvah, the bathing house, where she was unlikely to meet an acquaintance at this time of day. The little meadow where the river gently bends and where you can rub your washing clean so well would be deserted in the icy cold.

She walked quickly, on her short, always slightly waddling steps, a duck that's being driven on with sticks but still can't quite bring itself to fly. The wind swept particles of ice from the trees; they struck Golde's face like fine needles, and she enjoyed the stinging pain because it ennobled the purchase of a pound of meat for soup into a mission full of self-sacrifice. Where the alleyways narrowed again and the houses with their curious windows waited for her, she pulled the black headscarf tighter around her head, and actually managed to reach Naftali Pomeranz's shop without a single person talking to her.

Naftali wasn't there. Only Pinchas, his son, of whom Pomeranz was so proud, looked after the shop, a lanky lad, as long and thin as his father, with a thin growth of beard and a big gap in his teeth in which, when he was embarrassed, his tongue played. He was standing at the window with a rag in one hand and a book in the other, had probably started cleaning it and then immersed himself once more in his reading. When Golde addressed him, he started wildly, dropped his book, just managed to catch it, had to bend down for the rag and said at last that his father had gone to shul, to the synagogue, to prepare the Torah scrolls for the Pesach service, and could she come back later, he wouldn't be long.

'No wonder he's still single at twenty-five,' thought Golde. No, she said severely, she couldn't come back later, she had a sick guest at home who needed his strengthening soup, and as quickly as possible.

'I'd like to fetch my father, I'd love to,' said Pinchas and almost started stammering, 'but he expressly ordered me to stay in the—'

'Run!'

Sarah Pomeranz had come in, the woman whose cheesecake put Roth-schild's cook to shame. Even though she spent her life in the kitchen, she was just as gaunt as her husband and her son. It was almost part of her everyday outfit that her hands were covered with flour to the wrists, and she had to wipe them off on her apron before she was able to greet Golde properly. She closed the shop door behind Pinchas – 'Who buys meat in the middle of the week?' – and said in that way so characteristic of her: 'You'll have a coffee with me, no formalities, you give what you have.' Golde, feeling slightly sick after all the excitement, was happy to accept the invitation, even though she knew that there was as much curiosity as hospitality involved. He who keeps secrets makes no friends.

While Sarah ran a handful of beans into the coffee mill and, to show how much she valued this visit, added another half-handful, Golde began to deliver her report. 'He's the same age as my son,' she said, because sometimes, above all in events that violently stirred her emotions, she saw the child that hadn't been allowed to live now standing before her as a grown-up man.

'They say he's a foreigner.'

'A Frenchman, yes.'

'And how did he come to you?'

'He's mishpocha of my husband.'

'Ah, mishpocha,' repeated Sarah, as if that explained everything, and explain everything it did. 'And his name is?'

'Janki. Janki Meijer.'

Sarah put the big dough bowl on the floor to make room on the table and straightened a table for Golde. 'He wears a uniform, they say.'

'He was a soldier.'

'Wounded?'

'No, nothing – Baruch Hashem! – happened to him.'

'But he has a bandage. They say.'

'He only has it … for security.' There's nothing, Golde noticed, that connects someone more closely with a person than a shared secret.

While her hostess turned the handle of the coffee mill, only with her finger-tips as if that would make it quieter, Golde told her what she knew of Janki. As she did so she must have exaggerated slightly – when does one ever have the chance to tell such an adventurous tale? – because when the coffee was poured, a lot of coffee, not much water, as one does with honoured guests, Sarah sat down at her cup saying, 'Just imagine … No older than my Pinchas, and already he's survived Sedan!' She made the sound of Jewish astonishment,

25

a drawn-out hiss, the head moving back and forth so that the sound seems to ebb and flow.

'He didn't hear a single shot fired,' Golde tried to correct her.

'Not one? In such a big battle? Yes, God can protect a person wonderfully well.' And because she always saw her husband's shammes duties as her own, Sarah added, 'He will be summoned to the Torah and bentch gomel.'

Golde didn't contradict her any further. There are stories that are stronger than reality. And besides, she liked the idea that Janki, whom she already called her Janki in her mind, should be a hero and in the end: marching his feet bloody and sharing a kennel with a farm dog – is that any less heroic than fighting in a battle? She was already looking forward to the moment when he, healed once more, might stand on the almemor in the synagogue and bentch gomel. Who had more reason than he to speak as a thanksgiver for dangers survived? They would look down at him from the women's shul, and the other women would say, 'Without Golde's beef broth, heaven forfend, he wouldn't have survived.'

They drank their coffee, black and with lots of sugar, and Sarah flushed with pride when Golde told her how much the God-protected Janki had liked her cheesecake, how not a single piece of it had been left, indeed, he had pushed the crumbs together and licked them from the palm of his hand. 'He'll fit in well with us here in the village,' Sarah said out of deep conviction, and Golde heard herself expressing, to her own surprise, something that she had not yet even really thought: 'Yes, he will stay here. We will take him in. He has no one else, after all.'

Then Naftali Pomeranz came in and would have loved to hear all the news, but was sent to the shop to cut the meat. Sarah insisted – 'That's the least we can do!' – that Golde didn't take the little parcel home herself, but that Pinchas went with her. After all, doing something for a sick person was a God-pleasing deed, a mitzvah, and it would be a pleasure for her son, 'isn't that right, Pinchasle?'

Pinchas took such long strides that Golde almost had to scuttle her short legs to keep up with him. Out of pure politeness she tried to talk to the young man once or twice, and praised him for promising to be, as one heard, a worthy successor to his father, but couldn't entice a sensible word from him. It was only when they were standing at the door of the double-fronted house and he handed her the parcel that he suddenly blurted, 'Abraham Singer comes to see you often, doesn't he?' then turned and ran away without waiting for an answer.

'Strange,' thought Golde. 'Why would he care whether the marriage broker had called on Mimi?'

While the beef broth was still cooking – perhaps the smell alone, drifting through the house, would have an effect – Janki fell asleep. His breath, although it still had a quiet, papery rustle, was so calm, and his forehead was so much cooler, that Chanele dried his feet, covered them up and crept from the room on tiptoe.

Janki was quite alone now. Uncle Melnitz sat on the empty chair by his bed and talked to him.

'You're asleep,' said Melnitz. 'You think nothing can happen to you when you're here. But that's not true. Here is no different from anywhere else. Nowhere is different.

'Ten years ago was the last time it happened. Here in Endingen, yes. We were to get a few more rights. Not rights like the Christians, but almost like human beings. And they smashed in our windows. Not only the windows. Sometimes one of those stones lands on your head. Little Pnina had only herself to blame. She should have run away faster. Or made herself invisible. They would like us much better if we were invisible, yes.

'There are no guilty parties, because no one was there. No one anyone knew. They'd discussed that. They'd also agreed that everything would happen unprepared. From the people. From the moment.'

Uncle Melnitz had closed his eyes like someone only repeating a lesson learned long ago to be sure that he hasn't forgotten it.

'And at the start of the century we had the plum war here in Endingen, that's right. A little war. We live in a small country. The French had occupied Switzerland at the time. Napoleon. But they didn't wage war against him. He wouldn't have been afraid of their sticks. They fought against us. That's simpler. They had taught us not to defend ourselves long ago.

'They called it the plum war because the ripe plums were hanging from the trees. They like to wait until the harvest is over. Before, you have so much else to do. Afterwards you need something to do with your strength.

'There was another name for it. The ribbon war. Because they stole the bright ribbons from the dealers they beat up. They took other things too, but you saw the ribbons afterwards. Fastened to jackets. To sleeves. To hats. As medals, that's right. To show that they'd been there. Pride. Afterwards they always had only two possibilities. To be proud or be ashamed. They preferred to be proud.

'Someone from the village, a head of the community – his name was Guggenheim, like the inn – tried to talk to them. That was a mistake. If you talk, you're a human being, and they didn't want us to be human beings. Because you don't stick your pitchfork in a human being's face, so that a prong goes

27

in one cheek and out the other. Because you don't laugh at a human being when he tries to talk and can't because his tongue is torn. Because you don't hit a human being on the back of the head with a threshing flail just to make them stop screaming.

'Plum war, that's right. They called it war because the word made heroes of them. They're always heroes, every time they lay into us.'

Janki had closed his eyes. The blanket over his chest rose and sank only slightly, a ship that had reached the harbour and still remembered the waves from a distance. One hand lay beside his head, palm upwards, as if he were waiting for a present.

'You think you're safe now,' said Melnitz. 'But there is no safety. When he was lying on the floor and had stopped moving, one of them put his boot on his head. One that the girls liked because even after a bottle of wine he didn't touch them against their will. One who liked to play tunes on a comb with a sheet of paper folded over it. One who quickly picked dandelions for the rabbit whose neck he was going to break. A nice person.

'He put his boot on his head and pressed his face in the dirt because he wouldn't have been able to pull out the pitchfork otherwise. Tools are expensive, and the fork didn't belong to him. If he had been alone, he would have apologised as he did it. He was a decent person, yes. But he wasn't alone. They are never alone.

'There is no safety,' said Melnitz and told another story and another. He spoke without haste, someone who has a lot of time to fill. The way one speaks the Shemoneh Esrei at solemn festivals, one interpolation and then another. 'Sometimes they shout,' he said, 'and sometimes they whisper. Sometimes they are silent for a long time, and you think they've forgotten us. But they don't forget us. Believe me, Janki. They don't forget us.'

The smell of beef broth now filled the whole house the way incense, they say, fills a church.

4

'Horses?'

Salomon had been reluctant to take Janki along with him. First of all, people who have just been sick belong at home, and second...He hadn't been able to say the second to Golde. His wife had taken this relative, this unexpected visitor, as unreservedly to her heart as, many years ago, Mimi had the kitten that a farm hand had wanted to drown and which, facing perils that grew with every repetition of the story, she had rescued from the Surb River. Then as now, arguments would have served no useful purpose, and Golde would certainly not have accepted the actual reason for his rejection: Salomon didn't trust Janki. It was only a feeling, a grumbling in his belly, but Salomon had avoided many a bad deal because he had believed his belly more than his head.

So in the end he had given in, not because of Janki's pleading eyes, even though they had seemed as big in that sunken face as the eyes of a pregnant cow, but just to have some peace. He had even lent him a coat, his own old coat, which he always wore when he knew he would be spending the whole day in byres, and had been annoyed – 'Nu, it's going to smell of violet water!' – over the fact that Janki screwed up his nose and tested the heavy fabric as contemptuously between his fingers as a grain-dealer pulverising a dead ear of corn. He had lent him, no, given him, boots as well; why put off acts of generosity that you can't avoid anyway? 'It's nice', Golde had said, 'that he's so interested in your business. Who knows, perhaps it's something for him later on?' And Salomon, true to the principle that it's usually a good idea to hold your tongue, hadn't replied, 'A tailor as a beheimes dealer? Is he going to measure up riding trousers for the cows?'

So now they walked along side by side. Salomon's umbrella left its trail of holes, and Janki's boots, always a few steps behind, tramped them closed again. It was the first warm day this year; the spring dripped freshly thawed from the trees, on which the birds practised twittering as eagerly as if their beaks had been frozen shut throughout all those months. There was not a trace of romanticism in Salomon Meijer, he didn't even know the word, and yet today he would have preferred them to have walked in silence through the splashy morning.

But Janki talked. Still weakened by fever, he struggled to keep up, and talked. He stopped to catch his breath, ran a few steps behind, which left him even more short of breath, and talked. Salomon wasn't walking any faster than usual, but he wasn't walking more slowly either. He was on his way to meet master butcher Gubser in the byre that he had rented from the lea-farmer, and he would arrive on time for his appointment as he always did. Did Janki absolutely insist on coming? Nu, let him. If he wanted to waste his meagre strength chatting, instead of saving it for walking, then let him.

On the evening of his arrival, Janki had talked like a little boy coming home after his first day in cheder, and who has to get off his chest all the fears he endured from his strange new teacher. Now his breathless flow of chat had something of a quack doctor praising his home-made medicine in the marketplace, good against headaches, toothache and women's complaints, promising guaranteed healing as long as the patient was willing to swallow the brew for three weeks, every day at the same time – probably aware that he himself would be standing far away in a different market in three weeks, and that all promises are forgotten in a year or even in only six months.

'Horses? What would I want with horses? Cows are my trade.'

'Yes,' said Janki, 'I understood that, but you have to try out new things too.'

'Why?'

'To get on. Monsieur Delormes was forever designing new cuts. Wide lapels. Narrow lapels. None at all.'

'"None at all" is the one I like. Because cows don't wear coats.' He had had to keep his jokes to himself with Golde. But it wasn't Salomon Meijer's style to waste things.

'It would be a good time for horses.'

'Do you know that as a soldier or as a tailor?'

'I know it from the man from Muri. The man I spent a long time talking French to.'

'A horse trader?'

'He was a teacher.'

'At a school for horses?'

Salomon couldn't afford to be ironic with his farmers. He found the argument all the more amusing now for that very reason. He even complacently swung his umbrella once around his hand, as smitten farmworkers did with their walking sticks on Sunday.

'He told me something,' said Janki. 'It was secret, but he told me because he was proud that he knew all the words for it. Almost all the words, that is.'

'Well?'

Janki, apparently interested only in the cleanliness of his new old boots, carefully stepped around a puddle. Anyone else wouldn't even have noticed that he was only trying to hide his last hesitation before making a decision, but anyone who has engaged in lots of cattle deals learns to read such signs.

'Well?' Salomon asked again.

Janki coughed, although there was no coughing left in him. Then he stopped. 'We can get involved in the business together.'

'I should have walked on,' Salomon said to himself later. 'Just walked on and stopped listening to him. Then everything might have turned out differently.'

But he didn't walk on. He stopped as well and asked, 'What kind of business?'

'Horses,' said Janki, and now had a smile on his face that Salomon disliked as much as Mimi would have liked it. 'We will sell horses that we don't have.'

The business that Janki suggested when they stood facing one another among the dripping fruit trees, and which he over-eagerly explained as they walked along again, side by side, more slowly than before, which he praised with hucksterish eloquence, when they stopped again, gesticulating, having reached their destination far too quickly, this business went like this:

The French officers – 'whose boots we had to clean, even though they barely ever set foot on the floor' – all the lieutenants, capitaines and colonels, had not marched into their internment, but proudly ridden over the border, with freshly greased harnesses, had tugged the reins of their horses, which were fed significantly better than the infantrymen who dragged themselves wearily along, between the rows of Swiss soldiers, making them dance and traverse, in order to say: 'We have not come here as defeated men, we still have strength in abundance, and if we'd wanted things to be different, we would have done things differently.'

They had then – 'And like idiots we put up with it, at least on the first day' – taken all the steaming hay-bales that the exhausted soldiers had torn apart to make a comfortable camp for themselves, and requisitioned them for themselves, straw for the troops, hay for the horses, and had even ridden out in the first few weeks, had straightened their backs and held their reins loosely between two gloved fingers, but then the hay had started running out, not to mention the oats, and at last the horses had only stood there, in stables where that was possible, but also just under the open sky, tied in long rows; attempts had been made to light big fires to warm them a little, but the smoke had only made them restless and bad-tempered.

'There are some lovely animals among them,' said Janki, 'particularly the officers' private horses, but most of them are of course luggage pullers, dray and coach horses, and you're not going to win a show-jumping competition with those, but you might be able to drag a cannon out of the dirt. Hundreds of horses. Fodder for butchers.'

31

'Well?' said Salomon, and packed into that one syllable was a whole droosh, a sermon interpreting the verse of the scripture: 'You shouldn't tell a beheimes dealer, who's only interested in cows, anything about horses.'

'Now comes the bit that no one knows yet,' said Janki and took Salomon by the sleeve, an intimacy that not even Golde allowed herself. 'It's to be a secret for as long as possible, so that no one does a private deal with it. But this schoolmaster disguised as a soldier gave the game away to me. They decided to sell all the French horses to pay for part of the expense of the detention. There's going to be a big auction, in Saignelégier.'

'So?'

Janki stared at Salomon, amazed and sympathetic, the way you might look at someone who's been asked a riddle and is still looking for the solution even though it's staring him right in the face. '"So?" you ask? There will be so many horses on the market that prices in Switzerland are bound to collapse. They'll be so eager that they'll carry the animals to our door, as long as we buy them.'

'We won't buy them.'

'Yes, we will. After we've sold them.'

And then he described his plan to Salomon again, the plan he had hatched in the internment camp, he Janki Meijer, all by himself, the only thinking person amongst defeated, apathetic time-servers, the plan that had given him strength on his long march through Switzerland, that had warmed him in a stinking kennel, that had drawn him from his fever as if on a rope, because there was no time to lose, not a single day, because the opportunity was there now and it wouldn't come back.

They would sell horsemeat to a butcher, ideally to master butcher Gubser, with whom Salomon would have made an agreement to sell horsemeat, on contract, due in one month, one hundred kilos, two hundred, five hundred, what did Janki know, as much as Gubser would take from them, they would offer him a price so cheap that he would think they'd gone meshuga, a metsiya that no one could resist, certainly not a goyish butcher, because, as Janki remembered from the pub in Guebwiller they were always prepared to pull a fast one. But when the contract came due and the meat had to be supplied, the prices for horses would have dropped to their lowest ever, the butcher would be furious – 'But is that our problem?' – and they would make a reyvech, enough to set up as a tailor or a cloth-dealer or whatever you liked. Janki was so sure of his argument that he dared to parody the cattle-trader, whose support he after all relied on, with comical distortions.

'So?' asked Janki.

32

Salomon Meijer stroked his sideburn. 'A good sign,' thought Janki, who didn't know him. Salomon looked thoughtfully down the hill, at the stable less than two hundred yards away, where they were already waiting for him, then he rammed his umbrella into the soft soil, so that it seemed to stand all by itself, Moses' rod before the Pharaoh. He leaned against a tree, as Rav Bodenheimer sometimes leaned against the bookshelf when he began to explain something in a lesson, and said, 'Look at this umbrella!'

'The umbrella?'

'I always keep it with me, and I never put it up. Why?'

Janki helplessly spread his arms. He had no idea what Salomon was getting at.

'It's a mark. Something striking. Something that distinguishes me from all other Jews who deal with beheimes. Just as the pot in which I cook something in the inn when I have to stay there overnight, differs from all other pots. Because I make a mark on it. Three letters, a kaf, a shin and a resh, inside on the bottom. The word "kosher". If the letters are still there next time I know: I can use the pot. You understand?'

Janki didn't understand at all. How did they get from the horses to an umbrella and from the umbrella to a pot?

Salomon wouldn't be hurried. He finished his thoughts as slowly and carefully as the Rav did when he put two distant quotations together to clarify a disputed passage. 'I have assumed the habit of the umbrella so that people know who I am. The Jew with the brolly. The way you brand a mark on a horse's rump, if you want to talk about horses. It's been stolen from me twice, because there's a rumour among the farm boys that it's the place,' and he pointed to the belly of the umbrella, where the black fabric swelled in the gentle spring breeze, 'in which I keep my money. Nu, let them steal it. What does such an umbrella cost? I have three more like it at home.' When Salomon laughed he kept his lips closed, and his cheeks with their little red veins went round like two apple halves.

'I'm the Jew with the brolly. And people know: this Jew is honest. This Jew doesn't cheat. We can rely on the Jew. Not that I give them presents. Then they would say: the Jew is stupid. If they leave a cow that I'm supposed to buy unmilked in the byre for two days, so that the udder looks firmer, then I laugh at them. But it must be exactly the same the other way around. If they come to the Jew with the brolly for the milk cow and want to check the rings on the horn to see how often she has calved before, the horns aren't filed down. A beef bullock that someone buys from me won't have thirsted at the salt lick and then greedily drunk its fill of water, so that it weighs a few pounds more on the scales. People know that, and that's why they do their deals with me and not with anyone else. That's how I live, that's my parnooseh. And because that's the case, and because that's how it's going to stay...'

'But it's a unique opportunity,' Janki said pleadingly, knowing that he had lost the argument.

'Because it's how it's to stay,' Salomon went on, 'I will not sell butcher Gubser horsemeat on a contract that will only mean he loses money. Have I made a name for myself for all these years, only to buy it from me for a few gold pieces and then throw it away?' He pulled the tip of the umbrella out of the muddy ground with a quiet thwock and then went down the hill towards the byre, sticking the umbrella into the ground with every second step, as if to mark a boundary line.

There was something of the parson about master butcher Gubser, an unctuous tone that made him popular with the housewives who bought from his shop. He had the habit of repeating words that he didn't mean two or three times, putting his fleshy red hand on his heart as if making an oath before a court.

'Ah, the new relation,' he said, and half-bowed to Janki. 'I've heard of him. Welcome, welcome, welcome. A cattle trader too?'

'A businessman too,' replied Janki, and Salomon inflated his cheeks with his lips closed.

'From France, I hear. Been at the Battle of Sedan. Must have been terrible. Terrible.'

'There are nicer places to be than battlefields,' said Janki, and Gubser laughed as loudly and heartily as if he had never heard a more polished bon mot.

'Brilliant,' he said, 'brilliant, brilliant. But then you Jews have a way with words. That's why one has to take such care when one's doing business with you. But Herr Meijer knows I'm not blaming you. Everyone's as God has made him. A calf isn't a sheep, and a pig isn't a goat.'

Salomon, resting his hands on the handle of his umbrella, seemed to be counting the empty swallows' nests under the roof truss of the byre.

'Today I need a cow,' said Gubser. 'A cheap cow with a lot of meat on its bones. Could even be old and tough. Sausages are sausages, whatever you put in them.' He laughed loud and long, and when Janki didn't join in with his laughter, he asked, 'Didn't he understand that, this Frenchman of yours?'

'Doesn't he understand me, or doesn't he want to understand me?' Salomon said to Golde a weeks later. 'I ask him how he imagines his future, and he just looks at me and shrugs his shoulders and goes for a walk.'

'He needs to recover. He has been ill, and has to do something for his health.' Golde's voice sounded muted, because her head was in the big cupboard in the bedroom, as if in a cave. Crouching on the floor, she was fishing from the very back corner all the things that you never throw away, and only ever pick up at the Pesach cleaning. She held out to her husband a shard of painted porcelain, part of the plate that had been broken and distributed almost twenty-five years ago on the day of their engagement, and they exchanged a smile as one can only smile after long years of marriage, assembled from equal parts of contented memory and almost-as-contented resignation.

'Still,' said Salomon. He helped Golde to her feet and tried not to remember how much lighter in body and soul she once had been. 'He runs around the place, you never know where he's going next, and if you want to exchange a word with him he doesn't listen.'

'He's young,' said Golde. 'And he's disappointed, it seems to me. What sort of business deal did he suggest to you?'

'Not a clean one.' Business deals were men's affair. Salomon didn't ask Golde why all the handleless cups and cracked glasses had to be cleaned so thoroughly once a year, only to gather dust again for twelve months in the bottom drawer. 'I couldn't go along with it. But that's no reason to go walking around the world all on your own. People are talking.'

Golde filled her apron with cutlery, a peasant woman collecting pears in the autumn. She chewed on her lower lip, firmly resolved not to tell her husband, who always thought he knew everything and yet didn't understand a thing, a word of what people were really saying. But then, already half way out of the room, he was stronger than she was. She turned around again and said, 'He's not always alone.'

'My real name is Miriam,' Mimi had said. 'They call me Mimi because they treat me like a child. But I'm not a child any more.'

'No,' Janki had replied, 'you're not a child any more.' And he had looked at her with a look, 'with a look', Mimi had told the schoolmaster's daughter the same day, 'that would make you blush if he wasn't a relative.'

The friendship between the two young women went back to their childhood days. They had splashed together in the shallow water when they were still too little to understand that while they might have belonged to the same village they actually lived in different worlds. Anne-Kathrin had also played an important part in the episode with the rescued kitten; she had brought along the long-handled net that her father always took fishing, in the hope, never fulfilled, that the big, the really big pike would fall into his clutches. Now the two of them only ever met in secret, not because anyone frowned upon, or even prohibited, their having contact with one another, but because that secrecy had a charm of its own. A lock on a diary lends value to even the most trivial confession.

'He has eyes…' said Mimi. 'Very long eyelashes that stroke his cheeks. And then when he opens them…' She stretched her body as the kitten had once done when you stroked it behind its ears, and even the sound she made as she did so was like a miaow.

'You're in love,' said Anne-Kathrin, and was quite envious.

Mimi denied this with the vehemence of a guilty defendant. 'And most importantly, he is my cousin.'

'A very distant one.'

'Yes,' said Mimi and stretched her body again. 'Very distant.'

'My real name is Miriam,' she had said to him, and he had replied, not in Yiddish but in French for once, 'C'est dommage.'

Miriams, he had explained, were as numerous as the sequins on a ball gown, one more, one less, what did it matter? But Mimi, ah, he had only ever met one Mimi before, or rather: not really met, he had only read about her, in a novel, but even then he had thought: that is a very special name, and the person who bears it must be very special too.

'And *he* is in love with *you!*' When Anne-Kathrin was excited, her voice rose to a squeal. A pigeon flew up in alarm, and the two girls laughed at the silly bird as at that moment they would probably have laughed or cried over anything at all.

They were sitting in the round gazebo that Anne-Kathrin's father the schoolmaster, who placed great importance on being out in the open, had had built at the end of his garden. To get to it, you had to pass through the whole of the long garden, past all the flowerbeds that were fading away, bare and unused, at this time of year. The schoolmaster had only planted a few onions; he received his potatoes from the council, even though some people wanted to abolish this tribute on the grounds that it was old-fashioned. The flower beds were separated off by a row of rosebushes, and a big branch of an elder bush also obstructed the view. It was precisely because the gazebo was in seemingly such plain view that it was in fact an ideal hiding place.

'He wants to get hold of the book. He wants to go all the way to Baden, he says, just to find it for me. Even though he hates such journeys, because he had to do so much marching as a soldier.'

Anne-Kathrin brought the ends of her long blonde braids together in front of her nose and squinted slightly. 'Like a knight', she said softly, 'setting off to find a treasure.' She really wanted to say 'the Holy Grail', but she didn't think that was appropriate in the context of Mimi.

'And he wants to read it to me. We just have to find a suitable spot for it. Everything's upside down in our house at the moment, if only Pesach weren't coming up…My parents, you know.'

Of course Anne-Kathrin offered her friend the gazebo for her rendezvous. The adventures of others, when you have helped to set them up, are almost like your own.

5

'Mimi was a *fille charmante*,' Janki read, translating word for word into Yiddish and sometimes, if the right expression refused to come, simply in French. 'She was nineteen years old' – it said 'twenty-two' in the book, but as his listener was nineteen, the little change seemed appropriate – 'small, delicate and self-confident. Her face was like a preliminary sketch for the portrait of an aristocrat, but her features, delicate in their outlines and, it seemed, gently illuminated by the radiance of her clear blue eyes...'

'Anne-Kathrin has blue eyes,' thought Mimi, 'but she isn't an aristocrat. Certainly not an aristocrat.'

'...but her features,' repeated Janki, who had got lost in the novel's meandering sentences, 'sometimes showed, when she was tired or in a bad mood, an expression of almost wild brutality.'

'Brutality?' thought Mimi, and realised only from Janki's reaction that she had said it out loud.

'I haven't translated it very well. In her it's something positive. It means "strength" or "power".'

'That sounds better,' thought Mimi.

'...an expression of almost savage power, in which a physiognomist would probably have recognised the signs of profound egoism or a great lack of feeling. It's hard to find the correct words,' he added quickly. 'It sounds far too crude in Yiddish.'

'Go on!' Mimi pleaded and when Janki bent obediently over the book once more she felt something almost like savage brutality within her.

'Her face bore an unusual charm, her smile young and fresh, and her eyes filled with tenderness and flirtation. The blood of youth flowed warm and fast in her veins and lent her complexion, as white as camellia blossoms, a delicate pink tone.'

'Camellia blossoms,' Mimi thought and breathed in deeply. Hanging in the air of Endingen was the stench of the spring slurry that a farmer was spreading in his field. The bench in the gazebo was cobbled together from rough planks, the ground still covered with rotten leaves from the autumn, but Mimi lay stretched out on a sofa in an attic room, a gifted young poet sitting beside her, reading her poems that he had spent long nights writing, just for her.

'Her hands were so weak, so tiny, so soft on his lips; those childish hands in which Rodolphe had laid his reawakened heart; those snow white hands of Mademoiselle Mimi, who would soon tear his heart in pieces with her rosy fingernails.' Janki marked the spot with his own fingernail and snapped the book shut.

'Go on reading! Please!'

Janki shook his head, a gesture that Mimi sensed rather than saw. She had closed her eyes, and the warm spring sun stroked her lids.

'I'm sorry,' said Janki. 'It's not a book for young girls.'

'I'm not a child any more!' said Mimi, but not violently or challengingly as she did in her arguments with her parents, but quietly and with a hint of surprise.

'It was just because the name reminded me...Mimi.' She felt as if no one had ever called her by it. 'But then you're a Miriam.'

'Are you absolutely sure of that?' The kitten stretched its limbs again. 'If you breathe in deeply,' Anne-Kathrin had advised her, 'they look at your breasts.' Mimi breathed in deeply. It sounded like a groan.

'Are you in pain?' asked Janki.

'Only because you're treating me like a little girl.' She hadn't had to think for a moment for that answer, and was very proud of herself. 'How does the story go on?'

'She leaves him.'

'Oh.'

'And then she comes back to him. But it's too late.'

'Because she's married to someone else?'

Janki smiled. 'Marriage...The book is called *Scènes de la vie de bohème.*'

'Of course,' Mimi said quickly, because it had dawned on her that a book deals with fantasy, while a marriage, particularly in Endingen...The shadchen Abraham Singer had been to see her more than once, but every time she had asked Golde to send him away. What did she want with cobblers' sons and Talmud students? Gap-toothed Pinchas, the son of the shochet Pomeranz, made cow eyes at her every time he met her, and couldn't say a word. That was why you needed books, because in them everything was different. Because in them the right man was suddenly at the door, and you just had to let him in. 'Of course,' she repeated, and felt very wicked. 'Why should she marry?'

'She gets involved with men,' said Janki and looked her firmly in the eyes. 'Because they give her presents.'

'In the book?'

'In the book. But that happens in reality as well. I have known such girls.

The seamstresses at Monsieur Delormes...Your parents wouldn't want me to tell you about it.'

'My parents aren't here,' said Mimi.

'No,' replied Janki, 'your parents aren't here.'

Salomon Meijer was away again to see to a cow. And Golde – who can count all the things a Jewish housewife has to do, a few days before Pesach? She had to get horseradish for the Seder plate and cover it with soil so that it would stay fresh and hot, she had to attend to the matzos, and she didn't want, only lekoved Yontev, of course, to appear in the synagogue with the same ribbons on the same dress as last time.

Chanele was alone at home when the master butcher Gubser appeared at the door, and at first she didn't even hear his knocking. She had gone up to the attic to bring down the first box of Pesach crockery, and in passing – if she didn't attend to it, who would? – it had occurred to her that the little room needed to be cleaned and aired again. It was a matter of urgency, too. If you pressed your cheek firmly onto the pillow, you could distinctly smell Janki's male smells, of smoke and sweat and very slightly of cinnamon.

The room had been tidied, but the yellow neckerchief with the knotted coins was nowhere to be seen. 'He must have found a hiding-place for it,' thought Chanele, and felt hurt, only for a moment, by such mistrust. The foreign uniform hung stock-straight from a hanger as if still standing to attention. Although Chanele had brushed it out and aired it outside for several nights, a smell still clung to it, probably the smell of war: hay, gunpowder and tobacco. If you closed your eyes...

But Gubser was hammering more violently at the door now, with the heavy stick he always carried to drive on reluctant cattle, and which, if he met one of his good customers in the street, he liked to present as a rifle.

He didn't present arms to Chanele, he just gave a half-bow, impossible to tell whether it was meant politely or as an ironic insult and asked, 'Is Herr Meijer not at home?'

'They're all out and about.'

'I should have guessed. Busy people. Always busy. Like ants.'

'Can I give him a message?'

'That would be charming of you, lovely Fräulein, charming. I am most indebted to you.' Gubser placed his hand on his chest, where something bulged over his heart, probably his money bag. 'Tell him he is a clever man. What they say is quite correct: if a Christian is clever, he's prudent, if a Jew is clever, he's cunning. Tell him it worked.'

'Shall I also tell him what worked?'

'He'll probably know that himself, won't he? Perhaps he doesn't want everyone to find out. Discretion is what they call it. Discretion. He is an intelligent man. Tell him to call in on me. I have something for him.'

'What?'

But Gubser only shook his head, bobbed again in a half-bow and was already walking down the street. Before he turned the corner into Badweg, he gave a little skip, as if on the dance floor.

His path led him past the schoolhouse, where he saw Anne-Kathrin, that blonde with the heavy braids, sitting bent over a piece of embroidery in the bay of the schoolmaster's house. It was a picturesque, very Swiss picture, and Gubser could not know that Anne-Kathrin had neither the patience nor the skilful fingers for such work, and had never finished a piece of embroidery in her whole life. She was only using a pretext to keep watch inconspicuously for her father, who had gone off once again for one of his healthy outings into the open countryside, at a marching pace and with his walking stick over his shoulder. If he came back earlier than expected, she had arranged with Mimi, Anne-Kathrin would immediately run to her own room, which opened out onto the garden and, at the open window, knock out the heavy winter clothes which, now that it was getting warmer, had to be packed up and locked away safe from the moths. The carpet beater, and they had tried it out, made a satisfactorily loud noise that could be clearly heard in the gazebo.

Just behind the gazebo there ran a hedge in which Anne-Kathrin had, while still a schoolgirl, discovered a gap, which she had for various reasons repeatedly extended. You could force your way through there, to a narrow path that led to the river, and if you didn't forget to dab off telltale burrs from your dress, no one could guess how you'd got there.

Janki had flicked on through the book and was now translating a passage in which Rodolphe's enthusiastic eloquence 'by turns tender, stirring and melancholy' gradually won his Mimi over to him. 'She felt', Janki read, 'the ice of apathy that had for so long kept her heart unfeeling, melting from his love. Then she threw herself at his chest and told him with kisses what she couldn't say with words.' He fell silent, and Mimi, whose head, she didn't know how, had leant against his shoulder, made an impatient mewling noise.

'L'aurore – how do you say aurore?' asked Janki.

'Sunrise,' Mimi replied, and had to repeat the word several times. 'Sunrise.'

'Sunrise surprised them in a close embrace, eye to eye, hand in hand, and their moist, ardent lips...'

It had, Mimi later said to Anne-Kathrin, really just been a fly, a fly far too early for the season, that had landed on her nose and startled her, just a desire to get rid of it and shake it off and if her lips had touched Janki's mouth for a moment, had brushed against it only for a fragment of a second, it hadn't been intentional, *certainement pas* and he had, unlike a young man from the village would have done, reacted like a cavalier, which is to say not at all, he had acted as if he hadn't noticed anything, as if nothing at all had happened, and in truth nothing had happened, said Mimi to Anne-Kathrin, nothing at all, they had read a book together, that must surely be allowed, although her mother was always telling her off for her love of literature; if it was up to her, you were just supposed to waste away as a young girl.

Anne-Kathrin agreed and asked her to give a very detailed account of what hadn't happened, how Mimi had said 'Pardon!' quite calmly and coolly, as you do when you accidentally get too close to someone in the market, how Janki had only nodded, but how his eyes, those big, expressive eyes, had looked at Mimi – 'like when someone's thirsty, you understand?' – and Anne-Kathrin understood very well and wanted to hear the whole story all over again, just to be able to confirm to Mimi that it hadn't been a kiss, very definitely not a kiss.

Janki didn't read the sentence he had begun all the way to the end. He even left the book in the gazebo, and Anne-Kathrin later had to hide it under the pillow in her room. On the way home he walked beside Mimi like a stranger, a cousin beside a cousin that he doesn't know any more than that. For a moment Golde had the impression they had had an argument, but she forgot the thought again straight away, because she was much more preoccupied with another matter: master butcher Gubser urgently wanted to talk to Salomon, and Salomon had no idea what it might be about.

When Salomon arrived at Gubser's house, the butcher was still at dinner. His wife, an angular person who had developed a mechanical precision in her movements from cutting sausages and weighing slices, opened the door to the dining room for him, where Gubser and three red-faced sons were bent over their plates. All four looked up only briefly, as they would have looked up briefly from their hymn books if someone had tried to push their way along the pew. Gubser was first to finish his dinner, wiped up the sauce with a piece of bread and then said, still chewing, 'Ah, Herr Meijer! What a delightful surprise! Can I offer you something? A slice of ham, perhaps?'

'You wanted to talk to me, I've been told.'

'I did? I can't remember. But please sit down, my dear, dear Herr Meijer. Are you sure you won't do us the honour of having a little something? No? But you will have a drop of wine. Erika, a glass for our guest!'

They weren't playing the game for the first time. Master butcher Gubser knew very well that Salomon Meijer wasn't permitted to eat anything or drink wine at his house, and his digs had no more meaning than the compliments that he added to the shopping of his lady customers like free soup-bones.

'I don't want to keep you for long,' said Salomon. 'I only came because I was told it was an urgent matter.'

'Matter?' Gubser repeated. He stretched the word out in a questioning tone as if he were hearing it for the first time. 'What sort of matter would the two of us be…?'

'Chanele says—'

'Chanele?' Gubser imitated Salomon's singsong tone so convincingly that his three sons giggled into their plates. 'Ah, the young lady who was so kind as to open the door to me. Quite pretty, if it weren't for those eyebrows.'

'She says you have something to give me.'

'She must have misunderstood. Your people are supposed to be better at talking than listening, after all.' The eldest Gubser son, who was in fact already an adult, laughed out loud, which his mother, without looking up, rewarded with an accurate clip around the ear.

'Then please forgive me for troubling you.' Salomon took the hat that he had been holding in his hand all that time and put it back on.

'Not so fast, not so fast, dear Herr Meijer!' Gubser wiped his mouth with the sleeve of his coat and got up. 'Let's go into the office. The boys don't need to hear everything.'

The room that Gubser called his office was a cramped room with small windows that barely let in any light, because they were hung all over with tin-framed crests. On the table a paraffin lamp illuminated a muddle of bills and letters, the individual stacks weighed down with slaughtering knives and other butchers' utensils. On one of the stacks there was a heavy brass ashtray. Gubser – he had to squeeze in between the table and a standing desk with lots of drawers – sat down in a high-backed chair with carved legs, which would have looked more at home in an old castle than in a butcher's house, and pointed to a matching stool. 'Please!'

'I'd sooner stand, if you don't mind.'

'I do mind, my dear Herr Meijer. You lot must learn to make yourselves comfortable.'

Salomon sat down. As there was nowhere to put his hat, he hung it over the handle of his umbrella.

'Yeeesss…' Gubser leaned back in his chair, and hooked both thumbs in the arm-holes of his waistcoat. 'A farmer,' thought Salomon, 'who has cattle for sale when everyone else has to buy. Someone who looks forward to haggling, because he will always win. He'll be lighting a cigar next.'

'You have one!' said Gubser, holding out the wooden box. 'Or is that for-bidden too?'

'It is permitted. But I don't smoke. I take snuff.'

The lighting of the crude cigar was a laborious process. Gubser riffled through a packet of letters, chose one, rolled it firmly together, held it over the lamp and then, puffing away, twirled the cigar around above the burning paper. 'Yeeesss,' he said again, when the operation was finally concluded to his satisfaction, 'then let us try and discover how this misunderstanding came about.'

'You were at our house this afternoon...'

'Of course, of course. But even given the politeness for which your people are rightly renowned, I would not have expected you to pay me a return visit the same time.'

'You sent me a message...'

'You?' The butcher grinned like someone approaching the punchline when telling a joke. 'Herr Meijer!'

Salomon stared at him uncomprehendingly.

'Or should I say: Monsieur Meijer? What is he? A nephew, a cousin? You can never quite tell with you lot.'

'Janki?' A cattle trader only does good business if you can't see what he's thinking. At that moment Salomon was a very bad cattle trader.

Gubser laughed loudly and complacently.

'What do you want from Janki?'

The master butcher narrowed his eyes, pursed his lips, produced a series of fat smoke rings and watched them slowly floating apart in the gloom. It was only then that he replied, 'I don't know if I'm permitted to tell you this. You wouldn't be too pleased if other people knew about your business deals.'

Again Salomon gave no sign of his confusion. If someone wants to say something and is still playing coy, you will make him talk sooner with silence than with questions.

'But on the other hand,' Gubser said after a pause, 'you are family. Or – what do you people call it? – mishpocha. All one mishpocha.'

Salomon still said nothing.

'This Janki is a good man. Still very young, of course, but not stupid. Not stupid at all. He will go far. Above all he has a good nose...That's not supposed to be a double entendre, my dear Herr Meijer not a double entendre, for heaven's sake. You know that I would never mock the physical properties of other people. Never. He has a very good nose for the right people. A better one than you, if I can put it as directly as that.'

Salomon looked intently at a crest that showed half a red lily on the left and on the right a yellow field.

'He came to me and made me a proposal. A rather surprising suggestion, but an illuminating one. That's right, illuminating. It's about horses. Horsemeat, to be precise.'

Salomon hid his surprise behind a cough and waved the cigar smoke irritably away.

'He made you...?'

'You didn't want to have me in the business, he told me. I don't know why, when we have been working together, is this not so, dear Herr Meijer, so long and so well? You could easily have offered me the business with the contracts.'

The auction in Saignélegier, Salomon had known for two days, had taken place. So why was Gubser in such a good mood?

'How much?' asked Salomon, and his attempt to show nothing but harmlessly polite interest was not very successful, 'How much did you buy from him?'

The butcher laughed so loudly that the cigar fell from his mouth, bounced off the bulge in his waistcoat and, spraying a little volcano of ash and ember, landed on one of the piles of papers. 'Bought?' he panted. The words bubbled up from his laughter, like gas bubbling from a bog. 'I didn't buy!'

It turned out that Janki, after meeting Gubser, had visited him in his shop later the same day and made the same proposal that Salomon had so vehemently rejected: selling horsemeat on contract and then, after the price drop that might be expected, stocking up again much more cheaply. He didn't yet have any contacts here, he had explained, so he needed a partner familiar with the branch. He was prepared to put some of his money at risk, and he had brought his capital with him – 'knotted in a handkerchief, as gypsies do'. He had wanted to go fifty-fifty, but Gubser – 'We've learned Jewish ways from you' – had bargained him down to seventy-thirty; in the end he, the butcher, had had to do all the work. 'And earned the wrath of my colleagues.' It hadn't been hard to find takers, and even easier for Gubser than it would have been for Salomon. He had claimed that he had speculated with his purchases, and now that temperatures had suddenly become so mild, the ice he needed for refrigeration was costing him a fortune. He had sold a lot, and impressed on each buyer that he was to discuss it with no one. 'And they won't, now that they've fallen for it. No one will want to look a fool in front of the others.'

He had wanted to bring his share of the profits, calculated cleanly, or, as Gubser put it, in a correct and Christian manner, to Janki today, and he was sorry, terribly sorry, that he had caused this stupid misunderstanding and startled Salomon like that. 'You probably didn't even come for dinner. Can't I offer you something anyway? Really not?'

But perhaps, said Gubser, and looked for the next letter to relight his extinguished cigar, perhaps dear Herr Meijer would be kind enough to take the money to his nephew, or whatever the relationship between the two of them was, it was ready here in the office, and a decent businessman, strange as it might seem to Herr Meijer, didn't sleep easily when they hadn't paid their debts.

Gubser stood up and pushed his way past the edge of the table. He pulled open one drawer of the standing desk after the other while waving his other hand apologetically behind his back, which was probably supposed to mean: 'You must forgive a person who is involved in as many business deals as I am, if he can't remember every single insignificant detail all at once.' Bending lower he stretched his bottom out towards Salomon. The beginning of a wide, red-and-white striped pair of braces peeped out from below his waistcoat.

'Oh, that's it!' he said at last, in a voice that reinforced Salomon in his conviction that all this searching was a piece of theatre that he was staging for some unfathomable reason. Gubser straightened with a groan – he groan didn't sound convincing either – and held out a packet wrapped in wax paper to Salomon, with both hands, as if it was too heavy to carry it otherwise. The packet was tied tightly and the knot reinforced with a lump of sealing wax, so thick that it would have been enough for ten letters.

'Here!' A good deal for your relative. We could have done the same thing, just you and me. We wouldn't have needed him at all. I might even have given you forty per cent rather than only thirty. But you wouldn't have had sufficient trust in me. A poor knowledge of human nature, Herr Meijer. A very poor knowledge of human nature.'

When Salomon handed the packet to Janki, he didn't react. He went up to his attic room to check the contents, came back down as if nothing particular had happened, and didn't even want to notice the curious faces of the others. He sat down with them at the table, ate herring and potatoes, drank tea, passed the bread when asked to do so, and it was only sometimes – although perhaps Mimi was imagining it – that he didn't immediately notice when someone had asked him a question, and in order to reply he had to bring himself back from somewhere. 'It must have something to do with the book he was reading to me from,' she thought.

Golde held her knife and fork in her hands, two strange pieces of equipment whose purpose she couldn't quite explain to herself, sucked her lower lip deep into her mouth and was chewing around on it. 'There's something different about him,' she thought. 'If he was my own son, would I know what it was?'

'He's a man and not a boy,' Chanele thought and remembered the smell of the uniform.

'I shouldn't have taken him in,' thought Salomon.

Janki pushed his plate away from him and suddenly smiled. 'Is our neighbour Oggenfuss actually a good tailor?' he asked. 'I think I'll have a new pair of trousers made for Pesach.'

6

Three months later Janki had a shop.

He didn't set it up in peasant Endingen, where the Jews lived, as they did in Lengnau, not because the air was so healthy there, but because they hadn't been granted permission to live anywhere else in the Confederation, no, Janki set up his shop in Baden, which wasn't exactly Paris either, it wasn't even Colmar, but it wasn't a village, it was a small town whose inhabitants were interested in things other than the milk yields of their cows and the harvest from their fields.

The cellar, which in everyone's opinion he had rented at too high a price – 'I could get five byres for the same money!' said Salomon – wasn't very spacious. What Janki called 'just right for an exclusive clientele' was in Salomon's words as cramped as shul on Yom Kippur, when everyone forces their way in to clear their debts with God. You might serve perhaps two or three customers in there in elegant intimacy, but it was already getting too cramped for a fourth, and a fifth, if there ever was one, would have to wait pressed against the wall until room came free at the counter. Of course, Janki would have had more surface area for his money in a less prominent situation, but the Vordere Metzggasse, situated between the Weite and the Mittlere Gasse, was the precise spot that he wanted. 'If you want to impress people,' he said, 'you have to be on the Rue de Rivoli and not in some faubourg or other,' an opinion with which Mimi keenly concurred, even though she knew neither where the Rue de Rivoli was, nor what a faubourg might be. Salomon refused to be convinced, and insisted that where he was concerned, he wouldn't pay a higher price for a cow 'just because it shits on gilded straw'. Nonetheless, even if he would never have admitted it, he was starting to like Janki. There weren't many people who knew what they wanted.

One further disadvantage of Janki's new shop was the fact that both spaces had served as a grocer's store-room, and more particularly for his spices. Janki did engage a painter, and even had him come for a second time for good money, but the heavy aroma of ginger, cardamom and nutmeg resisted all attempts to dispel it, dug its way into cracks and crannies from which, particularly on hot days, it crept unsuspected and settled especially in the doors that Jani had fitted over his fabric shelves, so that he could dramatically display his goods by parting the curtains. Even decades later the smell of gingerbread and ginger nuts still reminded many of the residents of Baden of being led by their mother's hand to Frenchman Meijer's shop.

Janki also, after a detailed consultation with Red Moische, had the same painter who had painted the walls make a store sign, *French Drapery Jean Meijer*. As he had little room at his disposal on his narrow part of the façade, the letters were not as big as Janki would have wished, and for the same reason he did not take Moische's advice to leave a little space on the right so that he could later add the words *and Sons*. But there was one thing that Janki did not want on any account to do without: a coat of arms decorated with a little crown, like the ones that court suppliers had on their signs. As a sign for his coat of arms he ordered an orb, the result of which, dashed off unlovingly by the artist, looked more like an etrog, the citrus fruit needed for the rituals of the Feast of Tabernacles.

Even though the grocer would have let him have his own at a good price, Janki had a new counter made, wide enough for him to roll out a length of fabric on it. When the counter arrived, he locked himself in for a whole day and repeatedly practised a gesture that he had admired in Monsieur Delormes; he had had the knack of swirling the massive wooden pole the bale was rolled around through the air without any apparent effort, until the fabric assumed its own weightless life and floated towards the customer with metropolitan elegance. 'You must feel the dress just by looking at the fabric,' Monsieur Delormes had always said.

Janki had his first fabrics brought from Paris. As the cost of the shop's conversion had exceeded his budget, and he had to request a loan as an unknown businessman, there was so little that the doors over the shelves served to hide the gaps rather than present the goods on offer. The selection could have been much bigger had Janki not insisted on having only the choicest materials on offer but, Mimi explained to her hopelessly old-fashioned father, 'If you want to have the best customers, you must offer the best goods.' Along with the order, Janki had sent a letter to be passed on to Monsieur Delormes, in the hope that the famous man might give him a letter of recommendation which, printed in the *Badener Tagblatt*, would certainly make a big impression on the public. So far no answer had arrived, so that Janki had to settle for advertisements and notices, which he signed, 'Jean Meijer, formerly of the most important fashion houses in Paris'.

In spite of his new status as boss of his own company, Janki still lived in his attic room in Endingen. Golde wouldn't have allowed anything else, and with all the expenditure required by the shop, a flat of his own would really have been a needless waste of money. Every morning before six o'clock, without breakfast and with only a piece of bread in his pocket, he walked the two-hour journey to Baden; he had learned how to march, after all, and it was also, he explained, much easier, 'when you know that what awaits you at your destination is not a battle, but at worst a skirmish with a painter or a cabinet maker'.

On the long-awaited day of the opening he wanted to set off as early as possible, but he was held back by Mimi, who was normally extremely reluctant to leave her warm bed. She couldn't have got up early today either, because her hair still fell unkempt over the shoulders of her dove-grey dressing gown. That disorderly frame gave her face a wild, gypsy quality, an expression that suited her very well, as she had established at the mirror. Not without a certain embarrassment she held a present out to Janki, a money bag of soft, red Morocco leather, which she herself had embroidered with the letters J M. A little crown, like the ones on the signs of the court suppliers, hovered over the monogram. As she handed it over, their hands touched, and inside the money bag – was Janki trembling, or was it Mimi? – a coin moved. 'It's only a lucky rappen,' Mimi said quickly, 'so that you do good business and it is never empty.'

'Thank you. Merci. But now I should really...' The sentence lay there, a clock that nobody had remembered to wind.

'Yes,' said Mimi. 'You should.' Her lips were suddenly dry, and she had to run her tongue over them.

'I should be on time today of all days,' said Janki, and still didn't move.

'Today of all days,' said Mimi.

'The money bag is beautiful.'

'Yes,' said Mimi, 'it certainly is.'

'What does J M stand for?'

Mimi didn't understand him. 'Janki Meijer, of course.'

'Shame,' said Janki.

Only Anne-Kathrin, to whom Mimi reported the conversation word-for-word that same morning, could find an explanation for that strange reaction, an explanation so illuminating that Mimi burst into tears and repeated several times in a tone of self-reproach that she was a cow, a silly cow, and if Janki now thought she was a beef cow that you had to lead by a ring through its nose before it noticed where it was going, if he despised her now as a village clod, then she had only herself to blame. Not that she wanted anything from Janki, *certainement pas*, she wouldn't even think of it, but that she had not previously thought about the many ways in which such a monogram could be read, that she could not forgive herself, not if she lived to a hundred and twenty.

J M: Janki and Mimi.

So Janki said 'Shame', without guessing at the whirlwind of truly Talmudic interpretations those two syllables could produce. That Mimi did not immediately understand him certainly had something to do with the fact that at that precise moment Chanele arrived, she too bringing a present to celebrate the opening of Janki's business: a little bundle wrapped shapelessly in a cloth, which she pressed into his hand with an almost reproachful 'There, for you!' as one eventually, and reluctantly, yields to a child's endless pleading. Neither did she wait to see if he would unwrap it on the spot, but disappeared into the kitchen, where she was heard clattering pots and pans around as if they'd done something to her.

Janki shrugged, put the little bundle in the pocket of his coat and set off. Although Mimi stood behind the door for a long time, apparently completely fascinated by a sparrow taking its morning bath in the dust of the street, he didn't turn round.

'Why did you have to get involved?'

'Involved in what?'

'You know exactly what I mean.'

No proper friendship, or even a sisterly feeling, had ever arisen between Mimi and Chanele, contrary to what Salomon had hoped, when he had so unexpectedly brought home a second baby. If Chanele was to replace Mimi's stillborn brother, the plan was a failure; Mimi had, from the very start, resisted her rival, yelling herself sick and hoarse, had tried to peck her away as an old rooster would peck away a young one, had clung weeping to Golde for hours, and later, when she grew older, probably rubbed onions in her eyes to make the tears to which she seemed to lay claim visible for all the world. As Chanele – by her nature, or because no other possible role was open to her – proved to be a quiet, undemanding child, who allowed herself to be ordered about rather than issuing the orders – it soon became quite obvious which, in the old proverb, was the dog and which the flea.

Rather than playing with Chanele, Mimi had chosen to befriend Anne-Kathrin, with whom she could gather pearls and diamonds on the banks of the Surb, while Chanele insisted, with precocious maturity, that they were all only pebbles. When Mimi and Anne-Kathrin rescued the kitten that time, Chanele had only looked at the soaking creature, unmoved, her eyes small with concentration, and then said, 'You know it's a tom? We'll have to have it castrated.' But it then turned out, very much to Golde's relief, that she had just picked the expression up somewhere, and had no concrete idea of what it meant.

Over the years a tradition of mutual disregard had grown up between the two young women, a ceasefire marked on both sides by unspoken contempt.

Only sometimes, mostly begun by Mimi, were there violent arguments, although they didn't clear the air like summer storms, but just went on rumbling and stopped at the horizon with thunder and lightning.

'What do you want from Janki?'

'What am I supposed to want from him?'

'You're giving him presents.'

'Where does it say in the Shulchan Orech that I'm not allowed to?'

'You knew I was sewing a money bag for him! What have you given him?'

'Does that concern anyone but him?'

'I want to say something to you.' Mimi became so friendly that Chanele involuntarily lifted the pottery plate that she was holding in her hand like a shield in front of her chest. 'A man like Janki isn't interested in girls whose eyebrows meet in the middle.'

Chanele put the plate down on the table more violently than she needed to. And the cutlery that she took from the drawer clattered down more loudly than usual.

'What do I care what he's interested in?'

'You gave him something!'

'Don't worry! It isn't a red velvet money bag.'

'Morocco leather! It's Morocco leather!'

'Make Shabbos with it!' For the Sabbath you need very practical things: bread, wine, a piece of meat in your soup. Anything one might ironically compare with those is without reasonable value.

'What have you given him?' In her impatience Mimi held on tightly to Chanele's hand. Chanele pulled away and went on laying the breakfast table.

'A brush.'

'A brush?'

'And a rag.'

'What sort of present is that? A rag?'

So that he can clean his boots. By the time he gets to Baden he'll look as if he's just emerged from a pigsty. Is he supposed to greet his customers with mucky shoes?'

Whether Mimi started laughing out of relief or because she found Chanele's present so pitifully unromantic she couldn't have said in retrospect. Any more than Chanele had an illuminating explanation for why she threw the damp cloth with which she had just wiped out the pan for the breakfast eggs into Mimi's face. Mimi grabbed Chanele by the throat. Chanele clawed her fingers into Mimi's unkempt curls.

When he heard the cries, Salomon Meijer, with his phylacteries still on his forehead and arm, came running from the sitting room, stood helplessly in the doorway and said, because one may not, when one has put on the tefillin, engage in conversation with anyone but God, only: 'Now! Now! Now!' Golde had just been combing her hair, before hiding it once more under the sheitel for the day, and with the thin grey strands over her white nightshirt she looked, like a girl grown old, even smaller than usual. She pushed the two young women apart, a dog separating two cattle much larger than itself, slapped them both roundly and demanded to know – 'right now this minute!' – what evil spirit had possessed them and made them so meshuga in broad daylight.

In their embarrassment, and because they didn't really understand their own behaviour, Mimi and Chanele dismissed it as a harmless squabble between friends, which Golde didn't believe, but accepted for the sake of a bit of peace. Over breakfast the two of them even chatted together, but with empty courtesy, as the Prussian and French negotiators chatted when they interrupted the capitulation negotiations for a bite to eat. As is customary among diplomats, the actual subject was not once mentioned in the Meijer household.

Today the subject did not take the direct path via Ehrendingen, but instead came up through the forest, took a wide detour via the Nussbaumener Hörnli. The route was longer, but on the narrow path at least one did not risk becoming embroiled in a tiresome conversation by a bored market traveller. Today Janki wanted to be all alone, he wanted to savour the anticipation of his first day as a businessman, he just wanted to dream, as he seldom allowed himself to do. In his head he ran through all the polite and yet not submissive phrases with which he would welcome his customers from the very beginning. A first one, equipped with a great deal of taste and even more money, was stepping into the shop in his imagination and was greeted, as Monsieur Delormes had greeted all ladies who didn't look too matronly, with 'Bonjour, Mademoiselle', when a loud voice dragged him from his daydreams. 'The early bird catches the worm!' the voice blared.

It was the schoolmaster, Anne-Kathrin's father, a well-fed, pot-bellied man with a bushy beard, the only one in the village to practise movement for movement's sake, and who had set off at this early hour for a refreshing stroll through the forest. With his checked trousers and his jacket dangling over his shoulder – the walking stick hung in its arm-hole served as a counterweight – he might have been mistaken for an English summer visitor, had his unmistakeable Swiss not immediately destroyed that illusion.

'Ah, mon cher Monsieur!' said the schoolmaster. 'You are the Frenchman who has moved in with the cattle-trader Meijer, are you not? Exactly. Seek and ye shall find! I had no idea that you Frenchies' – he actually said 'Frenchies', a word that Janki had never heard before – 'have learned a lot from Jahn, our father of gymnastics. Amidst the mountain dew! I take this path every day, only in fine weather, of course. If it rains, I stand at the open window with my Indian clubs. Every day! I wanted to found a gymnastics club in the village, but the people here are not very open to new ideas. So be it! The strong man is most powerful on his own.'

'Don't let me hold you up,' said Janki, and pressed himself against a tree to let the other man pass.

'Not at all, not at all! Let's walk together! Anyone who loves walking in the open air is a good friend of mine!'

'Unlike you, I am not on the road for pleasure…' Janki began, but his objection was immediately washed away by the schoolmaster's next torrent of words.

'Pleasure? Well, perhaps it is that too. But above all it is a duty. To nurture your body like a sacred temple. That you may thrive here on earth. Fresh, pious, happy, free! You Frenchies haven't been nearly fresh enough, and far from pious, or else at Sedan the Prussians wouldn't just have…You were there, they tell me.'

'No, I…'

'You will have to tell is all about it! No buts! I'm thinking of setting up a local education association, for all social classes. It isn't just the lungs that need fresh air, the mind does too. *Mens sana in corpore sano!* I will invite you and you will tell us all about the great day. A massacre it was and not a battle. But you will have to excuse me. Words were exchanged enough, now is the time for deeds!' Elbows bent, the schoolmaster set off again and marched puffing up the mountain.

However hard Janki tried, his lovely dream of hordes of contented lady customers refused to come back to life, so he nodded quite crossly to the schoolmaster when, even before Janki had reached the summit, he came down towards him again in the winding gait recommended by Jahn, the father of gymnastics. 'As soon as the association has been founded.'

Even though the other shopkeepers of Baden didn't wait so long, Janki opened his shop at nine on the dot, in the Parisian style. With the chiming of the town bell he turned the key in the lock, left the door open so that the sunlight laid an inviting carpet on the wooden floor, and took his place behind the counter. From that position, since the salesroom was a few steps lower than the street, one could only see headless passers-by passing through the picture-frame of the door: black frock coats floating gravely over the cobbles, uniformed legs stamping as they marched past, once a whole colony of lace-up boots under identical dark brown coats. The only ones who stopped were the dogs. They sniffed after the new smell, and probably wanted to lift their legs to renew their claim to the territory, but were dragged away on their leashes by invisible hands and vanished from the field of vision.

The beam of sunlight on the floor wandered slowly from left to right, and anyone who had the time to concentrate on it could see its shape gradually changing, shortening the higher the sun rose, particles of dust floating above it, performing a gentle, courtly dance, disturbed by not a single draught of air.

You could rest both hands on the counter or just one, you could put your other hand in your pocket or shove it under your jacket like Napoleon, you could rest one forearm on the freshly painted wood, which conveyed an obliging and yet aristocratic impression, you could fold your arms in front of your chest or link your fingers behind your back and stretch inconspicuously, you could walk up and down, bob your knees or balance on one leg, you could open the glass doors over the shelves and arrange the bales of fabric yet more perfectly and enticingly, you could spot a dirty mark on the wall and rub away at it with your sleeve, you could polish your shoes again and, as you used the brush, think of Chanele's clever precaution, you could push the red money bag, the only object in the drawer under the counter, from the right to the left and then back again to the right, you could clear your throat and check whether your own voice hadn't lost all its power after such a long silence and, like the smell of cloves and peppercorns, crept into a dark corner, you could say 'Why?' out loud or shout or bring your fist down on the table, you could do whatever you liked, you were, after all, your own master in your own shop, and there was no one there that you could have disturbed by doing anything at all.

The chimes marking the hours or quarter hours seemed to be following one another more and more quickly, even though the time between them stretched out to infinity. The room, which had seemed so bright and inviting in the morning, now that the sun stood right over the house and no longer sent its rays through the open door, became more and more confined and oppressive. It was already almost midday, and the only visitor to Jean Meijer's French Drapery had been a little boy whose hoop skipped down the steps, bumped into the counter and lay there as if dead. The boy apologised politely and then, at the shrill cry of a female voice, ran quickly out again. Janki would have liked to hold him back, because in the end somebody – dear God, somebody! – wanted something from him.

Just before twelve, when Janki was adding up all the francs and Louis d'or that he had pointlessly and senselessly pulverised for the dream of his own shop, when he was already setting out the arguments for Uncle Salomon, who would, it was true, not welcome his failure, but would comment upon it with the benefit of hindsight, when he was already wondering whether the tailor Oggenfuss could use someone who knew something about fabrics, so, when he – he who lies to himself cheats doubly – was almost ready to admit his defeat, something unexpected happened. A man came into the shop, came down the steps like someone entering a house that he has just bought for the first time, peered attentively around, only then seemed to notice Janki and said with a smile that was more a baring of teeth, 'Jean Meijer – is that you?'

Janki nodded curtly, as Monsieur had done with dubious customers. 'With whom do I have the pleasure?'

'We will find out later whether it is a pleasure or not,' said the man. 'How many customers have you had today?'

'I'm not sure…'

'How many it was, or whether it's any of my business? I can tell you the answer to the first: not a single one.'

There was nothing special about the man. He was about forty, not big and not small, not fat and not thin. He wore a grey suit of heavy tweed, the jacket done in the German style with a belt at the back. An edelweiss made of fabric was fastened to the lapel of his frock coat.

'Did you want to buy anything?' asked Janki.

The man barked with laughter. 'You have a good sense of humour,' he said. 'Gallows humour. Which, as I see it, might be a very suitable expression.' He walked around the counter and, without asking permission, opened one of the doors. He ran two fingers along a dark brown Jacquard material woven with orange flowers, smelled his fingers as if the quality of what he had felt could be read from them, and then said appreciatively, 'Very pretty. Good quality. One might actually feel sorry that no one will be interested in it. Until it is placed on sale when the shop goes out of business.'

Janki clearly felt a blood vessel pulsing in his throat and wondered for a moment if it was the vein that the shochet had to sever cleanly if the slaughtered animal was not to be impure. 'I have no intention of abandoning my shop,' he said, and for the first time he had the feeling that the Yiddish melody made his German sound somehow inferior.

'Nicely put.' The man showed his teeth again. 'But sometimes in life we do things we don't intend to. Have you read the *Tagblatt* today?'

The question was so unexpected that Janki was stumped for an answer.

'There is a very interesting article in it,' said the man. 'Page four.' He pulled a folded newspaper from the inside pocket of his jacket and held it out to

Janki. 'Here. A little courtesy between colleagues. With the compliments of the local shop-owners.'

He stopped again in the doorway, looked around and sniffed. 'Hm. One might wonder: is that still the old spices, or is it already the new stench?'

7

The article 'from our Paris correspondent' sympathetically described the oppressive conditions in the French capital, which had had to endure not only starvation under the Prussian siege, but also the lawlessness of the so-called Commune and the horrors of its bloody defeat. 'Lutetia', the correspondent wrote in flowery terms, 'is like a virgin sorely tried by fate. Even yesterday she still skipped on rosy toes from delightful dance to delightful dance, and today she drags herself wearily through the streets, her features gaunt, more bowed by shame at her own frivolity than by longing for her former glory.' The article spoke of Castor and Pollux, the two elephants from the Jardin des Plantes, whose trunks had appeared, at the height of the famine, in the English butcher's shop on Boulevard Haussmann, 'to give a few wealthy profiteers the chance of one last debauch, while all around wailing infants sought in vain the withered breasts of their mothers'. With revulsion, but also with a certain relish, the author went on to describe the bloodbath at Père Lachaise Cemetery, at which French troops had once and for all put down the uprising of the Communards, 'their blood a bitter but necessary fertiliser, to let the tender sprouts of law and order flourish once more in place of the barricades erected by the deluded fanatics.'

The correspondent went into the greatest detail about the regrettable hygiene conditions in Paris. He described the prevalence of rats and other pests, explaining this not only with reference to the collapse of refuse collection, but also to the fact that their natural enemies, dogs and cats, had ended up in the pots and pans of the starving Parisians, 'and had indeed, even at the most noted restaurants, at Brébant and Tortoni, appeared on menus under the most fantastical names'. As scientists were agreed that rats could spread devastating plagues with their droppings – 'We need think only of cholera, whose hordes of vandals have time and again stormed across our own peaceful land' – the authorities had passed strict rulings to ensure that the two disasters of war and popular uprising were not followed by a third. All supplies of goods and products contaminated by rat droppings – after that hungry winter there were no food supplies left – were to be delivered by decree to the new government, and destroyed by fire under the auspices of the authorities. This draconian measure had led to great losses among many traders and manufacturers, driving some of them to ruin, but had nonetheless been accepted and obeyed in the interest of the health of the nation.

Only, and this passage was marked in red ink in the margin of the newspaper, only a few reckless businessmen whose own dirty profits trumped, as they saw it, the lives of their fellow citizens, had once again found ways and means to evade the law. These people – the correspondent, who had hitherto believed from the bottom of his heart in the natural equality of all peoples and nations, wrote it very much against his will – were almost to a man sons of Abraham. They smuggled contaminated goods, such as fabrics for clothes, out of the country where they were then, only superficially cleaned, sold on by the fellow members of their line, to credulous folk. What a rude awakening awaited these harmless customers, who could not guess that death and pestilence lurked in the goods that they had supposedly acquired at such a keen price! The correspondent had learned with horror that even in idyllic Baden, where one imagined oneself so far from war and revolution, a new shop was to be opened that would offer for sale materials from that self-same city of Paris. Without wishing in the present case to level at anyone accusations which might – and the correspondent's deep-rooted love of humanity led him to hope as much from the bottom of his heart – be unfounded, after weighing up the pros and cons he considered it his duty to raise a warning voice in the public interest. 'Caveat emptor!' he wrote in conclusion, and added for readers without a knowledge of the Latin tongue, the translation, 'May the buyer beware!'

Janki began to crumple the newspaper, then changed his mind and carefully smoothed it out again on the counter.

Pinchas Pomeranz only ever allowed himself to read the *Badener Tagblatt* when, after working in the butcher's shop, he had studied and understood the prescribed passage from the Talmud, his daily page of the Gemara. That Monday it was already after eight o'clock in the evening by the time he had finally battled his way through a particularly tricky passage from the Bava Basra tractate. It had been a hair-splitting and rather boring discussion about the correct level of restrictions surrounding wells, but in the middle the wise Rabba bar bar Chana had suddenly started telling fantastical tales. He talked of a crocodile the size of a city of sixty houses, and a fish so huge that seafarers confused it with an island.

Pinchas was strangely troubled by what he had studied, and picked up the newspaper with a certain relief. He had no real interest in the reports on the debates in the Great Council or the number of cattle at Zurzach Market, but just enjoyed the simplicity and directness of the subjects. He had toiled his way up a steep mountain, and now he was enjoying a few paces on the plain. Usually this reading left him calm and relaxed, but this Monday everything was different. Suddenly he leapt to his feet and ran, in his slippers and still clutching the newspaper in his hand, out of the house, 'like a meshugena', commented his mother, who had been about to bring a piece of fresh honey-cake to his study table.

After a number of detours he found Mimi on the little slope above the bend in the road, where one could sit on a toppled tree trunk and look over the way to Baden as comfortably as if sitting on a garden bench. Not that Mimi had been waiting for Janki with any particular impatience, *certainement pas*, but a letter had arrived for him, a letter from Paris, and it might contain something urgent, something that could not be postponed. And besides, and that would probably be permitted, she had needed to take a short walk in the open air; it was always so terribly stuffy in the house, now that the days were getting warmer.

Pinchas half-ran, half-hobbled towards her. He had lost a slipper on the way, and in his almost bare foot he had stepped on a sharp stone. Unused to running, and breathing heavily, he bared his teeth, making the gap between them look even bigger than usual. 'Miriam,' he struggled to say, 'you must... you absolutely must...'

Anne-Kathrin had always said as much. Shy men saved up their little bit of courage for years, and then wanted to spend all their savings in one go. Mimi sat up straight and held her head inclined slightly to the side, a gesture, she hoped, that would make her look at once incorruptible and unapproachable.

'You absolutely must...talk to Janki,' panted Pinchas.

'Meshuga,' thought Mimi, unaware that Pinchas's mother had said the same thing a quarter of an hour before. 'Does he think I need to request permission from something from Janki? Standing there with his slipper, waving his newspaper around in front of his face and talking nonsense.'

'On no account must he...'

'What?'

'Open his shop. Here! Pinchas waved the paper still more violently. 'Read!'

At first Mimi hadn't a clue what slaughtered elephants and revolting rats might have to do with Janki's drapery. Pinchas had to explain it to her, in a Talmudic singsong, with a lot of 'ifs' and 'thens'. And conclusions drawn from the general to the particular. 'And that's why Janki shouldn't open his shop,' he concluded his disquisition, having recovered his breath.

'He's already opened it. Today.'

'Oh,' said Pinchas.

'His goods are clean, I know that for sure. They might come from Paris, but he ordered them from the best dealer, even though I'm sure there were cheaper ones, and...'

'All goods from Paris are clean,' said Pinchas. 'At least so I assume.'

'But it says here...'

'If I wrote on a piece of paper, "Miriam is ugly", would that make it true?'

'Of course not,' thought Mimi.

'I could...' Pinchas took a deep breath and then said every quickly, like someone who doesn't want to pass up on his very last chance, 'I could use up a whole sea of ink, and it would still be a lie.'

Mimi no longer understood anything at all.

'Because you are fabulously beautiful,' said Pinchas. Anne-Kathrin's theory about shy and economical people wasn't so wrong after all. 'Like a herd of goats from the hill of Gilead.'

'What sort of goats?'

'Your hair. And your teeth... like sheep all of which bear twins. Besides, I've made some enquiries. The gap in my teeth can be got rid of. There's a doctor in Baden, he puts something in, it's called a pivot tooth, and then you can't see it any more. It's expensive, but my father would lend me the money, if you...'

'If I what?'

'If you...' But Pinchas had already spent his small amount of capital, and his voice subsided again. 'Most beautiful of all are the twin fawns grazing among the lilies.'

'What kind of fawns?'

'I'm sorry,' Pinchas whispered and turned bright red.

'You wanted to explain to me...'

'Of course. I'm sorry. What they are writing here—'

'Just sit down! You're making me nervous.'

Pinchas squatted on the very edge of the tree trunk, where there was no danger of accidentally touching Mimi. But he could inhale her smell, of youth and sweat and something he couldn't name. Pomeranzen – bitter oranges – must smell like that, a fruit that he had never tasted, but had looked up in the dictionary because of his name.

'Nu?' When Mimi grew impatient, she resembled her father more closely than she would have wished.

'This article in the paper...Someone has put it there to damage Janki. So that no one buys from him.'

'But if the rats...?'

'Into fabrics they will creep.' As soon as Pinchas was able to argue logically, he became noticeably more confident. 'Which are so tightly rolled that they have to eat their way in. And you would see it in the fabric. No, no, the whole story is one big lie. Except: people will believe it.'

'Why?' There was something pleading in Mimi's voice that touched Pinchas as if she had taken his hand.

'They believe bad things about us. And: it's a good story.'

'You think that's good?'

'I'm sorry. I mean: a good invention. Do you love him?' He hadn't wanted to say that. It had escaped him like a bird, which one has thought long tamed, escaping from a cage.

'Who?'

'Janki.'

'*Certainement pas!*' said Mimi and made her sharp face. 'He really is meshuga,' she thought.

'Because: if that's the case, I would try to help him.'

'You?'

'Yes,' said Pinchas and had to bend very low to examine his socks for holes. 'Because I would also be helping you. And for you...'

'Nu?'

Pinchas knew exactly how the sentence would have continued. But the last remains of his small courage were used up, and all that he could utter was: 'My mother doesn't like darning socks. She prefers baking cakes.' Which, as he reproached himself again and again throughout a long, sleepless night, Solomon would doubtless have left out of his Song of Songs.

After such a sentence you can only get up, walk away and never come back. He left the newspaper on the ground and didn't once look up when he, slouching along on a single slipper, set off on the endless journey home. Had his mother baked honey cakes? He would never be able to eat another honey cake as long as he lived.

When Janki came at last, it was almost dark. He moved as he had often done as a soldier, like an automaton, without a will of his own, impelled only by habit. His head was bowed and he walked straight ahead. Only sometimes, if a dandelion grew in the middle of the road, did he swerve to behead it with a kick. Mimi called him, and he stopped, as an exhausted army unit stops and waits for the next command: if it comes, you will carry it out, if not, you can stay like that until the end of time.

'How was it?' asked Mimi, although the back of his bent neck already told her the answer.

'If no customers come tomorrow, that will be twice as much as today.' He had thought of that sentence as a brave joke, but on the way from Baden to Endingen any humour had been stifled in the dust from the road.

'That newspaper article...'

'Yes,' said Janki. 'That newspaper article. I didn't hear a single shot in the whole war, and now I'm being killed with newsprint.'

'What will you do?'

Janki spread his arms, further and further, as if he wanted to take off and fly away. 'There are enough stables in the world,' he said at last. 'There is always room for someone who can hold a pitchfork. Then, in response to a command that he alone had heard, he set off once more, left, right, left, right. When he passed Mimi, his shoulders were weighed down as if by a kitbag.

Mimi ran after him. 'Here! A letter came for you. From Paris!'

Janki slit open the seal and unfolded the paper very slowly, a condemned man without hope that his request for pardon will be heard. He read the letter, nodded, nodded again, and on his face there appeared the same expression that the dead sometimes wore when their sinews contract and it looks as if they are laughing.

'That fits,' said Janki. 'Monsieur Delormes is dead.'

During the siege of Paris, François Delormes had eaten his fill. He knew a lot of diplomats and officers, and a man has as few secrets from his tailor as he does from his valet. François Delormes had known more than many others what was about to happen in Paris, and he had prepared himself. In the private dressing room reserved for the best customers, he had installed a shelf and filled it over the weeks, with bottles of wine, of course, champagne that makes the heart beat faster, and Burgundy that warms it, but above all with the delicacies that would soon cease to exist, foie gras from the Périgord, in yellow tins that gleamed like the purest gold, oval terrines, in which pheasants and hares slumbered under layers of fat as they awaited their resurrection, baskets of oranges and lemons, sugarloaves lined up side by side, with blue ribbons around their bellies, court officials before a state banquet waiting for the guests to arrive. On the stands, where in times of peace the hangers with half-finished clothes had jostled, there now hung whole hams and sides of bacon, fat sausages from the Ardennes and thin ones from the Belgian border. When the besieging army encircled the city and the roar of the cannons became louder and louder, François Delormes dismissed all his employers, the cutters and the seamstresses, the old ironing ladies and the young girls with the slender fingers who had sewn on the sequins for the evening gowns. He shut himself away in his studio, and while Paris starved he sat alone in his town house on the Rue de Rivoli and ate. When he was found, the leg of a confit guinea fowl was still stuck in his throat; in his greed he had tried to swallow it, all at once.

There was nothing of any of this in the letter, only that the writers regretted to inform Monsieur Jean Meijer that Maître François Delormes had not survived the siege of his city, and that Monsieur Meijer would unfortunately have to start his new business, for which, incidentally, they wished him the very best of luck, without a letter of recommendation. The letter was signed by one Paul-Marc Lemercier, whom Janki remembered as a dry accountant, and to whom the firm now apparently belonged.

'That fits,' said Janki bitterly. 'That fits precisely.'

Dinner time had passed long ago, but there was still a plate ready for Janki on the table. Chanele had kept some soup warm, which, if hours passed and the soup was to stay tasty, represented a lot of effort, but when Janki just sat there and didn't even touch his spoon, she didn't press him and asked no questions. It was Mimi who told her at last what had happened, not mentioning Pinchas once, and reacting furiously. Salomon wanted to know since when she read the papers.

'I'm not a child any more!' she said, thinking, 'You have no idea how little of a child I am.'

'People will forget,' Golde said consolingly, and didn't believe her fine words herself.

Salomon stroked his whiskers, shook his head and said thoughtfully, 'If it is said that a famer has had the plague in his byre—'

'This isn't about farmers!' Chanele cut in, Chanele who never normally involved herself in family discussions. 'It's about Janki.'

'You don't need to worry about me. I'll make my own way. That is: I'll make some sort of way. Somewhere.' As he sat there so dejectedly, behind Janki's narrow face one could sense the gaunt bird-like head that he would one day have as an old man.

'They'll forget,' Golde repeated. 'They'll definitely forget.'

'Why?'

Uncle Melnitz, whom no one had thought about while all the changes and plans of the past few weeks were going on, pushed his chair closer to the table. He was, as always, dressed all in black, and he enjoyed, as always, his own pessimism.

'Why should they forget? They never forget anything. The more absurd it is, the more clearly they remember it. Just as they remember that we slaughter little children, always before Pesach, and bake their blood in matzohs. It's never happened, but even five hundred years later they can tell you how we did it. How we enticed the little boy from his parents, how we promised him presents or chocolate, long before chocolate existed. They know every detail.

'They can describe to you the knife we used, as precisely as if they'd held it in their own hands. They know where we made the cut, at the throat or above the heart, they know what the bowl looks like, the one we caught the blood in, every year, everywhere, because matzohs aren't kosher without Christian blood. They know it all. They can tell you the name of the child, quite precisely. It says so on the saints' calendar. It's never happened, but they remember, they have a grave that they visit, an altar, and on feast days they stove in a few Jewish heads by way of commemoration.

'Forget? They forget nothing. The truths, perhaps, but not the lies. They still know the stories that the Babylonians and the Romans came up with against us, and they tell those stories and they believe them. Sometimes they say, "We are modern people so we know that none of that is true," but they still don't stop believing in it. It's stuck firmly in their heads. Lies have a lot of barbs, they surely do.

'Sometimes you won't hear the lie for a few years, but it's just sleeping then and collecting its strength. Until somewhere a child disappears, or someone remembers a child that did. Then it's wide awake again. Then we're holding the knife in our hands again, the long, sharp knife, then we gather in a circle again with our beards and our crooked noses, then we stab away again, and the child goes on screaming, the poor, innocent, fair-haired child, and we go on laughing as we always laugh, and the blood flows into the bowl again, and again we bake it into our matzohs, and everything is as it was. They don't forget.

'They can name the passages in the Talmud that aren't in it, and which they've all read anyway. They know our commandments, which don't exist, very precisely, they know them better than their own. Forget? Do you really think they forget anything?'

Janki's soup had gone cold long ago, but they were all still sitting around the table, sitting straight on their chairs and not looking at each other. Only Uncle Melnitz had made himself comfortable, had spread himself out and leaned back like someone who has decided to stay for a long time. He talked and talked.

No one listened to him.

Everyone tried not to listen to him.

8

Then Janki did go back to Baden, hopelessly, as one plays to the end a game one has lost, just to count up the points that one will have to pay. To general surprise Chanele went with him. She needed to buy something, she explained, and besides, she hadn't been in Baden for ages, and had an unclaimed day off. Salomon couldn't contradict her on this one, because if one wanted to look at it in those terms, Chanele had never had a day off; she was seen as a member of the family, and for that reason she wasn't paid a wage.

The two walked side by side in silence, so quickly that they repeatedly passed other, slower walkers, a peasant woman with a basket full of chickens, or a basket-maker balancing all his goods piled high on his back. As he marched, Janki kept his eyes fixed firmly forward, and yet he could have described quite precisely what Chanele was wearing: a brown dress of a fabric which was known in Paris as 'paysanne', and which Monsieur Delormes only bought so that he could give a few metres of it to a washer-woman or a seamstress. The fabric was too heavy to fall really loosely, but the tailor – if it had not been Chanele herself – had brought out the waist so skilfully that the skirt puffed out in a bell-like shape at the hips, and swung with every step she took. The round neckline and the sleeves were trimmed with something that looked at first sight like lace, but which was only folded white batist, a material that was normally used for petticoats and night-shirts, for everything, Janki had learned that touches the skin directly.

Chanele's petticoat, he was sure, was bound to be of less fine a material, and her blouse...

'You shouldn't have taken the trouble,' he said. 'I would have been happy to bring you whatever it is that you need.'

'Thank you,' Chanele replied. And then, ten or twenty paces later, 'It's something that men know nothing about.'

Her hair was, as always, rolled up in a bun and pushed into a net. For the journey she had put on a headscarf and sometimes, because she needed to cool down or was lost in thoughts, she put her hand to the back of her neck and lifted the bundle of hair a little as if to test its weight. Janki's father had always done that with his money bag when the last farmer had gone and he wanted to assess his takings.

Janki tried to imagine how long Chanele's hair might be, whether when she combed it it reached to her belt or even further, and whether in bed at night...

'It could be a hot day,' he said.

'Even hotter if you have to iron the laundry,' she said.

Chanele walked at the same pace as he did, left, right, left, right, without, as most women would have done, tripping along after his long soldier's stride. She must have had powerful legs, and yet, to judge by the slenderness of her arms, they were certainly not thick. You could imagine that Chanele...

'What are you going to do now?' she asked.

Janki had to reflect for a moment before he remembered why he was travelling to Baden.

'He could just as easily have stayed here and learned something from me,' said Salomon Meijer. He was sitting at the table in the sitting room and had set out a fat book and a stack of papers and notes. 'This business about blood lines is an extremely interesting matter.'

Golde, the hard working woman, considered Salomon's big project of drawing up the definitive family tree of all the Simmental cows kept in the district to be impractical nonsense, but she didn't contradict her husband. But as they had been married for a long time, Salomon still responded to her reservations.

'If I ever finish it...'

'If,' thought Golde.

'...one will be able to predict whether a cow is worth something even before it is born. And not only me, but someone who hasn't the first notion about beheimes. Like Janki, for example.'

'He isn't even interested in it.'

'He will be. He can forget all about his drapery store, that meshugas. But he has a head on his shoulders, and if he involved himself in the cattle trade...'

'Do you think he really likes Mimi?' Golde had skipped over a whole chain of 'ifs' and 'thens', but she had only arrived at the spot where Salomon was already.

'If he isn't an idiot...' said Salomon Meijer.

'No,' said Golde, 'an idiot he isn't.'

They could talk as openly as this because Mimi had gone for a walk again. 'You've been going for lots of walks lately,' Salomon had grumbled, but then he had decided not to enquire into the matter any further. He wouldn't have received an answer, or at least not an honest one. Because Mimi's path took her not into the countryside but into the middle of the village, to a door that she normally avoided if possible, to a very surprised Sarah Pomeranz.

Mimi had set out very precisely the story she wanted to tell: how her father had claimed she couldn't even make an omelette without burning it – he had actually once said something similar – and how she had then planned to surprise him, to prove her culinary arts, with a home-made cake. 'It will have to be a very special cake,' she was going to say, 'a cake for King Solomon in person. I only know one person in Endingen who can give me the recipe for such a cake, so...' But when Sarah opened the door, swathed in an aura of rosewater and bubbling oil, her concerns about Janki were greater than all her plans, and Mimi only said impatiently, 'Where is Pinchas?'

'Where do you think? In the shop.'

There can hardly be a less favourable moment to meet the woman you dream about every night than when you are precooking cow's intestines. Your hands aren't just dirty, they're repellently slippery, you look like an old maid because you've tied a cloth around your hair so that the smell doesn't linger in it, and worst of all you can't interrupt your work. Intestines precooked for too long fall apart and can't be used for sausages.

'You'll have to excuse me,' said Pinchas, 'but...'

'Don't stop!' He bent obediently over the steaming pot and stirred around with a big paddle with holes in it, the kind also used in laundries. The steam had covered all the surfaces with a pattern of tiny drops.

'Wouldn't it be better if we waited until...?' asked Pinchas.

But Mimi felt that she had a mission, and a mission can't wait. Not even if there's a sickly, rotten stench in the air and you've just stepped in some yellowish-green sludge. 'First of all,' she said, just as she had planned to on the journey, 'first of all' – she had at last found a relatively clean spot where one could stand without touching anything – 'first of all one thing must be clear: nothing can come of us. Ever.'

'But...' said Pinchas.'

'Never.' Mimi felt like a character in a novel.

'What if my father lends me the money for the pivot tooth?'

'It has nothing to do with that.'

'I fell because I was reading as I walked, and tripped. That's how I knocked my tooth out. But with a pivot tooth...'

'Enough about your wretched pivot tooth!' The conversation wasn't going as Mimi had planned.

'I know it looks ugly.'

'You're not ugly.'

'Do you really think so, Miriam?'

It wasn't easy to tell through the clouds of steam, but Mimi actually had a sense that Pinchas was blushing.

'I mean...' she said.

'You've just made me very happy.'

He just didn't seem to understand what she was trying to say to him. Luckily a sentence occurred to her, one that she had liked a great deal in a book and which suited the situation perfectly. 'Our hearts don't sing the same tune,' she said.

'What sort of tune?' asked Pinchas.

'No tune. Forget the tune!'

'You said...'

'I was going to say: you and I are just too different.'

'Of course we're different,' said Pinchas and bent low over his pot. 'I'm a man and you're a woman. So—'

'Are you even listening to me?' asked Mimi.

But Pinchas had stopped listening. He had spotted from some change in the stock pot that the right moment had come, so he hauled the paddle out, the pale white intestines snaking from it, laid it over the edges of the pot and then – Mimi felt a bitter taste rising in her throat and couldn't look away – then he grabbed the revolting, wobbly stuff with his bare hands, pulled it hand over fist out of the brew and hung it in dripping garlands on a stand.

'So,' Pinchas said at last and walked over to her, 'now we can talk.'

Mimi started retching.

In Baden, Chanele was being shown around the shop that she'd already heard so much about, and saying, because Janki seemed to expect as much, a few words of praise about the establishment. She felt as if she was being challenged to say something about the carpentry of the coffin-maker at a funeral. All the time when she was in the shop not a single customer appeared, and when she left to go shopping, Janki was standing forlornly behind his new counter, a little boy with a birthday present that the other children don't want to play with.

Red Moische, and also the pedlars by whom Endingen was sometimes overrun as if by ants in the spring, feared Chanele as an expert customer. She knew how to test the firmness of a hem with her teeth, and which colour the gills of a carp should have if it was really fresh. Golde even let her go shopping for the chicken on Shabbos, and Chanele only had to look at a bird to predict to within half a cup how much fat it would produce. Here in the town everything was different. The shops were strange, the traders unfamiliar, and Chanele didn't even know exactly what kind of shop she should do her shopping in. She stood for a long while in front of a shop window full of all kinds of tools, before walking on. She was already holding the handle to the door of the hardware shop, but she didn't like the look of the owner, who was smiling at her so expectantly through the glass. In the end she decided for a barber.

When the shop doorbell rang, three men turned their heads to her at once: the barber, his customer and a man dressed in grey who, *Tagblatt* in hand, was waiting to be served. Only the hairdresser's wife, ensconced on a high chair behind the till, didn't seem to notice her. The three of them studied Chanele for a moment, saw nothing worth looking at, and resumed the conversation they had been having when she came in.

'Now finish your story, Bruppbacher,' said the customer. When he talked, only the freshly shaven half of his face seemed to move, while the other, behind a thick application of soapy foam, lay dead next to it.

The barber was dressed like an artist, with a narrow neckerchief tied into a bow. On his upper lip there sat a waxed moustache that ended in a point, the masterpiece that a craftsman proudly puts on display in his window. 'Certainly, Doctor,' he said. 'So the man waits and waits. Eventually the landlord closes the book and says, "Sorry, we have only one very small room free. And I'm sorry to say that your nose wouldn't fit in it."'

The man with the foam on his face laughed.

The waiting man lowered his paper. 'Vulgar,' he said disapprovingly. 'Jokes don't solve problems.'

'Excuse me.' Chanele took a step into the barber's shop. 'Do you have razors?'

'No,' the barber replied, 'I shave my customers with a spoon.'

The man in the chair laughed so violently that he blew scraps of foam into the air.

'I mean,' said Chanele, 'what I meant was: do you have razors for sale?'

'Of course,' said the barber. 'I sell razors and tobacco and silk stockings. Welcome to the Baden emporium!'

The visible half of his customer's face turned crimson. He had choked on the shaving foam out of sheer delight.

'Have some manners,' the man in the grey suit said reproachfully and turned to Chanele. 'What kind of razor were you after?'

'I think I've come to the wrong place.' Chanele was about to turn to leave, but the man grabbed her arm and wouldn't let go.

'No, no, tell us! What kind of razor do you need?'

Chanele looked at the floor in embarrassment. She tried to free herself, but the man's hand was as firm as iron. Then she whispered almost silently: 'I thought a barber...If you want to remove facial hair...'

'Facial hair?' The man's fingers ran almost tenderly over the flower in his lapel. 'We can't help you there, I'm afraid. If you'd needed one to slit your

70

throat, we'd have been happy to help you.' He said it so politely, without raising his voice, that it took Chanele a few seconds to understand his meaning.

The man in the shaving chair only started laughing then as well.

The barber's wife, who had followed the whole conversation with an expressionless face climbed down from her high chair and pushed Chanele towards the door. 'It's better if you go now. Can't you tell that you're not wanted here?' she said.

Mimi would never have thought that she would one day be sitting with Pinchas in Anne-Kathrin's gazebo. But she had to talk to him, she needed fresh air, and there aren't many places in a village where you can go unobserved. They sat as far away from one another as the hexagon of the bench allowed. Pinchas stared out into the garden as if he was interested only in rosebushes and bunches of elderflower. Without noticing, he kept sticking the tip of his tongue through the gap in his teeth; it looked as if there was something alive in his mouth.

'Yesterday you said you'd try to help him. Help us. Help me.'

'I'd do anything for you.' The sentence had been waiting a whole night to at last be uttered, and it forced its way out of Pinchas like a prisoner from his dark cell.

'Even though you know...?'

'Not the same tune. I've understood.' Pinchas lowered his head. He would have had quite an attractive profile if it hadn't been for that sparse beard. And the gap in his teeth, of course.

'Janki and I, on the other hand...' She sensed that she was hurting Pinchas by saying these words, and it wasn't an unpleasant feeling. How had they put it in that Mimi novel? Savage brutality.

'Do you see any possible way of helping him?' she asked. 'That article...'

'I've thought about it.'

'And you could...?' Her voice suddenly sounded wheedling, a child that wants something it hasn't really deserved. He knew this voice was a lie, but he happily allowed himself to be lied to.

'You know what I learned yesterday in Gemara?' he asked and added quickly: 'It's relevant. I think it's relevant.'

And so it came to pass that Pinchas, in the gazebo of the goyish schoolmaster, told the story of Rabba bar bar Chana, who claimed that while on a sea voyage he had encountered a fish, entirely covered with sand and grass and so big that people thought it was an island, that they disembarked and lit a fire on the fish to prepare their dinner. Mimi didn't interrupt him until he had also told her how the fish, when it felt its back getting hotter and hotter, plunged into the water, and all the seamen would have drowned if their ship hadn't been anchored so close by. Only then did she ask, 'And what are you telling us?'

'Well,' said Pinchas, 'of course the story isn't true. Any more than the story in the paper is true. And even so, our sages in Babylon wrote it down and put it in the Talmud. Then the question arises: why?' Pinchas lapsed back into the tune of a Talmudic disputation. 'What could the reason be? Are we to learn something from the story? Are we to believe that there are fish that people can mistake for islands? Hardly. The Amoraeans who wrote the Talmud were practical people. They were concerned with barriers for artesian wells and things of that kind. They knew that history was a fairy tale and still they preserved it for later generations. What reason might they have had for that?'

'Nu?' thought Mimi.

'Might it not be that they simply liked the story? Because it was a good story? Because people like to believe good stories? Even though they know that they can't be true? What do you think?'

'I don't understand.'

'I've been thinking about it: they put a story in the paper so that no one would buy from Janki. So we have to come up with a better story to make them change their minds. They're lying? So be it. We'll just lie better!'

Chanele had spent a long time sitting on the edge of the fountain, dipping her arm into the water. She felt as if she had to wash the man's touch off her, as if his hand on her sleeve had left a stain that everyone could see on her. She herself didn't understand, couldn't explain to herself, why she hadn't just pulled away and pushed him off, why she had answered him, why she had answered him in front of those men, why she had spoken of something that didn't even concern Golde, why she had let him...

'There you are,' said an unfamiliar voice. Chanele spun round and lifted her arms as if to ward off a blow.

It was the barber's wife, a bony, matter-of-fact person that you could have imagined behind a market stall if there hadn't been a smell of talcum and face lotion about her. 'I've been looking for you everywhere,' she said.

'Leave me alone!' Chanele heard herself talking in a strange voice, fearful and insecure.

The woman sat down next to her on the edge of the fountain. 'Careful,' she said after a pause, 'you're making your dress all wet.'

Chanele defiantly plunged her arm even deeper into the water.

'They're men,' said the woman. 'Men need enemies. I don't know why. It seems just to be something inside them.'

'What do want with me?'

'If they speak,' said the woman, 'then you have to let them speak. There's nothing you can do. But I wasn't happy about the way they treated you. Why did you come into our shop, of all places?'

'I thought a barber...'

'There are six barbers in Baden. Five other barbers. Everybody knows my husband doesn't like Jews.'

'I didn't know,' said Chanele, feeling guilty. 'I just wanted...'

'I heard what you wanted.' It sounded like a reproach. 'Completely wrong. You don't do something like that with razors. You have to pluck. It hurts, but you'll survive. Here.' She held a tin out to Chanele.

Chanele folded her arms.

'As you wish,' said the woman. 'I don't care.' She dropped the tin into the fountain and got to her feet. 'But you'd really look a lot prettier without those eyebrows.'

On her own again, Chanele looked at the tin for a long time. It hadn't sunk, but floated, turning gently bobbing circles on the surface of the water. On the lid, two heads stared into the distance: an English officer with a bushy moustache and a dark-haired man in a turban. Above the picture it said in ornate writing: *Original Indian Macassar Hair Pomade*. The tin seemed to be trying to make its way towards her again and again, and each time it did, before it reached the edge, it was driven away again by the stream of water from the fountain pipe.

At last Chanele reached into the water, fetched the tin out and opened the lid. The tin seemed to be full to the brim with crumpled paper, the firm, light brown paper that is pulled over the head-rests of barbers' chairs. It rustled when she unfolded it.

When she saw what the strange woman had brought her, Chanele's eyes filled with tears.

It was a pair of tweezers.

'He fought in the Battle of Sedan,' said Pinchas.

'He says he never heard a shot.'

'Could be. But that doesn't make a good story. And of course he was wounded. A bullet went through his arm.'

'Heaven forbid!' Mimi cried in horror.

'You're right, Miriam,' said Pinchas, 'let's leave his arm alone.'

Mimi nodded with relief.

'He needs his arm for his work. They shot him in the leg.'

'What?'

'You choose which one.' Pinchas laughed. He was completely transformed, he talked uninhibitedly, gesticulated and kept interrupting Mimi.

'That tailor he worked for in Paris. What's his name?'

'Delormes. But he's dead.'

'Dead?' said Pinchas and nodded contentedly. 'That's good. Then he won't contradict us. And this friend of yours, what's her name?'

'Anne-Kathrin. Is she going to appear in the story as well?'

'She's going to lend us paper and ink,' said Pinchas. 'We've got to write it all down.'

9

'An interesting anecdote from the Franco-Prussian War. During the siege of Paris – our correspondent reported extensively on this in these very pages – a series of events began which will provoke shock and sympathy in the heart of any well-intentioned and sensitive human being. We have no wish to deprive our dear readership of the report that has only lately reached our ears, not least because the chain of events in its outermost link has also touched our lovely town of Baden, confirming the saying of the Greek philosopher Heraclitus that war is the father of all things.'

Pinchas, who read the *Tagblatt* every day, had insisted on the convoluted sentence construction. The classical quotation was supplied by Anne-Kathrin, who had a large supply of them thanks to her father.

'Our lady readers, particularly if they regularly study *Die Dame* or *Jardin des Modes*' (a contribution from Mimi) 'will be familiar with the name François Delormes. This master of the needle, as effusive admirers have praised him in the past, proudly refused, in spite of the requests of his many friends and admirers, to leave his beloved native city before the outbreak of hostilities. In a reversal of the cynical saying, he would dismiss all warnings with, *Ubi bene, ibi patria.*'

If it had been up to Anne-Kathrin, Monsieur Delormes would have added, '*Dulce et decorum est pro patria mori.*' But Mimi and Pinchas had firmly rejected that one.

'The steely grip of the siege was closing ever more tightly around the French capital, and soon the city of lights sank into leaden darkness. The fearful silence of a hospital reigned where once everyone had sung and danced so gaily. Where the Erinnyes rule, the Muses fall silent.'

Pinchas had to explain to the others what Erinnyes were, and Mimi, who had always taken him as a pure student of the Talmud, was surprised by his knowledge.

'Food supplies were growing increasingly scarce. Each inhabitant of Paris was given a daily allowance of just a hundred grammes of bad bread, and anyone who managed to acquire this pitiful amount for himself and his loved ones considered himself lucky.

'For François Delormes, who had been made rich long since by the popularity of his fashionable creations, it would have been an easy matter to escape the restrictions of these days of starvation and buy the choicest delicacies from the profiteers who, as everyone knows, multiply like bluebottles on a carcass in times of need. But nothing could have been further from this brave man's mind. He had the contents of his cellar distributed among the needy, and he himself settled for water and dry bread.'

Inspired by his newly discovered journalistic talents, Pinchas had also sketched out a passage in which Monsieur Delormes set one day each week aside for fasting, but the others deleted it again as being too Jewish.

'But that was not enough! When the siege was at its worst François Delormes gathered his closest colleagues around him—'

'Colleagues?' asked Anne-Kathrin. 'Doesn't he have any family?'

'That wouldn't be good for the story,' said Pinchas.

'—and informed them of something that was to shock them to the very core. In spite of his seventy years—'

'Sixty,' Anne-Kathrin suggested.

'Fifty,' said Mimi.

'In spite of his mature years he had volunteered for the national guard, to go to the front and face the foe who were making his beloved native city endure such hardships. Everyone tried to talk him out of his decision, knowing that in the given situation it would mean certain death—'

'*Dulce et decorum*,' said Anne-Kathrin.

'Sha!'

'—but François Delormes would not be dissuaded either by pleas or by tears. With admirable calm and circumspection he sorted out his affairs, determined a successor to carry on the business of the fashion house as well as possible, and gave this successor, one Paul-Marc Lemercier, his first and at the same time his final commission. "The best worker I have had in the last few years," he said, "the only one I found truly worthy one day to wear my mantle, is as I speak fighting somewhere in France against the mighty foe. I don't even know if this master pupil of mine is still alive, or whether an enemy bullet might not have whipped him away. But be that as it may: the best fabrics, the most artful materials from my studio, I leave to none other than to him. If he is no longer alive, then let them crumble to dust rather than belong to someone else less appropriate to the task. I therefore determine that a cart bearing this precious cargo be dispatched today on the way towards his native town—"'

'Where does Janki come from?'

'Guebwiller.'

'No one's heard of it.'

'"—on the way towards Colmar, and await him there until he or his coffin returns from the battlefield."'

'With the shield or on the shield!' said Anne-Kathrin.

At that point a problem arose which nearly defeated them: how do you transport noble material from a city hermetically encircled by the enemy? But Pinchas, inspired by Rabba bar bar Chana, who had a snake swallow a crocodile as big as a whole city, again found a solution here.

'That night Paris enjoyed a spectacle unparalleled in the annals of wars and sieges. A member of parliament appeared in the front box holding a white flag, and handed the German officer a letter addressed to his most senior commander. No one will ever know what the King of Tailors wrote to the King of Prussia, but it is well known that François Delormes supplied many royal houses, and that a manikin with the exact measurements of the Prussian monarch stood in his studio for many years.

'Be that as it may, it is a fact confirmed by a considerable number of witnesses that on that same night a heavily laden cart, drawn by four horses, rolled out of Paris and through a cordon of Hessian hussars on the road to Colmar.

'In the early morning of the following day François Delormes was mown down in a reckless grenade attack from a very short distance. Nothing was left of him but his hand, with which he had wielded the needle more masterfully than any other.'

Anne-Kathrin dried her eyes with the red silk ribbon that held her braid together, and Mimi too felt strangely moved.

'But the moving finger writes, and having writ moves on.' (Anne-Kathrin.) 'The receiver of this unusual transport, the only person that François Delormes had considered worthy as his successor, knew not the slightest of any of these events, for he lay unconscious in a German military hospital, his delicate yet manly face' (Mimi) 'aglow with fever. The Carmelites who tended to him self-sacrificingly, had long since abandoned all hope for him.

'How does a French soldier end up in a German military hospital? Many of our readers may rightly ask that question. But here too we must mention a whole concatenation of events behind which one may, however devoted one might be to the factuality of modern science, see the hand of providence.

'François Delormes' inheritor had been hit in the leg by a bullet in the great battle of Sedan, but dragged, with an effort that we can only describe as superhuman, another soldier who seemed to be more seriously wounded than he was himself, out of the deadly rain of bullets.'

'Wonderful,' said Mimi.

'There's better to come,' said Pinchas, delighted by her praise.

'This other man, whose life he saved with his heroic deed, was not a Frenchman, but a Prussian soldier. Seldom has it been possible to confirm so beautifully that the voice of humanity knows neither states nor borders. And so it came to pass that the two men, the rescuer and the rescued man, were operated upon the same day and lay bed by bed, in the same field hospital. One of them recovered. The other, whose wounds were inflamed, spent a long time waiting on the narrow ridge that divides this world from the next.'

'*Media in vita in morte sumus*,' Anne-Kathrin suggested, and Pinchas wrote it down.

From then on, the job became easier and easier. Pinchas, who was for the first time able to put his imagination, those pointless daydreams as his mother called them, to good use, wrote faster and faster. Only a paragraph later Janki opened his big sad eyes, modestly dismissed the attestations of gratitude from the soldier whose life he had just saved, and returned at last to his home town of Colmar – 'No, Miriam, absolutely not Guebwiller!' There to his inexpressible surprise he found the fabrics…

'…fabrics which have particular value not just because of their origins in the famous studio of the tragically departed François Delormes, but perhaps still more the fact that they left Paris even before the great plague of rats that our correspondent has so vividly evoked, and are thus hygienically quite unimpeachable.'

'Yes!' said Mimi and clenched her fist.

'Their owner who, after all the dramatic events that he lived through at such a very young age, yearns for nothing so much as tranquillity, decided to emigrate to the peaceful land of Helvetia, where he could offer his unexpected treasure-trove on sale to a select clientele. Avoiding any public brouhaha, he has asked us not to mention his name, a request with which we are of course more than happy to comply. So we must content ourselves with revealing to our honoured readership that Jean M. has set up his modest shop in one of the oldest and certainly one of the most beautiful towns in our Canton, and that the shop is open every day apart from Saturday and Sunday between the hours of nine in the morning and seven in the evening.'

'You're meshuga!' said Janki. 'What will I do if anyone asks me whether it's all true?'

Mimi smiled a conspiratorial smile. 'You deny it all, of course. Not a word is true, you say. Or it's about a completely different Jean M. Pinchas says if you say it's a lie everybody will believe it.'

It hadn't even been difficult to place the story in the paper. Anne-Kathrin, who as the daughter of a schoolmaster had the loveliest handwriting, copied the text out neatly, and a market driver who was going to Baden anyway dropped it off at the editorial office. The editor was a queer customer who saw himself as a bit of a scholar, and who devoted more attention to the four-volume *History of the County of Baden*, upon which he had been working for years, than he did to the contents of his newspaper. He scanned the article briefly and then sent the office boy to take it to the setter.

'"Master pupil!"' said Janki furiously. 'I was a shlattenschammes! I worked in the textile warehouse!'

'You want to sell textiles too,' Mimi replied, thinking, 'He should be grateful to me. Why's he getting so worked up?'

On the stroke of nine the first customer was waiting outside the shop door on the Vordere Metzggasse. When it remained shut in spite of her knocking, she went home again and said to her cook, 'He hasn't come today. His injury is probably causing him too much pain.'

'Sedan!' said Janki. 'I don't know anything more about the battle than the things people say about it!'

'Neither does anyone else,' said Mimi.

In a barber's shop in Baden a customer reading a newspaper was so startled by something he had just read that he jumped, jerking his head so violently that the razor cut deep into his cheek. 'Be careful, Bruppbacher!' he cried furiously. The barber's wife slipped from her high chair and brought alum and a cloth to dab the blood from his grey suit.

'And I'm not going to Baden!' Janki said for the third time. 'Never again.' He hooked his fingers together behind the back of the chair as if someone were trying to pull him away.

'So that man was right? Selling out because of the abandonment of the business?'

'No, of course not,' said Janki. 'But...'

'You have a visitor.'

Even before Chanele could ask him in, the schoolmaster had pushed his way into the room, flying out of the corridor like a cork out of a bottle, talking already. 'Mon cher Monsieur! And, oh yes, Fräulein Meijer. My compliments. I guessed as much! Is that not so? I felt it. Unless you feel, naught will you ever gain. If everyone is after you now, don't forget that I was the one who invited you first. My popular education association! You must be our first guest. You must. As soon as it has been founded. Oh, such furore there will be! Furore, I tell you. No smoke, no mirrors.' He waved a walking stick with a carved handle as if conducting an orchestra.

'I don't quite understand what you...'

The schoolmaster nodded, as if he had no intention of stopping. 'Discretion,

I understand. "Jean M." and not a letter more. My lips are sealed. Whether it's Meili or Müller or – I only suggest this as an example, purely theoretical – or Meijer, it matters not in the slightest. A rose by any other name would smell as sweet. But when I opened the *Tagblatt* today, it was clear to me straight away…Oh my apprehensive soul!'

'The article to which you are probably referring has nothing to do with me!'

Pinchas had not been mistaken: only now did the schoolmaster fully believe the story.

'Such exemplary modesty!' he crowed. 'I knew at once. But I should still like to make one request. If you happened to have a fabric in your storeroom that would suit a young girl…Do you know my daughter? Of course you don't. Why should you? She hardly ever sets foot outside the door. Full many a flower is born to blush unseen. A piece of fabric, as I say, for a dress. Not too dear, obviously. As a schoolmaster one doesn't have two pennies to rub together. Although: *Non scholae sed vitae*…But I don't want to hold you up. Please forgive the intrusion, Fräulein Meijer.'

He stopped in the doorway, came back and laid his walking stick on the table. 'Here. I nearly forgot this. For you. After such an injury you will certainly find walking far less strenuous with something to lean on. The handle is a lion. The most heroic of beasts for the most heroic of men. But never forget, my young friend: brave can be the merest slave. Discretion is the better part of valour. It has been a pleasure, Herr Meijer. A real pleasure.'

Janki's shop was not exactly overrun, but neither did he have to wait so much as half a day or even half an hour for custom. It was the old women and the very young women who discovered the French Drapery before everyone else. At first they visited the vault out of curiosity, and probably whispered when the elegant young Frenchman brought a heavy bale of fabric from a shelf – with *one* hand! – and hid his limp so bravely. At first Janki took his stick reluctantly to the shop, but soon he found himself reaching for it without even thinking, indeed, that he felt something was missing if he wasn't holding it in his hand. And what was wrong with that? If Salomon had an umbrella, why should Janki not have a stick?

Very gradually he became used, when walking, to letting one leg – not always the same one, until in the end he settled on the right one – drag very slightly behind the other and sometimes, particularly when he had been standing behind his counter for a while, it seemed to him that he could actually feel a dull ache in it. When his customers asked him questions, which – and this was a pleasant side effect as far as his revenue was concerned – they thought appropriate only after the third or fourth visit, he only shook his head and smiled wistfully, which could be interpreted either as regret over the persistence of a ridiculous story, or as a painful memory. It became customary among the better ladies of the town to try out on him the French that they had picked up in their afternoon conversation circles, and Jean Meijer not only understood them, but praised their pronunciation.

The cramped space of the cellar proved to be more and more of an advantage. In the French Drapery one felt as if one were not in a shop but in a salon, as if one were not a customer, but a guest, and if Janki, as sometimes happened, had to send a customer away because at that moment sadly, sadly, there was simply no more room for her, he filled all the others with pride.

There was also the fact that Janki really did know something about fabrics, and his goods, whether one really believed in their mythological origins or not, were of good quality. It was not long before he was able to order new fabric from Paris for the first time, and soon the doors over the shelves were to close only at the end of the day; there were no more gaps to hide, and as the press of customers grew there was no more time to be wasted on superficial fripperies.

The man in the grey suit was never seen again, but Janki sensed his undiminished interest behind the intensified attention that the market police paid him and his shop on an almost daily basis. Once when he offered the inspectors a special discount on purchases made by their wives, something that would have been par for the course in Paris, they even threatened him to report him to the governor for attempted bribery.

'I will have to engage a clerk,' he said in the kitchen one evening.

Very much to Salomon's annoyance the orderly rhythm of life in the Meijer household had been thrown increasingly out of kilter. At dinner they all waited until Janki was back from Baden, and he was often late, although lately he had been recognised more and more often, and was therefore given lifts by carts and even carriages. Salomon could drum reproachfully on the table top as much as he wanted, his impatient 'Nu?' was simply ignored. Once Golde even asked him, 'Is it too much to ask for you to wait a few minutes for the boy?' 'For the boy,' she said, as if this Janki weren't just a shnorrer who'd wandered in from somewhere, a shnorrer who happened to be a relative, fair enough, but a shnorrer none the less.

And when he did finally deign to arrive, in boots that Salomon had given him, and carrying that ridiculous walking stick, he didn't even apologise for keeping the head of the household waiting with his stomach rumbling, but let the three women of the house go clucking around him, dancing around him as if he were the Golden Calf, did all the talking at the table, talked about his constantly rising profits and the new, even bigger order that he planned to make over the next few days, and if he did once in a while ask about Salomon's business deals, the question had, in Salomon's ears, a certain condescending quality, like someone with twenty cows in the byre kindly inquiring about his neighbour's rabbits. No, in those first few weeks Salomon was not happy about Janki's success. He saw himself being displaced from the centre of the family, he sensed a hidden irony behind every politesse, an ageing territorial prince spotting conspiracies everywhere, unable to show his annoyance because it would have been interpreted as envy. But what Janki had said a moment before, That was going too far. Engaging a clerk! And perhaps a liveried coachman and a valet while he was about it?

'I have run my business on my own for a lifetime and it has done me no harm whatsoever,' said Salomon. He reached his hand out towards the bowl of coleslaw and noted with satisfaction that Golde, Mimi and Chanele all leapt up at once to pass it to him. 'Employees cost more than they're worth.'

'A textile shop and a cattle-trading business aren't the same thing,' Janki objected.

'Quite right,' said Salomon. 'Cows need to be fed and watered and milked. Even on Shabbos. Even at Yontev. Do you have to do that to your bales of fabric, too? Exactly! But does that mean I take on a stable boy? No. You pay a peasant a few francs. You organise yourself. You find a way. And you want a clerk for your little shop?'

'I could take better care of my customers if I had someone to do the little things. The till, for example...'

'The till?' Salomon was so worked up that he almost choked on his herb salad. 'Just put a sign on the door: "Ganev wanted!" Or put it in the paper. Maybe Pinchas Pomeranz will write you a nice article. "Since the battlefield of Sedan, where a bullet struck his red Morocco money bag" – Salomon had always known more about things than Mimi was entirely happy with – "since that time Jean M. has been uncomfortable in the presence of money, so he is looking for someone to take it from him." If I have learned something in my life, it is this: you do not let anyone, whether Jew or Goy, anywhere near your till!' God's voice from the burning bush could not have sounded more threatening.

'And what if he employed a relative?' asked Golde.

'What sort of relative? Uncle Eisik from Lengnau, who people only give work to because they have rachmones on him? Or do you want to go and work in Janki's shop, perhaps? Or Mimi?'

Chanele cleared her throat. She looked different lately, and no one could really explain why.

'I'd like to try something else,' said Chanele.

10

She plucked a few hairs every day, only a very few. She pinched each one individually with the tweezers, gripped it tightly as one grips the throat of an enemy that one has finally, finally managed to get hold of, pressed the ends of the tiny pliers together as firmly as she could, did it so violently that her whole arm quivered, and then pulled the hair out with a jerk. She enjoyed the short, stinging pain associated with it every time, couldn't wait for it and yet dragged it out just as Salomon like to draw out the redeeming sneeze after a pinch of snuff. Sometimes she let go of a hair she had gripped, granted it a reprieve without, however, lifting the death sentence, looked for another and a third, let the tweezers gently and with cold delicacy stroke the spot where the nose passes into the brow. On other days she was so filled with impatience, furious, painful impatience, that instead of a hair she gripped the skin and tore out whole chunks of herself and then had to cover the bleeding wound with a piece of gauze and tell Golde she had been sweeping crumbs and had bumped into the edge of the table when she stood up.

She did it all without light, just with the feeling in her fingers, just as a blind man, they say, if he is hungry enough, will find a handful of scattered grains on a gravel path. She bolted the door to her room, shut the shades in the middle of the day and, if too much light pierced the cracks, hung a bed-sheet over it and then sat down before the shell-framed mirror that Salomon had brought her from the market in Zurzach for her twelfth birthday. At twelve you were a woman, and women, he had said with a laugh at the time, like to make themselves beautiful. How little he knew her! She sat at the mirror, in which nothing was reflected, felt for the tweezers which – as long as you're hungry enough! – she always found as soon as she reached her hand out, and clicked the ends together a few times, making them sound like those insects that you hear on the leaves on quiet summer nights. Then, always slightly breathless, she began her ritual.

Afterwards she didn't look at herself in a mirror, on principle, she sought the change in her image only in the gaze of others, she was glad when their eyes rested on her for longer than usual and sought an answer without noticing the question. She didn't become vain, that would have been too out of keeping with her character, but in the morning she hesitated longer than usual when she had to choose between her few dresses. Once, only once, she had gone almost all the way downstairs with her hair down, her freshly combed hair that fell far below her shoulders, before hurrying back to her room and wrapping it again in her net.

At work in Baden she always wore the brown dress with the cambric trim. It was a kind of inconspicuous uniform, into which she slipped every day in the back room of the shop. By so doing she changed not only her appearance but also her name, because in front of the customers Janki insisted on addressing her as Mademoiselle Hanna. Mademoiselle Hanna took the ladies' coats and parasols, brought, if the choice between one material and another was taking longer than usual, a chair from the back room, or accompanied a lapdog to the nearest corner. And she handed out tea, not the proper, dark brown, sugary tea they drank at home in Endingen, but a thin, weak infusion for which she had to fetch hot water from the brewery next door, before serving it in tiny cups. Something that was taken for granted in Paris was an unheard-of novelty in Baden and soon, for the few families who constituted the better circles of the little town, it was considered the height of elegance to drop in for a little cup with Frenchman Meijer, to chat for a quarter of an hour, ask to see a few bolts of material more for the sake of entertainment than because one really needed something. Of course one bought, too; one could hardly steal the time of that good man who had been through so much.

The till alone, for which Janki had actually wanted a clerk in the first place, was not within Mademoiselle Hanna's territory. He himself attended to the financial side of things, and since Salomon's violent words he did so very secretively, even though in the evening Chanele, who had been present at all his sales, could have told him to the franc exactly what he had taken that day. The profits were considerable.

Chanele had always been quiet, but Mademoiselle Hanna was practically mute. She said 'yes' and 'no', she smiled politely when it was expected of her, and did everything to make herself as invisible as she was useful. She attended, whether she was asked to or not, to the tiniest matters, and had usually finished things by the time they occurred to Janki. Only once, when he asked her, using his constant argument that this was how Monsieur Delormes had always done things, to greet the customers with a curtsy, did she steadfastly refuse. They even had an argument about the matter, and it was only when Chanele said she would rather scrub the floors at home that Janki finally gave in.

But above all Mademoiselle Hanna listened. Even as a child, with her very unclear position in the Meijer family, Chanele had become used to collecting information from the conversations of others, drawing conclusions from tones of voice and gauging power relations, of vital importance for someone to whom no fixed place in the world has been assigned. She learned quickly that the top two hundred people in Baden behaved exactly as the Jewish community of Endingen did, that the haggling and fighting over tiny degrees of rank – who had to be invited to dinner, and who did you have to be invited by? – was just as stubborn as it was about the most desirable mitzvahs on the high feast days, and that heads under feathered hats produced thoughts no cleverer than those formed under headscarves and sheitels. She observed above all how skilfully Jean Meijer was able to manipulate his customers and flatter their vanities, how with only an apparently resigned shrug of his shoulders or a regretful shake of his head he persuaded them to choose the more expensive crêpe de Chine, even though the cheaper voile would have suited them much better.

No, she had to admit it, Janki wasn't really an honest person, not only because of the walking stick and the artificial limp. But the same quality also made him likeable again, because he fully inhabited all the roles he played; he might have lied, but he believe his lies. He played the businessman like an actor, and he played him well.

Chanele didn't share these observations with anyone, certainly not with Janki himself. Generally speaking, the two of them exchanged very few words, beyond the purely businesslike. In Endingen Janki had once come out with a story unprompted, about the pub in Guebwiller or the wonders of the city of Paris. Now on the way to Baden he would often walk along beside Chanele for half an hour, and if a milk-cart stopped for them and they had to push their way side by side onto the box seat to sit beside the driver, he seemed to find that contact disagreeable.

Mimi hardly ever got to see Janki now, at least on her own. In the week he left the house early and came back late. On Shabbos, when they would at least have had the right menucha for a reasonable conversation, Salomon almost always brought a business contact or a complete stranger along in his wake, with whom he then proceeded to have endless debates about God and the world over dinner – more about the world than about God, as was inevitably the case in the house of a cattle-trader. Janki always participated in these table discussions between tsibeles and bundel with an interest that Mimi couldn't quite believe in, he was avoiding her, and Anne-Kathrin thought so too. When he owed the rescue of his business and its obvious success entirely to her initiative. If she hadn't gone to Pinchas that time – and God knows going to him had not been easy – who knew whether there would still be a French Drapery at all?

On Sunday, without synagogue, without guests and without too rich a meal, which would have made everyone sleepy all afternoon, it was no better.

On the pretext of having to keep his business books, Janki locked himself in his attic room for hours at a time, even though there wasn't so much as a table in it. 'He can't look you in the eye,' was Anne-Kathrin's interpretation of his behaviour, 'and there can only be one reason for it.'

Not that Mimi was jealous of Chanele, *certainement pas*, but who else spent all week with Janki? Who had started plucking her eyebrows, clumsily, of course, so that her face looked plucked rather than prettified, with individual ugly clumps of hair, shrubs that have survived a forest fire? In fact one should feel sorry for Chanele, Anne-Kathrin thought, because she was dreaming a dream from which there could only be a rude awakening, as many novels told one.

But Mimi felt no pity within herself. And no hatred, of course, she would never have stooped to that, but she did feel a certain irritation, and if you said it in French, '*elle m'irrite*', the word had the unpleasantly scratching sound that corresponded precisely to her feelings.

In all likelihood, without that irritation, she would hardly have said 'Why not?' when Abraham Singer was at the door again, she would not, as if by chance, have joined the others in the kitchen and listened to what he had to say.

Abraham Singer was a trader with no goods, at least none that one could carry around with one in a basket or show to a customs man at the border. His business territory took in Alsace, South Germany and Switzerland, but on one occasion his travels brought him all the way to Frankfurt and in one very unusual instance he concluded a deal in Budapest. If anyone asked him – but no one who had to ask was a potential customer anyway – he firmly denied being active in the field in which he had a monopoly, and from which he lived quite well, not like a king, but not like a beggar either. 'Marriage broker?' he would say. 'I'm not a shadchen! Just a curious person who likes to get involved, and may that not be accounted a sin.'

He was a squat, short-legged little man with a crooked spine that kept him permanently bent. Consequently he looked at people from below, which was very useful to him, he claimed, in the profession that he didn't have. 'Everyone has learned to lie upwards, but downwards they all forget.' And then he laughed until tears came to his eyes, and had to take a checked handkerchief, big as a sail, from his pocket to wipe his face. His giggling, which he sometimes couldn't control for minutes at a time, was so well known in Jewish families that people would say to a mother who was taking too long to marry off her daughter, 'High time Singer came and laughed at your place.'

A doctor doesn't go to a house where no one is ill, and similarly Singer never came unplanned, but he always insisted on making his visit seem quite coincidental. Then he sat in the kitchen – 'No, the parlour would be far too elegant for me, I just dropped in, just for a minute,' spoke of this and that, told the gossip from lots of communities, talked about illnesses and deaths, but of course always about engagements and weddings too, about a shidduch that had been made here or there, 'with a dowry, I can't tell you how big, but the kind you would dream of for any Jewish child!' He inquired into the wellbeing of the family, he knew more about the smaller twigs of the family trees than Mother Feigele, drank a glass of tea and then another, told the story of the stupid coachman who has his horse stolen by the gypsy, wiped his face, got up to go, sat down again and then said quite casually, 'And your daughter, Frau Meijer? Soon to be twenty, if I remember correctly, and lovely as a flower. Quite the mamme, may my tongue fall from my mouth if I tell a lie.' That he didn't seem to notice Mimi, who was also sitting in the kitchen, was part of the game.

Golde, familiar with the rules, affirmed how glad she was that Mimi wasn't yet thinking of marrying, she thanked God for it every day. 'I don't know how I would cope without her, she is such a help to me and so gifted at everything to do with housekeeping.' Then she launched into a hymn of praise for Mimi's skills at cooking and sewing, a hymn in certain respects at odds with what Mimi normally heard on the subject. But how does the saying go? You don't shout in the marketplace, you bring your goose back home.

Abraham Singer sat on his chair like a doll, his feet far above the floor, and listened to the whole thing from below. He confirmed to Golde that she was very lucky, indeed that she was bentshed by heaven in having such a sensible daughter, there were too many girls who couldn't wait to come under the chuppah, he could name examples, more than one, in which it had not ended well at all.

Then he drank another glass of tea, told the story of the three pedlars who fall into the stream, laughed, wiped his face, rose to go, said, 'On the other hand…' and sat down again.

'On the other hand,' he said, 'I did happen to hear something, and I'm a curious person, what can I do, may it not be held against me. There is said to be a family, very, very bekovedik people, with a son, how should I put it, an only son, a pearl of a person.'

'Who?' asked Golde, but Abraham Singer would not have been so successful in his trade had he not had two particular abilities: hearing everything that might be useful to him, and ignoring everything that did not fit his plans.

'But he's supposed to be clever, so I have heard,' he went on, 'a real Talmud chochem. And a very practical person, too. Not like one of those Talmud students who can't button up their trousers without first looking it up in a sefer.'

He started laughing, but then, very much to the relief of his listeners, quickly regained control of himself and went on talking.

'He also has a parnooseh, a very good job, any Jewish child would be grateful for. One day he will take over his father's business, and he already works hard in it, even though he's so young.'

'How old?' asked Mimi, even though by tradition she should have left all the talking to her mother.

'Yes,' said Abraham Singer, 'you hear such things when you travel a lot. But I don't want to bore you. When your daughter is sensibly not yet thinking of marrying, why would you be interested in where someone was looking for a shidduch?'

'Where?' asked Golde. She had long been worried that she might have to marry Mimi abroad, knowing her only child among strangers, possibly so far away that she couldn't even hold her newborn grandson in her arms...

'Not that far,' said Abraham Singer, and Golde sighed with relief.

'Where?' asked Mimi.

Even if one is not a shadchen, only a curious person who hears something here and picks up something there, one still has to live, and he who announces his secrets in the street, this much was clear to Golde, finds many buyers but no payers. She was already standing up to get the little crocheted bag in which she kept her housekeeping money out of the cupboard, but to her surprise Abraham Singer resolutely refused, he even said, 'May my hand grow out of the grave if I accept anything from you!' And then, while Golde chewed around on her lower lip and Mimi wiped her suddenly damp palms inconspicuously on her skirt, Singer admitted, bowing even lower than usual, if possible, a little lie, 'may it not be held against me'. He had not come here by chance, he had been commissioned and paid. 'What do our wise men say? Woman is made of man's rib, and if your rib is missing, then off you go and find it.' He had been asked to call in at the house because this young man didn't want just any old bride but – heaven alone knew how he knew her – one in particular, who had to be called Miriam and Meijer and be his wife because otherwise he could never be happy his whole life long.

'How old?' asked Mimi.

'Twenty-six.'

'Where from?' asked Golde.

'Here in Endingen.'

'Who?'

'Pinchas Pomeranz,' said Singer.

*

Even though autumn was already coming to an end, it had been another hot day. When Chanele had emptied the mop bucket and put the scrubber away, she took off her brown dress and, in chemise and petticoat, stood quite still. The back room, into which only a very small amount of light fell from the courtyard, through a small window placed high in the wall, was pleasantly cool. It smelled of spices whose names she didn't know, of foreign places to which she would never travel. She ran her fingertips, as she had recently become accustomed to doing, gently over her face, from her hairline down her forehead to her nose, and it was as if she felt her touch not only on her skin but all through her body. She raised her arms above her head, her fingers interlocking, and pressed her head against her arm, first on one side, then on the other. The smell of her body mixed with the spice, a foreign land among many foreign lands. She moved her hips and stretched her arms still higher, it was not yet a dance, but she already sensed its rhythm in the distance, and she thought: 'Mademoiselle Hanna...'

'Sorry. I thought you'd finished.'

She hadn't heard the door open. Janki stood there, one leg hesitantly outstretched, a swimmer testing the temperature of the water with the tip of his toe. He held a chair in each hand.

Chanele turned away, her arms in front of her chest, but Janki only laughed, a laugh that she could sense on her skin like her fingers a moment before, and said, 'At Monsieur Delormes' shop, I was never anything more to the customers than a clothes stand. You don't have to hide from a clothes stand.'

He set the two chairs down, not against the wall, where they belonged, but in the middle of the room, and gripped Chanele by the shoulder.

She did not pull away. She let herself be turned around and led to the chairs that stood facing one another like two men who have stopped for a chat after the service in the square outside the synagogue. Then they both sat there, Janki in the flowery waistcoat that he had had the tailor Oggenfuss make from the leftovers of a very expensive fabric, Chanele in her petticoat, which was like a dress, indeed, but not one meant for men's eyes.

'This is fortuitous,' said Janki, as if there were nothing at all special about the situation. 'There's something I've been wanting to ask you for a very long time.'

But then he seemed to forget his question, and just looked at Chanele.

'It suits you,' he said. 'Only here...' and he reached out his hand and touched Chanele right on the sensitive spot above her nose, 'here you need to be more thorough.'

Chanele didn't reply.

'It's strange,' said Janki after a pause, 'I've only just arrived here, that is to say: it's more than half a year ago, but it feels as if it were yesterday. So much has happened, and so much has changed and yet – can you understand it? – I still have the feeling…'

His voice faded away as if it had got lost.

Chanele looked past Janki. On the shelf on the wall the boxes were stacked untidily on top of one another. They contained the button samples that Janki didn't sell, but which he had borrowed from a haberdasher so he could give examples to his customers. They needed to be put in order, thought Chanele, perhaps according to material, a system needed to be introduced.

'I will have a new chemise made for you,' said Janki, 'out of cambric. Everything one wears against the skin should be cambric.'

'Mademoiselle Hanna,' thought Chanele.

'I have this feeling,' said Janki, 'I often find myself thinking about it…That is to say: it isn't really a thought. It's more…more of a feeling, in fact.'

Or according to colour. That was better. If you organised the buttons according to colour, you'd always have them all together, the ones that matched a fabric.

'Can you understand that?' said Janki. 'No doubt I have years ahead of me, and yet…I don't know why, but I always have to do everything very quickly.'

'I don't even know what day his birthday is,' thought Chanele.

'It's meshuga,' said Janki, 'but I've decided to get married.'

There was a smell of cardamom, of cloves and of a new life.

'Yes,' said Janki, got up and pushed his chair against the wall. He was about to clear the second chair away as well, but Chanele just sat where she was. She grasped his outstretched hand, took both his hands, lifted her head with its new face and looked Janki in the eye for the first time.

'You wanted to ask me something?'

'Of course,' said Janki, embarrassed. 'I wanted to ask you…How much of a dowry do you think Mimi will get?'

11

Salomon only haggled out of cattle-trading habit, without any fire. With this future son-in-law, trading had stopped being fun. Janki had turned up formally, almost solemnly, for the discussion, he came from his room in yontevdik new trousers and his freshly brushed uniform jacket and marched as stiffly down the stairs as a general handing over a conquered fortress. He held his hand out to Salomon as if to a stranger, leaned his walking stick with the lion's-head handle carefully against the table and then sat ramrod-straight on his chair without touching the back.

Twenty thousand, he said, that would be the ideal figure. The textile store had luckily been very well received in the better circles, but the plain people of the town seemed to be put off by the exclusiveness of the clientele, probably because they were worried that they wouldn't find anything to suit their purses in the French Drapery. But Switzerland wasn't France, and Baden certainly wasn't Paris, elegant people were thin on the ground, so it seemed appropriate for him, Janki, for once not to follow the model of Monsieur Delormes, but to address his wares to a wider, even a peasant audience. That would, however, make the opening of additional branches necessary; by a happy chance the possibility existed of taking over the entire ground floor of the ideally situated house with the Red Shield, which belonged to the wealthy Schnegg family, with the option of buying the building itself. But even though he had given the matter his most serious consideration, he did not want to give up the shop on the Vordere Metzggasse, but rather to attempt to run both shops, each aimed at a different clientele, in parallel to one another. With the right staff – this too was an expense to be borne in mind – this could certainly be accomplished. He would in any case have to reorganise himself in this respect, after Chanele had found the daily journey to Baden too exhausting, and decided hence-forth to remain in Endingen again. Apart from rent, equipment and staff, the cost of a larger order from Paris would have to be taken into account, and to some extent the fittings for the new shop. Of course that could all be done with sixteen, or rather, on a tight margin, even fifteen and a half thousand, but Mimi – it was the first time that her name was mentioned in the context of this wedding proposal – had expressed a desire to settle in Baden, and the furnishing of a more or less suitable dwelling could not be had for nothing. All in all: twenty thousand.

Salomon offered ten.

'Your only daughter!' said Janki.

'If I had two,' said Salomon, 'I would have to divide the sum.'

Janki conceded that he might be able to try to raise the outlay required for larger amount of goods required for the new shop not in advance but, as a customer who was no longer entirely unknown, at least partly on credit, which would reduce the need for cash so that even with, let's say sixteen thousand...

Salomon offered eleven.

'You will be thought of as a tightwad,' said Janki.

'In my shop,' said Salomon, 'such a reputation can only be useful.'

One could of course, Janki reflected, keep the furnishing of the apartment as simple as possible, although he was reluctant to disappoint Mimi on a point that was so important to her. On the other hand some of her desires were very extravagant, he had to admit that, however much he loved her, like for example this fixed idea that the curtains in the drawing room had to be shantung silk, a material entirely unsuited to the purpose. If one were to cut back very severely in that area, one might perhaps with fourteen thousand...

Salomon offered twelve, and Janki shook on it.

Salomon had haggled for longer about many a cow from which twenty or, on a good day, thirty francs might have been made than he haggled over his daughter's dowry, and he was disappointed by his easy victory. He would have wished Mimi to have a husband with a more precise grasp of the realities of business negotiation. From the very start he had set aside the sum of eighteen thousand francs for his daughter's nedinye, not because eighteen is the numerical value of the lucky Chai, but simply because that sum seemed appropriate within his possibilities. Anything a son-in-law negotiated down from there, he had decided without talking to Golde on the matter, and even long before Janki's unexpected appearance in Endingen, anything left over from eighteen thousand would go to Chanele, for whose well-being he felt entirely responsible, albeit with little emotion. But he had not expected it to be six thousand francs, enough to provide Chanele with a respectable match.

So the family was called in. Golde came sailing out of the kitchen and wanted to hug Janki straight away, but hesitated because Mimi had precedence in this respect, and finally she just stood there, hopping from one foot to the other, sucking on her lower lip. Chanele followed more slowly, wiping her hands on her apron. Her 'Mazel Tov!' to Janki was, to Salomon's amazement, no more cordial than a 'Hello' to a chance acquaintance.

Mimi, in her room, seemed not to have heard all the shouting and had to be fetched. When she at last appeared in her mother's wake, she looked almost insulted by the disturbance, when she turned her cheek to her fiancé for the traditional first kiss she showed neither embarrassment nor extravagant joy, and it was only when Golde held her in an apparently endless embrace that she allowed herself a triumphant glance at Chanele over Golde's head.

'Now that you're a kalleh, a bride, I will have to get used to calling you Miriam,' Salomon said with a chuckle.

With a new and fully adult gesture, his daughter brushed her curls from her forehead. 'I'd rather stay as Mimi. It's more unusual than Miriam. N'est-ce pas, Jean?'

'Jean?' thought Salomon. 'Nu, so be it: Jean.'

The wedding was arranged for 17 December, a date when the farmers would be too busy too busy preparing for Christmas and New Year to need the services of a cattle-trader. Janki, for whom nothing could ever happen quickly enough, would have happily chosen an earlier time, but hoped – the house with the Red Shield would not be empty for ever – he would be able to ask Salomon for an advance on the dowry. In her head Golde was already drawing up lists of all the things that still needed to be organised for Mimi – clothes! Sheitel! All the monograms that would have to be embroidered into the linen for the trousseau! – and had already bitten her lip bloody out of pure excitement.

Only Mimi seemed as cool and calm as if she got engaged very day. In fact she had imagined this event with Anne-Kathrin so often and in such detail in the past that the actual process was almost a disappointment. Now at last she was standing next to Janki, they were what one calls a handsome couple, she even whispered something in his ear, but the two of them didn't, Salomon thought, look properly happy. On the other hand when he thought back to his own engagement to Golde, to young, dainty, irresistible Golde... 'Nu!' he said out loud, and in this case it meant: 'It will be what it is; one cannot expect too much in life.'

'There's one thing you must know,' Mimi whispered in Janki's ear. 'I will not serve your customers. I'm not an employee.'

Since Chanele, without supplying a sensible reason, no longer wanted to work in his shop and had even rejected the offer to raise her admittedly small wage, everyday life had become hard for Janki. If he had to do something in town, as he did increasingly often because of the planned expansion, he had to close his shop and then he didn't have a quite minute to himself. In the middle of a conversation with a joiner or a glazier – he wanted to put in big shop windows like the ones they now had in Paris – he suddenly imagined a customer deciding to buy her fabrics somewhere else from now on because of the closed shop door. Then he always concluded his discussion quite abruptly and hurried back to Metzggasse, where of course no one was waiting outside the door. In the end nothing had been done properly and half the day was lost.

It hadn't been hard to find a girl from the country to come and clean the shop in the evening after closing time, but as he didn't dare to leave a stranger alone with all those expensive fabrics, he always stood there impatiently as she worked, was in the way and at the same time felt irritation mounting in him daily. Monsieur Delormes had never had to concern himself with such trivia.

Janki's search for a clerk was more difficult than expected. The only people who responded to his advertisement in the *Tagblatt* were young pups who smelled penetratingly of patchouli or whatever else they had poured on their handkerchiefs to mask the smell of their unwashed necks, their hair plastered with too much pomade at the temples and their clothes of such vain tasteless-ness that they could never have been put before a discerning clientele. They knew nothing at all about fabrics, they couldn't tell French muslin from English tweed and showed so little interest in the material that it was quite clear: they didn't care whether they were selling fabrics or cigars, silk or soap. A single applicant, one Oskar Ziltener, was different from the others; he was a little older, conservatively dressed, and he asked questions that revealed a surprising knowledge of the field. But Janki thought he had once seen him in passing in Schmucki & Sons textile store, and so, for fear of providing a competitor with information, did not take him on.

In the evening, when he returned at last to Endingen, he was exhausted and bad tempered; the walk, which he had undertaken without much effort for all those months, now struck him as endlessly long, probably, he said to himself in an attempt to explain the change, because it was autumn now and he had to look for most of the path in the dark. There was no food waiting for him in the kitchen now either, and more than once he went to bed hungry. When he mentioned this to Chanele, she said quite amicably that she didn't want to deprive her friend Mimi of the opportunity to spoil her fiancé herself.

But Mimi was usually asleep, or had locked herself in her room. She spent exhausting days with tailors who had to be watched over so that they copied the patterns from the *Journal des Modes* properly, and with the wig-maker, not the quite good one from Schwäbisch Hall – Salomon had not approved the money for her – but the one from Lengnau who, if you weren't careful, made you a sheitel in which you looked as old as Mother Feigele.

But above all Mimi had social obligations, in so far as one could speak of society in a village like Endingen. It was neither customary nor necessary formerly to announce an engagement; no official proclamation could have kept pace with the speed of rumour. When Mimi walked through the village, and for the first few days there were many opportunities for such walks, people spoke to her and congratulated her on all sides. Furthermore, an old superstition from the days when people still believed in the evil eye, the name of her future husband was never mentioned, since to utter his name with hers before the wedding would have brought misfortune. People only talked about 'the man-to-be' or 'the happy one', and Mimi, enjoying every second at the centre of attention, became increasingly practised at turning her head away bashfully as a shy young bride, and even blushing.

At last, and she couldn't have said whether she was looking forward to the moment or dreading it, she bumped into Pinchas. She saw him coming from a long way off, long and gaunt, with a heavy package on his shoulder, his knee bending under its weight with every step he took. When he came closer, the package turned out to be a quarter of beef wrapped in sackcloth. One end protruded from the canvas, the obscene wound of a freshly amputated soldier.

They both stopped. Mimi arranged the curls at the back of her neck, a gesture that allowed her to bend her torso backwards and thus set off her figure to good effect. Pinchas vacillated back and forth as if he wasn't sure whether to walk towards Mimi or run away from her. But perhaps it was also partly because of the weight he was carrying. You could tell by his face that he was formulating one sentence after another, rejecting and choking it back, and immediately assembling the next one, which wasn't right either. In his cheeks, under his thin beard, muscles twitched as if his jaw first had to grind the words to tiny pieces, and his Adam's apple rose and fell as if it were having difficulty swallowing.

At last it was Mimi who opened the conversation. 'What were you thinking of,' she said reproachfully, 'sending Singer to my house?'

'I wanted...' Pinchas gulped again. 'I wanted you to know...'

'I've known for a long time, Pinchas.' She smiled at him and felt like that other Mimi, the one with the book who went with strange men without marrying them. 'But as I told you...'

'Our hearts don't sing the same tune.'

He had remembered the sentence and repeated it now, a pupil who may not have understood his lesson, but has learned it conscientiously by heart.

'That's exactly how it is, Pinchas.' A shame that Anne-Kathrin couldn't see her now, very much the grande dame, at once friendly and unapproachable.

'But...' Pinchas was swaying more and more under his burden. 'But... A person can learn to sing.'

'It's too late.' The sentence had appeared in many novels, and Mimi had always been touched by its finality.

'I would like...' said Pinchas. At one spot oxblood had seeped through the sackcloth and was slowly spreading. Mimi found herself being reminded of the bandage that Janki had worn on the very first evening. 'Luckily it's not my blood,' he had said.

'I would like...' Pinchas repeated. 'His tongue was playing in the gap between his teeth as if it had a life of its own. 'I need to talk to you again. Can't we meet? In the gazebo, at your friend's house? Please.'

'That's impossible!' But then Mimi saw that the bloodstain had already spread to Pinchas's shoulder, and for some reason she was so touched by the sight of it that she whispered something to him that she hadn't even wanted to say.

Pinchas would have reached his arms out to her, but he had to hold on tight to the quarter of beef.

It wasn't until the weekend that Mimi and Janki found time for one another. On Shabbos morning they walked to the synagogue side by side, Mimi with her hair pinned up, you had to exploit the fact while you were still allowed to show your own hair. They arrived as a couple and, when they entered the square, raised their heads together to look at the village clock, which in Endingen is mounted on the synagogue tower. From the women's shul Mimi could then watch Janki being summoned to read from the Torah, the first after Kauhen and Levi. After he had sung the blessing, a woman leaned forward to her and said, 'He has a beautiful voice.'

From her seat in the front row, right next to Golde, looking through the grid she could also see Pinchas and his father, two long, narrow figures who looked even more haggard in their white prayer shawls than they did in everyday life. Pinchas often stood alone at his lectern, because Naftali, the shammes, was constantly busy and scurried around the synagogue, here reminding someone of a mitzvah, there interrupting a noisy private conversation with a violent 'Sha!' None the less, Pinchas, who must have known exactly where she habitually sat, never turned his head upwards, as many men apparently stretch their necks at random before flicking to the next passage in the prayer book. He had pulled the tallis over his head and was rocking back and forth with concentration, someone with a very special request to make of God.

Mimi and Janki did not walk back together. It was the custom for the women always to leave the synagogue before the end of the service, so that the men, when they came home hungry, didn't have to wait for their meal, the traditional Shabbos seder.

At the seudah they now sat side by side at table. The place at the end, which had naturally fallen to the newcomer Janki back then, was now taken by Chanele. She seemed content with that. It was closer to the door from there, and she was often needed in the kitchen for quite a long time.

Golde, who had always been an impatient eater, now often left her plate untouched, so preoccupied was her mind with planning all the details of the wedding festivities. And not only that. She was already compiling courses of meals for circumcisions and drawing up lists of invitations for Bar Mitzvahs. At the same time she had to admit, and wasn't even ashamed of it, that she was even more pleased for Janki than for Mimi. He filled a hole in her life, a hole that she noticed only now that she was barely present.

Salomon hadn't seen his wife as happy and lost in herself for ages, and that did him good too. He was even more talkative than usual and told the stories he always told when he was in a good mood: the one about the farmer he had told that in Jewish byres the cows had to be fed with matzohs at Pesach, and who had asked in all seriousness if that didn't spoil the milk, and the one about the goyish cattle trader who refused to believe that the cow they were trading had only calved once, and whom he finally persuaded with the words, 'May my tochus go blind if I tell a lie!' and who had actually believed that the tochus was a relative and not simply his backside.

Janki laughed long and loud about each of those stories, which made Salomon like him more and more.

That the bridal couple talked very little to one another no one noticed – except perhaps for Chanele. But she kept having to jump up and attend to something urgent in the kitchen.

Salomon made Janki – 'Now that you are yourself a balebos, you will have to practise!' – say the table blessing, and even tried to find the right notes when Janki sang quite different tunes during their communal singing from the ones they were used to in Endingen. Afterwards Salomon stretched pointedly and explained that the old people – 'Isn't that so, Golde?' – had to go and lie down for a while now, that heavy food and everything, the young ones, he was quite sure, would – 'Isn't that so, Janki?' – be quite capable of passing their time without them. When Golde didn't come to the stairs with him quickly enough, he admonished her to hurry with a 'Nu!'.

Chanele had closed the kitchen door, whether for the sake of discretion or for other reasons; Janki and Mimi were alone in the drawing room. They were still sitting at the table, which had been cleared of dishes, but whose white tablecloth, a post-feast menu, listed all the delicacies that Golde had prepared for today, in hieroglyphics of sauce-stains and crumbs.

Mimi pushed her chair closer, until Janki could have put his arm around her waist without stretching. He didn't seem to notice the opportunity, or perhaps, even though it didn't quite seem part of his character, he was simply shy. She let her head drop onto his shoulder and closed her eyes. Janki made a movement that raised her hopes, but he had only been making himself more comfortable in his chair. Anne-Kathrin was right: men were like little boys, you had to show them the way.

Without opening her eyes, just pressing her head more firmly into the hollow formed by his shoulder and his neck, she started speaking, her lips on his skin, so that he could feel her voice more than he could hear it. 'Oh, Rodolphe,' she said, 'Rodolphe, Rodolphe, Rodolphe.'

'Pardon me?' asked Janki.

She straightened up and let her curls brush his cheek. 'Do you love your Mimi just a teeny bit?'

'Of course,' said Janki. There was something in his voice that Mimi took for arousal. Chanele, who had been able to observe Janki very precisely for a few weeks, would have described it as impatience.

'I love you too,' said Mimi and pursed her lips.

'Right,' said Janki, as one rounds off a not particularly important point in a business discussion. 'There's something I need to tell you.'

'At last!' thought Mimi. The clothes were ordered and the sheitel well on its way. Now it was time for the other thing that she always flicked so eagerly through Anne-Kathrin's books to find.

'It's like this,' said Janki. 'I've thought about everything very hard, over and over again.'

'Yes?' said Mimi.

'It's not going to work,' said Janki.

'What?'

'It's not going to work at all if you don't work in the shop.'

12

Not that Chanele was listening. As Mimi would have said, *certainement pas*. But she was busy in the kitchen, the kitchen was the place where she belonged, where she would always belong now, as long as she lived; she was a sensible person and she didn't dream of impossible things. She had come into the world to wash the dishes, she had come to terms with it once and for all, anything else was pointless woolgathering, pie in the sky. She wasn't in the kitchen to enjoy herself, certainly not, and if those two couldn't keep their argument any quieter, that was their problem. Mimi and Janki weren't exactly yelling at each other, you couldn't say that, but if you didn't exactly plug your ears – and why should Chanele have had to do that? Was it her fault if the wall between parlour and kitchen wasn't any thicker? If you weren't as deaf as old Schmarje Braunschweig, then you were practically forced to listen to the two of them hissing at each other. If that was the tone that young couples in love adopted with each other, then Chanele was glad, oh yes, really glad, that she had decided once and for all to have nothing more to do with men, they were as much use as a loaf of bread at Pesach.

Those two, you didn't have to listen at the wall to hear them, were arguing about whether Mimi was to be a housewife after the wedding, or a member of staff at the shop. Janki tried his well-practised sales patter at first, describing the joys of such shared activity as enticingly as he would have described an as yet untailored jacket to his customers. Mimi, for her part, reacted with the same childishly wheedling voice that she had always used when she wanted to wrap her parents, particularly Salomon, around her finger, she was entirely the helpless little girl who couldn't understand what the big bad world wanted of her. When that didn't work, she moved on to a tone of insulted injury, a sudden switch with which Chanele was all too familiar. She had actually thought that Jean had asked for her hand out of love – she still called him Jean, but she now spoke the name with a sarcastic undertone – and now she discovered that he hadn't been after a wife at all, just a cheap serving wench, a Jewish bishge, but she was too good for that, far too good, and she never wanted to hear another word on the subject. Janki answered with numbers, he talked about takings and running costs, and paced back and forth as he did so. You didn't have to have your ear to the wall to notice that; his footsteps could be clearly heard even in the kitchen, firm and regular, without the weekday limp that he had adopted for the benefit of his clientele. 'She's going to cry in a minute,' thought Chanele, and sure enough, she could already here Mimi sniffing as she had done even as a little girl when she threatened to lose a battle for a doll or the last piece of Shabbos cake. His demands were causing her pain, Mimi wailed, she had really expected better from her Rodolphe – 'What Rudolf?' thought Chanele – she had thought he didn't have the soul of a grocer like all the others, the disappointment was crushing her soul now, and he couldn't want his little Mimi to be unhappy, could he, he couldn't want that?

It was at that point that he began to hiss, at which the words 'spoilt little girl' and 'you can't do business sitting on your tochus' were uttered, and Chanele in her kitchen, probably unlike Janki, was not at all surprised when Mimi abruptly stopped crying and hissed back that a wife wasn't a commodity that you could buy and then do with what you liked until the end of time, and that people who had come here with nothing on their backs, with nothing at all, were in no position to redraft the laws of the land.

If one belongs once and for all in the kitchen, if that is the lot that one has been given in life, then one should do one's work thoroughly, so Chanele decided that the plates that she had just washed weren't clean enough, and started all over again from the beginning, purely out of a sense of duty, not, for instance, so that someone who came charging furiously out of the parlour into the kitchen, would find her at work and wouldn't find themselves wondering whether she might have taken the slightest interest in what was happening in the next room. *Certainement pas*, isn't that so, Mimi?'

The good Shabbos plates had to be treated with great care, so she didn't even look up when the door slammed behind her. That could only be Mimi, who liked to bring to a dramatic conclusion arguments she hadn't been able to win. At first Chanele didn't even notice Janki coming into the kitchen, picking up one of the freshly washed glasses and pouring himself some of the Kiddush wine which should really – but one is discreet, of course, and doesn't want to disturb the young betrothed – have been put back in the cupboard in the parlour ages ago.

'Can anyone understand a woman?' asked Janki.

'Not you.' Chanele bit her lip, because she hadn't actually wanted to say anything.

'What's that supposed to mean?'

'Nothing,' said Chanele, and rubbed away at a stain that she knew to be a flaw in the stone.

'Why don't I understand anything about women?'

'That's why.'

'And excuse me, but how do you know that?'

'Oh, I'm sorry,' said Chanele. 'I completely forgot I have no eyes. And no ears. And certainly no heart.'

'Don't you start!'

'Start what?' If you want to do it properly, washing up is not a simple matter, and requires a great deal of concentration.

'Mimi is so strange today. Is it so bad, working with me in the shop? Tell me!'

'It depends,' said Chanele, and examined a plate as carefully as if it had suddenly developed a completely new pattern, 'depends what you compare it to. Breaking stones is probably harder.'

'Why did you stop?'

'I'm more suited to a kitchen. You have to know your place.'

'You said the long journey...'

'You choose!'

Janki's right hand opened and closed again. In order to interpret the gesture, you would have had to study it as long and as closely as Chanele had. His fingers were looking for the walking stick with the lion's-head handle, which he didn't have with him because it was Shabbos.

'I thought you always understood everything,' said Chanele. 'Such a clever man. Who has experienced so much. Who was even at the battle of Sedan.'

'You know very well...'

'I don't know anything. I'm stupid. Fit for the kitchen.'

'You aren't stupid!'

'I am!' said Chanele, with profound conviction. 'Nobody could possibly be stupider than I am.'

Janki drained his glass of expensive Kiddush wine in one go. 'Now please explain to me...'

The Shabbos plates went in the cupboard in the parlour. Once it had been washed and dried, it had to be cleared away again. For someone destined by fate for housework, such a thing is more important than chatting to a man engaged to someone else.

Janki hurried after her. 'What are you doing, in fact?'

'My work. Does it say anywhere that you have to leave everything lying about the place because some posh gentleman suddenly feels like having a chat?'

'I'm not a posh gentleman!'

'Oh, Monsieur Jean, whence this sudden modesty?'

She just wanted to stack the plates on the second shelf from the bottom, and he just wanted her to listen to him at last. That it looked as if she was kneeling in front of him and he was pulling her up to him was just coincidence. And that he went on holding her hands when she was already standing before him meant nothing at all.

'Chanele, what's wrong?'

'Nothing,' she wanted to say, cattily and with great detachment. Her voice was supposed to be cold and firm, not cracked and tearful. And she certainly didn't want to say, 'I hate you.' Not in that tone.

'I don't understand...' Janki said for the second time.

'But it's true.' Chanele knew she would regret it, but it felt good, it felt so good not controlling herself for once, not being sensible. 'You don't understand anything. You look at a person and the person thinks you like something about them and really...You only ever see what can be useful to you. You knead away at a person and adjust them until they're what fits your purpose. You call them Mademoiselle Hanna when you want to impress the fine ladies, and Chanele if you need someone to put your dinner on the table. But they're not all like you, they can't all suddenly become heroes just by picking up a walking stick and starting to limp. Most people don't think they can be a soldier one day and trade horses the next and forever adapt and change and always be exactly what happens to be useful. There are people who think you really love them if you treat them as if you do.'

'You mean Mimi?'

'Yes,' said Chanele. 'I mean Mimi too.'

'Too?'

'Yes – do you think I plucked my eyebrows to please your customers?'

Pinchas Pomeranz could have explained to Janki what was going on inside him at that moment. Sometimes you sit for hours over a page of the Gemara, and nothing on it makes any sense at all. You've been through the text again and again, you've battled through Rashi's commentaries, and it's still all incomprehensible, a stormy sea full of words hurled together at random, from which only the names of wise rabbis loom like islands. And then, all of a sudden, the beginning of a sentence shifts in your head, questions and answers divide anew – because the Talmud, like a human being, has no punctuation to make comprehension easier – and everything is illuminating and clear, so simple that you can't explain to yourself why you didn't see it that way from the very start. Such moments are lovely, but also frightening, because they make it clear to you how easy it is to be blind with your eyes open.

'I had no idea,' said Janki.

'No,' said Chanele. 'You have no idea.'

'I would never have thought…'

'No,' said Chanele, 'you didn't think.'

'But again, I've never said anything to you that would have led you to imagine…'

'No,' said Chanele, 'you've never said a thing. And even though you're not going to understand this, Janki Meijer, thinking has nothing to do with it.'

The plates were still on the floor. But even though Chanele had to bend down very low to reach their shelf, it would never have occurred to anybody now to think that she was kneeling in front of Janki.

When she was finished she wanted to leave, but he stood in her way. 'I'm sorry,' he said.

Chanele slowly raised her shoulders and just as slowly lowered them. She looked at him with a smile which, now that her eyebrows no longer met in the middle, seemed to float on her face. 'Make Shabbos with it,' she said.

Outside the front door was opened and closed again. 'Your kalleh is leaving,' said Chanele. 'You should go after her. Not that you want to put yourself to too much trouble.'

Mimi hadn't wanted to leave, not really. She had only come out with all those things because she'd felt sorry for Pinchas for a moment, because she didn't want to leave him standing in the street like that. If you've started a book, you don't set it down mid-chapter. And if you really thought about it, she even owed Pinchas something, Janki owed him something and she was Janki's fiancée so she had her obligation. Yes, it really was a proper obligation. If Pinchas hadn't written that article, which was much more dextrous and imaginative than anyone would have thought him capable of, Janki might have been an assistant to tailor Oggenfuss right now, and wouldn't have been able to think of marriage. Of course, Janki wouldn't be pleased by what she'd done, but he didn't need to find out, and if he did, well, then he needed to learn from the start that a Mimi Meijer would not be ordered around by him like that, she had her own head, she could think for herself, after all she was the daughter of the respected Salomon Meijer and brought with her a nedinye that no one needed to be ashamed of.

There was no one else on the road in Endingen, at least not in the Jewish part of the village. At around this time most people were asleep, crushed by the weight of the heavy Sabbath dinner. Only later, when the men went back to the synagogue for Mincha, would the women visit one another to ruddel, to swap the latest gossip and rumours. What was wrong with meeting a girlfriend, a goyish girlfriend, fair enough, but is a girlfriend not a girlfriend? What was so wrong about sitting with her in a gazebo for half an hour, when there was so much to talk about and discuss before a wedding? Whose business was it if one took the path along the river and then – just because it was closer, why else – forced one's way through a hedge in one's fine dress?

Pinchas was already sitting there. He leapt up when he saw Mimi coming, he was about to dash towards her, but stumbled over the single step that led into the gazebo. His black Shabbos hat rolled to her feet, and as they both bent down for it at the same time, their heads were very close to one another for a moment.

'Here,' said Mimi and handed him the hat.

'Thanks,' he said.

Mimi was almost two heads smaller than Pinchas, and when she looked up at him now, he seemed to tower above the low roof of the gazebo. 'Let's sit down,' she said.

'Yes,' said Pinchas. 'Let's do that.'

The entrance to the bower was more than wide enough for two people, but Pinchas still took a step backwards, it wasn't clear whether he was politely letting her walk ahead, or whether he was afraid of touching her.

Left over from a patriotic celebration or some Italian party or other, ribbons with brightly printed paper flags, already slightly faded were strung below the roof of the gazebo, and a few wind-battered Chinese lanterns hung there too. Mimi was reminded of the brightly decorated Tabernacle in which they had sat only two weeks before.

Pinchas rubbed his hat with his sleeve, even though it wasn't dusty in the slightest. At the same time he wiggled his tongue in the gap in his teeth like a trumpeter going through a difficult piece in his head before putting the instrument to his lips.

'So,' said Mimi, when Pinchas showed no sign of starting the conversation. 'I came.'

'I didn't expect you to,' said Pinchas.

'Don't you trust me?' Mimi threw her curls out of her forehead in a playful sulk, a gesture which, and she had tried it in front of the mirror on more than one occasion, suited her very well.

'No, I do,' said Pinchas quickly, 'of course. But…' The tongue was now playing *prestissimo* in the gap. 'I thought perhaps you didn't want to hear what I…I mean: it's not seemly.'

'What isn't seemly?'

'For me to…When you and Janki…'

'So am I not allowed to talk to anyone any more?'

'Talk, of course. But…' When he swallowed, his Adam's apple moved up and down at least an inch and a half. Anne-Kathrin, who knew such things or claimed to, had once claimed that men with conspicuous Adam's apples were particularly tender. The purest nonsense, of course. It was easy to claim assert something that you could never try out or put to the test. Pinchas of all people.

'You're laughing at me,' said Pinchas.

'Not at all.'

'You smiled.'

'Don't you like that?'

It was like a game. Pinchas threw her the balls, and she caught them or batted them back, just as she wanted. There were little boys in the village who could make their hoops dance in the street, in a straight line or a circle, and barely had to use their whips. That was exactly what Mimi was like right then.

'Don't you like it?' she said again.

'I do. I like everything about you. You're …'

'Yes?'

'I've tried to tell you before. You're beautiful. Like a herd of…'

'Oxen, I know.'

'Goats.'

'Not any better.'

'Rashi says King Solomon…'

'Is this turning into a lesson?'

'I just wanted to…'

'Yes?'

'I just wanted to have told you once.'

'What?'

Pinchas stared at the paper flags with the faded Canton crests, as if there could be nothing more fascinating than the bears of Bern or the chamois of Graubünden. As he did so he murmured something, so quietly that Mimi couldn't make out the words.

'Well?'

'I love you, Miriam,' said Pinchas.

'What?'

'I wanted to have said it once. Just once. I have loved you. Really. You will marry your Janki and I will marry some woman that Abraham Singer will find for me, but at least I've told you. I would have loved you.'

There was a laugh that one was supposed to laugh at such moments, 'pearly', it is called in the books, and Mimi had always liked the word. But now, when it would have been appropriate, she couldn't do it.

'Are you crying?' asked Pinchas.

'Of course not,' said Mimi.

A gust of wind rustled the flags as if they had something important to whisper to them.

'And now?' asked Mimi.

'It will soon be time for Mincha,' said Pinchas. 'I should...' But he made no move to get up.

'I'm sorry,' said Mimi.

'Really?'

'Really.'

And then, because it was the last time, because Pinchas looked so unhappy, because she'd read so many novels, for one reason and for every possible reason and for none, because Janki demanded such impossible things of her, because it was autumn, because she would soon be a married woman, with an apartment of her own and a sheitel and a bunch of keys, because she was furious and surprised and touched, for whatever reason, she reached out her arm and drew Pinchas's head to her and pursed her lips and...

'So that's how it is,' said Janki.

He had run after her because Chanele had wanted him to. He had been in such confusion that he would have done anything Chanele had asked of him, that is: almost anything. You have to remain sensible and you can't lose sight of important concerns. He had wanted to set Mimi's head straight, perhaps in fact using the example of Chanele, who understood that some things were possible and some were not. He had wanted to make up with Mimi, they were engaged after all, and he had heard Monsieur Delormes say often enough, 'As a business relationship begins, so it usually remains.'

He hadn't come creeping after her, he hadn't hidden himself. That hadn't been necessary, either, because Mimi didn't turn around once, she walked through the narrow alleyways at a quick, defiant trot. At first he had thought she just wanted to be alone, as he himself had on the day the shop opened – less than half a year had passed since then, and it seemed so long ago. He had thought she was just after a bit of peace and quiet, just as he had taken the path via the Nussbaumener Hörnlio to think everything through once more, and it struck him as a good sign that she wanted to think about things again. But then it had quickly become apparent the she had a predetermined destination in mind. She was hurrying not away from something, but towards something.

Towards someone.

He hadn't heard what the two of them had said to one another. They were speaking too quietly, and he was standing too far away. The gap in the hedge was directly behind the gazebo, and because of the boards that formed the back of the bench that ran around in a hexagon, one couldn't have a complete view. But the kiss he had seen, it had been impossible to ignore, he had seen the look of surprise on Pinchas's face, and then the happy one, and the way his black hat tipped backwards and the way Mimi didn't let go of him.

'So that's how it is,' he had said, and now, in retrospect, he thought he might have phrased it better.

Mimi was crying; perhaps she was crying. She had thrown her hands to her face and sat crouching at her end of the bench, a child awaiting a smack. Pinchas had immediately leapt to his feet and placed himself in front of Mimi, but she had pushed him away, and now he was standing forlornly in the middle of the gazebo, exactly where the little table had been when they had written their article that time. He stood there, his tongue in the gap in his teeth, and looked as if he were about to launch into a speech. But he said only, 'It's my fault, Janki, all mine,' and Mimi lowered her hands for a moment, said, 'Oh, shut up, Pinchas!' and disappeared behind the cover of her hands once more.

And then the schoolmaster emerged from between the rosebushes and the elder bush, in his shirt sleeves and with a big green apron, beamed across the whole of his sweaty face and said, 'Ah, Monsieur Meijer! Dear young friend! You I had not expected in the antechamber. *Emilia Galotti*. And Fräulein Meijer! And Herr... Yes, yes, the later the evening, the lovelier the guests. Welcome to my Tusculum! Even though you, I fear, are waiting here not for me but for my daughter. I will fetch her at once. One second and she will be there. I go, I go. Look how I go. Swifter than an arrow from the Tartar's bow!'

13

It was a small event that made Janki's decision final, an event without any real significance of its own.

That Sabbath afternoon, after a very embarrassing encounter with Anne-Kathrin, he had come home with Mimi. Salomon had nodded knowingly to Golde when the two of them came in, and pointedly just happened to whistle to himself the song of the bride and groom, 'Chossen, Kalleh, Mazel tov'. That chossen and kalleh hardly exchanged a word with one another Salomon put down to a natural bashfulness, one could after all imagine that the two of them had not just chatted and talked about the weather on their walk together. From that point onwards Mimi and Janki were so strikingly polite with one another, saying 'Another drop of coffee?' and 'Will it bother you if I open the window?' that Golde whispered to Salomon that there was nothing lovelier than young happiness, and she could watch the two of them for hours.

A post horse trots to the next stop without a coachman, and so on Monday Janki was in Baden again, he opened his shop on time and smiled politely as he served his customers. He even went as agreed to view a flat, diagonally opposite the House of the Red Shield, where one would be able to look right across from the drawing room to the new shop windows. The owner of the house, a certain Herr Bäschli, was an old man in a grandfatherly frock coat, and had the habit of rubbing his hands constantly together, not in a circular, soapy way, but with his fingers outstretched as if it was winter and he just couldn't make himself warm. He had a hardware shop, as he called it, on the ground floor of the same house, more of a cabinet of curiosities, with shelves full of vases and paintings, but also old butter churns and broken spinning wheels. After the viewing – 'Think about it in peace, take your time, there's no hurry' – he insisted that Janki look around the shop with him, anyone starting a new household needed all sorts of things, and many a one had found quite unexpected objects in his shop, things they had been looking for all along without even being aware of it.

Janki itched to be back at Vordere Metzggasse, where, even though the early afternoon was usually a very quiet time, a customer might be waiting, but out of politeness he did as Herr Bäschli wished. First of all the old man offered him a pair of brass lamps, shaped like Ionic columns, their flutes still stuck with the wax of long extinguished candles. 'A Jewish household needs candelabras,' Herr Bäschli said with the pride of a scholar who is finally able to apply a bit of obscure book-learning to everyday life. Even the painting of a bearded man, so darkened as to be almost unrecognisable – 'It could be a rabbi!' – failed to attract Janki's interest. He was about to take his leave, when Herr Bäschli assured him, rubbing his hands together the while, that he still had something very special, something that he didn't show to every customer, it came from a very elegant house and Janki absolutely had to look at it. From a wardrobe painted in the rustic style – 'Also for sale, but I don't think it's something for you' – he took a strange silver device in which a crystal bottle was enclosed. 'A tantalus,' said Herr Bäschli proudly. 'I don't know if you have ever interested yourself in the Greek myths. Tantalus was the man who, standing in water, had to suffer thirst for ever.' He moved the enclosed bottle back and forth in front of the window. It was almost entirely filled with a shimmering, gold liquid that started to glow in the sunlight. 'A decent drop, I shouldn't wonder,' said Herr Bäschli. 'Far too decent to let any Tom, Dick or Harry get anywhere near. That's why there's this seal up at the top, do you see? However thirsty your maid might be, she won't be having a drink from this. Only someone with the key can take the bottle out.' He set the tantalus down in front of Janki and rubbed his hands still more violently together. 'That is the little catch of the matter. There is no key. But it also looks so very decorative, on a sideboard or in a cabinet. I will give you a very good price. A particularly good price because, to be honest, I imagine it must be terrible to spend a lifetime looking at something that one can never have.'

That was the moment, the precise moment, when Janki made his decision. Perhaps there was a logical connection between the tantalus that he bought from Herr Bäschli without haggling, and what happened next, but Janki didn't think about it. He was a person who was only really alive when he was in a hurry, and he couldn't remember ever being in such a hurry as this.

He didn't open his shop, he just went there for a moment to put the tantalus in the middle of the counter, he didn't even leave a message for that lump from the village who would wait outside the locked door, waiting in vain for his cleaning supervision. 'I will pay her for her trouble anyway,' he decided. That didn't matter right now.

On the country road his walking stick felt like a nuisance. You couldn't really take it round with you if you had no time to limp. Even though he was walking more quickly than usual, on the way he saw only things that had never attracted his attention before. One mossy end of an old border stone between two communities protruded from the ground; one could imagine a column sprouting from it, like asparagus. A garden fence, with a swallow sitting on each pole, smartly dressed petitioners in an official's antechamber. A nut tree, broad and massive, that reminded him of his grandfather sitting over his tomes at the table in the window, always knowing everything.

Untidy clouds drifted with him, and seemed to be in just as much of a hurry as he was himself, and in between them the autumn sun, faint now, was trying with one final effort to warm the world again, an old man realising far too late what he has missed in life. Hanging in the air was a smell of burnt wood; the hearths seemed already to be practising for the winter, which would very soon be there.

The journey had never been so quick. He must, without noticing, almost have been running, because when he saw the roofs of the village in front of him he was out of breath. He tried to collect himself, to find a posture corresponding to his decision, he used his walking stick again and even limped a little. By the time he arrived in front of the house with the two doors, he was Jean Meijer once more, a matter-of-fact businessman who knew how to make decisions and, if necessary, correct mistakes.

The front door was locked, and no one responded to his knocking.

Salomon was probably out and about doing business, Golde would be drinking coffee somewhere, at Picard or Wyler, and complaining, full of anticipatory joy, about the upheavals of the imminent wedding, and Mimi would either be sitting at Anne-Kathrin's, or would have found an illustration in the latest *Journal des Modes* that she urgently needed to show the tailor. But Chanele, surely Chanele must be at home!

Janki hammered on the door until Frau Oggenfuss poked her head disapprovingly out of a window on her half of the house. When she recognised Janki, she smiled politely, because since he had become not only a customer, but also a draper, she had the greatest respect for him 'All flown away,' she called. 'Can I do anything for you?'

No, Frau Oggenfuss couldn't do anything for him.

He found Chanele at Red Moische's. He could see them through the window in the door, standing by the barrel of pickled gherkins. The gherkins were sold by the piece and not by weight, and Chanele was checking with a severe expression on her face whether Moische wasn't taking unnecessarily small specimens out of the container for her.

She was wearing the brown dress that had hung on its hanger in the backroom of the drapery store for so long. The white cambric trimmings could only be seen at the sleeves, because the weather was cooler now, and Chanele had put a dark blue scarf around her neck. 'The colours don't go well together,'

Janki thought and noticed without surprise that this was the thought of an owner, not an observer.

He walked up and down outside the shop, paused now and then and threw his head back as if to etch on his memory the excessively long sign on the shop. *General Goods and Grocery Store Moses Bollag*, it said, and next to it, in a space far-sightedly set aside for the purpose, but in different writing: *& Sons*.

Chanele was now standing at the counter, and seemed to be haggling over something. Red Moische, known for his pettiness, was shaking his head and using, economical as he was, the same movement to scratch his head. His hair was no longer quite as red as it must have been in his youth.

There was not much to look at in the narrow alley, but Janki studied every door-arch, every ledge, every flowerpot on a windowsill. What was taking Chanele so long? They now had, he'd seen his customers with them, pocket watches for women. Perhaps one needed to...'One thing at a time, Janki,' he interrupted himself. 'One thing at a time.'

Red Moische, you could clearly tell from his slumped shoulders, even through the dirty window, had had to give in. He threw a handful of – what was that? Corks? – into Chanele's shopping basket and turned very ungraciously away. Chanele hung her basket over her arm. Janki took three very quick steps away from the door. And then they were facing one another.

'What do you need corks for?' asked Janki. It wasn't at all what he had intended to say, it had just slipped out.

'To rub the cutlery to stop it getting rusty,' said Chanele.

'I didn't know that,' said Janki.

'There's lots you don't know.'

She didn't seem surprised to see him, or at least she didn't ask any questions. She set off for home, and let him walk beside her.

'Shall I carry your basket?' asked Janki.

'I would never ask that of a war invalid.'

'I need to talk to you,' said Janki.

'If you need to, you need to.'

'Couldn't we...?'

'You want to talk, I don't.'

Chanele didn't slow down at all. And so he had to tell her in a great rush about his big decision, about the mistake that he had only just recognised – 'But it isn't too late to correct it!' – he had to divulge his reflections right there in the middle of the alley, that in the end what mattered was not the dowry, but that someone knew how to muck in, he had to jump over a puddle that hadn't quite dried, as he explained to her that Mimi loved someone else anyway – 'She kissed him in front of my very eyes!' – and that it would therefore be more correct if, when things still hadn't been made official, he followed logic to its conclusion and...

He hadn't finished his sentence when they arrived at the front door and Chanele stopped for the first time.

'What are you trying to tell me?' she asked, as if he hadn't been talking away at her all that time.

'Will you marry me?'

Chanele's only reaction was to switch the heavy basket from one arm to the other. 'Certainement pas, Monsieur Jean,' she said and disappeared into the house.

If Janki actually had been in Sedan, amidst the roar of the cannon and the hail of the bullets, he wouldn't have needed as much courage as he did for his conversation with Salomon. It was the fear of Salomon's reaction, of course, but above all he needed the courage for himself. He had wanted to switch from one ship to another, while he was still safely in the harbour, and now there was no second ship for him to switch to, and he still had to get out, that much was clear to him, he had to jump into the water and swim and he didn't even know where the shore was.

Salomon, the cattle-trader, didn't bat an eyelid, took a pinch of tobacco, sneezed, just drummed his fingers on the table and tried to read Janki's face.

'We'd agreed twelve thousand,' he said.

'It isn't about the money.'

Salomon went on drumming. In his experience it was always about the money.

'Is there a reason?' he asked.

Janki nodded.

'Nu?'

'I would rather not talk about it.'

'Mimi!' At lots of cattle markets Salomon had learned to be very noisy without making much of an effort. His massive body didn't move, his eyes remained fixed on Janki and his fingers went on drumming, without losing their rhythm. But in the other half of the house Frau Oggenfuss looked at her husband and said, 'There's fire in the roof.'

Mimi didn't allow herself any of the hesitations with which she otherwise liked to inflate her own importance a little, but a moment later she was standing in the room.

'Your chossen wants to cancel the chuppah. Do you know why?'

'I know why,' said Mimi.

'You don't know,' thought Janki.

'Do you want to tell me?'

Mimi shook her head.

Salomon ran his fingers through his whiskers, apparently looking for something that he'd lost and urgently needed to find. Mimi and Janki stood there and didn't look at one another.

'Nu,' said Salomon at last. And it meant: 'What we have here is a shlimazl, but at least no one has died.'

'I'm going to find myself a flat in Baden,' said Janki. 'That will be better.'

'Yes,' said Salomon. 'That will be better.'

'I'm sorry,' said Janki.

No one took the hand that he extended, so he walked in silence to the door.

'You forgot your stick,' said Salomon. 'And your limp.'

Only now did Mimi start to cry.

Abraham Singer giggled.

He was sitting in the kitchen of Sarah Pomeranz, and had had three pieces of her famous marble cake – 'The best I have ever put in my mouth, may all my teeth fall out if I tell a lie!' – had reported on a birth in Neu-Breisach and a funeral in Strasbourg, had told all his stories, about the coachman whose horse is stolen, and about the three pedlars who fall in the stream, and then, after all the usual detours, had actually come round to the actual reason for his visit, and had at that precise moment begun to laugh for no reason at all. He had been giggling so helplessly for several minutes now that his little body just shook, and coughed crumbs of marble cake into his checked handkerchief.

Singer's attacks of laughter were so well known that you could even make jokes about them, like the one comparing him to the famous Frankfur Cantor Lachmann. 'What's the difference between Lachmann and Singer? Lachmann sings, and Singer laughs.' Nonetheless, Sarah and Nafali had never seen him as he was now, sitting there wiggling his little legs with uncontrollable delight. And he seemed to want something important from them; he had insisted, not directly, of course, that wasn't his way, but with unmistakable hints, that Naftali be fetched from the butcher's shop to join them. And now that Naftali was there, he was doing nothing but laughing.

At last Singer calmed down, only little squeaks emerged from him from time to time, bubbles from a sunken ship, he wiped his brow with his huge handkerchief, which still had cake crumbs stuck to it, and at last said in a very weak voice: 'Forgive me, please. Be moichel. But the story is…You will laugh with me. Or cry. It's the same song, just with a different tune.'

'What story?' Sarah Pomeranz was a polite and hospitable woman, but if she ever became impatient it was not a good idea to keep her waiting.

Abraham nodded up at her and said, 'You will remember' – as if they wouldn't remember! – 'that you sent me, not sent me exactly, don't let me tell a lie, but neither did you forbid me to talk about it, that I told you about a shidduch that might interest you...'

'Nothing came of it,' said Sarah, 'and you kept your fee.'

'Fee?' Singer pulled himself up to his very modest height. 'Am I a shadchen? You gave me a present, your rewards will be in that other world, and I may have talked about the matter, here or there, the way one does when one travels around a lot.'

'I was opposed to the idea from the outset! Anyone with eyes in their head must surely see that Miriam and Pinchas are not made for one another.'

Sarah looked at her husband with surprise. It wasn't usual for him to say much in the Pomeranz house. 'Why?' she asked. 'Is our Pinchas perhaps not good enough for her? Just because she dolls herself up like Schippe Malke? Or is a beheimes trader something better than a shochet?'

Abraham Singer was already giggling again. He even had to bite into his handkerchief to control himself.

'Forget this shidduch. I have a better one for you. A much better one.' And already he was laughing again.

'I bet it's a good one!' Sarah Pomeranz didn't quite catch the right dismissive tone. A mother who offers a bride for her son has a lot of trouble feigning a lack of interest.

'A good family,' said Singer. 'And a nedinye – that any Jewish child would be pleased with. Twelve thousand francs.'

If Naftali had had a daughter, he couldn't have given her half of that as a dowry. 'And the parents are sending you to us?'

For some reason Abraham Singer had found that question irresistibly comical. 'No,' he giggled. 'The parents aren't sending me. The parents have no idea.'

'Who then? The Prophet Elijah?'

'The kalleh! The kalleh speaks to me in the street, offers me money – am I a shadchen? – and says to me, more or less like this, "Go to the Pomeranzes and inform them..." – am I a town crier with a drum? – "inform them," she says, and I'm thinking, why is she being so elegant? "Inform them!"'

'Who?' asked Sarah.

'I'm a polite man,' said Singer, 'please don't consider it arrogance on my part. If I am asked – why should I say no? So!' His hands were, in contrast to the rest of his body, a normal size, so they looked enormous. He hammered out a town-crier's drumroll on the table-top, and looked as if he would happily have climbed onto the chair to play his part to perfection.

'Hear ye, hear ye!' he crowed. 'I am informing you all!'

'He's drunk,' said Sarah.

'It's just a good thing that I'm a discreet person,' said Singer. 'Anyone else would want to tell the whole world.'

'You tell it!' Sarah Pomeranz was wringing her hands with impatience.

'Well then. A shidduch for your Pinchas. A very good shidduch. But with two conditions.'

'Conditions?'

'First of all,' said Singer, and beat the next drumroll, 'first he has to get a pivot tooth.'

'What does his tooth ... ?'

'I'll tell you. And secondly ...' – drum roll – 'secondly he is to move away from Endingen.'

'The woman must be meshuga.'

'No,' said Singer, and now he wasn't laughing any more, 'she isn't meshuga. More and more Jews, as you know, are living in Zurich, and they have no butcher's shop of their own. Not only could a shochet find a parnassah there ... he would need staff.'

'Zurich?' Sarah repeated the name as pitifully as if it were a city in America, unreachably far away at the other end of the world.

'Nowadays you just have to take the train from Baden. You'll be there in three quarters of an hour.'

'He's too young for a butcher's shop of his own.'

'What can I teach him?'

'Not nearly independent enough!'

'He slaughters a cow better than I do.'

'A dreamer is what he is.'

'Don't you have any questions for me?' said Singer, breaking into the argument.

'What?'

'Who the kalleh is.'

'Yes,' said Naftali, 'of course. Who ... ?'

'Leave him alone!' said Sarah and got up. 'He's a discreet person, he's not going to tell us. And besides, it's just occurred to me ...' She rapped her husband on the top of the head, as the teacher does at cheder when a pupil doesn't know the simplest answer. 'It's just occurred to me: I urgently need to pay a visit. To Golde Meijer. I imagine that the two of us have a lot to talk about.'

14

Anyone who suddenly makes the seamstress sew different monograms into the trousseau linen might as well book the drummer and announce his news in the village square. In Endingen, where people liked to spice the dry bread of everyday life with other people's excitements, everyone knew that. But they did Mimi the favour of playing along when she shook her curls with pearly laughter and said she still couldn't believe it, people had actually believed, her and Janki – and they were cousins, of course, he was like a brother to her, while Pinchas, well, now that the date for the chassene was set, she could admit it, she'd been wild about him ever since she was a little girl. And the meshugena was, said Mimi, with a yet more pearly laugh, that she herself had known nothing about the misunderstanding for a long time, people everywhere had congratulated her on her betrothed, on the lucky fellow, and it had never occurred to her – never occurred to her! – that someone might mean Janki, Janki of all people, who presumably wasn't interested in getting married yet, when he was only interested in his shop and nothing else at all. But that came from these old-fashioned customs, she had begged her father, practically begged him, to make the engagement as public as was customary amongst civilised people, with printed cards, but he'd refused to have anything to do with it, and so this crazy misunderstanding had come about, that she and Janki, of all people – you must forgive her for laughing out loud.

People were polite and said, 'Me neshuma!' and 'Is it possible?' and Mimi kept her head held very high when she walked through the village. At home she was as unbearable as she had been as a fifteen-year-old when she had discovered that Mimolette was the name of a cheese. She had made herself ridiculous, and because she knew that it was her own fault, she couldn't forgive the others. She locked herself in her room for hours, and when Pinchas, as custom thoroughly permitted, came by for a visit, she let him know that he would have plenty of time to fill her head with nonsense when they were married.

Then Pinchas would sit, often until late in the evening, in the parlour with Salomon, and they talked together about all the things that were needed for a kosher butcher's shop in Zurich, because people now found this plan, which Mimi had actually only concocted to get away from Endingen and from prying eyes, worthy of serious consideration. Salomon got on well with his surprising new son-in-law, and even taught him to take snuff, a habit that Janki had always resisted, and laughed warmly when Pinchas, trying to do it only too well, stuffed an enormous amount of Alpenbrise up his nose and then sneezed so hard that his yarmulke fell off his head. When he also started taking an interest in the breeding guide for Simmental cows and even made a very sensible suggestion for how the complicated lists could be drawn up more comprehensibly, Salomon was finally won over by him.

'He has a good head head on his shoulders,' he said in bed to Golde, 'even though you can't tell at first. But once they've given him that pivot tooth, he'll stop looking like Schippe Siebele. You could be a bit nicer to him, you know.'

Golde didn't reply. When Salomon had already been snoring for ages, she went on staring into the infinity of the dark ceiling and chewed around at her lower lip. Pinchas, and there was nothing she could do about this, would always be a changeling as far as she was concerned, an invader who had driven away her Janki, *her* Janki, that's right, there's nothing you can do about your feelings. And if Schippe Siebele, the lowest card in the game, had made the trick, well then, she would get used to it eventually, as she had got used to lots of things in life, but being pleased about it, no, unfortunately no one could demand that of her, not that. As she fell asleep she tried to improve her mood by imagining all the festivities of the impending wedding, but she saw only empty tables, a chuppah without guests and a musician who couldn't scrape a single note out of his violin.

Chanele had gone to bed, in her chemise, which wasn't made of cambric. Next to her lay Uncle Melnitz, who smelled of damp dust and cold earth, pressed himself against her back as a night-snail nestles against a green leaf, and talked away at her in his toneless, old man's voice.

'Good,' said Uncle Melnitz. 'Very good. So you've decided to become a martyr. How lovely. How delightful. You deserve praise for that, yes. We Jews love martyrs. We have to love them. We have so many. Sadly no one will sing for you. "Didn't want this man, allowed herself to be buried alive." Oy, oy, oy. You can be proud of yourself. Everyone will be proud of you. They will tell your story to the young girls when they fall in love with the wrong man. The story of Chanele from Endingen, who didn't take Janki because she wanted the big love and he had only the small one for her. A bad deal he offered you there, Chanele. You were right to turn it down.'

He embraced her with thin, cold arms and pressed her to him. 'You did the right thing,' he whispered to her back. 'You didn't compromise. Your honour is saved, that's the important thing, the only thing that matters. A martyr, just as we like them. Like the women of Massada who took their own lives before the fortress fell. Like the women of Worms who jumped off the roofs when the crusaders overran the city. Like the women of Lublin, who barricaded themselves in their burning houses lest they fell into the hands of the Cossacks. You are a heroine, Chanele. One of them. No, you're an even greater martyr than that, because you must go on living with your heroism, yes. You will be an old maid, you will go on washing your plates and scrubbing your pans and always saying to yourself, "I didn't take him because he didn't lay paradise at my feet and I wouldn't settle for less." Good, Chanele. Very good. If you can't have heaven, then you mustn't have the earth either.'

His hands, dusty parchment, slipped under her nightshirt, which was not cambric, and his voice went on whispering. 'We are gifted at martyrdom, we Jews. We carry it in us like a sickness. And do you know why, Chanele? Because we haven't the courage to drink dirty water, and would prefer to go thirsty. We are chosen, and he who is chosen may not want less than everything. You understand me, don't you, Chanele? You're proud of your renunciation? Is it not a lovely feeling, suffering like that?'

He crept inside her, he rubbed his desiccated body against her youthful one, fingered her breasts and her useless belly, and wouldn't stop talking. 'I'm proud of you, Chanele. They're all proud of you. They would be proud of you if they knew what you've done. No one will say, "She was stupid to let him go." Not a soul. Certainly not. They will admire you. Admire you. Children will be named after you. Other people's children, because you won't have your own. Are you proud of yourself, Chanele? Are you proud? Yes?'

When she woke up, she felt those musty hands still on her, pulled the nightshirt, which wasn't made of cambric, from her body and couldn't stop washing.

Janki had learned to pack, in Monsieur Delormes' drapery shop and in the army. He had got hold of a basket, a big basket with cloth handles that you could load on your back like a military rucksack. He hadn't borrowed it from Golde, but bought it at the market in Baden and taken it home. No one asked any questions when they saw him with it; one looks away when a coffin is carried into the house. When he said he had now rented a flat, not the big one from Herr Bäschli, just a garconnière with two cramped rooms, they nodded and quickly changed the subject. Only Golde said, 'Then you'll definitely need . . .' and left the sentence hanging in the air, a paper kite caught in a tree.

Janki folded his uniform trousers, each bend in exactly the right place. And the red and black jacket, with the flash that they had had to sew on themselves; the only time in the military that he had been better at something than his comrades. Chanele had washed the old bandage and rolled it neatly up again, and he packed it up too, a souvenir of times that he would only enjoy talking about when their reality was forgotten. The yellow neckerchief that no longer suited him; only pimply boys whom he woudn't take on as clerks put things like that around their necks, not a businessman with his own shop. He had more shirts than he needed. Three waistcoats with pockets, big enough for a silver watch – eventually he would buy one like the one Monsieur Delormes had had, with a pendant on the heavy chain. His shaving things. First he would have to buy a bowl for the soap. And towels of course. Bed linen. He had never thought about needing bed linen, he had only bought a bedstead from Herr Bäschli, and a mattress, and Herr Bäschli had rubbed his hands and said, 'Only one bed? Not very much for a new household.' And he would need plates, too, but that wasn't urgent, first he had to...

'Let me do that.' Chanele had come in without knocking, as if into a room where no one lives. She carefully inspected the clothes that he had neatly laid out side by side on the bed, picked up the uniform jacket, shook it out and set it carefully down again, folded slightly differently; in her concentration she looked as if she were bending over a patient.

'I can manage on my own,' said Janki.

'Of course, said Chanele. 'Who would dare to doubt it?'

'You know I'm moving out because of you,' said Janki.

'Not because of Mimi? After all, you were engaged to her.'

'Because I hadn't understood...'

'Ah,' said Chanele, very busy with a shirt. 'And now you've understood?'

'Except you don't want to,' said Janki.

Chanele gave a strangely incomplete movement of her head; it was impossible to tell whether it was a nod or a shake. 'No,' she said at last, 'I don't. But...'

'But?'

'Does it say anywhere in the Schulchan Orech that you always have to do what you want?'

Janki reached for her hands, which were at that moment laying out a shirt. Now it hung between them by its sleeves, a child forcing its way into its parents' conversation.

'Does that mean...?'

Chanele looked at him for a long time, two sceptical eyes under brows that no longer met in the middle. Then she freed her hands, turned away and smoothed the shirt on the bed, again and again, even though there was no need.

'You could have come to me a second time,' she said.

'Then would you have said yes?'

'You know,' said Chanele and unfolded the shirt, which she had already laid

119

folded on the bed. 'I have no nedinye. I have no family. I have no place where I really belong. Can I afford to turn down a job I'm offered just like that?'

'I haven't offered you a job,' Janki said furiously.

'That was how it seemed to me.'

'Just because I said I needed someone who knows how to muck in?'

'I have nothing against work.'

'What do you expect me to do? Declare my love?'

'Not any more.'

'Then what am I supposed to ...?'

'Nothing at all.'

Janki sat down on the bed, in the middle of a freshly folded shirt, and struck his forehead with both fists. 'I don't understand you.'

'I know.' Chanele nodded several times. 'You're stupid.' Then she sat down beside him, hunched her shoulders as if slipping into a dress a size too small for her, and said very quietly: 'But we can live with that.' And rested a hand on his.

'Can I kiss you?' asked Janki after a long moment.

'No,' said Chanele. 'Maybe later. We'll see.'

When Janki announced that he was going to marry Chanele, Salomon just said, 'Nu!' which in this case meant: 'Nothing in this house surprises me any more.'

Golde almost forgot to hug them both, because while Janki, less eloquent than they were used to hearing him, was still delivering his contorted explanation, it was clear to her that she would now have to prepare for a double chassene, a task whose like had never been seen in Endingen before.

Mimi's reaction to the news, and this might not necessarily have been expected, was friendly, practically relieved. 'Now I know at last,' she later said to Anne-Kathrin 'that it's not because of me that Janki ... I have, without knowing it, been nurturing ...'

'...a viper at your bosom!' Anne-Kathrin, who had read the same books, completed the phrase.

The two chassenes were to take place on the same day, which struck Salomon as only sensible. When the wedding was being planned, Mimi insisted that Janki and Chanele – 'It's unthinkable otherwise!' – come under the chuppah ahead of her, and told only Anne-Kathrin the reason: 'All the people will stay there to wait for me and Pinchas, and the others will be standing outside after their wedding, and nobody will be there to congratulate them!'

Janki had already decided to give up on the house with the Red Shield, and was pleasantly surprised when he learned that Chanele was to have a nedinye after all – and what a nedinye! Chanele even cried when Salomon told her, which was extremely unpleasant for the cattle-trader, who had never known her to do anything of the kind. To complicate matters even further, he didn't tell them that the sum was only as high as it was because Janki had negotiated badly the first time.

In such a short time a second trousseau could not be supplied, but they made do. 'Because of us,' Golde said, 'they should not lie on their bare tochus in Baden.' The garconnière was cancelled even before Janki had moved in, and Janki wrote to Guebwiller about the furniture that was still in storage with the coachman. When it was delivered, it was shabbier than he remembered, but for the time being – six thousand francs isn't the same as twelve, after all – they would have to do. Chanele made curtains, and in the end it was not a flat where you could impress elegant friends, but certainly one in which you could live.

Chanele had made it very clear that she wanted to have a parlour and not a drawing room, and the tantalus now stood on the old table from Guebwiller. If the curtains – not made of Shantung silk, but not exactly rags either – were open and the sun shone into the right corner, the yellow liquid gleamed like gold.

'One day everything in our house will be as elegant as that,' said Janki.

'Make Shabbos with it,' said Chanele.

On 17 December, two days after Chanukah, the chuppah was set up in Endingen synagogue.

It was a cold day, the coldest of the year. Anyone who wanted to be there – and who would have missed the double event – had to fight their way through heavy drifts of snow on the way to shul. The musicians who were to have collected the brides from home had appeared on time, but fearing for his instrument the violinist refused to play in the street, and the trumpeter and trombonist could produce nothing more than a gloomy rhythm, to which people could only slouch, and not march cheerily and proudly along.

Mimi and Chanele walked along side by side, and if anyone had been standing watching them by the side of the road – but no one was, it was far too cold for that – he would have taken them for the best of friends. Over the past few weeks they had treated one another with exquisite politeness, and only once, when they went to the ritually cleansing immersion bath at the mikvah, and met one another on neutral ground, they had talked of their true concerns. But no one had witnessed that conversation apart from Mother Feigele, who liked to make herself useful at the mikvah because it was always well heated, and Mother Feigele was deaf.

Mimi set one foot in front of the other in her expensive new boots, thinking as she did so about a historical novel that Anne-Kathrin had lent her, the story of the queens Elizabeth and Mary Stuart. They had walked along side by side and nodded graciously to the people, except that one of them was going to the scaffold and didn't yet know. 'I'm glad I'm getting Pinchas and not that chap Janki who wandered in from nowhere,' thought Mimi, and almost persuaded herself to feel sorry for Chanele.

During the first wedding she had to wait in a side room, next to a box of battered Holy Scriptures waiting to be buried with the corpse at the next levaya. A chair had been brought for her, but she thought it was dusty so she chose instead to stand and shiver in her white dress.

The noises in the synagogue hall could be heard only as a distant murmur, and it was impossible to make out voices or even individual words, and yet Mimi followed the sequence of the ritual in all its smallest details.

First the bride was led under the chuppah. As Chanele had not a single relative in the village, two women from the community had undertaken this task of honour: Hulda Moos, who always liked to push her way to the front at mitzvahs, and Red Moische's wife. The prayers and songs could not be distinguished from one another, but Mimi could still have spoken and sung along with them. It was in any case only a kind of rehearsal before they would then sound, with the same words and the same tunes, for her.

Now Salomon Meijer and Naftali Pomeranz were leading Janki to his kalleh. He was probably making a very pious face as they did, supporting himself heavily on his walking stick and dragging his right leg, the fraud.

They sang and prayed, and then the vague noise ebbed away and Mimi heard – she didn't really hear it, but she heard it all the same – Rav Bodenheimer uttering the marriage blessing to the chassen, and the chassen repeating every word individually. 'Herewith,' said Janki, 'you are made sacred to me, by the laws of Moses and Israel.'

It had been exactly as cold back then, as ice cold as it was in this bare room, back then when he had stood outside the house in his uniform, a pirate or an explorer, with his fake bandage and his fake eyes. She granted him to Chanele, she really granted him to her, and for that reason she smiled at the dead prayer books, with a majestic smile, and made a dismissive movement of her hand, just as Elizabeth did in the book, when she said, 'Cut her head off, but do it with respect, she is a queen like me.'

And then – the sudden noise surprised her, because she hadn't been thinking of that other marriage any more, and why should she have? – then the people in the synagogue were all making a great hubbub, 'Mazel tov!' they cried, and that meant that Janki had stamped on the glass that was stamped on at every marriage in memory of the destruction of the temple, that the ceremony was over or nearly over, that Janki and Chanele were a couple, a couple for the rest of their lives, according to the law of Moses and Israel.

It was really very cold.

'Have you been crying?' asked Golde when she came to collect Mimi.

'Why should I cry?' asked Mimi.

She allowed herself to be led between Golde and Sarah Pomeranz to the canopy. 'We must look ridiculous,' she thought, 'Sarah so long and thin and my mother so small.'

The people smiled at her, and she kept her head quite straight, like a queen.

When she stepped under the chuppah, something crunched under her shoe. It was a splinter of the glass that Janki had broken.

1893

15

Uncle Salomon never told anyone in advance when he was coming to Baden. Janki had often enough offered to send him a coachman, whenever he liked; as long as the information was received in time, a coach could be easily organised; after all, they delivered far into the Canton. But Salomon didn't want to be pinned down. 'All my life I've gone my own way,' he said in that cantankerous way he had, 'and now I'm supposed to know in advance when I'm where?'

The truth was that Salomon had become peculiar since Golde's death. Even Chanele had to admit that. Sometimes he locked himself up in the house for days at a time, no one knew if he was even eating anything, and when people dropped by to check on him, he wouldn't open the door. And it was quite a trek from Baden to Endingen, even if you drove it could easily take half a day, which was lost to the shop. And what about him? He left you standing in the street, you had to knock and shout, and once he calmed down and unbolted the door he refused to be disturbed, he had to work, he was on the track of major discoveries and under no circumstances could he interrupt his calculations. It was no longer the register of Simmental cattle that so intensely preoccupied him; he had completely abandoned the beheimes trade. Salomon's new passion – 'It's already more than an illness,' Janki said – was gematria, a Cabbalistic method of performing complicated calculations with the numerical value of Hebrew letters, to read hidden connections out of agreements and differences. Here too, Salomon was very much the cattle trader: he had practised juggling with numbers in a thousand cattle trades, and when he succeeded in wrestling a new meaning from a word with great computational skill, he was as happy as if he had purchased a cow at a knock-down price.

'My own name,' he would pontificate by way of example, Salomon, Shlomo, has a numerical value of three hundred and seventy five. Golde had a numerical value of forty-eight. Take forty-eight away from three hundred and seventy five – and what do you have left? Three hundred and twenty seven. And which word in the Torah has a numerical value of three hundred and twenty seven? Ho-arboyim, evening twilight. What is that trying to tell us? Since the Lord took my Golde away, evening has fallen in my life. All I have left is waiting for the night, for death.' When he said such things, he wasn't sad or anything, he smiled quite cheerfully as he spoke, as if providing an explanation and being right were consolation enough for him.

Golde had died quite suddenly, her death caused to some extent by motion. She had gone to Zurich, to see Mimi who – me neshuma! – had been through some difficult times, and who had found herself terribly out of her depth, had spent two days instilling the fear of God into that slut of a servant girl, had then got back onto the train to be at home in time for Shabbos preparations at home, and had just sat there, hadn't got out in Baden, or in Turgi, or in Brugg, and when the man who cleaned the carriages there poked her with his finger to wake her up, she had simply toppled sideways, 'like a bag of flour', the man said. When the chevra came to fetch the corpse, it was lying in the luggage store room. The right hand, which could no longer be opened easily, was still clutching a bag. In it was a large piece of smoked meat, the speciality of Pinchas's butcher's shop in Zurich.

Even in the cemetery, halfway between Endingen and Lengnau, Salomon had maintained his composure, and at the shiva, too, no one had noticed anything but the normal grief of a widower. It was only when Janki asked him, quite quietly and reasonably, on the last day of the week of mourning, whether he mightn't think of dissolving the household in Endingen and moving in with them in Baden, after all, there was plenty of room in the big flat, there was a sewing room that was never used, that Salomon had started shouting, all of a sudden and in a way that was most unlike him. They were to leave him alone, he had shouted, he wanted to stay with Golde, and apart from that he needed nothing and nobody.

Now he sat day after day over his calculations, visited by nobody but the shnorrers who buzzed around the double house in Endingen like bees around a particularly luxurious shrub. From Bialystok to Mir the address had been discussed as a place where you didn't first have to laboriously reel out your tales of woe about sick parents and starving children, where all you had to do was listen to the Cabbalistic ravings of the master of the house for an hour or two, stroke your beard and nod, before moving on amply piled with food and gifts. Janki repeatedly complained about this pointless waste of money, even though, as he stressed, it didn't affect him personally, because while his wife Chanele might have grown up in Salomon's house, nothing would come to her after his death.

Sometimes Salomon would take his umbrella at dawn and then walk the old paths for hours, to Zurzach, for example, on a day when there was no market there, or to the farming villages where he had once done his deals. There, as people were already saying all over the place, to Janki's irritation and Chanele's concern, he would enter some byre or other without a word of explanation, leave it just as silently, frighten the maids and be laughed at by the labourers, stayed whole nights away and was then, if anyone rebuked him for it, suddenly the old Salomon again, thoughtful and humorous.

'Of course I would rather come and see you unannounced,' he once said, 'ideally in the afternoon, when I can be sure that Janki is in his fabric store-room and Chanele in the other shop. Then I can sit down in the kitchen, fat Christine makes me coffee, a piece of bread or cake is found and I can talk at my leisure to my friend Arthur.'

Arthur, the late-comer, loved his uncle Salomon, because he treated him like an adult. 'You will soon have your bar mitzvah,' Salomon had declared. 'Thirteen years old, and thirteen is the numerical value of the word Echod. What does Echod mean? Echod mi yodea? Nu? Didn't you pay attention in cheder?'

'Echod means one.'

'Correct! And what does thirteen have to do with one? Very simple: when you are thirteen years old, you are no longer just a part of your family, you are a human being in your own right. An individual. A man. And I'm not supposed to talk to you seriously?'

If one has always been the youngest, always the one who understands the least, there is nothing more valuable than a person who gives you the feeling of being on an equal footing with you. Not that Arthur was jealous of his older siblings, that was not part of his character. He had a low opinion of himself, he knew that he would never smile as elegantly as Shmul or glow from within as Hinda did. He wasn't even dainty, which would have been the natural role of the baby of the family. Arthur was an angular child, he wasn't comfortable in his own skin and lost himself time and again in thoughts too complicated for his incomplete intelligence. He was often deemed to be precocious, but that wasn't right. Arthur was younger than his years, and that can be very painful.

Shmul, on the other hand, or actually François...The very fact that his brother had two different names profoundly impressed Arthur. He too would have liked a second personality that he could slip into, and sometimes at night when the leaves of the plane trees cast threatening lunar shadows on the wall of his room, he imagined himself as a Siegfried or a Hector, a broad-shouldered, fair-haired boy who could run faster than everyone else and throw a ball with-out his fellow pupils shouting 'Butterfingers! Butterfingers!'

If their eldest had two names, it was down to the fact that during the first week of his life, the eight days until the bris, Janki and Chanele had not, as so often, been of the same opinion. Janki argued for François, after his revered Maître Delormes, while Chanele, who had never known her own parents, insisted that the child should be called after Janki's late father, Shmul, because it's only if someone goes on bearing a name that the dead remain alive. And anyway, who had ever heard of a Jewish boy being named after a goyish tailor?

They never agreed on what the boy was to be called, but neither did they argue about it, as they seldom argued, each one instead imposing his or her own will, as if they had two different firstborn sons, Janki a François and Chanele a Shmul.

Shmul-François or François-Shmul learned early on to be one thing for one and another for the other, and to derive from this whatever he wanted. When he started talking, as he did very late, he talked about himself in a nameless third person, saying 'He's hungry' or 'He doesn't want to go to sleep,' and tacked as skilfully back and forth between his parents as if being a child had been merely a part he played, and the tousled head of curls no more than a theatrical wig. When his hair, in line with custom, was cut for the first time on his third birthday, it seemed to Chanele as if an entirely alien person were coming to light, someone she didn't know, and of whom she was strangely afraid.

By now François was twenty-one, he smoked Russian cigarettes in an almost authentic amber holder and had a moustache that he rubbed with wax every week. He also subjected his hair to strict discipline, using a pomade that he bought from the barber in colourful tins. The picture on the lid showed an Indian maharaja next to an English officer, and when the tins were empty, Arthur was given them for all the things he collected: stamps, of course, all schoolboys do that, but also the portraits of foreign races that came with certain cigarette packs, and optical illusions that seemed to change when you looked at them for some time.

Hinda also supported Arthur's mania for collecting things. It had been her who had given him his most precious possession: a ticket d'entrée with a picture of a Greek god listening interestedly but languidly to a muse. Janki had brought it for her, for her of course, as a souvenir of his first trip as a buyer to Paris, it was his ticket to the world's fair, where he had seen real-life savages and all of Thomas Edison's four hundred and ninety-three inventions. For his bar mitzvah, Arthur's dearest wish was for a microscope, because he too would have liked to be an inventor, and he was grateful to his sister for not laughing at him when he talked about it.

Hinda had slipped out of Chanele almost without causing her any pain. That was actually impossible, the midwife said, but she could have sworn that the child had, when it was barely born, smiled open-eyed into the light, and children seldom smile so early. At the holekrash, the naming ceremony for girls, Hinda allowed herself to be lifted up and carried around without crying once. Golde, Salomon told the story often, had kept wiping her eyes dry throughout the whole sude, while repeating the words, 'Like a princess!' Mimi, beside her, had drawn circles on her temples with her fingertips, because the happiness of other mothers always gave her a migraine.

Later, when Hinda was older, she wasn't afraid of anything, not even spiders. When her father fancied a particular bottle of wine she went to the cellar all by herself, just with a candle, and saw nothing of the ghosts that danced on the walls. Arthur admired her a lot for that. And even Janki, who normally saved the big words up for particularly good customers, admitted it: Hinda was a ray of sunshine.

Janki didn't have much time for Arthur; the business devoured him. When Arthur heard that phrase for the first time, when he was still a little boy, he had been terrified, and had clung weeping to his father until Janki shook him off and said to Chanele: 'You mollycoddle that boy.'

'Sometimes,' Arthur said to Uncle Salomon, and it was something that he had never confided in a single soul, 'sometimes I would rather be a girl.'

'Interesting,' Salomon said. He had crumbled a piece of cake into his coffee and was stirring the mixture around slowly, with great concentration. With each rotation the spoon hit the edge of the cup with a melodic chink. In the background Christine, the cook, provide a basso continuo on a chopping board full of onions. 'Very interesting. A girl. Why?'

'I don't know, it's stupid.'

'Nothing you think is stupid. Only not thinking at all is stupid.' Since Salomon had been preoccupied with gematria, he had become used to speaking in sentences.

'But it isn't really possible.'

'So?' Salomon waved his hand dismissively, and so violently that his coffee spoon skittered across the table top. 'What does possibility have to do with anything? Every day I dream that Golde is alive again.' The spoon had left a trail of coffee behind, and with his finger Salomon drew a snaking line in it. 'Why would you like to be a girl? Nu?'

'I don't know. It's...I think they have it easier.'

'Christine!'

The basso continuo broke off. 'Yes, Herr Meijer?'

'Do women have it easier than men?'

When Christine laughed, and she had a roaring, masculine laugh, she always kept a hand in front of her mouth, like a boxer feeling for a tooth that's just been knocked out. When she had a carp to kill for Shabbos, she didn't hit it on the head with a tenderising hammer, but stuck her wide thumb in its mouth and broke its neck with a jerk.

'You're a funny one, Herr Meijer,' she said in a strangled voice. 'We women do all the work.'

'That might be an argument against your thesis,' said Uncle Salomon. Arthur was flattered that he used such adult words.

'But girls don't need to have bar mitzvahs!'

At the bar mitzvah, the day when one becomes an adult in the middle of childhood, one has to deliver the sidra in the service, the Torah passage of the week, you have to learn it by heart, word for word and note for note, you have to stand up in front of the whole congregation as a singer, torture for someone who almost dies of embarrassment when he has, by way of punishment, to stand up in front of the class at school and recite Schiller's 'Veiled Image at Sais', in a quivering voice, every single verse. And then, if your voice assumes a life of its own, if it suddenly, without any advance warning, starts squeaking or growling...

'All our voices have broken,' said Uncle Salomon. 'And we still survived our bar mitzvahs.'

'Yes, fine,' said Arthur, 'but Shmul...' Shmul, whose big day he could still remember − there had been a whole table of cakes and a drop of wine, very sweet and warm − Shmul had trilled like a little bird in the prayer room, and Janki had been very proud of him, but that was it, Shmul was Shmul and Arthur was Arthur, and in his case, he was sure of it, the whole dreadful disaster would come about, the one they whispered about in cheder behind their raised copies of the chumash, his voice would finally break, on that precise day, at that very minute, he wouldn't be able to make a sound, not even a wrong one, he would just stand there and croak, and everyone would stare at him and shake their heads. Only Cantor Würzburger, with whom he had been studying this passage twice a week for months, would nod and say in his high, German voice, 'I always knew the boy would make me look a fool.'

And then there was the address, as well, the droosh that one had to deliver at major feasts, the learned speech that the listeners knew better than the speaker did, because Cantor Würzburger, who also rehearsed this part of the ritual, had only three addresses in his repertoire, which he drilled into his bar mitzvah boys in turn. Arthur had been landed with the one about those commandments which are time-bound, and from which women are therefore exempt, and he was sure − how could it be otherwise? − that he would falter or dry up, he simply wouldn't know how to go on, so that Chanele would lower her head, very slowly, as she did when she was really furious. And Janki would...

'You left out shitting your pants during the droosh,' said Uncle Salomon. 'That would be even worse, and it isn't going to happen either. If bar mitzvahs were really as hard as you think, the Jewish people would have died out long ago.'

'But...' said Arthur.

'You talk too much,' said Uncle Salomon. 'In the old days, if someone had offered me a cow and gone on the way you're doing, I wouldn't have bought it.' He licked his spoon clean, thoroughly and carefully, and then asked in a much quieter voice than before: 'Tell me, dear boy, what it is that you really want to say. Why would you like to be a girl?'

Arthur blushed. That happened to him often, the heat simply rose up within him and there was nothing he could do about it. He cast an anxious glance at Christine, but she had disappeared behind her veil of steam and was stirring her soup-pot with the concentration of an alchemist.

'My face is so ugly,' Arthur, feeling his eyes growing moist. 'If I had long hair, people wouldn't see it as much.'

Uncle Salomon didn't laugh at him. Neither did he say, 'You aren't ugly, mon joujou,' as Aunt Mimi would have done. He said nothing at all, just rested his big, heavy cattle-trader hands on Arthur's head and very slowly and searchingly felt its contours, ran one hand over the back of his head and the other over his nose, pinched his cheeks and tapped his teeth inquiringly with his fingernails. His fingers, with their rough tips, smelt reassuringly of snuff. In the end he wiped his hands on his frock coat, a gesture that he had acquired over many visits to cow-byres. Arthur waited for his judgement, like a seriously ill patient after a thorough examination, waiting for the diagnosis of the specialist.

'Nu,' said Uncle Salomon.

Arthur lowered his head. But two strong fingers gripped him under his chin and forced him to look up. Uncle Salomon puffed out his cheeks, lips closed. Where they weren't covered by his white whiskers, his many burst veins looked like colourful hundreds and thousands sprinkled on a cake.

'There is only one solution for your problem,' said Uncle Salomon. 'You will have to grow a beard.'

Arthur stared at him

'Not straight away, of course. Life has its rules. First come the pimples, then the beard. Shall I let you into a secret?' He tugged around at his own beard until the yellowish white strands pointed in all directions. 'I didn't like my looks when I was a boy either. In my case it was my hair, which I lost far too early. They called me "the galekh". But whether it's your hair or your face – no one likes themselves. Apart from stupid people. They like themselves a lot. So.' He rubbed his hands as if he were washing them without water. 'Now your parents can come home. I'm hungry.'

'But you won't say anything to them. Please.'

'About what?'

'What I told you.'

'You know,' Uncle Salomon said, with a lot of wrinkles around his eyes, 'I'm sometimes so lost in my own thoughts that I don't even hear what's being said to me. I've been working something out all the time. The difference between boys and girls. Are you interested in it?' He picked up his spoon like a pointer and began to pontificate. 'Son is ben, and has the numerical value of fifty-two. Daughter is bat – four hundred and two. A difference of three hundred and fifty. Does that mean that daughters are worth that much more than sons?'

'Perhaps,' said Arthur quietly.

'Wrong. Three hundred and fifty is, in fact, the numerical value of the word pera. And what does pera mean?'

'I don't know.'

'Pera means long hair! Like that grown by someone who has made a vow.' Salomon held the palm of his hand out to Arthur and made him shake hands as if concluding the purchase of a cow. 'So a girl, we can see from the gematria, is nothing more than a boy who has decided to stop cutting his hair. But if you add two hundred and fifty and four hundred and two…'

'What sort of maassehs are you telling the boy?' A maasseh is just a story, but the way Janki pronounced the word, it meant more than that: a stupid story, a superfluous story, a story that wastes valuable time, time that a little boy would be better off using to do his homework or learn his bar mitzvah address, so that he didn't make a fool of himself with it.

Janki hadn't come all the way into the kitchen. He stopped in the doorway, with the face of a Sunday walker whose path has led him around the edge of a bog, and who fears for his clean shoes. His light grey coat was cut quite generously, the way artists in Paris liked them at the moment. He held his hat in his hand, along with the lion-headed walking stick.

'Why don't you tell me when you're coming? So that we can at least send a carriage for you. What does it look like when you march down the main road on foot like a…like a…'

'Like a beheimes dealer, you mean? Nu, there are worse things.' Salomon rose from his chair and bent for the umbrella that had been lying at his foot the whole time like a faithful dog. His body looked smaller than before, bulky and less powerful. Golde's death had given the whole man a good shake and let him collapse in on himself.

'And why are you sitting in the kitchen and not in the drawing-room?'

'Because of Christine, of course,' said Salomon and winked at Arthur, as men do to one another. 'I've never been able to resist beautiful women.'

The fat cook, embarrassed, laughed her gurgling boxer's laugh.

'You shouldn't keep her from her work. Certainly not today, when we have guests.'

'I can go again,' said Salomon. 'It isn't all that far to Endingen anyway.'

'You know I wouldn't allow that.'

Arthur, who had a keen sense for things unsaid, looked anxiously back and forth between his father and Uncle Salomon.

'Of course you must stay,' said Janki. 'Although in fact today...'

'Important visitors?'

'A few business colleagues. Nothing special. Just a sandwich.'

'For which I've spent three days standing at the stove,' Christine grumbled into her soup pot.

'"Guest" is an interesting word, by the way,' said Salomon. 'In Hebrew it has the numerical value of two hundred and fifteen, exactly the same amount as...'

'Not now. Please.' Janki had great trouble keeping the polite smile on his face. 'I have a lot of preparation to do. And you need to...'

'What?'

'You aren't going to sit down at our table like that, are you?'

Salomon gripped the flaps of his old-fashioned frock coat and turned once in a circle on tripping footsteps. 'This is as handsome as I get,' he said.

'I'll fetch you a new shirt from the shop.' Janki had come into the kitchen after all. 'To what do we owe the honour of this visit, in fact?'

'I nearly forgot,' said Salomon. 'I've brought a letter. For Chanele.'

16

She must have run home five or ten times in the course of the day to give Christine one final instruction for the kitchen, and then one very last one; to be sure that Louisli, the inexperienced new serving girl, didn't try to polish the precious silver knives with scouring powder, as had actually happened in Mimi's Zurich house; to put out the big damask tablecloth for the two hired servants who helped out at all the big dinners in Baden, and entrust them with the key to the porcelain cupboard; to check this and correct that, because the formal events that Janki organised twice a year for his goyish business associates were battles that you could only fight successfully if you took into account every eventuality and every possible setback from the outset, and had prepared the correct strategy in advance. During the battle itself, once the guests had arrived, one had to be able to direct one's troops from the general's hillock at the end of the table with nothing more than the twitch of a finger and a nod of the head, and at the same time smile without meaning it, chat without saying anything and stress repeatedly that you hadn't gone to any trouble, and that what you were serving up was little more than a round of sandwiches.

If it had been possible, Chanele would have crossed these evenings out of the diary once and for all, not because they caused her too much trouble, but because she thought they were pointless, the mimicked ritual of a society to which one would never fully belong. It was a disguise, a masquerade that even involved her kitchen, because Chanele's house was of course run on kosher lines, and given that there was a prohibition on mixing meat and milk, one had to summon up a lot of imagination to find something appropriate to go with the butter sauces customary on such occasions.

She had run home at least ten times – luckily they only lived opposite, and only had to cross the little square between the Weite and the Mittlere Gasse – and ten times she had hurried back to the shop. To their shop, even though Janki's name was over the door in gold letters, Propriétaire Jean Meijer, and even though Herr Ziltener, the accountant, only ever said about any decision that affected them, 'I will suggest that to the boss.' But where everything else was concerned, Ziltener was anxiously meticulous, down to the tiniest detail; satirically minded commentators even said that he read his punctual 'good morning' from the paper frills that he wore to protect his sleeves. For all other colleagues there was no doubt who was really in charge at the Modern Drapery: Madame Meijer, and no one else.

Madame Meijer liked to be the last one left in the shop in the evening. She needed those undisturbed moments, she needed them more than ever. Chanele loved to stroll around the deserted sales rooms with the blouses laid neatly in piles, and shelves full of ribbons and haberdashery, here nudging a lady's hat on its wooden stand to exactly the right angle, there putting a forgotten tape measure back in its correct place behind the counter. She enjoyed those secret minutes, the only ones in the day that belonged to her alone, a young girl behind the bolted door, opening the trousseau for the hundredth time, counting the bedclothes and running her hand over the cambric undershirts. She had even ordered, or had Ziltener suggest to the boss, that the gas lamps were only ever to be turned off two hours after the close of business, a form of advertising, she had said by way of explanation, to signal to the customers that people in the shop went on working for them until late at night. You had to know how to deal with Janki.

Of course everyone in the company knew about that little foible the boss's wife had, and anyone who had to work longer at the shop, perhaps because a curtain ordered for the following day had to be stitched in a hurry, or a delivery that had arrived late had to be unpacked, stayed in the workshop or the store-room, kept the door shut, and wouldn't have dared to disturb Madame Meijer on her rounds.

Madame Meijer...

Chanele hadn't slipped into the new role on the day of her wedding. When someone is recruited to the military, you can dress him up on the spot, but under his uniform he is still a civilian at first. Inner feeling chases after outward circumstances, and we have all seen examples when the two never catch up. During the initial phase of her marriage Chanele had behaved as if she had merely switched servitudes, from one Meijer house to another. She ran her household quietly and inconspicuously, and even right at the start, when there was no question of hiring a servant, there was never a pan left unscoured nor an oven door covered with soot. Chanele cooked, she baked, and then when she came to her husband's table – still the old table, which Janki had had brought from Guebwiller, not the long, new one at which he would now entertain his guests – when she finally sat down, wherever she sat became the bottom of the table. Janki soon became used to issuing the mute commands that he had observed at Salomon's house in Endingen, reached his hand out without a word when he wanted to have a plate passed to him, or, when he came into the house, simply dropped his coat on the floor when he came into the house. But what for the old Meijers had been a wordless interplay, more an intertwining of forces than a sequence of orders given and obeyed, was slightly off in the young couple, like a wheel set not quite precisely on its hub. However, Chanele never seemed to be bothered by Janki's high-handed behaviour; at least she never rebelled against it.

She had also started to help out in the French Drapery Store again; it was as if she had never been away. She smiled politely and made tea, took the customers' coats off when they came in and handed them their hatpins before they left, wore the brown dress with the cambric trim and never contradicted when her husband went on calling her Mademoiselle Hanna in front of the customers. He also used that name, incidentally, when they were on their own, he whispered it into her body in bed, and although she generally responded to his attentions more or less dutifully, as she would have swept a cabinet-maker's workshop or harnessed a coachman's horses, during those moments she felt something like the memory of a feeling, a tone of thought that goes on vibrating after you wake up, even though you have long since forgotten the dream that goes with it.

All in all the young Chanele, even more severely trained by the awareness of her dependency than by the model set by Golde, was a blameless wife. At the 'Eshet chayil mi yimtza' Janki could have smiled at her, as Salomon always smiled at Golde, but he repeated the old words – and even that only for the first few years – without meaning them. Only on one single point did Chanele refuse to obey her husband from the outset. However much he tried to persuade her, whether he tried flattery or argued the duty of keeping up appearances, which she now had to perform by his side: never again did she pluck her eyebrows. The dark line across her face remained, and the more she became Madame Meijer, the less imaginable she was without it.

Chanele's transformation, if one wished to give a starting point to this slow process, began with the opening of the Modern Emporium at the House of the Red Sign, or in fact with a conversation that she had with Golde shortly before it opened. Old Frau Meijer – that was what she called herself, and she was proud of her mother-in-law title – hadn't come to Baden because of Janki and Chanele that time, but to take the train to see Mimi in Zurich. However, she had found time to be shown around the still unfinished sales rooms by Chanele. She had stopped in front of a mirror newly fixed to the wall, sucked her lower lip deep into her mouth and thoughtfully considered herself and Chanele.

'You need different clothes,' Golde said at last.

'What do you mean?'

'You're dressed like an employee. And you're the owner.'

'I am?'

'The shop's being set up with your nedinye.'

'But that doesn't make me the boss,' said Chanele and Golde laughed.

'Of course not. You must let your husband have his head. But who is the brains in that head?' She beckoned Chanele over with a bent index finger as if to whisper a secret in her ear, but just looked at her and spread her arms, as one does to emphasise the irrefutable conclusion of a long argument. 'Nu?' she said, and the impersonation was so perfect that Chanele couldn't help laughing out loud.

'In our house it was Salomon's head that decreed the rules,' Golde said. 'Things will be the same for you. And that's why you need different clothes.'

That had been the start. Without the new shop Chanele would probably never have become Madame Meijer.

Janki, who also saw himself as something of an artist where business matters were concerned, had only thought in the most general terms about the possibilities for further development that a wider clientele would involve, he fantasised numbers, and he liked those numbers, but it was Chanele who knew from her own experience the everyday life and the needs of the people who would buy at the new shop. Often enough she had suffered from the compulsion of having to talk her way at length into a discount of five rappen or a handful of free corks, so she was the first to see to it – later no one could imagine things being otherwise, but back in the 1870s it represented an unheard-of innovation – that all goods, without exception, were sold at an unchangeable price fixed in writing, so that from the outset there was no bargaining in the shop, no 'Jewing', as it was generally known. 'For every customer delighted with a good deal, you will get three who feel cheated,' she told Janki. 'And besides; we can't leave it up to each individual assistant to set the price from one case to the next.' But the argument with which she most thoroughly convinced him was a quite different one: 'I've heard that this is what they do now in the smartest shops in London.'

Furthermore, and this too was an unheard-of innovation at the time, the Emporium was the first establishment in the place that employed saleswomen as well as salesmen. Admittedly female assistants had not been anything unusual in the past, but they had their place, as seamstresses or ironing ladies, only ever in the back rooms. Now young women physically stood there behind the counters, in the uniform that Chanele had designed for them: a black dress with a narrow white collar, and a pale grey apron. When she herself went to work – and increasingly she felt that only what she did outside the house was real work – Chanele was dressed very similarly, although of course without the apron. Instead of the collar her dress had a white trim, no longer cambric but the best Brussels lace, affixed to which, like a kind of officer's flash, there was a brooch with a cameo that Golde had given to her as a wedding present.

If Chanele liked to employ women it had nothing to do with emancipation, a word that might have been known in Zurich, but certainly not in Baden. Women's wages were lower, that was one very practical reason, and the other: there are lots of things that women would never buy from men. What one might once have bought from a familiar door-to-door saleswoman was now suddenly available, with the same discretion but in a much wider selection, at the House of the Red Sign, and even in its first year of business the Modern Emporium sold considerable quantities of embroidered ladies' stockings and above all corsets, which in their simplest form could be had for as little as a franc. Janki was glad of the good profits he made in such everyday articles as children's pinafores or knitted striped socks for ladies, but those things were not the ones that really interested him. It would have been extremely embarrassing for him to walk through the shop and have a lady customer ask him about dress shields or waistbands.

So it was that the French Store and the Modern Emporium gradually became two very different shops, his and hers, each one with its own very particular character. On Vordere Metzggasse everything was French and elegant; Monsieur Jean Meijer held court among select fabrics, carried out sales as an act of mercy and received the money of his lady customers as a tribute quite naturally owed to him. Sometimes, and these were often the most lucrative afternoons, he didn't even open the curtains over the shelves, he only talked for an hour or two with the ladies of the town and, if heavily coaxed, related this or that experience from the Battle of Sedan.

In the House with the Red Sign, on the other hand, they got straight to the point, they talked not about heroic deeds but about indienne or muslin, they sold fabrics promptly by the metre or, for the older ladies, by the ell, and treated city women and villagers with the same routine politeness. Chanele – no: Madame Meijer – ran a tight ship, and woe to the assistant who dared to be sniffy when dealing with a customer from the country just because she wanted to buy nothing more than an antimacassar or a piece of Russian braid. 'We will have to gather everyone together again,' Madame Meijer made a mental note, 'and remind them that the smallest purchase is as important to us as the largest.'

Chanele ended her round and went back to her office, a modest room, smaller than that of Ziltener the accountant. The decoration was spartan, like the captain's cabin on a warship; there was only one shelf for files, and a plain writing-desk scattered with old ink stains, the last of the pieces of furniture that had come from Guebwiller back then. Here too she had developed a little ritual: every evening, as a final task, before she went home, she turned the little cardboard discs on her calendar so that they were ready for the next day. As she turned the ninth of May 1893 into the tenth, and a Tuesday into a Wednesday, the town clock struck the quarter-hour and Chanele thought, 'I must get a move on. Janki will go quite meshuga with waiting.' At the same time, spurred on by the same chimes, Madame Meijer was considering: 'Communion wreath. With cloth flowers and embroidery. That would certainly go down well at this time of year.'

'Excuse me.' The knocking had been so quiet that Chanele had at first ignored it. A woman in the spartan uniform of the Emporium was standing in the doorway.

Mathilde Lutz, née Mathilde Vogelsang, had been the very first saleswoman that Chanele had employed more than twenty years before. Now, with prematurely grey hair in a severe bun, she looked strict and superior, particularly when she put on the pince-nez that was fastened to her dress with a black velvet band. Back then – could it really have been more than twenty years ago – she had been a lively and, more particularly, a very pretty young girl, with a saucy little beauty spot on her cheek, and many a male customer had come into the shop just for her, on the pretext of having to buy something for his wife. She had soon left the company to marry, but had come back after her husband's early death, no longer at the counter – there were younger girls there now – but as a kind of governess whose job it was to ensure discipline and good behaviour among the female employees.

Madame Meijer and Frau Lutz were not friends; a general has comrades among his officers, not friends. But they were about the same age, they had experienced the rise of the Emporium together and, even though they had never said as much, shared the conviction that the unpleasant sides of life could not be improved by complaining.

'Excuse me,' Frau Lutz said again. 'I know you prefer to be alone at this time of day. But...'

'What is it?'

Mathilde Lutz was not otherwise inclined to shyness, quite the contrary. When she surprised a young couple kissing or in an even more incriminating situation, she was not lost for words; her sharp tongue struck fear into the shop assistants. But now she shifted uncertainly, almost fearfully, from one foot to the other, as only the young salesgirls normally did when they had been caught committing a small act of theft, and had under threat of immediate dismissal been persuaded to deliver a confession.

'I wanted…It's…'

'Nu?' Sometimes without noticing, Madame Meijer was very like old Salomon.

'We have known each other for a long time now, so I thought it better if I myself…'

'What?'

'You will find out, sooner or later.'

Chanele sat down, very carefully, as if she didn't trust the chair. In the gas light, the ink stains on the writing desk looked like dead insects.

'Mathilde,' she said, and Frau Lutz, whom her boss had not addressed by her first name in over two decades, tilted her head to one side in embarrassment. It looked as if she wanted to be stroked. The beauty spot on her cheek, Chanele had never noticed it with such clarity, had grown over the years into a wart. 'Mathilde, what am I about to find out?'

'The men…' In her embarrassment Frau Lutz had wrapped the velvet strap of her pince-nez as tightly around one finger as if she were trying to stem a haemorrhage. 'There's nothing you can do about it. The good lord just made them that way. And Marie-Theres is really very pretty. The one from the blouse department, you know.'

'I do know my employees,' said Chanele, and immediately abandoned her dismissive tone. 'Marie-Theres Furrer, is that right, Mathilde? What's wrong with her?'

It was hard to believe, but severe Frau Lutz blushed.

'Pregnant?' asked Chanele.

'Pregnant,' Frau Lutz whispered, and the word came straight from Sodom and Gomorrah.

Chanele – at that moment she was without a doubt Chanele and not Madame Meijer – laughed with relief. 'Bigger miracles have happened in the world.'

Frau Lutz did not join in with her laughter. 'But it's much worse than that,' she said.

'Twins?' Chanele was still laughing.

'The father. I've talked to Furrer, and she told me that the father…'

'Yes?'

'I'm so sorry that I have to be the one to…'

'Janki,' Chanele said very quietly and was shocked to realise that she wasn't surprised at all. Her husband hadn't called her Mademoiselle Hanna for ages, and she had assumed it was inevitable that he didn't always sleep alone on his business trips, and what the eye didn't see the heart didn't grieve over. But here in Baden, in his own shop...'Is it Janki?' she asked more loudly.

Frau Lutz looked at her uncomprehendingly. For her, who had only ever known Monsieur Jean Meijer, the name was meaningless.

'Is it my husband?'

Frau Lutz shook her head. 'No, Madame Meijer. Of course not. Monsieur Meijer would never...'

Chanele waited for a sense of relief and couldn't find it inside herself. 'Then who is it?'

The velvet strap tore. The pince-nez fell the floor with a faint clatter and broke. Frau Lutz bent down to collect the splinters and whispered into the floorboards, 'Young Herr François.'

'Shmul?' said Chanele.

17

'Shmul!' she would say. 'François!' she would say. 'Did you even think about what that would mean for the company...?'

No, that would be wrong. He would just look at her, contemptuous and weary at the same time, eyebrows raised, with that polite smile that he was so good at hiding behind, that smile that she didn't understand, and which frightened her, even though he was, after all, her own son, the smile of a man who has already lived a lot, when he was only...

Old enough to get a silly girl pregnant.

They would have to fire Marie-Theres Furrer.

No. That would make things even worse. They would have to take care of her, perhaps give her some money...

'The Jews always do everything with their money,' people would say. And if you didn't offer them any, 'The Jews are stingy.'

'Shmul,' they would say. 'We will sort this matter out somehow. But we will not tolerate...'

We?

Janki would be proud of his son. He wouldn't admit it, of course he wouldn't, he would blame him and reproach him, but he wouldn't be able to conceal his pride. 'My son! He has my hair and my face, and he is irresistible.'

'François,' she would say. 'You must promise me once and for all...'

No. Making promises was second nature to Shmul.

She would tell him what she thought, she would drown him in a mussar sermon until he couldn't see or hear, she would...

She managed not to get round to it for the whole evening.

First of all Janki was waiting for her, in the corridor, he came rushing towards her as soon as she had opened the door to the apartment, as if the guests, who hadn't even arrived, of course, had been sitting in the drawing room for hours, starving and shuffling their feet. He was so beside himself that for a moment Chanele thought an accident must have happened in the flat. But the faint smell of charred hair came not from a fire, but from the tongs with which Janki had been curling his hair. He came running out of the laundry room in his long shirt, legs bare, because he had retained the habit from his tailoring days of ironing his trousers himself before important occasions, because no one else could do it to his satisfaction. He still had no trousers on, but he was already wearing his tie, a black silk kerchief knotted into a flapping Lavallière.

'It's a disaster,' said Janki, already quite out of breath. 'You're far too late, and Salomon has arrived unannounced from Endingen. Of course I've invited him to dinner, that is: I had no option. But it means that now we'll have to…'

'The table is long enough.' Chanele looked around for Shmul, but he was nowhere to be seen. 'One place more or less…'

'…means we will…' Janki continued in a whisper. '…that we will be thirteen at table.'

'Does it say anywhere that that's forbidden?'

'Thirteen! Don't you understand? It's an unlucky number.'

'Not for Jews,' said Chanele.

'But all the guests are goyim!'

'Then don't invite your treyf friends.' Chanele had other concerns now.

'Are you even listening?' Janki raised his hands dramatically to the heavens. It looked as if he was about to tear his hair out. 'Thirteen! That means…'

'I've just been explaining that to Arthur.' Salomon now emerged from one of the many rooms into the corridor. 'The gematria of thirteen…'

'Leave me in peace with your gematria!' yelled Janki.

Salomon made a calming gesture, which had proved itself with many an over-eager guard dog. 'Nuuu!' he said, and in this instance it meant: 'Don't get yourself worked up!'

'I'm glad you've come to see us, Uncle,' said Chanele. She still used the old, formal style of address with him. 'Do you have everything you need?'

'The shirt is too tight. You wouldn't tie a rope around a calf's neck as tight as that.'

'It's your size,' said Janki. 'I have an eye for it.'

'But I don't have the neck for it.'

'Where is Shmul?' asked Chanele.

'François is in his room, I assume. He'll be getting himself ready.' His memory jogged, Janki grabbed his Lavallière and tugged the artful knot apart again in a gesture of desperation. 'Thirteen guests!' he wailed as plaintively as a cantor on Yom Kippur.

'Let Arthur eat with us. Then it'll be fourteen.'

'Thirteen and a half,' said Salomon and laughed.

Janki gave him an angry look. 'Arthur doesn't yet know how to behave in society.'

'He will soon. His bar mitzvah is coming up.'

'Why does Hinda have to be at Mimi's in Zurich today of all days?'

At that moment Louisli came into the corridor, already wearing the white bonnet and starched apron that she was supposed to wear to serve at table, saw the master of the house standing bare-legged in front of her, pressed her hand to her mouth and fled into the kitchen.

No, Chanele really had no chance of talking to Shmul.

When he heard what was wanted of him, Arthur tried to creep away. Until now, when they had important guests, he had always been allowed to eat in the kitchen, where not every facial expression and every movement were of crucial importance, and when it was just the family he only had to listen to all the thousand admonishments, to keep his back straight, to hold his spoon with only two fingers, to wipe his mouth before he drank from a glass. An official dinner seemed to be as riddled with obstacles as the suit with all the little bells with which Oliver Twist was supposed to learn to steal. Back then, when he had read the book, Fagin had appeared to him in his dreams every night, and Fagin had had Janki's face, the severe face that Papa made when he wanted to expose one of Arthur's shortcomings. He was convinced, and in such matters his imagination knew no bounds, that he would make a fool of himself, would knock over his soup plate or break a glass, that they would look at him reproachfully, all those strange people, and then nod like Cantor Würzburger when Arthur stalled while practising a droosh. 'We knew all the time,' they would say.

Chanele needed to persuade her son, needed to promise him a flexed nib for his collection because Arthur also collected nibs, which he arranged according to changing systems, a naturalist looking through a pile of various shells or snails for hidden affinities. Then, when she tried to make him wear the good trousers that had fit without any problems at Pesach, they were too small, the bottoms ridiculously halfway up his calves, and Chanele had to decide to get his bar mitzvah suit – which had already been prepared but not of course worn – out of the cupboard and thus exacerbate Arthur's anxiety still further. Any stain on that suit, he knew, would be a calamity that he would never live down for the rest of his life.

Then Louisli, who had been put in a flap by all the excitement in the house, had to be calmed down as well. The dining room had to be checked and instructions given for an altered seating plan. The big table was massive and imposing, and equipped with a modern mechanism that meant it could be extended to twice its length, 'with only one hand', as Janki proudly stressed. The table top – tropical wood! – was hidden under the white damask table-cloth, but one could very faintly catch the scent of the walnut oil with which it was regularly rubbed. When Arthur was even younger, Chanele had once caught him licking the top of the table with his tongue. 'It's an experiment,' he had said.

The table groaned, as it was supposed to, with nouveau riche abundance. The Sarreguemines porcelain – they had enough for twenty people – paraded in a double column, the silver cutlery gleamed and the crystal glasses whose fragility Arthur so dreaded waited around for the lighting of the candles, like debutantes in sequined dresses waiting to display their full beauty. The wine bottles were lined up on the sideboard, a guard of honour for the silver tantalus, which still lacked a key.

In the kitchen Christine had everything under control. She said it with the gritted smile of a boxer who doesn't want to show any weakness just before the victorious conclusion of a fight. The covered bowls and plates waited on the table like heavy artillery awaiting deployment in battle. Only one small gap was not occupied, just big enough for the two hired servants to act as food tasters for the party. They had hung their threadbare dinner jackets over the backs of the chairs and rolled up their sleeves, and when Madame Meijer came in they just lifted their bottoms an inch out of their chairs and greeted her with their mouths full.

And Chanele still couldn't talk to Shmul. She was already on the way to his room, but Janki was already coming towards her and cried in a despairing voice, 'You're not even dressed.'

So she dressed herself up, decorated herself as she had decorated the table in the dining room. Arthur was allowed to button up her dress; that privilege had been part of Chanele's promises, because Arthur loved nothing more than to be allowed to stand in his parents' bedroom, which was otherwise forbidden to him, Marco Polo in an exotic palace, and carefully finger all the little hooks into their eyes. As he was short-sighted, his head almost touched his mother's back, he was allowed to be quite close to her and inhale her very special scent of cleanliness, talcum powder and dependability, before he was dispatched to have his hair combed once more by Louisli.

Since Chanele thought vanity was only ever a waste of time, the rest of the preparations took a very short time; she put on her jewellery as one might hang a bunch of keys on a hook, and where her hair was concerned – well, there is one advantage to the Jewish tradition of wearing a sheitel: you can put your new hairstyle on like a hat.

When she came into the drawing-room, the whole family was already there waiting. Janki looked very elegant in the full glory of an evening suit. He had pinned the Lavallière over his silver brocade waistcoat with an artful careless-ness that must have taken a dozen tries. Shmul, whom she now had to spend an evening calling François, wore a velvet jacket that set off his narrow hips. The freshly waxed tips of his moustache stuck into the air like little knives, and he looked so elegant, in a bored way, that it was easy to imagine what young salesgirls found irresistible about him. Arthur, with a very unhappy face, waited beside his brother. Uncle Salomon had rested a reassuring hand on his shoulder.

'Shmul,' said Chanele, 'I need to talk to you.'

'Don't worry, Mama, I will act quite convincingly as if I'm enjoying the evening.'

'Frau Lutz came to see me today, Mathilde Lutz, and she told me...'

But the first guests were already being ushered in, and Chanele had to stop talking and put on her Mademoiselle-Hanna smile.

The first, as always were of course the accountant Ziltener and his wife. Ziltener, devoted to letters and numbers, had, in spite of all kinds of discreet hints, never been able to understand that etiquette required him to appear only ten minutes after the given time, 'to give the wife of the house the opportunity to carry out the last preparations', as it said in the books of manners. In his worn, dark suit and stiff collar he felt visibly ill at ease, and when he bent over his boss's hand like a folding ruler, she could see how carefully he had combed his thin hair over his bald patch. A sweetish smell of curd soap and mothballs rose from the back of his neck.

Unaccustomed to dealing with children, he was about to ruffle Arthur's hair, but then shied away from the contact at the last moment. His outstretched hand hung in the air as if he were about to bless the boy.

His wife, taller and bonier than he, came from a farming village near Lucerne, and didn't contribute a single word to the conversation. Ziltener had probably forbidden her to say anything apart from 'Good evening' and 'Thank you for the invitation.' They had both been invited only out of kindness, and were abandoned by Janki mid-greeting, when one of the two hired servants brought in the new guests.

Director Strähle, the owner of the Verenahof, had the engaging, eloquent manners of a hotelier who is used to saying exactly what the guest wants to hear. His voice, full of ostentatious cordiality, flowed from him as if freshly blended with oil, and seemed made for much larger spaces than the Meijers' drawing room. On the breast of his shirt, which swelled like the bow of a ship, there shone silver buttons with the coat of arms that he had had designed specially for his hotel.

Frau Strähle was German, and people in Baden said she had, when she had fallen in love with the attractive director of her hotel during a spa cure, abandoned an extremely advantageous engagement in favour of her new union.

Another rumour claimed that she had a different dress for every day of the season, all paid for from the tills of the Verenahof. Tody she was wearing a model in lime-green taffeta, which billowed with the suggestion of a bridal train each time she took a step.

Director Strähle kissed Chanele's hand, chatted to François, joked with Arthur, and could not get over the pleasant surprise of finding the honoured Herr Meijer senior here too. He had – and this too was part of the rituals of these invitations – brought an outsized bottle of champagne, the special cuvée of the Verenahof, as he stressed several times, and very popular among his guests. Life, he added, was in the end too short, hahaha, only ever to drink water.

'I didn't knew you *could* drink water.' Herr Rauhut, the editor of the *Badener Tageblatt*, liked to make little jokes about his own love of a decent drop of wine, and thus tried to gloss over the fact that he was generally drunk or at least slightly the worse for wear. He had come alone, and Chanele was already worrying that he had come without his wife and the seating arrangements would have to be changed all over again. But then Frau Rauhut was there after all, a sickly, reproachfully wheezing person with a bluish complexion. When her husband, as he inevitably tended to do after a few glasses, favoured the party with Schubert's Lieder – he had a powerful if not very tuneful voice – his wife had to accompany him on the piano, and every time she did one wondered if she really had enough strength to press down the keys.

The editor drew the hotel manager into a corner and began to talk at him in a whisper. Chanele observed them keenly to see if they were casting secret glances at Shmul, but they seemed to be talking about something else. The conversation fell quickly silent again, because the arrival of the Schneggs was announced. The Schneggs were, if there could be such a thing in democratic Switzerland, almost aristocrats, admittedly without a title, but surrounded by the almost equally elegant aura of old money. Herr Laurenz Schnegg was the biggest property-owner in town; the House with the Red Shield, in which the Modern Emporium was installed, belonged to him. He and his wife were dressed in a deliberately old-fashioned style, as if to demonstrate that they didn't need to adapt to the fashions or trends of the day. As they were welcomed into the house, Herr Schnegg held out his hand as devotedly to Chanele as if he expected that, in a reversal of the traditional roles of the sexes, she might kiss his; Frau Schnegg, with pursed lips and pointed chin, looked past her hostess and indicated to everyone that it was actually beneath her dignity to mingle with such society. She paid not the slightest attention to old Salomon Meijer.

Last of all, full of apologies and explanations, came Councillor Bugmann. Rauhut immediately wound himself around him as a loyal dog might his master, because alongside his many offices the councillor also had a seat on the board of the *Tagblatt*. A committee meeting had detained him for so long, and then there had been a case at his lawyer's office, a stupid story, a young man, in need of financial support, whose official guardian he was, had suddenly taken it into his head to get married, without a rappen in his pocket, and when he, Bugmann, had refused his consent, had had to refuse on the grounds of his responsible position, the young man had made a scene, indescribable, and used words that one really couldn't repeat in the presence of ladies – in short, it had taken a lot of time. He was sorry, really very sorry, to turn up late for such pleasant company, but he was sure Monsieur Meijer, as an equally busy man of the world, would have some understanding of the fact that the day sometimes needed to have twenty-five hours or even more. 'You just mustn't accept every honour offered to you,' his wife always said. Bugmann shrugged. It was a debate that the two of them had every day.

The councillor was a red-faced man of the apoplectic type. With his frock coat he wore an ascot of a grey material interwoven with metallic threads. Not really good quality, thought Janki as he assured his guest how honoured he felt that a man in such demand had even found the time in his busy calendar to accept his invitation to a modest sandwich dinner.

This was the prompt for Louisli, who, after a discreet nod from Chanele, shyly announced that dinner was served.

The meal passed without incident. Arthur didn't drop his cutlery and didn't knock a glass over, and as, out of fear of doing something wrong, he only ate tiny portions, he won general praise for his well-behaved restraint. Salomon discovered that he shared with Councillor Bugmann, most of whose voters came from rural communities, an interest in cattle breeding. François was charming, talked with Frau Strähle about jewellery and with Frau Rauhut about music, and even managed to make Frau Schnegg nearly smile once or twice. Janki leaned far across the table and discussed business matters with Herr Schnegg. Ziltener remained submissively silent. The hired servants performed their duties. Herr Rauhut drank.

The food was a great success as well. Christine had already outdone herself with the salmon mayonnaise; when the chicken soup with dumplings arrived Director Strähle swore that he would absolutely have to send his cook for the recipe, and the veal cutlets were prepared with so much goose-fat that no one missed the butter sauce. They washed it down with excellent wines, a Gewürz-traminer from Alsace with the fish, and then a heavy Burgundy that Janki had ordered specially from the Lévy cellar in Metz.

'I have one question,' said the editor, articulating each word with drunken concentration. 'Only one question, Herr Meijer. Tell me now, what is kosher about this wine?'

'That I hope it's going down particularly well,' Janki said evasively, waving to one of the hired waiters to refill Herr Rauhut's glass.

But the editor would not be distracted. 'No,' he insisted, 'I want to know now. A grape like that isn't slaughtered through shechita, at least not in these parts...'

'Hahaha, shechita, very good!' As a hotel manager, Director Strähle had become used to laughing uproariously at every joke uttered within his hearing.

'...and if it isn't slaughtered by shechita, what can be kosher about it? Or not kosher?'

'Our laws are sometimes very complicated.'

'Which laws are not?' Councillor Bugmann nodded knowingly. 'Only last week I had a case in my office...'

'One moment!' the editor cut in. His wife coughed anxiously. 'I haven't finished yet! We press men, the fourth estate, so to speak, want to have our questions answered. Now: what is kosher about this wine?'

There are things that cannot be explained without rudeness. A wine is kosher when it is produced by a Jew, and treyf when it is not. But how can one explain that to a drunken goy without insulting him?

It was Salomon who saved the situation, and saved it, indeed, with a gematria. And Janki had expressly asked him not to bother anyone with his chochmes.

'Listen, Herr Rauhut,' he said. 'Let me explain something to you about this matter. Wine, the Hebrew word for wine, of course, has a numerical value of seventy-five.'

'Numerical value?'

'According to our tradition, each letter corresponds to a number. So "the wine" has a value of seventy-five. And do you know what word has exactly the same value? Ganavcha, your thief.'

Rauhut looked at him uncomprehendingly.

'And what is that trying to teach us? That wine is your thief. And what is it stealing from you? Your intelligence and your manners.'

'Hahaha,' laughed Director Strähle. 'Very good. I'll have to remember that.'

When even Herr Schnegg nodded appreciatively, the others even joined in the laughter. No one likes drunken guests who disturb the polite insignificance of dinner-table conversations.

Herr Rauhut was so busy thinking about the problem of numerical values and thieves that he completely forgot his original question. He emptied his glass in one go and held it out to the hired servant to be refilled. 'But it's good, this kosher wine of yours,' he said, too loudly. His wife coughed.

Apart from that small event, the dinner went as perfectly as Janki had wished. No one noticed that Chanele spoke little, and kept looking anxiously across at her oldest son.

The evening would also have ended perfectly. But then the ladies withdrew to the drawing-room, Arthur said goodnight to everyone and disappeared with great relief to his room, the hired servants cleared the table and cashed up their tips. Then the gentlemen filled their brandy glasses and after thorough ritual sniffing and turning-around-in-the-fingers they lit the cigars that Janki handed around. Except François, who smoked a Russian cigarette in his almost real amber holder, and Salomon, who played in his pocket with his tobacco tin, because Janki had forbidden him to take snuff on the grounds that it was too rustic.

Then, inevitably, they turned to politics.

18

'What would interest me,' Councillor Bugmann said, opening the two bottom buttons of waistcoat with a groan of pleasure, 'what would even interest me very much, Monsieur Meijer: what do you actually think in *puncto puncti* of the popular initiative on which we will all be voting this summer?'

'An entirely superfluous innovation.' Herr Schnegg pulled a face as if someone had tipped vinegar into his brandy. 'Popular initiative! Even just the word! Making laws by collecting signatures from the rabble for any old ideas! What do we have a government for?'

That is pro...prog...progress.' It took Editor Rauhut three goes to clamber over all the consonantal hurdles, which didn't stop him from attempting another verbal mountain range. 'The further elaboration of the democratic rights of the...of the people.'

'The rabble,' Herr Schnegg repeated. Director Strähle rubbed earnestly at a non-existent stain on his shirt front. As a hotel manager he made it a principle never to involve himself in political discussions.

'I don't mean the popular initiative *per se*. This instrument of the decision-making process has been introduced, and we will have to live with it, *nolens volens*.' If his wife had been there, she would have known by these sentences that Bugmann too had had a great deal to drink. Where he was concerned, this always found expression in the Latin phrases of his student days floating to the surface. 'I mean the concrete case on which the people will have to vote in August. Article 25 bis.'

Salomon Meijer leaned forward and rested his hands on the table as if he were about to stand up. He began to drum very gently with his fingers, a musician who hadn't quite made up his mind which key was suitable for a particular occasion.

'25 bis,' Bugmann repeated with an expressive gesture, as if he wanted to write the paragraph in the air with the glowing tip of his cigar. 'A complement to the state constitution which might be of special interest to our host, who has entertained us so handsomely today. Please, Monsieur Meijer, tell us your opinion on the matter!'

This challenge was very unwelcome to Janki. He organised these 'goyish evenings' precisely to demonstrate, through natural social intercourse, that he had been accepted here in the town as an equal among equals, and that such important people as Herr Schnegg or Herr Bugmann simply saw him as the successful businessman, one of their own, or at least no longer primarily as a Jew. To this end he was prepared to listen to Director Strähle's genial boasts, let Herr Rauhut drink expensive cognac like water and talk happily about any subject they wanted to. Almost any subject. But why did Bugmann have to start on about this wretched people's initiative which, under cover of animal-protection legislation, sought to add an anti-Semitic article to the federal constitution and forbid the slaughtering of animals according to the Jewish rite?

'I have no opinion on the matter,' he said, attempting to evade the issue. 'After all, I am still a guest in this beautiful country. As a citizen of France...'

'*Quo usque tandem?*' Bugmann interrupted. 'How long do you plan to wait before you become one of us in terms of your papers as well? I have told you often enough before, Monsieur Meijer: people like you, people who promote our economy, are most welcome in the citizens' register. For myself, I would always be willing...'

'Citizens' register,' said Rauhut, drawing all the syllables together into a single one, 'such a word does not exist.' He nodded with satisfaction a number of time, as if he had just solved a big problem.

'We like being French, Herr Councillor.' François smiled so politely that his contradiction seemed like a compliment. 'In France égalité is just a word. A Captain Dreyfus has just been appointed to the General Staff. That same Dreyfus family also exists in Endingen. Do you think one of them could enjoy a similar career?'

'In principle, yes.'

'In principle perhaps, Herr Councillor,' said François, again with his friendly smile. 'But not in the Aargau.'

'Another drop of cognac?' Janki swiftly intervened. But only Rauhut held out his glass.

'Whether you be Swiss or French,' Bugmann insisted, 'you must have an opinion on the matter. You as a Jew...'

An old voice began to giggle. Uncle Melnitz was suddenly crouching with them at the table, right beside Janki. With his bony fingers, on which the skin sat loosely like an oversized glove, he had gripped a cigar and was bringing it to his wrinkled mouth. 'Come on, Janki!' he said, and with every word smoke rose up between his teeth as if a fire raged deep within him. 'Come on! Tell him your opinion. You as a Jew. Yes. Or did you think that ludicrous tie would make you an honorary goy?'

'Now,' Janki turned around, 'of course we can consider the problem from two sides. On the one hand...'

'On the one hand...' Melnitz mimicked.

'On the one hand, of course, I quite understand the desire to cause an animal as little pain as possible. But on the other...'

'On the other...' parroted Melnitz.

'...our religious laws require us...'

'I too have signed,' Herr Ziltener said all of a sudden. He had sat in his seat almost mutely for the whole evening, giving only given very curt answers to direct questions, so his unexpected intervention now seemed very loud. 'You may dismiss me if you wish, but I have a right to my conviction.' He held his brandy glass between the palms of his hands as a farmer might hold his warming cup of coffee on a cold day. He seemed to have said what he wanted to say, but after a pause he added, 'My wife loves animals too.' It was the first time in his life that Ziltener had found an opinion of his wife's worth mentioning.

If a domestic animal had suddenly started speaking, the general surprise could not have been greater. Herr Rauhut raised his glass in such impetuous agreement that the liquid, which had been poured far too generously in any case, slopped over the brim and he had to lick his fingers. Councillor Bugmann murmured something about 'Parturiunt montes', and Director Strähle, who had long since forgotten his school Latin, produced a short, barking laugh just in case it was supposed to have been a joke. Herr Laurenz Schnegg took a monocle from his pocket, held it in front of his right eye and looked at the accountant with such appalled surprise as a bather might look at an undesirable object washed up on the beach. François looked at the ceiling and twisted the tips of his moustache with ostentatious lack of interest.

Melnitz laughed until he choked on the smoke from his cigar.

'Why would I want to dismiss you, my dear Herr Ziltener?' asked Janki. 'I wouldn't have the faintest idea how to run my businesses without you.' He loved the phrase 'my businesses', that wonderful plural of social success.

'I couldn't care less.' Like many people unaccustomed to contradiction, Ziltener adopted an exaggeratedly combative posture. With his chin poking out from between his shoulders, he looked like an irritated lapdog.

'Woof!' said Rauhut. 'Woof! Woof! Woof!'

'Your cognac is really terrific,' said Director Strähle, trying to guide the conversational ship into less stormy waters. 'You will have to tell me where you...'

'Animal cruelty is animal cruelty, and we Christians have a duty...' Ziltener's courage failed him as quickly as it had taken hold of him. In his excitement he had half leapt from his seat and now shifted from one foot to the other with his bottom in the air, a guilty little dog begging for forgiveness with its tail between its legs.

'Oh, sit down,' said Councillor Bugmann, and Herr Schnegg hissed, 'Riffraff.' Ziltener lowered his head, a chastised schoolboy.

An embarrassed pause followed, which Herr Strahle tried in vain to fill with a chuckle.

Finally Councillor Bugmann tugged his ascot straight and cleared his throat. 'To be able to discuss something *sine ira et studio*,' he said, 'to weigh up the pro and contra serenely, that is the true trademark of democracy.'

'Trademark,' Rauhut repeated. 'Democracy.' He smiled proudly as the words left his tongue without stumbling.

'And the opinion of our charming host on this issue carries particular weight. *Sua res agitur*. So if you would be so kind, dear Monsieur Meijer...You have the floor.'

'Tell them, Janki,' giggled Uncle Melnitz and blue a perfect smoke ring in the air with each syllable of his laughter. 'You must be able to that. You as an honorary goy.'

'Well then.' Janki played nervously with the handle of his walking stick. 'There are certain traditions...'

'Certain traditions...' Uncle Melnitz bleated an echo.

'...which may not, by the standards of our enlightened times...'

'Heeheehee,' said Melnitz.

'...and under the aspect of a modern humanity...'

'Hehehe.'

'If slaughtering by shechita is forbidden,' said François, once again wearing the smile that struck terror into the heart of his own mother, 'then you will all have to make do with carrots at our next soirée.'

'Which would be a terrible shame,' Director Strähle used the opportunity to scatter a quick compliment on to the table, like salt on a red wine stain. 'The veal chop particularly...'

Rauhut nodded. 'And the Burgundy,' he said. 'With the shechita-slaughtered grapes.'

'There is only one point,' Councillor Bugmann insisted, 'on which *vox populi* strikes me as curious. The advocates of the initiative...'

'Riffraff,' said Herr Schnegg.

'The advocates of the initiative are arguing on the basis of their love of the tortured animals...'

'My wife also...'

'...and that is an argument that cannot quite...'

156

Salomon had been drumming on the table all the while, and now struck such a drumroll that everyone looked at him. 'I will happily explain it to you, Herr Councillor.'

'Please don't start with your gematria again!'

'Gematriwhat?' asked Rauhut.

Salomon rested his palms on the table. 'I am, as you know, a cattle-trader, and I have learned not to buy a cow just because it is offered with fine words. One should do the same, if I may give you some advice, Herr Councillor, in political matters as well.'

Janki saw with horror that Bugmann's face had turned crimson. But perhaps that was simply down to his apoplectic nature.

'The thing about the tortured creature, my esteemed Herr Councillor, is this: no one is as kind to animals as a butcher without anything to slaughter.'

'I don't understand,' said Herr Schnegg.

'It often happens that an animal, although it corresponds to all health police requirements, turns out after shechita to be ritually impure and can therefore not be eaten by Jews. So it must be sold to a Christian butcher. Hence the people's initiative.'

'Aha!' said Director Strähle, and tried to make a face as if he had understood.

'As the animal has already been slaughtered, the sale must go through quickly. And hence at a very low price. The butcher who does the deal is of course delighted; everyone else is envious. They are all fearful that their more fortunate competitor might bring their prices down. And out of that fear they suddenly discover their love of animals and want to ban shechita entirely. It's as simple as that.'

'Are you trying to claim that concern for the welfare of the tortured creature is only a pretext ...?'

'The purest hypocrisy,' said Salomon. 'You as a politician must know something about that, Herr Councillor.'

'Omeyn!' said Uncle Melnitz.

Herr Bugmann stood up, and it was not simply a man rising to his feet, it was a demonstration. 'I am going home now,' he said.

Director Strähle immediately followed suit. 'It was an extremely pleasant evening. Really, very, very pleasant.'

'I am most grateful to you for the hospitality you have shown me,' said Herr Ziltener.

As he left, Herr Schnegg stopped in front of Salomon and studied him through his monocle. 'You could be a man after my own heart,' he said. 'It is really a shame that you ...'

He didn't finish the sentence, but Janki thought he heard Uncle Melnitz laughing.

At last Herr Rauhut, the newspaper editor, rose unsteadily. 'I shall now sing a few Schubert Lieder,' he said. But there was no audience left to hear him.

When all the guests ad been helped into their coats – 'allow me, Frau Strähle, it was an honour, Frau Schnegg' – when the last compliments had been paid, like tokens being put back in their box after an evening of card-games, to be distributed again on the next occasion, when even the exhausted Christine had received her traditional thank-you present – a pair of fine embroidered gloves, which she had asked for but would never wear – Chanele went back to the dining room in search of Shmul. She had still not had a chance to talk to her son.

Janki was sitting all alone at the long table. No, he wasn't sitting, he was slumped in his upholstered chair, a general after the battle has been lost. The black silk kerchief hung like a funeral crape from his shirt collar. His mouth was pursed, as if to whistle or sing, his left hand was flat on his belly, and with his right he tapped impatiently and furiously against it, as one goes on hammering at a door that should have been opened long ago. Chanele, who was all too familiar with this pantomime, filled a glass with water from a jug, took the tin of sodium bicarbonate prescribed by Dr Bolliger from the drawer in the sideboard and set them both down in front of Janki. He tipped too much of the white powder into the glass and looked at Chanele reproachfully when the mixture foamed over the brim. After he had drunk, he burped without putting his hand over his mouth. It didn't matter any more.

'It was a disaster,' he said.

'Even though we weren't thirteen at table?'

'A social disaster.'

'There's something else you should know,' Chanele began.

But Janki wasn't listening. 'A disaster,' he said over and over again. It sounded like one of the prayers with the many repetitions that one growls to oneself on certain feast days, until the last shred of meaning has been worn away. 'A disaster that can never be rectified.'

'Mathilde Lutz told me...'

If, after the defeat at Sedan, Napoleon III had been asked which shirt he wanted to wear the following day, he could not have looked at the questioner with greater contempt. 'I'm not interested in that,' said Janki, stressing each syllable individually.

'Do you understand? I don't want to know! Right now your little problems with the shop are as unimportant as...as...as...' In search of a suitable comparison his eye fell on an ashtray. He tipped the mixture of grey ash and wet, chewed cigar butts onto the good damask tablecloth, where it formed a dirty little heap, of the kind that street-sweepers make in the early morning. 'There!' he said. 'That's how unimportant it is for me right now.'

'It's not about the shop,' said Chanele.

'I don't care what it's about.' The dramatic gesture – or the stomach powder – seemed to have given him new strength, and the apathetic despair that he had just revealed turned to voluble fury. 'You weren't there! You don't know what has happened! While you were chatting peacefully with the ladies, about sewing or recipes or who knows what all else, while you were having a lovely evening...'

'Nebbish!' said Chanele.

'...while you've been enjoying your life, everyone's been tearing into me. Even Ziltener! And it wasn't a coincidence, believe me, things like that don't just happen on their own. They must have agreed in advance! Did you see Rauhut, that toss-pot, that shassgener, whispering with Bugmann? Of course you didn't. You wouldn't notice anything like that. They come to my house, they eat my food, they drink my wine, and then...'

'What's happened?'

Janki's fury subsided as quickly as it had flared up. 'There's no point,' he said, and pressed his hand to his body as if he were suffering not from heartburn but from a deadly wound. 'You can do what you like, you're never a part of it.'

'What a ridiculous party.' François came into the room with the ostentatiously springy elegance of a ballet dancer who goes on striking poses after the curtain has fallen.

'Shmul, I need to talk to you straight away about...'

'One moment,' said François and looked searchingly around. 'So much politeness makes you thirsty.'

'Right now!'

'I will be at your disposal straight away.'

And he had gone out again.

'It's all Salomon's fault,' Janki complained. 'If he hadn't got involved! Why, today of all days, did he have to...?'

'Ask him!'

Salomon had come in, his new shirt unbuttoned so that the tzitzits of his arba kanfes hung over his trousers. 'It's a shame the word "tie" doesn't appear in the Bible,' he said. 'I'm sure it would have the same numerical value as "goyim naches".' Goyim naches are all the things that non-Jews for some unfathomable reason find pleasurable.

'It's your fault,' said Janki.

'I don't know what it is,' Salomon replied, 'but if it makes you feel better I'll happily take the blame for it.'

'Why did you have to attack him like that? Councillor Bugmann of all people.'

'He asked a question, and I answered it for him. Should I have been rude?'

'You shouldn't have been there at all!'

'Believe me,' said Salomon Meijer and smiled peacefully, 'if I'd known who you'd invited I'd have stayed in Endingen. I prefer my shnorrers.'

'You called them hypocrites!'

Salomon spread his arms. 'Nu,' he said. And in this instance it meant, 'I've grown as old as this and I'm not allowed to tell the truth?'

'What did you want here anyway?'

'To bring this letter to Chanele.' Salomon drew a piece of paper, folded several times and no longer quite clean, out of his trouser pocket. 'I'll soon have been carrying it around for two months.'

'It must be an anonymous letter,' was Chanele's first thought. 'About the pregnant salesgirl.'

But it was something quite different.

'Since Golde, may she rest in peace, is no longer with us,' said Salomon, 'every day I have the feeling that I have to put things in order. My life. Has it ever occurred to you that the word "viduy", the confession of a sin, has exactly twice the numerical value of the word "love"? That is trying to tell us: only if we admit our mistakes...'

'Leave me in peace with your gematria!' cried Janki.

Salomon laid the letter on the table and took Chanele by both hands. 'Throughout your life I have always been in your debt,' he said.

'You have always been good to me.'

'Perhaps this will change your opinion,' said Salomon. 'Here...' He held the letter out to her. The paper rustled as she unfolded it.

There was complete silence in the room.

Until Shmul came in. He had opened the outsize champagne bottle that Strähle had brought, and was drinking it from the neck. 'I know,' he said, no longer elegant, 'I know this stuff's not kosher. But I need it now.' He planted himself, legs apart, in front of Chanele. 'So. What did you want to say to me?'

'Nothing,' Chanele replied. 'It doesn't matter any more.'

19

Mimi loved spoiling Hinda.

The girl wasn't really her niece, admittedly, and strictly speaking she wasn't even a relative, but who else could you call *ma fillette* if you didn't have any children of your own.

Had it been meant to be, back then, it would have been a boy. 'It was a boy,' they told her, and with that single sentence a living future had become a dead past. Golde tried to console her by telling her of her own misfortune, but Mimi didn't listen. During those days she hated her mother, who of all the qualities she could have left to her, had passed on precisely this one: the inability to conceive a son. 'It doesn't necessarily mean anything, the doctors said and nodded encouragingly. 'Next time everything might be fine.' Mimi didn't believe them, They just wanted to comfort her, they wanted to prettify the gloomy picture of her life, but she wasn't one of those weak people that you have to lie to, not her, she could look facts in the face, and if that was how it was to be, then that was how it was to be.

And she had been right.

Pinchas, who was a dreamer, a hardworking shochet, but a dreamer, told her stories about women who had become mothers only after ten or twenty years, and she let him slog away at the topic and thought, 'Just go on talking!' She didn't even wonder whether he got his chochmes out of the Talmud or from one of the many newspapers that he read every day. He loved arguing, except it didn't change the facts. It was the way it was.

She had adjusted her life according to it. Childlessness filled her days as completely as motherhood would have done. She brought up her sorrow, let it grow and develop, became ever more familiar with its demands, sometimes struggled with it, as with a child that threatens to suffocate you with its constant demands for attention, then pressed it to her again and couldn't have lived without it, not for so much as a minute. When other women talked about their children or even brought them on visits – often they didn't – then Mimi's fingertips drew circles on her temples and she talked about her migraine.

Childlessness gave her life content, and herself a role. She wasn't like all the others, she had something to endure and did it bravely, and her misfortune, although she would have contradicted anyone who had dared to say as much, made her happy. She had – one went to the new municipal theatre and knew the specialist terminology – become a character actress, no longer the naïve young girl no one remembers once the performance is over. She had found her theme, and now lived it out in ever new variations.

When Hinda came to visit – and it was only right that she came often, her aunt was a lonely woman with a sorrow, and needed company and distraction – then Mimi experienced all the motherliness she assumed lay within her, she was a best friend and a discreet confidante. She would have liked to give Hinda advice in matters of love, and was repeatedly disappointed that her niece still seemed to show no interest in the matter. 'That will be down to Chanele,' Mimi thought often. 'Such a dry old stick – where would the daughter get it from?'

It was Mimi's greatest dream to find Hinda a shidduch, not just anyone, but the perfect shidduch, an affluent, educated, very special husband. Chanele would have to thank her, and she would say, 'Mais de rien, ma chère. You live away off in Baden, so remote from polite society – someone had to take care of things.' Janki would see them standing side by side, his Chanele, as colourless as the headmistress as a girls' boarding school, and Mimi, a lady of the world who knew how to behave and dress herself. She would smile at him, smile at him as a sister might, and say, 'I hope you've found happiness.' She also knew exactly which hat she would wear to that chassene, nothing conspicuous, certainly not, a childless woman whose life is filled with sorrow doesn't doll herself up, but she had seen black swan feathers at her milliner's, soft, sad feathers.

'I am a black swan,' thought Mimi.

At a tea party she had sat Hinda next to Siegfried Kahn, who studied law and who, given the importance of his family in the silk importing trade, would soon be a successful lawyer. Furthermore, apart from his sickly sister, he was an only child and would eventually inherit the lot. But after their meeting Hinda had only laughed, and imitated the way the student twisted his head, in its high starched collar, back and forth like an owl, 'as if he had no neck'. Mimi had had no more success with Mendel Weisz from the matzo baking dynasty; Hinda had submitted to his awkward compliments and then said, 'A matzo factory might be very useful at Pesach, but what would I do with him for the rest of the year?'

Chanele really hadn't prepared her daughter very well for life.

Today there were no young men on the agenda, but who knew whom one would meet in town? Hinda's clothes were all of good quality, after all she was the daughter of the biggest drapery in Baden, but all très simple, more suited to a provincial backwater than for a proper city. Luckily Mimi had taste, and you can do lots with a nice cape and a parasol.

She herself wore a very plain twin piece in dark blue silk satin, the jupon cut straight, with a wide pleated flounce and a sewn-on twill ribbon, and the long jacket was very simple too, with a little plissé ruching and with a barely noticeable inset of silk twill. Hair was worn very severely that year anyway, with the tiniest of hats. Her umbrella alone was slightly extravagant.

'Where are we going?' Hinda asked.

'We'll have a cup of hot chocolate later in the Palm Garden. But first... You'll see.'

The flat was in Sankt Anne Gasse, directly above the butcher's shop. Mimi didn't really like living there. Having a shop in one's house was, in her opinion, très ordinaire, but of course it was practical too. Since Pinchas had taken on an assistant, young Elias Gutterman, a very efficient shochet, and luckily one who could stand on his own two feet, he was often able to absent himself from the shop for an hour or two, and then only had to climb a flight of stairs and he was sitting at his desk. Over the last few years he had been writing more and more little articles, which had appeared under the abbreviation – pp – in a few German newspapers and now even in the newly founded Zurich Tages-Anzeiger. A financially unrewarding art, of course, but the butcher's shop was going well, and Mimi, as she often stressed, didn't get involved in it.

They didn't head towards Löwenstrasse where, only a few yards from the butcher's shop, the synagogue was, but went first to Bahnhofstrasse and then along one of the little alleys up into the Old Town. Mimi still wouldn't say what she had planned, but for some reason she was very excited. 'You don't need to be afraid, Hinda,' she said impetuously, 'nothing at all can happen.'

Hinda laughed. It was hard to imagine that anyone in Aunt Mimi's milieu might do anything serious, let alone anything frightening.

They came to a house in Wohllebgasse, a building so narrow it looked as if the neighbours had reluctantly shifted sideways a little to make room for it. On the ground floor was an upholsterer's workshop. A group of tatty chairs with their innards spilling out stood in the street in a semicircle, as if awaiting unloved guests.

To get into the house, you first had to enter the workshop and then leave it again immediately through a rough wooden side door. The pungent smell of boiling glue made way in the narrow, dark stairway for the intense smell of cabbage soup, a poor-people smell that Mimi would have on any other occasion described as dégoûtant or affreux. Now she just pulled up her skirt and climbed the creaking stairs ahead of Hinda, past a door behind which the cries of a baby and a cross woman's voice could be heard, and a second, behind which a dog was furiously barking and repeatedly hurling itself against the wood with a dull thud.

On the top floor, where the walls were already beginning to slope, Mimi stopped by a door to which a brass lion's head was fixed. It was probably intended as a doorknocker, but its mouth lacked the appurtenant ring.

'What...?' Hinda began to ask.

Mimi put a finger to her lips. 'Take your gloves off,' she whispered.

Even without a knock on the door, their arrival was noted. A gaunt woman of perhaps fifty, but perhaps much older, opened the door a crack. She wore a light grey skirt and a high buttoned blouse in the same colour, fastened at the neck by a silver brooch. Her hair was covered with a scarf of starched material, also grey. Her eyes were narrowed, as though even the gloomy light of the stairwell was too bright for her. Without a word of greeting she nodded to Mimi, as matter-of-factly as if she were ticking off a sheet on a laundry list, and then turned her suspicious gaze on Hinda.

'Who is that?' she asked tonelessly.

'My niece,' answered Mimi. 'Madame Rosa knows.'

'She mentioned nothing to me.' The gaunt woman seemed at first not to want to let them through, but then finally stepped aside. 'You're late,' she hissed reproachfully.

A smell of cabbage soup hung in the corridor too, mixed with a sickly, penetrating smell that Hinda couldn't identify. In big plates, ordinary soup plates, arranged on the floor along the walls, candles flickered, sooty smoke rising from their wicks.

Hinda coughed. The woman in grey walking in front of her turned to her and cast her a reproachful look. Then she opened the door to a room whose windows, in the middle of the afternoon, were covered with heavy velvet curtains.

Five or six people, Hinda couldn't tell straight away in the half-darkness, sat around a circular table. The room was tiny, even smaller than the maid's room under the roof in Baden. Four people had to get up and push their way into the corner of the room and the window niche so that Mimi could sit down. As they did so, the curtain was pushed aside for a moment, bright sunlight flashed in and lit an unframed oil painting, hanging on an unpapered wall, depicting a fogbound crevasse.

Hinda, always ready for an adventure in spite of her irritation, wanted to follow Mimi, but someone held her back. The gaunt woman had grabbed her parasol and didn't seem to want to let go of it. It was only when she saw that the woman also had Mimi's parasol hanging over her arm that Hinda realised she was trying to take it away from her. She pushed her way along the edge of the table to her seat, and all the others sat down again with much scraping of chairs. No one said a word.

Hinda was horrified to feel something touching her legs; but it was only the worn, dark brown table-cloth that reached to the floor. On her left sat Mimi, on her right an asthmatic-sounding, heavily breathing woman who smelled unhealthily of sweat. They had both rested their hands on the tablecloth with their fingers spread. Hinda looked around and established that everyone else had assumed the same posture, so that their little fingers touched and the whole thing formed a kind of chain. Hinda joined them; it seemed to be expected of her. The strange woman's finger was cold and damp.

For almost a minute nothing happened. Then the gaunt woman, the only one to have stayed standing, said, 'Let us close our eyes.' Although she was still whispering, the sound of her voice reminded Hinda of a strict governess.

She obediently lowered her eyelids, but only half. When the kauhanim appeared before the congregation for the priest's blessing in the prayer room, looking was also forbidden, and there was even a rumour among the younger children that a stolen glance could make you blind. Arthur, fearful as he was, had always obeyed the prohibition, but Hinda had once been unable to resist the temptation. Nothing bad had happened to her, but neither had she seen anything exciting. Only Mosbacher the businessman with his son and old Herr Katz, all three with arms outstretched, tallises pulled over their heads.

What she saw now around the table from beneath her lowered lids was even less exciting than that.

With one exception, all the people gathered around the table were women. The only man was sitting right next to Mimi, an elderly man with a narrow white beard, whom one might have imagined as an academic, or perhaps a grocer who liked to pick up a book in his free time. The woman beside him wore glasses with very small lenses, which sank into the fatty wrinkles of her round face like raisins in fresh dough. Her eyes were so tightly shut that she looked like a bawling baby. Then came a younger lady with an arrogant expression; one had a sense that she had only closed her eyes so that at least she didn't have to look at the unworthy society in which she found herself against her will.

Next, diagonally opposite Hinda, sat a small, cosy woman, who looked a bit like the wife of Pfister, the baker on the Church Square, who not only sold the best Spanish rolls, but who was also first with the latest gossip. She was the only one of the ladies who was not wearing a hat, but had instead hidden her hair under a colourful turban, with an enamelled medallion resplendent on the front. That, of course, was Madame Rosa.

Next to her was a women entirely in black, with a half-length widow's veil pinned to her hat, covering her eyes, and then came the woman who was having difficulty breathing. To look at her more closely, Hinda would have had to turn rudely and look at her.

'Is there a good spirit there, who wants to speak to us?' asked the woman with the turban. She said it in the coarse dialect of a suburban village, and as unceremoniously as someone asking if the post has arrived. Hinda, with her gift for seeing the ludicrous side of everything, had to struggle not to explode with laughter.

'I ask again: is there a good spirit there, who wants to speak to us?'

Even afterwards, Hinda couldn't explain what happened next. The table seemed to move under their hands, seemed to rise in the air and fall again, like someone turning in their sleep and then coming to rest again a moment later. There was a clearly audible knock as the foot of the table touched the floor again.

'We greet you,' said Madame Rosa, and all those present repeated: 'We greet you.'

'What is your name?' asked Madame Rosa.

As in shul, when the moment has come, the people around the table began to murmur. Hinda thought for a moment that it was a prayer, but then she understood the strange sounds.

A B C D E F G

In a muttered chorus they recited the alphabet.

H I J K L M

Like little children at school.

N O P Q R

A knock.

'R,' said Madame Rosa.

The speaking chorus started again.

A B C D E F G

This time the knocking came after the O.

And then after the D.

And again after the O.

R. O. D. O. L. P. H. E.

'Rodolphe,' said Madame Rosa. A particularly violent knock confirmed the name.

Next to Hinda, Aunt Mimi started sniffing.

'It's him,' she managed to speak between her tears. 'I would have called him Rodolphe if he ... if he ...'

An impatient knocking interrupted her. Under Hinda's hands the table was bucking like a restive horse.

'Do you want to say something to us?' asked Madame Rosa.

Knocking.

And the murmuring began again from the start. ABCDE.

M. the table spelt this time. M. A. M. A.

'He's talking to me,' sobbed Mimi.

There was still a smell of of cabbage soup.

Afterwards, when they were sitting in the Palm Garden, Mimi admitted that while she didn't believe in any of it, of course, there was without a doubt a lot of hocus pocus involved and she felt a little bit ridiculous, but on the other hand how could the table, or how could somebody, if there was deception involved, how could they have known the name Rodolphe, not just Rudolf, as people spelt and pronounced it hereabouts, but Rodolphe, in French, such an unusual name, how could anyone have known? And even if – she could see that Hinda was laughing again, she didn't even need to hide it and perhaps she was right – and even if it was all a lot of theatre, a show put on for the credulous, it had done her good, so much good that Hinda couldn't begin to imagine. Anyone who has not known true sorrow, Mimi said, anyone who does not know proper tsuris, cannot understand, but if someone has been through as much as she has, one clutches at straws. And what the voice had said – for her it was a voice, even if all you actually heard, of course, was the knocking noises that Madame Rosa then had to interpret – what the voice had said had been so correct, so clearly and unambiguously meant only for her, that he was well, that he was happy and that he loved her, ah, Hinda had no idea what that meant for a mother who had never been able to pick up her child or bentsh it on a Friday evening. Rodolphe was the name she wanted to give him, after a book that someone had once read aloud to her, it was so long ago that she sometimes thought she'd only dreamt it all.

Then Mimi poured the hot chocolate, very daintily, with gloved fingers, and ordered two slices, because spiritual excitement always gave her an appetite.

When the séance was over – 'This is a scientific experiment, which is why we call it a séance,' Hinda was told by the elderly gentleman who, it turned out, had been a teacher all his life, a professor of Physics and Chemistry at the high school for girls – when the gaunt woman had drawn the curtains and revealed the little room in all its petit-bourgeois shabbiness, they had stood around for a while, very uncomfortably, because even after the chairs had been carried out they had still kept their backs pressed against the crooked wall and made conversation. Most people's interest was directed at Hinda, the new adept, in the words of the heavily-breathing woman, who introduced herself as Hermine Mettler, wife of high court judge Mettler. She herself, she confided in Hinda, had been seriously ill and long since given up by the doctors, but in contact with the beyond she kept finding new strength, and her spirit guide had even promised her that she only needed to experience one proper ectoplasmic phenomenon to become quite healthy again.

The woman with the little glasses and her arrogant neighbour were mother and daughter and came to every séance, because Madame Rosa had discovered that they both had quite special clairvoyant powers, which the circle of hands required to make contact with the other world. The veiled woman didn't take part in the conversation, just dabbed her eyes with a little black lace handkerchief and sometimes said into a silence, 'Yes, yes.'

Madame Rosa was the only one to stay seated. She looked, to use a term from Mimi's lexicon, *très ordinaire*, like a washerwoman after a long day in hot steam or like Christine after the last course of a big dinner. The enamel medallion on her turban represented an open eye. She was, as Mimi explained on the way to the Alpenquai, a distant relative of the upholsterer who owned the house, had discovered her special abilities only very late and only by chance, and in principle accepted no money for running the séances; one just gave the gaunt, grey woman something to cover the costs, with no compulsion at all, one could give what one wished.

When they were saying goodbye, Madame Rosa had rested a cabbage-smelling hand on Hinda's cheek, had looked at her and then said with a shake of her head, 'Today is a very special day for you, my child.'

They had gone down the stairs – the baby had stopped crying, and the dog was barking only very faintly – and when they stepped out of the workshop door and breathed fresh air again, Hinda had laughed so hard that she had thrown herself into one of the broken chairs and kicked her feet.

On the way through the city her laughter had kept bubbling up again, and in the end it had infected Mimi, too. They both giggled like schoolgirls sharing a secret, and even – 'But you mustn't say that at home, it will not be considered polite!' – had to find the ladies' convenience on Bürkliplatz, because Mimi was weeping with laughter, and without freshly powdering her face she couldn't show herself in the elegant surroundings of the Palm Garden.

20

The Palm Garden in the Tonhalle was the most fashionable place in Zurich to enjoy a cup of hot chocolate. Well, in fact, the hall of the Hotel Baur en Ville on Paradeplatz was perhaps a little more exclusive, but it attracted a quite different clientele, predominantly foreign travellers, and Mimi had never understood why one should put on one's best for people one didn't even know. In Palm Garden one always saw familiar faces, particularly in the afternoon, when the orchestra played on the low platform, 'under the baton of the eminent conductor Fleur-Vallée', as it said in the advertisements. Monsieur Fleur-Vallée was a regular customer at the butcher's shop, and his real name was Blumental.

The four huge palm trees that gave the café its name grew from metal-studded tubs which had to be turned every three months by the whole staff, all pulling together and people shouting 'heave!', so that they didn't grow towards the light from the plate-glass window on all sides. Mimi knew that from Monsieur Fleur-Vallée, who had complained that they actually expected him, a sensitive artist, to join in with such a coarse operation.

For someone who didn't know, the Palm Garden might have looked like an undifferentiated sea of little round tables, washed together here and then into random groups of islands for larger parties. But just as one did not move just anywhere when choosing a place to live, but sought the proximity of one's peers – small craftsmen in the Old Town, workers in the recently incorporated district of Wiedikon, Jews around the synagogue on Löwenstrasse – here too one had to respect a clear social demarcation which might not have been recorded anywhere, but with which the habitués were nonetheless very familiar.

The most sought-after seats were on the bright south front – 'but not right by the window,' Mimi had explained to Hinda, 'that's cheap. It shouldn't look as if we need to display ourselves in a shop window.' They found a seat in the second row, not too far from the wide entrance; they wanted to be able to see who was coming and going, after all. In the Palm Garden there was a quarter of elderly couples, an arrondissement of newspaper readers, and so on. Right in front of the orchestra platform sat students in their best clothes and young ladies who wanted to be near them. Non-residents had to content themselves with a seat in the no-man's-land somewhere in between.

Today there were a lot of untypical guests in the Palm Garden, noisy, often colourful figures, 'not really elegant people', as Mimi established after a glance at the frayed collars and hats that hadn't been brushed for ages. Around their tables, on which pamphlets were stacked, the chairs were crammed so close together that the heavily laden waiters could hardly make their way through. Some of the men hadn't even sat down, but, bottles and glasses in hand, were getting in the way, gesticulating and talking at one another.

'Those are the socialists,' said Monsieur Fleur-Vallée. After his own arrangement of popular folk tunes and the concluding 'Circassian Tattoo', he had joined Frau Pomeranz and her guest at their table, and had greeted them both by kissing their hand, once again prompting Hinda to burst out laughing. When he was conducting on the platform, the conductor looked like a figure from a musical box, all tiny, regular and finely turned out. Seen from close to he was just a little man with a big nose, not the curved, Levantine kind that people like to ascribe to Jews, but swollen through illness and purple in colour, a defect that Monsieur Fleur-Vallée attempted to conceal with a lot of powder. Consequently the lapels of the tailcoat that he wore as a work uniform always bore a white dusting.

'The socialists,' he repeated, pulling a face as if a trumpeter had parped in the middle of one of his finest pianissimo passages. 'They are holding their world congress here in the Tonhalle. It's been going on for three days. People without any feeling for music. They even go on talking during "Åses Tod", and that's really almost like Kol Nidre.'

As if to confirm his words, at that moment the discussion at the crammed-to-gether tables rose to a dissonant crescendo. 'They'll come to blows again,' said Monsieur Fleur-Vallée. 'It wouldn't be the first time.'

'Where do these people come from?' Mimi asked.

'From Germany,' said Monsieur Fleur-Vallée, drawing a loop in the air with his index and middle fingers pressed together each time he named a country, as if conducting a map. 'From Austria-Hungary. From France. From England. From Italy. From Russia. From Poland. And from America, I assume.'

'You do seem to know a lot about these socialists,' said Mimi, threatening him with her finger, a saucy gesture that she had copied from the soubrette in the municipal theatre.

'I have established it through music,' said the little conductor, rising on tiptoe as if pride at his own cleverness had made him taller. 'By means of a little exercise from my days as first violinist with the spa orchestra in Bad Kissingen. A pot-pourri of national anthems, performed in the style of Rossini, all very light and *scherzando*, but with very daring transitions. Do you play the piano at all?' he asked Hinda without transition.

'Sadly not.'

'That's lucky, believe me. Very lucky! Stay that way! It's better not to play an instrument than to do it in a dilettante manner. So many times have I had to accompany so-called music lovers at parties. Lovers, heavens above!' He threw his hand to his face in dramatic despair. It looked as if he was trying to hide his swollen nose. 'But what was I about to . . . ? The national anthems, of course. Listen.' Still standing by the table, he leaned down to the two women, like a waiter taking an order, and slowly began to sing the Austrian Kaiser anthem. '"Gott erhalte, Gott beschütze unsern Kaiser, unser Land, mächtig durch des Glaubens Stütze führt er uns mit weiser Hand! Allons enfants de la patrie, le jour de gloire est arrive." A daring transition, don't you think?'

'And what does that have to do with the socialists?' Hinda asked.

'A little game that we used to pass the time in Bad Kissingen. You're not really artistically stretched in a spa orchestra of that kind. Before we played the pot-pourri, we always bet on the individual countries. We looked at the people in the audience and tried to guess where they came from.'

'And then . . . ?'

'The fact is that people applaud when their national anthem is played. I don't know why; they just do. At least on this point the socialist comrades seem to be exactly as patriotic as everyone else.'

Because they all turned their heads at that moment – pointlessly, because if people don't actually happen to be swinging flags, you can't see their patriotism – so because at that moment they were looking over at the tables of the congress participants, they were able to see quite precisely what was happening there, and what would even appear in the newspaper the following day under the title 'Riot in the Palm Garden'.

They didn't catch the words of the discussion, they had no idea what it was about, but one of the men involved must have said something that so enraged his listeners that they no longer knew how to reply with arguments, resorting instead to brandished beer glasses. The result was that in the middle of the archipelago of crammed-together tables a volcano seemed to be erupting. A surge of chairs, cutlery, fluttering pamphlets and flying hats poured in all directions, and in its midst, fish washed on to the shore by the storm, fighting men thrashed around, fists flailing, even as they fell.

It all happened so quickly that Mimi and Hinda didn't even have time to be really frightened. They hadn't had time to explain the sudden flurry of excitement, when a young man, pushed by another, crashed backwards into their table and knocked it over. The cups of hot chocolate and the plates of cream slices went flying through the air as if slung from a catapult. The man himself, as he stumbled, landed half in Hinda's lap, and nearly dragged her from her chair.

Hinda heard Mimi screaming beside her, a long, high note like the one blown by a tekiyoh on a shofar, except that it wasn't in fact Mimi, it was Monsieur Fleur-Vallée.

The strange man slipped very slowly from her knees to the floor, tried to cling on to something, reaching blindly into the air, grabbed the sleeve of Hinda's dress, pulled himself up by it and, as he did so, tore the sleeve from its stitches, with a noise which to Mimi, who had by now recovered from her shock, sounded like a shot from a cannon.

The man struggled to his feet, smiled at Hinda with big, white teeth, as if the whole thing had been only a harmlessly amusing diversion, said something incomprehensible in a foreign language and hurled himself back into the fray. Hinda tried to watch after him, but the churning floods of humanity had immediately swallowed him again.

The whole thing lasted only a few minutes. Tempers cooled as quickly as they had flared. The men brushed the dust from each other's suits, lost hats were sorted, undented and put back on, toppled plant tubs were set back up again. The injured were carried out on table-tops, the legs having probably served as clubs. When at last two policemen, as quickly as their official dignity allowed, came into the Palm Garden, the previously so disputatious conference participants were already calmly helping the waiters clean up.

Monsieur Fleur-Vallée took considerably longer to calm down. He was a sensitive artist, after all, as Frau Pomeranz would surely confirm, and not made for excitements of this kind. But more than his own wellbeing, it had been concern for Hinda that had led him to pass the remark, and it was his most fervent hope that the young lady had not been hurt in any way, and that she had soon recovered from her unpleasant experience.

He had to ask his worried question twice before Hinda heard him. Lost in thought, she was observing two delegates as they picked up scattered pamphlets. Neither was the man who had collided with her so roughly. Perhaps he had been one of the injured men.

'At least put your cape on!' said Aunt Mimi. What will people think if they see you in your torn dress like a gypsy?'

She actually wanted to go home straight away, but the landlord of the Palm Garden, who was rushing from table to table to apologise in person to his regular guests for all the unpleasantness, insisted that they first be served another hot chocolate, with cream slices, on the house, of course.

'Well, all right,' said Mimi, 'the refreshment might do us good after all that excitement.'

'As you wish,' said Hinda, who hadn't been listening.

Monsieur Fleur-Vallée was still quite pale, and Mimi insisted that he join them and also have a hot chocolate, on the house.

The socialists, as if nothing had happened, were already sitting back at their tables talking. Mimi looked on, with respectable disapproval.

'Such people shouldn't even be allowed in the country,' she said. 'He could have broken all your bones, Hinda.'

'I'm sorry?'

'He could have crippled you.'

'He didn't do it on purpose. And nothing really happened.'

'He tore your dress. Is that nothing? Well, if you ask me, it doesn't matter very much anyway, it's hardly the latest fashion, but still…What is the world coming to?'

'Still, he did apologise,' said Monsieur Fleur-Vallée.

'Did you understand what he said?'

'Did you not, Frau Pomeranz?'

'Can I speak Russian or Polish or whatever it was?'

'It wasn't Russian,' said the conductor, and rubbed his hands together in a know-it-all manner, spraying powder all over the place. 'And it wasn't Polish.'

'So what was it?'

'Yiddish,' said Monsieur Fleur-Vallée.

'Seid mir moichel,' the man had said, 'Forgive me.' He had spoken not the Yiddish that was customary hereabouts, but the Eastern European variant that served the Jews as a lingua franca from the Baltic down to Bessarabia. There were many Jews from different countries among the delegates at the socialist congress, said Monsieur Fleur-Vallée, which was hardly a surprise, after all, Karl Marx, who had invented the whole thing, if you liked, had himself not been a goy.

'Herr Blumental', Mimi displayed her newly acquired knowledge later over dinner, 'has even met Karl Marx's daughter in person. She is an interpreter at the congress. And August Bebel, the top socialist, has a son-in-law in Zurich. A doctor. And you, Pinchas? Did you even know that there was such a congress here?'

'Well, yes,' said Pinchas, 'I kind of suspected as much. Because of all the articles that have been appearing in all the newspapers for weeks.'

'As a housewife one has no time to sit around for half the day reading newspapers.'

'Of course not, my dear,' said Pinchas, and there wasn't the slightest trace of irony in his voice. He loved his wife as she was, and happily allowed her all her superficiality and little vanities, although without ignoring them. He didn't disapprove of her spending too much money on clothes. After more than two decades Pinchas still felt it was his greatest good fortune that Mimi had married him and not Janki; sometimes when he thought of her, he had to interrupt his work for a few seconds and just stand still and rejoice.

Pinchas had changed a lot since the Endingen days, not just because he had got that pivot tooth. He had grown into himself, physically, too, his gangling frame had become rounder, and his movements less agitated. Only his beard was still thin, but that was no longer so striking since it was cut and trimmed into shape once a month. At dinner he wore a soft brown housecoat in whose pockets – how many times Mimi had complained, but the man wouldn't listen! – he carried far too much paraphernalia. He had covered his head with a small black silk cap.

'You two had a real adventure today,' he said. Mimi started in alarm, because she was thinking of Madame Rosa, but her husband was bent over a slice of cold meat with such concentration that he didn't notice.

'At least I'll have something to talk about at home in Baden,' laughed Hinda.

'But don't exaggerate too much!' For Mimi it was unimaginable that someone could pass on an experience without embellishments. 'Otherwise they'll stop you coming to see me.'

'I hardly think Hinda lets people stop her doing anything very much,' Pinchas said.

'It really looked very dangerous. Imagine: our little Hinda and that huge man—'

'He wasn't that big,' Hinda said.

'—comes charging at us as if he's about to rob us, with his hair dishevelled and those black, black eyes—'

'Green eyes,' said Hinda.

'How do you know that?'

'I know,' said Hinda.

'Perhaps I should go along to this congress as well,' Pinchas considered. 'Talk to a few people and write an article about it.'

'Are you a shochet or a journalist?'

'Both.'

'Can I come along?' asked Hinda.

'To the congress?'

'It might be quite interesting.'

'*Certainement pas!*' said Mimi. 'That's absolutely out of the question! I would reproach myself for the rest of my life if anything…'

The front doorbell rang in the corridor. Not twice, which according to local minhag would have meant a customer turning up when the shop was shut, after remembering something he absolutely needed from the butcher's shop, but just once.

'At this time of the evening?' said Mimi.

'Maybe Guttermann wants to know something. Or else it's someone from the community.' Pinchas who, say what one liked, was far too easily persuaded to perform his duty, had been elected to various committees, and it wouldn't have been the first time that someone had dropped in unexpectedly at an inconvenient time to discuss a problem with him.

From outside came the sound of the maid thundering down the stairs to open the front door. The staff changed often in the Pomeranz household. Mimi wasn't terribly successful at dealing with the staff, one day treating the young things like best friends, and then being unnecessarily strict with them the day after. The 'speciality of the month', as Pinchas called each incumbent, was called Regula, and was of rather limited intelligence.

'Frau Pomeranz,' she said, when she came into the dining room – and Mimi had dinned it into her a thousand times! – without knocking. 'There's a man here.'

'What sort of man?'

'I don't know him,' Regula said as if that was an end to the matter.

'Then please ask him his name.'

'As you wish, Frau Pomeranz.' Pinchas had only to dart a glance at his wife to know that Regula too would not remain long in her job.

'It's so hard to find good staff,' said Mimi. 'You have no idea, Hinda.'

'I've asked him now,' said Regula, coming back into the room.

'And?'

'I didn't catch his name,' Regula said. 'It's something foreign.'

'Then please ask the gentleman for his visiting card.'

'Perhaps it would be better if I just . . .' said Pinchas and was about to get to his feet. But Mimi wouldn't let him.

'How is she to learn if we always do her job for her?'

'He says he hasn't got a visiting card,' Regula said a few moments later.

'Then give him a sheet of paper, and tell him to write his name on it.' Things were never as complicated as this in the social novels that Mimi always liked to read.

After a further short exchange – Regula asked in all seriousness where she could find some paper, when she dusted in the study every day! – the impro-vised visiting card lay on the table in front of Pinchas. 'It's not even such a difficult name,' he said.

'But it is foreign,' Regula insisted. 'I'm quite sure of that.'

'Zalman Kamionker,' Pinchas read. 'Do you know who that is?

'Probably a shnorrer. Regula, does he look like a shnorrer?'

Regula didn't know what a shnorrer was.

'We can play this out all evening,' said Pinchas and stood up. 'But perhaps there's another, easier way. Regula, bring the gentleman in.'

'I don't think he is a gentleman,' Regula said. 'He looks more like a man.' And she went out to fetch the gentleman, or the man.

'Kamionker,' Pinchas repeated thoughtfully. 'Where can I have heard that name before?'

'In Galicia.'

It certainly wasn't a gentleman who had come into the room. He wasn't even holding a hat, just a greasy leather cap.

'That's him!' said Mimi, pointing an accusatory hand. 'The man from the Palm Garden.'

'Yes,' said Hinda. 'That's him.'

21

'The musician gave me the address,' Zalman Kamionker explained, without the slightest embarrassment. He spoke German in a curious Swabian accent, mixed with scraps of Yiddish. 'The klezmer, you know the one. The one who was standing by your table. He didn't want to let me have it, but I shook him. I didn't really shake him, don't worry, I just told him I would shake him. I'm a peaceful person.'

'That's not how it looked this afternoon,' Mimi said severely.

'There are times when words aren't quite enough. What is one to do?'

He had rough shoes on and his trousers had been darned, but he stood there in the room quite at his ease, legs splayed like a sailor's, solid on his two feet and prepared for any storm that might come his way. He had put his cap back on and buried his hands in his trouser pockets, not out of embarrassment, but like a craftsman who only unpacks his tools when he needs them. He didn't seem bothered that they were all staring at him, he just looked back with friendly interest, from Hinda to Mimi, from Mimi to Pinchas and back to Hinda, and then said: 'Nice place you have here.' It was an observation, not a compliment.

'So you're ... ?' Pinchas began.

'Guilty as charged,' said Zalman Kamionker and didn't look guilty in the slightest. 'I didn't start the brawl, but neither did I run away. Such things happen. What's a person to do? That's how it is in politics.'

'I don't think I find this way of conducting political debates very correct,' said Pinchas.

'Me neither. I am, as I said, a peaceful man. That's why I came to apologise again. To Frau Pomeranz and to her lovely daughter.'

'She isn't my daughter.'

'Of course not,' said Zalman Kamionker and took a hand from his pocket to strike himself on the forehead. 'Where is my seichel? You're far too young to have such a grown-up daughter.'

'*Il fait des compliments*,' Mimi said, but was still flattered.

'This is our niece,' Pinchas explained, although strictly speaking it wasn't true. 'Fräulein Hinda Meijer from Baden.'

'Fräulein Hinda,' said Zalman Kamionker. He put a hand on his heart in an old-fashioned gesture and bowed. 'Will you accept my apology?'

'Nothing happened,' Hinda said dismissively, feeling her face suddenly becoming very hot. 'I'm not going to blush,' she thought. 'I'm not Arthur.'

Kamionker seemed not to have noticed anything. He turned to Mimi with the same formal gesture – he had the quality of only ever paying his full attention to one person at a time, as if that person were at that moment the only one in the world – and asked: 'And you, Frau Pomeranz? Are you moichel too?'

'You tore her dress,' Aunt Mimi said, trying to look severe.

'It can't have been a really good stitch.' The young man laughed, showing big teeth. 'But never mind. Give me the dress and I'll do a double cap stitch, an elephant could pull on it and it wouldn't tear.'

'You're a tailor?' Mimi asked with surprise.

'What else?' said Zalman Kamionker. 'Did you take me for a street-sweeper?'

He wasn't very well brought up, that much was clear to Mimi very quickly. If you burst into someone's house at an impossible time of day when people are having their dinner, and the lady of the house asks you purely out of politeness whether you might perhaps be hungry, you have to say no, even if your stomach is rumbling. You certainly don't just say thank you, push your cap back on your head and just plonk yourself down at the table. And if you do, then you wait politely until you're offered something, you don't just reach into the bread basket and then grab a piece of cold meat before the lady of the house has time to call the maid and set a fourth place.

But on the other hand, if a young man is hungry…And he praised everything, the cold meat and the bread and even the tea, which he sipped in the Russian way through a lump of sugar. He knew himself that he was eating greedily, and apologised for it. 'The people from my union put together the money for the "Eintracht". But as for food…I'm the ox who's doing the threshing, and whose mouth has therefore been bound.' And for a while he said nothing more, although silence, and this was now clear to anyone, was certainly not his way.

'He doesn't look like a tailor,' Pinchas thought. 'Herr Oggenfuss, who lived next door to the Meijers in Endingen, he was a proper tailor, narrow-chested and thin as a reed. This Kamionker is far too strong for the job, his suit fits so tightly over his muscles that you could imagine him as a bricklayer or furniture packer, if they weren't such goyish professions. And his shirt is a worker's shirt too, out of that thick, not quite white fabric – what's it called again? – that farm labourers wear. But one can be mistaken. Perhaps practices are very different where he comes from, over there in the East.'

'He doesn't really have green eyes,' Hinda thought. 'Not in this light. Where did I get that idea? He has brown eyes. Brown with little light specks. Or are they green, in fact? One would have to look at them from close to. He has a little scar on his forehead. Maybe he gets into fights a lot, this peaceful man. No, he has too friendly a face for that. A sweet face. One might imagine...' And then she pulled herself together, sat up quite straight and was fully resolved not to imagine anything at all.

Mimi saw Hinda looking and looking away and looking again, and was reminded of another young man who had once stood simply outside a door, had just sat down at a table, who had also been hungry and also knew how to talk, someone who even read novels out loud, and in the end it had been nothing but empty words. No, she didn't like this Zalman Kamionker after all. He just took his knife and cut off a piece of bread for himself! 'I'm glad you like it,' she said sharply.

Pinchas heard the undertone and smiled to himself.

'The smoked meat,' Zalman Kamionker said, before he had even swallowed down the last mouthful. 'The smoked meat is excellent. In my country we don't get things like that any more. When the people come off the boat the first thing they do is to cut off their payos, and the second thing is to forget how to eat respectably. But that's just how things are in America.'

'America?' Pinchas said in amazement. 'But you said...'

'I'm an American from Kolomea who speaks German like a Swabian. A muddle, as befits a Jew. A Galician Yankee with an Austrian passport. I only came to New York two years ago. Some people say I'm still a greenhorn.'

'A green what?'

'He *does* have green eyes,' thought Hinda.

'A greenhorn is someone who's only just arrived in America. Who doesn't yet know his way around. Who thinks there's money in the street in the golden medina, and you just have to bend down and pick it up. But bending down is the biggest mistake you can make. You have to defend yourself. Hence the union. Hence the Congress.'

'I'm interested in this Congress,' Pinchas said. 'You'll have to tell me more about it. How did you end up there?' And Zalman Kamionker, who was now full and content, was not the man to need cajoling when offered a challenge such as this.

So he told them about Kolomea, that little town in the Imperial Crown Land of Galicia, where every second inhabitant was a Jew, where there had even been a Jewish mayor – there had been dancing in the street when Dr Trachtenberg was elected – and where the nationalities were all mixed up together as if in a big pot, the Austrians and the Ukrainians, the Huzules and the gypsies, there were even Tartars, and in Mariahilf the Swabians from whom he had learned his German. He described the chaos of churches and synagogues, where the various religions lived together in a great whole – 'Although sometimes we had to fight, what are you going to do?' – where there weren't even any real tensions after the pogrom in Kiev, which wasn't all that long ago, where it was only difficult to find a parnassah, unless it was in Simon Heller's tallis weaving mill, where he too had worked, but not for long – but, he said, that was all part of it, if you wanted to understand why he was no taking part in his Congress.

Because this man Simon Heller was a Jew, a very pious one, in fact, with a seat right against the eastern wall of the synagogue, but also a capitalist, and therefore paid wages that weren't real wages but a joke. In the end they had to found a union – 'not a real union, we didn't even know what that was' – and because no one else wanted to do it, they had appointed him, the young Zalman Kamionker, as their spokesman. He had tried to negotiate at first, quite peacefully, but old Heller had had him thrown out of his office, twice and three times, and so in the end they had called their strike, the famous strike of Kolomea, they must have heard of it, even here?

No, no one here had heard of it.

'That's how it is,' said Zalman Kamionker, and laughed, showing his teeth, 'you think you're shaking the world, but the world can't be shaken so easily.' He was used to talking in front of other people, it was obvious. He had the sort of calm that people only have when they're sure no one is going to interrupt them.

They actually won their strike – 'To tell the truth, we hadn't really believed we would' – and old Heller had to grit his teeth and pay every weaver and every tailor a few more Kreuzer for the working day, but they weren't a real union, not the kind they had in America, everyone thought only of himself, of his own little advantage, and when the strike-leaders were fired a short time later and couldn't find work anywhere else, no one fought for them. Still – 'He who has a bad conscience gives tzdoke' – enough money was raised for a crossing to New York, and eventually he had disembarked in Castle Gardens, a total greenhorn, and had looked for work and found it – 'You take what you get, what are you supposed to do?'

So he had – 'Beggars can't be choosers' – learned to sew coats, by hand and with the machine, he had even had a talent for it, but it hadn't made him rich, he'd come just too late for that. 'The coat factories all belong to the German Jews who have been in the country already for twenty years; the Russians and the Galicians can only sit at the machines.'

He was a good storyteller, and when it was already getting dark outside and they had had to call in Regula to light the gas lamps in the room, they were still listening. He told them about the two seasons that existed in the coat-making world, two months of winter in the summer, and one month of summer in winter, and laughed at their uncomprehending faces. 'In the summer you sew coats for the winter season, two months' work, that's when the orders are issued, and the manufacturer doesn't need any more cutters or stitchers or finishers. When it's hot, fewer coats are sold, so in the winter there's only half as much work, and during those three crucial months, two in summer and one in winter, you have to earn enough money to live off for the whole year. But I'm boring you with stories.'

'You're not boring us at all,' said Pinchas.

'Not at all,' thought Hinda.

'So they had founded a union in New York as well, but this time a real one, the Jewish Cloak Workers Union, and because all the stitchers were in it, whether they wanted to be or not – 'We weren't friendly to scabs!' – because everyone was pulling together, they didn't even have to strike, just threaten to strike – 'which I preferred, I'm a peaceful person.' Because of his experiences in Kolomea he was elected onto the committee, and then when the International Socialist Workers' Conference was called in Zurich, the Jewish cloak makers had chosen him as their delegate. They were proud because of their victory, and they wanted to have a say. 'I didn't push to come,' said Zalman Kamionker, 'but what are you going to do?'

Pinchas nodded. The community kept making similar demands on him.

The Congress itself, Kamionker said, getting more and more into his swing, the whole event so far had been a big disappointment. Even the room where they met was far too elegant. As solemn as a church. There was even an organ on the stage – 'What do we need an organ for? Have we come to pray?' Although on the walls in sixteen different languages – 'Even in Yiddish!' – was the motto of the proletarians of the world about how they should unite, 'but they don't want to unite, they just want to be right, each one individually, like in a little shtetl, where there are three different prayer rooms and each one has a different minhag, and each one is broyges with all the others, and even if Khmelnitzky in person came riding in with his Cossacks, they would all go on arguing, instead of pulling together and defending themselves.'

The German delegates above all, Kamionker said contemptuously, had nothing in their heads but debates about first principles and amendments to the rules of procedure. For a whole day, and this was just one example among many, for a whole long day they had argued only about the admission of delegates, who they wanted to have there and who not, and in the end only the majority socialists had been allowed to stay, the decent, orderly ones, and the independents, who were all a bit meshuga, but who at least wanted to do something – 'There don't need to be barricades in all the streets' – had been sent home, as had the anarchists. But they wouldn't accept it, so the first fights of the Congress had broken out, and they hadn't been the last. 'They could ban them from the big hall, but the Palm Garden is a public place, they're still sitting there every day.'

Meanwhile everything at the Congress was running like clockwork, but it was a soup without pepper, they all delivered their well-phrased speeches and applauded one another, they had even taken – 'Typical!' – the big cowbell from the chairman, the one he had had the beginning, to drown out any dissent, and instead given him a delicate little bell that tinkled so delicately that no one could hear it, and the whole Congress was like that! Now the only people who had the floor were the ones who always had the same opinion anyway and admired one another; if Friedrich Engels walked past – yes, he was there too – they were inches away from falling on their knees and crossing themselves like goyim when they carry the Yossel Pendrik through the streets on his cross. Engels, of all people, who was a manufacturer and not even a worker! And anyway, if you asked him, they were none of them socialists anyway, they were all bourgeois in disguise, who wouldn't last a season in New York, twelve or fourteen hours at the sewing machine and then a mattress that you had to share with two others in shifts! August Bebel even had a villa on Lake Zurich! Need he say more? With gas heating!

Nothing would come out of this Congress, said Zalmon Kamionker, nothing at all, apart from a pile of resolutions and decisions. All just paper. 'You are a shochet, Herr Pomeranz, are you not? If you go to the slaughterhouse and stand beside a cow and say, "Dear cow, we have democratically decided that you are to give up your meat for the Shabbos roast" – will you then have anything to eat? Will you hell! You have to take the knife and slaughter the cow, it's the only way. I am a peaceful man, but all that talking brings up my bile!'

'When he gets worked up, there's something of the hero about him,' thought Hinda. And she had never thought before about what a hero might look like.

'What I'd really like to do is let the Congress be the Congress. But that wouldn't be the decent thing. I've been sent here at great expense, so I sit on my seat every day. I listen to the speeches, and they go in one ear and out the other. If someone has any money, I allow him to buy me a beer...'

'And then do you fight there?' It wasn't a reproach, just something that interested Pinchas.

'What are you going to do? For example today—'

But he didn't get round to saying what had happened today, because the

Neuenberg clock that hung on the wall beside the misrach panel was already striking half past nine. Zalman Kamionker glanced at the fine timepiece, not because he was shocked by the lateness of the hour, just matter-of-factly, as if he wanted to buy the clock – 'Or steal it,' thought Hinda – and quickly stuffed another slice of smoked meat in his mouth, he really did have no manners, wiped his moustache, just like that, with the back of his hand, even though there was a napkin beside his plate, and explained, as he got up, that the door of the 'Eintracht' was unfortunately open only until ten o'clock; and that if you wanted to get into the dormitory after that you had to pay five rappen key money. He thanked them for the food, not extravagantly, but with a certain formality, a guest of state who knows the importance of etiquette, even though he is entitled to the most generous hospitality, and then said to Pinchas, 'If you're really interested in the Congress, I'm happy to give you a guided tour. The session doesn't start till two the day after tomorrow. The committees meet in the morning and decide what's to be voted on in the afternoon. Most delegates will be there at about twelve. We can meet in the Palm Garden if you like, and I'd like you to meet a few people.'

'That would be very kind of you.'

'I even know which delegates I have to introduce you to. You'll have loads to talk about, since you're a shochet. Dr Stern from Stuttgart.'

'Is he a Jew as well?'

Kamionker spread his arms and moved his torso back and forth as if trying to keep his balance on a narrow plank. 'Ask him yourself,' he said. 'He will give you such a thorough answer that you won't get a word in for an hour. He likes the sound of his own voice.'

He turned to the two women and held out his hand to them. 'So, Fräulein Hinda Meijer, are you moichel?'

'If it matters so much to you.'

'It matters a great deal.'

'Well then, if you wish.'

'Fine, then that's everything sorted out.' He took Hinda's hand and held it tightly for a long time. And then, before he let go of it again, he said quite surprisingly, 'Yis'chadesh!', the blessing for a new dress or a new flat, which seemed totally out of place.

'And you, Frau Pomeranz?'

'*Alors je vous pardonne.*'

Kamionker laughed at Mimi – an impudent laugh, in fact – and said, 'Don't talk French to me. Otherwise I'll talk English to you, and then *you* won't understand.'

Mimi raised a threatening finger, but then she said, 'I forgive you.' She held out her hand so that he had no option but to bend down and press his moustache to it.

'He didn't kiss my hand,' thought Hinda.

'It's time for the maid to finish work,' Mimi thought out loud, 'and the front door will be locked. Pinchas, would you...?'

'Of course. More than happy.'

'Don't stir yourself, Uncle Pinchas,' Hinda said quickly, and if anyone suspected anything more than simple helpfulness behind her words, then that wasn't her problem.

Zalman Kamionker just stopped in the open doorway and looked at her expectantly.

Just stopped.

'Is there anything else?' Hinda asked at last.

'I'm waiting for the dress. So that I can sew the sleeve back on.'

'That's out of the question.'

'I'm a good stitcher.'

'Be that as it may.'

'The best double cap stitch in New York.'

'No, I said.'

'I'm a peaceful person and I will not argue with you. But if you give me the dress now, I can come by tomorrow and bring it back to you.'

'No!'

'As you wish,' said Zalman Kamionker. 'I'll come by tomorrow anyway.' And he laughed with big white teeth and went into the night, with his hands in his pockets.

22

Poplars grew on either side, haughty, self-contained trees that cast no shadows. It was a cloudless day, and even though it was only May the sun glowed as if it were trying to burn a hole in the sky.

Chanele was dressed far too warmly. And she had, quite out of character, spent a long time thinking about what to wear that day, she had stood by her own wardrobe as if by a stranger's, had tried to see herself with the eyes of a stranger, no, not a stranger, different eyes, eyes that might be the same colour as her own, who knows, it was possible.

It was possible.

When Hinda had her tonsils taken out that time, she had been given a paper doll by way of consolation, the cardboard figure of an angelically blonde girl in a white blouse, surrounded by a whole wreath of different dresses. Its colours were slightly faded, because the sheet had been in the window of the stationer's for a long time, but that only made the dresses all the more elegant. You could cut them out and fold them up and put them on the paper girl, so she looked different every time and had different plans, going shopping in town one time, another time going to a ball or to her own wedding.

Faced with her own wardrobe, Chanele had felt like that cardboard figure. A toy.

In the end she had opted for a grey travelling outfit, a practical dress for all weathers one could put on all by oneself, and on which even small flecks of dust from the locomotive would not be noticed. The dress had big, brown pockets with brown borders on either side, although they were only for decoration and you couldn't put anything in them. She hadn't brought a suitcase; she had only packed a bag of absolute necessities. 'You're travelling like a serving girl,' Janki had said. 'Are you sure you don't want me to come with you?'

'No, I have to do this one all on my own,' she had replied, and perhaps that had been a mistake.

The poplars stood on either side like sentries.

In the little hotel whose address Janki had written down for her, she had not at first been given a very friendly welcome. Hoteliers are used to gauging the importance of a guest by the amount of luggage they have. But then she had given her name, and the porter, a cheap popular edition of Herr Strähle, had personally ushered her into his room with 'Bienvenue, Madame Meijer', and 'Quel honneur, Madame Meijer'. Janki seemed to be a valued guest here, even though his business didn't bring him to Strasbourg very often.

But what did she know about Janki's business?

The room smelled of withered flowers, as if at a goyish levaya. For a whole sleepless night the dress hung before her eyes on its hanger, an alien body that she would just have to slip into the following morning to become someone else.

She just didn't know who.

The fabric was far too heavy. Everything was far too heavy. The shirt stuck to her body, like the wet canvas that Golde had wrapped her in back in the old days when she had a fever, so tightly that she couldn't move her arms, that she got scared and tried to wriggle free, to hit her arms out and tear at everything. Until Golde turned it into a game, a test of courage. Mimi, even if she was perfectly healthy, was also wrapped up, and then the two girls lay side by side, and every time Chanele held out longer than Mimi did, every time, and was so proud that she forgot her fear and even her illness.

In the hotel they had told her to take a cab, it was too far to travel on foot, but she still had them explain the directions to her, through the city and out of the city. She had brought nothing but her handbag, a simple linen bag with which Mimi would never have been seen dead.

The bow-fronted houses here leaned curiously into the street. Chanele bought an apple from a market stall, but then threw it into the gutter after the first bite. She stopped for a long time in front of the cathedral and couldn't have said a thing about it afterwards.

When she had reached the edge of the city, where the houses grew smaller and the vegetable gardens bigger, she also stopped in places where there was nothing at all to see. She wanted to gain time, she wanted to postpone the encounter for which she had waited so patiently.

As a child, of course, as a child she had dreamed of it, she had imagined herself into all the fairy stories, she was the child who was lost, the one who was found, she had put her foot in the glass slipper and it had fit, it had fit her and her alone, she had slept for a hundred years behind a hedge of thorns until the prince came and recognised her as his princess.

As a child you can simply dream up things you don't know.

But she was now forty-one years old.

Without being aware of it, Chanele had begun to count her steps — ninety-six, ninety-seven, ninety-eight — and once she was aware of it, she couldn't silence the voices in her head.

Ninety-nine, a hundred.

In the military, she knew this from Janki, they counted like that to make unbearably long marches manageable. 'I'll survive for another thousand steps. Another hundred.'

Back in the days when she had marched by Janki's side from Endingen to Baden, and from Baden to Endingen, her journey had never seemed so long.

The avenue was not designed for people who came on foot. It was a road for coaches and horses, for noble men and grand gestures, a path from the past.

Past.

She had once asked Golde about it, just once, and Golde had sucked her lower lip into her mouth and stroked her hair and said, 'It was the Lord God.'

Whenever someone doesn't know the answer, it's always the Lord God.

Perhaps she should pray.

But a prayer just because you're scared is nothing but counting your steps to make a difficult journey easier.

Shema. Yisrael. Adonai. Eloheinu.

A hundred and thirty-four. A hundred and thirty-five. A hundred and thirty-six.

If Salomon were here now, he would find a meaning for each number.

What is the numerical value of fear?

The avenue between the trees which provided no shade rose slowly to a mound behind where the row of poplar trees seemed to sink into the ground, only the trunk of the first, then the haughty branches of the next.

From the mound you could see the asylum.

Little remained of the castle's former elegance of the castle. An ungainly building of yellow and red brick spread out from the old white stone façade, the wealthy associate of an old established firm. The red bricks were arranged in the form of gable windows and turrets, so that the new building, for all its modern functionality, had a vaguely castle-like quality, as if it were mocking its neighbour and its old-fashioned demeanour.

Most of the windows were barred.

There were unhealthily bare, apparently dried-up patches in the expansive, deserted, stubbly lawn, although there had not been many really hot days that year. The borders of the long-untended flowerbeds, mossy and overgrown, marked vanished forms on the ground, sunken graves in a long-abandoned graveyard.

There was no one to be seen for far and wide. Only one old man raking leaves, with unchanging, concentrated movements. When Chanele approached, she saw that there were no leaves there.

'Excuse me . . .'

The man ignored her.

'Can you tell me?'

He went on scratching away at the ground.

'I'm looking for...'

The same spot, over and over again.

Perhaps the old gardener was hard of hearing. Chanele touched his shoulder, and he started screaming, the breathless, terrified screams of a little child. Arthur too had often screamed like that when he had woken from a bad dream.

Chanele tried to calm the old man in the way that had worked with her youngest. She put her arm around him and repeated several times, 'It's all right. It's all right. I'm here.'

The man only screamed all the louder. Apart from two brownish stumps his wide-open mouth was completely toothless.

'Our Néné doesn't like being touched.'

The woman in the starched, pale grey linen uniform must have been watching from a window. With two pointed fingers she removed Chanele's hand from the screaming man's shoulder. Then she bent for the rake that he had dropped and held it out to him. 'There are lots of leaves left, Néné, you keep on working.'

And sure enough: the man calmed down. He gasped for air a few times, gathered his breath for one last scream and then suddenly seemed to forget his panic. He started raking again. Carefully and regularly and always on the same spot.

'I'm staff sister Viktoria,' said the uniformed woman. She rolled her Rs the way people from the Baltic do. Her face was friendly, but it was a professional friendliness that she had put on with her uniform.

'My name is Meijer. I have come from Baden...'

'I know,' said the staff sister, and her tone left no doubt that she knew everything that went on here. 'We expected you sooner.'

'I walked from the hotel.'

But that wasn't what the staff nurse meant. 'We wrote the letter weeks ago.'

'I've only just received it.'

'There was a lot of work involved in finding out your details. A lot of work.'

'I'm grateful to you.'

'With good reason, Frau Meijer. With very good reason. The files from the French days are extremely chaotic. You go on working, Néné!' She turned away, walked a few steps towards the brick building and then stopped again. 'Come,' she said, and her friendliness was no longer such a perfect fit. 'I have other things to be getting on with.'

After her long march, the corridor in which Chanele waited was pleasantly cool. The light came from a series of narrow openings very high in the wall. The brightness penetrated the room in well-defined beams, like in the women's gallery in Endingen synagogue when the colourful glass windows were opened.

Except that there were no bars over the windows in the synagogue.

And the walls weren't freshly whitewashed and bare, as if in a prison.

The bench to which staff sister Viktoria had shown her was right against the wall. To keep from dirtying her dress, she had to sit with her back ramrod straight. She tried to shift forward, but the legs of the bench were fastened solidly to the floor. So she stood up again and walked back and forth on aching feet.

Sixteen. Seventeen. Eighteen.

A display case was fixed to one wall, like the trophy cupboard full of laurel wreaths that Chanele knew from the Guggenheim inn back in Endingen. The hooks behind the glass door were empty. She tried to open the box, but it was locked. The inscription had been scratched from an enamel sign, and all that remained was an arrow pointing into the void. On each of the many doors, at eye level, there was a lighter, faded patch where there had once been a sign. Chanele thought of a story from Janki's days as a soldier. He and his company had once had to pull road signs out of the ground and burn them to confuse the advancing German troops.

Fifty-two. Fifty-three. Fifty-four.

Somewhere far away someone began to speak. Chanele couldn't even have said whether what she heard was German or French, or a language that didn't exist, but she understood very clearly that the voice was trying to persuade someone, was talking away at someone who didn't want to listen, constantly presenting new arguments, listing reasons, delivering proof and then, when the other person stayed mute, beginning to plead, to beg, to wail and at last to weep, to whine. And fall silent.

Everything was still once more, so still that she could hear a beetle that had got lost beating against a window time and again in search of an exit.

She had no watch, but it was already the afternoon.

She had had the impression that the corridor simply stopped at its furthest end, but there must have been another one off to the side. From it a man now emerged, looked searchingly around and bore down on her with clumsy haste, a bear walking on its back legs. Even before he had reached her, he started to speak.

'I'm sorry, I'm really sorry. It isn't usually my way to keep guests so long... Not that we have the opportunity to welcome many guests here. Far too few.

Most of our patients are…Out of sight, out of mind. Regrettable, but one cannot hold it against people either. Sometimes it's hard to bear when somebody…I am Dr Hellstiedl. Hello, pleased to meet you. And you are…? Stupid of me. Staff nurse Viktoria told me…Frau Meijer, of course. Interesting spelling. I know e-i, a-i, e-y, but I've never seen the name spelt like… From Baden, is that right? Baden in Switzerland? Very nice. Then please come to by office, so that I can…'

He had opened one of the many doors and disappeared into his room, before Chanele had had a chance to say a word. Then he stuck his head out of the door again, like the jack-in-the-box that Hinda had always liked to play with, and which had frightened Arthur every time, and finished his sentence, '…make the necessary preparations.'

Dr Hellstiedl's unease, Chanele soon noticed, had nothing to do with impatience. Rather, he was constantly distracted by his own thoughts, found each new idea worthy of note and kept interrupting himself as a consequence. Conversing with him was a little like following the conversation at an animated dinner party, a dinner party where the conversation was more intelligent than it had been at Janki's goyish evening.

When she entered the office, he was standing by an open filing cabinet, flicking through the cards in an index box. Papers and books lay around on every available surface, and in among them were objects whose function in this room could be explained only if one used a great deal of imagination: a pine cone, a soup tureen, knitting needles with the beginnings of a sock.

'Meijer,' Dr Hellstiedl murmured. 'Meijer, Meijer, Meijer. I will shortly… Just one moment. The classification system of my French colleagues… Although I don't believe that each people has typical qualities…It is more the external circumstances that create the appearance that…Meijer, Meijer, Meijer. Please sit down!'

Chanele stood where she was, because even the chair by the desk, the one meant for visitors, was covered with papers.

'And my predecessor – a most capable specialist, I never had any doubts on that score – cleared out everything French so painstakingly when he took over the clinic that now…Even the signs on the doors. An excess of thoroughness, which in a patient one would see as…One might really wonder whether patriotism should not be considered an illness…Although presumably it would be incurable. Meijer. Meijer. Meijer. Where on earth is the…?'

At last they sat facing one another, and Dr Hellstiedl had abandoned his search for the index card.

'An interesting case. A most interesting case. Although of course all cases are fundamentally...One is inclined only to take the most spectacular...Did you know that in London they used to take the whole family to see the mentally ill as if going to the theatre? A spectacle, in fact. The asylum was called Bedlam. Bethlehem. Suffer little children to come unto me. A very interesting case, our Ahasuerus.'

'Ahasuerus?'

'I shouldn't allow the giving of nicknames to the patients. I tell the nurses off and then do it myself. Only human, I fear. But these nicknames are often very appropriate. Insights are not always expressed in intelligent terms. Perhaps it's wrong of us to give our children names when they are born. We might be better off waiting until we know them better.'

'François,' thought Chanele. 'Shmul.'

'Ahasuerus.' Dr Hellstiedl ploughed through the chaos on his desk. 'He already had the name when I inherited the institution from my predecessor... It probably wasn't a nurse who came up with it. They're more inclined to think of simple...We have an inmate that they call "Fox". One woman is called "the queen". But "Ahasuerus"...The eternal Jew. An intellectual reference. He lives and would like to be dead.'

'Dead?'

'Of course. How stupid of me. You don't even know...So: Ahasuerus. You will forgive me if I don't further explain...Although of course...Your name is Meijer, isn't it?'

'Hanna Meijer.'

'With e-i-j, of course. Unusual spelling. I should...' Suddenly he tapped his temple, so clumsily that he knocked off his glasses and had to look for them again amongst his papers, and said, 'How stupid of me! You grew up with foster parents...didn't you? And you've taken their name? So why am I looking under...? There isn't going to be a card for "Ahasuerus". And right now the correct name isn't coming to...'

'Are you sure it's him?'

'We assume so. The dates tally. But we have no precise details left from those days. Our French colleagues were here in those days, and my predecessor...A most excellent specialist, but unfortunately also very rigorous. Well, there is nothing to be done about that now.' Dr Hellstiedl sat down at his desk again. 'To answer your question; we assume that it's him. And of course we hope that his encounter with you...I'm no devotee of shock therapy, by no means, but if such a shock is of a purely emotional kind...So I would ask you not to say anything at first. Just don't say a thing. Sit down with him and let him...Perhaps there are some outward signs that...Such cases are sometimes basically frozen in an experience, and their memory has remained correspondingly fresh. As if time had stood still, if you know what I mean. We know very little about these mechanisms. One would need to... Let's do it like this: I will take you to the section – all men from whom we expect no progress – and let you go in on your own. Don't worry. There are no aggressive or dangerous patients in there.'

'So I'll be alone when...?' Chanele said, and her mouth was dry. 'How will I recognise him?'

'He'll probably be lying on the floor. He often does that. Sometimes he lies there motionless for hours. We used to try and get him out of that compulsive state. Forced him onto a chair and even tied him to it. My predecessor...I gave instructions for him to be left alone. He doesn't do anyone any harm, and perhaps...' With a gesture of resignation he pointed to a crowded shelf. 'We have so many books, and we know so little.'

'He lies on the floor?' Nothing was as Chanele had imagined.

'Sometimes for hours at a time. Then in between he's quite unremarkable again. Hides in his corner and watches the others. They recognise him by his white doctor's coat. One of these modern things. I gave it to him. I let him talk me into it once, because lots of colleagues in Berlin...But I'll have to get used to it now. He's happier when he wears something white. He says that's how it has to be.'

'Why?'

Dr Hellstiedl spread his arms wide, a movement that made Chanele think of Salomon. 'Ask him!' he said. 'It's almost always possible to talk to him. When he's on his feet he even talks to the other inmates. Tells them he will soon be a father.'

'A father?'

Dr Hellstiedl nodded and shrugged at the same time. '"In case it's a boy", he's invited me. To that party that the Jews have at a circumcision. But if that's the case, as we suspect, Frau Meijer...? If that's the case there will be no circumcision. Because you are not a boy.' Dr Hellstiedl rose to his feet. 'Let us postpone it no longer,' he said. 'Come, Frau Meijer, I will take you to your father.'

23

They walked – thirty-six, thirty-seven, thirty-eight – along a corridor on whose walls red tiles framed non-existent windows, turned – seventy-four, seventy-five, seventy-six – into a second corridor so similar to the first that Chanele almost expected to meet herself waiting there, left the building through a back door and crossed a deserted courtyard, followed – one hundred and twenty-one, one hundred and twenty-two, one hundred and twenty-three – a narrow gravel path that crunched under their shoes, and then, through a side entrance that Dr Hellstiedl had to open with an outsize key, entered the old castle – one hundred and seventy-three, one hundred and seventy-four, one hundred and seventy-five – through two rooms in which decommissioned plank beds were stacked into towers, reached a staircase, once the magnificent entrance to the castle, climbed up one curved flight of stairs and then another – two hundred and twenty-six, two hundred and twenty-seven, two hundred and twenty-eight – then Dr Hellstiedl unbolted a grille, pointed to an open door and said to Chanele, 'So, do you dare?'

Two hundred and forty-seven.

Two hundred and forty-seven is the gematria of moyreh.

Moyreh means fear.

'Frau Meijer?'

If you don't speak, your voice can't fail. Chanele nodded. And went inside.

The room was high and bright. Over the windows were curtains of dirty tulle, which did little to keep out the harsh sunlight. The crossed bars of the grille appeared as dark lines on the pale fabric. Protruding from the ceiling was a big iron hook, from which a chandelier would once have hung, and on the walls the remains of stucco ornaments in the form of woven wreaths could be discerned. The floor was covered with roughly planed boards that creaked when someone walked over them. Hanging in the air was the smell of sweat and old clothes.

There were about fifteen or twenty men. Most of them sat at a long table with benches lined up beside it, the others stood around somewhere in the room, singly or in groups. One man had put a broom handle over his shoulder like a rifle, and was marching repeatedly from one wall to the other in a military goosestep, performing a ragged turn every time he got to the end. Without the disturbance of his movement, the atmosphere would not have been much different from men's shul at the start of prayers.

None of the men were lying on the floor, and Chanele couldn't see anyone in a white overall.

The patients weren't dressed identically. A few of them wore quite proper suits, as if they had been invited to an official gathering, others, like poor relatives, only peasant trousers and coarse shirts. Some of the patients' clothing had bizarre features, as with the marching man who had fastened several spoons as medals to his jacket. Another wore a tatty tailcoat over his bare chest.

Chanele had stopped in the doorway. A few of the men at the table had their heads turned towards her, but looked in such a way that any sign of perception glided over her, giving her the confusing sensation of being invisible. It was some time before anyone noticed her. Two men, both similarly tall and gaunt, like brothers, came towards, stopped close in front of her and looked at her with such harmless curiosity, such childish shamelessness, that Chanele couldn't help smiling at them.

'Hello,' she said and then, when no reaction was forthcoming, she rummaged through her memory for one of the few French words she had picked up from Mimi: 'Bonjour'.

The men looked at her with as much amazement as if she had performed a circus trick for them. A third man, the strange figure in the tailcoat, hurried over on tripping feet and tried to push the two others aside. They let him do so, but kept pushing their way over again as if attracted by a magnet.

'You're a woman,' said the man in the tailcoat.

'That's true,' said Chanele.

'I thought so,' said the man, as satisfied as a scientist whose experiment has proved a disputed theory. He turned to the two curious men and explained in the tone of a museum curator presenting the treasures of his collection to some visitors: 'She's a woman.'

The two men stood there wide-eyed. Some drool fell from the corner of one of the men's mouths.

'You don't belong here,' said the man in the tailcoat. 'Women are on the other side.'

'I'm visiting.'

With a reproachful shake of his head the man pushed the others a few steps back and explained to them, 'She's visiting.'

'I'm looking for...' Chanele began, but the man with the bare torso raised his hand majestically. Under the armpit of the tailcoat, where the seam had come apart, a big hole gaped.

'I know who you're looking for,' said the man. 'Of course I do. People often come here looking for me. But I'm here incognito.' In an exaggerated pantomime he looked around just to be sure, and then winked at Chanele.

'I'm not looking for you.'

The man nodded in agreement, as if she had said exactly the right thing, winked at her again and explained to the two importunate onlookers, 'She isn't looking for me.' And he added with a triumphant giggle, 'She didn't recognise me.'

In the meantime they had been joined by a fourth man. He was poorly dressed, with a pair of trousers several sizes to big for him, which he had tied together with binding twine, and a jacket that was missing all its buttons. Before Chanele could dodge him, he had gripped her by the upper arms, pulled her to him and kissed her on the forehead. He smelled like old potatoes.

'I have blessed you,' the man said. 'Now nothing more can happen to you.' He wiped his hands thoroughly on his trousers for a long time and walked away again.

The two curious men pushed closer, and the man in the tailcoat pushed them away. 'You're a woman,' he said to Chanele. 'That's what I thought.'

On either side of each window hung heavy, drawn night-blue curtains. From behind one of them a man who had been hiding there stepped forward.

A man in a once-white doctor's overall.

He was old, at least as old as Salomon, and Chanele saw nothing familiar about him. His face had deep wrinkles like those that come from hunger or from many tears, and his cheeks were covered with stubble. He had covered the thin strands of his hair with a white linen cap, of the kind that men wore to service on high feast days. He was barefoot. Below the seam of his coat, thin calves could be seen.

The man was now standing right below the window, and the bright light delineated the outlines of a thin old man's body.

He was ugly.

And he was a complete stranger to Chanele.

None the less, without thinking, and as if her legs had a will of their own, she walked up to him. She just pushed the two curious men aside. There was no sign now of the man in the tailcoat.

Walked up to him.

He saw her coming, and on his face, that lived-in, broken, old face, the emotions alternated as quickly as the light changes when a wind lashes scraps of cloud past the sun. Surprise. Amazement. Disbelief.

And love.

He stretched out his hand, not like an old man looking for support, but like a young man who can be a support to others, he stretched out his hand to her, a hand covered with brownish patches, so that she had no option but to hold out her own, and he gripped it, his skin like paper, like the pages of an old book that falls to bits when you read it, took her fingers between his own, rubbed them with thumb and forefinger to see if there was really something there, if there was really someone there, opened his mouth, moved his lips, soundless at first, the way one speaks a prayer or a magic spell, gulped and said in a voice full of tenderness and full of fear, said with an old, young voice, 'Sarah, my darling, why are you not in bed? You should lie down.'

And then, startled by his own words, he let go of Chanele and darted back as if he had burned himself on her. He put his hands side by side, palms up and fingers bent, as if drawing water from a well, lifted them very slowly to his face and covered his eyes with them.

She still hadn't even seen what colour they were.

He stood quite still for an endless minute. Then he began to rock his torso back and forth, at first quite undiscernibly, then faster and faster, he rocked, he shockelled, began to hum, a prayer without words that was part of no service and no feast day, assembled from scraps of melodies, from all nigunim and none, moved his head back and forth as if someone had gripped it and was forcing it to move, pressed the balls of his hands into his eye sockets, never wanted to see anything again after he had seen Chanele, and then, after a minute, after an hour, he became calmer, he stopped humming, stopped shockelling, slowly lowered his hands and splayed his fingers in front of his eyes as little children do when playing their favourite game of making the world disappear and reappear, and asked very quietly, in an almost inaudible voice full of disbelieving hope, 'Sarah?'

'I'm not Sarah.' Chanele didn't know if she'd said it or only thought it.

Either way, he had heard. He reached his arm out towards her, a thin branch in a white sleeve, moved his hand back and forth, as if to wave away steam or perhaps a ghost, approached her forehead very slowly, the contact, when it came at last, as tender as when one bumps into a cobweb on a dark staircase, stroked her forehead, her temples, ran his hands along her eyebrows, that straight line along the edges of her nose, moved back and forth, Chanele had never stroked herself more tenderly there, and a smile crossed his face, a loving, enchanted, young smile that sat on his wrinkled face like a colourful painted mask. 'You're Sarah,' he said. 'No one has such beautiful eyebrows as you.'

Chanele was forty-one years old and only now did she know what her mother's name had been.

His hand was on her cheek now, it had found its place there like a butterfly on its final flight. She moved her head very slowly up and down. It could have been a nod, it could have been assent to what was happening to her, but perhaps too it was just the desire to be stroked by this hand.

'Are you well?' he asked, and answered his own question. 'You are well, my darling. The sun is shining, even though it's January.'

She was born in January.

The smell he gave off was not pleasant. It was a smell of illness, of decay. A smell of destruction.

Behind her back the man with the broom handle marched back and forth. Back and forth.

'Your time will soon come,' said the old man. His eyes were directed at her, but she had the feeling that he was talking to someone very different. 'Everything will be as it must be,' he said. 'Everything will be fine. If it's a boy we'll call him Nathan. After your father.'

Nathan. Another name that belonged to her. Once upon a time she had also had a grandfather.

'And if it's a girl...You say, Sarah, my darling. What shall we call it if it's a girl?'

'Chanele,' she said.

And he repeated: 'Chanele.'

The soldier marched back and forth. Every time he stepped on the wooden floor on which Chanele stood she was lifted slightly into the air, because the boards had only been loosely laid and had shifted over the years, and underneath there was a very different floor, probably a much finer one, which no one had seen for a long time.

'It will be a big simcha,' said the old man. 'A simcha that people will talk about. Eating and drinking and singing. We will invite everyone, and they will all come. Even Dr Hellstiedl. He is a goy, but a good man. We will invite him. Won't we, Sarah?'

'Yes,' said Chanele. 'We will invite him.'

'You will still be weak.' His hand lay on her cheek as if it had gone to sleep. 'For the first few days one is weak, and that mustn't alarm you. I will carry the child for you. I will hold it. I will never drop it. Nothing will happen to it. Nothing will happen. I know.'

'No,' Chanele said. 'Nothing will happen to anyone.'

She will die, your Sarah that you loved so much, and you will lose your mind. A strange man will come, a beheimes trader called Salomon, and he will take your daughter away and bring her up in his own home. After many years he will write letters and look for you, and you will meet your daughter again and you won't know.

Nothing will happen to anyone.

Suddenly and for no external reason the old man shouted out loud. His voice was suddenly much louder than it had been. He drew his hand away from Chanele's cheek and stared wide-eyed at his fingers. Then he hid his hand behind his back. 'It doesn't mean anything,' he said, and repeated twice more: 'Means nothing. Means nothing.'

Chanele had never seen anything sadder than the reassuring smile he tried to put on.

With his eyes still on Chanele – but who could have said whom he really saw in front of him – he walked backwards, walked away from her on tripping little steps to the window and stuck his hand in the folds of the heavy curtain.

'You mustn't be afraid,' he said, speaking faster and faster, someone using the last of his strength to run for help, and yet knowing that he won't find it. 'The blood means nothing. Nothing at all. It is quite natural. The doctor will come and make everything good again.'

His voice was fragmenting more and more. The wrinkles in his face waited for water like dried up river beds.

'The doctor will come. He has already been sent for. He will come and say, "There is no need to be afraid." He is a good doctor. He is called Dr Hellstiedl. He is the chief doctor. He can determine everything. Everything. Everyone has to obey him. He will determine that you are not dead. That you are not dead. That you are not dead.'

His body had disappeared into the curtain. Only his face was still visible, becoming older and older and stranger and stranger.

'He will determine it,' he repeated. 'If I ask him to, he will determine it. You don't need to be afraid. He is a good doctor. A good person. He gave me this shroud. He is a goy, but he gave me a sargenes. I have more need of it than he does, he said. Because I have already died.'

He cried, letting the tears flow down over him like rain. She would have given anything to know how to comfort him.

'You will not die, Sarah. Dr Hellstiedl will heal you. You will not be dead. Only me. Only me. I gave my life for yours. Because it was meant to be.'

He had now crept all the way into the curtain. The endless, disembodied echo of his voice could only be made out in scraps.

'Not die…means nothing…determine everything.'

A strange hand tapped Chanele on the shoulder. The two curious men were standing there, hand in hand now, two children egging one another on. With them was the man in the tailcoat.

'He is dead,' he explained kindly. 'When they are dead they have to wear white shirts. That's how it is with Jews.'

Chanele wanted to push him away, but her body wasn't strong enough to move.

'He will sing in a minute,' said the man in the tailcoat. 'They have to sing, even when they are dead.'

And true enough: behind the curtain Chanele's father started singing in a high, thin voice.

'I thought he would,' said the man in the tailcoat and winked at Chanele. 'I know all about them, but they don't know me. I'm incognito here.'

'Yisgadal,' sang the old man. 'Yisgadal veyiskadash shmey raba.' It was the kaddish, the prayer for the dead that one speaks in memory of one who has died, sons for their fathers and fathers for their sons.

He sang it for himself.

He sang the whole long prayer, and in the places where the congregation has to join in, Chanele silently said the Amen.

The heavy fabric moved. The head of the man they called Ahasuerus here, and who was her father, became visible, not up where it had disappeared into the curtain, but down on the floor. He must have knelt down and lain on the floor and was now crawling, lying on his back, into the room, he pushed himself away from the wall and lay motionless on the raw floorboards, his arms by his sides, his sightless eyes wide open.

'They put them on the floor when they have died,' explained the man in the tatty tailcoat. 'They wash them, and they lay them down, and then they put them in the coffin.'

Chanele crouched down by her father, by this strange man. She would have liked to pray, but none of the many blessings that Judaism keeps ready for every possible event and opportunity suited the situation. At last she murmured what people say when news of a death arrives: 'Praise be the judge of the truth.' The old man didn't stir, but she had a feeling he was content.

She closed her eyes and would have crouched for a long time like that beside the motionless man, if there hadn't been a sudden smell of wet potatoes, a smacking kiss on her forehead and a voice saying, 'Nothing more can happen to you now.'

Then Dr Hellstiedl was with her. Perhaps he had arrived at that precise moment, but probably he had been watching the whole thing from somewhere.

They must have had observation windows up here, where not even a nurse was paying attention to anyone.

The doctor took her arm and led her silently out. It was only when he had opened the grille and closed it again that he said, 'I have found the old index card after all. His name is Menachem Bär.'

Menachem.

Menachem and Sarah Bär.

And their daughter Chanele.

When they were walking across the courtyard that already lay in the shade of the brick building, he asked her, 'Is that your father?' She didn't reply, and he didn't press the point.

They walked down the long corridor where there were no names on the doors, through the corridor with the windows that weren't windows, down the other corridor where the arrow on the enamel sign still pointed into the void. There was something consoling about the chaos in his office, like a warm, untidy bed inviting one to climb in. Dr Hellstieldl lifted the cosy off a pot and poured a glass of tea. He did it clumsily with the pot in one hand and the cosy in the other. Chanele watched him, as one might observe an event in the street that doesn't concern one. When he held out the glass, she had first to think before she understood his gesture.

He sat down opposite her and said nothing. Saying nothing was plainly a considerable effort for him. More than once he made as if to speak and then left his words unsaid.

The tea was hot, and Chanele was grateful for it. The sun was still shining, although lower in the sky, but her whole body was shivering with a kind of cold that she had never felt before. Old people sometimes complained that they could never get warm any more. For the first time Chanele understood what they meant.

'I called for a cab for you,' Dr Hellstiedl said at last.

She nodded, grateful not to have to make any decisions for herself.

'If you wish, I can keep you informed about his condition. In case a change … It could be, or it could not be. We know so little. And to combat our ignorance we have Latin and Greek names.'

He topped up her tea and then asked again: 'Shall I …?'

'No,' Chanele said. It was the first word she had spoken since her meeting with her father.

She took the cab back into town. In the avenue, the poplars now cast long shadows.

In the square in front of the Minster a feast day was being celebrated, with happy people and cheerful music. Chanele thought of the big simcha that Menachem Bär had been so looking forward to, and to it she devoted every laughing face she glimpsed from the cab window.

The hotel porter welcomed her with chummy curiosity. How had her day been, he wanted to know, had she found the way and how did the esteemed Madame Meijer like Strasbourg? She silenced him with a tip.

That night she slept deeply and dreamlessly.

The next morning she took the train back to Basel and from there on to Baden. She went straight from the station to the shop and worked there as she did every day.

When she got home in the evening and Janki questioned her, she replied, 'They made a mistake. It was someone completely different. He has nothing to do with me.'

24

Pinchas had to grab his shirt collar again to get some air, and that had nothing to do with the fact that the sun was beating down far too hot for the second day in a row. This man that Zalman Kamionker had introduced him to, this Dr Stern from Stuttgart, Congress delegate of the Württemberg Majority Socialists, was driving him completely insane. And he looked quite harmless, an outwardly inconspicuous man of middle age, not very tall, with a cosy, round little bourgeois belly, on which his watch chain did a skipping little dance each time he laughed. And he laughed a lot, in an unpleasant way. He said the most dreadful things, concluded them with a wobbly 'Hohoho!' and then wiped the back of his hand over his moustache. 'God,' he said, for example, 'God does not exist, of course. I should know, I'm a rabbi.' He made his belly wobble and looked at Pinchas with the natural expectancy of someone who already has a counter-argument ready for any objections.

He had in fact once been a rabbi, in Buttenhausen, a small congregation in the Swabian Jura. 'I learned the job thoroughly,' he said and laughed again, as if at the best possible joke. 'No half measures where I'm concerned. Even today I can cast a glance at the innards of a chicken and tell you unerringly whether it's kosher or not. Admittedly it's an utterly meaningless skill, but I can still remember how to do it. The way other people can balance on their hands or walk a tightrope.'

Pinchas wouldn't have been surprised if his interlocutor had performed one of those tricks on the spot. Dr Stern's manner had much of the fairground barker about it, one of those men one sometimes encounters outside travelling theatres of curiosity, except that the attractions in his booth were not six-legged calves or women with fishtails, but the treasury of mysteriously glittering theses and the mirror-maze of brightly polished paradoxes. 'Every true believer is proof that there is no God,' he would say, for example, rocking springily back and forth on the balls of his feet, as if he was about to turn a somersault and shout 'Hoppla!'.

He liked talking, almost compulsively, about how he had lost his faith, 'freed himself from it', as he called it, and it seemed that he often addressed large gatherings on the subject. He never had to search for a word, and his perfectly formulated sentences always sounded as if they were read from a manuscript. He had not been a rabbi for ages, but was the first chairman of the German

Free-Thinkers' Union, and he could, when he spoke of this association and its goals, adopt an expression every bit as unctuous as if he were still wearing the cassock. He put his unbelief on display in his buttonhole like a medal, he was proud of it as one might be proud of a doctorate acquired after a long period of study. There was something crusading about his atheism. Godlessness was his religion, and he advocated it with the fire and enthusiasm of the convert. When he said, 'God is nothing but an invention of man,' he beamed like Moses at the sight of the Shechinah on Mount Sinai.

The two men had met in the Palm Garden at around midday, and Kamionker had introduced them to one another. He did that with a sly smile whose meaning Pinchas only now understood. It was noisy and stuffy in the Palm Garden, so they decided to take advantage of the fine weather and take a short stroll in the park by the lake. Pinchas had prepared a whole list of questions about the Socialist Congress – the *Israelit* in Frankfurt would certainly be interested in an article on the subject – but he never got around to asking them. No sooner had Dr Stern learned that the actual profession of his new acquaintance was that of shochet, than he only wanted to talk about religion, or rather about the non-religion that was his deeply held credo. 'Man should know and not believe,' he said with devout emphasis, spreading his arms to welcome the whole world with a fraternal kiss into the newly founded alliance of the godless.

He must once have been a good pulpit speaker, even though Buttenhausen, as he said, had only a tiny synagogue, where it was often possible only with a great deal of difficulty to assemble a minyan. 'But what was I to do? Rabbinate positions were thin on the ground, and as a theologian fresh out of college one had to take what one could get. An interesting word, by the way, 'theologian'. If one returns to the Greek root it actually means nothing more than a person who talks about God – and one can of course also talk about things that do not exist. About unicorns, about dragons or indeed about the Lord God.'

'But our world must . . .'

Dr Stern interrupted Pinchas with an expansive gesture. 'My dear friend,' he said, and it sounded like 'My dear congregation', 'My dear friend, I hope you are not going to bother me with one of these proofs of God's existence. Which one were about to take out of your pocket? The cosmological? The ontological? The teleological? All of them refute long ago. Read Kant! Read Schopenhauer! "The fourfold root of the principle of sufficient reason." The world does not need a first mover. It bears its laws within itself! We need only recognise them. Voilà!' He gave a little hop, a circus artist returning to terra firma after a daring tightrope walk, and expecting applause.

'And who made those laws?'

'Nobody.' Dr Stern, the man whom one could as little imagine without his title as without his trousers, dabbed his forehead dry with his silk handkerchief. Pinchas had a sense that he had practised the elegant movement in front of the mirror. 'When the sun is shining, no one sits there heating an oven. Natural laws need no almighty creator to set the first ball rolling. The universe is as it is. Our fate is what we make of it. The world – to bring it down to its lowest common denominator – is as we form it. It is only because we are afraid of this responsibility that we invent punitive deities and in their name draw up laws for whose consequences we may thus not be held to account.'

'But the Torah…'

Dr Stern caught this objection in mid-air as well, a juggler whose hand is always in the place to which the next ball is about to fly. 'The Torah is literature,' he said. 'Very fine literature, in fact. Like many of our writings, incidentally. I myself have brought out a small volume with Reclam's Universalbibliothek: *Rays of Light from the Talmud*, a collection of quotations valuable not least from the pedagogic point of view. One had only to pick them carefully out from among all the silly legends – I am thinking for example of the woolgathering tales of such a one as Rabba bar bar Chana – and the overheated sophistications of the interpretations of the law. The moral clarity of our scholars is strangely at odds with the logical confusion of Talmudic ritual. One might even say: where Judaism manages without God, it can serve as an excellent model for other people.' And, inspired by his own eloquence, he made the watch-chain on his belly skip, laughed deeply from his throat and ran the back of his hand over his moustache.

Pinchas, who took part in the shiur of the Talmud-Torah Association twice a week, had the feeling that he knew a thousand arguments against such blasphemous talk, but not a single one came to mind. If he could have led this debate in the familiar evening classroom, protected by the bulwark of a shelf full of ancient tomes…But here, in the bright light of the lakeside promenade, under the fresh green of the trees, here, where a disobliging-looking nanny in a starched blue and white blouse led two little girls in pink by the hand, where an old lady was scattering cake-crumbs into the water from a greasy paper bag, for swans and ducks to dispute over with belligerent gulls, here, where a teacher had assembled his whole class around him so that he could name all the peaks of the alpine panorama, clearly visible today thanks to the föhn air – here he felt helpless. Debating the nuances of a word, the finer points of the interpretation of a law – that he was used to. But someone simply wanting to tear down the whole intellectual edifice on which so many generations of scholars and their pupils had taken such trouble – that left him speechless. He walked along in silence beside Dr Stern, who kept dancing with excitement at the abundance of his own self-confidence.

Their path led them past the improvised geography lesson, where the teacher was just saying, 'Over there, still shrouded in fog, you will see the Grosse Mythe and the Kleine Mythe.' Dr Stern chuckled, a rich man winning the lottery on top of everything. 'You see, my dear friend,' he said, wiping his moustache with the back of his hand, 'this bold pedagogue has just summed up my whole argument in the most concise form. We humans come up with myths, big ones and small ones, we claim they are as solid as fortresses, and mask our own doubts with a fog of traditions and rituals.'

'It's easy to believe in nothing at all.' Pinchas felt unfamiliar fury welling up in him.

'On the contrary, my friend.' Dr Stern had also been expecting this sentence, like a practised dancer taking his partner's hand without looking at the end of a complicated figure. 'Believing in nothing is difficult! What is easy is to swallow down without resistance the mush of ideas, pre-chewed a thousand times, of previous generations. It is easy to bend the knee obediently, to cross yourself, put on the tefillin, jump over a burning pyre at midnight, or whatever strange rituals our forefathers came up with in the name of their self-invented deities. It is easy to accept holy scriptures as God-given, to accept the premises of a religion uncritically and use one's intelligence only to draw constant new conclusions from it. We Jews are true masters in the art of gnawing our way through the finest ramifications of supposedly divine laws, like woodworm in a long-dead tree. Night after night we study medieval commentaries, just to understand debates pursued fifteen hundred years ago, we talk ourselves blue in the face about the rituals of sacrificial services in a temple destroyed two thousand years ago. We waste our intelligence because we lack the courage to question ancient fairy-tales. Fairy-tales, yes indeed! But in fact: he who does not wish to think must believe.' He was so pleased with that last sentence that he performed a little dance on the spot. Two elderly ladies peered at him disapprovingly from under their parasols.

'You know what strikes me?' Pinchas asked and felt rising up in him the combative anticipation that emerges from the sense of a watertight argument. 'You know what even strikes me a lot about you? You still say "we". "We Jews." So for all your protests you are still part of it.'

'Let's say: I don't exclude myself from it. Or only as long as the concept refers to the community of a people and not of a faith. But otherwise…In this connection I can tell you a funny story.' He pointed to one of the wooden benches that the Beautification Society had set up along the promenade. 'The sun will do me good, after all those long hours in the Congress Room.' He carefully wiped a trace of pollen off the green painted slats, made himself comfortable in the middle of the seat, his arms spread out on the back, and when Pinchas continued to hesitate, tapped invitingly on the narrow free space beside him. 'Sit down next to me, my dear friend! I promise you, you will enjoy yourself royally.'

Pinchas sat down. What option did he have? His interlocutor, that much was clear to him, was not one of those people who can be deterred from telling a story once they have started it.

'This is already...' Dr Stern began, and adopted that artificially reflective face that loquacious people often put on in order to give often-repeated stories the appearance of spontaneous authenticity. 'In fact, more than ten years ago now. How time passes! It was clear to me at last, once and for all, that I could no longer reconcile it with my conscience, telling my little flock...A lovely term, isn't it?' he interrupted himself, and even that interruption seemed to be part of his manuscript. 'Little flock. It so accurately describes the submissive lack of criticism with which even thoroughly intelligent people credulously trot along with the herd of their religion, always encircled by the barking dogs of the punishments of hell and eternal damnation. As I say, it was clear to me that I would be being unfaithful to myself if I went on interpreting laws to my congregation that I no longer believed in myself – even though the interpretations themselves were still entirely correct. Utterly meaningless, like all religious mumbo-jumbo, but correct. If you consider: a God who is concerned in all seriousness with the question of whether the pitum is broken off an essrog, such a detail-obsessed heavenly trifler, can only be an invention of humanity! Only we humans are stupid enough to glue our view of the world together from mere trivia.'

'And your view of the world, Dr Stern?'

The free-thinker heard the irritable undertone and seemed to be pleased, a conjuror who has directed his audience's attention exactly where he wants it. 'I deal with the main issue, and flatter myself that I have thus achieved something greater than all those regulation-obsessed Talmud greats. With one exception. Does the name Elisha ben Abuyah mean anything to you?'

Pinchas nodded. 'Acher,' he said. 'The Other.'

'Very good.' Dr Stern nodded to him with schoolmasterly condescension. 'Excellent. That is how he is always referred to in the scriptures. "The Other." And why? Because he was not even granted that name after he, the great teacher of the Law, had reached the only possible conclusion: that there is in fact no God. And do you know how he lost his faith?'

Pinchas had studied the relevant passage of the Talmud not long before. It concerned a boy ordered by his father to fetch eggs from the nest, but first to chase away the mother bird, as it is written: 'You shall let the mother fly and take only the young, that you may thrive and that you may long endure' – the same reward that the Torah promises for the keeping of the Commandment to honour one's father and mother. In spite of that twofold promise, the boy fell and broke his neck. And that is supposed to have been the moment when Elisha ben Abuyah became an apostate.

'You cannot use that argument,' Pinchas said, 'if you bear in mind what Rashi says about the passage "that you may long endure"...'

'I'm impressed.' Dr Stern applauded ironically, and Pinchas could have slapped him. 'So you know that passage from kiddushim. But I like the explanation that Talmud gives in the treatise of Khagiga – 14b, if you want to look it up – much better.'

'I know that passage too,' said Pinchas, but Dr Stern had closed his eyes as if to remember better, and recited, almost singing, as one does during a lecture. 'Ben Asai, ben Soma, Elisha ben Abuyah and Rabbi Akiba meditated long enough over the glory of God until they could glimpse the uppermost sphere. Ben Asai died. Ben Soma lost his reason. Elisha ben Abuyah fell from faith. And only Rabbi Akiba...'

'I see no reason to make fun.' Pinchas had spoken much more loudly than he had actually intended. A young woman who was walking past the bench with her pram, quickened her pace in alarm.

'I'm not making fun,' Dr Stern said. 'On the contrary. I have always felt a great affinity with this Acher. Perhaps he actually did glimpse heaven, and established that it was empty.'

'I have to go now. I can't leave my butcher's shop alone as long as this.' Pinchas was about to get up, but Dr Stern would not let him. He held him back as a circus barker might an indecisive peasant.

'Wait, dear friend. I haven't yet told you my story.'

'I don't know if I want to hear it.'

'Of course you want to hear it. You are a curious person. Did you not come here just to ask me questions?'

'Not these questions!'

'Because the answers might shatter your picture of the world?'

'No!'

But Pinchas stopped making as if to stand up, and Dr Stern laughed, making his watch chain skip, wiped his moustache and said, 'Let's wait a moment! So, as I said, I had understood at last that I could no longer perform my office.

Because – unlike most people, as I have been forced time and again to observe – I am not afraid of drawing conclusions from my discoveries, I decided to draw a clear line. So I wrote to the Supreme Royal Württemberg Rabbinate and declared to them, to my superior authority, that I was abdicating from Jewry.'

'What nonsense!' Pinchas had raised his voice too loudly again, and really had to force himself to utter his next sentences in a more moderate tone. To his annoyance it now sounded as if he were about to confide an intimate secret to the man beside him on the bench. 'You can't step down from Jewry! We're not a club!'

'That's exactly what the Supreme Rabbinate said to me. Amongst some very wordy admonitions. But I am a consistent person, and someone who doesn't want to play the game no longer needs to adhere to the rules. So at the next Yom Kippur I went and stood with a bag of ham rolls outside the main synagogue in Stuttgart, and when all the dignitaries walked out of the door with their black top hats on...'

'You should be ashamed of yourself!' Pinchas had leapt to his feet, and he no longer cared in the slightest that passers-by were staring at him. 'You should be thoroughly, thoroughly ashamed of yourself.

Dr Stern smiled in friendly challenge at the man who stood so furiously before him. 'A pity you aren't Catholic. "Apage, Satanas" would simply sound better.'

'Ashamed!'

'You have said that before, my dear friend. But perhaps you should consider whether you yourself might not have more reason to be so. A man of your profession.'

'What does my profession...?'

'You are a shochet, are you not? And thus a professional, approved animal-torturer.'

'I'm not a...'

'You shouldn't shout so loudly. The two policemen coming along the path over there already look quite suspicious.'

Pinchas had no choice but to sit down again.

'How can you claim that a shochet...?'

But Dr Stern had suddenly stopped enjoying the debate. He drew a watch from his waistcoat pocket and let it spring open. 'So late? I'm neglecting my duties as a delegate. Do you know what, dear friend? Read my brochure. *Animal Torture and Animal Life in Jewish Literature*. Available in every bookshop. With a rabbinical-theological appendix about shechita. It might interest you. I have been told that this little essay will play a big part in the coming plebiscite in these parts. Now farewell, dear friend, farewell.'

25

At the same time as Pinchas was talking to Jakob Stern or, as he later said only half ironically, arguing with the devil, his wife received an unexpected visitor.

Mimi wasn't feeling well that day. It was probably because of the much too sultry weather that she felt dizzy when she tried to stand up, and had to lie down in bed for an hour again with a cloth soaked in lemon water over her forehead. Regula, the great lump, wanted to open the curtains without the slightest delicacy, when a beam of light would go like a knife through the head of a sensitive person in such a condition. Later Mimi even had to throw up, and it was already almost eleven when she finally summoned the strength to leave her room. In a peignoir of salmon-coloured crêpe Georgette had lined with matt silk, which set off the pallor of her face to extremely good effect, she crept through the flat like a ghost. Nothing was moving anywhere. Even the breakfast plates were still on the dining-room table. If one wasn't constantly chasing them – Pinchas had no idea! – the servants immediately became slapdash.

She found Regula, Frau Küttel, the cleaner, and last of all Hinda in the kitchen where they all, at a time when the preparations for lunch should really have been far advanced, were drinking coffee with lumps of bread and, as far as Mimi could tell from the sentence that broke off mid-word as she appeared, discussing Regula's favourite topic, the question of whether the tram driver at whom she had been making eyes for weeks now, might have more serious intentions. Mimi had to become quite fierce, although that was far from easy in her condition, and she also had to tell Hinda, who often had quite déclassé tendencies, off for socialising with the staff. Hinda merely laughed and said that in all honesty she found Regula's love story more interesting than any novel, at least she had never yet come across a novel in which a gallant had slapped his sweetheart on the backside and said appreciatively, 'You're better padded than my horses.'

Later – she still lacked the strength to get dressed – Mimi went through the contents of her clothes cupboard with Hinda. The Hachnasat Kallah Association, which supplied dresses for impoverished brides, had organised a collection of cast-off clothes, and as wife of the community shochet – 'You can't imagine how people watch you!' – Mimi felt obliged to contribute something. But it was actually only a pretext to spread out the treasures of her wardrobe once again.

She had just taken out a day dress of greyish brown silk twill with a maroon rose pattern, a dress that had always suited her very well, but the skirt of which she really couldn't wear any more, because it still had a *cul de Paris* cut, and that was truly out of fashion once and for all, and she was busy persuading Hinda that the tight-fitting jacket with the little collar and the *jacquard* trimming on the cuffs would actually suit her youthful figure very well, although obviously with a different skirt, they would donate the old one to the impoverished brides, and in all that activity she had begun to forget how poorly she was actually feeling, when there was a ring at the flat door. 'I'm not at home to anyone!' Mimi called and, pained by the wound of her own voice, had to draw little circles on her temples with her fingertips.

'Frau Pomeranz isn't at home,' they heard Regula explaining a little later. And then, in response to an inaudible objection from the visitor, the maid added. 'She definitely isn't! She just told me herself.'

Hinda bit her hand so as not to burst out laughing. Mimi rolled her eyes with a long-suffering expression.

Regula's protest, increasingly uncertain and hence increasingly shrill, made it clear that the uninvited guest would not be fobbed off as easily as that, and at last the maid knocked at the room of the door and said, 'I'm sorry, Frau Pomeranz, but there's a lady here who absolutely...'

'It's me!' a voice rang out from the corridor.

'Mama!' Hinda exclaimed and pulled the door open.

Regula watched the embrace between mother and daughter with disapproval. 'I told her you weren't here,' she explained reproachfully to Mimi. 'But she came in anyway.'

'It's fine.'

'Well, there's nothing I can do about it,' Regula grumbled, as insulted as someone whose cake has been a failure because of a deliberately incorrect recipe, and withdrew to the kitchen again, to continue analysing the presumed intentions of the tram driver.

Chanele must have come straight from the station; the smell of the locomotives still clung to her. She was not, however, as the rules of etiquette would have dictated, wearing a travelling suit, but her 'uniform' that she usually wore in the shop, and a hat that had not been *en vogue* at least since last season.

'You haven't even put on gloves!' Mimi said reproachfully.

'Nor you a dress.'

'You have no idea how dreadful I feel.'

'Have you come to pick me up?' Hinda asked, and didn't seem at all keen on the idea.

'Let's talk about that later. Now I have something to discuss with Mimi. Alone.' Chanele said it in a tone that her daughter had never heard before: not actually severe, that would have been the wrong word, but such that it wouldn't have occurred to one to contradict her.

Hinda curtsied obediently. 'Then I'll be in the kitchen.'

'Tell Regula to clear away the breakfast things,' Mimi called after her. 'And that lunch…' She put her hand to her brow and sighed. 'Although I myself couldn't eat a single…I can't even think about it.'

'Are you ill?'

'Ach!' said Mimi, and the *dame de salon* at the municipal theatre could not have outdone her bravely dismissive gesture. She was about to lead her guest into the dining-room – 'Although everything is still standing around in there; I don't know how I end up with such terrible staff!' – but Chanele shook her head.

'Let's go into your room. It seems…how shall I put it? It seems more appropriate to me.'

There wasn't even room for the two of them to sit down; the bed and both chairs were covered with clothes. Automatically, as she would have done in the shop, Chanele started clearing things away, while Mimi squatted on the Turkish pouffe by her dressing table and dabbed her temples with *eau de cologne*. For a while the only sound was the rustle of fabric and the click of hangers.

'Mimi,' Chanele said at last and studied the *moiré* effect on a yontev dress as intently as if she had never seen anything similar in all her time in the trade. 'Mimi…Did it bother you very much that we never wanted to call you Miriam?'

'What makes you think that?'

'There was a time when that was very important to you. Back then I never understood, but today…It would have been your real name, you had a right to it, and all of us – whether out of habit or cosiness – only ever called you Mimi.'

'But I'm called Mimi.'

'Of course, today.' Chanele held the dress high to shake it out. It looked as if she were dancing with a life-sized doll, the gently rustling material a curtain between the two women. 'But you never wondered whether you might have turned into a completely different person if you had had your own name?'

'I don't understand what you mean.' Mimi said it in the pitiful voice of a child that doesn't want to go to school. 'I have a headache.'

Chanele hung the dress in the cupboard and said, more into the black opening that smelled of old experiences than to Mimi: 'I don't understand it myself.'

She had already cleared a chair, and now she carried it over to the dressing table and sat down opposite Mimi, so close that their knees almost touched.

Janki, long ago now, had once sat opposite Chanele like that. She had been afraid to look at him, but she had felt his breath. She had been almost naked at the time, so wonderfully naked. And then he had asked her...

What had she expected? If you have notions, it's your own fault.

She took Mimi's right hand, leaned over, breathed in the smell of bedroom and eau de cologne and suddenly kissed those strange fingertips.

'What on earth are you doing?' Mimi asked and drew her hand back.

'I don't know. It's just...We aren't sisters, you and I. We have never been friends, either. No, don't contradict me. There was no friendship between us, not even when we were sleeping in the same bed. They stuffed us together the way I've just stuffed your dresses into the cupboard, velvet next to duchesse and black next to olive, as they happened to come. We didn't choose each other. We got along, somehow, you with me and I with you. And when we laughed together – one also laughs with random acquaintances. But we told our secrets to others. You to your Anne-Kathrin and I to my pillow. It worked quite well, didn't it, Mimi? It worked quite well.'

'I don't know what you want.'

Sometimes Mimi still had the same whining voice that she had had as a little girl, when she answered everything that sounded like criticism with a precautionary wail.

'Everything was fine until Janki came. You remember? The bandage with the blood that wasn't his? Of course you remember. We both did everything wrong, back then, me too. And so we never became friends. I regret that now. Because after all that time we belong together. Don't you think so, Miriam?'

Mimi had never been able to hide her emotions. Even now Chanele could read everything happening in her on her face: surprise, the beginning of an argument, the beginning of a reconciliation and then a sly don't-show-a-thing expression. As children they had often played 'scissors, stone, paper', and that was exactly what Mimi had looked like every time she had been determined not to be gulled. 'Did you come to Zurich to tell me that?' she asked.

'No, that's not why. And I don't want you to give me an answer, either. That will grow eventually. I came because I need your help.'

'What for?'

Chanele took two of the colourful bottles from the dressing table and tinkled them together like wine glasses. 'You need to find a shidduch,' she said.

Mimi was a bit disappointed that Chanele had anticipated her secret plan before she'd been able to put it into operation, so she argued against it. 'Hinda has no interest whatsoever in that kind of thing.'

'A shidduch for François.'

Mimi was so startled that her tongue hung out of her mouth.

'Shmul?'

'His name is François. Whether I like it or not.'

'But he's far too young to get married!'

'Believe me,' said Chanele, 'he's old enough.'

'The boy is twenty-one.'

'And he isn't to get married straight away. But soon. As soon as possible.'

'How could Janki come up with such a meshugena idea?'

'Janki knows nothing about it.'

'And you want…?'

'If you help me.'

Mimi looked at Chanele in amazement, thought – scissors? stone? paper? – and then held her hand out. 'Tell me everything,' she said.

It was good to talk about it. About François's smile, in which the eyes didn't smile too, that fake, polite smile with which he had always frightened Chanele, even when he was still a little boy, because even then his face had been like a book in a foreign language. How he had once, at five or six, persuaded another little boy, the godson of a cook, to put his hand on the red-hot oven door and how then, when the boy wept and screamed, he had said quite unmoved, 'I just wanted to see if I could make him do it.' How he had always brought good reports home from school, without really doing anything for them, because he always found someone to do his homework for him or let him copy it; how on Shabbos, when he was forbidden to do any kind of work, three or four of his fellow pupils would often be waiting for him outside the front door, practically beating each other up to be allowed to carry his schoolbag. One of his teachers had once, when he went with his wife to the Emporium and Chanele introduced herself to him, actually raved about what a gifted, yes, he had no qualms about putting it like that, what a blessed son she had, and François, when she mentioned it, had smiled his smile and said, 'He's a pushover; he has podagra, and on the days when he limps particularly badly, you just have to ask him how he is.' Then, when he started helping in the shop, in the Drapery Store with Janki rather than with Chanele in the Emporium, he made a game of bringing the customer unsaleable pieces, goods from last year or with small flaws, and was pleased every time he talked someone into a sale and they were grateful to him. Chanele also described François's very idiosyncratic way of speaking, which she called 'poisoned', because he was apparently able to say the most challenging things very politely, with a smile and a bow from the hip, and she told of how he felt superior to other people and despised those people for it.

For once Mimi was a good listener. She nodded or tilted her head back and forth in a amazement, said, '*Vraiment?*' or '*Mon Dieu!*' and didn't let go of Chanele's hand all the while.

But then when Chanele got to the evening of the goyish dinner, when she told of how Mathilde Lutz had knocked at her office door and told her that a young salesgirl was pregnant, and by whom, in her excitement Mimi forgot to speak French, exclaimed, 'me neshuma!' and 'Shema beni!' and patted Chanele's hand as one does on a sickbed visit, when one wants to give the patient more hope than one actually feels.

In forty years the two women had never been so close.

'What are you going to do about the girl? Mimi asked at last. 'Such a thing could be a scandal, particularly in a small town like your Baden.'

'I know,' said Chanele, and didn't seem to be particularly worried about a scandal. 'But I've already got something under way.'

'Sometimes,' thought Mimi, 'sometimes Chanele has a smile not that unlike her son's. Except that she would be horrified if she knew.' She felt a sudden urge to take Chanele in her arms and press her very, very firmly to her. But of course she didn't, she just asked, 'And Shmul...?'

'His name is François.'

'Do you think he loves her?'

Chanele shook his head. 'He just wanted to see if he could make her do it.'

'And now you want to marry him soon?'

'I think it will be the best thing. Because it will rein him in. It's not a good solution, but it's still the best one.'

Mimi stroked her friend's fingers. Her friend? So be it: her friend. Those hands that had worked for so long in Golde's kitchen had become no less rough during the years when Chanele had been Madame Meijer.

'I've got a secret to tell you,' Mimi said, and her sudden courage turned her cheeks quite red. 'The loveliest thing for me, the loveliest thing ever, would have been to have children of my own. But if I can't have any, if it simply isn't to be, then the second loveliest would be to make a shidduch for others. I sometimes think: I'm God's experiment to see if one can make a mother-in-law from scratch.' She laughed as she said it, but she meant it in all seriousness.

On the dressing table, among all the fashionable fripperies, there was a diary. Its pages were still quite empty, even though it was for the year 1887. Mimi hadn't bought it then because she needed it, but because it was bound in such beautiful Morocco leather, exactly the same leather as the money bag that Janki had used so many years ago to open his own shop...Anyway. It had a little silver pencil which she now picked up, flipped the diary open and said like a waiter taking an order: 'So, Madame Meijer! I'm listening!' She looked girlishly dainty, sitting there with her head tilted expectantly to one side, and the sight made Chanele feel slightly sad in a not disagreeable way, like entries in an old poetry album.

'What's it to be?' asked Mimi, and moistened the tip of the pencil with her tongue, as she had once seen the clerk do at the post office counter. 'Young? Pretty? Rich?'

Chanele didn't respond to the facetious tone and answered the questions very seriously. 'Rich will be necessary. Yes, I think so. At least well-to-do. Otherwise Janki won't agree with me. Young? That's not so important. As far as I'm concerned she can be older than François. He isn't supposed to fall in love with her, he's just supposed to marry her.'

Mimi couldn't believe her ears. For her, having grown up with novels, Chanele had just said something monstrous. 'Not fall in love?'

'I don't think François can. That's why it wouldn't be good if the girl was pretty.'

'You're joking now.'

'I'm just trying to see things as they are.'

'And you see your son with an ugly old bag?'

'I see François. As he is. And I know: if he's married, he will cheat on his wife.'

'Chanele!' In a play, Mimi had heard an actor say something similarly dreadful. But not in such a calm, natural voice.

'There's no point pretending,' Chanele said. 'If you don't accept reality, eventually you go mad. Believe me, I know that. François will always want to have everything, especially the things he's not supposed to. And he will get them. That will make him a good businessman and a bad husband.'

'So...'

'I've thought about it very hard. A pretty young woman who's always been accustomed to compliments, whose suitors have always been queuing up outside the front door – she would be destroyed by a man like François. First she would blame him, then herself, and then she would be unhappy for the rest of her life.'

'You're meshuga!'

'You think?' Chanele took the diary out of Mimi's hand and set it back down in its place. Only then did she go on talking, so quietly and tonelessly that Mimi had to lean forward to understand her. 'If Janki had married you then – could you bear being treated as he treats me?'

'Does he treat you badly?'

'No,' said Chanele. 'Does one treat one's desk badly? One's cigarette case? He isn't interested enough in me to treat me badly. It's enough for him that I'm there and do the things that need to be done.'

'I'm sure that's partly...' – 'your fault,' Mimi had wanted to say, but the Chanele who was siting opposite her was no longer the same Chanele she had known all her life. And she herself, it seemed to her in her bedroom right now, was no longer the same Mimi. 'I'm sure it's down to work,' she said for that reason. 'A man like that has a thousand things on his mind.'

'Of course,' said Chanele and didn't mean it. 'But what matters is this: I've never expected much from my life, so I can cope with the fact that I haven't had much. While you...'

'While I have no children. I'll soon be an old woman, and I become more and more superfluous with every year.'

'You aren't superfluous,' said Chanele. 'I, for example, need you a lot.'

Mimi rubbed her temples and then her eyes as well. She still had headaches, but that had nothing to do with it.

26

Mimi was needed, so she forgot all her complaints.

Admittedly Chanele's plan was meshuga, she thought, and if she, Mimi, had ever come up with such an idea, people would have said she was wool-gathering again, but sometimes she had the feeling that we live in a meshugena world, and being crazy was perhaps the only reasonable option. Chanele had been very right to come to her straight away with her wish, not just because they were friends – 'That's what we are now, aren't we, Chanele?' – but above all because here in Zurich she knew every Jewish family, really every single one, that was the advantage, but also the curse, if you owned the only kosher butcher's shop in the city. She could list every marriageable girl in the community, she could write a list if necessary, right now on the spot in the diary with the red binding. And she could introduce her to the families at any time, very discreetly and as if by chance. It was only a shame that Chanele hadn't come up with her plan a few days earlier because today, today of all days, as a day for such introductions would have been a good one, surprisingly good, in fact, she herself believed in such hints from fate, and at some point, in a quiet minute, she would have to confide something in Chanele – one couldn't talk to Pinchas about such matters – about one Madame Rosa and certain messages that one received at her house, but now was not the moment. She sometimes got lost in her thoughts like a child in a room full of enticing toys. Chanele had to ask her twice what was so special about this day, and she didn't immediately understand Mimi's answer. The clothes collection of the Hachna-sat Kallah Association, she explained, clinging to the bedpost so that Chanele could tighten the laces of her corset – 'Much tighter, I can take it!' – this clothes collection to which she, Mimi, had to go anyway, in fact she was already far too late, would have been the ideal opportunity to take an initial look, one could meet most of the women with eligible daughters, and shidduchim, whatever men thought, were always made by the mothers. When she talked about it, Mimi was entirely in her element, and the rustic red patches on her cheek became so pronounced that she had to hide them with foundation cream; one didn't want to look like a milkmaid, after all.

She could just come along, Chanele said, but at first Mimi didn't want to let her. Chanele was certainly not dressed for such an occasion, and when shad-chening the first impression was often crucial. People in Zurich were aware of Janki's successful business deals, but Chanele herself knew most of them only from hearsay, and if she turned up in a dress, that...She didn't want to be mean, she understood that with three children and a shop you didn't have time to pay proper attention to your wardrobe, although it wouldn't have done anyone any harm to be elegant.

Chanele refused to accept these reservations, and in the end Mimi, not unwillingly, allowed herself to be persuaded. But she demanded categorically that Chanele change her clothes, there were enough dresses there and something was bound to suit her. Chanele resisted the idea of changing, after all it wasn't Purim, and it didn't say anywhere in the Shulchan Orech that as a future mother-in-law you had to be got up like a maypole. Then Mimi had pulled out for her a cream satin afternoon dress from the pile that still lay on the bed, and a petticoat of starched taffeta with plissée flounces, and it was only the fact that the skirt was quite plainly far too wide around the waist that made Mimi relent. As a girl Chanele had been able to wear Mimi's cast-off clothes without altering so much as a stitch, but recently, in spite of the best corsets, Frau Pomeranz had become somewhat matronly. Still, at least she could still do this, she quickly offered Chanele the hat that she would have lent her to go with the dress, a city model that Mimi herself had never worn, with a brightly coloured ostrich feather that hung delicately over one's shoulder.

'But there's one thing I must insist on,' she said as she put the hat carefully back in its box, 'if you really are determined to come as you are, then you should talk very little and on no account are you to be polite.' Chanele, she explained to her startled companion, was after all a woman from a wealthy business household, and that was exactly how she would have to appear. 'If you think you're too refined for them, they'll all want to be involved with you.'

For herself Mimi chose an inconspicuous pale blue dress, very slightly enhanced with a few decorative buttons of carved mother of pearl. She was only in the background today, she thought; Chanele would have to make the big impression, that was what counted in such situations. To hear her lecture like this one might have thought she had become the successor to Abraham Singer, and whole hordes of young couples owed their happiness only to her intervention.

She pulled two more dresses from the pile, the maroon one with the cul de Paris and a dark blue one with slightly worn velvet buttons, those were the ones she wanted to sacrifice to the good cause. Regula was to bring the dresses down to them, no, they would certainly not just carry them down in their arms, even though it wasn't far to the synagogue, certainly not, in that case she would tolerate no objection, such an appearance would create completely the wrong impression.

Hinda would have liked to go too, out of pure curiosity and even though she had no idea what Chanele and Aunt Mimi had in mind. Mimi brusquely rejected the idea. What was it that Golde, who knew lots of Jewish proverbs, had liked to say? 'If you want to sell a rooster, you don't go to market with a goose as well.'

On the way there Mimi held her head very high, as if the servant with the big parcel wrapped in pressing cloth were only walking behind her completely by chance. She even forced a driver to rein his horses violently in by walking right in front of his cart without looking to left or right. He went on swearing at her long after she had turned into the Löwenstrasse.

Because of the hot weather the doors of the synagogue were open. The shrill soprano of Frau Goldschmidt, the synagogue choir soloist, mixed with the sound of carriages and passers-by. She was rehearsing for Shavuot: the two women recognised – by the words, if not by the unfamiliar melody – the songs that accompany the bringing out of the Torah. At the 'Raumamu' she fluffed her notes twice in a row.

'That is the reason why Pinchas is seriously thinking of leaving the community,' said Mimi.

'Because she sings so badly?'

'Because of all these innovations in recent times. Women in the chorus and a harmonium. They're talking about having a secession community like the one they have in Frankfurt.'

They entered the synagogue building through the side entrance on Nüschelerstrasse. The small hall served every possible purpose; there one could offer the community the traditional Kiddush after a bar mitzvah or hold the annual general meetings of the many social and charitable associations, whereby these two functions could be pleasantly combined. Today the tables were pushed together into two long rows at an angle to one another, at which volunteer helpers were sorting through the donated items of clothing. Most of them were what Mimi, with French discretion, liked to call *ne plus vraiment jeunes*, generously ignoring the fact that the women she so described were no older than she was herself. There is a stage in the lives of respectable bourgeois ladies when the children no longer make demands on their time all around the clock, when the well-oiled machine of the household produces clean washing and regular meals all by itself, and one has enough time and energy left over to devote it to culture, superstition or philanthropy. And gossip, of course. The practised eyes of the well-to-do ladies read the most detailed information from the donor, her generosity and her fashionable taste, and as their sharp-tongued commentaries were generally directed against absent friends, the Hachnasat Kallah Association never had the slightest trouble recruiting enough honorary workers.

The highest-ranking of the ladies present was Zippora Meisels, the widow of a former community president, who was known on the quiet as 'the young old woman' because in spite of her advanced years she could not be deterred from wearing a Titian-red sheitel. The youthful hair colour and the artfully curled hair contrasted with the sharp outlines of her weathered face in a ridiculous way. Even though she unusually had no official function in this association, she had got hold of the best seat, and sat precisely where the two rows of tables met at an obtuse angle, and from where one could not only follow all the conversations but also keep an eye on the door to the hall. Consequently she was the first to spot Mimi and Chanele. When she saw Regula coming in behind them with her parcel of clothing, she ironically raised her eyebrows – 'We're very elegant today!' – giving her face a clownish appearance: she had painted the eyebrows on her face herself, and not quite matched the line of thinning hairs.

Malka Grünfeld, with whom she had just been talking, followed her gaze, apologised and went to meet the two new arrivals with outstretched arms. Frau Grünfeld was the president of the Association, a position that she owed not so much to her popularity as to a large donation from her husband, who had recently made himself rich by speculating on railway shares. Malka who for many years, as Mimi knew only too well, always bought the very cheapest pieces of Shabbos roast, now gave herself aristocratic airs and, if she honoured an occasion with her presence, always dragged a whole host of getzines-leckers behind her like a train.

'My dear!' she said in the singsong voice she had adopted as a wealthy woman. 'How nice that you found your way here at last.'

'You're late,' that meant, and, 'I'm not used to being kept waiting.'

'I was held up, pardonnez-moi.' Mimi knew that Malka spoke no French, and was discreetly referring to that shortcoming. 'I had a surprise visit from Baden. May I introduce you? Frau Grünfeld, Madame Meijer.'

'I have wanted to meet you for a long time.' Malka Grünfeld had put on this sentence along with her chain of pearls and high-buttoned gloves, and found that in its affable condescension it suited her down to the ground.

'Madame Meijer, I'm sure you know, my dear Malka,' said Mimi, repeatedly putting a smile between the words like a piece of punctuation, 'is the wife of Janki Meijer, who runs the French Drapery and the Modern Emporium in Baden.'

Malka Grünfeld smiled back just as artificially. 'I have heard that one can find some very nice things there.'

'Quite nice for a provincial backwater like Baden,' that meant.

'And in what field does your husband work?' Chanele asked. She had only wanted to make polite conversation, but Malka Grünfeld threw back her head and was insulted. She was used to people knowing who she was.

You would have had to know Mimi very well to notice that she was smiling contentedly.

'Shall I go now?' asked Regula, who had put her parcel down on one of the tables.

'Do that, my child.' When she put her mind to it, Mimi could be at least as aristocratic as any *nouveau riche* Association President's wife. 'And see to it that you make some progress with the silver polishing. Is it not énervant?' she added, turning to Malka. 'By the time you've polished the last pieces, the first are always dirty again.'

'We have silver cutlery as well,' that meant. 'And we've had it longer than you.'

Then the other ladies had to be greeted, with Mimi mentioning the Drapery Store and the Emporium every time an introduction was made. The better sort of people met in the Hachnasat Kallah Association to confirm to one another through demonstrative benevolence that they were also in fact superior. Chanele did not really know what to say in such society, so she created precisely the detached impression that Mimi would have wished.

'That is Delphine Kahn,' said Mimi, and led Chanele to a severe looking woman who wore her high-corseted bosom before her like a suit of armour. 'You will have heard of Kahn & Co. The biggest silk importers in the country. The Kahns have a very charming son, Siegfried is his name, a very promising future lawyer. I think your daughter Hinda once met him by chance.'

If Hinda had been there, she would immediately have noticed the similarity between mother and son. Frau Kahn too had the habit of moving her head back and forth like a neckless owl. A pair of spectacles with round lenses further intensified the impression.

'I am delighted to make your acquaintance, Madame Meijer.' She couldn't have uttered the phrase more precisely with an etiquette guide in front of her.

'Frau Kahn also has a very charming daughter,' Mimi said, and nudged Chanele with her knee in a very unladylike manner.

'She is here,' said the owl. 'My Mina is such a good child that she wouldn't dream of missing an opportunity to be present at a charitable event. I'm always telling her, "Young as you are, you don't need to worry about such things!" – but it's like talking to a wall. Over there – you see how hard she's working?'

The daughter of the biggest silk importing business was easy to spot among the volunteers. A skinny girl, younger than all the others, was folding clothes at one of the tables. In her concentration she had bent her head so far forward that her long black hair hid her face like a widow's veil. Chanele could only see that she wore glasses, like her mother. Her movements showed that indecisive caution that arises either out of short-sightedness or out of a lack of confidence. There didn't seem to be anything really striking about her, but when she carried a stack of folded clothes to the laundry baskets, she seemed to swing a stiff right leg forwards in a semicircle with each step she took, and her body swung back and forth in counterbalance, as if she were drunk.

'Polio,' said Frau Kahn. 'The poor child has to wear a metal brace.'

When all the clothes were sorted and all the comments on them passed – on the subject of Mimi's donation, everyone agreed that she displayed both good taste and a tendency to wasteful frivolity – liqueurs and cakes were passed around, a generous and unanimously applauded donation from the esteemed President. The seating arrangement at the two long tables seemed to happen quite naturally, but followed strict rules of rank and age, with Zippora Meisels and Malka Grünfeld naturally holding court in the middle. Chanele, the unadorned simplicity of whose dress was interpreted, perfectly in line with Mimi's plan, as the whim of a wealthy woman who doesn't need to show off, was given the seat of honour beside the president, and pulled the resisting Mina Kahn down onto the chair beside her.

'Perhaps I should really …' the girl began to protest, but she wasn't used to contradicting people.

Seen from close to, Mina had an unusually interesting face which, like the optical illusions that Arthur collected with such enthusiasm, seemed to tell a quite different story from one glance to the next. At one moment Mina was an intimidated girl who hardly dared look up from the floor, and a moment later an adult woman who had had to experience far too much already.

'Perhaps it's because of her illness,' Chanele though. 'Suffering can make you old. Or childish.'

They talked about unimportant things, passing the obligatory trivia to one another, as one passes salt or the bread basket at the dinner table. Only one thing that Mina said made Chanele prick her ears up. 'Do you sometimes have the feeling,' she asked out of nowhere, 'that people only talk so they don't have to listen?'

The general chat meandered like a river without waterfalls, through the most varied subjects, and landed at last with the plebiscite which was due that summer.

'What will your Pinchas do,' Mimi was asked, 'if shechita is banned in Switzerland?'

'He's quite sure that the initiative will not be passed. Shechita is one of the most painless methods of slaughtering that there are. If one only explains that sensibly to people...'

'Sensibly?' Zippora Meisels grimly shook her head with its flaming red wig. 'It would be the first time reason had achieved anything against rish'es.'

A whole row of wigs was seen to nod thoughtfully. Rish'es, the collective word for every kind of anti-Jewishness, is always a convincing argument.

'My husband's business friends', Malka Grünfeld said with the pride of a woman for whom it always comes as a pleasant surprise that her husband even has any business friends, 'all assure him that they will vote against the plebiscite.'

'Initiative,' a voice corrected her. 'It's an initiative.'

'It doesn't matter what it's called,' Malka said loftily. 'The matter will be rejected in any case.'

'If people had to state their opinion publicly, perhaps.' Mina had so far only spoken when she was spoken to, and the surprised reactions clearly showed that in this particular circle they did not like it when unexperienced young things opened their mouths. Nonetheless Mina went on, although she avoided looking anyone in the eye. 'But such a vote is not public. You just have to put a Yes or a No on your piece of paper and no one sees what they throw into the urn.'

'My husband's business partners...' Malka Grünfeld began again.

'One must take things as they are,' Mina said, actually interrupting the president of the Hachnasat Kallah Association. 'There's no point in pretending.'

'Quite right!' said Chanele, so loudly that everyone looked at her. Then she apologised to the ladies because she absolutely couldn't miss the train to Baden.

When Pinchas came home at last from his conversation with Dr Stern, Chanele had left again, taking Hinda with her.

'She came with me to the clothes collection,' Mimi said, concealing behind voluble lists of trivia the things that she wanted to keep to herself, 'although she really hasn't been brought up for such occasion. And afterwards she was suddenly in a great hurry, you know how she is. Hinda wasn't happy to go with her. They even had an argument about it. Even though there's a fair in

Baden at the weekend, the little one absolutely wanted to stay in Zurich for Shabbos, one might have imagined there was nothing more important to her in the world. It's always so cosy at our house, she says. But do you know what I think? You'll never guess! Do you know what I think?'

'My dear,' said Pinchas, 'if I could translate every page of Gemara as easily as I can your face, I would be the greatest Talmid Chochem in the world.'

'So, what am I thinking?'

'You're thinking: Zalman Kamionker.' He put his arm around his wife and drew her to him. 'Don't look so disappointed. It wasn't a very hard task. The young man inquired so insistently after Hinda today...'

'But you don't know about the other story,' Mimi consoled herself, feeling her new-found friendship with Chanele as a precious warmth within her.

Pinchas too had something to report, the crazy tale of a rabbi who had become an atheist, and now tried to prove the worthlessness of the Talmud using Talmudic quotations. On the way home he had firmly undertaken, when telling it, to stress only the comical aspects of the story, and to give no sign of how troubled he had been by the discussion. But he didn't get round to it for the time being, because at that moment Regula brought in a letter that had arrived that afternoon. She didn't bring it in on a tray, as Mimi had been trying to teach her for weeks, but had set it down on a perfectly ordinary plate like a slice of bread.

'Ah, *les servants!*' Mimi sighed, and Regula marched out, insulted. You don't have to know foreign languages to notice when someone's talking disparagingly about you.

The letter was addressed in old-fashioned writing and green ink. In a skilfully embellished hand it said, 'Pinchas Pomeranz, Esquire.' Pinchas tore open the envelope – with his fingernail, even though Mimi had given him a letter opener with an ivory handle! – cast his eyes over the contents and frowned in puzzlement.

'Do you know who's written to me?' he said, imitating Mimi's voice. 'You'll never guess.'

'Who?'

'The letter is from Endingen.'

'Who?'

'The father of your friend Anne-Kathrin!'

'The schoolmaster?'

'He signs his letter as chair of the Popular Education Association. Which he always talked about. So he actually did set it up.'

'What does he want from you?'

'He's planning a public event: "Arguments pro and contra shechita slaughtering." In the hall at the Guggenheim. He wants to invite me as a speaker.'

'Are you going?'

Pinchas carefully folded the letter and put it in his pocket.

'Do I have a choice?'

27

He hadn't played truant, Arthur said to himself, not really. You had to go to school, it was even a law. Even if you were two minutes late, there was one on the hand with the ruler, and sometimes even if you just made a face that a teacher didn't like. He'd never dared just to stay away from school. Even after the chickenpox, when he had a letter excusing him, signed by Janki Meijer in person, even then he had gone back trembling, and even dabbed spots on his face with white zinc ointment so that people really believed he was ill.

But the bar mitzvah instruction, he persuaded himself, that was something else completely. It was voluntary, as you could tell from the fact that it took place not in a classroom but at Cantor Würzburger's house, in a room that always smelled of sal ammoniac pastilles that the cantor sucked for his voice. Otherwise, for ramming the Torah passages and the droosh down people's throats, Würzburger was paid a fixed sum; Arthur always had to bring him the envelope at the start of the month. Surely he would be pleased to have to give one lesson less for the same amount of money.

Arthur hadn't just stayed away, either, he had hatched a plan which, if everything went as it should, would make him invisible in a way for an hour or two. Immediately after lunch, at a time when the cantor, to relax his vocal cords, always took a little nap, he had called in with Frau Würzburger and, coughing violently, told her he was unfortunately a bit feverish, and hoarse as well. His voice had been quite quiet and weak, half out of dissemblance and half out of fear. Did she think, he had asked, that he should still come to the lesson after school? She had most strictly forbidden him to do so, because Frau Würzburger knew, exactly as Arthur did, her husband's terror of everything to do with hoarseness. So everything had gone as he had expected.

Arthur had worked everything out very precisely. Even if Frau Würzburger were to inquire of Mama, on Shabbos in shul, perhaps, whether her youngest was feeling better, it wouldn't prompt any suspicion. Arthur was often sickly, and Chanele would only think he'd had his headaches during the lesson again.

He was not practised in these matters. Shmul wouldn't have had so many scruples; in his school days he had played truant as a matter of course, and always found a fellow pupil to lie for him. And Hinda wasn't afraid of anything anyway. She had even, when she was as old as Arthur was now, come up with tests of courage, had once gone into a shop where Jews were treated in an unfriendly way, and asked for a hundred grammes of 'Klaff Tea', before running away, laughing loudly. Of course the shop-owner couldn't have known that 'klafte' is more or less the worst word in Yiddish that one can use about a woman, but Arthur would never have dared to do anything like that. He suffered from the fearfulness that goes hand in hand with an overactive imagination: it was too easy for him to imagine all the things that could go wrong.

But today he simply had to play truant. On the Gstühl – it had been the main topic of conversation at break-time that morning – the Panopticon had arrived, a first herald of the spring fair at the weekend, and he knew: if he didn't go there straight away, today, he would have lost his chance. At the autumn fair the same company had once been in Baden, two of his classmates had visited it and reported the most marvellous things, but then the rumour had spread in town that there were objects on display in there that endangered public morals, and all the pupils at the pro-gymnasium had been forbidden to go there. Some had crept in anyway, but Arthur had been unable to summon the courage to defy such an emphatic prohibition, had stood for a long time in helpless longing outside the colourful booth, repeatedly listening to the barker's patter: 'Thirty rappen entrance! Children pay half!' His imagination had had six months to dream of the marvels he had missed, in ever more glowing colours, and meanwhile the pictures in his head had become entirely irresistible. Early in the morning he had pinched three five-rappen coins from his savings box; Shmul had once shown him how to do that with a knife and a knitting needle. All day he had been restless and impatient, for fear that there might be another prohibition this year too, but there had been none as yet, and the old one, or at least one might convince oneself that this was the case, must no longer be valid. So there was something like a gap in the law through which he had to slip today, because tomorrow was Friday, when he went home straight after school to prepare himself for the service, nothing was possible on Shabbos anyway, and at this time of year it got dark so late that he wouldn't be allowed out after Havdole either. And by Sunday . . . Not only did the time till then seem unbearably long, the fear of missing the great event for a second time was for once stronger than any prudence.

The Gstühl Square, where the donkeys waited in the summer so that the spa guests could ride on the Baldegg and drink milk still warm from the cow, was almost empty. Only a few particularly early market traders had already secured the best spots for themselves and, with their carts, marked out the future thoroughfares of a town of booths and stands, as adventurous and transient as the gold-digging settlements in California that Arthur had read about.

227

Two staked bony horses snuffled morosely around in the feedbags around their necks before the Panopticon, which stood there still almost in its undergarments, like Mama before someone's deft hands fingered all the little hooks into the eyes. The front of the booth was still bare, a forbidding surface of stained canvas, quite without the brightly painted panels that Arthur had gazed at so longingly in the autumn. They had shown a Roman gladiator blocking the path of a charging lion, while a woman in white knelt in the sand with her hands folded in prayer; a man in a turban had whipped along a column of dark-haired slaves with heavy shackles around their necks; a martyr, bleeding from countless wounds, had smiled mildly and forgivingly from below his halo; a knight had fought a dragon and a stag carried a flaming cross in its antlers. All these wondrous pictures were still stored in one of the two huge carts in which, it seemed to Arthur, a whole world could have been transported. They were not, like ordinary removal carts, simply painted with water-resistant dark green paint, but with an oversized portrait of the barker that Arthur remembered so clearly, an imposing man in an admiral's uniform decorated with all kinds of ribbons and medals, with a majestically twirled moustache, beside which Shmul's looked as childishly insignificant as a rocking horse beside a dashing steed. The painted promoter pointed with a stick at a panel bearing the inscription: *Staudinger's Panoptikon, Johann Staudinger Wdw*. Under that someone had added, in a different colour and in letters that jostled one another in the tight remaining space, *Owner: Marian Zehntenhaus*.

The till had already been set up on the low podium next to the entrance. In the autumn it had been draped with an embroidered green velvet blanket with gold sequins; the woman who took the money from the visitors and put it in a heavy iron box was wrapped in a veil of the same colour, and a row of golden coins hung over her forehead. Now the table was stripped of its magic, as ordinary and everyday as the wrapping table in the Emporium, and that made Arthur strangely sad.

He had walked quite close up to the table the till sat on, but there was no one there to take his fifteen rappen. He even knocked on the scratched wood with one of his precious five-rappen pieces, as Papa did on Sunday outings to call the waiter over, but nothing moved. The only sound was the rustle and snap of the lengths of canvas. After all the calm, sunny days, over the last hour a strong wind had risen up, chasing dark clouds across the sky.

'What are you doing there, you little beggar?' called a voice.

A man came climbing down from one of the wagons, big and strong, with loose trousers stuck into the top of his boots, with braces that stretched across his shirt with the rolled-up sleeves, as wide as an arba kanfes, and above all with a device strapped over his face which, at first glance, looked as if it was made of metal, as if the man in the iron mask had managed to escape from the Bastille and in some inexplicable manner found the way to Baden. But on closer inspection it was only a leather moustache strap. It was fastened so tightly that the man could not really move his mouth; when he spoke he sounded as if he had no teeth.

'What do you want?' the man asked again and came menacingly closer.

Arthur held out the three coins on the open palm of his hand. 'I want to go to the Panopticon,' he said, and because he felt he needed to explain the fifteen rappen, he added unnecessarily, 'I'm a child.'

Two suspicious eyes looked at him so keenly that Arthur's muscles were already tensing to run away. Then the man scratched himself carefully under his open shirt for a long time, spat, turned away and returned to the cart. 'Come again tomorrow. We're not open yet.'

'Tomorrow I can't.' There is a kind of despair that feels almost like courage, and it was that despair that sent Arthur running after the man. 'Please,' he said, and realised that tears were welling up in him as inexorably as storm clouds in the sky. 'Isn't there a possibility even so that I might...? I'll even pay the adult price. I can bring you another fifteen rappen, but not until Sunday.'

The man thought for a moment and then stretched his hand out. He didn't take the money, however, but rested his fingers on Arthur's upper arm and pressed it as if performing an examination. 'Are you strong?' he asked. 'My old woman has drunk too much and is no use for anything. If you help me shift the last few things, you can look at everything for free afterwards.'

It was the most exciting thing that had ever happened to Arthur in his whole life.

The whole cart had been almost cleared. If you climbed in – the loading space was high up, and Arthur had to lie on his stomach before pulling in his legs and then his feet – it was as if you were in a cave; footsteps echoed on the board floors, and it smelt musty, as Arthur imagined bats did. The cart was empty, there only a few figures wrapped in coarse sackcloth at the very back, some of them secured with straps that looked like dirty white belts. The protective packaging hid their shapes; it was impossible to tell whether they represented men or women, whether they were queens, murderers or Indians. Arthur recalled the poem about the veiled picture in Sais that he had had to learn by heart for school: 'A youth there was who, burning with a thirst for knowledge, to Egyptian Sais came...'

His task was to loosen the straps and push the figures to the edge of the cart where Herr Zehntenhaus – for it was the owner of all these precious objects in person who had taken him on to do the job – tipped them over his shoulder and carried them inside the booth. Arthur was worried at first that he might break something, snap off a finger or even a head, but the figures were much more stable and also much heavier than he had expected; with the bigger ones he had to make a huge effort even to move them. 'Only the outer layer is made of wax, there's always a plaster core inside,' explained Herr Zehntenhaus who, every other time he came back with the empty sacks, liked to break for a chat to get his breath back. When he did he took the moustache strap off his face, wiped off the sweat underneath and then let it spring back into place with a damp smack. 'Basically I hate moustaches,' he said, 'but it's just expected of a fairground barker.'

At last the cart was cleared. Only one single figure, smaller and wider than the others, was left. 'The Holy Virgin got broken on me,' said Herr Zehntenhaus. 'I haven't yet found anyone who can fix her.'

He helped Arthur down from the cart and led him to the rear of the booth, where a corner of the canvas was held up and fasted on a nail. 'Then I'll just look in quickly on my old lady,' he said, pushed Arthur through the opening and let the makeshift door fall shut behind him.

Arthur felt he was in paradise. He wasn't just in the forbidden Panopticon, he was there as the only visitor, before everyone else, and today all these unimagined treasures belonged to him alone. At that moment he wouldn't even have swapped places with Janki, who had been at the World's Fair in Paris and seen all of Edison's inventions. The sky outside had turned gloomy. Not so much light was filtering in through the gaps where the canvas had been folded away into triangular windows. Arthur enjoyed the mysterious gloom in which one could be fearful without being really frightened.

The treasures of the Panopticon were even more exciting than they had been in his dreams. There was the 'Spanish Inquisition' (a half-naked man being stretched on the rack by a hunchbacked torturer), the 'Medieval Scold's Bridle' (two old women fastened to a kind of yoke by the neck and wrists), 'Witch Torture in the Middle Ages', the 'Indian Widow-Burning', 'Mary Stuart's Final Walk' and the 'Oriental Harem'. Each exhibit was accompanied by an explanatory panel, and Arthur studied these as carefully as if he had had to sit an exam about them at school.

He also visited the medical cabinet, at whose entrance there hung a panel which could be turned to face one way or the other, 'Now only for Gentlemen', or 'Now only for Ladies'. This cabinet, he had no doubt, had been the reason for the headmaster's ban. Filled with guilt and curiosity he contemplated the 'Siamese Twins', the 'Osman Eunuchs', and did not fail to linger over the pedagogical displays warning about 'The Damaging Effects of Self-Abuse' (a man with tumours all over his body, his hands thrown to his face in despair), and the 'Consequences of Corset Wearing' (a woman with a naked torso, whose waist was no wider than a napkin ring).

Only then came the modern section, with 'Gorilla Abducting Farmer's Daughter', 'Moltke and MacMahon in the Battle of Sedan', the 'African Explorer Casati Imprisoned by the Bantu Negroes', the 'Chicago Triple Murder' and...

So filled was Arthur with images and impressions that at first he didn't understand what he was looking at.

A man dressed in black, with a big hat and long locks on his temples, had grabbed a little girl by the back of the neck, as one holds a cat before drowning it, and cutting open her throat with a long knife. A second man, identical in appearance, was catching the blood in a silver bowl.

On the cardboard sign under the pane of glass it said: 'The Ritual Murder of Tisza-Eszlar.'

Lightning flashed outside. In the sudden change of light the man with the knife seemed to be winking at Arthur.

It had grown so dark, in the middle of the afternoon, that the explanatory panel wasn't easy to decipher.

'On Easter Sunday 1882,' it said, 'in the Hungarian town of Tisza-Eszlar a desperate father and mother reported the disappearance without trace of their daughter. All attempts to find fourteen-year-old Eszter Solymosi, a particularly alert and lovable girl, were fruitless. No corpse was washed up on the banks of the Theiss, which has particularly dangerous currents in the region. The case would probably have remained a tragic mystery for all time, had not five-year-old Samuel Scharf, the son of the Jewish synagogue servant, been driven by the voice of his conscience to a terrifying confession. His father, he explained, had together with his older brother Moritz, lain in wait for the innocent girl, dragged her into the synagogue, and there, with the knife ordinarily used for the slaughtering animals, slit her throat. The blood of Christian virgins was known to be used by the Jews in their ancient ritual for the making of Pesach bread. The body of the girl, whose life was so horribly taken from her, was never found, so that the violently disputed trial ended with the acquittal of the synagogue servant, a judgement that provoked great rage in Hungary.'

A choking sensation rose in Arthur's throat and filled his mouth with a sour taste. He heard thunder that was meant for him alone. It was his fault. He had known that the Panopticon was not allowed, and he had gone anyway. He had wanted to unveil the forbidden picture, and now he was being punished for it.

When day appeared, the priests
Found him extended senseless, pale as death
Before the pedestal of Isis' statue.

There were mysteries, he had always known, things that went on in the shadows, which one only glimpse out of the corners of one's eye, and which one must on no account turn around to see. And if one did ...

His happiness in life had fled for ever
And his deep sorrow soon conducted him
to an early grave.

Every time he was asked to recite that passage, he felt as if it referred to him.

Again the sky flickered outside. Arthur closed his eyes tight and waited for the thunder as if it were a judgement.

The man with the bowl of blood was suddenly empty handed, and he was no longer a wax figure: he was Uncle Melnitz, whom Arthur knew so well, even though Papa always said he was dead and buried long ago.

'That's how it is,' said Uncle Melnitz. 'You will never be quite sure whether the story might not be true after all. Of course it is a lie, you know it is a lie, but if the same lie is told again and again, and believed again and again ...You will never be quite certain.

'You know Uncle Pinchas, who is also a shochet and has a long knife. You know that he cuts the throats of cows, with a single long slice and without flinching. Cows and calves and sheep and sometimes a chicken. But not children. But not little girls. Not Uncle Pinchas. You know that. You think you know. But you can't be sure.

'You sat on his knee and he told you stories. About a fish, as big as an island, so big that a ship moored by it and the seamen lit a fire on its back. You liked the story, because you knew it could not be true, that the big fish was made up and couldn't do anything to you. You knew, but you weren't sure.'

Uncle Melnitz was now holding the long knife in his hand.

'It is well known,' he said, 'that the blood of Christian virgins is used by Jews to make the Pesach loaves. Well known.'

He drew the knife, without flinching, along his own throat, and no blood came.

'You have unveiled the picture,' said Uncle Melnitz, 'and you will never be able to tell anyone about it. "All that he saw and learned, his tongue ne'er confessed." You won't be able to talk about it, and you won't be able to fight it. Because you're not sure. You will go to the library at school and you will ask your teacher for the big atlas, you will seek the land of Hungary and the town of Tisza-Eszlar on the Theiss, you will find both, and you will not be sure.'

It had grown dark behind the canvas walls, but Arthur could still clearly see Uncle Melnitz.

'You will not be able to get rid of the fear,' said the old man, and had long locks at his temples, 'the fear that there might be something inside you which you've never been aware of, and which is still a part of you. Until it suddenly comes out of you, from one day to the next, and is stronger than you. Eventually. It could be, yes. If everyone tells the story, it could be. Although it isn't true. Or else it is true. How could you know? How could anyone know?'

Outside the thunder crashed, like a rock fall or an avalanche, the lengths of canvas bulged inwards, hailstones rattled down like gunshot, as the bullets had rattled at Sedan in Janki's stories, something sharp caught Arthur in the back of the neck, an ice pick or a knife, a long knife for cutting the throats of cows, and not only cows.

As was well known.

He couldn't find the exit, he couldn't find the spot where you could simply lift the canvas, in the darkness his face collided with a figure that might have been a torturer or a murderer or a shochet from Tisza-Eszlar, he bumped into a hand that wanted to grab him and hold on to him, he wanted to flee and couldn't, he crept on all fours over sand and trampled grass, whining and trembling, eventually, somehow, found himself outside, lay with his face in the mud, the storm hammered down on his back and he was grateful for it, it was like a cleansing, he imagined that his jacket was in rags, and his trousers, that his skin was shredded and his trousers, that he was bleeding from a thousand wounds like the martyr in the painted panel, that he was smiling mildly and bravely, but without a halo, because Jews didn't have such things, that he endured unbearable pains and thus redeemed everything, the truancy and the lying and the curiosity, that he was innocent again, or newly born, or turned into a girl, that he was maybe even dead and they found him and said, 'He was a good boy, such a good boy.'

The hail stopped as suddenly as it had begun. Arthur raised his head. The black clouds were fleeing the sky as if they had a guilty conscience. It was not night, but still bright daylight.

He drew up his legs and straightened his torso. The hailstones under his knees were hard as gravel. Where the wind had driven them against the canvas of the Panopticon, they were piling up into white cushions.

He stood up and noticed that he had lost his cap. It was somewhere in the booth, and he would never have the courage to look for it.

The two horses stood with their legs spread and their heads in between them. They were probably not trying to shelter from the storm any more, however, just rummaging for the remaining oats at the bottom of their feed bags.

Arthur was hungry.

In one of the two trucks a lamp burned behind a window, exactly as if it were in a house. He remembered that it was late, that everyone had been waiting for him for ages, and that, drenched and dirty as he was, no one would believe that he was coming from bar mitzvah instruction with Cantor Würzburger.

But that wasn't what frightened him most.

28

By the time Arthur finally came home, he had come up with an excuse. He had been on his way home from bar mitzvah instruction, exactly, that's how he would put it, when suddenly a whole gang of boys he'd never seen before jumped out at him from a doorway and beat him up and threw him in the dirt. Of course they would ask him if he recognised the faces, and he would reply: They certainly hadn't been from his school. They would believe his story, he hoped, because something of the kind had actually happened once before, except that it hadn't come to blows. They'd just shouted 'Schiissjud, Schiissjud!' – 'Fucking Jew! Fucking Jew!' and ' – 'Jewboy, Jewboy, fetch your cap, or else pay us seven rapp'!' They'd taken his cap from him and thrown it from hand to hand while he dashed helplessly and breathlessly after it. He had only told Mama the story; Janki got so cross so quickly, and he himself had felt strangely guilty, as if he had somehow deserved this torment because of some special quality he had. This time, this was the story he had come up with, they had run off with his cap, had put it on the end of a stick and waved it around like a flag. They had also shouted something else while they laid into him, not 'Judebübli', but 'Tisza-Eszlar!', 'or something like that', he would say, he hadn't really understood. It had all happened so quickly. He had defended himself as best he could…No, he had been too scared to put up any resistance; that would make the whole thing properly convincing, he reflected.

But when he crept into the flat, there was no one there to ask him questions. Only fat Christine heard him coming and pulled him out of the corridor into the kitchen, where the oven was always hot even in summer. There he had to sit down on the bench, and she sat down beside him and rubbed him with a cloth until he had stopped shivering. The cloth smelled of fresh bread.

The cook, who was otherwise very curious, didn't want to know why he was only coming back now, dirty and drenched. She didn't ask where he had left his cap. She just let her hands do the work, as they would have rolled out pastry or tenderised a tough piece of meat, and was meanwhile elsewhere. Suddenly she let go of him, went to the door and opened it a crack. She stood there for a few moments, then she furiously slammed the door close again, and Arthur couldn't see who she was so furious with. She pulled a hand-kerchief out of her apron, with the same red and white pattern as the meaty kitchen towels, and loudly blew her nose in it. Arthur couldn't help thinking of the two horses near the booth, and the way they had buried their heads in their feed bags.

Then Christine turned to him, looking as if she had just discovered him in her kitchen and wasn't happy about the discovery. 'Are you hungry?' she asked.

'No,' Arthur said quickly, although it wasn't true. Little boys who have been beaten up, he had imagined, lose their appetite for ages afterwards.

Then they sat together in silence. Christine seemed to be listening out for something, she kept lifting her head and lowering it again straight away, as if she'd caught herself doing something forbidden. The kitchen smelled of soup, burnt wood and secrets.

Then, very slowly, as if time had gone rusty, and was only reluctantly getting going again, the door handle lowered itself. Christine too, it seemed to Arthur, had to struggle from her chair, bend her torso a long way forwards and rest her broad hands on her thighs to get to her feet.

In the doorway stood Louisli, the young maid, strangely holding a small framed oil painting, *Rabbi in the Sukkah*, it was called, and it actually belonged on the wall in the corridor.

Louisli was really still a girl and not a woman. When she brought the breakfast coffee to the table her eyes were sometimes quite red from crying, because she had been homesick for her village during the night again. Now her eyes were wide open. 'As if she had seen a ghost,' Arthur thought.

As if she too had seen a ghost.

'So, what is it now?' Christine asked.

'I hate him,' said Louisli.

'They're really arguing over you?'

'No,' said Louisli.

And then something happened that Arthur had only ever seen in very small children: her face folded in on itself, it actually crumpled, she closed her eyes and twisted her mouth as if she had eaten something revoltingly sour, and then she started to wail, quite noisily without warning, just as the hail had begun today, still in the doorway she stood and howled, sobbed with her whole body, the lion from the Panopticon sat inside her and tore her to shreds.

Christine went over to her, laid a heavy arm around her and drew her into the kitchen. Arthur closed the door. He had the feeling that had to be done right now.

'There, there,' Christine said consolingly, and again and again, 'There, there.' 'A Jew would say, "Nu, nu,"' Arthur found himself thinking, and the very difference in the words of consolation represented an unconquerable obstruction between him and the rest of the world.

The two women were now sitting side by side on the bench by the stove, where Arthur had previously been sitting, and Louisli still clutched the painting as if rocking a new born baby.

'There, there.' Christine repeated the words regularly and without the slightest impatience, just as she could stir a sauce at an unchanging pace for half an hour until it had exactly the right consistency. Louisli's face smoothed itself out very gradually; she sniffed and wiped her nose on her sleeve. Arthur could clearly see the revolting glistening trail on the black material.

'It's my own fault,' said Louisli. 'I should have known.' Her body heaved again, but not violently this time, as if the lion were already full and had only bitten her one last time out of habit.

'What should you have known?' Christine asked. Her voice was quite soft.

'That he was lying to me.' And then, placing each word as carefully as one places the good porcelain on the table, 'He said I was the only one for him.'

Christine laughed, a short, snorting, boxer's laugh, as if after far too obvious a feint, from which one cannot be lured into dropping one's guard.

'And he said he loved me.'

'They always say that. I know that one. Men can hurt you very badly.' Arthur, pressed invisibly into the corner by the door, stared at the cook. He had never heard her say anything like that before, not Christine, who could break a carp's neck just with her thumb and then, with bloody hands, calmly scoop its guts out of its belly, not fat Christine, who in Mama's opinion was a pearl precisely because no suitor was ever going to distract her from her duties. 'Oh, yes,' she said now, and made a face like Aunt Mimi when she had a migraine, 'I know men.'

In spite of all the excitement he had experienced, and the fresh excitement that was happening right now, that was the moment that Arthur would later remember most clearly, 'the precise moment', he was still saying fifty years later, 'when I stopped simply being a child. I realised for the first time, at that exact second, that all the people I knew weren't there just because of me, but that they had a life of their own, a life I knew nothing about, and which had absolutely nothing to do with me.'

'I know men,' said Christine. 'They're all the same.'

'He knocked at the door, did young Herr François, I pretended to be asleep, but he just didn't stop. I put my head under the pillow, but that doesn't help.' Louisli said all that in a very small, tearful voice, but Arthur with his fine ear still had the impression that she was enjoying the story, just like the martyr on the panel outside the Panopticon had been happy with his wounds, 'I only let him in so that he didn't wake everyone up,' she even smiled.

'I was awake.' Christine, like Louisli, had her bedroom in the attic.

'He said he loved me. That he couldn't sleep because he kept thinking about me. That I was the only one in his life.'

'Ha,' said Christine, who would never have fallen for such a move.

'And then...and then...' Louisli started crying again, but this time the lion was gone.

'Nothing happened,' said Christine, and although Arthur couldn't imagine what had gone on between Shmul and Louisli, it was clear to him that that was a lie. Something had happened.

'Have you bled this month?' Christine asked. And when Lousli nodded through her tears, 'Then everything's all right.'

Arthur, quite confused now, thought once more of the martyr with all his wounds.

Christine had been speaking comfortingly and attentively to Louisli, but now her tone suddenly changed, just as one doesn't go on stirring a sauce once it has started to set, and she said quite soberly, 'So tell me! What's going on over there?'

There's nothing one can do if one has simply been forgotten and then hears things not meant for one's ears. Christine herself had brought him into the kitchen, and no one had told him that the conversation between the two women was none of his business. If he had cleared his throat or otherwise drawn attention to himself, he could only have disturbed them at a moment when they certainly didn't want to be disturbed. So Arthur just stayed in his corner and listened.

Papa, he learned, had come home in a rage, more furious than anyone could remember, had shouted for Chanele and later for François, and had then locked himself in with them both in the dining room, had slammed the door so violently that a picture fell off the wall in the corridor, the painting of the bearded man in the funny shack. 'It's a sukkah,' Arthur thought, 'a rabbi in a sukkah,' and nearly said it out loud. This painting – Christine now leaned it carefully against a chair – that couldn't just have been left lying on the floor, would have been an excuse for Louisli if someone had caught her listening at the door. Christine, the first to go out and check what was going on, had actually heard Janki yelling something about fornication, about shame being brought down on his house, and when she said that in the kitchen Louisli had turned quite pale. She had then crept out herself, even though her legs were trembling with excitement, and at first she hadn't understood anything, not just because Janki's voice kept breaking with fury, but because he had lapsed into a language that she didn't know, it sounded like ordinary German, and then again it didn't, and it was only the answers that François had given that made her understand that they weren't talking about her. She had been so worried about being sent home under a cloud of shame and insults, that her people would never, never have forgiven her, and she would have been seen as the village slut for ever and ever, but then, when she realised that they weren't even talking about her, it had actually been much worse, to know that François had another and perhaps many more, a salesgirl in the Emporium who was even expecting his child.

It was, even before his bar mitzvah, really the day when Arthur grew up.

Louisli stood for a long time at the dining room door, still holding the painting, but she couldn't hear much more. Then she had had to run away because she had heard footsteps, probably Hinda. Her room was right at the end of the corridor, but such a racket must have been audible all the way there. And there wouldn't have been any point listening any longer, because what she heard went around in a circle, so to speak, always the same: Janki swore and threatened, François made excuses, didn't understand why everyone was so worked up, and Chanele only spoke occasionally, always very calmly and in very few words. And then Janki started shouting again.

Christine, who knew men, was a little surprised, because in her estimation of Janki, she said, she would never have thought that he could get so worked up about such a matter.

Louisli sniffed into her sleeve and said it wasn't just such a matter, it had broken her heart at any rate, and she would never get over it her whole life long.

Christine said, 'Ha!' and smiled her boxer's laugh.

But in the kitchen they didn't know everything, and even Janki and François, the ones most affected, knew only a part.

In fact what had happened was the following:

In the afternoon, just as Janki was serving two particularly good customers, Frau Wiederkehr – 'of the rich Wiederkehrs' – and Frau Strähle, the wife of the manager of the Verenahof, Herr Rauhut the editor came into the shop, never having been in it before, and demanded to talk to Janki, right away, he would not be put off. 'In private, please: I'm sure you don't want everyone to know what I have to discuss with you.' Janki explained to him that he really had no time right now, he said it quite politely, and even made a little joke, to the effect that the customer was queen as far he was concerned, and anyone who didn't want to fall out of favour would be well advised not to leave his monarch rudely in the lurch, but Rauhut insisted, he even became impertinent – 'When he is sober, which isn't often, the chap's even more unbearable!' – and said at last that he didn't care himself, as far as he was concerned they could go on talking in public, because sooner or later it would appear in the *Tagblatt* anyway. And then he asked, in front of Frau Wiederkehr and Frau Strähle – who of course would tell her husband, and then one might as well put it in the paper without further ado – just asked straight out: 'Is it true, Herr Meijer, that the salesgirl Marie-Theres Furrer of the Modern Emporium is expecting your child?'

Janki had never heard the name – 'You are aware that I don't know all the women who work in my shops!' – but Rauhut refused to believe him, he had it from a good source, a very good source, that there had been some hanky-panky, if he might use the term. And he had been told that the girl was pregnant, one could in fact see it with the naked eye. He as an editor was at the service of the public, and the public had a right to be informed and warned regardless of the status of the person if things happened in town which were irreconcilable with public morals.

Janki contradicted, denied, even pleaded. He remembered only too well the newspaper article that had almost ruined him on the day of the Drapery opening. But Rauhut stood his ground and referred repeatedly to his source, whom he could not name, but who was reliable, absolutely reliable. And all that in front of the greedy ears of Frau Wiederkehr and Frau Strähle, who clearly couldn't wait to pass on the story and spread it around, not as an unproven accusation, of course, but as a documented fact.

At last, and even that had – me neshumah! – not been easy to achieve, Rauhut declared himself willing to wait another few days with his article, but if by then he had no proof to the contrary, clear and unambiguous proof to the contrary…Verbatim, he said, 'I will have no option,' and anyone who speaks as pompously as that, Janki said, has evil on his mind. And generally speaking: how, excuse me, is one supposed to prove that something hasn't happened?

Chanele heard all of this very calmly, so calmly that it made Janki really mad, and then said only a single sentence.

And Janki leapt to his feet and yelled for François.

His son came in smiling, and when Janki noisily slammed the door shut, his polite smile grew even wider, as when one tightens the rubber string of a carnival mask. Because Janki demanded as much, he sat down, but only with half his bottom, as though purely out of courtesy.

Janki set the walking stick with the lion's-head handle down at an angle on the table in front of him, and rested both hands on it. 'If you were a goy…' he began, and had probably, while waiting for François, honed his rebukes to a very sharp point. But his rage was greater, and he started shouting in a voice that was constantly on the point of breaking. 'But you aren't a goy! You're a Jew, and a Jew must behave respectably!'

'So?' said François, looking in his pocket for his case of Russian cigarettes. 'You're not going to smoke now, are you?'

A shrug. 'If it bothers you, Papa...'

Chanele noticed without any great surprise that something had changed in her. Francois' smile, which had frightened her so because of its strangeness, was no longer threatening since it had reminded her of something. The man in the insane asylum, the one with the tailcoat over his bare chest, had smiled just like that when he had said, 'I'm incognito here.'

'Why did you have to go and start something with the nafka?' Janki yelled.

'Louisli?' François asked the question in an off-handed, throw-away manner as if to say, 'What are you getting worked up about? It's nothing more than a coffee stain on a tablecloth.'

'Her too? This has got to stop! Is that clear? It will stop right now! No, I'm talking about this...about this...Chanele, what's her name again?'

'Marie-Theres Furrer.'

'Oh, that one. You'd like her too.' François nodded to his father as if to say, 'If you wanted, we could have a nice little secret together.'

'I don't even know her!' roared Janki. 'And the whole town is saying I've got her pregnant. Don't laugh! Stop laughing this instant! It's going to be in the paper! And all just because you...because you...'

'Is she pregnant?'

'Yes,' said Chanele.

'Well, it'll cost a bit of money. We're not poor people.'

Janki brought his walking stick down so hard on the table that the handle came off. The lion's head turned a number of somersaults and then came to a stop in front of François, sticking its tongue out in mockery.

'We will become poor people!' yelled Janki. 'If people boycott us, we might as well shut up shop! You have no idea of the damage such an article can do. You are nothing and you know nothing and you haven't experienced anything! The only thing you can do is unbutton your trousers and be an idiot!'

Janki's rage, even though François was its butt, was directed much more at Herr Rauhut, against all the Rauhuts, against the whole town, against a world in which one could take as much trouble as one wanted, in which one could pedal frantically and do everything correctly and then all it took was a rumour, a single unmerited suspicion, to destroy everything one had built up over twenty years. François was not yet a real man, he could afford to make a mistake; at his age such things were practically expected of him. 'Young blood', people would have said, half in blame and half in admiration, women would have given him sidelong looks and dreamed up stories in which they themselves played the lead role, men would have been a bit envious and then, if word had got out that they had treated the girl decently, with an appropriate sum, the matter would have disappeared, once and for all, forgiven and forgotten. But now people thought *he* had been messing around with the girl, a girl twenty-five years younger than he was himself, and an employee to boot, which made it doubly contemptible. Above all it would now become public, not just something one talked about over brandy and cigars after the ladies had withdrawn. Now it would have consequences. Janki was not François. He was no longer a young rake, he belonged to society, or he nearly did, he would have belonged to it long since if he only went to church on Sunday and not to the prayer room on Shabbos, and in society the rules were stricter. His customers, those arrogant small-town queens whom he had been courting for two decades, would stay away, and if they didn't stay away they would turn up their peasant noses, they would look at him like...like...like a salesman, a quite ordinary tailor, someone who has to be subservient, whom one uses when one needs him, but that's all. Now he would never belong to it.

That was why Janki shouted so loudly.

Then when Hinda came in and wanted to know what was going on, he was already quite out of breath, he had cursed François a thousand times and forbidden him a thousand things – he was not allowed to go out of the house except to work, they would soon see who was in charge around here – but he had not solved the actual problem: how does one make a rumour disappear?

'Don't worry, Hinda, my ray of sunshine,' he tried to lie. 'We are only discussing a business matter. An unpleasant matter, but nothing for you to worry about. How were things in Zurich?'

But Janki's veins were swollen, and he was as red in the face as Councillor Bugmann. François had fixed his eyes on a point where there was nothing to see, and the smile was frozen on his face. Chanele sat straight-backed on her chair and seemed to be waiting for something.

'I would prefer to tell you about Zurich later,' Hinda said quickly. 'For now I want to check that we're having dinner this evening.'

When she had left, Janki picked up the broken lion's head and tried hopelessly to fix it back to the stick. 'Do you think I can glue it back on?' he asked in a sad voice.

'If you let me do it,' said Chanele, 'I'll sort everything out.'

29

'Three thousand francs?'

Herr Ziltener's hands were clenched behind his back in an attempt to ensure that he didn't touch Chanele's desk even by accident. Her office was so small that any conversation carried out behind closed doors assumed an inadvertently intimate character, a kind of familiarity with which this sober accountant was extremely uncomfortable.

'Three thousand francs? The boss said nothing to me about that.'

'Because he doesn't know anything about it.'

'In that case I can't...'

'Yes, you can, Herr Ziltener,' said Chanele, and realised to her own surprise how much she had been looking forward to this moment. 'You have authority to deal in sums up to this figure.'

'But...'

'My husband granted you that authority on the assumption that you are capable of conducting transactions of this magnitude without having to request his instructions.'

'Three thousand francs...not a small matter.' Herr Ziltener wasn't stammering, but he wasn't far off.

'If you feel it's too much for you,' Chanele went on, a little ashamed that she was enjoying the situation so much, 'my husband and I will fully understand if you prefer to leave our company and seek a less demanding post elsewhere.'

'You're going...?' The stammer was threateningly close. 'You want to dismiss me?'

Not at all, Herr Ziltener. Certainly not. Who would want to dispense with such a reliable and discreet member of staff?' Chanele waited until Ziltener's shoulders relaxed with relief, and then added as if in passing:

'Unless, of course, you found that you were not in a position to follow my instructions.'

Ziltener silently moved his lips, a schoolboy going through a calculation over and over again so as not to reach the wrong result. 'I could...I could...'

'Yes, my dear Herr Ziltener?'

'I could of course fetch the money from the bank and then have it confirmed by the boss later on...'

'That would not be a good solution.'

The schoolboy had worked out the calculation so carefully, and still no praise from the teacher.

'Not a good...?'

'I do not wish my husband to know anything about this sum.'

'That's impossible!' In his excitement the accountant had repeatedly clutched his head; his thin hair, which he had combed over his bald patch with painstaking precision, was now standing up in all directions.

'Regrettable. But if you say so. Many thanks, Herr Ziltener. That will be all.'

Ziltener didn't go, of course he didn't. He stopped by the desk and uneasily fiddled with his paper sleeves. For a moment the nervous rustling was the only sound.

'If the boss finds out, he will fire me,' he said at last, and his eyes were huge with anxiety.

'If he finds out, I will fire you.' Chanele had borrowed Francois' smile for this conversation, ruthlessly polite and politely ruthless.

One could actually watch Ziltener struggling with the problem. His jaw worked; he had to chew on the bitter pill that she had given him to swallow.

At last he lowered his head and gave in. 'But it's all in order?' he asked.

'Of course, my dear Herr Ziltener,' Chanele said in a friendly voice. 'It's all in order.'

During the time that the accountant needed to go to the bank, contrary to all custom, Chanele sat idly at her desk. If someone had come in unannounced – which of course no one would have dared to do – he would have wondered why Madame Meijer was smiling so dreamily.

Madame Meijer. Yes, she had finally grown into that name.

The first part of her plan had worked exactly as she had planned. Simply rebuking François, telling him that things could not go on this way, that he had to change his life, would have been utterly pointless. No support could have been expected from Janki either. He wouldn't have taken the whole matter seriously, she was sure of it, he would have seen Francois' affair as a little slip, as he saw everything his golden boy did, he might even have been proud of him. For men such stories were like a game, and everyone wanted to be on the winning side.

But now that Janki himself had fallen under suspicion...

And when he was firmly convinced that François was to blame...

It had not been easy to persuade Mathilde Lutz to join in. She hadn't at first wanted to play the part that Chanele had assigned to her, but of course in the end she had given in. It wasn't hard to manipulate people; one only had to take the trouble to find out how they worked.

And one mustn't feel sorry for them.

So that evening Mathilde had gone to the Crown. It could equally have been the Golden Eagle or the Edelweiss, because Herr Rauhut the editor was bound to turn up at each pub in town sooner or later in the course of the evening. She had sat down alone at a table, as far as possible from the hustle and bustle of the regular guests. She had put on a hat with a thick black veil, an old hat that she had kept from her husband's funeral, even though that was already many years ago. The veil had been Mathilde's own idea. It wasn't customary for decent women to visit a pub unaccompanied, and anyone who has a rumour to spread does not want to fall victim to another.

Rauhut arrived at half past eight, sat down at the regulars' table where he was greeted with a loud 'Hallo', and was served his half of red without having to order it. As if merely continuing a conversation that had just been interrupted, he had immediately involved himself in a violent debate in which he outdid everyone, in the loudness of his arguments at least. He seemed to have settled at the table, and in the end Frau Lutz had to ask the waiter, who was already on his way with his next half litre, to tell the editor as inconspicuously as possible that there was someone here who had interesting information for him.

When he joined her, she began by complimenting him, exactly as Chanele had commissioned her to do, told him that she never missed one of his articles signed 'fr' (his first name was Ferdinand) in the *Tagblatt*, and had often thought how nice it was that at least one person in this city had the courage to say in the newspaper how things really were. Rauhut accepted the praise as no more than his due.

'Then, when you tell him the story,' Chanele had further instructed Mathilde, 'do it haltingly, like someone who might have decided to reveal a secret, but who is tormented by her conscience.' Mathilde didn't have to dissemble to create this impression. One does not betray one's king without palpitations, and she still saw Monsieur Meijer, with his elegant manners and his injury from the Franco-German war, as having something majestic about him.

Dissembling would have been pointless in any case. It was so noisy in the Crown, and Herr Rauhut already so intoxicated that she practically had to bellow the sensational news in his ear. 'A salesgirl, a young thing, and the father is...No, not the girl's father, the child's father! – the father is...'

When he had finally understood her, there was a fat grin on his face, 'a really fat great grin,' Mathilde said to Chanele the following day, and she would have liked to take it all back again.

Yes, so far the plan had worked. The rumour was in the world, and had done its duty. Now the important thing was to make sure it was forgotten again.

Herr Ziltener now came with the money, and Chanele took the envelope as if he had brought her nothing more than a pair of gloves that she had forgotten somewhere. The receipt that he laid next to it she left untouched on the desk, and Ziltener didn't dare remind her.

She thought for a moment about going home again and changing her dress, but that would have felt like disguising herself, and that was something Chanele had firmly resolved never again to do. So she stayed in her black shop uniform, put a coat on over it and fastened her hat to her sheitel. That was the least she could do; what she planned was an official visit.

She had already sent a messenger that morning. If Herr Councillor was in his office at about three o'clock, she had something that she wanted to discuss with him, and the reply had come that of course he was available to the esteemed Monsieur Meijer at any time. She had not mentioned Janki in her letter, but Herr Bugmann had – as Chanele expected – assumed as a matter of course that where business matters were involved it would naturally be the husband who came to see him.

On the way to the Weite Gasse, she met the wife of Cantor Würzenburger, who inquired after Arthur's health, 'the poor boy looked very ill on Thursday.'

'I must make more time for Arthur,' thought Chanele, murmured something along the lines of 'everything's fine,' and apologised, saying she was in a hurry.

'Are you going shopping?'

'Yes,' Chanele said, 'you could call it that.'

Anyone who stepped into Councillor Bugmann's law office found themselves at first confronted by a wooden barrier that made a petitioner of every visitor. Behind it a scrawny office boy sat by his desk on a high stool, in a distorted, boneless posture. He had wedged his pen behind his ear, something which, to judge by the ink stains on his face, was probably a regular habit.

'Please tell Herr Councillor that I'm here.'

The young man twisted his head to look at her, visibly indignant at her presumption. 'Herr Bugmann is busy right now,' he said in a nasal voice and hunched once more over his open ledger.

The old Chanele would have patiently explained to the upstart that his boss was expecting her or, if she had been kept waiting for too long, she would have shouted at him, as she sometimes had to do with her employees. The new Madame Meijer simply opened the little door in the barrier and walked towards the door with the metal sign saying 'bureau'.

In his excitement the gawky youth almost fell from his stool. He was one of those people who like to exert authority but don't know how to defend it when it's called into question. 'You can't do that,' he said, sounding just like Herr

Ziltener. He walked over to Chanele with a strangely elegant gait, and blocked her path with spread, waving arms. 'Herr Bugmann said quite emphatically...'

'What did I say?' The councillor had heard the commotion in his ante-chamber, and was now standing in the doorway.

'Your young man was about to announce my presence. And by the way, a very committed employee you have there.'

Bugmann looked back and forth between the two of them and then tapped his clerk sharply on the head. The youth, probably used to such treatment, took the punishment with a kind of bow and slouched back to his stool.

'The nephew of a fellow party member,' the councillor said apologetically as he took off Chanele's coat. 'I was urgently requested... You may know how that is. Sometimes you have no option.'

Bugmann's office, with its big bow window looking out on the Weite Gasse, was furnished like a living-room, with heavy doors and landscape paintings on the walls. Of course there was also a desk, but the place of honour, where the light was best, was occupied by two chairs and a three-seat sofa, all upholstered in red velvet, with white crocheted antimacassars, a fashion that had spread from England. On small tables, of which there were at least half a dozen, photographs were crammed together, jostling with other souvenirs and knick-knacks. A massive bookshelf took up almost one whole wall. The leather backs behind the glass doors emphasised the twofold character of the room: apart from collections of legal writings and the thick volumes of a dictionary there were also the collected works of Goethe, Schiller, Hebbel and Pestalozzi.

Bugmann offered Chanele a seat on the sofa – 'There you won't be dazzled by the sun!' – propped another cushion behind her back and displayed the over-eager bustling activity often used to cover over awkward situations. He fetched a tray of bottles and glasses from the credenza, and tried to offer her a little glass of advocaat. Chanele declined politely, whereupon he apologised at length for having nothing else to offer her, after all, he couldn't really expect a lady to drink cognac or even a proper schnapps. 'Of course I would have made tea if I'd known you...I had been expecting your husband. He isn't ill or anything, is he?'

'Don't worry, he's fine. I'm sure he would pass on his kindest regards if he knew I was here.'

The councillor tried not to show his surprise, which only made it all the more apparent.

'My husband has asked me to sort out a delicate problem for him, and would prefer not to be personally involved in the details. Perhaps you know how that is. Sometimes you have no option.'

She hadn't planned to use Bugmann's own phrase; the words had simply been hanging in the air. But he nodded as if she had said something extremely significant, sat down in an armchair opposite her, propped his chin in his hand and drew one eyelid slightly down with his index finger.

'I'm listening.'

'You are, amongst your many obligations, also an official guardian, is that not so, Herr Councillor?'

'I am guardian to an orphan. That is correct.'

'And you told us, when you recently did us the honour of being our guest, that you must sometimes reveal a certain severity in this capacity, which actually contradicts your well-known philanthropic character.'

Bugmann did not dismiss the clumsy flattery, and proudly inflated his red cheeks. 'Like a fish that has just swallowed a lure,' thought Chanele.

'I think I remember,' she went on. 'You also spoke in this connection of a young man whose desire to marry you could not grant consent to because he didn't have the necessary means to establish his own household.'

'There are many such cases,' said Bugmann and made a solemn face, as if he were about to deliver a public address. 'Sad for those involved, of course, but I must bear in mind my responsibility.'

'That cannot always be easy.' Chanele had almost laughed out loud, it was all going so easily. 'I have now found myself thinking that it could not be wrong – not least in the interest of a certain popularity, upon which one depends, after all, as a politician – if you would nonetheless make a marriage possible in one or other of these cases.'

Bugmann tried to appear quite nonchalant, but his torso leaned far forward in curiosity. Salomon had taught his foster daughter to read such signs.

'It would certainly create a very positive impression in public,' Chanele said, delivering her prepared speech. 'The guardian to an orphan paying his charges the dowry they need out of his own pocket…'

'His own…?' There was something breathless about Bugmann's voice.

'So, my husband and I place great value on discretion when it comes to good works. One does not wish to boast. So we would insist that the foundation set up by us should remain anonymous or, even better, that it should not be mentioned in this connection at all.'

'Foundation?' Councillor Bugmann's face had turned even redder than it already was naturally.

'We thought a sum of three thousand francs. To begin with. And you alone, of course, would decide the amount to be paid in the individual case.'

'And to whom,' Bugmann said quickly.

'And to whom, of course. With a man such as yourself no checks would be necessary.'

Bugmann breathed out slowly. It was a sigh of relief.

'Although if I might be permitted,' Chanele said, 'to say a small word on the selection of the recipients. It concerns a salesgirl in the Modern Emporium. A very respectable girl, fundamentally, who has unfortunately – how can I put this – strayed once from the path of virtue. With certain...certain consequences, if you understand my meaning.'

'Of course,' Bugmann said, and thought he understood much more than Chanele had said.

'She is one of my best workers, and a man who asked for her hand would certainly not regret the proposal. Above all if she had an appropriate dowry.'

'Which you would not wish to put personally at her disposal.' One could not say that Bugmann grinned, but his facial expression could certainly have been called complacent. 'You would prefer a neutral foundation...'

'As I said: we place great value on discretion. We would be only too happy if you yourself would appear in public as the noble donor.'

Councillor Bugmann poured himself a big glass of cognac and drank it down in one gulp. Then he stood up, walked to his desk and opened his ink bottle.

'The name of the young lady?'

'Marie-Theres Furrer.'

Bugmann wrote and waved the paper in the air to dry the ink.

'So the whole thing will go through as quickly as possible?'

'As quickly as possible.'

'And the money...?'

'I have brought it.'

Bugmann carefully folded up the sheet of paper, halved and quartered it and then put it in the bottom of a briefcase. Chanele opened her handbag and took out the sealed envelope that Herr Ziltener had brought her.

When the transaction was complete and they sat facing each other again on the red velvet, Chanele said, as if it the idea had only just occurred to her, 'Ah yes, Herr Councillor, there is one other small thing...'

'What?' Bugmann had now set aside all politeness, a farmer who doesn't quite trust a cattle-trade that is far too cheap, but who is willing defend his advantage with tooth and claw.

'You are one of the directors of the *Tagblatt*, are you not?'

'Why?'

'Herr Rauhut, the editor, you know him, the man who was so unpleasantly drunk at our little supper, seems to have been taken in by certain rumours.

As I have learned by chance, he is linking my husband in a certain way with the unfortunate girl I just mentioned to you.'

'This Marie-Theres Furrer?'

'Entirely without foundation, of course. But such a story could have unpleasant consequences for the poor young thing. Particularly when she will soon be marrying.'

'And even more unpleasant consequences for Monsieur Meijer.' Bugmann was now quite relaxed. He had got to the nub of the matter, and discovered that it referred to someone else.

'But the article will never appear.' Chanele assumed François's smile again. 'Will it, Herr Councillor?'

'You can rely on me,' said Bugmann.

'I know I can rely on you,' said Chanele.

Everything that needed to be said had been said, but they went on chatting for a few minutes, scattered harmless commonplaces around about their secret as one throws sand over one's traces if one doesn't want to be reminded where one has been.

'I'm already looking forward,' said Councillor Bugmann, when he held out her coat, 'to being able to enjoy another of those delicious meals in your lovely home.'

'I am sorry,' said Chanele, walking through the door that he held open for her. 'My husband and I have decided not to continue with the tradition of our evening invitations.'

The office boy from the antechamber still hung on his stool like a crooked question mark. Chanele stopped beside him for a moment and said benignly, 'By the way – you have ink on your face.'

30

'No article is going to be published,' was all she said, and Janki asked no questions.

They were sitting around the oversized dining room table – tropical wood! – as if to depict a living picture entitled *Family at Dinner* for some invisible spectator, without the slightest notion of how such a thing would be done. Janki had rested his walking stick against the table, and was still clutching the freshly glued-on lion's head. He sat where he always sat, no one had secretly moved the table or switched the chairs, and still, although he couldn't have explained his feeling of unease to himself, he didn't really feel as if he was sitting at the top of the table any more.

François had made a show of not being hungry, and had only sat down at the table on an order from his father. He had pushed his plate listlessly aside and instead put the tantalus with the yellowish fluid in front of him, the one that was normally on the sideboard. With one of the ivory toothpicks that were only put on the table for big meals – a soapstone knave held a dozen ready, like spears before the battle – he ran his finger, as if there nothing more important in the world, around the tiny silver lock whose key had been missing for ever. 'If I am going to be kept prisoner here,' said every one of his movements, 'then at least I can do something useful and try to get this thing open at last.'

Hinda, who normally chatted merrily away over any ill humour, had for once been infected be the general gloom, and stirred her soup with a face as stony as if the soup had been prescribed her by her doctor against her will.

No one noticed that Arthur said not a word and did not once look up from his plate. They were used to him being like that. He was often so preoccupied with his own thoughts that you had to ask him questions three times before he finally heard you. When he was in a good mood, Janki would laugh, calling him, 'Our little philosopher!' On other days he struck his glass with his spoon, and when everyone looked at him, he would say with cutting friendliness, 'If the professor would like to give us the honour of his attention...?'

Louisli's eyes were red from weeping when she set the soup tureen down on the table. In her case at least one didn't have to look for an explanation.

After a long silence Chanele finally cleared her throat. 'Janki, I think you should give Herr Ziltener a small raise. He hasn't been having a very easy time lately.'

Janki didn't contradict her, as he would automatically have done on any other day, but said only, 'If you think so…' and reached again for the handle of his walking stick to check it with his fingers.

And then they had a visitor. At a time of day when no one paid visits in Baden.

Louisli announced the visitor as if announcing a death. 'Someone would like to speak to the lady and gentleman of the house. A Herr Kamionker.'

In the books that Arthur devoured in his every free minute, people were often said to be gasping for air. He had always thought it was just a figure of speech, like 'He got cold feet' or 'His hair stood straight up on end.' But when Hinda heard the visitor's name, she did exactly that: she gasped for air.

Even in Zurich, at Pinchas and Mimi's, Zalman Kamionker had been out of place. In Janki's dining room, which was furnished not to be comfortable but to impress, with his clumsy shoes and patched trousers he looked as out of place as Herr Bischoff, the goyish caretaker, at Yom Kippur, when all the men were wearing their white sargenes, and he crept through the prayer room in his worn dark suit to open or close the windows. Except that Herr Bischoff always drew his head in to make himself invisible with his hunched posture, while Zalman Kamionker stood in splay-legged confidence on the green carpet as if he were the man in charge and the others the incomers. He had pushed his greasy leather cap a little back from his forehead, a craftsman who is about to perform a difficult task.

'I have come here,' he said in his strange accent, half Swabian, half Yiddish, 'I have come here because Fräulein Hinda has already left Zurich.'

Hinda stared into her plate as if there could be nothing more interesting in the world that a lump of potato and a fibre of meat.

'By the way: Frau Pomeranz isn't very well. At lunchtime today she was as white as a sheet. But you are not to worry on her account, she said to tell you.'

Who was this strange person, thought Chanele, bringing her news of Mimi?

'I have something I would like to tell Fräulein Hinda, if you will permit me,' Kamionker continued.

'If you will permit me,' he said but his whole posture made it clear that he would still have said what he had to say whether anyone minded or not.

Janki sat up very straight, as Monsieur Delormes had done in the event of unwelcome disturbances. This was still his dining room, and he had not invited this strange man. 'Whatever it is – couldn't it wait until tomorrow?'

The question was clearly meant rhetorically, but Zalman seemed to be deaf to undertones. He thought for a moment, with the serious face of a man who has a serious decision to make, and then shook his head. 'No,' he said. 'It can't wait till tomorrow.'

And without anyone asking him to, he took a chair and joined them at the table.

'He's not one to stand on ceremony,' thought Chanele.

'Would you perhaps like a plate as well?' Janki asked sarcastically.

'That's very kind of you.' The uninvited visitor shook his head. 'Maybe later.' He put both hands on the table cloth the way one prepares a tool that one is going to use later. His fingernails weren't quite clean.

Hinda was still holding her spoon. A grey thread of potato soup dripped unnoticed back onto the plate.

'*Alors?*' said Janki patiently. Monsieur Delormes had always said '*Alors?*' in exactly that tone as well.

Kamionker nodded gratefully, as if he had just been given the floor at a public assembly. 'So it's like this,' he said, 'I was in Zurich at this Congress, and now it's over.'

Only now did Chanele match him up with the man Mimi had told her about. 'You're the man from America,' she said.

'The Yankee from Kolomea, that's right.'

'And you've come all the way to Baden just to say goodbye to my daughter?'

Arthur glanced at Hinda out of the corner of his eye. Her teeth were sunk firmly into her lower lip, as he had seen at Aunt Golde's. 'That must hurt,' Arthur thought.

'So it's like this,' Kamionker repeated, 'for the last few days I've been at this Congress, and I met a man from Vitebsk. A shoemaker, but a nebbish as weedy as a tailor. His brother emigrated to New York, and so did two of his uncles.'

'Could you kindly explain to us why that should interest us?' François interrupted him in his most rudely polite voice.

Kamionker looked at him with unexcited curiosity, as a tourist might look at an unusual piece of local architecture. 'It wouldn't interest you,' he said. 'But it might interest your sister. Mightn't it, Fräulein Hinda?'

'I've no idea why,' Hinda said.

Arthur was surprised. He had a fine ear for such things, and there was something in her voice that he didn't know.

'I'll happily tell you,' said Zalman Kamionker.

Hinda threw her head back; it wasn't clear whether she did so in a gesture of rejection, or because it set off her hair.

'This shoemaker,' Kamionker continued, 'Jochanan, is his name, by the way, like Rabbi Jochanan out of the Talmud who was also a shoemaker, so this shoemaker has his whole mishpocha in America. And he himself is sitting there in Vitebsk, where a socialist is as popular as a flea in a marriage bed. We know what a shoemaker earns: less than nothing, and from that he still has to make Shabbos. By the time he has enough money saved to go to America, he will have a beard to the ground. Although he has no beard. When he read Karl Marx for the first time, he cut it off. The same day, he told me.'

Kamionker told his story without haste, a man who is used to speaking in front of an audience and not expecting to be interrupted.

'For ten days he moaned at me about how much he missed his brother, every day it was about this unnecessary Congress. His krechzening was unbearable in the end.' The Meijers were Swiss Jews, and the word wasn't familiar to them, but they all understood it anyway. 'What was I supposed to do?' asked Kamionker. 'I had to shut him up somehow.' He spread his arms as if to hug somebody. 'So I gave him my ticket.'

The Jewish cloak-makers of New York had given money, each according to his ability, to send Zalman Kamionker as their delegate to the big Congress in Switzerland. A crossing – in the cheapest steerage class, of course, but a crossing is a crossing and you're not handed it on a plate – and a ticket for the railway. Only in fourth class, obviously, but it still cost money. And what did he do with it? He gave it all to someone he'd only just met. To a shoemaker from Vitebsk.

'He's already on the way,' said Kamionker. 'Zurich-Paris. Paris-Le Havre. Le Havre-New York. Although, there, God knows, they have quite enough shoemakers already. Yes, Fräulein Hinda, that's how it is.'

Hinda didn't look at him, ignored him with all her might, as one can only do with a person who interests one more than anyone else does, and so it was Chanele who asked him. 'And you?'

'I'm staying in Switzerland,' said Kamionker. 'A tailor has it easy. He can starve anywhere.'

'Then go ahead and starve!' said François icily. 'Just please don't do it here.'

Kamionker gave him a friendly smile, as if he'd just been paid a compliment. He had delivered lots of speeches at lots of assembles and knew how to deal with hecklers.

'That's an interesting moustache you have there,' he said. 'I didn't know Purim was celebrated so late in Switzerland.' Purim is the festival of ridiculous disguises.

If Chanele hadn't laughed so loudly, François would doubtless have come up with a brilliant riposte.

Kamionker turned a contemptuous shoulder towards him, as one does to a defeated opponent upon whom one doesn't even have to keep an eye, and turned to Janki. 'And as I'm going to be staying here,' he said, 'I have something I'd like to talk to you about, Herr Meijer.'

'He's looking for a job,' thought Janki. 'He's a tailor, and I have a clothes shop. But like hell am I going to put such a louse in my fur.'

'I'm sorry...' he began. But Kamionker cut in.

'Perhaps you'd rather we withdrew to a different room?'

'I wouldn't dream of it,' said Janki, and reached for his walking stick as if for a weapon.

'That's fine too.' Kamionker struck his hands together, so loudly that Arthur gave a start, and stretched, making his joints crack.

'He has strong hands,' Hinda thought, and waited with bated breath to see what he would say next.'

'Do you have a union in your company?' said Zalman Kamionker.

A union? Was that why he had come?

'Why do you want to know that?' asked Janki.

'Well,' said Kamionker, 'it would make things easier to understand.'

'My employees don't need a union.'

'Maybe,' said Kamionker, 'or maybe not. We could argue about that. But another time. We'll have other opportunities.'

'The hell we will,' thought Janki.

'It's like this,' said Kamionker. 'If you'd negotiated with unions, you would know that there are only two kinds of demands: the ones you can talk about, and the ones that are non-negotiable. Is that clear?'

'The man is meshuga,' thought Janki. 'Simply meshuga.'

'In our case, Herr Meijer: we can talk about anything.' Kamionker held his open palms out in front of him, as chiefs did in Arthur's books about Indians, when they wanted to show that they hadn't unburied the hatchet. 'I'll go still further; you can determine how you want to have it done, and it will be done like that. I am a peaceful man. Only one thing is not negotiable.'

'What's he actually talking about?' thought Hinda.

'Absolutely non-negotiable,' said Zalman Kamionker.

'What are you actually talking about?' asked Janki.

'About Fräulein Hinda, of course. I'm going to marry her.'

Had he said 'marry'?

Fat Christine had spent the whole evening in the kitchen consoling the weeping Louisli. The two girls knew nothing at all about what was going on in the dining room. And this time there really would have been something worth listening to at the door.

Janki said no, of course he said no. Here was a complete and total stranger, a man who was nothing and had nothing, and he just wanted...'Out of the question,' said Janki, and because Kamionker who'd dropped in out of nowhere didn't seem to hear it, he repeated it again, 'Out of the question. Absolutely out of the question.' One had heard a few things about Galician customs, that they were rougher than elsewhere, in the East such rag-and-bone-man behaviour might be common practice; he was unable to judge. That is: his judgement was firm, absolutely firm, and no further discussion was required for that reason. They were not in the Balkans, and certainly not in America, so the issue was not open for debate, it wasn't open for debate, and there was an end to it, full stop, period. By the way it was probably the best for all if Kamionker took his leave forthwith.

Herr Kamionker smiled, quite peacefully, as he had once smiled quite peacefully at Simon Heller of the tallis-weaving mill in Heller's office, and said Herr Meijer must not have heard him correctly, he had said quite clearly that this point was non-negotiable.

Janki raised his stick and was about to bring it down on the table, but lowered it again straight away, not out of fear, of course, after all, he'd been in the war, but he'd just had the lion's-head handle glued back on, and if it happened again, they had warned him in the turner's workshop, that fine piece of craftsmanship might no longer be reparable.

At that François leapt to his feet, the tips of his moustache on end, and grabbed Kamionker by the collar, grabbed the thick material of his jacket with his fist and was about to throw out this unruly guest, but Kamionker just sat there as if no one were tugging away at him, and it was only when François grabbed him with his other hand as well and tried to pull him up as a clumsy person might try to lift a heavy piece of luggage, that Kamionker flicked him away, there could be no better word for it, he just flicked him away, wearing an expression as if it were just a piece of high-spirited banter among friends.

That was exactly how he had smiled, with big white teeth, in the Palm Garden, when he had tripped over Hinda and landed right in her lap.

'The police!' François gasped breathlessly. 'We need to call the police.'

'Police? Narrishkeit!' said Zalman Kamionker. That was another word that people in Switzerland didn't know and yet understood. He picked a crystal carafe off the table and weighed it in his hand as if checking its suitability as a missile. François took shelter behind his chair.

Arthur noticed with some pride and a little disbelief that he wasn't scared at all, even though he would have had every reason to be.

Kamionker looked at the carafe thoughtfully and set it back down on the table-cloth. 'You are rich people,' he said Janki. 'All right then. It's not something I've chosen myself, but there's nothing I can do about it. So if it's about the dowry – we don't need one. I've always made everything in my life with my own hands.'

'It's not about the dowry!' said Janki in too loud a voice, and propped a hand on his hip as Monsieur Delormes had always done.

'As you wish. I've said before: on all these points I am happy to abide by your wishes.'

It was the second time in only two days that Janki began to shout. Louisli would have had more to eavesdrop on today than yesterday, but she was too busy pouring her heart out to the fat cook. You can pour out a full heart for as long as you like, it doesn't get any emptier.

And neither did Janki's fury subside just because he gave it such noisy expression. On the contrary: it just went on growing until he could only make little yapping noises, as when one runs out of breath on an over-inflated stomach. Except that in this instance there was no sodium bicarbonate powder to grant him relief.

Eventually he fell completely silent. The eruption was over. Zalman Kamionker had waited quite calmly, a specialist in pyrotechnics who knows exactly when a Roman candle has burnt itself out. Then he turned to Chanele. 'And what do you think, Frau Meijer?'

Chanele looked at him for a long time, from the greasy leather cap to the peasant shoes, from the unkempt hair to the fingernails with the black edges. She raised her eyebrows so that the black line seemed to occupy the middle of her forehead, and then asked the question that Arthur would have asked long ago if he had not been a little boy but an adult just like the others. 'Have you talked to Hinda about it?'

Hinda was still holding her soup spoon, and now set it down as carefully as one might set a lucky ladybird that had landed on one's hand from a leaf.

'Nu?' asked Chanele, when Kamionker didn't reply.

Zalman was embarrassed as only someone can be for whom embarrassment is an entirely unfamiliar feeling.

'So it's like this,' he said and hesitated. 'I thought I had to ask the parents first.'

'Narrishkeit,' said Chanele, already knowing that this would become one of her favourite words.

'I wanted...' said Kamionker.

'Ask her!'

Meanwhile Janki had recovered the use of speech. 'It's absolutely out of the...' he began.

'Scha!' said Chanele.

Zalman Kamionker, who had been so confident until this point, now studied his hands, like an instrument that he had never learned to play. Then he held them out to Hinda, as shyly as a little child handing a bouquet to a queen. 'Fräulein Hinda,' he asked, 'will you...?'

Hinda kept him waiting, and only after a few endless seconds she said, 'What am I supposed to do? If it's non-negotiable...'

31

It was June already, and Mimi still wasn't feeling any better. She was so bloated that she couldn't bring herself to look in the mirror, although – '*Comme ça me dégoûte!*' – she couldn't keep anything down. Pinchas sometimes heard her retching when he got up very early in the morning to lay tefillin.

Sophie, the successor to the unfortunate Regula, was something of an expert in herbs, and treated Mimi with teas whose exact recipes, as she proudly explained, were in her family only ever passed on to the oldest daughter, to some extent as a dowry. She herself, she said with a significant expression, would probably pass on the secret knowledge to her niece, because Sophie didn't like men. Pinchas often hadn't even heard the names of the plants and roots that she boiled up in his kitchen, and who passed on their penetrating smell to his food. Mimi at first swore by Sophie's arts, and a tea from a garden weed called cinquefoil – Sophie called it crampwort – even brought her a certain relief. But then, after a visit to her home village, Sophie made a brew of buckthorn bar that gave Mimi diarrhoea for several days. That was the end of the herbal cures, and a new maid called Gesine Hunziker was taken on.

Mimi was also – although Pinchas wasn't allowed to know anything about it – again attending séances at Madame Rosa's. But the voices from beyond could give her no advice, quite the contrary. The only message she received was, 'There is much youth in you,' and Mimi perceived this as transcendental mockery, because she was secretly convinced that her problems had to do with a feared time in the life of a woman, which Golde had prudishly referred to as 'the change'. Mimi was far too young for that, in fact, but she had always been particularly troubled by such things, other people had no idea how.

For weeks Pinchas had wanted to seek advice from Dr Wertheim, but Mimi categorically refused; she didn't like dealing with doctors. At the time when she lost her chid, no one had been able to help her, and spending a pile of money just so that someone can explain in Latin that he hasn't a clue? *Certainement pas!*

'I'm not sick,' she said, 'I just don't feel good, and it wouldn't be half as bad if you didn't make such a fuss about it.'

That Sunday, when Pinchas had to go to Endingen early for a debate, her feeling of nausea wouldn't subside. In fact Mimi had wanted to go with him; she hadn't seen her childhood friend Anne-Kathrin for ages, and it would have been a good opportunity. Anne-Kathrin still lived in Endingen, but hadn't lived in the school house for a long time. She had married the eldest son of master butcher Gubser, and had since then written Mimi regular letters, in which, in her tiny handwriting, she had told her of all the amazing progress that her four unusually gifted children were making week by week. The terrifying perfection of these offspring had been reason enough for the childless Mimi to put the trip off time and again, and secretly she was quite glad to have the state of her health as an excuse to herself. More than an excuse, God knows, because the very thought of the smoke from the locomotive filled her mouth with such a bitter taste that in the end she gave in and promised to call the doctor, 'yes, definitely today'. Dr Wertheim was part of the community, he shouldn't have been sent for on Shabbos, but on a Sunday that wasn't a problem. And now if Pinchas would be so kind as to set off on his trip, Mimi said, and not miss his train on her account, because his excessive concern would eventually turn her into a truly sick woman.

Pinchas had to stop outside the flat door and take a deep breath with his eyes closed. My God, how he loved that woman! She simply had to regain her health!

He had prepared well for the debate in Endingen, had even collected far too many arguments until he finally he thought he had a retort for every possible objection. After all, he wasn't just a shochet, he was also a journalist. He was good with words, he was a modern person, even though he took the traditions of his faith seriously, and that made him – he had reached the conclusion after initial doubts – the ideal representative of the Jewish perspective. He could counter the animal-protection people who thought shechita was an unnecessary cruelty with the experience of his professional life. In the abattoirs where Jewish and Christian butchers worked side by side, he really knew better than all these sensitive do-gooders. There was no place there for the delicacies of the drawing-room, either on the Jewish or the Christian side. Sausages and chops didn't grow on trees. And what was far more important: he could prove to them with concrete examples that the modern captive bolt method that had been given such publicity over the last few years by no means guaranteed a painless slaughter. In the end, regardless of which method one used, it all depended on the sure hand of the slaughterer. And who did his work more carefully? The uninterested Christian butcher's boy who could always improve matters with a second attempt, a stab to the neck or a blow to the head, even with two or three blows when the animal was still twitching, or the Jewish slaughterer who could turn the whole animal into treyf with a small mistake, who risked his own parnooseh at each individual slaughter, and who therefore...No, he couldn't say 'parnooseh', he told himself, he had to speak the language of the people in the hall, and not make himself an outsider.

So he had put on his most goyish suit, grey virgin wool and actually far too hot for this time of year. He had taken the suit as settlement of an unpaid meat bill from tailor Turkawka, who had actually made the piece for a professor at the Confederate Technical College, who had wanted to wear it at his inaugural lecture. But then he hadn't been appointed after all, and had never collected the suit. Mimi had told Pinchas off at the time for being too easy-going and allowing himself to be exploited, but basically she had been proud of him, he had seen that she was. Turkawka had adapted the suit for him; it fit perfectly, and Pinchas didn't look at all Jewish in it. Apart from his little black silk cap, of course. Perhaps in the service of the good cause he should just...

Pinchas gave a start. He had been completely lost in his thoughts; that happened when you had the train compartment all to yourself. And on the journey he had planned to go through all the precautionary measures that were to be observed in a correct shechita; there could, he thought, be no more convincing proof of how much care was taken in shechita slaughtering to ensure that the animal was caused no unnecessary pain. First of all, he counted them off to himself, the blade was to be carefully checked, because even the tiniest nick on which anything could get caught or on which the tissue might tear would make the whole slaughtering process invalid and the meat unsellable. The cut itself must be carried out in one go, without pressure and only with the sharpness of the blade; the windpipe and the oesophagus had to be completely severed one after the other. 'These are all precautionary measures,' he would say, 'to cause the animal as little pain as possible. So you see,' he would say, 'you may not be anti-Semites yourselves, but your vote would still confirm those people in their belief that things can be achieved with prejudice and harassment.' Yes, that was what he would say.

But then his thoughts drifted away. What was he doing delivering speeches? Was he a politician? He would have been better off staying at home and looking after Mimi. What was wrong with her? She had always liked to complain and enjoyed her little ailments, she had turned every molehill into a mountain and every crisis into a drama. It was precisely because she was behaving differently this time that he was worried. Every time he asked her about her condition she evaded the issue, accused him of making her ill with all his endless questions, and one didn't have to be constantly singing and dancing just to prove to one's dear husband that one was feeling well. As long as it wasn't anything danger-ous! This evening, immediately after his return, he would talk to Dr Wertheim and refuse to be satisfied with the empty, comforting phrases that doctors were so good at. No, he would insist...

He had arrived in Baden without noticing.

To his surprise, it wasn't Janki waiting for him at the station, but Chanele. Janki preferred not to come to Endingen, he had said to tell him, after mature consideration it seemed more correct to him as a Frenchman not to get involved in such purely Swiss matters. Chanele delivered the message in a tone which left no doubt that Janki really had different reasons. It was simply that he chose to avoid situations in which his role was not entirely clear.

She as a woman, Chanele said, was not a desirable presence at such political assemblies, but no one could prevent her from visiting her foster-father, and then to take him, if Salomon wanted to go, to the Guggenheim in the afternoon, he was an old man now, after all, and needed the support of an arm. The idea of a frail Salomon Meijer made Pinchas chuckle; in spite of his years, the cattle-trader went walking across country for a few hours every day, swinging his umbrella as he had long ago.

Chanele hadn't ordered a coach for them, and instead waited with a box-wagon and pair. Gold letters on a green background sang the praises of the Modern Emporium and its comprehensive range. 'At the weekend the carts are just parked in the shed,' Chanele said by way of apology. 'Why throw money out of the window to no good end?'

So the three of them squeezed onto the coach box. The coachman subserviently made himself very small and actually leaned over to the side to leave enough room for Chanele, and sometimes asked solicitously whether Madame Meijer was really sitting comfortably. He smelled of the stale smoke of his curly Virginia cigar, which had gone out when he was waiting and which he didn't dare relight, and his presence made conversation impossible. Chanele inquired after Mimi's health, and Pinchas shook his head dubiously. Then they fell silent again.

It was Sunday, and no one was working in the fields. The weather was calm, and the few clouds drifted slowly across the sky. One might have thought it wasn't just human beings who were taking a break, but nature as well, a breather between blossom and fruit.

Chanele felt reminded of the time – was it really more than two decades ago – when she had worked in the newly founded French Drapery. Back then, too, they had often sat crammed in the coachman's box, whenever a friendly driver stopped for her and Janki, early in the morning or on the way home to Endingen. Then Janki had tried not to touch her, but she had always been very aware of his body, so close to hers. She hadn't been happy in those days – where does it say in the Shulchan Orech that you have to be happy? – but it had been a vivid unhappiness, a pulsating sadness, not the impersonal coexistence that had become her fate. Chanele would have liked to be properly sad once again, just to know that she hadn't lost the ability.

The houses of Endingen came into view, and when he approached his parents' house, where someone else had been running the butcher's shop for a long time now, Pinchas armed himself against a surge of homesickness and melancholy. But when they drove past he saw that the place meant nothing more to him. He had grown out of Endingen once and for all.

The carts and coaches were parked so densely around the Guggenheim that there was no room for the broad box-wagon to get through. 'As if there was anything for free,' the coachman grumbled sullenly. He couldn't force his way through to the entrance to the inn, but had to let Pinchas climb down first, and was quite disappointed when Chanele too decided to walk the few streets to the old double house. He would rather have driven his boss up like a princely postilion, with snorting steeds and a bright rosette on his top hat.

In the pub room there was hardly an empty chair to be found, even though the meeting was due to start at three o'clock. The wave of conversation, laughter and shouting swept over Pinchas so loudly that he took an involuntary step backwards and had to take a second run even to enter the room.

He didn't often visit inns, he wasn't really familiar with these places, and yet he immediately had the feeling that there was something different here, something that you didn't usually see in such places. Only at first he couldn't quite put his finger on what that different thing was. Until all of a sudden he understood: usually one sits in an inn at night, it's dark, and in the lamplight all you see is faces, hands and glasses. Here the sun shone through the windows and gave the clouds of smoke from the many pipes and cigars an almost festive glow. The guests, all men, also seemed to be in a holiday mood. While normally in the country people carefully nurse their beers or wines to derive the greatest possible amount of comfort from their invested money, here they were boisterously clinking glasses, no sooner had they been given their schnapps than they ordered another one. The mood was more like a victory party at a gun-club party than the meeting of a Popular Education Association.

The door to the hall where the actual event was to take place was wide open, but two sturdy young men, dark blue ribbons around their muscular upper arms, flanked the entrance and made sure that no one entered the holy of holies prematurely. They stood there motionless as sentries, with severe expressions, visibly impressed by their own importance.

'Seek and ye shall find,' said a voice directly beside Pinchas. 'Herr Pomeranz! I recognised you immediately. Yes, yes, true beauty stands the test of time.'

The schoolmaster himself had changed a lot. Above all he seemed to be much smaller than Pinchas remembered, the miniature copy of a vanished original. In Pinchas's day Jewish children had only gone to the cheder and not, as they did quite naturally these days, to the community school too, but that had not diminished the authority of the schoolmaster. On the contrary: precisely because one had not experienced them personally, one believed all the horror stories that the village children told about his teaching methods.

Now an elderly little man was standing there, with thin legs and a pot belly that looked as if he had stuffed a pillow up his waistcoat. His beard was just as bushy as before, but now it looked as if it had been stuck on. His voice had got shriller and thinner as well, just as a bottle, when being filled, reaches its highest note just before overflowing.

'The good endures,' said the little man. 'Slow and steady wins the race. It took me a long time to found my Popular Education Association, but then my son's stepfather said to me: Let's just do it. And look at this onslaught, this enthusiasm. This delight in the competition of opinions and arguments! *Arma virumque cano!* Do you understand Latin?'

'Enough for that,' Pinchas said.

'Who would have thought that in such unusual circumstances we would...? You remember the last time we met? It was in my garden, in my modest Tusculum, and you...But I see you don't like to be reminded of it. Don't worry, I am as quiet as the grave.' He put a finger to his pursed lips and blinked at Pinchas with unpleasant familiarity. 'Come, come, they'll keep a chair for us, but not for long. So many people have come to hear the song and see the chariot-fight.'

He took Pinchas by the arm and pulled him along in his wake. When they made their way through the inn, conversations fell silent as they passed. People nudged one another and whispered.

Pinchas didn't recognise any of the faces, however hard he tried to think back twenty years. They all seemed so young to him, but of course that was ridiculous. He himself had got older.

The first familiar face was that of master butcher Gubser, whom he had often met in the abattoir when his father had taken him there. Gubser had hardly changed, had if anything become more dignified and vicar-like. He leapt to his feet when Pinchas and the schoolmaster approached, and although it was very noisy in the inn, the many little pendants on his watch chain could be heard jangling.

'Young Herr Pomeranz,' he exclaimed, putting his hand on his heart. 'How lovely that you could come. I'm so glad, so glad, so glad.' He took Pinchas's hand and shook it as if he had just met up with a long-lost friend. 'Sit down, please, sit down! I had to fight like a lion for a chair. Will you drink a glass of wine with us?' And when Pinchas politely refused, 'Of course not, how silly of me. Our wine isn't clean enough for you, or however you put it in your books. But we don't have such sensitive stomachs, what do you think, people?'

The two men at the table laughed loudly. You could tell: they would have laughed at anything Gubser said.

Pinchas would have preferred to find a seat elsewhere, but the schoolmaster wouldn't let him. 'Herr Gubser helped me so much with the preparations,' he said, and was childishly delighted by the success of his Popular Education Association. 'I myself would have expected the setting – what blessing it is to be modest! – to be much smaller, in the schoolroom, perhaps, but Alois…'

'One does what one can.' The master butcher bowed slightly to the schoolmaster. 'Did you know, dear Herr Pomeranz, that Anne-Kathrin and my eldest…? Oh, you did? Of course. You people are always well informed. Then you will also now that I have passed on the business to my son and now devote myself only to important matters. The truly important matters.'

The men around the table nodded. Yes, there could be nothing more important.

'Alois,' the schoolmaster said in his piping voice, 'Herr Gubser is in fact the chair of our local league—'

'Cantonal!' one of the men corrected him with an important expression, and again they all nodded.

'You?'

'Who knows more about the suffering of animals than a man of my trade?' said Gubser piously.

'—and he will also be representing the viewpoint of the organisation on the podium today,' piped the schoolmaster. 'I am already looking forward to an informative and peaceful debate, relying only on the power of the superior argument. How does our beloved Goethe poet put it? "With words we can our foes assail."'

Pinchas was not at all happy about the prospect of having to stand up against master butcher Gubser, who was so popular in Endingen, and his facial expression revealed as much with great clarity.

'I cannot imagine a better pairing than the two of us,' said Gubser, and put his hand on his heart again. 'When we are professional colleagues. A *Schlächter* and a *Schächter*. Two types of work with only an L between them. And do you know what that L stands for, my esteemed Herr Pomeranz? For what the *Schächter* sadly lacks. For Love.'

The men at the table applauded.

Pinchas felt himself turning very cold inside. 'If the L does not stand for what the *Schlächter* has too much of,' he said. 'Lies, I mean.'

'But that's—!' one of the men began, but a gesture of Gubser's was enough to silence him.

'Gentlemen!' The schoolmaster would probably have liked to smack them all. 'These are not the tones I wish to hear hereafter. Sober and peaceful, that's how it's to be done. Who lives by the sword dies by the word.'

'Of course,' said Gubser and smiled. 'Peaceful. Absolutely peaceful.'

32

When, in response to an invisible sign, the two doormen stepped aside, allowing access to the hall, there was a great rush, as if there were really – how had the coachman put it? – something for free in there. An elderly man lost his hat in the crush and tried to bend down for it, but the flood of people would not be stemmed by a single individual. Still bending, unable to straighten up in time, he was simply swept along.

In an instant, the table at which Pinchas had so reluctantly taken his seat became the only one where people were still drinking. On the others the glasses and jugs stood empty or at best half-full, so sudden had the general decampment been. Only the men from the league – it had taken Pinchas a while to notice the badge that they all wore on their lapels – sat motionless, like dignitaries on the platform of honour in a festival procession. 'No one takes our seats away,' said Gubser, and the schoolmaster beamed all over his old face and said Alois always thought of everything. It would never, he had to admit, have occurred to him on his own that one would need ushers at such an event, but then he was more a man of intellect than a man of action.

The two ushers who had been guarding the door for so long were stood a beer each by Gubser. They drank them standing to attention in the military style, and had exactly the same foam moustaches above their mouths afterwards.

'Don't we also need to . . . ?' Pinchas was about to get to his feet, but Gubser shook his head.

'Not yet. Keep the people waiting for a while, and they'll pay more attention.

'In school it's exactly the other way round,' said the schoolmaster. 'If you leave them alone too long they become unruly.'

Everyone ignored him.

The door of the inn opened and a few stragglers came in. Because the sunlight was behind them, they were at first seen only as silhouettes. It was only by his umbrella that Pinchas recognised Salomon Meijer. Chanele had come in with him, and a man he didn't know. He must have been from the East, because he wore a kaftan tied with a black cord. The red payot that framed his bearded face seemed to be fastened to the brim of his oversized hat.

'This is Reb Tsvi Löwinger from Lemberg,' said Salomon, introducing the stranger. 'He has come to Switzerland to collect for his yeshiva, and has done me the honour of being my guest over Shabbos.'

The shnorrer nodded his head loftily.

'Reb Tsvi is interested in this event that you are having here. So if no one objects . . . ?'

'We welcome all those who for knowledge strive!' squeaked the schoolmaster. 'What does it say in *Faust*? "I may know much, but I would fain know all."'

'Yes,' said master butcher Gubser, and looked the man in the kaftan up and down. 'I'm happy for him to be here. You can't imagine how happy I am.'

His animal-protection friends giggled, even though Gubser hadn't said anything the slightest bit funny.

Loud laughter echoed from the hall, as if the people in there had been listening to what there were saying.

Salomon turned his face to the door of the hall. 'A lot of people?' he asked.

'You will find a seat, Herr Meijer,' said Gubser. 'I have no worries on that score. You people are practised enough at pushing your way in anywhere.'

Laughter from the hall again.

Salomon waved Pinchas aside. 'It's not looking good,' he whispered.

'I know.' Everyone at the table now drained their glasses as if on command. 'It's not going to be easy.'

But Salomon's concern had nothing to do with the League. 'Reb Tsvi and I took a look at the gematria. You're going into a discussion, a pilpul. Numerical value two hundred and twenty six. But it will be a discussion without a lev, without a heart.'

'It's time!' called Gubser.

'Nu!' said Salomon, and in this instance it meant, 'They will be able to wait a moment longer.'

'I really have to . . .' Pinchas began, but Salomon wouldn't let him finish.

'Take care,' he said, talking more and more quickly. 'Lev has the numerical value of thirty-two. Take that away from two hundred and twenty-six and it leaves one hundred and ninety-four. And what word in the tenach has the gematria of one hundred and ninety-four? Nu?'

'Perhaps you could tell me later, after the . . .'

'Vayiboku,' Salomon said triumphantly. '"And they were parted."'

Pinchas stared blankly.

'The waters of the Red Sea. During the exodus from Egypt.'

'Herr Pomeranz!' cried Gubser.

'You understand what that means,' Salomon said. 'In a discussion held without a heart, there can be no agreement.'

'Enough words have been exchanged, let us at last see deeds.' The school-master had pushed his way between them and pushed Pinchas in front of him like a schoolboy who ignored the bell for the start of the lesson.

'So let's go in,' said Chanele, and wanted to hold out her hand to Salomon. He looked at her as if she was a meshugena, gripped his umbrella more firmly and nodded to Reb Tsvi. The two of them formed the rearguard of a little procession making its way into the assembly.

In the doorway Gubser let Pinchas step in ahead of him.

In the hall of the Guggenheim the men sat closely packed together at long tables; their shoulders touched, and they could hardly reach for their freshly filled beer glasses. They stood side by side along the walls as well, obscuring the sight of the laurel wreaths and club flags in the glass cases.

On the stage a big Swiss flag hung from the ceiling. The man standing in front of it at the lectern looked almost tiny in comparison.

'Has it started already?' Pinchas asked, baffled.

'Of course not,' said Gubser. 'Of course not. It's just a bit of entertainment so that people don't get bored.'

A wave of laughter made it clear that people actually weren't getting bored.

The man at the lectern was reading a poem from a slender volume:

'Here stands the Jew, with dross to sell,' he recited,

> To his Christian clientele.
> And though he knows for trash they pay
> Herr Levi sells it anyway.

'Exactly!' called a voice somewhere in the hall, and the agreement of the others was one big shared exhalation.

> And while the Jew counts out his gold,
> The Christian's produce goes unsold.
> You fool! Behave like Jacob's seed!
> Devote yourself to fraud and greed!

This time it was not an exhalation, but a common shout.

'This is wrong,' Pinchas said furiously.

'Why? It has nothing to do with the subject at hand.' Gubser assumed the suffering face of a man who is constantly obliged to explain the simplest things in the world to others. 'Or did you want to talk about Jewish shops?'

'Of course not!'

'Then I don't understand what you're getting so worked up about, Herr Pomeranz. You people are always so thin-skinned.'

To sit more comfortably, the audience had pushed their benches far back, and now, a rampart in its Sunday best, blocked the passageways between the table. If two ushers had not created a path for the speakers, it would have been impossible for them to get through.

The little man in front of the big flag saw Gubser coming, snapped his book shut and held it aloft. 'This is all in the songbook of Ulrich Dürrenmatt,' he called into the hall. 'Get hold of it if you want to learn something!' Then, to thunderous applause, he stepped away from the lectern.

The long tables that stood at an angle to the stage, didn't reach all the way to the front. Right in front of the steps was a single row of unoccupied chairs, guarded on either side by young lads with blue and black arm bands. They stepped back simultaneously, as precisely as if they had been practising, and freed the path. The schoolmaster sat down in the middle, flanked on each side by Pinchas and the master butcher. The gentlemen from the league sat down in this row as well. There were a few chairs free on both sides. None of the people who had failed to find a seat dared to use them.

Pinchas looked searchingly around, but there was no sign of Salomon and Chanele now. They had probably stopped by the door.

One could sense that the people in the hall were impatient, albeit in a disciplined way. Pinchas was reminded of Simchas Torah, how, in his childhood, the silence required during the service had also been kept only with difficulty, in the knowledge that a bag of sweets was waiting for him at the end.

When the schoolmaster climbed up onto the stage, he was initially greeted with applause. But then the mood quickly changed, when his words of greeting turned into a long address. In an effort to remain on the level of his audience he only quoted Swiss writers, and kept weaving a pithy quote from Gottfried Keller or Conrad Ferdinand Meyer into his remarks. Except that the people hadn't come to hear him set out the goals of his Popular Education Association. A buzzing noise, as if from an irritable swarm of bees, swelled from the back of the hall to the stage, and because the schoolmaster would not be deterred and had now reached Pestalozzi, they started calling for another speaker, at first only a few voices and then more and more. 'Gubser! Gubser!' they shouted.

In a bid to drown out the catcallers – how he would have put them in the corner of his schoolroom, the lines he would have given them to write! – the old schoolmaster's voice grew ever shriller, and so squeaky that the people eventually started laughing at him. When he resignedly announced the first speech and then climbed back down to his seat, it was as if he were running away.

Gubser took the four steps to the stage very slowly, like a parson climbing to the pulpit, collected and calling the assembly to silence. He didn't step behind the lectern straight away, but stood right at the front by the steps, looked into the hall and shook his head sadly. 'You should be ashamed of yourselves,' said master butcher Gubser. 'Just laughing at a man like our schoolmaster. Are you all children?'

That was not what they had expected of him.

'What will the world think of us if you behave so badly?' asked Gubser, and seemed to mean it quite seriously. 'It isn't as if we're just among ourselves here. We have visitors from a long way away. People want to check if we're doing everything correctly, we simple Swiss. Someone has come to us from Lemberg. That is somewhere far away in the East, where the garlic grows. The gentleman's name is Lowy. Or Löwental or something of the kind. I am too stupid to remember those foreign names. But it's something to do with a lion, I'm sure of that. He certainly has a wild mane, at any rate' He pointed to the hall entrance, and people craned their necks round or even stood up to see who he meant. The sudden attention so startled Reb Tsvi that he took shelter behind Salomon, which prompted laughter in their immediate vicinity.

'So, do not shame your country,' said Gubser. 'Or do you want people in Lemberg to say that people in the Aargau don't know how to behave themselves? In Lemberg, of all places, that centre of civilisation, compared to which Paris and London are only shabby little backwaters?' They showed clear signs of relief that Gubser hadn't been serious after all. Those unaccustomed to irony are twice as pleased when it opens itself up to them.

Gubser laughed too, just for a moment, and then made his serious pastor face again. He stepped out from behind the lectern, took a manuscript from the inside pocket of his jacket and carefully aligned the pages. Then he poured himself a glass of water from the carafe that stood ready for the purpose, and took a long sip.

'Dear friends,' he began, reading from his manuscript, 'the reason for meeting here today is a very serious one. In a few weeks we Swiss will be summoned to the urn to vote for a very serious matter that touches the innermost heart of our state. It is not simply about the pros and cons of the duty of stunning before blood is drawn, no that is only the outward occasion. On that Sunday we will all be called to answer a much more fundamental question. Can there, in our country, can there, in a state in which laws are made for all, be special rights for a single small group?'

'No!' cried the hall.

'With all respect for traditions, even if they are not our own…'

271

'This is still a Christian country!' a voice called out.

'With all due respect: can customs which – I do not wish to dispute this for a moment – might have had a certain justification thousands of years ago, can such practices carry more weight in our modern times than the suffering of a tortured animal?'

'No!'

'Let us take another look at the facts!' said Gubser, and began to list all the arguments that Pinchas had expected. He himself, said Gubser, making sentimental eyes, he himself was a friend to the Jews, a friend who welcomed with his heart, with all his heart, the fact that in Switzerland the old narrow-minded barriers had fallen, and that the Israelites were now granted the equal rights that should be nothing more than their due in a modern state. However, he said, and made a long, significant pause after that word, however, it must also be possible to demand that the Jews for their part also acknowledged their newly acquired equality, and did not behave like pettifogging lawyers and only try to pick the raisins out of the cake.

'That's what they're like!' The heckler seemed always to be the same one.

The Jews, and this was not an unreasonable demand, Gubser continued, must accept the duties that came with their new rights, which applied to all the other citizens of the country, and not, as in the question of animal slaughter, insist for a long time on an outdated practice. Indeed, his fraternal feeling towards the Jews went so far, he said, and put his hand on his heart, that he felt compelled, indeed obliged, to voice a warning here. Clinging to Medieval practices could only, in uneducated circles, encourage the belief in unproven tales of horror, as the ritual murder trial in Tisza-Eszlar had demonstrated once again only recently. He himself, and he had thought about the problem for a long time, could only say, 'Only in the stuffy air of outdated practices can such superstition flourish!'

Then Gubser turned his attention to the various methods of animal slaughter. As a butcher of long standing he was confident in all modesty, yes, in all modesty, that he could deliver an expert judgement on his question. He himself had witnessed shechita countless times from close to, and the Jewish shochet Naftali Pomeranz, who was incidentally the father of his adversary today, had always been, if not a close friend, then at least a valued colleague, and he had to admit that the bloodthirsty process had always shaken him to the core. And even though he was not, as anyone who knew him was aware, an old maid who only had to cut her finger with a letter opener to fall into a faint straight away.

The audience, who would have welcomed a little more ribaldry, received his little joke with grateful laughter.

Even throwing the animals down, said Gubser, caused them unnecessary pain, and it was not rare for horns or ribs to be broken, or for innards to be crushed. He would not describe the actual process of shechita in detail, to spare his audience's sensitivities, but only quote what the royal-court veterinarian Dr Sondermann of Munich had said on the subject. One could but admire, he had written in an essay, anyone who could perform this act of human senselessness without internal outrage.

But in order to find a reliable witness, one did not have to go all the way to Munich, Gubser continued, because there were enough experts here in Switzerland who enjoyed an international reputation.

'I hope he's going to mention Siegmund here,' thought Pinchas, because he could easily discredit this entirely biased crown witness of the opponents of shechita. Siegmund was the inventor of a cattle-bolt mask that he was trying to promote across Europe, and therefore had a very personal pecuniary interest in disparaging other competing methods of slaughter.

'The abattoir administrator and veterinarian Siegmund from Basel,' Gubser said, 'has established that the death of an animal in shechita takes between one and a half and three minutes. One and a half to three minutes! And killing slowly, when one could do it quickly, is in my view, gentlemen, nothing but animal torture.'

The first row applauded, and the rest of the audience joined in.

Gubser counted out a whole list of authorities, all of whom described shechita as unnecessarily cruel and no longer in line with the times. During his list of names, titles and the same unchanging arguments, certain of the guests' heads were starting to sink to their chests when Gubser switched direction.

'Anyone who knows me,' he said with his hand on his heart, 'knows that I am a simple person, a man of the people, and I like to call a spade a spade. If it were up to me, I would say at this point, "That's it, that's enough, you know how you have to vote in August."' He raised his hand to stop the incipient applause. 'But here we are, not at an assembly of our league, as one might think in the presence of so many dear and familiar faces, but at the inaugural meeting of the Endingen Popular Education Association. That means that it is not only one side that has the floor; the other side must speak too. How do we say that in Latin again?'

'*Audiatur et altera pars*,' squeaked the schoolmaster.

'You see how much more intelligent that sounds if you don't understand it?'

The audience laughed gratefully.

'So I shall now hand the lectern over to a man who has opinions quite different to my own about shechita.'

273

Somewhere in the hall a shrill whistle rang out.

Gubser shook his head disapprovingly. 'Please, gentlemen,' he said. 'What will our adjudicator from Lemberg think of us?'

Again all heads turned to Reb Tsvi.

'I shall now pass the floor...'

Pinchas straightened his tie.

'It is my great pleasure to pass the floor to...'

Pinchas made a sudden decision. He took his kippah from his head and put it in his pocket.'

'...I shall pass the floor to a man who has studied everything to do with shechita from the bottom up.'

Pinchas got to his feet.

'No Jewish haste, Herr Pomeranz,' said Gubser. 'It isn't your turn yet.' His smile was one of toxic friendliness. 'It is our honour to be able to greet a real rabbi, who will explain to us everything that we do not yet know.'

For one confused moment Pinchas thought that Gubser, unaware that a reb is still a long way from being a rabbi, had suddenly decided to invite the shnorrer Tsvi Löwinger to the lectern.

But it was far worse than that.

With the elastic gait of a tightrope-walker, his watch chain dancing merrily on his belly, a man whom Pinchas would never have expected to see here skipped onto the stage.

Dr Jakob Stern.

33

The defeat was worse than anything that Pinchas could have imagined in his worst nightmares.

Dr Stern, who was also impertinent enough to greet him from the stage as if they were old friends and sparring partners, knew exactly how to get a meeting going. He was a Jewish scholar of the Talmud, he said by way of introduction, a modern Talmud scholar, please note, one who fully and completely accepted the duties of the modern world as Herr Gubser had just accurately described them; after all, we were no longer living in the eighteenth century, but in the nineteenth, and there was no room now for bigoted hypocrisy and wrongheaded piety. (A shout from the first row: 'Quite correct!')

It was with a heavy heart that he had to admit that if truth be told, of course there were still many fellow holders of his office who, in what they called their faith – but faith was not the same as knowledge – were so stubbornly blockheaded that they couldn't even spell the word 'progress'. But such people had, if he might put it in the clearest of terms, no business being in modern, enlightened countries like Switzerland, and might be better off retreating as quickly as possible to those dark realms where their medieval world-view still prevailed. To Lemberg, for example.

Heads turned to the back.

Reb Tsvi, who spoke only Yiddish, hadn't quite been able to follow the speaker's words. But he had understood the name of his home town, and when everyone looked at him now he thought he was being welcomed, and waved back.

The hall growled like a watchdog.

He himself did not come from a metropolis exactly, Dr Stern continued, but from the little town of Buttenhausen in Swabia, which could easily be compared to Endingen. But it was his experience, he said, and bowed to his audience, a magician who is about to pull a rabbit from a hat, it was his enjoyable experience that in smaller places of this kind practical common sense was at home precisely among the so-called simple folk, who weren't afraid of a bit of hard work, and who had acquired everything they owned through the sweat of their own brow.

Yes, said the hall, that was exactly how it was, and if people at the top would only listen to them more often, lots of things would be better.

In the big cities people liked to believe, Dr Stern said, that they were the navel of the world, when in fact they were a quite different part of the body, of which one might only be aware if one looked backwards.

He had often used the joke before, and knew that he would have to give the hall time. But then they exploded with laughter and struck the tables with the palms of their hands.

Dr Stern gave a complacent little skip. His watch chain skipped with him.

So he knew, he continued, that the people before him today were not the kind who would allow their minds to be obfuscated in the long term with big words and complicated theories.

Certainly not, the hall opined, and waved the waiters over with their beer glasses, which were empty yet again.

But it was precisely that kind of obfuscation being practised from a particular direction, and it was urgently necessary that a fresh wind be allowed to blow in. The whole debate was in fact entirely without foundation. Absolutely unnecessary. To prove this to them, he invited them to take an excursion into the world of the Talmud, an obscure and strange world, he must say without further ado, in which many people had got lost in the past. The man from Lemberg – heads turned – in his outmoded garb was a good example of the kind of people who flourished in that world. But he promised his listeners, Dr Stern said, that he would take them by the hand and guide them safely out of the labyrinth of pseudological pitfalls. Were they brave enough to follow him on this expedition?

The people in the hall didn't quite grasp what it was that he wanted of them, but they were certainly brave, and they liked this speaker. They had only known him for a few minutes, but they were putty in his hands.

All the fat volumes of the Talmud, Dr Stern said, were concerned only with using all kinds of logical convolutions and distortions to derive from the Old Testament laws and prohibitions that were not even mentioned in it. One must imagine such a Talmud rabbi as a less-than-pure lawyer, who liked nothing more than to talk to pieces the clear and intelligible text of a contract until it seemed to mean the precise opposite of what was actually agreed in it. Would anyone who has endured such legal acrobatics to his own detriment in real life now please raise his hand?

It had happened to all of them at least once.

Then they would easily be able to understand what he was about to explain to them. In the Mosaic Law, to which rabbis referred constantly as the supreme authority, there was in fact – and this would come as a surprise – not a single word to say that animals destined for consumption need to have their throats severed with a long knife. Not a single word!

The hall was amazed.

'Only in the fiftieth book of Moses, chapter twelve, verse twenty-one, does it even mention the subject. You are certainly all Bible-reading men, and you know the passage off by heart (laughter), but for the few who might not be able to remember it right now, he would happily repeat it: "If the place which the Lord thy God hath chosen to put his name there be too far from thee, then thou shalt kill of thy herd and of thy flock, which the Lord hath given thee, as I have commanded thee, and thou shalt eat in thy gates whatsoever thy soul lusteth after."' As soon as Dr Stern quoted verses from the Bible, in spite of all his unbelief he assumed once more the god-fearing expression that had certainly served him well in his time as a pulpit orator.

'"Thou shalt kill of thy flock as I have commanded thee," it says, and nothing more. Not a word about long knives or severed throats. Only "as I have commanded thee". But *how* God commanded is recorded nowhere in the Bible, you can read the Old Testament from cover to cover and the New straight afterwards. And because it doesn't say anywhere, interpreters and exegetes set about referring to an oral tradition that no one could prove and no one could refute. This is more or less as if, to put it in the simplest terms, one were to write in a contract with one's neighbours: "we want to keep it as we have always kept it." Then at some point a lawyer and twister of the law would come along and slip the most impossible things into the clause, until eventually one had not only granted the neighbour a right of way, but signed over one's house and chattels.

'"Thou shalt kill of thy flock as I have commanded thee."' In a religious sermon, the exception rather than the rule in the Jewish tradition, the orator would quote a verse from the Bible over and over again, to highlight a different interpretation and suggest an even deeper wisdom could be gained from it. Dr Stern, delivering a kind of sermon of his own, did the same.

'"Thou shalt kill of thy flock as I have commanded thee."' However, slaughtering was also mentioned in another passage of the Old Testament, where it was expressly stated that one had to spill the blood of the animals. '"Thou shalt offer the blood upon the altar of the Lord Thy God."' But in those verses they meant only sacrificial animals, not everyday slaughter, which is something quite different. The Bible also made a linguistic distinction, and they were to forgive him if he now had to make a slight detour into philology. 'You know how we scholars are: we always want to prove that we've actually learned something at university.' (Laughter.)

It was really only in those passages discussing the slaughter of sacrificial animals that the Bible used the word 'shachat', which meant the slicing of the neck, and whose linguistic root was also present in the word 'shechita'.

But where the everyday killing of animals was concerned, as in the verse he had just quoted, the word was 'sabach', and anyone could see that two very different words also meant two different things, that much was obvious to anyone who hadn't twisted his brain into a knot studying the Talmud. Where it said 'shachat', the animal's throat had to be sliced. The word 'sabach' also included any other method of killing.

Of course the rabbis had noticed this contradiction as well, and as religious shysters they had tried to magic it away with an argumentative somersault. Ramban, for example, who was one of the most important Talmudic commentators, had seen fit to interpret the clear word of the Bible thus: 'When God said "Thou shalt slaughter as I have commanded" he did not mean "In everyday life", but: "As I have commanded in the case of sacrificial animals." Hence Ramban, believing that he knew better than God himself, claimed that what the Lord had really meant was, "Grab your knives and slash away!"'

The hall cried, 'Boo!' and was proud to have caught a medieval scholar cheating.

'Of course this is quite a hairy argument,' said Dr Stern, and was now unable to stand still with delight at his own brilliance. 'But then these gentlemen sometimes are quite hairy, like our friend from Lemberg who is so industriously taking notes at the back.' Laughter and general head-turning.

RebTsvi hadn't been taking any notes at all, just trying to follow the address as best he could. But in the heads of the participants he was now a spy, someone who had come to keep an eye on them, and they really didn't know why they should put up with such meddling.

'I'll sum up,' said Dr Stern.

Perhaps they should just throw the interloper out the door. What was the point of having bouncers?

'I'll sum up!' There was no bell with which they could have called the meeting to order, but Dr Stern hammered on the lectern until they listened to him again. 'According to Mosaic law, and I say this to you as a trained Jewish theologian, there can be no question of so-called shechita as a religious duty. All rules in that direction are an invention of medieval Talmudic Judaism, and cannot be derived from the word of the Bible itself. So there is no reason to agree to any exceptional laws on the basis of a false understanding of religious tolerance. Thank you for your attention.'

The hall cheered him, and as he left he thanked them for the ovation with a series of tripping little steps and bows that would have befitted a circus performer. He looked as if he would have liked to come on stage again and deliver his whole speech again *da capo*.

But now it was Pinchas's turn to speak.

It was a disaster.

They didn't listen to him at all, and why should they have? The shopkeepers and craftsmen and farmers in the hall had all suddenly become specialists in religious history as well as ancient Hebrew linguistics, and wouldn't have their heads muddled up any further. Every time Pinchas tried to start talking about the moral obligation of a tradition many thousands of years old, they bellowed *sabach!* and *shachat!* to drown him out. He had only to say, 'In my experience!' and already they were shouting, 'Experience as an animal torturer!' and the roaring started up again. Master butcher Gubser had shown them that shechita was nothing but bloodthirsty carnage, and this Dr Stern had also told them that the Jews had even forged the Holy Bible. So why should they listen to him?

Gubser's comparison of methods of slaughter had been one-sided and partial. But how to refute it? He would no longer be able to find anyone to listen to that kind of evidence here. You can't halt the storm with your bare hands. And Dr Stern's distortion of the Talmud? How was Pinchas supposed to argue with that? With Rashi and Onkelos and other sages? They would have mocked him as a medieval sophist. No, the hall had delivered its verdict, and was announcing it in drunken chants.

Then they started singing too, only to drown him out at first, and then because they liked it. 'Hail to Helvetia,' they sang, and all bold sons they were, as once St Jacob saw, ready for fight. Their mouths opened and closed as if all by themselves, and no longer belonged to them, they drummed out the beat on the tables with their beer mugs, and would probably have marched off somewhere if they could, no matter where.

In the front row the schoolmaster had stood up and was waving his arms around, trying to calm everyone down. But the song was stronger than he was, and his waving gradually turned into conducting, he picked up the rhythm, and guided it and for the first time really belonged to this founding evening of his Popular Education Association. Master butcher Gubser and his animal protectors sat there with their arms folded and had nothing to do with the whole thing.

The people were just singing for themselves now, and had completely forgotten Pinchas. He carefully took one step aside, and then another, the alley was quite close by, and then he had reached it and disappeared behind the stage. On a small table beside the curtain pull was a half-empty beer mug. Here Dr Stern had probably given himself Dutch courage before and after his performance. A small door leading straight to the street was open.

They were still singing in the hall. 'Standing like rocky cliffs,' they sang, and so they did, upright and manly and swollen-chested. Ne'er did they peril shun, bold mortal risks did run, and they were happy because they had found something to defend, if only an animal protection league.

Some of them knew all the verses, others started again with the first one, until their voices became a jumble and finally fell silent. But they had sung enough now, and wanted to do something at last. There was no one on the stage now, and they weren't surprised. That Jews are cowards and run away as soon as you put up any opposition, they had known for ever. But at the back of the hall, there was still that foreigner, that spy, and they wanted to show him what was what and how the land lay. No one needed to tell them what to do to him, they knew already. If someone like that thought he could just come from Lemberg and obstruct their freedom of speech, he could face the consequences.

The bouncers were waiting for an instruction from master butcher Gubser, but in the hall everyone was on their feet, they were even standing on the benches, so they had to take the initiative and do as they saw fit. With arms linked they blocked the people's way, but weren't able to hold them back for long. But it was long enough for Reb Tzvi Löwinger to get himself to safety, slam the hall door behind him and run across the floor of the tap-room and out into the street.

Then the charging crowd came to a standstill all by itself, because someone was lying on the floor right outside the hall door, legs twitching. It wasn't the foreigner from Lemberg, but cattle trader Meijer, whom almost all of them knew, another Jew, but a decent fellow, and they knew the woman kneeling beside him as well, her name was Chanele and she had grown up here in Endingen.

No one had done anything to Salomon Meijer, certainly not with a fist or a beer mug. He had just fallen over all by himself, without anybody even touching him. Dr Reichlin, who was also in the animal-protection league, said it must have been a sudden stroke, as could happen to anyone at any time; it needn't have anything to do with the excitement of the moment. He couldn't supply a good prognosis, sorry though he was, he knew of cases that had gone on for months, but bringing such a patient back to life was beyond the medical art.

Then they carried him out to the back, carried the still heavy boy across the stage past the Swiss flag. The other way wouldn't have been such a good idea, because there was a noisy post-meeting party on the go, and the people were singing again.

'The moving finger writes, and having writ moves on,' said the school-master, and even the master butcher was very sorry about the whole affair. It was really an unfortunate coincidence, he said, that it had had to happen here of all places.

Chanele had run ahead to look for the coachman.

They laid the old cattle trader on a bed of fabric bales ready for delivery in the cart the following day. Salomon was still breathing, quite regularly, in fact, but eyes had rolled back in their sockets and his tongue hung out of his mouth.

When they were about to set off one of the bouncers came hurrying out of the Guggenheim, his black and blue armband still around his sleeve, and brought Salomon Meijer's umbrella out after him.

They drove to Baden, where Janki had long offered his father-in-law a room in the big flat.

The last words of Salomon Meijer, beheimes dealer and gematria artist, had been these: 'Why is the numerical value of "shachat" so much higher than "sabach"?' Then he gave up the ghost.

On the train back to Zurich Pinchas shared his compartment with two men who talked about their culinary preferences throughout the whole of the journey. They didn't recognise him as a Jew and tried to involve him in a conversation about the relative merits of brawn and calf's head. He only answered in monosyllables, which prompted a sniffy reaction. It seemed that this gentleman was too refined to talk to them.

All along Löwenstrasse Pinchas drew out each step, and yet the way to the Sankt-Anna-Gasse seemed shorter than ever. Sometimes he even simply came to a standstill, out of pure cowardice, even though he excused himself by staying that he still had to find the right phrase. At the same time he was aware that there are no painless ways of telling a woman that her father is dying.

He had reached the house before he was ready, and rummaged awkwardly in his pocket for a key, even though the door could not have been locked at this time of day.

In the stairway the steps creaked far too loudly with each step he took.

When he stepped inside the flat, Mimi was already in the corridor waiting for him. She had hectic flushes all over her face, as she always did when she was agitated. She wanted to say something but couldn't get a word out and started sobbing.

Chanele must have sent her a telegram.

Pinchas took his wife in his arms. Although it wasn't really the moment for such thoughts, he was struck by how good she smelled. Under all the perfumes and eaux de Cologne that she liked to use, there was still the young girl that he had fallen in love with all those years ago.

Pomeranzes.

Gradually her sobbing subsided and faded away as a summer storm fades away, with one last gust and then one very last one. She sniffed like a child, and then, without freeing herself from his embrace, she opened her tear-filled eyes and looked up at him.

Her face was very soft.

'It's a miracle,' Mimi said.

Pinchas stroked her back helplessly. At that moment he perceived everything with exaggerated clarity that he could hear the material of her dress rustling.

'*Un vrai miracle*,' Mimi said.

Her sheitel had gone slightly askew and sat crookedly on her head as if she had only donned it as a playful disguise.

'In this state one has no pains,' Pinchas said comfortingly. 'I'm quite sure of that.'

Mimi took the tip of his nose between her fingers and slowly moved his head back and forth. That had once been a game between the two of them.

'You men!' Mimi said. 'What do you know about these things?'

'The doctor said...'

'You've already talked to Dr Wertheim?' Her tear-damp face was very disappointed.

'Dr Reichlin. I don't know if you know him. He was at that meeting too, and—'

'I don't want to hear a word about your stupid meeting,' said Mimi. '*Certainement pas*. Dr Wertheim says there's absolutely no doubt about it. Pinchas, I'm pregnant.'

34

Salomon Meijer died on 20 August 1893, the day of the plebiscite. His condition hadn't changed during all those weeks. They had taken him to the little room that was called the sewing room even though no one ever sewed in it – if you own a business with its own tailor's shop you don't need such a thing – and he lay there on his back for all those days, breathing without apparent difficulty, was there and yet not there.

At first they still talked to him, or talked at him, thus keeping to the un-spoken agreement that this was still Uncle Salomon lying there and not just a lump of old meat. Very gradually, in imperceptible stages, the language that they used to the patient became increasingly childish, as if the old man were getting younger and younger with each day of his death throes, turning back into a baby, as if at the end of his journey he would not die, but would instead slip back into the warmth of the womb.

But this reverse transformation was not complete, because at the same time Salomon's face got older and older. His beard sprouted as if gaining additional power from the motionlessness of the rest of his body, and shaving his sagging skin proved difficult. So stubble turned to hairs, and hairs to clumps. The side-burn, so carefully groomed for so long, lost its contours, an island swathed in seaweed. The little red veins that for as long as Arthur could remember had always made his cheeks look so cheerful now disfigured that face like a rash.

Even they themselves didn't notice that they were treating Salomon more and more like an infant. When they had wiped away his drool, it struck them as perfectly natural to pat his cheeks and say, 'Yes, yes, yes, that's better, isn't it, that's better.' Later they didn't talk to him at all, they did what needed to be done quickly and in silence, and left the room without looking round.

Although looking after the sick is not really among the duties of a cook, fat Christine proved particularly efficient at such tasks. The performed the most unpleasant duties as naturally as she might have scrubbed the scales from a carp or pulled the innards from the abdominal cavity of a freshly shechita-slaughtered chicken. 'If you cook every day, nothing repels you,' she once said to Arthur, and the longer he thought about that sentence, the worse food began to taste.

In the end he was the only one to spend long hours by Salomon's bed. Janki looked into the room once a day when he came back from the Modern

Emporium, stood in the doorway still in coat and hat and didn't actually come inside. 'Is everything all right, Salomon?' he would ask, or, 'Do you have everything you need?' When no answer came, as indeed no answer could, Janki cleared his throat two or three times, executed an almost military turn and left. He never closed the door behind him, it was as if he feared the finality of a lock clicking shut.

Chanele came more often, but only ever when Arthur wasn't there and she could be alone with Salomon. Once Arthur had come into the room without knocking – and what would have been the point of that, when Salomon could hardly have shouted 'Come in!'? – and Chanele had been sitting there with Salomon's hand in hers, crying. Arthur was quiet, and went out again without her noticing; there was something indecent and forbidden about seeing his own mother crying.

Only Hinda treated Uncle Salomon as she always had, even after weeks. Every time she visited she chatted away about the trivialities of her everyday life, as one does with a dear friend whom one sees so often that everything important has already been said. If Uncle Salomon really had still been able to hear anything, he would have known more about her than anyone else, including things that Hinda didn't confide in anyone else, that she had kissed Zalman Kamionker, and that it had been quite different from kissing father or mother after bentching on Friday evening. He had put his tongue in her mouth, an idea only that meshugena could have come up with, but it hadn't even been unpleasant, 'like a little soft animal', Hinda confided in Uncle Salomon, and if she blushed he couldn't see it anyway. Kamionker had already found work in Zurich; he knew how to use a sewing machine, and nobody could have predicted that. 'He can do everything,' said Hinda.

François never came. Worrying about someone who wasn't even aware of it and couldn't be grateful for it was utterly pointless as far as he was concerned.

Twice Pinchas and Mimi came from Zurich. There was something out of the ordinary about them, Arthur noticed immediately. Pinchas now walked along very close to his wife, as if to protect her, and Mimi was unusually nice to Arthur, stroked his head and mussed his hair. She even brought him some presents, once a red and white candy cane, and once a kaleidoscope with little coloured shards of glass that kept assembling themselves into new patterns. She called him 'Cousin Arthur', and then had to hold a handkerchief up in front of her mouth, it made her laugh so much. When she saw her father lying there, his eyes rolled back in their sockets and his tongue hanging out, she burst into tears and said, 'Mon Dieu, ah, mon Dieu.' But she didn't cry for long. Then she had to shut herself away with Chanele in Chanele's room and talk to her for ages.

Mostly Arthur was alone with Uncle Salomon. He sat for hours on a chair beside his bed, always bringing a book along and never reading it. He had understood that Uncle Salomon was going to die, and he wasn't even afraid of it. In fact he was afraid of missing the exact moment when someone was living and then they weren't, because Arthur had decided to become a doctor, not just an ordinary doctor, but the kind who makes discoveries and whom people travel from far away to come and see. If you managed to observe the moment of death, it seemed to him, if one could observe it very precisely, it must also be possible to find a cure for it. Thomas Edison had made 493 inventions, probably even more than that by now, and every time he had started with a very simple observation.

Now Arthur always ran home after school as quickly as he could, and was first to go into the sewing-room. Then when he heard regular breathing he was reassured and relieved.

He had already made one discovery, and a very important one, in fact. Dr Bolliger, who had come every day at first and later only twice a week, had even said to Chanele, 'He's extended your father's life with that.' Uncle Salomon wasn't Chanele's father, but it would have been too complicated to explain that to the doctor.

Arthur's discovery went like this: at first it had been impossible to feed Uncle Salomon. He didn't notice if you put a spoon into his mouth, and the soup or milk just flowed back out of it. Or if it didn't run back out his breath would suddenly stop, and he had to straighten the heavy body and slap it on the back. 'You're not the kind of woman one has to mince words with,' Bolliger had said to her, and Arthur had pressed himself very quietly into the corner lest he be sent from the room. 'Your father will not die from a sudden blow, but from a lack. And not from hunger, but from thirst. Man can survive for a very long time without food, in India there are supposed to be fakirs who don't eat a mouthful for forty days, but thirst is something quite different. If your father can't take any fluids...' He had moved his head meaningfully back and forth, and Chanele had said, 'Perhaps it's better that way.'

But then Arthur made his discovery. He had experimented, just like Edison, he had tried out all possible methods and then happened upon it: if you pressed the full spoon down on the tongue a little, at a very precise spot very far back, Uncle Salomon swallowed, or rather: his throat swallowed. It didn't work every time, but Arthur became more and more skilled at it, so Uncle Salomon didn't go thirsty, and Dr Bolliger said, 'You have quite an unusual boy there, Frau Meijer.'

One could not have said that Arthur took over the care of his uncle all by himself; without fat Christine, who could straighten Uncle Salomon up or turn him over as if he were no heavier than a bag of onions, he couldn't have done it. But it was Arthur who spooned fluid into the helplessly gaping mouth, mostly luke-warm broth whose recipe came from Aunt Golde, made from a whole pound of stripped flank. Arthur suggested trying the special drink that was known in his family as Techías Hameisim tea, but Dr Bolliger explained that the cloves and schnapps would be too irritating for the unconscious man's throat. 'The swallowing reflex is still there, but we don't want to check whether the coughing reflex is still working.' Arthur was proud that the doctor addressed him as an equal, almost as one specialist to another. The only other person who had ever taken him so seriously was Uncle Salomon.

Chanele praised him for looking after Salomon so touchingly, but the truth was that Arthur enjoyed the long hours by the dying man's bed. Just sitting there and listening to the even breathing gave him a feeling of usefulness with which he was otherwise unfamiliar. Arthur, the late addition, in fact considered himself superfluous, someone who had only come into the world when everything was already finished and distributed. Now at last he had a function, a task that he hadn't had to take away from anyone, and which was entrusted to him gladly and even gratefully. He always pushed his chair very close to Salomon and sat there quite still, often long past his bedtime. And because his bar mitzvah was approaching, he chanted the whole of the sidra to Uncle Salomon again and again, with all the blessings and haftorohs; he recited the droosh, of the mitzvot that are bound to time, and from which women are therefore exempt, and repeated the whole thing so many times that Cantor Würzburger rapped him on the head with his knuckles in astonishment and said in pointed High German, 'Look at this one, has the little door opened?'

If anything changed in Uncle Salomon's condition, Arthur was always the first to notice. Even before anyone else spotted anything, his nose told him it was time to call Christine to clean the bed again. Uncle Salomon had been put in nappies, extra large and specially made for him in the tailor's shop at the Modern Emporium, and when they were being changed, Christine would often pat the old man's backside and say, 'Yes, yes, yes, that's better, isn't it, that's better.'

Salomon was looked after with great attentiveness, 'in an almost exemplary fashion,' said Dr Bolliger, you could tell that amongst the Jews the family still meant something, say what you like. None the less, one day there was that rotten smell, which Arthur was of course the first to catch. It was an open sore that came from lying down for a long time, and which ointments did nothing to help. Uncle Salomon regularly had to be turned, from his back onto his side, and from his side back onto his back, 'like a piece of meat to be roasted on all sides,' Christine said to Louisli. Even so, the smell got stronger, Dr Bolliger's face grew thoughtful and Arthur felt guilty.

And then, on the morning of 20 August, on the eighth of Elul of the year 5653, Salomon Meijer stopped breathing. It didn't happen as Arthur had expected, there was no gradual weakening or fading away. Uncle Salomon's last breath was no different from all the others before, it was sure and steady, but no others came after it. Otherwise nothing at all had changed, the eyes were open, and the tongue that hung out of the mouth was still damp, but under the canvas the ribcage no longer rose and fell, and the rotten smell, to which Arthur had almost become accustomed, suddenly acquired a completely new meaning.

Nothing had happened that could have become a discovery. It was only that something had stopped happening.

Arthur came out of the room, 'very quietly', as Chanele later told Mimi, and said, 'I think we should call the chevra.'

The men of the funeral fraternity were soon there; they had been expecting Salomon Meijer's death, and everything was ready. One of the men screwed up his nose and said, 'It was high time.'

That Sunday evening, when the corpse had long since been carried from the house and old Herr Blumberg, who had drunk away his fortune and now performed any duties asked of him, was keeping watch over him in the cemetery, the news came in that the vote had been lost, and the prohibition on shechita was now part of the constitution. Janki said, 'That's all we need!' and later, whenever anyone talked about shechita, Arthur couldn't help thinking about his dead Uncle Salomon.

Nothing unusual happened at the funeral, except that Herr Strähle, the hotel director, in ignorance of the more austere Jewish practices, sent a big wreath. Fat Christine and Louisli later plucked the flowers from it and used them to decorate their attic room.

For the shiva, Janki had the big table with the tropical wood top taken to the store-room; in its place the low stools for the mourners were arranged. Then the family sat there for a week, as people in Biblical times had sat on the floor as a sign of mourning, but what one sensed in them was less grief than relief.

Many visitors came, including some who had never known the beheimes trader Salomon Meijer. Arthur opened the door to everyone and pointed them to the dining room. No one had told him to do this; he had simply got used to having a task. Janki was delighted with every new arrival. He liked to be an important man in the Baden community, someone to whom respect was paid by participating in his loss.

None of the guests had put themselves out at home and cooked a meal for the mourners. Given that the family had its own cook, the old custom no longer really made any sense. But they did bring bread and cakes, more than could be eaten.

Although Chanele was not a real daughter, she sat with them there for the whole week, and no one was bothered by the fact. On the other hand some people raised objections to Mimi. Frau Pomeranz, they said, was not making the sort of face suitable for such an occasion. And in fact it could not be denied that Mimi was happily and absent-mindedly smiling away to herself the whole time.

Uncle Melnitz arrived with the visitors too, sat down and didn't get up again. Pinchas, who had entrusted the butcher's shop to his co-partner for the whole week and stayed in Baden, nodded to him, while Janki assiduously ignored Melnitz and looked at him only very covertly out of the corner of his eye. 'If we just don't take any notice of him,' he thought, 'sooner or later he'll have to work out that he has no business here, that he's dead and buried once and for all and no longer belongs in the present.'

But Uncle Melnitz sat where he was, and even if he didn't say anything, he involved himself in the conversations by his mere presence.

Such a shiva is not only devoted to the shared commemoration of the dead, but also gives the bereaved the chance, in the long hours that they spend sitting together, to discuss everything that needs to be sorted out after a death. They quickly agreed that Chanele should take over the closure of the flat in Endingen, and that the small profit to be taken from it should go to the shnorrers that Salamon had so liked to look after in the last years of his life. A few of them had even turned up at the shiva, confident that grief might open the money bag.

Pinchas asked to be able to pick out anything useful to him from the books of the deceased. There would not be a great deal, that much was clear, because Salomon had not been a scholar in matters religious, and the writings that he had bought in his dotage on the subject of gematria belonged largely in the sphere of superstition.

The only argument centred on the Shabbos lamp that hung over the dining table in Endingen, and which both Mimi and Chanele would have liked to own. This good piece was made of brass and fitted with a device whereby the lamp could be lowered – 'lamp down, worries up!' – and then hung higher again after the end of Shabbos. It was filled with oil, and then the seven wicks burned from Friday evening until Saturday night, because on the Sabbath itself lighting a new light is of course forbidden. For Mimi, this lamp symbolised everything to do with home, all the security of her parents' house, and it had a special significance for Chanele as well. For all those years it had been one of her tasks to prepare the lamp every Friday and clean it again every Sunday. The two women engaged in their debate in unusual manner: each insisted that the other should take the lamp, and out of pure concern and generosity they nearly came to blows. In the end they agreed that the lamp would go to Baden for the time being, but that it should not be hung there; in that way the difficult decision was put off until later.

When everything had been discussed and sorted out, and when, as is often the case during the last days of a shiva, a little boredom was already beginning to spread, Pinchas suddenly cleared his throat and said he had something important to tell the family. Now of course everyone knew about Mimi's pregnancy, even if no one had officially mentioned it, and they were therefore preparing to put on the expressions of fake surprise that people like to wear so as not to spoil the joy of the bearer of good news. But Pinchas wanted to say something quite different.

'Now that the prohibition on shechita has been introduced – and we have the anti-Semites to thank for that! – much in my job will change. One will have to travel abroad once or twice a week, to Strasbourg, perhaps, that remains to be seen, to perform shechita there and then import the meat back into Switzerland. That will take a great deal of time. Or else we will not be able to do our own slaughtering at all any more, and will have to prepare meat brought in from somewhere else. Either way, I will no longer be able to be a butcher as my father was.

'He could still be proud of the fact that he was a shochet. But I...After that meeting in Endingen, after the terrible atmosphere there, which may be partly to blame for Salomon's death, who can say, after all that hatred that one encountered there – Chanele, you were there and can confirm it – and now, after the result of this plebiscite, after this decision, which was not made for the protection of animals, we all know that, and not out of love of God's creation, but simply out of a dull feeling of hostility because the Jews are bad people who need rapping over the knuckles...After all that I simply don't want to do it any more. I will sell the butcher's shop to my co-partner. Elias Guttermann is a hard worker, and he makes smoked meat even better than I do.'

'And you?'

'Kosher groceries. There's also a need for such a shop. I've discussed it with Mimi. She thinks I'm meshuga...'

'Un tout petit peu fou,' said Mimi without a hint of reproach.

'...but I think that now is the right moment to start something new. One will perhaps earn less, but what is very important to me right now: I will have more time. For Mimi and...Well, I'm sure you've all noticed.'

Now at last they were allowed to say 'mazel tov!', they could slap Pinchas on the shoulder and kiss Mimi on the cheek.

Only Uncle Melnitz made a serious face and said, 'You're running away. But that's our style, of course.'

35

Arthur's bar mitzvah wasn't as big a party as might usually have been expected. On Friday they had still been sitting shiva and receiving visits of condolence, and on Shabbos they were supposed to be suddenly cheerful? What sort of impression would that make? The people in the community would think their grief for Uncle Salomon hadn't been genuine. 'We'll do what's absolutely necessary and not a step beyond,' Janki had decided. 'Arthur will understand that, he's a sensible boy.'

The actual reason was that they had just had enough of shared experiences, happy or unhappy. On Sunday morning Salomon had died, and that same afternoon Mimi and Pinchas, summoned by telegram, had arrived in Baden, and since then they had all been crammed into the same flat, which while it might have been spacious, wasn't in fact all that spacious, they sat side by side on their mourning stools all day and got far too close to one another at mealtimes; at the little tables that were only really designed for drinking tea, you almost bumped each other's elbows. On Friday afternoon, when the men from the chevra at last collected the low stools again, and kindly helped bring back the long dinner table from the store-room, everyone tried to hide their relief, but each one of them in his own way longed for the everyday. Chanele wanted to get back to her shop and Pinchas to his butcher's business, where much needed to be discussed because of the planned handover to Elias Gutter-mann. Mimi worried at length about whether Gesine Hunziker, who hadn't been working for her for long and had not been properly introduced to her tasks, whether this girl from the country had paid due attention to business, perhaps they would return to a veritable brouhaha, 'et tout cela dans mon état'.

Throughout these days, François had worn his guardedly polite expression, the mask he always took out when something wasn't to his liking. For him, the week of mourning was only a continuation of the strict regime that Janki had imposed on him and which, quite contrary to François's expectations, hadn't simply been cast into oblivion. When he wasn't even allowed to go to the pub in the evening, with a few other young people who all had exactly the same moustache as he did, when it was quite certain that no more mourners were due to arrive, he complained that in this family you were treated like an under-age child, at any rate he couldn't wait to get out of this musty prison as soon as possible, regardless of how. When Chanele merely smiled, he was insulted and didn't say another word all day. The visitors who saw him sitting there with a pinched face took it for grief.

Janki had been given the task of informing all outside guests who had been invited to the bar mitzvah seudah that they very much regretted not being able to enjoy their company, but in view of their tragic loss they had decided to spend this day in thought, and in the closest family circle. The letter was also sent to Herr and Frau Kahn from Zurich, who were on the list along with their daughter Mina. Even though Chanele had taken a great deal of trouble to persuade Janki that personal contact with the biggest silk importer in the country might be useful for his companies, she didn't protest when he declined. One must take things as they are. On the other hand, Hinda, who was otherwise always the family's little ray of sunshine, did not seem to have responded well to her enforced proximity to her relatives. She argued with her father about the letter of refusal, and even raised her voice. All because the same letter had also been sent to Zalman Kamionker.

But Kamionker came anyway, just turned up at the door on Friday evening and explained quite harmlessly that the letter had never reached him, so he would have to have a serious word with the postman, he was indeed a peaceful man but such a thing simply could not be allowed to happen. He couldn't even be sent away, because how could he have travelled back to Zurich, so soon before Shabbos? In any case, he had brought a present for Arthur, wrapped quite casually in a Yiddish newspaper whose front page showed the picture of a worker bursting his chains. The present was a tallis, not a new one, but made of wonderfully finely woven material, and with a decorated collar the like of which no one here had ever seen. He had made it for himself in Simon Heller's weaving mill in Kolomea, Kamionker said, and only the best had been good enough for him.

Arthur had had the whole week off school, even though the religious rules did not oblige him to take part in the shiva. Chanele had talked to his class teacher, because she was worried about her youngest. At his age, experiencing the death of a person in such proximity, let alone with the dying man in a room, such a thing could not help but leave a trace on a child, she argued, let alone so sensitive and even often sickly a child as Arthur. Her request was not in line with school policy, but because of the outcome of the plebiscite the teacher had a vaguely guilty conscience with regard to all Jews, and therefore made an exception on this occasion.

In the night before his bar mitzvah Arthur slept badly. His big day fell on the Jewish date of 14 Elul, in the middle of the month and on a full moon. He was no longer afraid – he was a man now, after all – of the shadows of the plane trees, hadn't been for ages, but the fading light still kept him awake, and his thoughts turned endlessly in a circle. When he had got to sleep at last, the shrill cry of a bird outside his window woke him up again. It was a magpie, which actually had no business being in town. He had learned to tell the birds and their calls apart from Uncle Salomon, just as he had learned everything important, it seemed to him at that moment, only from him. Salomon had also told him a story about magpies: a farmer had once caught one and put it in a cage which he took into the field, so that it would lure its fellows with its tuneless cries for help. A second magpie flew down, the farmer grabbed it and wrung its neck. 'And at that moment,' Uncle Salomon had said, 'at that precise moment the magpie in the cage keeled over and died as well. And do you know what it died of? Of a broken heart.' Perhaps Salomon's heart was broken too, Arthur thought, you couldn't tell by looking.

Then at last it was day and time to put on the new suit that had had a kind of dress rehearsal at the big party. A white shirt went with it, with a very tight collar, and a tie with glittering silver threads woven into it. Janki stood behind Arthur to tie his tie, just as Arthur had often stood behind Chanele to button up her dress. It was almost an embrace, and Arthur would have liked to lean back into his father's arms and be held tight by him. But of course that was impossible. At thirteen you're ready to stand on your own, Uncle Salomon had said, because thirteen is, after all, the numerical value of Echod, or 'one'.

Fat Christine, this had been agreed, would later help him unpack the presents, and in return he had had to promise to show himself to her before he went to the prayer hall, in his suit, tie and black hat. When he came into the kitchen in all his glory, she propped her arms on her hips the way she did at the market when offered a fish that she didn't think was quite fresh, looked Arthur up and down and then said to Louisli, 'Yes indeed, those young Meijers are good-looking men all right.' Whereupon Louisli burst into tears; Arthur couldn't tell why.

In shul, the prayer-hall at the Schlossberg that the community had rented from the Lang brothers who ran the factory, Arthur was definitely the focus of interest. When they came in, Janki and François and he, it was almost like when the Torah scroll is carried through the synagogue, when everyone throngs in on all sides to touch the velvet cover with the tzitzits of the prayer shawls. They clapped him on the shoulder or pushed him companionably and said, 'Well? Very excited? Nu, you'll be fine.'

In general Arthur liked 'going to shul', as attending synagogue was called. In his case it had nothing to do with piety, absolutely not. Arthur had even – during Kol Nidre, in fact – thought quite firmly, 'Perhaps there is no God!' He had done it very deliberately and thus called for a very severe punishment, but nothing had happened. No, he wasn't even concerned about religion, he just liked the hubbub of the voices, the familiar tunes, the murmuring, that had something pleasantly soporific about it. If you only held the prayer book open in front of you and didn't entirely forget to turn the pages, you could devote yourself to your thoughts here, wonderfully undisturbed. François – no, Shmul, of course, in religious context he was Shmul – always complained that the services went on too long, but as far as Arthur was concerned they could have been endless.

Today everything was different, uneasy and unfamiliar, not just because it was his bar mitzvah and he would soon have to show what he had learned, but also because of the suit and the tie and the tallis. The soft material smelled very slightly of tobacco, which was strange, because who puts on a tallis when he wants to smoke?

Shacharit passed quickly , and the repetition of the Shemoneh Esrei was over so suddenly that Arthur almost believed Cantor Würzburger had skipped something.

Already the Torah was being held aloft. François, as a relative, was allowed to hold it in his arms. The expression on his face suggested that the office was not an honour, but a punishment for him. He was already carrying the Torah scroll to the lectern, the men were already crowding around to touch and kiss it, its crown was already being removed, the silver shield and the embroidered cloak, it was already being unwrapped and unrolled, it was all happening so quickly, far too quickly. And then Herr Weinstock, the shammes, was already calling out in his thin, bleating voice for Herr Katz, who, as a priest, was the first to be summoned to the Torah, and then it was the turn of Cantor Würzburger, who was a Levi, and therefore second. It made perfect sense, people said at every bar mitzvah, because it meant that he was already on the almemor when it was the turn of the bar mitzvah boy, and could help him if he got stuck. Because now it was already Arthur's turn, so quickly, far too quickly.

'Chaim ben Yaakov, ha-bar mitzvah,' bleated Shammes Weinstock, and Chaim ben Yaakov was him, it was his Jewish name. He was called Arthur every day, but in shul he was Chaim, which means life, and his father was Yaakov, or Jacob, but where the Lord is concerned there is no Janki and certain no Jean.

They all looked at him as he walked to the almemor, all the men in their white prayer shawls, and behind them in the women's shul – he didn't dare turn his head, but he could feel it very clearly – stood Chanele and Hinda and Mimi wearing her new hat with the black swan-feathers, they were all looking at him, and he knew his voice would fail, that he would get stuck in the middle of the sidra, that he would bring shame, terrible shame, on himself and the whole family.

But then when he started his first blessing it was as if he could hear his Uncle Salomon breathing beside him, steadily and regularly, and he was singing only for him, as he had sung for him again and again in the sewing room, he didn't forget a single word or a single trill, and afterwards people said it was very rare for a bar mitzvah boy not to be agitated in the slightest.

At the reception, which they hadn't been able to cancel because that would have looked mean, they stood side by side, son and father, and every time someone said 'mazel tov!' to Arthur and 'you sang beautifully,' Janki put his hand on his shoulder and was proud. Chanele stood there too and knew by heart all the gifts that Arthur had received but hadn't yet been allowed to look at. When it was the turn of the people in question to shake hands, Chanele poked Arthur inconspicuously in the back and then he would say, 'Thank you very much for the lovely present.'

There were little cakes and pastries, arranged on real silver dishes, which attracted a great deal of attention. The dishes had been provided by Herr Strähle from the hotel; when the sweets had all been eaten, the coat of arms of the Verenahof became visible. The women dank sweet wine and the men schnapps; they filled the little crystal glasses to the brim and raised them to Arthur. 'L'chaim!' they cried, and even the familiar Jewish toast sounded strange to Arthur today, because 'l'chaim' actually means 'for life', but today, which was his day after all, it could also have meant 'for Chaim'. Arthur felt as if they had been keeping the word ready for generations, just to use it in his honour today.

Then the reception was over. They had all eaten far too many sweet things, but the seudah awaited them at home, it was simply a part of it.

As she had promised Arthur, fat Christine was already standing ready with a sharp knife, even though there was quite enough for her to be getting on with in the kitchen. All the parcels had been put in the sewing room, which smelled strangely of fir twigs. Arthur only knew the smell from school, when Christmas was celebrated in class every year and he had to sit there in silence at the side until the others had finished. The fir needles had been Louisli's idea, because in spite of their assiduous attempts to air the room, a memory of Uncle Salomon's rotting wounds had hung in the air. The bed had been moved out; instead there was a table in its place, with a whole mountain of presents on it, waiting for Arthur.

'Where shall we start?' Christine asked, waving the knife around as impatiently as if she were looking at a heap of potatoes that all had to be peeled for lunch.

Arthur would have preferred to leave the unwrapping until after Voch, when he would once again be allowed to cut the ribbons and tear the paper all by himself. But something would not be put off, there was something he had to know straight away, there and then. The one present, the one that was the most important, far too precious – was it there?

The first parcel that seemed to be the right size and the right weight was a disappointment. Christine's knife revealed only a slipcase of black books, the prayer books for all the feast days of the year, in the Rödelheimer edition with the German translation. His name was embossed in gold on every siddur: Arthur Chaim Meijer. It looked elegant, and it was an expensive present, from Uncle Pinchas, of course, the member of the family most devoted to tradition, but Arthur set it carelessly aside.

The next package was far too light; he took it out of Christine's hands and put it back. She was quite indignant about the fuss he was making. But the third – ah, the third!

A box made of elegant stained wood, no, not a box: a proper little cupboard, with two wing doors like the Torah ark in the prayer room. There was even a lock, small enough to seal a diary, and for a moment Arthur panicked because he couldn't find the key for it straight away. But below the little cupboard there was a drawer with a moveable brass handle like the one on the chest of drawers in Mama's room, and when Arthur pulled it open, there lay the glass plates wrapped in silk paper and, sure enough, the key. He put it in the lock and for a moment – probably because of the special day – he had the feeling that he had to say a prayer before he opened it up. Then the two wing doors flew open, and there it was.

His microscope.

'Which one shall we open next?' asked Christine, and Arthur felt as if someone had suddenly started talking loudly about the weather or his business deals at the most sacred moment of the service.

'Tomorrow,' he said. 'I'll do that tomorrow. Otherwise Papa will get impatient.'

Christine was happy to go. She had, it was true, given Louisli precise instructions, but many a soup has been burnt at the very last moment because someone didn't stir it with the necessary care.

His microscope.

It couldn't simply be lifted out, there was a fastening that first had to be released with a tiny wing nut, but then, once you had wiped your fingers, moist with excitement, on one's trousers, you could hold it in your hands, very, very carefully, you could set it down in front of you, ideally on the window sill, the light was brightest there, and you could look at it in peace, no longer as a picture in a book. Arthur wasn't aware of it, but he was making the same face as Hinda did when she looked at Zalman Kamionker.

The viewfinder with the three lenses looked a little like the kaleidoscope that Aunt Mimi had brought him, except of course that it wasn't wrapped up in childish, brightly coloured paper. It was made of brass, only the ring around the eyepiece was made of a lighter, gleaming metal with a matt finish. There was a regulating screw at the side which you could turn, and then the tube became longer and still longer, and if there had already been a glass plate on the bracket it would have broken there and then.

Arthur would, he had firmly decided, perform his first scientific experiment on his own blood, he would prick his finger with a needle and squeeze out a drop. A true researcher and discoverer doesn't balk at pain.

When Chanele came to get him, he was sitting on his chair by the window, the same chair on which he had always sat by Uncle Salomon's bed, stroking the microscope with his fingertips as if it were a living creature. 'Are you happy now?' she asked.

He was so happy that he couldn't put it into words. And at the same time he had a guilty conscience because Uncle Salomon was dead, after all.

They were all sitting around the table already; it was laid for a feast, because even though one might not have wanted to make a fuss about it, it was still a bar mitzvah. The good Sarreguemines crockery rested on the best tablecloth, the knife with the silver handle lay beside the board with the Sabbath loaves, and the wine for Kiddush had already been poured.

Janki looked younger than usual, perhaps because he was proud of his son. Pride always made him sit up straight, as befits an old soldier. He gripped his walking stick with the lion's-head handle, and when Chanele ushered Arthur in he gave a signal with it, and everyone began to clap.

François did so only with his fingertips, and held his head at a slight angle as if to say, 'This might all be superficial theatre, but if it has to be, I won't flinch from it.' But he also winked at Arthur, and it was like a mark of distinction, like being accepted into a secret society of which the others knew nothing.

Hinda clapped loudest, no, second loudest, because Zalman Kamionker was sitting next to him, and each time he brought his hands together it sounded like a shot ringing out. He also tried to strike up a song, but when no one joined in he just laughed and let it pass. Kamionker had come to Baden without shabbosdik clothes, and Janki had insisted that he put on one of Uncle Salomon's old jackets. Although Salomon had been a burly man, the tailor's broad shoulders almost burst the seams.

Uncle Pinchas whispered something in Aunt Mimi's ear, and she turned bright red in the face and slapped him on the arm and said, '*Mais vraiment*, Pinchas!' Then she pursed her lips and blew a kiss to Arthur, and he nearly thanked her for it and said as he had done at the reception, 'Many thanks for the lovely present!'

The only guests who weren't part of the family were Cantor Würzburger and his wife, who couldn't have been left out because Arthur still had to deliver his droosh over lunch, and it was better if someone was there just in case he stumbled. The cantor, applauding, cried 'Bravo!', and because the sound of his voice didn't strike him as sonorous enough, he reached into his waistcoat pocket with two pointed fingers, took out a sal ammoniac pastille and popped it in his mouth.

Chanele had sat down too now, at the other end of the table, opposite her husband. It must have been Mama who had persuaded Papa to buy the microscope even though it was so expensive. Arthur was sure of it, and loved her for it very much. It was because of his mother that he had never understood why, in the morning prayer, one thanks God for not creating one as a woman.

Christine and Louisli stood in the doorway and would probably have applauded as well, if they hadn't had to hold onto the plates with the salted carp.

'It's lovely to belong to a family,' Arthur thought, and decided that he would have three children as well one day, at least three, and that he would give them anything they wanted.

'Now sit down,' said Chanele. 'You're dreaming again.'

1913

36

'It's lovely to belong to a family,' thought Arthur. He took off his glasses, closed his eyes and rubbed the bridge of his nose between his thumb and his middle finger. Such a young doctor, who can't afford to turn down night-time house calls, has trouble staying awake during a long ceremony. The gesture inconspicuously concealed the fact that his eyes had once again filled with tears, with that inexplicable stirring of emotion that suddenly came upon him, time and again, in situations where he should really have been happy.

And he was happy. Of course he was happy. Why shouldn't he have been happy?

As they did every year at Pesach, almost the whole of the Zurich family had gathered together. They had got used to the fact that two of them were missing, that there should really have been two more chairs around the table, each with its cushion, that there should have been two more glasses on the white table-cloth. One was left with no other option but to get used to it.

It was now seven years since François . . .

It was seven years ago, and it still didn't seem natural. On the contrary: the silence about the thing no one wanted to mention got louder every year. 'As if we were all patients,' Arthur reflected, 'still feeling a limb that was amputated long ago.'

All the other Meijers were there. In fact it wasn't at all correct to call them 'the Meijers', because they were called Pomeranz and Kamionker, but if one had asked them that was what they would have called themselves too. On the sideboard, as if by way of proof, stood the photograph for which Salomon and Golde had once reluctantly posed, she with her sheitel, which sat at an angle like a wonky tea cosy, he supporting himself on his umbrella like a general on his sword, both their faces contorted, by the requirement to stand still for a long time, into stern masks, as if to intimidate posterity. The photograph had faded; Hinda kept planning to put it in a different place where the sun wouldn't shine on it so directly, but she kept forgetting. There were too many other things to do in this household.

Today of all days, when the Seder needed to be prepared for the whole mishpocha, she needed four hands or at least a maidservant. At the Kamionkers' they only had a cleaning lady, for a few hours a day, and even she sometimes had to wait longer for her wages than was strictly respectable. Frau Zwicky wasn't very efficient, and she certainly didn't show a great deal of initiative, she didn't see the work if you didn't hold it up in front of her nose, but she had two little children at home and a husband who hadn't earned any money since an accident. You don't fire someone like that; Zalman would never have allowed it. 'Can't you stop being a trade unionist at least at home?' Hinda had once asked him, and received the answer, 'Then I would be someone else, and getting involved with a strange man is adultery, Frau Kamionker.'

In the end Hinda didn't care if her household wasn't run perfectly. As long as her husband was amused by the inevitable little disasters – why should she get worked up? Once, when the children were still small, they had had a visit, a preannounced visit, please note, and there had been a full *pot de chambre* – in such delicate cases Mimi wasn't the only one who spoke French – in the middle of the room. The ladies of the Russian Refugees' Relief Committee talked about the matter for ages afterwards, and didn't know what they should be more outraged about: the unspeakable object itself, or the fact that that Hinda had only laughed at the embarrassing event.

Zalman, who was an extremely hard worker, could have forged a career for himself, he should have been a cloth preparer or even a shop-floor manager, instead of going on sitting by the sewing machine like a simple tailor, ruining his eyes, but sooner or later he always ended up having a row with his boss over some kind of injustice that didn't even affect him personally, but only ever affected other people who couldn't defend themselves or didn't dare to. Most of them were Jews from the East, many of whom had fled to Zurich after the Tsarist pogroms of 1905, and who came quite as naturally to Zalman Kamionker as the shnorrers had once come to Salomon Meijer in Endingen. Zalman found them jobs, fought their battles for them and often won them, too, and when after a victoriously fought battle he was thrown out on the street, he always reported proudly on his dismissal when he got home. 'You're meshuga,' Hinda would say, and Zalman would reply, 'Luckily so – otherwise you'd get far too bored with me.'

It was a good marriage, even though money was always in short supply in the Kamionker household. But what's money? When Hinda saw her husband sitting in the place of honour as Seder host, having the bowl and towel for the washing of the hands passed to him, in this setting he was Croesus, and the Seder would have been unthinkable anywhere else, not at the Pomeranzes', where sickly Mimi could never have done all the work, and not at Arthur's, because his bachelor flat didn't even have a big enough table. And of course not at Mina's, poor Mina who deserved such sympathy after her husband and son...

Don't think about it. Not today.

Today was Pesach, a joyful celebration, a day of liberation and redemption. 'All who are hungry, come and eat; all who are in need, come and celebrate Seder.' They had told the story of the flight from Egypt, they had asked the traditional questions – 'What distinguishes this night from all other nights?' – and given the traditional answers, they had heard about the four sons, the clever one, the bad one, the stupid one and the one who doesn't know how to ask questions, they had listed the plagues of Egypt and for each plague spilled a drop of wine from their full cups – if others are suffering, one should diminish one's own joy – they had eaten the things that one eats on this evening, the symbolic foods, sweet, gluey charoset and bitter horseradish, as well as the worldly ones, matzo balls and gefilte fish, they were already singing the Shir Hama'a lot that introduces the table prayer, they would have been a Jewish family like any other, a happy family, even though François...

Don't think about it.

As always, the singing turned into a friendly little competition. From Kolomea, Zalman had brought with him a different pronunciation and tunes different from those familiar in Switzerland, and was now drowned out by the rest of the family. The result was a cheerful cacophony that made even Pinchas chuckle, even though he took the religious traditions more seriously than anyone else.

Zalman sat at the head of the table like a king – 'no, like an emperor', thought Hinda, because the more his moustache invaded his cheeks, the more Zalman looked like the Habsburg Emperor Franz Joseph.

He was an enthusiastic father, who would have loved to bring a whole dynasty of little Kamionkers into the world. When Ruben was born, nineteen years ago now, Zalman had loudly declared at the bris, inspired by paternal pride and mazel tov bronfen: 'I already know the names for the next ones,' and had started listing them all, 'Simon, Levy, Yehuda, Dan, Naftali...' to indicate that he, like the patriarch Jacob, wanted to have thirteen children, twelve sons and a daughter. There had only been three in the end, Ruben and the twin girls, but the number thirteen had retained its special secret significance for Zalman and Hinda. Even now, when they were a long-standing couple and far beyond such silliness, he could still make his wife blush with embarrassment at dull social occasions by whispering in her ear, 'Wouldn't you rather go home and complete the thirteen?'

Ruben saw his mother smiling and thought reproachfully, 'Her mind isn't on it.' Uncle Pinchas, to whom this honour fell at every Seder, had just struck up the table prayer, and for the fulfilment of the commandment it isn't enough just to join in with the communal singing out of habit, while following one's own train of thought, no, one must speak the text word for word along with everyone else, and be aware of its meaning. For some time Ruben had felt obliged to think rigorously about religious matters, because after the feast days he would be leaving Switzerland for at least a year to study at the yeshiva. Not one of the big, famous yeshivas, he wasn't such a brilliant student as that, but still a real one, meaning one in the East. At first Zalman, for whom the traditions of his religion meant more than their study, had not been at all keen on Ruben's wish, and had even hurt Uncle Pinchas, who often studied with Ruben, with the accusation that he was determined to turn his son into a rebbe, when he didn't have the mind for it. But in the end he had yielded – 'If someone wants to be an apple tree, you'll be waiting a long time for pears!' – and had organised a year's study for Ruben in his home town of Kolomea, along with lodging at the home of a friend from his tallis-sewing days, who was even willing to put Ruben up in his house for nothing. 'I would do anything for a son of Zalman Kamionker,' the friend had written. This generosity had something to do with a fight with drunk Ruthenians, who had considered it pleasing in the sight of God to break the nose of a young Jew one Sunday after church. 'There were six of them, and he was alone,' said Zalman. 'I am a peaceful man, but I really had to get stuck in.'

Ruben cast a disdainful look at the twins, who couldn't even stop squabbling during the table prayer. In the excessive zeal of his new-found religious severity, he even felt obliged to put an admonitory index finger to his lips, which sent them both into a fit of giggles. Girls were silly, his sisters especially.

The twins had got their names because Zalman had said when they were born, 'I'm like the patriarch Jacob. If I'm not going to have twelve sons, at least I've got a Lea and a Rachel.'

Anyone who didn't know them would never have thought the two seventeen-year-olds were sisters, let alone twins. Lea took after her grandmother, she had inherited Chanele's unbroken monobrow, and a dark complexion that nothing would lighten, however much she tried to stay out of the sun. Rachel, a quarter of an hour younger, was almost a head taller than her sister and had – never in living memory had such a thing appeared in the Meijer family – flaming red hair. Her freckled face and bright green eyes didn't match the rest of the family at all, which was why Zalman affectionately called her 'my goyish daughter'. In one respect, however, Lea and Rachel conformed precisely to the image that people have of twins: they were inseparable. They would have liked always to wear the same clothes, but that was a luxury the Kamionkers couldn't afford. They had to make do with what Zalman was able to procure cheaply from his employers, either rejects or last year's models. So on this Seder evening Lea was wearing a dark red velvet dress cut far too old for a seventeen-year-old, while Rachel, in a white cheviot dress with a Bengaline collar, looked even more pale-skinned than usual.

Déchirée, on the other hand...

A late arrival in Mimi and Pinchas's life, their daughter wasn't really called Déchirée. Her name was Désirée, the longed-for one. For Pinchas, Deborah, his daughter's Jewish name, would have done just as well – Désirée and Pomeranz were two worlds that didn't really fit together – but as the French elegance made his wife happy, he didn't resist.

Although...French names...If François had stayed plain Shmul, perhaps he would never...

Such thoughts were to be avoided.

After the difficult birth Pinchas had fulfilled Mimi's every wish; the torture had lasted over twenty-four hours, and Désirée had been an unusually big baby. Mimi had been poorly for all those years. Sometimes she didn't leave her bed for days at a time, drank only camomile tea, ate chocolates and played patience on the bedcovers. She nurtured the complaints of her motherhood as devotedly as she had once tended the torments of her childlessness. Today, for example, when they sat down at the Seder table, stressing her weakened state, she had had Pinchas and Arthur give her their cushions, and made herself a proper little sofa, on which she now reposed in splendour, a sovereign long weary of ruling and who still refused to give it up.

From childhood Désirée had been a model daughter, a child who caused few problems, and yet if she did anything to discomfit Mimi, laughed too loudly or wanted to play the piano when Mama was resting, she was put firmly in her place with the same rebuke, '*Ah, ma petite, mais tu m'as déchirée!*' Mimi used this irrefutable argument so often that it eventually became a nickname, and even Désirée had stopped minding when it was applied to her.

Today, once again, she was wearing a dress that couldn't help but make Lea and Rachel envious. Although she was only nineteen, just two measly years older than her cousins, it wasn't an outfit for a flibbertigibbet, but a very grown-up, hand-embroidered crêpe-voile dress with Valenciennes insets, a model, Zalman had established with his first expert glance, that must have been imported from France; nothing of such quality was produced here in Switzerland. Her dark hair, parted severely in the middle, was held in place with an ornamental comb that actually seemed to be made of real silver. In spite of all her finery, Désirée, mollycoddled and always, since childhood, put to bed for the slightest indisposition, had an attractively helpless quality.

She sat there with her eyes lowered and her hands in her lap, and during the communal singing her lips moved only silently.

The second-last sentence of the table prayer, observant practice decrees, is only whispered, because the words 'I have been young and now am old; yet have I not seen the righteous forsaken, nor his seed begging for bread' might hurt the feelings of a needy dinner guest. But today there was no one who had been invited out of pity, apart perhaps from Mina, who as a married woman and mother had to go alone to someone else's Seder because her husband...

There was an extra cup on the table, filled to the brim with wine, waiting not for François, but for the Prophet Elijah. It was more likely that the prophet would seek out this flat – 12 Rotwandstrasse, third floor – and this date – 21 April 1913 – to announce the imminent arrival of the redeemer, than that François Meijer, store-owner and successful businessman, would once again celebrate such a feast in the family circle.

For that was what they were being so noisily silent about at this Seder table: François Meijer had had himself baptised.

Had had himself 'geshmat'.

Had rid himself of his Jewishness like an annoying pimple.

It was seven years ago now, and the question of 'Why?' after 'How could he?' and 'Why did he do that to us?' still prompted the most violent debates in the little circle. Not today, of course, because today Mina was sitting at the table. Mina, Francois' wife. It had been hardest of all for her, everyone agreed, a Jewish wife with a goyish husband, and still she hadn't divorced François, but had gone on living with him as before. The cynics among the Zurich Jews – and there was no shortage of those – said she probably couldn't part from his money, because François Meijer had become rich more quickly than others and, it was whispered, hadn't always kept his hands clean in the process. Milder temperaments traced Mina's surprising fidelity back to quite practical difficulties: 'How can a goy write a Get?' A Get is the letter of separation that a husband must issue to his wife to make the divorce legal and enable her to marry someone else, and as it is also a religious document, of course it cannot be issue by a non-Jew.

The true reason was that Mina didn't want to lose her son, because François – and Hinda resented this more than anything else – had also dragged Alfred along into being geshmat, an innocent twelve-year-old at the time, who couldn't have guessed at the momentousness of the event. 'He didn't even allow him a bar mitzvah,' she said every time she talked to Zalman about it, as if this particular detail was the most contemptible aspect of the matter.

Arthur, the brooding theorist, was the only member of the family who thought it possible that François – even though it didn't fit with his calculating nature – had experienced a genuine epiphany, that a sudden insight, whether genuine or putative, had led him to renounce his ancestral religion and adopt another. But Arthur, as everyone knew, had always admired his brother beyond all measure, and was far too easily inclined to find an exculpatory explanation for the errors of others, 'as if he himself were hiding something he hoped to be forgiven for,' as Chanele had once thoughtfully observed.

The affair had taken its toll on her and Janki; Chanele because she feared that her eldest son would never be able to find equilibrium as long as he lived, and Janki out of concern for his reputation in the community. In the first flush of his fury he had even sworn never again to exchange a word with his son, and would have stuck to his principles had it not been for all those unavoidable business meetings. Francois' shop had been set up with Janki's money, an investment that had made Janki a wealthy man. But for seven years he had repeatedly turned down the invitation to come to Zurich for the Seder, and preferred to endure a joyless ceremony on his own with Chanele in their echoing Baden dining room. In Zurich he would have had to go to the synagogue, where he would have met the Kahns, Mina's parents, who always looked at him as reproachfully as if he had personally dragged his son to the font. Mina herself had never reproached anybody. She endured her husband's decision as she had endured her polio as a young girl, patiently and without complaint.

For Pinchas, François's conversion had been a cause for mourning, and he preferred to avoid the theme: one does not put a strain on a painful body part. Mimi had come up with a pun on 'chrétien' and 'crétin', which she repeatedly threw into the debate, even though no one had laughed even the first time she had said it.

'Some people try to get things by being a nice guy,' he said. 'François will try and get them by being a nice goy.'

The table prayer was over, the third cup drunk and the fourth poured. In the ritual of the Seder evening they were now reaching the point where the flat door is opened to admit the prophet Elijah who, it was promised, would arrive the evening before the Pesach feast to announce the time of redemption. Désirée was sitting closest to the door, so she was the one dispatched. It was already nearing eleven – such a Seder evening can go on for a long time – and she had to feel her way along the corridor. Behind her, Zalman was intoning the prayer in which God is exhorted to rain his fury down upon the unbelievers. The gas light was burning in the stairwell, and through the frosted glass it looked for a moment as if someone was standing outside the door, just waiting to be let in.

'They have devoured Jacob,' Zalman recited in Hebrew, 'and destroyed his dwelling place.'

Someone – probably Mimi, who was always afraid of burglars, had put the security chain on the door. It took Désirée a moment to free the hook.

'Pursue them in indignation, and destroy them from under your heavens.' The door creaked as it opened, like a dying man struggling to breathe.

Someone was actually waiting on the step: a young student in full regalia, with cap, ribbons and sash, all in the green and white colours of his fraternity. He was tottering slightly, and when he started talking his breath smelled of beer.

'Hello, Déchirée,' the student said. 'Déchirée,' he said, as if they knew each other. 'Today's the day when the hungry are invited. So I thought I'd just drop by.'

'Who...?' asked Désirée and gulped before she could finish the sentence. 'Who are you?'

'Don't you recognise me?' said the student. He belched, almost brought his hand to his mouth and then waved it away wearily: completing the movement was too much of an effort. 'I'm Alfred. Alfred Meijer. The goy.'

37

'Scandaleux,' said Mimi.

She said it for the fourth or fifth time during this late breakfast, while buttering her matzo with such furious ardour that it crumbled to tiny pieces on her plate. The satin bow that fastened her dressing gown of Turkish-patterned muslin at the throat with gaudy elegance fluttered into the void for a moment and then settled once more on her bosom. Mimi had not grown fat, *certainement pas*, but she had, the closer she came to sixty, assumed certain matronly qualites, 'statuesque' would have been the word in the novels that she still liked to read, and it gave her, as she repeatedly noted in front of the mirror, a certain dignity. Her face was still smooth, a condition that she eagerly supported with powders and creams; only on either side of her mouth, below her slightly doughy cheeks, did two deep wrinkles stretch down to her chin, the kind that life draws on the face if one has had much to endure; other people have no idea.

'*Scandaleux*,' Mimi repeated. 'Of course he was drunk. At their pub crawls, or whatever they call them, they drink beer like pigs from a trough. Such impudence, simply coming in and joining us at the table! As if he were part of the family!'

Désirée had lowered her eyes and was concentrating hard on a tiny chip in her coffee cup. You don't use your very best crockery for Pesach, it just sits in the attic all year waiting for someone to bring it down for a week. If you ran your fingernail along the edge of the cup, it always made a quiet, almost inaudible clicking sound when you reached the crack. 'He is a relative, though,' said Désirée without looking up.

'Not one of mine. Kinship is something different. You have to bear in mind where he comes from, this...this student.' Mimi uttered the word with such revulsion as if she couldn't find a more contemptuous one in the dictionary. 'Even Chanele – you know I love her, may she live to be a hundred and twenty, but she'll only ever be a foster-child. And Janki...a grandson of an uncle of a grandfather. If that's mishpocha, then I'm related to the whole world. A stranger. Stood outside our door in Endingen in the middle of the night like, like...'

'Like Alfred yesterday?'

'Alfred!' Mimi's fury had immediately found a new direction, like a dog chasing a new odour trail. 'What sort of a name is Alfred!'

'He can't do anything about that. My name is Désirée, although...'

'Although? Although?' When Mimi became annoyed, she got bright red cheeks like a stout market trader.

'Sorry, Mama,' said Désirée, although she had said nothing she needed to apologise for.

'Just outside the door.' Mimi's rage went on bubbling away, as milk goes on foaming even after you've taken it off the flame. 'And he was so bold as to sing along.'

During the Hallel, Alfred had sat there in silence. A chair had been found for him, and Rachel had even had to fetch a pillow, from her own bed, because pillows and cushions are part of a Seder evening. But he didn't lean back, he sat there with his back straight, both feet planted firmly on the floor, like someone who was about to get up and leave at any moment.

They had all tried not to stare at him, whether out of politeness or embarrassment, who could say? Only Ruben stared at his cousin the whole time, as he might have stared at a piece of pork that had landed on the Seder table after an intricate sequence of chance events – more unusual situations arise in the elaborate examples in the Talmud. 'You are a treyf goy and have no business here,' the expression was supposed to say.

Had anyone looked at him like that in his fraternity's regular haunt – although Ruben could not have known this – Alfred would have immediately challenged him to name his second. Here he didn't even notice the looks. Nor did he seem to hear the twins exploding with mirth time and again, however much they pressed their napkins to their mouths in a vain attempt to control themselves. He just sat there, rocking gently back and forth. Back and forth.

Like someone shockeling.

Once, just as the others were chorusing 'Omeyn!', a belch escaped him. He leapt to his feet, clicked his heels together and seemed about to launch into an apology. But then he forgot what he had wanted to say, looked around with confused eyes and sat down again.

Arthur took off his glasses and pressed his fingertips against the bridge of his nose. 'The poor boy doesn't know where he belongs,' he thought. 'That's the most terrible thing that can happen to anybody.'

Hinda had taken Mina's hand and was gripping it very tightly. The gesture said, 'I know how you are feeling right now,' and Mina was grateful for the pious lie. Of course Hinda, to whom nothing really bad had ever happened in her whole life, couldn't begin to imagine what was going on in her sister-in-law's mind, but consolation draws its power not from understanding but from good intentions. So Mina's son was suddenly sitting at the table, an only child, in the wrong place at the wrong time and in the wrong world, drunk and chaotic and ridiculous, and she couldn't throw her arms around him and press him to her, she couldn't just kiss away his confusion, as she had kissed away his little hurts when he was a little child. She could only look at him. All her life she had had to look at everything.

Zalman, the master of the house, tried to act as if nothing at all had happened. He didn't really succeed. He sang the Hallel more loudly than necessary, and after the fourth cup he wiped his lips with ostentatious nonchalance. Then they had come to the very last part of the Seder, the medieval songs that no longer have any ritual significance, and which you only sing because they've always been sung and the evening would be incomplete without them. They sang the 'Adir hu' and very suddenly, at 'bimheyro, bimheyro', Alfred joined in with the song. He hadn't been at a Seder for seven years, and he had only sung with his fraternity brothers, 'Gaudeamus igitur' and 'When the Romans got too bold'. But now a memory had welled up in him, perhaps because he was too drunk to avoid it, and he sang along with the others as if it was the most natural thing in the world.

Ruben immediately fell silent; in his severe youthful religiosity it felt like a sin to sing a song praising the mystical qualities of God along with someone who had been baptised. But not even Uncle Pinchas wanted to be a part of this silent protest, so at the next refrain he joined in with the chorus with renewed vigour. Ruben had a rough voice into which the occasional squeak crept, as if, even though he was old enough for the yeshiva, his voice hadn't quite finished breaking.

Alfred, on the other hand, intoned the old melodies with a velvet-soft baritone that made you forget his beer breath and inappropriate suit. He had closed his eyes now and smiled to himself as he sang. 'A little boy,' thought Désirée.

They sang the songs with all the repetitions. Towards the end of the next song, an Aramaic round about the lamb that the father bought for two zuzim, they all fell silent as if by mutual agreement and let Alfred sing the last repetition on his own. He actually remembered – seven years! – the whole backward chain of events by heart, he had the slaughterman kill the oxen, and the oxen drink the water, the water put out the fire, the fire burned the stick, the stick struck the dog, the dog bit the cat because it had eaten the lamb that the father had bought for two zuzim, the lamb, the lamb.

After the last song of Seder there is always a moment of awkwardness. One has followed the prescribed ritual for a whole evening, one has pursued a familiar path and must now find one's own direction again. On this evening – what distinguishes this night from all other nights? – this feeling was particularly strong. They all looked at Alfred, who still sat there rocking gently and listening to his own voice. Then Alfred opened his eyes, not like someone waking up, but someone who's been startled, he looked at them and got to his feet, clicked his heels and said, 'Please forgive me, I don't belong here.' And walked to the door, as bolt upright as drunks sometimes walk, and belched once more and was gone.

'*Scandaleux*,' said Mimi.

Désirée's fingernail circled the rim of her cup.

With any luck Papa would be home soon.

In the prayer room of the Israelite Orthodox Community morning-service ended a little later than it did in the big synagogue on Löwenstrasse. Here all the traditional interpolations and additional prayers were treated with great precision; after all they hadn't only split from the big community because of the harmonium and the women's voices in the synagogue choir. They wanted to preserve the traditional Ashkenazi traditions, without exception, because if one stops filling up the holes in a dam for as much a day, sooner or later the floods will be unstoppable.

Pinchas had not joined the religious society at first. With excessive correctness he had feared he might be accused of self-interested motives, because of course the Orthodox members of the dissident congregation were the best customers a kosher provision merchant could have. But that had been almost twenty years ago, and there had been no tensions between the two communities for ages. He had even been offered the chance to stand for the board, but – again for fear of losing one half of his customers – he had so far always turned it down. Perhaps if they asked him again . . .

The sun was already quite warm on this spring morning, so the little groups chatting outside the prayer hall broke up slowly. It was a perfectly normal day all around, an apprentice was pushing a trolley-load of parcels to the post office, a drayman was heaving barrels from his cart, and in the middle of this sea of workaday bustle, two solemnly dressed men stood on an invisible island, holding by the hand two children in their party clothes, doffing their gleaming top hats in a gesture of farewell.

As they did so they revealed the little black caps that they wore under their hats, lest they stand disrespectfully bareheaded for as much as a moment. Arthur was almost the only one wearing an ordinary black hat. That was usual among bachelors, except that in this community very few men of his age were still bachelors. Even though he wasn't a member, he had recently taken to accompanying Pinchas to the prayer hall on Füsslistrasse, where he was considered pious in his own way, because he was still often seen standing there even after the congregation had finished its prayer, eyes closed, apparently deep in worship. In reality Arthur was just mechanically turning the pages in the prayer book when his neighbours did the same, and using the murmuring regularity of the service to pursue his own thoughts, thoughts that turned in a circle, in an endless circle around the same central point that he didn't dare to approach.

He had of course – it didn't even have to be stated openly, so obvious was it – been invited to Pesach breakfast by the Pomeranz family. 'The ladies won't have waited for us,' said Pinchas. 'When Mimi is hungry, she is hungry, and Dr Wertheim says she should eat when she feels like it, she needs that in her condition.' Arthur knew Dr Wertheim as an elderly colleague, who was particularly popular among patients who weren't really ill, because he recommended spa cures rather than diets. Mimi's 'condition', he assumed, would not be found in a medical handbook but was, in spite of all the strains that her late motherhood had brought with it, no more than a handy excuse to avoid unpleasant duties and always to do exactly what she happened to feel like doing. But he just nodded and said, 'Maybe we could do a little detour. There's something I'd like to show you.'

On the way to the other side of Bahnhofstrasse, of course, their conversation turned to Alfred's surprising appearance at the Seder. It was one of those events that you have to bat back and forth over and over again until it has found its suitable place in the museum of family memories. 'If I had been in Zalman's place,' Pinchas said, 'I would have thrown him out. But I wasn't the master of the house.'

'Why would you have done that?'

'Such a thing is inappropriate,' said Pinchas, and among Jews that is a formulation that brooks no argument.

They walked a few steps in silence, side by side. Arthur greeted a patient who came towards him with a shopping basket over her arm, and she looked in surprise at the young doctor who had put on such a solemn suit on a perfectly ordinary day. 'Someone close to him must have died,' she thought.

'I have some sympathy with the boy,' said Arthur.

'He isn't a boy any more. He must feel extremely grown up in his student finery. We should be grateful that he didn't bring his sword as well.'

'He can't do anything about who he is.'

Pinchas looked at Arthur in surprise. 'Why so vehement?'

'You're all attacking him, while in fact...'

'It was Pesach, and he's a goy.'

'Because he's been turned into one. It's bad not to know where one belongs.'

'You're not going to find out by getting drunk.'

They nearly had an argument, but as always in such situations Arthur relented. Afterwards, he knew already, he would be unhappy with himself for doing so. Luckily they had reached the window display that he wanted to show Pinchas. It belonged to a tiny shop on one of the alleys leading up to the Rennweg, and was hardly big enough for the magnificently embroidered flag displayed in it. It was white and blue, the shimmering matt silk run through with gold threads. 'Take a look at that!' said Arthur. 'That's exactly what we need!'

'Herrliberg Rifle Guild,' Pinchas read. 'What do you have to do with them?'

'Not this flag, of course. A flag like it. The same quality, I mean. I've looked into it. It has to be cotton velvet, with a particularly thick nap, and flag rep, pure silk. The thread is called Japanese gold. It's the most expensive, but it will still be shiny in a hundred years.'

'Why do you need...?'

'For the Jewish Gymnastics Association. Without a proper flag we'll look ridiculous at any gymnastic festival.'

'I didn't think you were still a member?'

'No, in a way I am,' Arthur said, looking surprisingly embarrassed. 'That is: very involved, in fact.'

It had been three or four years ago that Arthur, who had always dreaded gym class at school, suddenly took a great interest in sport. He had joined the Gymnastics Association, newly founded and much derided, and become a very active member. His family had only shaken their heads, particularly when he chose wrestling as his personal sport, because Arthur had never shown any particular talent in physical matters. 'He considers each step until he trips over his own feet,' Uncle Salomon had once said of him. Surprisingly, he turned out not to be particularly clumsy, perhaps because his specialist anatomical knowledge proved useful in wrestling, and there was a special hold, the neck wrench, with which he had on more than one occasion felled an opponent stronger than himself. He even won the Association Championship in the Greco-Roman style, even though his opponent, a sturdily built apprentice called Joni Leibowitz, was generally held to be the favourite.

And then, just as suddenly as it had begun, Arthur's enthusiasm for the sport had vanished again, and if you talked to him about it, he just replied with a shrug and an embarrassed smile.

'I'm no longer active,' he explained now, 'haven't been for ages, but an association like this needs a doctor, and I said I was willing...'

'Is it one of the doctor's duties to organise a flag for the association?'

'I just thought...' Arthur had blushed for no reason at all, a weakness from which he had suffered even as a child. 'You could help me,' he said. 'You write for the Israelite Weekly News every now and again. If they published an appeal...To raise some money. A flag like that is expensive.'

'How expensive?'

'Very expensive,' said Arthur and blushed again.

It was quite customary to save the money for an advertisement by placing a free classified, and there was no reason why Pinchas shouldn't do him that small favour. 'That can be done,' he said. 'But right now I'm hungry. Every year for days in advance I look forward to the first matzo breakfast. A thick layer of butter and then strawberry jam on top.'

Outside the house – Mimi and Pinchas now lived on Morgartenstrasse – a deliveryman stood squinting at the doorbells like someone who can't read and is using his short-sightedness as an excuse.

'Can I help you?' asked Pinchas.

The deliveryman pushed his red and black cap, whose brass letters identified him as number forty-six, to the back of his head, and rubbed his forehead dry with a stained handkerchief, even though it wasn't at all hot. 'I'm supposed to drop off a letter,' he said at last, 'But he doesn't seem to live here.'

'What name?'

'Meijer,' said the deliveryman, and added, with the face of a scientist who has just made a great discovery, 'You know, it's funny. There are so many people called Meijer, but when you have to look for one, you can't find him.'

'Could I see the letter?'

The deliveryman pulled an envelope from the inside pocket of his uniform jacket, took a step back and, facing away from Pinchas, his torso bent shelteringly forward, studied the address, a schoolboy who doesn't want his neighbour copying from him. 'His name is Meijer,' he said after a while and nodded several times. 'With a very odd first name.' He held the envelope so close in front of his eyes that his whole face disappeared behind it. 'Pinchas Meijer.'

'In that case the letter must be for me,' said Pinchas.

'Is your name Meijer?' the deliveryman asked suspiciously.

'My name is Pomeranz.'

'The letter is for Meijer.'

'My name is Meijer,' Arthur butted in.

'And you live here?'

'No,' Arthur began. 'I'm ...' The deliveryman started turning his head back and forth, very slowly from left to right and back again, as if to say, 'I'm far too clever to fall for con-men!' so Arthur decided a white lie was called for. 'Yes, I live here.'

'And your name is Meijer?'

'Yes.'

'Pinchas Meijer?'

'To an extent,' said Arthur.

As he left, the deliveryman was convinced that something not quite right had occurred. He hadn't even been given a tip. He couldn't have known that on feast days Jews aren't allowed to carry money in their pockets.

They opened the letter at the dining room table, where Mimi and Désirée were still sitting over their late breakfast.

Dear Uncle Pinchas,

I remember so much, and I still can't remember your surname. I'm just writing 'Meijer' on the envelope. You were always Uncle Pinchas to me, and I hope you won't mind if I continue to call you that. I still remember the stories you told us when I visited you to play with Désirée. One of them was about a fish so big that sailors lit a fire on it and had a picnic. Back then I believed in that fish, and in a way I still do.

You once told me you had a tooth missing, and the doctor gave you an artificial one. I was to guess which one it was, and I couldn't find out. They all looked the same, and yet one was false and the others were real. I couldn't understand that at all.

I also remember that you promised me a very special present for my bar mitzvah. I never got it.

I'm no longer drunk, even though all this may read as if I am. We had to celebrate the opening of the new university building with German colleagues, and didn't leave the pub for three days.

I'm writing this letter to apologise to you and Aunt Mimi and Désirée. I behaved incredibly badly, and it didn't just have to do with the drinking. Sometimes there are moments

The sentence ended there, without a full stop or a comma, and what came next had plainly been added later: the same handwriting, but in a hand much more angular and controlled.

I beg you to forgive me, and promise that I will never again trouble you with such a ridiculous performance.

Respectfully yours

Alfred Meijer

Pinchas carefully folded the letter as one folds a document that one is going to need for a trial. Arthur had taken off his glasses and was rubbing his nose. Désirée seemed to be counting the matzo crumbs on the tablecloth.

'*Scandaleux*,' said Mimi.

38

François had only employed his chauffeur because his name was Landolt. He had previously been his coachman, and François had bought him a chauffeur's cap and a pair of leather gloves and organised driving lessons for him.

'Where can they be, Landolt?' he could say now, or, 'Faster, Landolt', and because it was a sour joke, pickled in vinegar, as it were, it stayed fresh for a long time. He could equally well have got himself a dog, some mutt off the street, and called it Landolt, but dogs just whine if you treat them badly, and put their tails between their legs.

A human being was better.

His Landolt had sticking-out ears. From the back seat it looked as if the grey cap was wedged in between them. The shaved back of the head above the collar of the dust coat was pimply and inflamed. He was an ugly person, this Landolt.

That was another reason why Janki had employed him.

'Everything satisfactory, Landolt?'

'Yes, Herr Meijer.'

If he leaned forward, he could see beyond the back of the driver's seat how tightly Landolt had to grip the steering wheel. Sometimes, after a long journey, he had blisters on his hands.

Which was fine.

Of course it would have been more comfortable to take the train to Baden. One wouldn't have got so dusty, and Mama would have picked him up at the station. She always enjoyed being on her own with him for a few minutes, even though they usually didn't talk, but just walked along in silence side by side. Sometimes he thought, 'One could explain to her how everything came about.' But he owed no one an explanation.

No one.

The car was a Buchet, with a radiator that looked like a gaping mouth. French quality. François had never become Swiss, unlike Arthur, and he had no plans to do so, either. Why conform when you get nothing from it?

Once they had covered the journey from Zurich to Baden in three quarters of an hour. François loved those moments when the cloud of dust that you pulled behind you gave you a sense of speed. If necessary, the car with its heavy iron springs could also cope with potholes and bumps in the road. A car was something for people who refused to be held up. It was all about power.

Twenty-five horsepower. François liked the thought of twenty-five horses having to strain to take him to Baden.

Buchet engines were even put in aeroplanes.

'Faster, Landolt!' he said, and had to repeat it in a louder voice because the engine was making such a racket. Landolt.

They had met twice, and on both occasions Landolt had been polite. He had got to his feet when François came in, had offered him a chair and held out his cigarette case. Dark brown leather with an engraved gold family crest. François hated him for it.

'You have made me a very interesting proposal,' he had said.

Landolt owned a plot of land – he owned a lot of them, but there was this one, this particular one – a plot of land that had always belonged to his family. 'Always,' he said, and it sounded almost like an apology, as if the Landolts had stood outside of history without having to do anything, once rich, always rich. There was a squat, elongated building on this particular plot, a former workshop or factory, with narrow windows, long obscured, and dirty green, moss-covered roof tiles. A ruin in a prime location, just a stone's throw from the Paradeplatz. Forgotten and abandoned, because you didn't need to do anything with it.

Not if you were a Landolt.

François had walked past this plot so often that it almost belonged to him. He knew exactly where the entrance to his new department store would be, two massive double doors that had to be open whenever the weather permitted, so that you had no option but to walk in, not just into a shop, but into a world where you could stroll around and gasp with amazement and buy lots of things. He had paced out the length of the shop windows, each one four and a half metres long, and had already envisioned the displays, not goods crammed together as if in a general store, but generous ensembles, designed by artists.

He had already counted the customers.

Business wasn't going badly, far from it. None the less, it was all very limited. It was called a department store, but when it came down to it you were still standing behind the counter and had to bow and scrape each time you made a sale. That wasn't what he wanted, he had other plans, he had always had, much bigger, and he would see to it that they were realised. One man walks on foot, another buys a Buchet. Eventually, he had firmly decided, he would get hold of the property near the Paradeplatz, regardless of the cost. Even then Landolt had been an old man, a sickly old man, and his inheritors would...

One of Landolt's grandsons was in the same student fraternity as Alfred. They were getting closer to one another.

Once Alfred had his doctorate...Dr. jur. Alfred Meijer. He should have been given a second first name, as was the practice in America. Dr. jur. Alfred D. Meijer.

D for Department Store.

Our junior head, Dr Meijer.

Eventually.

For now Alfred was a freshman, and François was almost prouder of the term than his son was. And he didn't mind if Alfred stayed up all night with his fraternity and couldn't get out of bed in the morning. That was bound to happen. For now the important thing was that he was meeting people there. One had to belong.

That at least had been right.

That at least.

The Buchet had slowed down, and now came to a standstill on the main road, still pulsing and quivering as if the machine could sense François's impatience. Two cows whose ribs could be counted blocked the way, and the farmer's boy who was supposed to take them to the field, or to the butcher or the knacker, just stood there, switch in hand, and stared at the automobile as if he'd never seen one before.

François leaned out of the car and had to stretch until his hand reached the rubber bulb of the horn. The noise was too loud, half bleat and half groan. The cows didn't even look up – as if their own horns were too heavy to lift, they were so thin – and then at last they set off, leisurely old ladies who stretched out each movement to fill as much of their empty days as they could with their few errands.

'Now drive, Landolt!'

He had made a quite respectable offer. Nothing trivial. Mina's dowry had not been inconsiderable, and had grown still further along with the business. Janki was also prepared to top up his silent partnership. Everything had been discussed with the bank, even though Herr Hildebrand there had said, 'They won't sell you the property; you'll see.'

And then Landolt coughed into his handkerchief and said, 'A very interesting proposal that you've made to me.' And offered him a chair and held out his cigarette case.

How he hated that man.

'You can do your sums, that much is obvious,' said Landolt. 'Everything you've written there makes sense. It's almost a shame...' He turned his cigar around in his fingers, puffed on it and had all the time in the world. Studied the glowing ember as if he had just invented fire.

'...almost a shame that we can't go into business together.'

The plot, Landolt explained, belonged to a family trust. He himself, and this had been stipulated, as the eldest of his generation, had sole discretionary power, he could sell if a sale seemed appropriate, but he had certain rules to observe.

Superannuated rules, perhaps, he wouldn't argue about that right now, but none the less binding for that. And one of those rules – 'It really is almost a shame!' – was that one did not do business with people of the Mosaic faith.

'Is it really laid down in those terms?' François had asked.

And Landolt had studied his cigar, whose ember still didn't strike him as perfect, and had replied, 'There are things that you don't have to write down.'

'That's the only reason? If I weren't a Jew, would you sell me the property? At that price?'

'In principle, yes.'

That had been the moment. The precise moment.

It was seven years ago now.

Already seven years.

There was suddenly a rotten smell in the air. Probably the rapeseed that was already blossoming in a field.

'Drive faster, Landolt!'

It was the first time in his life that François had thought about his Jewishness, and he moved the vague sense of his membership of the community around in his personal accounts book, entering it now in one column, now in the other, and got a different result every time. He weighed up loyalty against usefulness, compared old habits with new opportunities and started one new calculation after another. Nothing like faith appeared in any of them, because he had never had faith. If such philosophical concepts had been part of his world, he would probably have described himself as an agnostic, someone who considers it a waste of time to ask questions for which there are no answers. According to ancient Jewish practice the name 'God' was never put down on paper out of sheer awe of the sacred, one writes 'G-d'. For François, this traditional lacuna had always meant something quite different from respect: there was simply nothing there. Or to put it another way: everyone was free to put whatever they liked in the gap.

These were unfamiliar trains of thought for him. All through his life he had given more thought to his moustache – for years he had worn it short, no longer as striking as it had been in Baden – than to his religion. For him, being a Jew had been just as natural as the fact that he had brown eyes, or that his hair had turned grey far too soon.

It was just how it was.

But hair could be dyed, and he could hide his eyes behind a pair of glasses.

Mina had a paralysed leg, but as long as she stayed sitting on her chair, no one noticed.

Not that his Jewishness was the same as a handicap, of course not. But a handicap it sometimes was. The business with the plot of land was just one example among many. Situations had repeatedly arisen in which it would have been more useful to be called Huber or Müller. Things were easier for a Meier than for a Meijer.

And a Landolt could afford to do anything he liked.

A stone thrown up from the road struck the spokes of the back wheel. It sounded like a string breaking in a piano.

'Be careful, Landolt!'

He didn't talk to anyone about it, not even to Mina. Even though they'd been talking to each other more and more often for some time, and that had been unexpected. At the time he had married a dowry, and Mina had come with it, a bale of satin fabric with last year's pattern that you have to take if you also want the fashion material currently in demand. Their marriage had been a business deal, an honest, clean transaction. She had acquired a husband, and he the chance to start a company at a young age. He had fulfilled his part, he had always been a decent husband, even though Mina, with her paralysed leg, wasn't really presentable. If he cheated on his wife, he did it so discreetly that she didn't have to notice if she didn't want to. But then, very gradually, he had got used to her, the way people who keep pets get used to a dog; he had even started missing her if he came home and she happened not to be there.

At first he had only sometimes thought out loud, had summed up in words a problem or a decision that needed to be made, and he had certainly not expected a comment from Mina, let alone a solution. But Mina could listen the way other women play the piano or arrange flowers, she had turned it into an art form, so that when telling a story one found the answers one had been looking for all by oneself, before having them confirmed by Mina. She was a good person to talk to.

An outsider would probably have observed that in the course of his marriage François had gradually fallen in love with his wife, that familiarity had gradually turned to affection. But there was no more room for the word 'love' in François's vocabulary than there was for 'faith' or 'blind trust'. Human beings – and this reflection would also have been alien to the businessman François Meijer – can feel more than they can say.

He told her nothing about Landolt. Only that the purchase of the property had fallen through. But another solution would be found sooner or later.

There was nothing to discuss, either. For the time being he was only collecting information. Purely theoretically. Just in case. An imaginary manoeuvre, nothing more. A general doesn't go straight into battle just because he's working on a strategy.

Even the conversation with Pastor Widmer had been nothing more than that. A conversation, nothing more. Just because you're talking to people doesn't mean you're making plans with them.

He had just happened by the church. If the property by Paradeplatz was not to be had, he would have to look for another one. He would have to stroll through the city without a precise goal in mind. Look at the people and see them as customers. Where did they keep going? Where did they stop? If you want to cast a net, you have to know where the fishes swim.

He had gone in purely out of curiosity. A tourist passing an interesting ruin in a strange city. He had never been inside a church before. It wouldn't be all that different from a synagogue, but since there was one there…He just had time.

Entirely by chance.

His first impression was a great disappointment. He had always imagined a church as something magnificent, all colours and paintings and fragrances, but apart from the brightly coloured windows this was just a bare hall, high and narrow and forbidding, a building with pursed lips, you might say.

No incense in his nostrils, just dust and the waxy solution that was rubbed on the pews. It was how his schoolroom had smelled after the summer holidays.

You entered by a side door; they probably opened the main entrance only on Sunday. The first thing you caught sight of was a wooden stand holding texts and brochures. 'Too many goods in too tight a space,' François noted with a practised eye. Bad for profits. Over-filled shelves signal to the customer that there's no special hurry to buy.

Grey unadorned walls, stone blocks that looked damp but weren't. At the back a loft with organ pipes. No galleries to the side. Men and women weren't separated here during the service.

François couldn't imagine sitting next to Mina during prayers. But that was out of the question in any case. He was just here by chance.

Purely out of curiosity.

They didn't have individual seats for the members of the congregation as they did in the synagogue, just long benches in which, François imagined, people probably came unpleasantly close to one another.

No little desk to set down books and tallis.

Stupid. As if they would need a tallis here.

Why shouldn't François just sit down? He had been walking through the city for ages, and his legs were tired.

There was even a special board to rest your feet on. Not really comfortable, it seemed to him. But perhaps the construction had another purpose.

Of course.

'I would never kneel,' thought François. 'I would feel ridiculous.'

A pulpit had been fitted to one of the pillars that held up the barrel vaulting. Stuck on like an afterthought. Among the Christians, François remembered, you weren't born a priest, you could become one.

You could become anything you liked.

Old Kahn, as his name suggested, was a Kohen. François had always found it hard to see Mina's father as being in any way holy just because he pulled his tallis over his head when giving the priest's blessing. Perhaps the Christian system wasn't all that silly.

Purely theoretically. Not that it had been his intention.

At the front to the right, where the rabbi would have sat in a synagogue, a panel of numbers was fasted to the wall. '124, 1–4, 19, 1, 2, 6.' Every religion had its secrets.

The same panel on the left as well.

In the middle the cross.

The tseylem.

An empty cross, with no one hanging from it. They no longer needed the image because it was already in their heads. Later on, that was also an important factor in his decision. François could never really have got used to a naked man on the cross.

So this was a church. Disappointing, all in all. Well, anyway, it had nothing to do with him.

'It's customary to remove your hat,' a voice said. It was the first sentence that Pastor Widmer uttered to him.

Widmer was as unadorned as his church. He might have been mistaken for the shammes, or whatever they called it here. A black suit and a black tie. A peasant face, far too healthy for the murky room. His round glasses didn't fit the rest of his face, as if he'd only put them on to make himself look more dignified.

'I've never seen you here before,' said Widmer.

That was how they fell into conversation.

Quite by chance.

If Widmer had had anything even slightly priest-like about him, anything solemn or unctuous, François would have put his hat back on and left. He would have continued his walk and thought no more about the matter. Or thought about it and done nothing. If Widmer had been just slightly different. If he had shown the merest hint of the thrill of the chase. The slightest bit of interest in winning a new sheep for his flock.

But it wasn't like that. Not at all. He wanted nothing from François, and François wanted nothing from him. Two reasonable human beings talking reasonably to one another. Talking about similarities and differences, possibilities and impossibilities. Very generally. As if it didn't really concern either of them.

And it didn't concern either of them. It concerned a property. The perfect property in the perfect spot. It concerned Landolt.

When it could no longer be kept a secret, François said to Mina, 'No one converted me. It's not about that at all. There's no point clinging to outmoded traditions that bring you nothing but disadvantages. That was always your opinion. You have never worn a sheitel, and the world didn't end. My father stops eating kosher as soon as he's out of the house. Such things aren't important these days. We're living in the twentieth century. And what does it change? I haven't been to synagogue for two years. Now I won't go to church instead. Now say something!'

But Mina was only listening. She had sometimes expressed her opinions as a young girl, but had grown up in the meantime.

'If you think about it properly, these are all just outward appearances. I no longer get dressed like Grandfather Salomon. You have to conform. You have to forge ahead, not creep along behind. We will have the most modern department store in Zurich, if that property ...'

'Ah, yes,' said Mina. 'The plot of land.'

'That was just the pretext. Even without it I would sooner or later ... If only because of Alfred. You want him to have the best chances too. You want him to be able to study and join a fraternity.'

'There are Jewish student fraternities.'

'They're not the same thing. I want him to be able to do anything he wants. And so do you.'

'I want my son to know where he belongs.'

'He'll get used to it. At his age it isn't a problem. You put the candles on a fir-tree instead of a Chanukah menorah. The difference isn't that great. A child does what its parents do.'

'I'm not going to get baptised,' said Mina.

'But ...'

'And another thing, François: I'm not going to get divorced.'

39

What do you wear to your own baptism? They don't tell you that sort of thing. Frock coat and top hat? That would have given the matter a fake solemnity. When a businessman starts working with a new partner, he doesn't go into the office in morning dress and striped trousers. On the other hand: you can't look too everyday either, it would have been impolite. People mustn't think he didn't know how to behave in church.

But there wouldn't be any people there. Just Widmer and Alfred and him. Don't make a fuss, he had insisted on that. No fuss, on any account. Ideally he would just have signed a piece of paper, a declaration under oath, and that would have brought the matter to its conclusion. But if Widmer was also a reasonable person and not a creeping Jesus, certain forms, he thought, should be simple. Of course in the end it came down to faith and nothing else, Herr Meijer was right about that, but the church was made for people, and people needed rituals. 'On this point the Catholics are far ahead of us. I sometimes think the organ converted more people than the most eloquent sermon ever did.'

Please God no organ! François had put his foot down on that one. He couldn't have borne organ music, and although the similarity would never have occurred to him, in this respect his thinking was not very different from that of Pinchas, who had switched congregations because of a harmonium. 'Plain and simple,' he said when they discussed the ceremony, 'above all I want it to be plain and simple. And with no people.' He had even been able to talk Widmer out of having a sponsor. They weren't really indispensable, he had admitted in the end.

That was one advantage of the new religion: you could strike deals with it.

In the end they decided on a Tuesday morning at half past eight. 'The men are still being shaved, and women are at the market.' François opted for a plain single-breasted suit of salt-and-pepper Marengo, with a silver-grey tie, which was quite solemn enough. Alfred wore his sailor suit; at his age that was always correct. François had requested a day off school for him, on the grounds of unpostponable family matters.

Mina could just have slept a little longer, could have let them go and get the thing out of the way and never talk about it again afterwards. But when the time came she was standing in the doorway, quite naturally, as if she were just going to the shops or to school, she smoothed the ribbons of Alfred's sailor cap and straightened François's tie. Then she stopped in front of him and said, 'You can still change your mind.'

François didn't change his mind. When a reasonable person has made a reasonable decision, it would be unreasonable of him not to carry it out.

Widmer was already waiting for them. He was wearing the same black suit as always, in which he looked like his own sacristan. Yes, François had learned the word for a Christian shammes in the meantime. The parson had assumed a solemn expression that suited his peasant face no better than his wire-framed glasses. He kept his hands folded in front of his belly as if to hide from François the black book that he was holding ready in preparation. His jacket stretched across his torso. 'Badly cut,' thought François.

The three of them stood around the font. The basin, polished red granite, grew from a pair of carved hands, the only graven image that François had been able to discover in this austere church.

Judaism, he reflected, had no graven images either. The difference wasn't so great.

When you thought about it rationally.

'Shall we start?' asked Widmer.

François switched his hat from his right hand to his left. He didn't know if he would have to cross himself later, and he didn't want to look clumsy.

'Let's start,' he said.

Alfred held his head lowered, a schoolboy before an exam that he hadn't revised for.

Widmer opened his book. Between the pages there were lots of silk ribbons in various colours. François hoped he wouldn't need all the marked passages.

'I shall read from the gospel of Matthew,' said Widmer. 'Chapter twenty-eight, verses eighteen to twenty.'

Now he did have that unctuous priestly voice. Had he been pretending until now?

'And Jesus came and spake unto them saying, All power is given unto me in heaven and earth. Go ye therefore and teach all nations, baptising them in the name of the Father, and of the Son, and of the Holy Ghost.'

'He's explained that thing about the Holy Ghost to me five times,' thought François. 'I've never understood it.'

'Teaching them to observe all things whatsoever I have commanded you; and lo, I am with you always, even unto the end of the world.'

Parson Widmer closed his book with such vigour that the silk ribbons flapped. 'That didn't take long,' thought François, and felt slightly disappointed.

But Widmer hadn't finished yet. It was just that he didn't need a template for what came next.

'Our Father, which art in Heaven. Hallowed be Thy Name.'

François had grown up with Hebrew prayers, of which he had understood only scraps. 'That makes it easier,' he thought now.

'Thy kingdom come. Thy will be done on earth as it is in heaven.'

The organ struck up with a great roar of thunder. A storm in the empty church.

'Give us this day our daily bread.'

François knew the tune. It is sung three times on the eve of Yom Kippur, the most solemn prayer of the whole year.

The prayer with which one frees oneself from religious vows. So that God does not lay claim to promises made to him too lightly. So that he does not punish one.

The organ played 'Kol Nidre'.

The organist was sitting somewhere up in the loft, screened by the handrail, but François saw him sitting there, all in black, and his hands, hammering down on the keyboard, were those of an old man.

The organ sang 'Kol Nidre'. 'Ve-esarei, vacharamei, va konomei.' François knew the voice, he had always known it.

As he played, Uncle Melnitz rocked his torso back and forth, as a devout person would do, or a musician immersing himself in his music, he stretched his arms aloft, as one dances behind the Torah scroll, he clapped his hands, ay, ay, ay, and didn't leave out a note, not one, he made the organ sing and he himself sang along, and François understood every word, even though it was in Aramaic and foreign and concerned him not at all.

'Vechinuyei, vekinusei ush'vuot,' sang Uncle Melnitz.

A little louder each time, as custom decrees.

'All vows, prohibitions, oaths and consecrations,' he sang, 'let them be permitted, abandoned, cancelled and null and void.'

'And forgive us our trespasses,' said Widmer.

'I regret them all,' sang Uncle Melnitz.

And sang it again and then again.

'As we forgive those who trespass against us.'

And then Melnitz stood next to François and clapped his hands in time to the music, the organ played a dance and Uncle Melnitz took François by the shoulders and whirled him in a circle and kissed him on the forehead and was glad because the oaths were not oaths and the vows not vows. 'You can have your Jewishness washed away,' he said – a step to the left, a step to the right – 'but it will do you no good. It has never done anyone any good. They have always waved it around in front of our noses with the greatest freedom,' he said – a step forward, a step back – 'but when we tried to touch it, they had always meant it differently.'

'The Jews in Spain,' said Uncle Melnitz. 'You remember? The proud Sephardim. "Have yourselves baptised," they said to them. All smiles. "It will spare you the pyre and purgatory, and everyone will love you. Just a few drops dripped on your foreheads, and you will be Spaniards like all the rest. Then you can be doctors and ministers and whatever you like. You can buy plots of land and build department stores with doors that stand open to everyone, with sales staff who are always friendly, and paternoster lifts. Just a few drops," they said.'

'And lead us not into temptation.'

'And then they called them Marranos, which means swine, and all that lovely baptismal water did them no good at all.'

Uncle Melnitz stuck his bony finger in the font and licked it. At home in Baden fat Christine had tested the soup like that.

'It tastes bitter,' said Melnitz and pulled a face. 'If you pour salt water into a person, keep pouring one jug and then another and another, if you hold his nose closed so that he can decide with his God-given free will whether he wants to drink or suffocate, and then if you ask him if he has secretly remained a Jew, at least in his thoughts, then baptism will protect him no longer. Then the Jew comes back out of him again. You may have to jump on his belly, but he will come out.

'You can also pull out his nails or break his fingers. You can hang him up by his arms and twist his joints apart until he dances in the air and sings the song that goes with it, ay, ay, ay. There are lots of things you can do to tickle the Jew back out. Fat books have been written on the subject. When you have to hang him up and when twist him apart. So that everything has its order. And then, if he is burned – and he was always burned – then they didn't do it themselves. They left that task to the worldly courts, full of regret, and they themselves always stood sympathetically by his pyre, Bible in hand, and said to him, "Repent! Convert! So that you go not to Hell as a dead Jew, but to Heaven as a dead Christian." They didn't even keep that promise, oh no.

'No ministerial hat did any good. No doctorate, and no bright fraternity ribbon. And no department store in the best location, with the most beautiful window displays in the whole city. None of it did any good. A Jew remains a Jew remains a Jew. Yes. Regardless how often he has himself baptised.'

And he sat back down in the loft and rocked to the tune, ay, ay, ay, hammered his ancient hands down on the keys, trod the pedals with his feet and pulled out the stops, vox humana and vox angelica, and made the very deepest bass notes thunder.

'Kol Nidre', he made the organ sing. 'May our oaths be no oaths and our vows no vows.'

'And lead us not into temptation,' said Widmer, 'but deliver us from Evil. For Thine is the kingdom, the power and glory, forever and ever. Amen.' He looked expectantly at François.

'Amen,' said François. And nudged Alfred, who also said, 'Amen.'

'And now the declaration of faith.' Widmer made that solemn face again. 'If you don't mind, I will speak it on your behalf. For you too, Alfred. It's enough that you think along with the words. God recognises his own by their hearts.'

By their hearts.

'I believe in God, the Father Almighty, creator of heaven and the earth,' said the man with the peasant face.

'Think along with the words like a nice chap,' whispered Melnitz.

'And of Jesus Christ, his only son, our Lord, who was conceived through the Holy Spirit, born of the Virgin Mary, suffered under Pontius Pilate, was crucified, died and was buried, he descended into hell, on the third day he rose again from the dead, he ascended into heaven, and is seated at the right hand of God the Father; from there he will come to judge the living and the dead.'

'Remember all that,' whispered Melnitz.

'I believe in the Holy Spirit, the holy Christian Church, the communion of saints, the forgiveness of sins, the resurrection of the body, and life everlasting.'

'That's a lot,' said Melnitz, and made the organ sound again.

'Amen,' said the man with the round wire-framed glasses.

'Amen,' said François.

And Alfred repeated, 'Amen.' But only after his father had given him a nudge.

'Omeyn,' said Uncle Melnitz.

When Widmer poured water over his head for the third time, some of it dripped onto his silk tie. François would have liked to wipe it off, but didn't know if that would have been correct or not.

All of a sudden it was so strangely quiet. Or had it been as quiet as that for a long time?

'Why are you stopping, Landolt?'

'We're there, Herr Meijer.'

The flat smelled of chremsels, the sweet pastry without which Pesach can never be quite complete – 'Ah, yes, Pesach,' thought François – and from the kitchen, where fat Christine had not reigned for some time, there came the distant clatter of a frying pan.

Time and again the room in the Baden flat had assumed new functions, like a person without any particular gifts whom life drives from job to job. It had been a sewing room and the dying room of Uncle Salomon. When Chanele had had her kidney complaint and needed round-the-clock care, the nurse had lived in it, a severe woman who, it turned out later, had the curious habit of marking her presence with a pencilled line on the wallpaper beside the bed, a prisoner waiting to be released.

Now it was Janki's office; by the window there stood a desk covered with papers, and hanging on the wall was the picture of François Delormes that had hung for all those years in the back room of the French Fabric Warehouse, the portrait of a saint. It wasn't a painting, just a cutting from an illustrated magazine, but Janki had still had it very lavishly framed.

'Where is Mama?' asked François.

'She's bringing Arthur to the station.'

'Arthur?'

'He paid us a surprise visit. Because it's Chol HaMoed. You remember?'

Of course François remembered. Chol HaMoed is the time between the 'front' and the 'back' feast days, where the yontev takes a break but everyday life isn't yet quite in control again.

'And what did he want?'

'To convince me that the French Fabric Warehouse should donate a flag to his gymnastic association. That would be a good advertisement, he said.'

'Did you tell him you don't need any more advertisements?'

Janki shook his head. 'It's not signed yet.'

'But you're going to sign?'

'I want you to take another look at the contracts. You know these things better than I do.' Janki took a narrow bundle of papers from the desk and walked to the dining room ahead of his eldest son.

'He's getting old,' thought François.

The walking stick with lion's-head handle was still the same, but when Janki Meijer used it to support himself, it was no longer an elegant gesture, but instead an unpleasant necessity. His right leg, which had always dragged a little, had been really painful for some time, and had simply bent several times for no discernible reason. The stick, once an ornament and now a tool, proved less than suited to its new task. When Janki, fighting to keep his balance, gripped the handle too tightly, the carved mane of the lion's head left painful marks in the palm of his hand. None the less, Janki would never have swapped his stick for another; it would have been like giving up a part of his character.

'Pain?' asked François.

'Everything's fine.'

'Even your leg?'

'Couldn't be better.'

'I had the impression...'

'That's the old war wound. It's only natural that I should feel it from time to time.'

Janki had never been in a battle in the war of 1870–71, and had certainly never been wounded. But François didn't contradict his father. Everyone has the right to turn himself into whatever he wants.

The dining room, he was always surprised to notice, was much smaller than he remembered. Even the table – tropical wood! – was a perfectly ordinary table. The tantalus still stood on the sideboard, the half-full crystal jug in its silver prison. Since his childhood the level of the golden liquid locked in it hadn't changed. 'What's actually in there?' asked François.

'I don't know. I've never had a key for it.'

The contracts were sound. The French Warehouse and the Modern Emporium were bought by Paul Schnegg, a son of the rich Schneggs who also owned the House of the Red Shield, and whose parents François had once met at an unfortunate soirée. Schnegg took over the shops as they were, and wanted to go on running at least the Modern Emporium. There wouldn't even be a closing-down sale. The price was good, and Janki would invest the money in François's firm.

'What does Mama have to say about that?'

'I've been working for forty years,' said Janki. 'Haven't I earned a bit of peace?'

'So she didn't agree.'

'It's a purely business decision.' Janki carefully arranged the papers that François hadn't even discomposed. 'And it will do her good too. We will travel. A spa treatment by a lake, and later perhaps Italy.'

'So everything's all right?'

'Everything's all right.'

There must have been violent arguments between his parents, François was quite sure of that. The store had been the content of Chanele's life. What was she supposed to do without her shop?

But the decision was sensible, and good sense has to govern decisions in business matters. Just good sense, no emotions.

Clear conditions. Clear rules. Clear decisions.

Anything else was unfair.

Damn it, it was unfair.

He had turned up at Landolt's the following day. With his baptismal certificate in his pocket.

Landolt smiled, offered him a chair and pushed the cigarette case with the family crest over the table.

The family crest that made him something better just because it also hung in some guildhall or other.

How he hated this man.

'What brings me this unexpected pleasure, Herr Meijer?' asked Landolt and coughed into his handkerchief.

Cleaned his glasses awkwardly before putting them on again.

Then studied the baptismal certificate as thoroughly as a scholar studies a document in a foreign language.

Even held it up to the light.

Folded the paper up again and set it precisely in the middle of the table. A poker player putting down his bet.

But games have rules, and Landolt wasn't sticking to them.

He took his glasses off again and said:

He said it in a very friendly voice.

As if it were really a question.

Said: 'May I ask why you're showing me this?'

'The property. You couldn't sell it to a Jew.'

'Ah,' said Landolt and shook his head regretfully. 'It's really almost a shame. But you see, my dear Herr Meijer: even a baptised Jew is still a Jew.'

'Damn it, Landolt! Drive!'

40

Mimi ate liqueur chocolates for medical reasons. Dr Wertheim had actually prescribed port for her frail constitution, but Mimi couldn't stomach alcohol – 'I will never understand how anyone can enjoy getting tiddly!' – and actually had to force herself at least to take the recommended stimulant in this form. If she now put the fourth of these balls of sweetness into her mouth, it was entirely Désirée's fault.

You trust your children, you make sacrifices for them, and then something like this happens!

She had become quite dizzy with excitement, and her migraine was announcing its presence again. She drew little circles on her temples with her fingertips, leaving fine traces of chocolate.

'Good that you're back, Désirée,' she said and smiled tragically. 'So you've been out with Esther Weill?'

'Yes, Mama,' said Désirée, looking rather surprised. Esther Weill, of the shoe-shop Weill's, was her best friend, and Mimi had never before objected to the two of them going walking or visiting exhibitions together.

'And you really saw a big fish in that booth, at the top of the square?'

'Not a fish, Mama, a whale. A whale is a mammal.'

'How nice,' said Mimi in a worryingly benign voice. 'How considerate of you to enlighten your stupid mother about such matters. So it's a mammal? How interesting.'

Her hand reached for the next praline.

'Of course it's only a skeleton. But massive! Much bigger than I'd imagined. They have to transport it on three carts and reassemble it in each new town. The skull alone …'

'The skull,' said Mimi and turned a chocolate wrapped in shiny silver paper around in her fingers like a missile. 'I'm particularly interested in that. What does it look like, this skull?'

'Very long and narrow. Like an enormous bird's beak.'

'A bird's beak. Very interesting.' The little ball turned rotated faster and faster.

'Are you quite all right, Mama?'

'Me? Why ever not? I just always like to hear about all the things my daughter experiences. With her best friend. Describe this whale's lower jaw?'

Désirée stared at her mother. 'It's lower jaw?'

'Or do whales not have things like that? Perhaps because they're mammals?'

'I don't understand what's up with you, Mama.'

'But I understand very well.' Mimi had planned to remain quite calm, but now she struck the table. Brownish juice dripped from her fist onto the good table-cloth. 'I understand that my daughter is lying to me.'

'I…'

With an extravagant gesture that had something of a practised air – and she had actually tried it out two or three times as she waited for her daughter – Mimi set down the *Tages-Anzeiger* down in front of Désirée. The gesture didn't have entirely the dramatic effect that she was looking for, because her fingers stuck to the paper. She irritably took her handkerchief from her sleeve and wiped her hand clean.

'Read!' she said. 'Page four. "Miscellaneous news".'

Now it would not have been true to say that Mimi studied the newspaper every day. The small letters put too much of a strain on her eyes. But the new bishge, who had an urge for higher things, read the paper, which Pinchas subscribed to, every morning from cover to cover during her coffee break and, if Mimi was unable to avoid her, liked to repeat her newly acquired wisdom. Today it had been a very small news item, which she was absolutely unable to get over. 'Who would do such a thing?' she had asked, shaking her head.

'A curious theft,' read Désirée, 'took place the night before last in Zurich. From the travelling natural history cabinet currently attracting the attention of the educated classes behind the Museum, the lower jaw of the skeleton of a sperm whale (Physeter macrocephalus) on display there was pilfered. According to Herr Marian Zehntenhaus, the owner of the booth, the missing piece of bone was almost three metres in length, and can only have been carried away on a cart. So far there is no trace of any perpetrator, but it is assumed that irresponsible night-time gangs lie behind this low crime. A reward of fifty francs is offered for any information about the location of the nobbled piece of skeleton. This generous sum is explained by the considerable scientific damage done by this senseless act of vandalism. In the view of Herr Zehntenhaus, an incomplete skeleton is entirely worthless and no longer suitable for exhibition purposes. So the booth on the Platzspitz remains closed until further notice. Tickets already purchased may be returned to the booking office.'

Désirée looked up from the newspaper, her face bright red.

'Can you explain to me,' said Mimi, her voice as sweet as her pralines, 'can you please explain to your stupid mother how you and Esther Weill visited an exhibition that isn't even open?'

'We…' said Désirée, fingering the piqué collar of her blouse. 'We went…'

'I don't deserve this.' Mimi's powdered cheeks quivered like those of a wine connoisseur testingly sloshing a good wine around in his mouth. 'If I were one of those mother hens who go around checking up on every single little thing their children do, then perhaps I might understand. But I'm not like that. *Certainement pas.* I have never in my life got involved. Never. That's why it pains me so much that you have lately begun to consider it necessary to lie to me.' She darted an exploratory glance at her hand and then, when it was seen to be satisfactory free of any traces of chocolate and liqueur, she brought it to her bosom. 'It hurts me deep in my heart.'

'I'm sorry, Mama.'

'And you think that's enough?' Mimi dabbed the corners of her eyes with her handkerchief. 'All my life I have sacrificed myself for you, you have no idea how I have suffered just to bring you into the world, *tu m'as déchirée, ma petite*, and this is the thanks I get now. You have secrets from me. See-crets.' She stretched the word out as long as it would go.

'Today Esther and I were...'

'No, don't say anything.' Mimi, red-cheeked, was enjoying the drama of the scene. 'I don't want to know. If my daughter no longer trusts me, if I no longer have a daughter, then I must live with that. It breaks my heart, but if it is to be my fate, then I shall endure that too. That too,' she repeated in a quiet voice, tilted her head to the side and, in a gesture that she had lately seen in the Municipal theatre, laid the back of her hand to her brow.

It took ten minutes and two more liqueur chocolates before Désirée was finally prepared to deliver her confession.

'But you must promise me not to tell anyone.'

'You know me, ma petite. No one can keep a secret as well as I. Lots of people have told me that.'

'You swear?'

'All right then,' said Mimi. 'I swear.'

And then, with a lot of fidgeting and blushing, it suddenly came out: Esther Weill, Désirée's best friend, had an admirer.

'A real admirer,' said Désirée.

They met in secret, took long strolls, hand in hand, drank coffee in places that decent people didn't go to, and where for that reason people weren't afraid of being surprised by someone they knew, and Désirée supplied their alibi, nodded in agreement when Esther lied as brazenly to her parents as she herself had been lying to her trusting mother for weeks, invented details about events that they had never visited, even acquired brochures just to lend more credibility to their lies, had, for example, bought a flyer about the prepared whale skeleton for five Rappen, so many metres long, so many tonnes in weight, just because she didn't trust her mother, who had once been young herself and knew very well what it's like when your heart beats faster because of a man, a mother who had, after all, sympathy for the aberrations of young souls, whom one could confide in, in whom one should have confided long ago instead of coming up with silly fairy-tales that would sooner or later...

To the point: 'Who is the man?'

But that was precisely what Désirée could not tell her mother. She had promised her friend absolute confidentiality, and Mimi must surely see that one could not break such a promise, 'Isn't that so, Mama?'

Mimi was not a curious person, *certainement pas*, and she didn't even think of interrogating Désirée. If she didn't want to talk about it, then that was fine, completely fine, and Mimi was even properly proud that her daughter was so dependable.

'However...'

She threw her objection into the room as a fisherman casts a fish-hook in the water. 'However you are also assuming a great responsibility. If the young man, I'm only saying this as an example, were to come from an entirely unsuitable family...'

'He comes from a very good family,' said Désirée.

'And he is a Jew, I hope.'

'From a very good Jewish family.'

'That does reassure me. Although...I would actually be obliged to inform Rifki Weill that her daughter...'

'You mustn't!'

'I'll think about it,' said Mimi and wanted to know some details, as many details as possible, so she could reflect on the matter. This really was a novel from real life.

Mimi loved novels.

Désirée couldn't say how the pair had met. 'It must have been by chance,' she said, and Mimi nodded meaningfully and murmured something about chances that one could help along if one put one's mind to it.

'At first she didn't even like him.' Désirée seemed relieved to be able to talk at last about something she had had to keep quite for so long. 'At first she couldn't stand him. She thought he had notions about himself. But then she realised that he was only shy. And unhappy. He's terribly unhappy, Esther says.'

'Why?'

'He's been through a lot. Says Esther. I myself don't know him very well. Not at all, in fact.'

'But you're there when they meet?'

'Well, yes,' said Désirée, her cheeks now as red as her mother's, 'I can't leave the two of them all on their own. That wouldn't be respectable.'

'However.'

'But I stay in the background. I don't sit at the same table when they go to a café. Or when they go for a walk I keep my distance. I don't want to listen in on their conversations.'

'Of course not,' said Mimi, very slightly disappointed.

'I'm so glad that you're not cross with me any more.'

'How could I be cross with you, ma petite? But from now on you tell me everything. You hear me? Everything.'

And so began the little conspiracy between mother and daughter. Not that Mimi approved of her daughter's behaviour, quite *au contraire*. She had read enough novels to be able to paint for Désirée in the most garish colours the terrible, deadly consequences that could follow on from a secret dalliance, and she did so over and over again, adding new variants each time she did so. But she did not expressly forbid her daughter's discreet favours as a friend, and above all: she didn't tell anyone, not even Pinchas, who – men don't grasp such things – found out nothing at all about the affair. If Mimi met Rifki Weill at the women's association or at some other occasion, she always inquired with the most innocent expression in the world how her charming daughter was, already so grown-up and yet so girlishly innocent, and did so in such a conspicuously inconspicuous way that Frau Weill said to her husband, 'If I didn't know that Mimi Pomeranz had only a daughter and not a son – I would swear she was trying to make a shidduch.'

In return Désirée had to tell her mother everything, absolutely everything, about Esther Weill's adventure, she had to report in the tiniest particulars on each bit of hand-holding and whispering-in-the-ear, and above all she had to describe in detail any moments of threat, which were by no means a rarity. Once, for example, because they thought an acquaintance was coming towards them, they had escaped into a tobacco shop, and the young man, whose name Mimi was not allowed to know, had bought a cigar purely out of embarrassment, and then actually tried to smoke it. Another time, on a walk in the Zurichberg Forest, Désirée had lost sight of the pair purely out of discretion, and then she couldn't find them for ages, and when Esther and the young man – 'No, I'm not going to tell you his name, please don't ask me, Mama!' – reappeared from a completely unexpected direction, the pair were so embarrassed that they couldn't even look at each other, no, Désirée didn't know if they'd secretly kissed, and that was really something that you couldn't even ask your best friend, 'isn't that right, Mama?'

And once...

Désirée seemed to be having more and more fun talking about these strange adventures. Sometimes she even drew her mother aside when she was in the middle of some activity or other, to update her on a forgotten detail, and over dinner she even suddenly uttered the sentence, 'He wants to grow a moustache, but it doesn't suit him.'

'Who wants to grow a moustache?' said Pinchas, baffled.

'No one,' Désirée said quickly, and bent down for her napkin, which had fallen on the floor.

'An actor in the Municipal theatre,' Mimi whispered to her husband. 'She saw him in a play and now, it seems to me, she's *un tout petit peu amoureuse.*' She put a finger to her lips, and when Désirée reappeared in a state of terrible embarrassment, Pinchas quickly changed the subject.

'I'm even having to lie for you,' Mimi later said reproachfully to Désirée. And was very proud at how skilfully she had rescued the situation for her daughter.

Generally speaking, Mimi took charge of the whole affair, came up with meeting places where disturbance was unlikely, and was particularly imaginative when it came to finding occasions that Esther and Désirée could use as an excuse for spending the afternoon together. 'The new autumn collection is being presented at Seiden-Grieder today,' she said for example, 'that might be something for you girls.' When she winked, fine cracks appeared in the powder around her eyes. 'And in any case it's high time that you finally started giving some thought to your appearance.'

She said those last words purely out of habit. In truth – perhaps her involvement in these strange adventures had something to do with it, or else it was simply down to the fact that her daughter was gradually turning from a girl to a woman – either way; recently Désirée had developed a great interest in fashionable matters, had even once burst into tears just because Mimi refused to buy her a pure silk azure sequined dress that she had discovered in François's Store. But thirty-four francs fifty for a dress that would be out of fashion in a year was really too much. Mimi was already spending far more money on her daughter than was sensible. Perhaps if Pinchas had still had the butcher's shop rather than the general grocery store, which was only doing ho-hum business, while Elias Guttermann, so it was said, had made a mint with the butcher's shop.

Désirée had also stopped parting her hair normally in the middle, although that girlishly simple cut had rather suited her even face. She tried out a great variety of hairdos, and even gave her mother a great deal of fun by trying out all the hats in Mimi's well-equipped wardrobe. But they were all too fussy, and a simple bolero with a little blue Atlas silk wing trim suited her much better. The hat was also from François's shop, which now had the best selection, even though one had actually decided not to shop there any more.

The interesting thing about this matter was that Désirée changed more and more, while Esther Weill showed not a sign of her mysterious liaison. She remained what Mimi called an 'uninteresting girl', not pretty and not ugly, not particularly clever and not particularly stupid. Sometimes when she dropped by to play piano duets with Désirée – she had to take piano lessons too, although unlike her friend she really hadn't the slightest talent for it – Mimi would drop a tiny hint, although without picking up so much as an echo. Such a one as Esther Weill was just wrongly cast as the novel character whose adventures Mimi experienced in sometimes daily instalments.

Even though Mimi wasn't curious at all, she was tormented by the fact that she still didn't know the male lead in this novel. But on this point Désirée remained stubborn. 'I have given my promise,' she said, 'and no one will shift me from it.'

Mimi was really annoyed that Pinchas had switched to the Orthodox Community, because it couldn't be one of them, they were all far too pious. She would really – but this would have attracted attention – have liked to seize the opportunity to go to the synagogue on Löwenstrasse to look from the women's loft with her Argus-eyes at the young men of the community. 'But I'll find out in the end,' she thought, and was by now already firmly convinced that she had uncovered the story simply thanks to her superior knowledge of human nature. She had already completely forgotten about the coincidence of the closed booth.

Until Pinchas mentioned that precise story over dinner, just by chance.

'I don't know if you know about this,' he said. 'A very strange crime was committed a few weeks ago, right here in the city. In a booth on the Platzspitz some circus person was exhibiting some sort of giant fish…'

'A whale,' said Mimi. 'It's a mammal.'

'Do you remember the story?'

No, said Mimi, she didn't remember, it had just been a general observation.

'At any rate, this whale, which is said to have been so big that you could actually have had a picnic on it – anyway, one day the skeleton was no longer complete. Someone had stolen the lower jaw. Do you really not remember?'

Désirée had never heard of it either.

'This bone, which must have been almost a metre long…'

'Almost three metres,' said Désirée, and quickly added that someone in school had been talking about whales and that she seemed to remember that their jaws...

'In any case: one day this bone had suddenly disappeared.'

'Really?' said Mimi, and Désirée was very surprised as well.

'This skeleton was to an extent the exhibitor's livelihood, so he had had it insured. With Sally Steigrad. It was insured for a considerable sum, and now he wanted to claim on it on the grounds that an incomplete skeleton had lost all value. But now a witness has been found, I have this from Sally himself, who saw this famous Herr Zehntenhaus himself dragging the jaw out of the booth and throwing it in the Limmat. Business wasn't going very well, so he wanted to...A simple case of insurance fraud! What do you think of that?'

It was unbelievable, the things people came up with, said Désirée. And Mimi added, 'Secrets like that are utterly pointless. Everything comes out sooner or later.'

41

For the first holiday trip of his life, Janki had himself measured for three new suits. In one, with a black frock coat and striped trousers, he looked like a diplomat, and also, when trying it on, checked that the sleeves didn't slip back too far if one doffed one's hat politely on a spa promenade. With the second he opted, after a long, expert discussion with the tailor, for a sporty, American style, with a matching button-down waistcoat, which was worn this season with shirts with a Caruso collar, not particularly comfortable, but the high cut forced one to hold one's head very straight, and that gave one's whole figure an elegant air. Thirdly, he ordered a very light beach suit: trousers of white English flannel and a double-breasted navy blue jacket, along with a sailor's cap with an embroidered ribbon and white beach shoes, which François had to order him specially from a supplier in England. In case of high winds – and on the North Sea one had to expect such things – there was a tennis coat of heavy white frieze, and while he was about it, he also bought a few small items, not absolutely necessary but elegant, a small box containing some particularly soft travelling slippers, for example, or a practical double clamp with which one could fasten one's straw hat to the lapel of one's coat on hot days. What was the point of co-owning a store if one didn't take advantage of it?

Chanele, in her intractable way, didn't want to buy anything new at all at first, she already had more than enough unworn dresses in her wardrobe, and where did it say in the Shulchan Orech that you had to dress up like a trained monkey only to get sand in your shoes on some godforsaken island? She wouldn't listen to any of Janki's arguments, either that after working for so many years one could allow oneself a treat, or that one couldn't turn up at the table d'hôte like a nebbish from the provinces, and only gave in when she was persuaded by Mina, who was much more sensible about these matters than her mother-in-law. In the end she had a bathing costume of heavy napped cheviot forced on her, a dress and jacket made in silk according to the latest Paris fashion, and for bad weather a rubber mackintosh in a Raglan cut. Janki also tried to persuade her to have a loden suit in the Bozen style, but Chanele said she didn't intend either to go climbing mountains or to learn to yodel.

Then, of course, their two trunks weren't enough, and at the last minute François also had to buy a big leather suitcase for them. It was so new that all the contents later smelled as if they had had Russian leather perfume poured all over them. François didn't come to the station; he avoided meeting his Jewish family more than absolutely necessary, they had nothing to say to each other, and every time his mood was spoiled by the way everyone tried so hard to talk to him normally and without reproach.

But the others were there. Mimi, as excited as if her friend and her husband were setting off on an expedition to the sources of the Nile, kept saying over and over again: 'Be very careful, please be very careful.' She found it hard to cope with the August heat, and every time she dabbed away the sweat she tried to pretend it was tears of farewell.

Pinchas had brought a food parcel with him for their journey, including a dry sausage which smelled so strongly of garlic that Janki, even when he was thanking him for it, decided to leave it in the compartment at the first possible opportunity. 'So that you have something kosher with you,' said Pinchas, and it could also have been heard as a reproach. In Westerland – they didn't talk about it, but everyone had thought about it – everything would be chazer-treyf. Mimi darted him an accusatory glance – 'Sometimes he can be so tactless!' – and by way of distraction began to complain about her housemaid, whom she would probably have to fire because the goy preferred to read the paper rather than dust under the furniture.

Désirée had appeared in an embroidered white voile dress which made Lea and Rachel so envious that they whispered to each other that they wouldn't want to be given something like that, it made you look like a little doll, and the slightest stain would ruin the marvellous thing in a second. Of the Kamionkers, only Hinda and the two girls were there; Ruben was already studying in Kolomea, and Zalman, who had just taken a new job, couldn't just stay away from it in the middle of the week.

Arthur had assembled a little travelling pharmacy for his parents, 'just in case', and Mimi found that so touchingly considerate of him that she had to dab away her tears or her sweat all over again and say, 'Take care, for heaven's sake take care.'

'What's going to happen to them?' Mina didn't like emotional outbursts. Since having polio as a child, she had had to watch and listen to far too much, and like someone with a subscription ticket who goes to the same theatre three times a week, she had become more sensitive to wrong notes with every passing year.

The locomotive spat smoke. Lea and Rachel were already waiting with mischievous delight for the first specks of soot on Désirée's white dress, when all of a sudden Alfred turned up as well. He didn't greet anyone, he didn't even look his relatives in the face, but only held out a package of gingerbread to Chanele, 'for the journey', doffed his student cap and then, because the stationmaster was already trilling excitedly on his whistle, and slamming the doors to the compartment with an official expression on his face, he gave his mother his arm and walked along the platform with her to the exit, he ramrod straight and she bent-backed, Mina hobbling from side to side as always, as if she were drunk. She had always worn very wide skirts so that people couldn't clearly see how she had to swing her paralysed leg around in a semi-circle with each step she took. The whole family watched the ill-matched pair with such fascination that at first no one noticed the train setting off. And then they all ran after the carriage, waving furiously.

'A terrible person, that Alfred,' said Lea to Désirée, but a speck of soot had just landed on Désirée's white dress, and she had to concentrate on removing it again with her fingertips.

The Meijers were travelling first class. It was meshuga expensive, but they could afford it, and although Chanele protested – 'Since when have we been called Rothschild?' – she was quite glad that they had a compartment all to themselves for the very long journey. In Baden-Oos, where the train stopped for a few minutes, she looked yearningly out of the window; if Janki hadn't set his sights on Sylt, of all places, they would have been at their destination already. A cure was a cure in the end, and whether you were getting bored in a thermal spa or on the beach, it didn't really make much difference, at least to her.

Janki's leg hurt from sitting down for so long, and even his travelling slippers brought him no relief, but because he had been the one who decided that this beach resort and no other was the right one, he couldn't show his complaints.

He had never admitted the true reason for his choice to Chanele: in the *Journal des Modes*, which he studied each month from the first page to the last, it had said that the Austrian imperial court tailor Kniže spent the summer months on Sylt in Westerland every year, and Kniže was, where elegance and social correctness were concerned, the measure of all things at the time. He was even – and this had only ever previously been reported of François Delormes – said to have refused to make a pair of trousers for Archduke Franz Ferdinand, just because the successor to the throne had insisted on a cut that Kniže considered unsuitable.

Eventually – 'I'd rather clean up for Pesach three times in a row than ever endure such a journey again!' – they ended up in Hamburg, where Janki had reserved a room with running water at the Vier Jahreszeiten, another waste of time, and just for an overnight stay. He had firmly resolved to spare nothing on this journey. You don't sell your business only to mortify yourself afterwards.

The next day they had to cram themselves back onto a train, a little branch line to a backwater called Hoyerschleuse, from where the steamer left for Sylt. There was only one first-class compartment, with ancient upholstery that smelled damp and rotten as if a few farmers had been comparing samples of manure on the previous journey. The railway official Janki wanted to complain to about it spoke such broad dialect that no normal person could have understood a word.

To top it all, they didn't even have the compartment to themselves. Just before the train set off, they were joined by a distracted-looking man, immediately identifiable as an old soldier even though he was wearing civilian clothes. He excused himself very correctly for the disturbance, but in such a clipped and flippant voice that his apology, for all the politeness of the words, sounded more like an attack.

Their new fellow passenger sat down opposite Janki and Chanele, and at first there was one of those unpleasant pauses in which etiquette dictates that one pays no attention to a person even though he is sitting right in front of one. The man, about Janki's age, wore a hunting suit of dark-green loden, and his hat, which he had raised briefly to Chanele when he got in, was decorated with a little feather. An ugly, brownish, discoloured scar ran from his left eye almost all the way to his chin. 'It must be a schmiss from one of those idiotic student fraternities,' thought Janki. 'It's a shame we can't show it to Alfred, he'd soon lose his taste for such goyim naches.'

The man noticed Janki's gaze, probably read his thoughts as well, and said in a booming voice, 'Grenade splinter. 1870. Sedan.'

And without thinking, Janki replied, 'Sedan? I was there too.'

'Really?' The man could not have beamed more happily at Janki if he had been his long lost brother. He immediately leapt to his feet, which meant that Janki couldn't help getting up too, and because the compartment wasn't very spacious, the two men were standing as close together as if they were about to hug and kiss. But in the end they only shook hands and sat back down in their seats with the awkwardness of people unaccustomed to intimacy.

'No one will ever believe it!' said the man. He had shed his parade-ground voice as abruptly as one loosens a tight collar among friends, and a South German twinge could now be heard in his voice. 'Absolutely mind-boggling.' There could be no doubt. This was the strongest expression of surprise that he could think of.

He stared in amazement at Janki, shaking his head, as if Janki couldn't possibly exist, let alone in this train, and then leapt back up again, he couldn't stay in his seat, doffed his hat and introduced himself, 'Staudinger'.

'Meijer,' said Janki. To be quite correct he should probably have got to his feet as well, but there was simply too little room between the seats. So he just inclined his head and gestured vaguely to Chanele. 'My wife.'

Staudinger pulled his hat from his head again and clicked his heels together. Then he bent over Chanele's hand and pressed a kiss upon it, not an elegant hint at a kiss, but a real one, smacking and damp. 'It is an honour, Frau Meijer,' he said. 'It is a joy. The wife of a comrade-in-arms.'

'Do sit down,' said Chanele, who was already feeling ill from the shaking of the train and the mouldy smell of the upholstery.

Staudinger sat down, repeated once again that the hen in the pan would go crazy, and then leapt back up again. 'Fifth Royal Bavarian Infantry Regiment, Second Battalion,' he announced this time. 'Based in Aschaffenburg. And you, Comrade?'

'Twentieth Corps. Second Division. Fourth Batallion of the Régiment du Haut Rhin. Based in Colmar.'

'Colmar? But that wasn't even ...'

'I am a Frenchman,' said Janki.

Staudinger sat down again as suddenly as if someone had kicked him in the back of the knees.

'You were ...?'

'On the other side,' said Janki, gripping the handle of his walking stick more firmly.

But Staudinger was enthusiastic. 'This is amazing!' he said. 'Absolutely mind ... Where did your regiment fight?'

Chanele held her handkerchief in front of her face, probably because of the unpleasant smell. Janki had been asked so often by admiring lady customers to tell them about his heroic warlike deeds that he was not lost for an answer. 'A soldier goes where he is sent,' he said. 'When the bullets are flying around your head, you don't ask questions about geography.'

'Correct,' said Staudinger. 'Absolutely correct. We were all young at the time, and didn't know that we'd have to talk about it for the rest of our lives.'

'Which you probably enjoy doing more than I do.'

'Why?'

'You won the war.'

Staudinger let out a barking 'Ha!' which was probably supposed to be a cordial, comradely laugh. 'Very good. Really very good. I'll have to remember that one. "You won the war."' Again he said 'Ha!' and that seemed to get the preliminaries out of the way as far as he was concerned, and he started relating his own experiences of the war. 'We were standing at the Porte de Mézières.

Have you heard of it? No? Well, it wasn't right at the front as such, but it was a strategically very important point that absolutely had to be held. I can list the positions if you like. Well, perhaps another time. We will see each other again, I hope. Are you bound for Sylt as well? Westerland? Me too. We'll absolutely have to…Which hotel? The Atlantic? On Herrenbadstrasse, I know. An elegant place, very distinguished, not everyone can afford it. I certainly can't. Ha!' He performed his laugh as if it were a duty, and then continued with his monologue, which he had doubtless delivered many times, word for word. 'So our emplacement was at this gate, along with the first Battalion and a company of riflemen that had been assigned to us, and the grenades were flying over our heads. If you were there, you know the sound, that whoosh that gets louder and louder until you want to bury yourself in the ground. But we had an old colonel, Niedermayer was his name, a proper, cosy old Bavarian, never promoted beyond a certain point because of some old story or other, even though he was very hard working, he just laughed when we threw ourselves down, and said, "If you can hear them, they've already gone past." And that was exactly how it was with me. I never heard the grenade that got me. Didn't hear it at all, just imagine. Only my face was suddenly very hot, no pain, nothing at all at first, just that feeling of heat, and something damp ran over my hands; at first I thought my flask had been hit. But it was my own blood. So I was only vaguely aware of most of it, the French waving their white flags like mad, I don't want to be rude, but that was how it was, and the peace negotiator coming through our ranks…But you'll know all that. Until at last the medical corps came and…' He suddenly broke off and looked at Janki with a slightly suspicious expression. 'Were you injured too?'

'In the leg,' said Janki. 'But the pain is bearable. I only feel it when the weather turns.' Chanele was holding her handkerchief in front of her face again. The smell from the old upholstery was really very unpleasant.

By the time the train arrived in Hoyerschleuse the two men were the best of friends, and had firmly agreed to see one another on the island very soon. Staudinger, who planned to meet a few comrades here before travelling on to Sylt on the same ship, found them another porter for their luggage – he could put his booming, order-issuing voice on and off like a coat – gave Chanele another smacking kiss on the hand and bade farewell to Janki by resting his hand against the brim of his rifleman's cap in the military style.

It was only when the luggage had been counted – two trunks, a new Russian leather suitcase, four hatboxes – and the porter had been paid, that Chanele managed to speak to Janki.

'What sort of shmontses are you telling that man?' she said. 'The ladies in

Baden might believe your adventures, but this fellow Staudinger was really at Sedan. An unpleasant person, by the way, with that scar.'

'I can't see it that way.' They were standing side by side leaning on the railing of the *Freya*, watching the burly sailors untying the ship's hawsers with insulted expressions, as if the ferry service for guests at the spa was far below the dignity of a true Christian seafarer.

'Janki Meijer, the hero of Sedan!'

'Scha!' Janki turned round in horror. Luckily no one had heard.

'Just a shame you forgot to pack your medals.'

'What medals?'

'The ones awarded to you by Napoleon the Third in person. For special bravery in the face of the enemy.'

For all those years Chanele hadn't worried when Janki described the few glorious memories of his time in the military more colourfully each time. It hadn't really bothered her, and in the company there was, God knows, enough to do that was more important. But since Janki had sold the Modern Emporium over her head, she no longer felt obliged to take his sensitivities into account. Chanele had grown bitter, almost from one day to the next, not argumentative, but obstinate, and as Janki had a very bad conscience about giving up the business, and could therefore not admit a mistake, there were more and more violent arguments between them.

Like a wine stored for too long, after forty years their marriage had turned sour.

'You don't understand,' said Janki. 'In a spa town like this you have to know the right people or else you're left alone. So now we have an entrée into high society.'

'Make shabbos with that!' Chanele turned her back on her husband and for the next few minutes was very busy observing the flock of seagulls following the ship out of the harbour as a screeching escort.

Chanele's unconcealed disapproval and the quiet anxiety that she might be right spoiled Janki's delight in the preferential treatment they received as they put in at Sylt. While other passengers had to take pot luck with coaches, or even had to linger forlorn and abandoned beside their mountains of luggage, they had a liveried chauffeur waiting for them, with the word *Atlantic* emblazoned on his cap in gold letters. They were the only new arrivals who had booked in at this hotel in the very top category, and Janki was almost slightly disappointed that his new friend Staudinger was nowhere to be seen. He would have liked to wave at him in comradely fashion from the automobile that stood ready for the journey to the hotel, or even offered to take him into Westerland. There would have been enough room, because the car, at least as grand as François's Buchet, had two spacious rows of seats as well as the chauffeur's seat. Their cases, and Janki found this particularly elegant, were not simply tied on at the back, but jogged along behind them on a luggage car pulled by two horses.

They were welcomed at the hotel with much bowing and scraping, and that subservient attitude continued like that all day to such an extent that Chanele said ironically that you learned to tell the different employees apart by the backs of their heads. Their suite, 'the best in the whole hotel', said the fawning porter, had all the comforts of the modern age, electric lights, a bathroom of their own and a whole row of bell-pulls with which the correct employee could be summoned for any special wishes they might have.

'You see how we're welcomed here?' said Janki, when they were on their own at last.

'Like anyone else who's expected to provide a decent tip.'

'Better than anyone else.' He had assumed a mysterious expression, but Chanele didn't do him the favour of showing any curiosity, so he had to report the chachma that he'd thought up, and of which he was very proud, unasked. 'I asked Herr Strähle, the manager, to notify his colleague here that we were particularly important guests. What do you think of that?'

'Narrishkeit,' was all Chanele had to say on the matter.

42

A lady's maid could be summoned with the buttons on the bell panel, who would be willing to help madam get dressed at any time, the cringing porter had assured them upon their arrival. To Janki's annoyance, renewed every day, Chanele strictly refused to take advantage of this service, even though it was included in the price of the room and would thus be paid for anyway. Every time he demanded that she change her outfit for the promenade, the table d'hôte or a drinks party – he liked, since it was after all his field, to decide which dress was right for which occasion – he had to open all the complicated ribbons himself and tie them all again, and manoeuvre the thousand little hooks into the tiny eyes. Where does it say in the Shulchan Aruch that if a man wants to belong to fine society in his dotage, one has to help him in his meshugas?

Unlike Arthur, who as a child had loved to use every opportunity to get closer to his mother by giving her a helping hand of this kind, Janki hated this toilet service. But Chanele forced him to do it, precisely because she knew that her body, now old and flabby, was unpleasant to him. Janki loved the external, the effect; he had not had his suits tailored to be comfortable to wear, but so that he would look good in them. What he admired most about court tailor Kniže, who was increasingly easing out his old master Delormes from his personal Pantheon, was his ball suit, which, according to the *Journal des Modes*, he had once produced for a misshapen member of the imperial household, 'so perfectly cut that the hump was no longer apparent'. When she wore one of her expensive dresses, Chanele was as he wanted to see her: the well-to-do wife of a successful businessman. In blouse and corset the woman standing there was just a grandmother with withered skin, and if Janki had bought her an expensive *eau de toilette* on their first stroll around Westerland, he had not done so by chance. He thought he smelled age and decay on her, and he couldn't bear it because it scared him.

Janki was not unskilled as a dresser. He was familiar with fabrics and dresses, and when Chanele was fully disguised, as she herself put it, he also tried to find the right jewellery and accessories to go with it. It was the only part of the ritual that he enjoyed.

Today he had taken a summer outfit in ivory crépon from the wardrobe. For a reason that he never talked about, he was particularly fond of this dress.

It was more than a dozen years ago now that he had once involuntarily listened in on the conversation of a couple he didn't know, but he could still hear the wife's loud voice. 'What bothers me most about these Jewish women,' she had said, 'is that they are all so fat.' The crépon dress was accompanied by an unusual patent leather belt that stressed Chanele's narrow waist and made it clear to any observer that she didn't need to hide her figure behind pleated tulle or artfully draped floral garlands. If Janki imagined who that imaginary observer was, he now thought always of his new friend Staudinger.

The spa orchestra in the Music Shell on the promenade now wore theatrical uniforms from the time of the Napoleonic War; there was a 'Fatherland Concert' on the programme, which meant that the eight musicians would have to play one military march after another, even though their instrumentation wasn't really suited to it. But the sole trumpeter tried gamely, and the band leader – whom Monsieur Fleur-Vallée would have mocked as as a pitiful dilettante – had for once set his violin aside and instead rattled the instrument known as a Turkish crescent. The spa guests seemed to like it; the ladies hummed along with the memorable tunes, and sent the flower arrangements on their hats bobbing rhythmically; the men tapped their walking sticks on the ground in time with the music. A few children had shouldered the little spades with which they usually built castles on the beach, and marched eagerly back and forth under the orders of a twelve-year-old.

Chanele's toilet – why did she object to being helped by a lady's maid? – took time, and then Janki himself couldn't decide between three different ties. When at last they reached the Music Shell, at a comfortable stroll as befitted the spa promenade, even though they had allowed good time, all the white painted chairs were already occupied. They were not the only ones who had to stand, but Janki, who was staying in the most expensive hotel in town, was extremely dissatisfied with the lack of foresight from the spa administration. There was not a sign of Staudinger, even though the selection of music would have been to his taste.

While Janki looked searchingly around, ready to doff his hat at any moment, even though no one knew him here apart from his railway acquaintance, Chanele gazed with fascination at the orchestra's cellist, an elderly gentleman with fine, narrow features. The tunes of the Fatherland Programme were all written in the same 4/4 march rhythm, and the cellist seemed visibly to be suffering from the undemanding qualities of the music that he was having to play. He was indeed scraping his bow quite correctly – one, two, one, two – across the strings, but he kept his eyes closed, as if he could no longer bear to see the conductor with his Turkish crescent. He bobbed his head back and forth to a quite different rhythm, moving his lips as he did so. Chanele imagined that as he did his duty he was singing an inaudible counter-melody to himself, a song that belonged to him alone, and which no one could take from him.

After each individual piece of music the gentlemen applauded, and the ladies patted their fine gloves together. The short break produced each time the pages were turned was suddenly broken by a piercing cry, and a little boy in a sailor suit ran from the troop of drilling children, who were at that moment presenting their spades in file, and pushed his way through the rows of seats in search of his mother. Now children on the spa promenade were thoroughly tolerated; as long as they remained cute and silent even complete strangers patted them on the head and gave them a sixpence for their piggy-banks. But this little boy was noisy, his cries were penetrating and to top it all he carried behind him a spade that was doubtless full of sand and dirt, without paying the slightest heed to the dresses of the ladies that he was barging into. He drew behind him a trail of disapproving comments and severe pedagogical glances, just as the dust of the street hangs in the air when a car has driven past. The boy was aware of none of this. He couldn't find his mother, and had a terrible outrage to complain to her about, so he yelled at the top of his little lungs.

'Mamme!' yelled the little boy. 'Mamme!'

Chanele handed Janki the parasol on which he had insisted, pulled her arm out from his as one pulls a thread from a needle, and left him standing. Her laced ankle-boots were made for elegant promenading; it was not so easy to reach the other side of the audience quickly enough. She was watched with looks of disapproval; this must have been the unfortunate mother who was incapable of keeping her child under seemly control.

The little boy came shooting out of the rows of seats headfirst; he must have tripped over a slyly extended parasol, or even over his own feet. He had lost his spade, but he didn't care, he just wanted to be hugged and hidden and comforted.

'What's happened?' asked Chanele.

'I want to be a soldier too!' the boy wailed. He said it in Yiddish, of exactly the same hue that Chanele knew from her son-in-law Zalman.

With a ching of the Turkish crescent and a boom of the kettledrum the music started up again, and the sound seemed to make the boy so miserable that he buried his tear-stained face in Chanele's dress and clung to her desperately with his hands. She would never get the stains out of that delicate crépon.

Chanele bent down to him and picked him up with the sure grip of a woman who has consoled many children and grandchildren in the past. The boy's hair smelt of sun and sand, and Chanele couldn't help hugging him. 'Hush now,' she whispered to him, 'hush now. We'll find your Mamme.'

It had all happened so quickly that Janki didn't know whether he should go running after his wife or wait for her exactly where he was. A voice with a Southern German inflection relieved him of the decision. It addressed him with such noisy cordiality that some of the spa guests looked around disapprovingly for the source of this new disturbance.

'There you are, Meijer,' roared Staudinger. 'Where have you been hiding yourself all this time? I would like to introduce you to a few comrades.' If you're holding a walking stick in one hand and a parasol in the other, it's hard to lift your hat as form decrees. The four men who accompanied Staudinger didn't seem to be bothered by this. They had just emerged from an early drinking session that had carried on over lunch, and cared nothing for formalities. They clapped Janki on the shoulder and shook him, regardless of walking stick and parasol, by the hand. One of the men, as awkwardly as if he had copied his movements from the drilling children, presented his hiking stick, covered with little metal crests, with great military precision, and they all talked over each other so excitedly that Janki couldn't even hear the names by which they introduced themselves. The man with the hiking stick, that much he understood, had even mentioned an aristocratic title.

They insisted that Janki accompany them to the Strandcafé, where the beer was particularly good, straight away and with no dawdling, because drinking, they thought, was like artillery fire – it was only when you stopped that things got dangerous, ha! They put him in the middle, and no one who met the group on the way to the café really knew whether someone was being flanked by a guard of honour or led away as a criminal.

They drank beer. Janki's suggestion that he celebrate their encounter by buying a good bottle of wine or even champagne was laughed at like a good joke, absolutely mind-boggling, but then he was a Frenchman, they said, so allowances had to be made. But they recommended that he abandon such dandified cravings forthwith, lest they find themselves forced to resume hostilities.

'Ha!' said Staudinger.

Janki laughed with them. He would have laughed at anything, so happy was he to be included in this company, of which one member even had an aristocratic title.

Staudinger, whose scar had been turned bright red by the sun or by the beer, must have described the encounter in the train to Hoyerschleuse in all its details to his four colleagues, and he exaggerated proficiently. He had clearly turned Janki into a Gallic hero fighting with courage born of desperation, who might have turned around the fortunes of the Battle of Sedan single-handedly, had a bullet not struck him in the leg and injured him with potentially fatal results. He did not necessarily wish to assert that this bullet actually came from the ranks of Staudinger's Second Battalion, but it was still a possibility, which was why the two men – a soldier is a soldier, regardless of which side he is fighting on – were linked by a kind of mystic blood-brotherhood, which had to be celebrated at all costs, and to which glasses must be raised.

They celebrated, and they raised the glasses.

Janki, who wasn't used to beer, couldn't hear everything that the comrades told him, only that all five of them, albeit in different units, had been at the Battle of Sedan, that they had met much later at a Sedan Day celebration on Sylt, and had decided henceforth to meet in the same place every year and commemorate the day together, as a kind of veterans' reunion or even just as a men's group outing, 'any excuse to leave the old woman at home, I bet you feel exactly the same, don't you, chum?'

They were by now on first-name terms, they had solemnly included Janki in their circle in a drunken ceremony in which Chanele's parasol had to stand in for the sword in the dubbing ritual, and when they walked him back to the Atlantic they all had their arms around each other's shoulders, out of comrade-liness as much as a lack of balance, and together they sang the song about an old comrade, and how you'll never find a better one.

Janki had left the parasol in the Strandcafé.

Even though it would soon be evening, hence time to change for the table d'hôte, Chanele wasn't yet back at the hotel. While Janki was learning to drain a glass of beer without setting it down, she had found the little boy's mother.

'Your dress,' was the first thing the woman had said, 'for heaven's sake, your beautiful dress! Motti, what have you been up to this time?' And then she had been very relieved that Chanele hadn't been looking for her because of the stain on her dress, but because it was high time the little boy was finally, finally able to wail out his woes.

They hadn't let him play.

He had wanted to join in with the company of drilling children, with spades over their shoulders and sailors' caps at an angle, as they all did, he had paid close attention and followed the orders, 'Right turn!' and 'At ease!' and 'Pre-sent...arms!', he had done everything right, he'd definitely done every-thing right, and still the twelve-year-old, who was the officer and who was able to issue whatever orders he liked, had pushed him away and said, 'Not you.' Just: 'Not you.' And when he had tried to join the ranks again anyway, the elbows had spread and the spade-handles had been used as bayonets, and the officer had grabbed him by the ear and pulled him out of the formation and said, Jews can't be soldiers.

And now his mother was to come, right now, and tell the others they had to let him join in with the game.

'I'm sure it's been over for ages,' the woman said comfortingly, even though they could still here the jangle of the Turkish crescent. She blew her son's nose, straightened his sailor's cap and promised him that Tata would buy him a new spade for the beach, a much, much nicer one.

Then she sighed deeply and said to Chanele with a sad smile, 'You don't know how people sometimes treat us Jews.'

'Me neshuma, I know,' replied Chanele.

'You too?' the woman said with relief. 'I should have known, with those eyebrows.'

Of course they fell into conversation, and of course they had lots to tell each other. Or rather: the little boy's mother told Chanele's lots of things. She was one of those people who are usually quiet out of shyness, but who then, when the person they are talking to proves not to be a threat, let the flow of words surge over the banks like a flood.

Malka Wasserstein came from Marjampol in Galicia, no need to have heard of the town – town? It was a backwater, a fly-speck on the map, nothing at all. Her husband had made a certain amount of money there with a sawmill – 'We're no Rothschilds, but God willing we found ourselves very well off' – and that had caused a problem – 'A problem? May all Jewish children have such a problem!' – that would never have occurred to them before: there was no husband for their daughter to be found for far and wide. Little Motti had an elder sister, and he himself had been a latecomer, an afterthought – 'born when I already thought my time was over. But Riboyne shel Oylem must know what he's doing.'

Chanele could hardly interject that she too had had a latecomer, and that she sometimes even found herself thinking that Arthur was the nicest of all her children. Malka's words had spread their elbows too, leaving as little room for other words as the drilling children had for little Motti.

So there was Chaje Sore, almost fifteen years older than her brother – 'Motti, leave that, we don't play with things like that!' – a girl of already twenty-one, God willing, and still unmarried. Of course there had been proposals – 'The shadchonim overran the house, she could have had anyone in the district, a golden key opens every lock' – but why should Chaje Sore marry a chandler or a herring trader or – 'God preserve us!' – an innkeeper who has to drink l'chayim with every customer and stinks of bronfen by the time he eventually crawls into bed? Not that we thought we were finer than other people – 'May my tongue fall from my mouth if I ever said such a thing!' – but one wants the best for one's children, otherwise why would one break one's back a whole life long?

'How many children to you have?' asked Malka, but didn't wait for the answer, her sluice-gates were too wide open, but instead reported on how her husband Hersch – 'I sometimes call him Hershele Ostropoler after the famous jester, because he has such meshuganeh ideas' – had hit upon the notion of crossing the sea, not for a holiday – 'I need that like a corpse needs suction cups!' – but because he wanted to meet people, voyleh Juden, who also had children and who were on the lookout for a shiduch, and who one knew for certain moved in the right circles, precisely because such a summer resort cost a lot of money and not everyone could afford it.

When Malka Wasserstein talked like that, she sounded a bit like a schoolgirl hoping to impress her teachers with undigested phrases from her parents' conversation. Outwardly, too, she looked like a little girl dressed as a grown-up, because – only in Marjampol could it have been considered elegant – she had chosen a street dress of very colourful, broad-striped silk fabric that swathed her chubby figure like casually tied-up wrapping paper. With it she wore a hat with a heron-feather, which Chanele would never have sold anyone for afternoon wear; heron feathers belonged in the ballroom, where it was this season's fashion to let it bob along when dancing the tango.

But much more than her clothes, it was her movements that made Malka's origins in the Galician provinces unmistakeable. She talked with her hands, and with her gestures even the story of her holiday turned into a dramatic event.

So they had set off – 'The cost! The bother!' – but of course Hersch hadn't looked into everything in advance, he always liked to get things done quickly, he plunged into everything he did like a bridegroom into a mikvah, and he had actually booked their holiday on Borkum, Borkum of all places! Did Chanele have any idea how they did things there?

No, she could have no idea, and she should thank God that she didn't! He had destroyed Sodom and Gomorrah, but he must have overlooked Borkum, because that place was far, far worse than the two biblical cities, an island full of reshoim. Malka never wished harm on anyone, but if a flood came and washed the whole pile of sand into the sea, she at least wouldn't weep a tear for it, and when she passed the graves of the people, she would dance on them, yes, she would dance.

On Borkum the following had happened...

But now Malka had been so busy telling her stories that she had forgotten the time, and she had only left the spa concert very quickly to go in search of Hersch and Chaje Sore, she had thought that her Motti – 'Put that down, Motti, who knows who else might have picked it up!' – was playing peacefully with the other children, you never had a moment's peace, and why people went on holiday for pleasure she would never know, even if she were to live, touch wood, to a hundred and twenty.

They would absolutely have to meet again, her husband would want to thank Chanele for her kindness in person, and who knows, perhaps Chanele might even know someone who…How old had she said her youngest was, the latecomer? Thirty-three? Then it was high time he thought of getting married. 'Being alone puts stupid ideas in your head!' Yes, they would certainly see each other again, tomorrow would be best of all, but now Malka had to go and look for her husband and her daughter. They had wanted to sit down in the patisserie garden, where you could see and be seen, but all the tables there had been occupied, they must have gone somewhere else and were bound to be wondering where she'd got to, she would really have to go. 'Shake hands with the lady like a good boy, Mottele! You must be moichel to him, he's all over the place today, normally he's quite well-behaved.'

When Chanele came back to the hotel room, Janki was lying on the bed with his dirty shoes on, fast asleep. He was snoring and smelled of beer.

43

Janki didn't mind Chanele leaving him alone; in fact it suited him. His new friends – by now he also knew their names: Hofmeister, Neuberth, Kessler and von Stetten – took up all his time, almost around the clock. They expected him at eleven o'clock in the morning, when one had barely struggled out of bed, for a buffet breakfast, where one had to eat smoked eel – treyf, but not at all bad – and other fatty things because it was traditionally believed that they more than anything else helped to absorb the alcohol from the previous evening, and then, to clear their heads, they went for a healthy walk along the beach, but they never got any further than the Strandcafé, where they were already expected and their beers were served without them even asking for them. There, over the course of the next few hours, they became first patriotic and then emotional, they sang under the direction of Neuberth, who was a member of a men's singing club, romantic songs so mellifluous that they were moved to tears: 'In the tower at Sedan a Frenchman stands, clutching his rifle in his hands.' But they were never again as drunk as they had been on the first day; they saved that up for the evening. They said their goodbyes at the door of their hotels, none of which were nearly as smart as the Atlantic, as elaborately as if they weren't going to see each other again for years, when in fact they were only parting for the duration of the table d'hôte where, each in his own price category, they lined their stomachs ready for a night spent drinking in Tacke Blecken's Cellar. The place was otherwise avoided by the spa guests, because in this drinking den, the last refuge of locals and sailors, one occasionally came across ladies whose faded charms might only have seduced a seafarer who hadn't set foot on dry land for many months. They had commandeered the round table for the duration, right under Tacke Blecken's celebrated chandelier consisting of an old model galleon and a set of elk antlers. Tacke, who was said once to have been a captain, until he had run his cutter aground on a reef while three sheets to the wind, poured a drink that might have been called grog, but which contained, along with rum, sugar and water, other ingredients that made one seriously philosophical after the first glass.

Apart from a few hasty adventures on business trips, Janki's life had never presented him with the opportunity to let his hair down properly like this. All the greater then was his enjoyment of his late-blossoming bachelor life, he called for one round after another, and was in the meantime able to give such a detailed account of his experiences at Sedan that the battle would have had to last three days to include them all. So he thought he remembered – and each glass of grog made the memory clearer – how he had rescued an injured comrade from enemy fire at great risk to his own life, and from whom he had later received the walking stick with the lion's-head handle by way of thanks, a distinction, he claimed, that was far more precious to him than any medal that the state might have been able to award him.

Of course the others noticed that he was exaggerating, but they weren't bothered; they were doing exactly the same thing themselves. The Wound Badge awarded to Hofmeister, for example, which he always wore proudly on the lapel of his coat on Sedan Day, a picture of King Karl of Württemberg with the caption 'For loyal duty in war', was really a simple silver medal of the kind that was generously distributed at a time of general triumph. Hofmeister, a cosy innkeeper from Nürtingen, had been part of a supply unit in the war, and as he stood over his cooking pots had heard nothing more of the whole battle than the distant roar of cannon. Why should he have doubted other people's accounts of the battle, as long as they didn't call his own heroism into question?

Von Stetten, the oldest of the group, was the only one of them to have been an officer at Sedan, a dashing lieutenant, as he put it who, if he hadn't been so discreet, could have told them stories about his conquests with the ladies, 'it would make your hair curl, gentlemen!' He had preserved the custom from those days of twirling his moustache at the conclusion of each sentence, so that the ends stood up like confirmatory exclamation marks.

Every night they drank Tacke Blecken's mysterious grog, smoked the cigars that Janki was allowed to bring and, behind a curtain of smoke and male laughter – 'Ha!' – they created their own world, into which only warriors were allowed, no civilians and certainly no women.

Chanele, for her part was not unhappy to see her husband occupied, although the stench of smoke and grog that he brought into the room in the early morning was thoroughly repellent. But that was a small price to pay for the fact that she was free of the need not just to be in a summer resort, but also of having to play the role of the summer resort guest. By the time Janki rolled out of bed with a hangover, she had long since put on one of her simple Liberty dresses in which she felt most comfortable, had had breakfast and left the hotel.

She even discovered a new passion for which she had never in her life found time: the Atlantic had a reading room, and there she picked a book from the shelf at random, a different one every day, took it with her to the water, sat down in her wicker beach chair and enjoyed the luxury of problems and entanglements that one could snap shut and set aside whenever one wished. So even though she wasn't aware of it, she spent her holiday much as Janki did: in a world that didn't really exist.

But her peace was repeatedly disturbed by the Wassersteins, who had set up their rented beach chairs – not one, not two, but three! – in her immediate vicinity, and were firmly resolved not only to nurture Chanele's acquaintance, but to appropriate it entirely to themselves.

Hersch Wasserstein was smaller than his wife, a squat, curly-haired bundle of energy. On this beach spending time in the water was not considered truly healthy, but still he wore a black bathing costume all the time, from whose neck curly chest hair sprouted, and a straw hat with a coloured ribbon of the kind sold in all the souvenir shops of Westerland. His arms and legs were burnt bright red, but in spite of his wife's warnings he never spent long in the shadow of his beach chair, and was instead constantly doing something, either fetching glasses of lemonade – 'You have one too, Frau Meijer, do me the honour!' – or helping Motti set up a water wheel in the moat of his sandcastle, exactly the same system, incidentally – 'This is bound to interest you, Frau Meijer!' – on which the sawmill in Marjampol operated.

His wife, who had talked away at Chanele the first time they met as if words were going to double in price the following day, said little in her husband's presence. Apart from, 'What do you mean, Hersch?' and 'Quite right, Hersch!' she was hardly ever heard. But that was still more than her daughter said.

Chaje Sore Wasserstein was insulted, not for any concrete reason, but in principle. The lemonade wasn't cold enough, the sand too hot, the young men one met here no better than the ones in Marjampol – and she said all that without words, she just let the corners of her mouth droop, studied her fingernails and groaned every now and again as if the whole world had conspired to turn her twenty-one-year-old life into a living hell. From childhood onwards her parents had assured her that things would get better, and Chaje Sore Wasserstein was of the view that they certainly had not kept their promise.

Hersch was a very talkative man and insisted on telling Chanele in great detail about all the dreadful things they had experienced in their first resort of Borkum. Little Motti's sandcastle had been trampled to pieces, there had been a map on the wall of their hotel showing the route from Borkum to Jerusalem, a brazen message to them that they should go there and not come back, and at the spa concert everyone had sung a song, the Borkum song, whose last lines he would never forget if he lived to be a hundred and twenty years old, God willing. 'But those who approach you with flat feet,' they had sung, 'with noses crooked and curly hair, they should not enjoy your beach, away with them, away with them!' They had left very quickly, they had fled, in fact, to be honest, and here on Sylt it was really much better, 'don't you think, Frau Meijer?'

Chanele would have preferred to withdraw behind her book, but the insistent attention of her new acquaintances repeatedly kept her from doing so. Sometimes when she dozed off for a few minutes in the midday heat, characters from the two worlds merged, a Bedouin prince from an adventure story assumed the features of Hersch Wasserstein, and the beautiful countess that he was holding prisoner had the same pinched little mouth as Chaje Sore.

Janki dreamed too, or rather: the six musketeers, as they called themselves, pursued a common dream. They couldn't remember which of them had had the idea first, most likely it had been Staudinger, who was something like the chairman of their association. For days now they had all been weaving away at it and, inspired by beer and grog, drawing ever brighter colours through the beautiful picture. In Westerland, they knew from before, 2 September was decked with bunting in honour of Sedan Day, and the mayor laid a wreath for the fallen on the victory monument, but was that really enough for such an important day? The fact that the hotels decorated their dining rooms in black, white and red, and the chefs invented new patriotic names for their old recipes – Hofmeister, who knew about such things, remembered very ordinary Büsum shrimps which had appeared on the table bearing the name 'Field Marshal Moltke prawns' – that the spa band had played patriotic tunes and that the battle flag had flown on many a sandcastle, that was all well and good, but not enough for true veterans, who had risked life and limb in that battle.

'Someone', Staudinger said, 'should organise a central event, with speeches and honours...'

'...and', Kessler went on toying with the idea, 'hire a hall in a hotel...' and of course Janki cried, 'In the Atlantic, where else?' There was in fact a big ballroom there, where meetings and dances were held, and the manager – 'Don't worry, I'll see to it!' – was sure to make it available to them, the spa newspaper would publish big advertisements, the house band would play something dignified rather than the inevitable tangos – 'The Hohenfriedberg March', suggested the musical Neuberth, 'composed by Old Fritz in person' – the war veterans would march into those sounds and then...Yes, they weren't quite clear about what would happen then, so they ordered the next round of Tacke Blecken's mysterious grog, rested their heads on their hands and gave it some thought.

'I have given it some thought,' said Hersch Wasserstein, 'and in fact it could all be done very quickly and without any fuss.' He had sent his family on a walk and was now kneeling in the sand beside Chanele's beach chair, as Sir Walter Raleigh knelt before the throne of Queen Elizabeth in the book she was just reading. 'How do you like my Chaje Sore?'

'Charming, quite charming,' said Chanele, for where does it say in the Shulchan Aruch that you are supposed to rob a proud father of his illusions?

'She is a pearl of a child, of the kind all Jewish parents would wish. A little quiet, perhaps, but then silence is golden, isn't that right?'

Chanele, holding her index finger impatiently between the pages of the book, confirmed that his observation was quite correct.

'And she will have a nedinye...We are not rich people, but God willing, we are fine.' His wife had said the same thing word for word; she had the tendency of quoting her husband's words without divulging the source, as one quotes a proverb or a well-known aphorism. 'Yes, my Chaje Sore is a good match, and angel, God willing, and at twenty-one she is exactly the right age. Your son is a doctor, isn't he?'

'Arthur? You mean that Chaje Sore and Arthur...?'

'He's thirty-three, my wife tells me. Exactly the right distance between them. Of course my Malka sees shidduchim everywhere. What do they say? "God couldn't be everywhere, so he created the Jewish Mamme." But I like the thought. A doctor from Zurich – it's a far cry from a chandler or a trader in Herring. Everyone thinks they're something, while in fact...In a little village it's easy to be a king. So, Frau Meijer, what do you say? Are we agreed? Shall we shake on it?'

Chanele didn't pull a face and it wasn't easy. Hersch Wasserstein looked so ridiculous, kneeling in front of her there in the sand, in his bathing costume like the ones that wrestlers wear at the funfair, and with the straw hat that he had bought two sizes too small. He actually held his hand out to her the way Salomon had done when a cattle trade had been concluded and only needed to be sealed, he really thought he could do the deal here on the spot and then move on to truly important matters like the prices on the lumber market and how last winter's storms would affect them.

But he was also a father, who wanted the best for his daughter.

Chanele remembered Zalman asking so clumsily for Hinda's hand, that had been ridiculous as well, and the pair had been happy together, she thought of all the things she herself had done to marry off François, so she didn't laugh, but just said, 'Not so fast, Herr Wasserstein. You don't even know my son.'

'I know his mother!' he said and with an elegant motion that would have suited a frock coat better than a sweaty bathing costume, Wasserstein put his hand to his heart. 'If the son is bentshed with only ten per cent of your charm…What am I saying?' he broke off and began to negotiate with himself to hike up the compliment, 'If he has only five per cent, only one per cent…'

'You don't know him,' Chanele repeated, 'and in any case: you would have to discuss such matters with my husband.'

'Very sensible,' said Hersch Wasserstein. 'Business is men's affair. I have also made some inquiries. Tell me: this Meijer who has that fine store in Zurich – is he mishpocha of yours?'

'Meijer,' said von Stetten, 'that is a good German name. We had a Meier in our regiment, he even became a district president.'

They were sitting at their regular table in the Strandcafé, and the first round of beers stood still untouched on the table. The six musketeers had a lot of things to discuss, because something that had originated as an idea prompted by beer or grog had quickly assumed concrete forms, so quickly that they were quite alarmed. The management had made the ballroom available to them, for free, and had undertaken, at its own suggestion, to ensure that it was appropriately decorated. The editor of the *Kuranzeiger*, with whom they had very cautiously discussed their plan, immediately went great guns for it, and contacted all the associations on the island, all of which now wanted to take part in the parade. At that point the mayor of Westerland had suddenly realised that he had long ago conceived this plan himself, and offered not only to greet the heroes of Sedan with a word of welcome, but also to award them the Sylt badge of honour, a distinction normally reserved for hoteliers celebrating their anniversaries or for particularly meritorious wine suppliers.

It would all have been wonderful, if the editor of the *Kuranzeiger* hadn't announced in bold letters that a real veteran would deliver a speech for the occasion, relating his own experiences in the great battle.

None of the musketeers wanted to be that speaker, and each of them had a different excuse. Von Stetten argued that the memories of a private soldier would be much more effective than those of an aristocratic officer. Kessler mentioned a stammer that always afflicted him when he appeared in public, Neuberth, he had learned that trick in the men's singing club, suffered from hoarseness, Staudinger had witnessed none of the crucial events because of his injury and Hofmeister blushingly admitted to his comrades that he had been with the baggage train and not with the fighting troops. So that left only Janki, whose detailed accounts of the battle they had all listened to with such fascination.

'But he's a Frenchman!' Kessler protested. His objections were eloquently demolished by the others. The former enemy being allowed to speak on such an occasion, von Stetten said, was a proof of genuine chivalry, and Neuberth supported him, saying that after the Battle of Sedan even Bismarck had treated the defeated French emperor with exquisite politeness. And in any case, said Staudinger, Comrade Meijer wasn't really a true Frenchman, because after all he came from Alsace-Lorraine, and that had been a solid part of the German Reich for over forty years.

Which prompted von Stetten to observe that Meijer was also a good German name.

Janki demurred, but not very violently. He already saw himself marching into the ballroom to the sound of the *Hohenfriedberger*, limping but brisk, he already saw himself standing behind the lectern, supporting himself on his walking stick, whose story he would of course tell, he already saw the expectant faces and already heard the applause. So he drained his beer glass in one go, as he had learned, rose to his feet and said, 'Comrades! When duty calls, a soldier cannot shirk.'

At the table d'hôte Chanele wanted to tell her husband the funny story of Hersch Wasserstein's surprise offer, but Janki's thoughts were so focused on the planned party that he didn't hear her words. He was very disappointed – he hadn't expected otherwise, but he was disappointed none the less – that his wife was not at all enthusiastic about his plan, and was even trying to put him off the whole idea. She had never understood, he said, how important it was in this world to be accepted, and what acceptance could be more complete than to be allowed to give the ceremonial address at a Sedan Day party?

'But you weren't even at Sedan!'

Janki gave his wife a censorious look and then said in his most charming voice, which had previously been reserved only for his best lady customers, 'Why don't we order another bottle of wine, my dear? We have something to celebrate.'

The next day, when the six musketeers were in the Strandcafé again, discussing the details of the big day – in what sequence were they to march in? Did one shake the mayor's hand after the badge of honour had been awarded, or did one give a military salute? – a strange man approached their table. He was wearing a white linen beach suit with brown street shoes that didn't match. A straw hat a couple of sizes too small sat ludicrously on his curly hair.

'Please excuse me,' said the man, 'but I had something urgent to discuss with Herr Meijer.'

His voice had an unpleasantly foreign accent.

'As you see, we are very busy,' Staudinger said dismissively.

'It won't take long,' said the man, who was clearly used to having things that he had got into his head sorted out on the spot. 'Five minutes, if we agree. And if we don't – well, we will have finished even more quickly than that.'

'We really have no time for business right now,' said Staudinger.

'Which one of you is Meijer?' asked the man, and when everyone looked at Janki, he shook his hand like that of an old friend and said, 'Be moichel me, I should have explained straight away. I'm sure your friend mentioned it to you.'

'May I ask what it's concerning?'

'Chaje Sore, of course. A pearl of a daughter. Exactly the right one for your Arthur. A shidduch – made in heaven, God willing.'

Von Stetten rose to his feet, a judge getting up to deliver his verdict. His voice suddenly had the same booming commanding tone that Staudinger had used on the train to Hoyerschleuse. 'Comrade Meijer,' he said, 'Do you know this Jew?'

'I have no idea.'

'No idea he says he has, this Herr Meijer,' said the persistent stranger, 'when our children are to marry.'

The echoing laughter that these words provoked around the table faded quickly away. They saw Janki's embarrassed face and knew that there was nothing to laugh about here.

'Meijer,' said von Stetten – the 'comrade' had been lost along the way – 'Meijer, I have just one question for you: are you a Jew?'

'What does that have to do with anything? I'm also a Frenchman, and you said…'

'I would prefer it, Herr Meijer,' said Lieutenant von Stetten, 'if you would address me formally from now on.'

44

Afterwards, Arthur couldn't and wouldn't forget, afterwards, which was always a before as well, when they were able to breathe again, and their hearts no longer hammered as if they had climbed a summit, and it was a summit, every time, an impassable summit which one fears, while it draws one irresistibly, different each time and each time more familiar, with paths that one would yearn to walk again, and again and again, were one not afraid that one might exhaust oneself before exploring others, afterwards, when one did not yet wish to open one's eyes, as one tries to prolong a dream even though one already knows that one will not be able to bring it back, not until the next time, when it will be different again, yet more beautiful, yet more mysterious, yet more dangerous, afterwards, when the fine hairs on the skin still bore that charge, and drew sparks beneath the wandering fingertips – wait! not now! not yet! – afterwards, when the everyday seeped once more through the closed shutters with its weary smell, that stench of reality that one can drown out for a few minutes but not really expel, when self-evidence fell from them like a badly stitched coat, when their nakedness was nakedness again and liberation no longer, afterwards, when they got up and lingered for a few seconds, afterwards, when they sat side by side and dangled their feet in the air, as if it were not the couch in Arthur's consulting room, but a shore, a lake, a sea, and really cold water into which they were now to jump – not yet! please not yet! – as they both stared at the glass cabinet of medical books because they did not yet have the courage to let their eyes meet, afterwards, when it was over and slight disappointment rose up in them, the kind that belongs to happiness as age does to life, afterwards, when time stood still and yet must start again, they covered over the seconds of their sweet embarrassment with the unchanging sentimental ritual.

'Oh please, Doctor,' Joni had to say, 'when can I have another appointment with you?'

And Arthur had to take the black diary from the desk, had to flick through it as if he didn't know the answer, as if he were not the only answer in his life that he did not doubt, and had to say, 'Whenever you like.'

They had met here, here in this room with the smell of disinfectant and the freshly printed diploma on the wall. Arthur had just furnished the room, but it felt too old for him, he felt like a little boy putting on his father's trousers, far too long for him, and a jacket his arms couldn't find a way out from, who paraded like that through the flat and imagined he's grown up. Back then Janki had shouted at him for dragging the carefully ironed trouser legs over the freshly waxed floor, and he had only wanted to try out what it was like if you...

He had just wanted to try it out.

No, that wasn't true. It had been more than curiosity.

Much more.

Joni had come to him with a pulled muscle, nothing serious, not even particularly painful, but the next weekend there was to be a competition, and he wanted to know if there wasn't a remedy for it, something to rub in or something, because this particular competition was particularly important. 'Are you interested in wrestling, Doctor?'

And Arthur had said, 'Please slip out of your things.'

Sometimes quite ordinary sentences, sentences that one has said a thousand times, suddenly acquire a new meaning, the words come freshly coined from the mint, gleaming and new.

Please slip out of your things.

Open, Sesame.

He had used, 'du', the informal form of address, of course he had. The boy was seventeen, no longer a child, but not yet a man either. Why shouldn't he have called him 'du'?

There was no ulterior motive.

And then Joni had been standing naked before him. For the first time.

His muscles weren't particularly powerful. Not for a wrestler. A brutal fighter could have grabbed him and broken him. Could have hurt him. Quite slim hips. And his belly...Tense, as if a clenched fist were hidden in there, just waiting to be...

Stop. Jonathan Leibowitz. A patient. Rectus abdominis well developed. Legs perhaps slightly too sturdy for real symmetry. Flat feet? No, it was just the way he was standing. Combative was the wrong word. He wasn't just ready to fight, he was ready for anything.

'Did you say something, Doctor?'

His voice. Like running a hand over your arm without quite touching it, just brushing the fine hairs so that they stand up and yearn for more – that was the sort of voice that Joni Leibowitz had.

'Did you say something?'

A strain in the levator scapulae, hence the slight pain when he had to move his shoulder. Arthur showed Joni the muscle on one of the coloured posters that he'd been given for the opening of his own practice. The flayed man, one arm resting, the other held aloft, always reminded him of the bloody martyr in the poster for the panopticon all those years ago. That had been another such day, a day that had changed everything, when nothing afterwards was where it had been, when one suddenly understood...

'What can we do about it, Doctor?'

He had prescribed him an ointment that would help or not, and said, 'Can you come back a week today? I would like to take another look at you.'

All of a sudden the most natural sentences were no longer so natural.

I would like to take another look at you.

Then he had gone to the fight. Just like that. In the *Israelitisches Wochenblatt* there had been a small advertisement requesting support for the Jewish Gymnastics Club, so why shouldn't he go, when he had nothing better to do on that Sunday afternoon? He would just say he'd dropped by at the schoolhouse on the Hirschengraben, he would just mingle among the spectators, but there were hardly spectators there, there was no real competition, and the wrestlers – this made it much easier for him later on – didn't have many fans anyway. The people looked around when he came into the gym, and Sally Steigrad, the chairman of the club, hurried towards him, garrulous as befits an insurance salesman, and greeted the young doctor as a welcome guest of honour.

Joni was sitting on a bench next to three other wrestlers, all four of them in long white gymnastic trousers and tight vests. A curl had fallen into his forehead, he threw his head to one side and his eye caught, by chance – but nothing that Joni did involved chance, it wasn't possible that this could all be chance – his eye, as if by chance, caught Arthur's. Then he smiled, and seemed to lose interest in the new spectator.

As Arthur was to discover, Joni had two kinds of smile, a public and a private one.

In the middle of the vast gym the mats had been laid out, a raft in the sea, and the spectators arranged themselves around it in almost indecent proximity. They were competing in only four weight categories, the young Jewish gymnastics club did not yet have any more wrestlers to offer. It was a very unequal competition: inexperienced rookies against confident veterans, who knew all the holds and counterholds and gained their points routinely, as a matter of course. Joni's turn was last; the score was already three-nil, and his fight was no longer significant. But he was to be brought out anyway, Sally Steigrad had agreed with the chairman of the opposing team, 'My boys need experience.'

Joni's opponent had very hairy arms, far too coarse to be grappling with this slender boy's body.

Far too coarse.

When the two of them stood facing one another and entered the first clinch, when they pressed their torsos against one another, golem and angel, when their heads touched as if in a caress, Arthur had to take off his glasses and rub his nose. He had been seized by a strange emotion, a not unpleasant sadness that brought tears to his eyes.

Then the fight was over. Joni had been knocked off his feet, his opponent left the raft of mats, had finished his job, which had been strenuous but not particularly difficult, and Joni was still lying on the mat with his face contorted, pointing at his shoulder, which his opponent had tugged at like a farm hand straightening a sack of corn before getting a proper hold of it and throwing it on the pile with the others.

'Would you be so kind, Doctor?' asked Sally Steigrad.

It was as if Joni had no smell of his own. The sweat of his hairy opponent rose into Arthur's nose, the dust of the mat he knelt on, and the sour aroma of effort and exhaustion common to all gyms in the world. But Joni? Even when he bent over him to examine the injury, there was no scent for him to catch. Or was it so close to his own that he wasn't even aware of it, as one isn't aware of one's own smell?

'The same spot again?' Arthur asked.

Joni turned his head towards him and smiled at him from below, with his very private smile.

'Oh, please, Doctor,' said Joni, 'when can I have another appointment with you?'

It was the first time he had said it.

That was how it started.

Arthur would have done anything to be close to Joni, and Sally Steigrad was proud of this new, academic member whose suddenly awakened interest in wrestling he attributed to himself, or at least to the appeal that he had placed in the *Wochenblatt*. Arthur was not a really gifted athlete, but he tried, and as a medic he had the advantage that he knew about bones and sinews, and didn't need to have the holds and their effects explained to him in great detail. He just had to overcome the inhibition of applying that knowledge practically in a fight.

In training, his partner was usually Joni Leibowitz, who was in the same weight category. They were a good pairing, Sally Steigrad thought, as he looked at them. They often worked together on their technique, when the others were already getting dressed again.

Arthur couldn't have explained what happened between himself and Joni during this time, although in sleepless nights he analysed every look caught by chance – by chance? – and every offhand remark for hidden meanings.

He had never been in love before, and could not interpret the condition that assailed him, could not begin to interpret that illness. No one had ever told him that love is confusion above all.

Joni was only seventeen, an apprentice in his uncle's stationery shop, and reacted with much greater calm than the doctor with all his book-learning. He interpreted Arthur's vague feelings before he really understood them himself, and seemed to fee neither hurt nor threatened by them. He played quite unselfconsciously with the power they gave him over the older man, and he did that without any malice, just as a cat feels no hatred for the mouse that it allows to escape and catches again and allows to escape and catches again. Whether Joni returned his love – yes, it was love, Arthur had had to admit it, and since then felt strangely relieved – whether he felt the same or at least something similar, that was a question to which Arthur never found a certain answer, right until the end.

Arthur won his first bout, quite to his own surprise. It was in the return round of the championship – the more modest the sporting achievements, the more seriously one takes rules and plans – and the Jewish Gymnastics Club was already abjectly at the bottom of the table. The opposing team was the same one as the one at Arthur's very first visit to the gym, the Workers' Gymnastics Club from Wiedikon, all people who did hard physical work in the factory day after day, and who had chosen wrestling as a sport because they needed an outlet for their surplus strength at the weekend as well. Arthur faced the same man who had defeated and injured Joni, who had dared to hurt Joni, and when he felt the man's hairy arm against his body, he was suddenly assailed, for the first time in his life, which had hitherto always been mild and theoretical, with such boundless fury that they had had finally to drag him off his opponent, because he refused to relax his neck wrench long after his opponent had knocked on the mat as a sign of giving in.

'Now we've taught you how to give it an edge,' Sally Steigrad said, and attributed this success to himself as well.

Afterwards they stood side by side at the wash basin. Joni threw his curl out of his forehead and said, 'I know what you want from me.' They called each other 'du', of course, fellow sportsmen call each other 'du', there's nothing special about it. 'I know what you want,' said Joni, 'but you'll only get it if you defeat me.'

Arthur lay awake all night and tried to grasp what he thought he had understood.

They faced one another at the Club Championship. It wasn't an important title, a single bout would decide it, there were no other competitors in their weight category, and it would actually have made more sense to award Joni the victory wreath without a fight. Arthur hadn't beaten him in a single training session so far. There were, in fact, real bronzed oak-leaf wreaths with blue and white bows; Sally Steigrad placed a lot of value on such outward appearances, which was also why he complained about the fact that the Club still didn't have a flag.

Luckily no one from the family had come, even though Hinda and Zalman had offered to support him. Arthur felt as if he had been caught every time someone asked him about his new-found passion for the sport, and sometimes became really bad-tempered, as if someone were touching the open wound of his bad conscience.

They stood facing one another on the mat, they established their holds, and Arthur's hands trembled as they did every time he touched that body. It was a battle of wait-and-see, a clumsy dance, and soon, after hold and counterhold, their heads were quite close together, cheek to cheek, and Joni suddenly smiled his smile, a very private smile, and Arthur whispered, 'A promise is a promise.' Then he let himself fall in such a way that everyone would think Arthur had pulled him off his feet. The fight was over, and Arthur had defeated Joni.

When the put the wreath on his head – 'Completely ridiculous, such decorations!' he had always said, and never let it go for as long as he lived – when Joni stood in front of him and shook his head, surprising victor and fair loser, he heard the words for the second time. 'When can I have an appointment with you, Doctor?'

It was a very ordinary consulting room, with the smell of illness and cleanliness and fear of death. The couch was narrow, so high that your legs dangled in the air if you sat on the edge, and a thick roll of paper was fastened at one end, the same rustling hygienic paper that hairdressers used for their head-rests. There was a desk in the room, an armchair behind it, a chair in front of it, a screen that concealed a clothes-stand, and a white-painted glass bookshelf in which textbooks jostled with specialist journals, and at the back in the second row, where it couldn't be seen, Professor Hirschfeld's *Yearbook of Sexual Intermediary Stages*, which Arthur scoured in vain for explanations for his own confusion. He had found only questionnaires, with which one was supposed to measure the female proportion of one's own physicality: 'Are your fingers pointed or blunt?' 'So you give off a noticeable smell in hot weather?' 'Do you think logically?'

No, he wasn't thinking logically, and it worried him, and it gave him courage, and he couldn't wait for the day he had agreed to see Joni.

It was a quite ordinary consulting room, but it was the most beautiful room in the world.

Joni had been just as uncertain as he, just as curious, and afterwards just as happy and exhausted.

Every time.

Afterwards, which was always also a before.

Arthur had immediately given up wrestling. He knew he couldn't have gone on touching Joni without everyone noticing the way he was touching him. Once he had started awake from a dream in which they had met for a training session, the mat in the middle of his consulting room, onlookers had jostled all around, Sally Steigrad and Cantor Würzburger and also Uncle Salomon, even though he had died long ago, they had walked towards one another, Arthur and Joni, and Joni had thrown the curl out of his forehead, and Arthur had kissed him, he had kissed him in front of everyone, and Joni had smiled and said, 'Oh, please, Doctor, when can I have another appointment with you?'

'There's something I have to discuss with you,' said Joni.

The wrong words.

'It has nothing to do with you,' said Joni, and didn't look at him, just stared at the glass book-case, which couldn't provide any answers either, 'just with me, and the fact that I'm nineteen now and have to think about what happens next.'

They had been the best years of Arthur's life, and even before Joni went on talking he knew they were over.

'I'm going into army training,' said Joni, 'so we won't see each other for a long time anyway, and afterwards I may be going abroad. My uncle knows someone who has a paper factory in Linz, and there I can ...But that's not the reason. None of that is the reason. The reason is ...'

The reason is that there are no miracles.

The reason is that one cannot be happy without being punished for it.

'I've done a lot of thinking,' said Joni. 'The way you always think about things before you do them. I've learned a lot from you, you know. I'm grateful to you for that. Honestly: I'm grateful to you. But I've done a lot of thinking and reached the conclusion ...It really has nothing to do with you.'

Your heart is torn from your body, but it has nothing to do with you.

'I have reached the conclusion ...' said Joni, still sitting beside Arthur, he would only have needed to reach out his hand to touch him, to hold him, never to let him go.

But he didn't have the right to do that.

'I have reached the conclusion,' said Joni, 'that I'm a perfectly ordinary person. One like all the others. Nothing special. Not like you. Just a man who wants to have a family and children and ...yes, and a wife. The way you do.'

The way you do.

'It would also be the best thing for you. A family, I mean. You'd be a good father. A wonderful father, I'm sure of it. It's always been lovely with you, really, it was lovely, and I'm not levelling any reproaches at you.'

Reproaches.

'But it isn't going anywhere. You understand what I mean? It isn't going anywhere.'

And Arthur did the bravest thing he had ever done in his life, he did the most cowardly thing, the most contemptible, and said, 'Yes, Joni, I understand you.'

Joni slipped from the couch and stood in the room as much of a stranger as if he had only come here by accident on his way to a quite different destination. Arthur saw him naked, one very last time. The physique was no longer that of a boy, now it was a man, just a man, a man like many others. He walked as if he was flat-footed, his legs were slightly too short and his bottom...

Gluteus maximus. Just a muscle. Which started here and here and stopped there and there and moved that and that.

The screen was a three-part metal frame stretched with pleated beige material, and Joni disappeared behind it, as all patients did after their examination, they disappeared, you heard a rustle, and eventually they reappeared and were dressed and armoured and belonged only to themselves.

Arthur sat on the edge of the couch for a long time. He touched the leather covering where Joni had been sitting and thought he felt a last trace of his warmth.

45

Joni didn't return to the gymnastics club after military training. Neither did he go to Linz, which had just been an excuse; he now had other interests, he had broadened both inwardly and outwardly, had lost his narrow-hipped youthfulness and grown into a shape of which there were many copies in the world. Of course they met repeatedly, Zurich was small and Jewish Zurich still smaller, but Joni only had his public smile left for Arthur, he had decided not to remember the other smile. When he greeted him, he was polite and detached, a pupil meeting a teacher long after the end of his school days.

Eventually Sally Steigrad contacted Arthur, visited him at home and brought with him two bottles of beer which they – 'No ceremony among fellow sportsmen!' – drank without glasses. Sally was a long, thin man, for whom the club was more important than his family. not because he didn't have one, on the contrary, the Steigrad family comprised countless siblings and cousins, and their policies brought him, an insurance salesman, a decent income as if it were the most natural thing in the world. But policies don't make life interesting. It was in the competitions he made his gymnasts take part in as often as possible that Sally sought excitement; in terms of his character, he said, he was a global traveller or conqueror, and he liked to complain that everything in his life was so orderly and regulated, he sometimes felt as if all he had to do before he died was tick off due dates, and no surprises of any kind were factored into his life's plan. Although of course one always had to reckon with surprises, even unpleasant ones. And while they were on the subject: had Arthur ever thought of taking out life insurance?

But that wasn't what he had come about, it really wasn't, although they should have a quiet talk about the topic another time, 'better safe than sorry' as the English said, and they were hardly stupid people. When Sally turned to the topic of insurance, there was something automatic about his words, a gramophone that starts singing away from wherever the needle happens to fall in the groove. As he talked, he bobbed up and down as if an over-abundant temperament wouldn't leave him in peace for a moment, and appraised Arthur's modest furniture like an auctioneer evaluating an inheritance. But insurance wasn't the reason for his visit today, it really wasn't, Sally said and sat down at last, today he didn't want a signature from Arthur, but something quite different – to get straight to the point – he wanted to win him back to the gymnastics club.

'No,' said Arthur.

Never again.

'Not as an active member,' Sally reassured him. Arthur had never, and he wasn't to be offended by his frankness, been a Karl Schuhmann, he would recognise the name, only five foot six and four gold medals. Arthur's mind, Sally had often observed, had never been entirely on the subject, 'as if you were thinking about something other than victory', but that was what intellectuals were like. He, Sally, imagined the medical profession as a big adventure, something that demanded the whole person, not like insurance, in which everything was already planned out and prescribed by central office. Arthur should, just by the by, think of taking out household insurance, he didn't own much now, but the leather armchairs they were sitting in were very pretty, and if he ever got married they could ramp up the premiums.

But back to the topic at hand. He didn't want to bring Arthur back into the club as a wrestler, but as a doctor. It had recently become customary, and he thought it made perfect sense, to have a representative of the medical profession on the spot, mostly they were only nurses, and once, which he had found completely ridiculous, a dentist had even turned up at a wrestling competition, could Arthur imagine? if someone had dislocated a joint he would probably have reached for his drill, ha ha ha.

Little jokes like that had helped Sally conclude many a deal.

So, to get to the point: what did Arthur think of the idea of making himself available as the club doctor? It wouldn't take as much time as active sport, he trained to a certain extent in his daily practice, ha ha ha, and perhaps – it didn't have to be so, but it was a timely thought – perhaps he could occasionally give the young people a kind of course, medically correct relaxation before training, the anatomical foundations of competitive sport. Just things like that.

To his own surprise Arthur heard himself saying 'yes', not 'yes, he would think about the suggestion,' but quite rashly and directly 'yes'. Sally Steigrad attributed this spontaneous agreement to his own powers of persuasion and saw, once again, confirmation of his credo that arguments in the insurance trade are more important than forms.

Arthur assumed his new duties for two reasons. On the one hand he felt a debt towards the gymnastics club, and it was part of his character always to feel most himself when he thought he was atoning for something, and on the other hand he hoped – an essay in the *Yearbook for Sexual Intermediate Stages* had led him to this thought – that regular harmless contact with young men would have an inoculating effect on him, just as a dilute pathogen protects the body against the outbreak of illness.

And he knew that there would be no second Joni among the gymnasts, because there could never again be a second Joni.

If it was a penance that he had taken upon himself, it was one of a not unpleasant kind. Arthur had only just celebrated his thirty-third birthday, but since Joni had ended their relationship he had aged, not exactly like Rabbi ben Ezra, who was said to have turned overnight into a dignified old man, but like someone for whom memory has become more important than the future. The young gymnasts treated him, out of respect for his profession, and indeed for or his age, with a certain distance, and he appreciated that. It was part of his character always to re-examine himself, just as there are people who turn around three times just to check that the front door is locked, and each time he did so he established, reassured and a little disappointed, that there was nothing there.

There would never be anything there again.

When Sally Steigrad, in the pub where they drank beer after training, started talking about the need for a club flag, whose acquisition was indispensable because one would otherwise simply make oneself ridiculous at gymnastics festivals – 'we can't just tie a tallis to a stick and carry it around in front of us, after all' – Arthur voluntarily assumed the task of drumming up the money. He would, he reasoned, dedicate the flag to Joni, only in his own thoughts, of course, but they were what mattered in the end.

He was so pleased with the idea that he didn't even contradict Sally when he wanted to fix a date for the consecration of the flag. They agreed on 28 June of the following year, 'which gives you nine months', Sally said, 'and nine months, I don't need to explain to a doctor, is enough to create something with functioning limbs, hahaha.' That was a joke that he liked to trot out for young married couples.

However the self-appointed task proved almost impossible. Arthur did the rounds of Jewish businessmen, but hardly won a concrete agreement from anyone, even though he was always given a very polite welcome. People are always polite to doctors, perhaps for fear of not being treated properly should they fall ill.

Typical of the increasingly long list of his disappointments was his visit to Siegfried Weill, the father of Désirée's friend Esther.

'Bureau', it said on the door; the French spelling was probably supposed to upgrade the desk squeezed between the shelves to something more elevated, but it was just a store-room directly behind the shop, and the chair that Herr Weill had offered him was actually meant for salesmen, who tend to stay too long if they're sitting comfortably.

With his deep voice and black beard, Herr Weill looked like a licensed German rabbi. He radiated imposing dignity, which he was well aware of, and which he liked to deploy as a sales technique. He would confirm hesitant lady customers in their decisions with such a sermon-like 'A very good choice, Madame!' that afterwards they rarely dared to go and look elsewhere. He used a pair of ladies' buttoned ankle-boots, chevreaux leather with patent toecaps, to explain to Arthur why – 'to my great regret, and even though I see great value in supporting the gymnastics club as such' – sadly, sadly he could not take part in the collection of money. 'Look at this shoe,' he said, and with a solemn gesture held out the open cardboard box to Arthur, 'one of our most popular models, American in origin. On sale for eighteen francs. And now tell me, Doctor: what does this shoe cost me? If I include everything, transport, rent, wages, taxes? What does the shoe cost me?'

Arthur had no idea. 'Fifteen francs?' he said hesitantly.

'Fifteen francs! Halevei! If I were to buy a pair of shoes for fifteen francs and sell them for eighteen, twenty per cent rewech, it would be a hanoe to me to pay for your flag, and the flagpole too!' He shook his head, like a sage over the sins of this world, repeatedly lamenting, 'Fifteen francs, he says! Why not make if fourteen?'

And in any case, said Herr Weill, one had been so overrun of late by shnor-rers – 'Do not take the word amiss, Doctor!' – like wasps in a hot summer they were, and then of course there were the regular obligations too: if you was called up to the Torah in synagogue, you had to shnoder something, and apart from those charitable donations he also paid his shekels for the construction work in Palestine – he wasn't one of those diehard Zionists, but one didn't want to stand aside completely – and otherwise there was always this and that, in short: sorry thought he was, in this case he would have to say no. But if the Jewish Gymnastics Club undertook to buy all its sports shoes from him in future, then he would offer a ten per cent discount, what was he saying, fifteen per cent! Just so that the doctor could see that he was very positive on the subject.

That was the response that Arthur got wherever he went; the money simply wouldn't come together. When he had gone all the way through the list of businessmen, the firm commitments came to less than a hundred francs. And a flag, even a modest one, cost at least four times as much as that.

Next June, which had seemed an infinite distance away only a short time before, was now suddenly, it seemed to Arthur, practically on his doorstep. Sally Steigrad called meetings in which the design was discussed, he had also already drawn up a list of the halls where the big ball might be held – 'Of course there must be a ball, if you're going to do something, do it properly!' – and at the flag-makers' they had told Arthur that three months was the least, the very least, he could expect; now that everyone was thinking about the national exposition in Bern, they were drowning in commissions.

Arthur didn't dare knock on his father's door again; Janki hadn't recovered at all in the summer resort on Sylt, and had been constantly depressed since then. Being separated from his shop, with its smell of old spices, was harder for him than he had expected.

There was only one last possibility.

Arthur's relationship with François had never been easy. As a child he had been unable to put into words the breathless admiration he felt for his big brother; even then he had found it hard to talk about emotions. Later, when he had perhaps found the words, the opportunity never arose, even though by now they both lived in Zurich. An ambitious businessman, who is already married and has a son, is worlds apart from a young medical student, and Arthur had felt as if the age difference between them was distancing them further and further; the more adult François seemed to him, the more immature he felt himself.

And then François had had himself baptised, and that had introduced such awkwardness into their relationship that nothing cordial could arise to combat it. One of Arthur's teachers at grammar school had had a flaming red growth on his forehead that everyone had to ignore and yet couldn't ignore, and that was exactly what he felt about François's Christianity: the effort not to mention it all the time silenced all conversation.

But it was possible to talk to Mina.

François had had a villa built on the Zurichberg, in the new quarter near the university. The building was generous but lifeless, a mere stage, and Mina, who was supposed to be the mistress of the house, moved around the big rooms like an actress who hasn't been given the script of her play. A janitor who looks after other people's properties without having any claims to them herself.

'No, Arthur, you aren't a burden at all. This house is arranged for guests. We could have twenty-four people to dinner if there were twenty-four people who would accept an invitation from us.' She said such things without bitterness, she was just establishing facts, and in her uncomplaining directness she resembled her mother-in-law Chanele.

A maid with a cap and apron served them tea. They had taken a seat at a little cast-iron table in the conservatory, where in spite of the cool autumn day it was almost too warm. Arthur admired a little orange tree with perfectly formed fruit hanging from its branches, and Mina followed his gaze and said, 'As long as you don't try to eat them...'

She thought it entirely possible that François could be persuaded to make a donation.

'Even though...?' Arthur couldn't bring himself to ask the question, but Mina answered it anyway.

'That's why. François likes to stress that nothing has actually changed for him, that people are just too narrow-minded, too fixated on outward appearances to understand that he's still the same person he was before... So why shouldn't he support the Jewish Gymnastics Club?'

'And? Is he still the same person?'

Mina poured a few drops of milk from the silver jug into her tea, added sugar, stirred it and drank. 'Have a piece of cake,' she said.

'Is François still the same person?'

'I fear so.'

'Strange,' thought Arthur, 'that one can feel more closely related to a sister-in-law than to one's own brother.'

When François came home he was in an excellent mood, and treated the presence of Arthur, even though he hadn't seen him for months, as if it were the most natural thing in the world. 'Good to see you here. I have something to show you. I've just got it.' He waved a long green cardboard tube, a child proudly presenting a new toy, and in his enthusiasm almost knocked over one of the many flower-holders that turned the conservatory into a little civilised jungle.

He was in such a hurry that he didn't even take the time to remove his jacket; he just threw his hat on one of the ornate wicker chairs. They had to follow him into the drawing-room, where he pushed the low table aside to make enough room on the floor. He knelt down, still in his coat, took a long parchment-coloured roll of paper out of the cardboard packaging and had Arthur pass him two heavy, polished ashtrays to fix one end of it down on the carpet. Then he unrolled the paper so carefully and almost tenderly that Arthur was reminded of the unrolling of the Torah in the service, although that comparison was more than out of place with François.

What François had brought was the plan of a store, a colourful architectural drawing, lovingly prepared down to the smallest details. Smiling mannequins, dressed in the latest fashions, already paraded in the window displays, and outside the double front door a line of carefully sketched customers waited impatiently to be allowed in.

The three-storey building was in the classical style, the wide shop windows separated from one another by half-relief Corinthian columns from whose capitals chiselled acanthus leaves flourished. On each of the two columns which, twice as broad as the others, flanked the entrance, there sat a stone lion

379

with the crest of Zurich between its claws. On the upper storeys the windows were bigger than usual, which produced the idea of inviting, light-flooded spaces inside.

On either side of the plan a row of medallions was arranged, drawn window frames through which one could see as if through a window all the things that were actually going on in the store. A salesman was helping a customer in his shirt-sleeves into his new jacket, a woman was trying on a hat decorated with feathers, a young couple with a bashful expression considered a selection of cots.

'This is it,' François said proudly. 'The most beautiful department store in Zurich.' He looked so happy that Arthur felt closer to his brother than he had for ages.

'You're planning a new building?' he asked.

'Eventually. Eventually.' François said it in such an exaggeratedly dismissive way that it was clear: he couldn't wait to be asked about further details.

'And where?'

'Right beside the Paradeplatz.' François rubbed his hands. He was still kneeling on the floor, and it looked as if he was praying.

'So you got the land after all?'

'Not yet,' said François, his face radiant with anticipation. 'But it can't go on for much longer. I have it from an impeccable source that old Landolt is on his death-bed.'

They had to admire the drawing, and François couldn't stop revealing more and more details to them: 'the whole thing has three underground levels – the store-room on its own has more floor-space than the whole shop! A garage specially for home deliveries – all motorised vehicle, of course, and the chauffeurs in uniform! An annual catalogue with a mail order service covering the whole of Switzerland!' In his enthusiasm he was, without knowing it, an exact copy of his father. Janki had once, when he was bargaining over Mimi's dowry, described the planned Modern Emporium to old Salomon Meijer.

Arthur made the right noises, said, 'really?' and 'impressive!', but he might just as well have said nothing at all, because François was basically just talking to himself. Mina, as was her way and special talent, listened to her husband as attentively as if he hadn't described his plans and ideas to her a hundred times.

'The most modern steam heating that closes off the entrance with an air curtain, so that the doors to the street can stay invitingly open even in cold weather! A tea-room in the fabrics department, so that one can look at the swatch books as if in the comfort of one's own sitting-room! Four paternoster lifts and also...'

François got no further with his enthusiastic account, because there was suddenly a noise outside the door, a violent argument, a defensive voice could be heard, and another, furious voice that would not be fobbed off, and then the door to the drawing room flew open and Mimi stormed in, tramped over the rolled-out plan, her heels tearing holes in the paper, pushed Arthur aside and grabbed François by the arm, pulled him up from his kneeling position and grabbed him by the lapels of his coat so that he was forced to stand facing her, her face very close to his. The terrified maid appeared in the doorway and tried to explain that she had simply been pushed aside, that there was nothing she could do about it, but she couldn't get a word out because Mimi was shouting at François, shouting at him so violently and so furiously that she spat as she did so, shouted and shouted and wouldn't let go of him the whole time. He didn't defend himself, just put up with it and tried unsuccessfully to understand what it was that Mimi was saying over and over again, and which made absolutely no sense.

'I will never forgive you for that!' Mimi shouted. 'Never, never, never will I forgive you for that.'

46

In the end it was a delivery of English gentlemen's boots that brought the whole structure of lies crashing down.

The two wooden crates full of shoe-boxes, which had arrived two days earlier than expected, were too big for the door of the warehouse marked 'Bureau', so they stayed in the salesroom and compromised the sales-promoting elegance on which Siegfried Weill placed such value in his shop. So he decreed that the crates be emptied immediately, and the boxes placed on the shelves, an operation for which he had to call upon the services not only of his two members of staff, but of his whole family, 'yes, you too, young lady, you can take that elegant coat of yours off right this minute and put on an apron instead.'

That afternoon Esther Weill had arranged to see her friend Désirée, and had been on the point of leaving the house when her father stopped her and dragooned her to work for him in spite of all her protests. An hour previously, and this was among the precautionary measures they had agreed, she had dropped in at the Pomeranz household as if by chance, and had discreetly confirmed to Désirée that nothing stood in the way of their autumn walk together. Only then had Désirée confided in her mother that Esther Weill was meeting her suitor again, and that as her best friend she had once again to act as chaperone and alibi in one.

In the event of last minute obstacles, they had agreed this, the rendezvous was to be cancelled straight away and rearranged for a different time. But Désirée was too much in love to be sensible. More than a week had passed since the last time, and this week had been an eternity.

They had already missed far too many years together. As if everyone and everything had conspired to keep them apart. When in fact they were meant for one another.

From childhood onwards.

Désirée and Alfred.

Alfred and Désirée.

They had arranged to meet on the Dolder, in the deer park behind the Grand Hotel. It was a long walk there from the hut in the forest where the rack terminated, so one could be fairly sure, at least on weekdays, that one wouldn't meet anyone.

When she arrived he was already there. He was always already there, he missed her so much every minute. Even from a distance he could see that Désirée was carrying her hat in her hand, and that made him happy because he knew what it meant. Mimi insisted that Désirée wear wide-brimmed hats because of her sensitive complexion, and they got in the way of kissing. They kissed each other for a long time, and no one was watching them. Only a stag, no more timid than a cow stood behind the bars of its enclosure, seemed like them to be waiting for something.

Esther didn't come; it was already twenty minutes past the agreed time, and she had never been as late as this before. 'She mustn't have been allowed to get away for some reason,' said Alfred. 'You'll have to go back straight away.'

But his face was so sad, and Désirée couldn't bear to see him sad. 'Just five minutes, just three, just one.'

His tongue tasted of peppermint. Before they met he always sucked these little pastilles; it made her laugh at him, and love him all the more.

And then a whole hour had passed, and there was no getting around it; she had to deceive Mimi one way or another. Sometimes Désirée completely forgot that she lied to her mother every time, it become so natural to let Esther Weill play the lead in her own love story. It was so easy to forget everything in the few hours they had together.

It was so beautiful.

'Nothing will happen,' Désirée whispered. They whispered often when they were together, even if there was no danger of anyone hearing them. She laid her head very close to his and whispered in his ear, and then there was his earlobe, which had to be kissed as well, sometimes she nibbled on it and even bit into it. Once she had tasted his blood, just a drop, and it had made a magical connection between them.

But they were magically connected anyway.

When they had met again anyway, just by chance, she had been dismissive of him, really quite brusque. Alfred continued to hold it against her, and claimed he was still angry with her about it. Only as a joke, of course, in truth he could never have held anything against her. Then he tried to pull a severe face, which he couldn't do at all, and after that he imposed a punishment on her that had to be kissed away, kiss after kiss. 'I am a lawyer,' he said, 'I cannot let lenience prevail.'

She had been quite brusque with him.

Her piano teacher lived and taught in Stockerstrasse, an old Frau Breslin who actually had a much more complicated Russian name, and who seemed to hate the music she hammered out of her piano every bit as much as she hated her pupils. No one liked going to see her, but her unfriendliness had won her a reputation of particular capability, and Mimi wouldn't hear of her daughter giving up her lessons or switching teachers. 'You just have to practise more,' she said.

Désirée hadn't practised that day either, and she was late as well, which would lead to a tirade half in German and half in Russian. At the Conservatoire in St Petersburg lazy pupils were rapped on the knuckles with the conducting baton, and Frau Breslin was very sorry that she wasn't allowed to introduce this method in Zurich as well. Désirée had wedged the thin music folder under her arm, turned the corner far too quickly – 'A lady doesn't run!' – and almost knocked him over. Her music fell to the ground, he bent down for it and only when he handed it to her did they recognise each other.

'Where are you off to in such a hurry, Déchirée?' asked Alfred, and she wrenched the folder from his hand as reproachfully as if he had been responsible for the collision, and walked on without a word.

She had been really brusque.

And then, an hour later, when she left the house in Stockerstrasse again, he was already standing outside the door, he had just walked after her and waited for her and said, 'Hello, Désirée.' But the tone in which he said it sounded arrogant, and she didn't like him at all, not at that first meeting, and not the next time either.

Because a week later he was there again. 'I've waited for you every day,' he said. 'Except on Shabbos, of course.' The word sounded artificial coming from his lips.

She didn't like him, she really didn't. She threw her head back and left him standing. He had watched after her for ages, he claimed later, but she hadn't turned round. And why should she have? It wasn't as if he thought she was interested in him.

She didn't care about him, that's right, she didn't care about him in the slightest, but then she couldn't stop thinking about him, she was all over the place, and dreaming with her eyes open. Mimi was already starting to worry because Désirée was always so careful and reliable about everything, she gave her cod liver oil, and Désirée had to gulp it down because she couldn't tell her mother what was really wrong with her.

She didn't understand it herself.

Eventually, and she would have burst if she hadn't done it, she talked to Esther Weill about it, and Esther immediately got very excited. Esther was the kind of person to whom nothing dramatic or extraordinary can ever happen, because they don't have the talent for recognising the extraordinary.

That Désirée was experiencing secret love – 'I don't love him, what would give you such a meshuganeh idea?' – and this love of all loves, which was so impossible and forbidden – 'If you say "Love" one more time, I won't talk to you again as long as I live!' – that her best friend had fallen head over heels in love with this baptised relative – 'Esther, really!' – thrilled her so much that she was scared by the idea that this second-hand experience might soon be over. 'You have to accept his invitation,' she urged, because he had actually asked Désirée to meet him, just so they could talk, really, just talk, nothing more, he had so much to say to her.

But Désirée couldn't go on meeting this strange man – all right, not really strange, but it made no difference – couldn't just go on meeting this man, what would people think? Esther offered herself as an alibi, as a chaperone and a co-conspirator.

If you really thought about it, it was all her fault.

The first time they went walking along the Sihl The spring was almost over, and beneath the chestnut trees there lay a carpet of blossom. Esther always stayed a few discreet paces behind the others, but even though she couldn't hear what they were saying to each other, she could still see how Désirée changed during the walk, how her posture became increasingly soft and yielding. And she was walking more and more slowly, too; at first she had actually been walking away, and by the end, as they approached the Selnau again, she had become so slow that Esther almost had to come to a standstill lest she catch up with the others. Désirée no longer held her arms folded, but let them dangle by her side, almost as if she were hoping that Alfred would grab her and hold her tight. But he didn't do that, he just said goodbye without a handshake, with a small, still bow, and when he had gone Désirée said, 'He's very different.'

He was unhappy, but he said so without complaint, he just stated the fact, a doctor diagnosing an illness. Had Désirée ever heard of Kaspar Hauser? That was exactly how he felt, as if he had lost part of himself and no longer knew where he belonged. 'I'm always in between,' he said. 'Do you understand what I mean?'

He had never been able to talk to anyone about it before, not even with Mina, who understood everything. Never had he found anyone he could confide in about everything. Until all of a sudden Désirée had been there again, little Déchirée, who he had played with as a child.

Not that he only ever talked about himself, far from it. He even apologised for bothering her with his problems, and generally treated her with such care it gave her the feeling that she was something particularly valuable.

She often wondered when she had actually started loving him, and could find no answer. It hadn't been right at the start, certainly not at first sight, and yet she felt as if it had never been otherwise. It had been going on for almost five months now, next week it would be five months.

Five months since Désirée had had finally redeemed the promise of her name. Désirée, the desired one.

When the story of the booth and the whale skeleton had happened, she had almost died of fear. But then in her desperation she had come up with the idea of attributing the whole story to Esther, and since then there had even been a second person to whom she could describe her feelings. It was almost as if she had told Mimi the whole truth.

That she had only seemingly drawn her mother into her confidence was the most unforgivable thing of all.

Mimi had happened by the Weill shoe shop just by chance, had seen all the boxes through the window and, as she liked to be the first where fashion was concerned – not that she was vain, *certainement pas* – she had gone in. To her disappointment, the new delivery consisted entirely of gentlemen's boots; Mimi was about to leave again, but was held back by Herr Weill. He absolutely had to show her an extremely elegant clasp shoe that only women with very narrow feet could wear and which was therefore, he dissembled in his best rabbi voice, could have been made specially for dear Frau Pomeranz. Mimi knew he was lying to her – 'No one has ever been able to deceive me' – but she liked the compliment, and she had no urgent plans.

She had just sat down – 'but really just a moment' – when to her surprise she caught sight of Esther, who was on her way to the store-room with a stack of cardboard boxes.

'Oh, so you're both back already?'

'Yes, we're. That is: we didn't…we hadn't arranged to see each other.'

Herr Weill shooed his stammering daughter into the store-room. As proud of his educational principles as he was of his talents as a salesman, he was about to launch into a lengthy sermon on the text, 'First work, then pleasure,' but Frau Pomeranz was suddenly in a great hurry, had forgotten an important appointment and would have to try on the elegant clasp shoe, narrow foot or no narrow foot, some other time.

'Never interrupt another sales conversation of mine!' Herr Weill told his daughter, and couldn't understand why Esther kept bursting into uncontrollable tears over even such a mild reproach.

When Désirée came home, Mimi was lying on the chaise-longue, with a damp cloth on her forehead.

'Headache, Mama?'

'Ah, if only it were a migraine…Did you have a nice day, ma petite?'

'It's getting a bit cool, up in the forest.'

'I can imagine,' said Mimi in a pained voice, 'and it will soon get much colder.'

'Shall I bring you a cup of tea?'

'Not necessary, ma petite.' Mimi took the cloth from her forehead and put it back in the bowl of cooling lemon water. 'Sit and join me for a moment, there, on the cushion, and tell your mother all the things you've done today.

And so Désirée told the story of how Esther and her nameless admirer had met at the deer park, and how happy they had been to see one another again. It had been another nine days since the last time, 'and nine days is a terribly long time if you're in love, I think.'

'So you think they love each other?'

There could be no doubt whatsoever as far as Désirée was concerned. She herself had not yet experienced anything of the kind herself, she wasn't the one who was in love, it was Esther, but if you saw the way the two of them held hands and wouldn't let go, the way they kissed…

'Ah,' Mimi cut in, 'So they kiss?'

Désirée had promised her friend never to betray that to anyone, 'but you can keep a secret, can't you, Mama?'

'*Certainement*,' said Mimi, no one could be more discreet than she. She had sat up, and only her hand, which kept clenching on a handkerchief, showed that there was anything wrong.

Désirée described how shy the two of them had been the very first time they kissed, how clumsy they had been for a long time. 'Once he almost knocked the hat off her head, just imagine!' – and how they then gradually, and more and more…

'Practice makes perfect, you mean.'

Yes, you could put it that way.

'And you watch them?'

No, of course not. Désirée was discreet, and left the two of them alone. She preferred to go back around the corner and warn the lovers if a walker was approaching. She had developed a special whistle, like the one used on Shabbos when you're not allowed to use the doorbell. No, she didn't watch them kissing, she certainly didn't, what was Mama thinking of, but Esther was her best friend, and had told her exactly what it was like when one…

'And? What is it like?'

Wonderful, Esther had said, it wonderful. You came so close to one another, and at that moment you knew that you belonged together, 'I don't think you can kiss a man if you don't love him.' Because you also tasted and smelled, and there's that expression, 'someone not being to your taste', and if someone wasn't to your taste, Désirée assumed, then you couldn't kiss him either. Yes, and then there was a funny story to tell: the young man, Esther's friend, always sucked peppermint pastilles before they met, 'isn't that very funny, Mama?'

Mimi didn't laugh.

'So the two of them know that they belong together?'

Désirée was quite sure of that. She had seen the two of them often enough, and they complimented each other as well as ... as ... 'As well as you and Papa. I'm sure you knew from the beginning as well ...'

Not quite from the beginning, thought Mimi.

And they would overcome all obstacles, Esther had said. Even if their families were firmly opposed to the idea, nothing could ever tear them apart.

'Why should their families be opposed?'

'Beause he ...'

'Yes?'

But Désirée had promised her friend not to tell, or else she might as well tell Mimi the name straight away. And she had already told her far too much.

'Non, ma petite,' said Mimi, and her voice had suddenly shed all its migraine and weakness. 'You've talked quite enough already.'

And then she talked about a delivery of English gentlemen's boots – she said 'gentlemen's boots' in the same frighteningly friendly tone in which she had said 'whale jawbone' not so long ago – a surprise delivery that had had to be cleared away immediately, first work, then pleasure, which was why Esther Weill had stayed at home for the whole afternoon, without a rendezvous, and without a walk and hand-holding and kissing. And now Mimi wanted to know, she wanted to know right now, who had met whom by the deer enclosure, who had kissed whom, and who the man was, this strange man whose name she was not allowed to know because the families would be opposed. 'No more lies!'

Désirée's resistance held out for only a few minutes.

She had always been an obedient daughter; even as a baby, if you believed the stories, she had cried less than others. Mimi had waited for a child for two decades, and had – she had so much to catch up on – been resolved from the first day to be a perfect mother. She shielded and protected Désirée so zealously that Pinchas had said to her more than once that even falling over was something that such a child needed to learn. Even later, when Hinda's children, who were of a quite different temperament, turned the whole flat upside down, Désirée showed so little interest in pranks and adventures that

Lea and Rachel derisorily called her 'Mammatitti'. She had never learned to stand up to her mother, and if she tried to, a reference to the tortures that Mimi had suffered during her labour was quite enough to make her give up again straight away. All the lies of the past few months had only been possible because had been telling the truth the whole time, she hadn't invented anything, she had just given her experiences a different name, had said 'Esther' when she meant 'I', and had been happy somehow to be able to confide her secret in her mother in this way.

She tried silence, pressed her eyes firmly shut the way little children do when they want to make something threatening disappear, and couldn't keep the tears from flowing down her face.

'Don't ask me, Mama, please don't ask me,' she said again and again, but Mimi was more furious than Désirée had ever seen her, not so much with her daughter, even though she had told her monstrous lies, but much more with herself for allowing herself to be lied to, for having been blind and stupid, for having played along like an idiot, for giving good advice, for being led around by the nose. There could never be forgiveness for it, not for her and not for Désirée either.

At last she gave in.

Yes, it had been her, she herself, Désirée sobbed, it had been her the whole time, but she hadn't been able to say so, because it would have been forbidden her, and she wouldn't have survived that, no, she would rather have jumped from a bridge than give this man up. 'You don't know what it's like when you love someone, Mama, you can't know, or you wouldn't look at me like that. But it's my life and not yours, and I'm not going to let anybody break it.'

'Who is the man?' asked Mimi.

Désirée swore that she would never give it away, never in her life, and yet she knew that she didn't have the strength to resist her mother.

'Is it a goy?' asked Mimi.

Désirée nodded and said at the same time: 'No, no, he's not a goy,' but he was one and he wasn't one, and now everything was broken, destroyed for all time.

'What's his name?' asked Mimi.

Désirée cried and pleaded and then said the name after all.

Mimi locked her daughter in her room and set off for François's house. If someone had himself geshmat and made himself unhappy for the rest of his life, that was his affair. But if his son, this goy Alfred, wanted to destroy Désirée's life as well, that was something quite different. Something for which she would never, ever forgive him.

47

The whole flat smelled of the cheesecake – Mother Pomeranz's old recipe – that Hinda normally only baked on Shavuot. She hadn't let them take that away from her, although Zalman shook his head disapprovingly and said, 'They're not coming for coffee.'

'Still,' Hinda said and fetched the yontevdik tablecloth out of the cupboard. It was so heavily starched that its folds cracked slightly when it w,as laid out. 'The whole family is meeting at our house! Do you want them to think they're at a poor person's house?'

If it had been up to Zalman, they could have sat at the empty table, with a glass of water in each place and nothing else. He had taken part in lots of negotiations as a trade unionist, and it was his experience, he said, that one reached an agreement more quickly if the circumstances were niggardly. 'You think better on an empty stomach.'

'You're more peaceful with a full stomach,' Hinda replied and of course she was right again.

Lea and Rachel were unusually helpful out of pure curiosity and, as on Seder evening, they carried in chairs from all the rooms.

'Too many,' said Zalman. 'There are only nine of us. Janki and Chanele aren't coming.'

'There are still eleven of us,' Lea contradicted him and started counting: 'Three Meijers, Uncle Arthur makes four, three Pomeranzes makes seven and four Kamionkers...'

'Two Kamionkers,' Zalman corrected her. 'You're going to stay in your room. This is nothing for children.'

Lea protested, as outraged as one can only be outraged at the age of eighteen to be described in those terms, and Rachel, who out of sheer high spirits often talked more quickly than she wished she had in retrospect, tried to support her sister. 'If we aren't allowed to then how come Désirée...?' And wished she could have swallowed the sentence straight away.

'Exactly,' said Zalman.

Then Arthur rang breathlessly at the door, had in his haste already taken his coat off on the step, and to his own surprise he was still the first. 'And I thought...I couldn't get away from the practice. Everybody's got a cold in this weather. And it was summer only a moment ago. Can I go and wash my hands again, Hinda?' At work he didn't notice the smell of carbolic on his hands, but in any different surroundings he felt as careless as if he were bothering his fellow men with private matters.

They all wanted to postpone the unpleasantness that awaited them, which was why no one wanted to sit down first. They remained standing very formally behind their chairs, and talked about all kinds of things, but not about what vexed them.

'Have you heard anything about Ruben?' asked Arthur.

'He writes every week.'

'Are things going well for him in Kolomea?'

'He has become even more pious.' It was impossible to tell from Zalman's tone whether he was pleased or annoyed about this.

'Good,' said Arthur, and then, after a pause, again. 'Very good.' Like an old man, he reflected irritably, who has to keep his own company and fills his empty days with pointless scraps of language. He coughed with embarrassment, pulled out his watch, which he wore on an old-fashioned chain from his waistcoat pocket, and let the cover spring open. 'They're all late.'

'There are two methods in negotiations,' Zalman lectured. 'Either you come first and are to some extent the balebos who determines the rules, or you keep the others waiting to demonstrate that you don't need to be on time.'

'This isn't pay bargaining, Zalman!'

'You're right there, Frau Kamionker. In pay bargaining each side knows what it wants. Today they'll just know what they don't want.'

The Pomeranzes appeared next. Mimi, all in matronly black, was breathing heavily, in a reproachful way, as if it were a personal affront to her that the Kamionkers could only afford a flat on the third floor. 'You should lose some weight,' Arthur thought, 'then climbing the stairs wouldn't be so hard for you.'

Pinchas's beard had turned greyer over the previous few weeks, but perhaps Hinda was only imagining that. He rested his hand on Désirée's shoulder the whole time, either to bolster her courage or just to hold on to her.

Désirée had parted her hair in the middle again, which gave her the girlish appearance of someone who needed protection, and she was wearing a very plain white dress that must have been freezing for her in the street. She held herself very straight, like someone who is afraid of a fight and yet doesn't want to show any weakness. She greeted her relatives with a certain formality – 'Hello, Uncle Arthur, hello, Uncle Zalman' – shook hand with each of them and avoided everyone's eyes. 'She's decided not to cry,' thought Hinda.

The new arrivals didn't sit down yet either, and also stood behind their chairs. Désirée gripped the back of hers so firmly that her knuckles turned quite white. For a few moments no one said a word. As in the service, when the whole congregation waits for the rabbi to bring the Shema to an end.

And now, out of nowhere, Arthur couldn't help laughing.

'I'd like to know what's supposed to be so funny here!'

'I'm sorry, Aunt Mimi. But I was just thinking: we're standing around here like…'

'…like at a wedding sude,' he had thought, 'where no one is allowed to sit down before the bridal couple have taken their seats.' And he hadn't been able to hold back the laughter, because the comparison that presented itself to his head was so odd. This family meeting on the neutral terrain of the Kamionkers' flat had been organised not to celebrate a chassene, but on the contrary to prevent one.

'The Meijers will be here at any moment,' Hinda said into the embarrassed pause. 'Would anyone like a piece of cake in the meantime?'

No one answered. Only Mimi reached her hand out towards a plate with what was almost a gesture of longing, and quickly lowered it again.

The place where Hinda and Zalman lived wasn't exactly a slum, but no one had ever seen a Buchet here before, let alone the latest model. The car hadn't even come to a standstill before a group of children had gathered at the side of the road, commenting expertly on the vehicle and its occupants. When Landolt wanted to open the car door for his employers, a boy of about fourteen got in ahead of him. His knees were scraped bloody from some adventure or other, and a cigarette behind his ear demonstrated his premature masculinity. He opened the car door, dramatically pulled the cap – wherever he had learned the gesture – from his head, wedged it under his arm and held out the hand thus freed in a demanding manner. The three Meijers got out, François very correct in top hat and grey Ulster greatcoat, Mina in her usual over-sized skirt, and Alfred in a suit with such an adult cut that it made him look particularly young. Ignoring the outstretched hand, they walked through the cordon of curious faces to the front door. The disappointed tip-hunter nodded as if he had expected nothing else, and said, 'Typical Jews – they're all tight.'

'Herr Meijer is a Protestant,' said Landolt.

'Of course,' the boy answered and spat artfully just in front of the chauffeur's feet. 'And this is a horse-drawn carriage.'

With her lame leg it was hard for Mina to climb the stairs. None the less, she would have nothing of Alfred's proffered arm. The rejection seemed to upset him, and she regretted her own inflexibility. 'It's not you,' she said quickly. 'I've just got used to doing things for myself.'

When at last they reached the third floor, François had already rung the bell and gone in. Mina took her son's head between her hands – she practically had to stretch, because Alfred was already far taller than she was – drew him down to her and tried to smile encouragingly. 'Things will go on somehow.'

'Somehow,' Alfred repeated. It didn't sound convinced.

When he came into the room, Désirée gave a start as if she wanted to run towards him or away from him, but Pinchas hand still rested on her shoulder and wouldn't let go.

They greeted one another formally and without warmth, delegates from enemy countries who are forced for diplomatic reasons to meet in a last bid for peace, even though both sides are already arming for war. Zalman was right: this was not a coffee party, it was a conference.

'Let's sit down,' he said. Chair-legs scraped like gun carriages along the parquet floor.

The seating arrangement arose quite naturally: on one side the Meijers, on the other the Pomeranzes, Alfred and Désirée each flanked by their parents, just as miscreants are guarded by severe police officers in court. Désirée kept her head lowered the whole time and ran her fingernail repeatedly along a starched fold in the table-cloth. Alfred studied the mizrach panel on the opposite wall. Zalman, as master of the house and, as an experienced negotiator, moderator of the discussion, had taken his seat on the narrow side of the table by the window. Arthur was left with the seat at the opposite end of the table, with his back to the door, and unable to push his chair too far back in case anyone suddenly came in. Hinda sat down at a corner of the table, ready to get up at any moment and fetch something they'd forgotten from the kitchen.

'Who will have a piece of cake?' she asked.

François pushed his plate aside in a gesture of refusal, the others mutely shook their heads, and only Pinchas was polte enough to say, 'Thank you very much, Hinda. It's very kind of you, but ... this really isn't the moment.'

'In that case ...' Zalman began.

'I'd like a piece of cake,' said Alfred.

It was a challenge, quite clearly. He wasn't concerned about the cake – how could one be hungry in such a situation? – he just wanted to demonstrate that he was not prepared from the outset to accept any decisions that were made here.

'Stop it!' his father hissed at him.

Alfred didn't seem to hear him. He held his plate out to Hinda and said, 'I loved your cakes even as a child.'

François brought his fist down on the table.

Hinda, with the cake slice already in her hand, looked from one to the other and didn't know what to do.

François slowly opened his fist again, one finger at a time. His face twisted into a smile, although one that didn't reach his eyes. Hinda was familiar with his apparently friendly expression. Even as a child her brother had always put it on when he was genuinely furious. 'Can we start now?' he asked. His voice was flat, he was probably trying to hold his breath to keep from shouting.

'In that case...' Zalman tried to start again, but Alfred cut him off again.

'One moment, please, Uncle Zalman,' he said, and his smile was as ruthlessly polite as his father's. 'There are temptations that I cannot resist.'

Arthur was the only one who noticed Désirée blushing at these words.

'So if you will be so kind, Aunt Hinda,' said Alfred, and held his plate out to her again.

Hinda hesitated. Like everyone else at the table she sensed: there was an argument going on here, in which one didn't want to take sides.

Désirée raised her head into the silence. Her voice quivered slightly. 'I'd like a piece of cake too,' she said quietly, looking only at Alfred.

To gloss over the tension of the moment, apart from François everyone suddenly said they actually did want some cake after all, and of course they would have to have coffee to go with it. Under the pretext of making themselves useful, Lea and Rachel used the opportunity to welcome their relatives, who had gathered together for such a sensational occasion, and at the same time to inspect them as inconspicuously as possible. Back in their room they then had a violent discussion about whether Désirée's eyes had really been red with tears.

It was only when the plates and the pleasantries – 'Your cake gets better all the time, my dear Hinda!' – had been finally cleared away that they got to the subject. It quickly became apparent that apart from the couple involved, everyone shared the same opinion: what was happening between Désirée and Alfred was impossible. Absolutely impossible. Admittedly the pair were not so closely related that an association between them needed to be ruled out for that reason, but, well, all right, it simply didn't fit.

But the reasons that the two fathers gave for this shared conviction were completely different.

François, the businessman, based his argument on the chances that Alfred would throw away his whole life through an ill-considered liaison. He listed all the advantages that his son enjoyed at present: freshman in an exclusive student fraternity, links with the best families in the city, endless business contacts, just because he no longer bore the stigma of...

'Stigma?' Pinchas spat the word out like a stone that's found its way into the jam. 'I must ask you not to use such treyfeneh expressions.'

'Call it what you like. It won't alter the facts. As a Christian Alfred has all the opportunities that I never did.'

'You pauper! One can see that you're on the brink of starvation!' said Hinda, even though she had made a firm resolution to stay out of the debate.

'This isn't about me!'

'Ah,' said Mimi, 'then that would be the first time!'

'It's about my son.'

'You should have thought of him before you dragged him along to be geshmat.'

'I'm not willing to talk to you about this matter. That I had myself baptised that time...'

'Geshmat,' Mimi insisted.

'...is no one's business. It was my quite personal decision!'

'But not his.'

Alfred adopted such an studiedly indifferent expression that the argument at the table might have been about some insignificant namesake.

'I did what was best for him,' said François, and Mimi laughed the pinched laugh used to express contempt in social comedies at the Stadtheater. '*Chrétiens* – cretins,' she murmured, and nodded several times, as if the profound truth in this similarity between the two words had only just struck her.

'We won't get any further like this,' Zalman tried as chairman to bring order to the debate. 'We have to speak sensibly and in turn...'

'That's exactly what I'm trying to do,' said François. 'As a Christian – whether you like it or not, Pinchas – Alfred has the best prospects for a glittering career. And they would be destroyed at a stroke if he married Désirée.'

'Married? Ha!' said Mimi, her cheeks already combatively pink.

'Which is of course out of the question,' said Pinchas.

'Then we agree.'

'No, François, we don't agree at all.'

'Don't call him François,' Mimi barked. 'His name is Shmul.' And repeated, because she knew how much François hated his old name: 'Shmul! Shmul! Shmul!'

'This is impossible,' said Zalman.

Mimi pursed her red painted little mouth and leaned back in her chair with her arms folded. 'If my opinion isn't wanted here – please, I don't need to say anything. *Certainement pas*. I can be silent too.'

'Listen to me, François,' Pinchas began again. 'I want to present you with my point of view without excitement, but also with great clarity. Deborah is a respectable Jewish girl...'

'Deborah? Since when has she been called Deborah?'

'It was the name of my late grandmother, may she rest in peace.'

'You see? That's exactly your problem. You want everything always to be as it was for your forefathers.'

'Who are also yours.'

'Perhaps. But they lived back then, and we live today.'

'Some things are always valid.'

'And some things change.'

'At any rate I will not let my daughter marry a non-Jew...'

It didn't happen often that Mina got involved in debates. But when she did, you listened.

'Alfred isn't a goy,' she said. 'He's my son.'

'He's baptised.'

'He's my son,' repeated Mina, and even Pinchas had no objection to raise to this, because the child of a Jewish mother always remains a Jew, regardless of what detours his life might take.

'But he's also my son,' said François with the menacingly quite voice of someone who can barely contain himself, 'and I forbid...'

'I don't care what you forbid or what you allow!' Désirée wasn't used to raising her voice in front of other people, and her voice, like a flute being blown into too violently, immediately tipped over into shrill. 'And I don't care if Alfred goes to synagogue or to church or nowhere at all! I don't care. I love him.'

'Nebbich,' said Mimi. 'What does anyone your age know of love?'

'At what age is anyone supposed to know about it?' asked Arthur, but no one listened to him.

François spoke of the necessary adaptation to society in which his son was not to become an outsider again. Pinchas quoted passages from the Talmud, none of which really applied to the situation. Mimi repeated her *bon mot* about *chrétiens* and cretins, and even Arthur, who normally always found something worth supporting on both sides of an argument, took a position for once and said very sadly that some relationships, however painful it might be to those affected, were condemned to failure from the outset, it pained him to say it, but that was his experience. Only Mina said you had to take things as they came, and sometimes she had the feeling that some people only talked so that they didn't have to listen.

They threatened and they begged, Mimi even wept and sobbed, '*Mai tu m'as déchirée!*' But the old accusation had lost its power. Désirée just went on repeating over and over again, 'I love him,' a magic phrase that suspended all reality. And Alfred, the law student, explained stubbornly that he was an adult now, and as soon as Désirée turned twenty-one nothing would stop of them from doing what they thought was right.

'And what are you going to live on?' cried François. 'You won't get a rappen from me.'

'You can't buy everything,' Alfred replied, and Désirée, with a courage that scared even her, reached for his hand across the table and said, 'The really important things are free.'

The more often the same arguments were repeated, the more everyone talked at the same time. You could hardly make out a word, even though Lea and Rachel had now opened the door to their room wide, curious passers-by standing outside a circus tent without tickets, and trying to guess from the reactions of the spectators which sensation they had just missed.

'What if we made them some more coffee…' Rachel wondered aloud, but Lea shook her head. 'Papa will kill us.'

At first Rachel seemed entirely willing to take even that risk into account. She had – 'It'll be her red hair,' Zalman always said – a fiery temperament and was inclined to rebellion. But then she stayed sitting next to her sister on the bed after all.

'What kind of person is Alfred?' she asked.

Lea shrugged. 'Would you have thought Déchirée capable of such a thing?'

'No,' Rachel replied, and added yearningly after a long pause. 'But I'd like to be able to love someone as much as that one day.'

48

They finally agreed on a compromise that satisfied nobody.

'If no one has really won,' Zalman said afterwards to Hinda, 'then no one has really lost.' Even though it had been not a piece of pay-bargaining, but a love story, he was probably right.

The solution, which wasn't a real solution, and which could therefore be accepted by everybody, consisted in putting off the decision. The two lovers were obliged not to see one another for a whole year; then, if they were still sure of their cause — 'Which God forbid!' — then they would see what happened next. At worst they would be allowed to do as they pleased, although it was to be hoped — 'Very much to be hoped!' — that they would have come to their senses by then. Désirée and Alfred claimed that nothing, nothing at all, could part them? Then fine, now they would have the opportunity to put their conviction to the test.

But as long as they both remained in Zurich, the Meijers and the Pomeranzes were agreed, they could not be relied upon to keep their word on anything. They were practised at secrecy, and even without Esther Weill's help they would find ways and means of getting round any arrangement. Over the last few months Désirée had demonstrated that she was able to lie shamelessly to her parents, above all to her mother, who had — 'Tu m'as déchirée, ma petite!' — sacrificed herself for her all her life.

So the family council decided that Arthur, during this cooling-off or probationary period, would interrupt his studies and go abroad. Perhaps it had been a mistake to let him study so young, and the spoilt rich sons in a fraternity had probably not always been the best models for him. A thorough dose of practical work, François hoped, would drive the fancies from his mind. In Paris — that was far enough away — François had a business friend, a certain Monsieur Charpentier, who also ran a department store; he would get in touch with him and ask him to take his son on as an apprentice.

Mimi, who liked things to be dramatic, suggested that the two of them shouldn't be allowed to write letters to each other either during the agreed year, but everyone thought that was too harsh. 'But I will read every letter that comes to our house,' said Mimi, having the last word after all.

The arrangement with Monsieur Charpentier was soon in place. He didn't just agree to taking Alfred on in the various departments of his store and, if he proved his mettle, even giving him some responsibility, he also personally found him a little lodging, nothing luxurious, but with a good reputation, where the young man could suitably stay. In a long letter full of solemn French *politesses* he promised Mina to keep an almost paternal eye on Alfred, and in a second, significantly less formal letter, he agreed with François that he would keep him discreetly informed if his son did anything stupid. Whereby the two businessmen agreed that a particular kind of stupidity in this special case was thoroughly desirable. In Paris, according to François's secret plan, the women weren't nearly as buttoned up as they were in Zwinglian Zurich. A young man would find enough distractions there to forget any kind of romantic nonsense.

Désirée wasn't even allowed to accompany Alfred to the station. Mimi even tried to keep the date of his departure secret from her, but in contrast to the image that she had of herself, she had no great gift for dissemblance, and chattered with such incredible excitement about trivial matters that Désirée set down her knife and fork and said, 'He's leaving today, isn't he?'

'He's gone already,' said Mimi, and was prepared to take her weeping daughter comfortingly in her arms. But Désirée just nodded silently as if the news had no particular importance for her.

Mimi had undertaken to spend a lot of time with her daughter now. 'After all,' she often said to Pinchas, 'it's all my fault and mine alone. I have paid too little heed to Désirée, and am a very bad mother!' Pinchas then contradicted her, and that comforting contradiction, they both knew, was the true purpose of her self-reproach.

Although Mimi repeatedly stressed that she, in the goodness of her heart, was entirely willing to forgive and forget, the old friendly intimacy between mother and daughter did not reappear. When Désirée had confided her secret adventures to her every day, even though she did so under the pretext that it had all happened to her best friend, they had got on better. She was now forbidden to see Esther Weill, much to the amazement of Esther's parents. But if one didn't want to be the talk of the whole community, one couldn't let anyone in on the whole sorry story.

Contrary to Mimi's expectations, Désirée showed no sign of seeking her forgiveness or consolation. Quite the reverse: it was as if they had swapped roles, and now Désirée, as the adult, had to overlook some of her mother's immature behaviour. Her whole life long Mimi had preserved the egocentricity and whining tones of a little girl; Désirée had grown up almost overnight.

Pinchas was not unhappy with the change in his daughter. He had been worried about her, and now comforted himself with the thought that with her increasing maturity she would soon see what a pointless flirtation she had wandered into; one only had to give things time. At first one could be pleased that she was developing very new interests and was no longer content simply to tick off the social diary of a daughter of the affluent middle classes.

Désirée even tried to make herself useful around the house, although that only led to difficulties. Mimi's maids, if they didn't leave the house at the first possible opportunity, very quickly developed a high degree of independence. Every now and again they stoically endured a monologue from the mistress of the house, but they were also well organised, and Désirée's sudden interest in household matters was perceived as bothersome spying. Mimi too didn't really think it appropriate for a daughter from a good house to be bustling around in the kitchen, and even trying to join in with the cleaning. She herself liked to complain how exhausting it was running a household – Pinchas had no idea! – but she preferred to leave these things to others. The current holder of the post was very efficient, and Mimi did not want to give her cause for complaint under any circumstances.

So it was that Désirée sought a new field of activity in Pinchas's shop. He had only a single employee, one Frau Okun, whom Zalman had once sent him with the request to do something for her. Frau Okun, a young widow, had fled from Russia in dramatic circumstances, and liked to talk in a quavering voice about the persecutions that one had to endure there as a Jew. She was extremely efficient, but treated the customers in a very unfriendly manner. Having grown up in a country where shortages prevailed, she could not be dissuaded from the conviction that customers were basically only supplicants. So there were repeated complaints, and anyone else would have sacked her long ago. Pinchas saw it as a mitzvah to keep her busy, but he was also to some extent happy to use the opportunity to move her from the front to the backroom. So Frau Okun filled bottles up with sweet wine from Palestine in the cellar, pulling the lever of the corking machine with such force that the dull blows could be heard even in the shop. Désirée stood behind the counter wearing a white apron, selling red horseradish coloured with beetroot, or strictly kosher chocolate produced under supervision.

She never mentioned Alfred, which Pinchas, who knew more about the Talmud than he did about psychology, took as a good sign. Alfred's letters, which Mimi always censored, as she had threatened to do, became duller each time and often contained nothing more than the dutiful greetings one fills the back of postcards with in the summer holidays. 'You'll see: the affair will die down,' Pinchas said optimistically, and Mimi herself already believed that the idea of the cooling-off period and the traineeship in Paris had actually come from her.

They were both mistaken. Désirée, who had to ask permission every single time she went out – very much to the satisfaction of Lea and Rachel, who had to endure the same thing – met Aunt Mina at the tea-room of the Huguenin restaurant once a week. Mimi would have liked to forbid even that; Mina was François's wife and thus on the side of the enemy. But again Pinchas would hear nothing of it. He felt sorry for Mina. After everything she had had to put up with in her life, now her son had been taken away on top of everything.

The Huguenin was a very respectable place with many Jewish customers. In the summer, when the days were long, one could even sit there on Shabbos afternoon, although of course without money in one's pocket, which would have been forbidden. One went back on Sunday to pay the previous day's bill. None the less, the suspicious Mimi checked with a few friends who also went there that it really was Mina there with whom Désirée drank her hot chocolate. One never knew.

There was one thing that her spies didn't tell her, because they didn't notice: the two women did more than just talk about Alfred. Mina also brought Désirée his real letters, which he sent to a box at the main Post Office, and which she collected there for her daughter-in-law. Yes, daughter-in-law. Mina, few of whose wishes life had fulfilled, considered Alfred's baptism as something like her own polio, a misfortune about which the boy could do nothing, and was firmly resolved that it wouldn't stop him from being happy in exactly the way he wished to be. It was the first time in her life that she wasn't just an onlooker and a listener, and to her own surprise she enjoyed the conspiracy, a model pupil carrying out all the pranks she had missed in her obedient school days, all at once.

Alfred's real letters did not consist of empty postcard phrases. They were, if one wished to apply literary standards to them, even quite overblown. He described his life in Paris as nothing but endless waiting; when he went to the museum at the weekend, he saw only Désirée's face in every portrait, and he asked every cloud that drifted eastwards over the city to carry greetings with it. If one is young, in love and parted, one isn't very troubled by kitsch.

Désirée read the letters so often that she knew whole passages by heart. She kept the precious pages in the shop, in a drawer full of bonbons that Pinchas had once ordered in large quantities, but which no one wanted to buy. The paper soon assumed a sweetish scent, as if Alfred's emotional phrases smelled of almonds and rosewater all by themselves. Désirée even took the perfume home with her; in the drawer of her bedside table there was a handful of the sweets, and when she opened the drawer and closed her eyes she felt Alfred quite close to her.

In her diary, which she kept only because she knew very well that Mimi would read it in secret, she wrote, by way of disguise, apparently disappointed sentences like: 'Alfred seems to cool towards me,' or reminded herself to work harder on her French conjugations. The conjugation she meant had been in Alfred's last letter: 'Je te desire, tu me desires, nous nous désirons.' Mimi had, without knowing it, given her exactly the right name.

François also kept himself discreetly informed. His business friend was able to tell him about an industrious, serious young man, who showed a great talent for department stores. 'One can tell all that he has learned from you,' wrote Monsieur Charpentier. He hoped to be able to do a lot of business with François in future, and was therefore not sparing with his compliments. To François's regret he could tell him nothing about love affairs, even though, as Monsieur Charpentier flatteringly wrote, Alfred was a very good-looking young man, whose good future one could see at first glance. 'At this age fidelity doesn't last long,' François consoled himself. 'Something is bound to happen.'

People didn't come to Pinchas's shop just for the kosher food; it was also a place where one was bound to meet – and this was at least as important to many of the lady customers – someone who knew the latest gossip from both communities. The stories that appeared in the *Israelitisches Wochenblatt* on a Friday had already been discussed long ago in the shop, and in fact many articles signed 'pp' had only come into being because Pinchas, a freelance worker for the 'rag', had kept his ears open while filling bags with flour or sugar. Even the better sort of lady, who liked to send their maids to do the shopping, liked to drop by in person to discuss marriage prospects, exchange sickness reports or just have a good ruddel. Frau Okun, with her brusque, impatient manner, had often spoiled the fun of these cosy chats; Désirée, the ladies were delighted to note, was quite different in this respect. As her thoughts were mostly far away, she was in no hurry to take their money, and didn't get involved in their conversations, which won her the reputation of being a very sensible and intelligent girl.

Male customers seldom came. Only old bachelors or widowers dropped in every now and again, to buy the meagre portions that they then prepared on their gas cookers at home. Young men attracted attention here, particularly when one of them turned up on a regular basis and seemed not to know what he actually wanted to buy. He hadn't just happened to be in the neighbour-hood, either, the well-informed ladies observed, he worked in a stationery shop on Schaffhauserplatz, and it was a good half-hour's walk from there to Pinchas's kosher shop. And besides – the ladies had not only keen eyes, but also good noses – he always arrived smelling of freshly applied *eau de Cologne*, which was an unambiguous sign in young men. 'He is interested in Mimi's daughter,' the rumour soon circulated, and everyone waited to see when and how the young man would make his first step.

Désirée was probably the only one who heard nothing about these speculations. Two months of the long year had already passed, and Alfred's letters were stacking up in the drawer with the sweet bonbons.

Mimi, on the other hand, knew all about it – what are friends for? – and immediately started making investigations. Not that she wanted to get involved, *certainement pas*, that really wasn't her style, but as a mother one was obliged to know, above all since Pinchas, like all men, was terribly naïve in these matters. He hadn't even been aware of the affair with Alfred.

The young man's family, she had soon discovered, was not 'one of our people', which meant that he didn't come from Endingen or Lengnau but had, a few years before the big wave of Russian refugees, come from the East. Mimi was proud of her tolerance in these matters, and even Eastern Jews – *pourquoi pas?* – could be very respectable people. The parents belonged neither to the religious community nor to the Orthodox Community, but visited a 'schtiebel', a kind of private prayer circle, where religious service was performed according to Hassidic custom, and where, above all at Simchas Torah, there was a lot of wild, exotic singing and dancing. The son, however – an only son, incidentally – had adapted very well to Zurich manners, and was even a member of the gymnastics society. So what could be more obvious than to invite Arthur to dinner and then ask him a few questions afterwards?

'I wouldn't mind', said Mimi, after she had reassured herself that Désirée was in her room and couldn't hear anything, 'such a kosher admirer. The child needs a distraction. What do you think, Pinchas?'

'He has never said a word to suggest that he is interested in Désirée.'

'What do you expect? That he should buy a mitzvah and then wait until he is called upon? He was in the shop five times over the last three weeks. *Cinq fois!*' she repeated, as if the number were much more imposing in French.

'And? Frau Wyler comes five times a day.'

Mimi waved her hands in despair. 'Tell me, Arthur, are all men so helpless?'

'It also seems to me that you're reading a bit much into the situation.'

'Bella Feldmann once saw him standing by the shop window for a quarter of an hour. And you're not going to claim that there's much to see there!'

Pinchas chose to say nothing on the subject. He had already had heated discussions with Mimi about his shop window. He was of the opinion that the customers already knew what they wanted to buy from him all by themselves, while Mimi dreamed of artistic arrangements of soaps based on the Tower of Babel, or the outlines of a Hanukkah candlestick in white and brown beans. She took Pinchas's silence for resignation and returned to Arthur.

'You could tell us a bit about the young man, I think. He's in the gymnastics association as well, and you know everybody there.' She looked at him so expectantly that Arthur couldn't help laughing.

'You would make the job much easier for me, my dear Mimi, if you could tell me his name.'

'His name is Leibowitz. Jonathan Leibowitz. But everyone calls him Joni.'

The night was cold. A biting wind that heralded winter had cleared the streets, and the few people who were still out and about preferred to switch pavements rather than pass one another, as if everyone but themselves must be up to no good if they weren't at home in a warm flat in such weather.

Arthur hadn't buttoned up his coat, and felt the cold like a hot iron. The wind blew the first fine particles of ice, sharp needles that hit his face. Just not hard enough.

Not hard enough.

He had given no reaction, just taking his glasses off and rubbing the bridge of his nose, and then talked about Joni Leibowitz, as if he were struggling to remember the name. Yes, yes, he was quite a respectable young man, at least nothing negative was known about him, his father worked as a cobbler, he believed, and his mother brought in a little extra money with embroidery. He and Joni had even trained together at one point and in fact, now that Pinchas said it, it occurred to him again, they had once fought in a competition, he couldn't quite remember who had won. Joni had still been a boy at the time, no more than seventeen or eighteen. Was he now actually old enough to ...? Well, why not. It was a long time since they had seen one another and – 'I'm sorry, Mimi' – he couldn't tell her much more about him. Joni was no longer active in the gymnastics association, and they had lost contact long ago.

They had lost contact.

Somehow, without noticing, he had reached the riverside facilities. Thick clouds covered the moon, and the water, sheltered from the wind by the Engen harbour mole, could be neither seen nor heard. A few lights shone on the other side of the lake, but before that the darkness was like an abyss. The chain of a ship rattled.

'One should really jump in,' Arthur thought, and knew that he would never do anything so final.

And he had no reason to, either. No reason at all.

The affair was long over.

No, thought Arthur, nothing dramatic would happen, the world would go on turning, he would go on doing his work, he would remain friendly, helpful Dr Meijer, he would go on explaining to the young people in the gymnastics association how to warm up their muscles before training and then to relax them again, somehow he would drum up the money for the association flag, and if Joni came to the flag consecration ceremony, they would say hello, friendly and detached.

Nothing dramatic would happen.

If Mimi was right in her assumption and Joni was interested in Désirée, he wouldn't get involved. Perhaps she would forget Alfred, perhaps she wouldn't, 'love is not something that lasts,' Arthur thought, and if what had to happen happened, he would go on playing his part, he would be the kind uncle who sends an original present for the engagement and a tasteful one for the wedding. Eventually the family would stop wondering why he didn't have a family himself, even the most eager matchmakers would stop coming up with shidduchim for him, he would have found his place, he would just be harmless, slightly odd Uncle Arthur, and eventually he would be as old as he had always seemed to himself.

Nothing dramatic.

With a sudden movement he slung his hat in the water. A quiet splash, then all was still again.

49

The entrance to the offices, François had explained to him on the telephone, must be in the bed-linen department on the second floor, somewhere among the shelves full of dressing table accessories, guest towels and wall coverings on which the predetermined legend 'hard work brings blessings' had yet to be embroidered. In the end, Arthur asked a salesgirl the way, and she showed him the little door, which bore no sign. He had walked past three times without noticing it.

When one stepped through this door, one suddenly found oneself in a quite different world. In the spaces meant for the public, François's department store had something of the brilliance of a stage set, a superficial magnificence that was supposed to give the customer the feeling of being one of those lucky people for whom a few rappen or even francs make little difference. Behind the door everything was bare and matter-of-fact. One was welcomed by the musty smell of a room that no one took the time to air, like a lackey switching back from the staterooms to the servants' passageway.

The door wasn't locked, but when it opened it bumped against an obstruction: right behind it, in a narrow corridor, was an old sofa, as if temporarily dumped there by removal men during a move and then never picked up again. The man sitting on it seemed to have been forgotten as well. He had fallen asleep in an uncomfortable seated position, his head sunk on his chest, and presented the visitor with the pimples on his reddened nape. It was only the uniform cap lying next to him on the seat that reminded Arthur where he had seen the man before: he was the chauffeur whom François seemed to hate for some reason, and yet never sacked. Landolt snored quietly. He was probably waiting here for his next assignment.

The doors on either side of the passageway bore no inscriptions, and through the little frosted-glass panes it was impossible to tell what lay behind them. Arthur stopped indecisively until one of them opened directly behind him. A woman with a severe hairstyle – 'I am something important,' her facial expression said – came out and looked suspiciously at Arthur. Her buttoned-up black satin blouse had a collar that reached up to her chin, so tight that her eyes bulged slightly. 'Or perhaps she just has a slight case of Basedow,' thought the doctor in Arthur.

'Can I help you?' said the lady. Her tone left no doubt that if it was up to her no one around here would be helped at all.

'I'm looking for François,' said Arthur and corrected himself straight away under her disapproving governess gaze: 'Herr Meijer, I mean. I'm his brother.'

She looked at him as dubiously as if every day she had to deal with con men, claiming some kind of family relationship in order to trick their way into the chief executive's holy of holies.

'Do you have an appointment?' she asked.

'I have an appointment.'

'Then follow me.' She had the ability to turn even apparently polite sentences into accusations just with the tone of her voice.

'So, how do you like my Cerberus?' asked François when the two brothers were alone.

'Let's say: she isn't excessively polite.'

'That's as it should be.' François clapped his hands together as if he had just concluded a profitable business deal with himself 'She has to keep people off my back. Otherwise I won't have a minute's peace here, and won't get a stroke of work done.'

'Sorry to disturb you, then.'

'I didn't mean it like that.' François must have been in a particularly good mood, because apologising wasn't normally his way. 'Make yourself comfortable. As best you can, I mean. I'm not set up for guests here.'

Unlike his house, where he had commissioned the architect to design everything as impressively as possible, regardless of the cost, François's office was practically Spartan in its furnishings. The furniture wasn't as old as the pieces in Chanele's office in Baden, but with the best will in the world one could not have called them distinguished. There wasn't even a chair for visitors. The only place to sit was a couch covered with greenish material which reminded Arthur of the treatment couch in his surgery. Mina had once told him that François slept in his office if there was a lot to do there. He hadn't made it very comfortable for himself.

François followed his gaze and laughed. 'Not exactly luxurious, is it? But I'm not putting another rappen into it. It's going to be very, very different anyway.'

'You plan to rebuild?'

'Perhaps.' François made the wouldn't-you-like-to-know? face that Arthur knew from childhood. Then, when François had something particularly good on his plate, a chicken leg, for example, or the slice of birthday cake with the sugar icing, then he had always left it there for a long time and waited, with exactly that face, and it was only when Hinda and Arthur had eaten their portions and stared enviously at his still-full plate that he asked, 'Would anyone like some more?' Woe to anyone who said 'yes', because it was only then that he ate it all himself, cut very small pieces off to prolong the torment of the others, chewed carefully and noisily, like a wine connoisseur savouring the taste of a good wine, and it was only the fact that they had to watch him enviously that made his relish complete. It was only if one didn't answer, and acted as if one were far too full to take an interest in what was left on his plate, that one had any kind of chance.

So Arthur asked no more questions, and instead got straight to the reason for his visit. 'I have wanted to talk to you about this for three months, but then this business with Désirée and Alfred got in the way.'

'That's all been sorted out. I hear from my friend Charpentier that Alfred is working very sensibly in the shop. I asked him to introduce the boy to the various houses, you know what I mean. That will distract him. Until he has forgotten the girl in a year.'

'Do you really think so?'

'You'll see. So, what did you want from me?'

'Well…The thing is this…'

'Yes?'

'It's a bit embarrassing to have to ask you for money, but…'

'Is the practice going so badly? From what one hears, you aren't very popular with your patients.'

'I don't need the money for me!'

'Oh, back to the good? Is my brother out to improve the world again?' François didn't mean it nastily, but almost with a hint of pity, as if Arthur's inclination to be concerned about other people were a regrettable weakness, which one must accommodate in a brother, but with a heavy heart.

'It's about the Jewish gymnastics association.'

'Not this business with the flag again! Papa told me about your begging. I've never understood where your sudden enthusiasm for the sport comes from, but each to his own.' François sat down behind his desk, straightened his notepad and screwed off the cap of a thick fountain pen. There was something condescending about it, as if he were granting an audience, and Arthur wondered if he himself came across like this to his patients as he prepared to listen to their case histories.

'So you've bought this flag.'

'Not bought as yet. We would like to, but…'

'Hang on! The flag consecration ceremony has already been scheduled. I read that in the *Wochenblatt*.'

'You still read that rag?' Arthur asked in amazement.

'Just because the occasional baptised reader looks into it, it doesn't make it treyf. So you're having a flag consecration ceremony, but you have no flag. In other words: your collection campaign was unsuccessful.'

'I would have expected it to be easier,' Arthur admitted with embarrassment.

'It's never easy to get hold of other people's money.' François said that like an art critic who wants to win back an unjustly undervalued work into the canon. 'It either takes a lot of skill, or ...'

'... which I plainly lack ...'

'... or a miracle. But perhaps...' François laid both index fingers to his upper lip and from there ran them along the sides of his cheeks. Arthur knew that gesture as well. It dated back to the days when François had worn his moustache long, in the dandy style, and meant that he was very contented with something, usually a business deal. 'Perhaps today is one of those miraculous days.' He bent over his notepad and looked quizzically at Arthur. 'How much does such a flag cost? And how much have you managed to get together?' François wrote the two sums down, one below the other, drew a careful line and then announced the result of his calculation: 'You will have to put off your ceremony. By about fifty or a hundred years.'

'I had hoped you might be able to help me.'

'As a goy?' François raised his eyebrows.

'As a brother.'

'I will have to think about that.' Carefully and without haste he removed a bit of fluff from the gold tip of the pen, drew a few experimental curlicues on his note pad, and only went on talking when the line was clean and slender again. 'Such a flag always has a sponsor,' he reflected. 'I won't say "godfather", because I'm sure you would find the connotations unpleasant.'

'Sponsorship is customary, that's right,' Arthur said carefully. He didn't yet know where François was taking this.

'And this sponsor – correct me if I'm mistaken – is generally the donor who made the biggest contribution. Is that not correct?'

Arthur nodded with some anxiety.

'Fine, then I will now write you a cheque, and at your big occasion I will solemnly hand the flag over to the association.'

'You?'

'Perhaps with a nice little speech.'

'That's impossible!'

'Why?'

'You...'

'Yes?'

Arthur didn't reply, and François suddenly started laughing. 'Why don't you just say it? You would take money happily enough, but a baptised god-father – sooner not.'

'I thought,' Arthur said awkwardly, 'we could appoint the department store as the donor. That would be a good advertisement.'

'Of course.' François smiled with ironic politeness. 'If you all buy your gym vests from me, my turnover will reach unimagined heights.'

'Then please forgive me. I'm sorry to have taken up so much of your valuable time.'

'Just wait a moment. You're always very quick to take offence.' François grinned. He had once again been playing one of those games to which only he knew the rules, he had won and was very pleased with himself. He took a chequebook from a drawer of his desk, opened it, wrote in a sum and signed with a flourish. Then he tore the paper from the book, waved it in the air to dry the ink, and held it out to Arthur. 'Here. I've rounded up the sum. Things always cost more than it says in the estimate.'

'It's really out of the question, having you as flag sponsor.'

François carefully screwed the lid back on his fountain pen and put it back in its case. 'I'm not interested in that,' he said. 'I just wanted to see your face as you imagined the potential embarrassment. Jus tell your people you got the money from Papa. Let him make a ceremonial appearance at your party. He likes that kind of thing.'

Arthur still didn't take the cheque. 'Why are you doing this?'

'Because I'm in a good mood,' said François, and let the cheque flutter to the desk. 'Because today I've had a piece of news for which I've been waiting for a very long time.' Again he clapped his hands as if applauding the successful conclusion of a business deal. 'Old Landolt has died at last. Isn't that wonderful?'

Waiting in the corridor was a man with a big portfolio tied with black ribbons, which he was holding on to with both hands. He might have been waiting there for a long time and hadn't even been able to sit down because the chauffeur was still snoring on the old sofa. The severe woman whose blouse collar was too tight came shooting out of her room and glared at Arthur; he had probably taken a schedule that had been puzzled over with a lot of time and effort and recklessly thrown it into confusion by having too long a discussion. She pulled open the door to François's office and said to the man with the portfolio, 'Please, Herr Blickenstorfer!' Arthur noted with surprising relief that she was just as unfriendly to other people as she was to him.

François had the sign painter rest the cardboard against the wall, where the best light fell on it from the window behind the desk, and looked at the drawing for a long time. He felt Blickenstorfer looking at him anxiously, and enjoyed not showing how pleased he was straight away. And in fact it was perfect. Just perfect. That was exactly what the trademark of his new department store should look like. Solid, elegant and memorable. No garlands or ornaments of the kind that was so fashionable nowadays, but a clear form. He would have them painted on all the windows of the new building, not too big, but quite understated. Stylish. A company like his didn't need to boast. 'The form is like a seal,' he thought, and he liked the idea. 'The seal of quality.' He would have to write the phrase down later.

He wasn't superstitious, but he thought it was a good sign that the designer had brought it today. The day he had had the news of Landolt's death. The young heirs would come round. He had already put out some discreet feelers, and they didn't seem unwilling. They were modern people, for whom business was more important than hand-me-down prejudices. Of course they weren't going to give him a special price, but that was fine too. Money shouldn't be the clincher. It would be hard to pay off the debts, but then debts were nothing but figures on a balance sheet. The plot of land was the important thing. The perfect plot of land for the perfect department store. Nothing would get in the way this time. Not this time.

He must have been absently shaking his head, because the sign painter asked in alarm, 'Isn't this what you wanted, Herr Meijer?'

No, it was. Exactly what he wanted.

A circle, and in it, horizontally and vertically, the letters M-E-I-E-R, arranged in such a way that the two words shared the central I. Meier. Trustworthy and local. A Swiss name. 'Let's go to Meier's,' that slipped off the tongue nicely. Or, before one went shopping somewhere else, 'Let's go and look in Meier's first.'

'Well done, Blickenstorfer,' said François. And he added the highest praise he knew. 'You can send me your bill.'

There was already someone else waiting outside, but this visitor didn't knock. He just walked through the door without first opening it, and sat down on François's desk with his legs crossed.

'Pretty,' said Uncle Melnitz, holding the drawing with the new company insignia in his hand. 'Really very pretty. But haven't you forgotten a letter?'

'You're dead,' said François. 'I don't have to talk to you.'

The old man shook his head as only a dead man can shake his head: the loose skin stayed where it was, and only the skull behind it moved. 'I've died many times,' he said without moving his mouth. 'This is something quite different.'

'What do you want from me?'

'I want to remind you of your good name.' said Melnitz. In his mouth his faded teeth formed the shape of a smile. 'Your name is Meijer.'

'I know what my name is.'

'One becomes forgetful when one has oneself baptised. You've forgotten the J. Or the yud, if you want to write it in Hebrew. You've lost a yud. You didn't want to be Meier with a yud.' He laughed as if reading his laughter from a book, one syllable at a time, in a language he had never learned.

'I've just simplified the name,' said François. 'For business reasons.'

'You've simplified a lot of things for yourself, haven't you? Were you at least able to sell your yud? Did you get a good price for it? Such an exclusive letter.' The old man held the cardboard with the new company insignia up to his face and moved his jaws under his weary skin as he spelt it out. 'Meier. How ordinary! Mass-produced goods from the bargain bin. Couldn't you have come up with more noble material? Silberberg? Goldfarb? Or something fragrant? Rosengarten or Lilienfeld? In the old days people scraped together all their money to buy themselves a pretty name. I remember it very clearly. I remember everything.'

'It was back then,' said Melnitz, making himself comfortable in François's director's chair, 'when the law suddenly decreed that everyone must have a new name. Not the good old one, which linked one's own first name with that of his father, just as you are called Shmul ben Yakov, or your son's fiancée Deborah bas Pinchas. It had to be a modern name, one that could be recorded neatly in a list and a family tree, that's right. You had to go to the register office, stand in front of a desk and make a deep bow, and then the official dipped his pen in the ink bottle and assigned you a name.

'My name is Melnitz, and there's a special reason for that – but I'll tell you another time. I didn't have to go to the register office, but many people had no other choice. You could have a name given to you for free, you only had to pay the fees, but something that costs nothing is also worth nothing, and that was what those names were like. In such offices people got bored, of course, and to pass the time those officials came up with funny jokes, or jokes that they thought were funny. "Your name is now Stiefelknecht" – Boot-jack – they would say when a little Jew stood in front of them and hadn't even brought them a gift out of politeness, or, "You're now the Futtersack – Feedbag – family." And there was always some underling who would laugh loud and long and praise their humour because he wasn't a Jew, and already had a name that no one could take away from him.

'But the people in the offices were human beings too, and human beings can be talked to. Not that they were corrupt or anything, officials never are, but crossing a line out of a list and writing another one, that takes effort, particularly if it's to be a pretty name, and no one could possibly object if they liked to be rewarded for that effort. Anyone who brought enough money could be called Blumenfeld or something else nice, and when he came home with a new name a bottle of bronfen was opened to celebrate the fact that they had got off so lightly.

'Yes, Shmul Meijer,' said Melnitz, 'buying a name is an old Jewish tradition. But buying oneself a Meier, a quite ordinary Meier, is something I have never heard of.'

'You're dead, Uncle Melnitz. I don't have to listen when you talk.'

'You've written your new name in an original way,' said Melnitz and studied the drawing. 'So wonderfully symbolic. Your name as a cross, how appropriate. And such a pretty circle all around it. Is that the circle you're moving in now?'

'You're dead!' shouted François, and wasn't sure if he had really shouted or not.

Uncle Melnitz put the drawing very carefully back against the wall. Where he had touched it, the bones of his hand were depicted as if on an X-ray. 'I wish you the best of luck with your new name, Shmul Meier,' he said. 'Yis'chadesh. May you wear it gesunderheit.'

50

The stage curtain smelled musty, like an old woman's dress. The soft, dark red fabric of the curtain condensed the chatty chaos on the other side into a broth of words and laughter; you could imagine that down in the auditorium everyone had only mouths, but no faces.

'Where have you got to?'

Since the success of the evening was obvious – more than six hundred tickets sold, when the gymnastics association would have covered its costs with five hundred – Sally Steigrad had started adopting an unpleasantly bossy voice, like the one the regional director of his insurance company used when he gathered the representatives together for their annual conference. 'I have had enough of having to check every single detail myself,' this tone said, 'but with staff like these I have no option.' Even a few weeks previously, when 28 June was approaching at great speed, Sally had been secretly anxious about the association's finances, but now, with a full house, he saw himself as a born organiser, and was already planning new feats, a tournament with Jewish sports clubs from all over Europe, or at least an association trip to the Olympic Games in Berlin.

'All the parents are asking after you, Arthur,' he said crossly. 'They want to know when their little ones will have their turn.'

The children had been another of Sally's ideas. In the name of the festival committee he had put an advertisement in the rag – 'For the arrangement of a flag ceremony we need a large number of boys and girls' – and had given Arthur's surgery as an address for applications without asking him first. 'People are happy to entrust their children to a doctor,' he said when Arthur complained, 'and besides, who knows, you might even get some new patients out of it.'

Then, of course, Arthur had had to do all the work. Sally had thousands of even more important things to think about, the decoration of the hall, the list of guests of honour to be invited, but above all the collection of donations for the big tombola, which for an insurance salesman was very discreetly associated with customer care and acquisition. He had also raised a considerable number of attractive prizes, from three pairs of almost high-fashion lace-up boots (Schuhhaus Weill) to twelve bottles of sweet wine from Palestine (Pinchas's contribution). The main prize, presented in the foyer on a pedestal decorated with colourful crêpe, was a very respectable bellows camera with tripod.

'Why are you hiding yourself here on the stage?'

'I just wanted to…' Arthur fell silent. He couldn't tell Sally the truth. 'I'm hiding', he should have said, 'because I'm afraid of meeting Joni. Because I'm even more afraid of not bumping into him. Because I don't know what I should say to him. Because I don't want to say the wrong words. Because there are no right words.' But as it was, he just shrugged, took off his glasses and rubbed the bridge of his nose.

'Come on, come on!' Sally clapped his hands as his regional director always did. 'Into the hall with you!'

So many people had come – 'From both communities!' Sally observed with satisfaction – that even the big Volkshaus hall was full to the rafters. The tables had had to be pushed forward again, and in the end there was hardly enough room, once the official part was over, for dancing or, as Sally had called it in his small advertisement in the *Israelitisches Wochenblatt*, paying homage to Terpsichore. Apart from those for the few official guests – the community presidents, the rabbis, the gymnastics association delegation and of course the generous donor Janki Meijer – there were no reserved tables, so when the door opened at seven o'clock in the evening an amusing competition for the best seats had begun, in which the yontif-suited men and the heavily made-up women in their glittering dresses had to pretend not to be in a hurry, and were only moving more quickly than usual out of a sudden excess of energy.

To Hinda's displeasure and Zalman's secret amusement, Rachel had no ladylike inhibitions. Holding up her skirts, she had been the first to charge off and had conquered a table for eight for the family, right beside the dance-floor, and was now successfully defending it with Lea's help. Zalman who, as a good tailor, didn't just know about coats, had conjured two evening dresses for the twins out of remnants from one of last year's collections, and they looked irresistible. So they had to sit in a spot where they could be seen. When was one to make conquests, if not today?

Zalman and Hinda were wearing the same clothes as they had on Seder evening, the suit and the twice-altered skirt which they'd also worn to synagogue, and which they would take out of the wardrobe again for the high holidays. Admittedly Hinda had seen a beautiful dress in a shop window and made eyes at it for a few days, but in the end a wooden-barrel washing machine with a crank drive had been more important.

On the other hand, Aunt Mimi rustled into the hall in a new black dress embroidered with diamante, and with a hat the size of a wagon wheel full of ostrich feathers. She ignored Rachel's achievement in finding a family table, and sat down in the best seat as if it were the most natural thing in the world.

Uncle Pinchas had refused to put on anything more solemn than his black lustrine jacket, but Mimi had compelled him to put on a silk cummerbund, and had tied it so tightly that in the course of the evening he had to keep pulling it out with his index finger so that he could breathe.

And Désirée...

She hadn't even wanted to come along at first. When Mimi insisted she gave in, but explained that she wouldn't dance, not so much as a step. As long as she was parted from Alfred, it would have seemed as inappropriate as going to an operetta in the 'terrible days' between New Year and the Day of Atonement. Then she also refused to put on a ball-gown, even though, much to Lea and Rachel's envy, she had two in her wardrobe. Now she sat with the others at the table in a plain linden-green dress, drawing attention by being so conspicuously inconspicuous.

The last chair was meant for Arthur, but for the moment he had no time to sit down. The children he had trained for the flag ceremony came charging at him from all directions, and their parents seemed to be waiting even more excitedly for the great moment. He had to repeat over and over again that they still had plenty of time, first there would be the prologue and all the gymnastic demonstrations, and then, at nine o'clock at the earliest...

Someone tapped him on the shoulder, and it wasn't the next impatient father, but Joni.

Joni.

Joni, who gave him a smile, half public and half private, and said, 'I've been looking for you.'

His dark blue suit was slightly too small for him, and it made his upper arms look particularly powerful. Since meeting Arthur for the first time he had grown a vain moustache that sat on his upper lip like a stuck-on little brush. His face had the puffy look that athletes often get when they stop training. He wasn't, if you took a proper look, an extraordinarily attractive man, but Arthur saw only Joni, his Joni, and had to take off his glasses and rub the bridge of his nose before he could say, 'Nice of you to come.' His voice barely quavered.

'You have to do something for me,' said Joni.

'Yes?' The question was over-eager and far too quick. 'I'm not a waiter fighting for a tip,' Arthur thought irritably, and felt the heat rising into his face.

'This Désirée Pomeranz,' said Joni. 'She's something like mishpocha of yours. Can't you give me an official introduction?'

Luckily they were joined at that moment by Sally Steigrad, who needed Arthur very urgently. The stage manager was causing problems about the torches that they'd planned to use for the big pyramid in the finale, something to do with safety regulations and permissions. 'Deal with it,' said Sally, who had recently adopted a Napoleonic tone, so Arthur was able to escape behind the stage with an apologetic gesture.

The flag consecration, or at least the first part of it, was a complete success.

Sally had written a prologue in verse, in which he rhymed 'high aspirations' with 'gymnastic sensations' and 'mighty hand' with 'fatherland', thus reaping enthusiastic applause. Then he announced the gymnastic work – among athletes it was customary in this context only ever to speak of work – and the men's squad began their free exercises. Sally had had the idea, or had taken it from a report in the gymnastics newspaper, of having the rhythmical elements accompanied by the band, and the old conductor Fleur-Vallée had arranged a pot-pourri of well-known and well-loved melodies especially for the occasion. At particularly daring transitions, as when the folk-song 'Ramseiers wei go grase' suddenly modulated into a nigun from the Simchat Torah liturgy, a murmur went around the hall. Apart from that, Sally noted with satisfaction from behind the scenes, the beat of the music effectively covered up the inevitable little slips made by the gymnasts.

The bar and stretching exercises were rather tedious, but were still loudly applauded, as is customary at family occasions. The appearance of the newly-founded ladies' squad even prompted actual cheering, although some guests from the Orthodox religious society shook their heads disapprovingly over their skimpy costumes.

Then at last it was the turn of the children.

Monsieur Fleur-Vallée, who was becoming more and more modern with increasing age, had had the impudence to rearrange 'Entrance of the Gladiators' into a solemnly synagogical minor key, and when the boys and girls marched in, not from behind the scenes, as expected, but through the doors from the foyer, a general 'Ah!' ran through the hall. They were all wearing white shirts or blouses, and had knotted a scarf in the blue-and-white colours of the association and the city around their necks. The display that Arthur had rehearsed with them over four evenings in the gym hall did not create its full intended effect for want of space; the additional tables had made the dance floor shrink considerably. But that did nothing to dampen the general enthusiasm. In the finale, when the children, to the notes of the Hatikvah, formed a Star of David, Pinchas recorded for his report in the 'Blättchen' that the cries of bravo sounded as if they were never going to end.

A break followed, during which the children had another important task to perform: they had to sell the lottery tickets, without which no association event could cover its costs. After long consultation, Sally Steigrad had set the prices very high: one ticket for twenty rappen, six for a franc. 'They all know each other,' was his argument, 'so no one can afford to be stingy.'

Only now, in the break, did Arthur manage to greet his parents. Although a major argument in favour of selling the shops had been that they would have more time for their children and grandchildren, Chanele and Janki had not been in Zurich for ages. Instead they hid themselves away in their flat in Baden, which was far too big for them, and Janki for one didn't seem particularly pleased if one paid them a visit there. He was finding it increasingly difficult to walk; the war wound that he had never had was now very painful, just as a bad dream can pursue one into real life. Chanele, one could tell by many little gestures, had grown into the role of nurse, and if she considerately adjusted Janki's sash or encouragingly handed him a handkerchief, there was always something triumphant about it, a collector unnecessarily straightening a valuable item that he has at last acquired after a great struggle, to confirm to himself that it now really belongs to him.

Arthur noticed that his father was repeatedly clutching the left side of his chest, and the doctor in him was already looking for the illness to match this symptom. But in fact Janki was only reaching for the manuscript of his speech as flag sponsor. 'Just don't talk too much about the Battle of Sedan,' Arthur said as a joke. His father looked at him severely and replied: 'I wasn't even at Sedan.'

The old Kahns, Mina's parents, came by and congratulated Arthur with pointed cordiality on his production of the children's display. They ignored Janki and Chanele, the parents of a son-in-law who had had himself geshmat, equally pointedly. Mina herself, of course, hadn't come.

When Arthur had finally fought his way through to the family table, his seat was already occupied. On the last chair, right next to Désirée, sat Joni Leibowitz.

'I have taken the liberty of introducing myself,' he said. 'I've already told Fräulein Pomeranz that we are very good friends. We are friends, aren't we?' The threat in his voice could not be ignored.

'Of course,' said Arthur. What else was he supposed to say?

'Then I'm sure you won't mind if I occupy your seat for a little longer.' Joni stroked his young moustache, took a drag on a cigarette and smiled at Désirée from behind the smoke with slightly narrowed eyes, just as the lovers did in the picture house. 'One seldom encounters such charming company.'

Lea and Rachel looked on enviously – 'Not even a ball-gown, and already an admirer!' – and in the shade of her ostrich-feather hat Mimi smiled as contentedly as if she had created Joni Leibowitz in person.

Arthur would have liked to flee, but he couldn't immediately find an excuse. Luckily Sally Steigrad had become accustomed to treating him as his personal adjutant, to whom all unpleasant tasks could be passed, and just at the right moment – in the form of a hastily dispatched young gymnast – a messenger appeared on Sally's behalf, urgently summoning Arthur back behind the stage. A noisy argument had broken out there between two young ladies, a Fräulein Horn and a Fräulein Jacobsohn, about the home-made donation from the ladies' squad. They were both supposed to hand over to the flag-bearer the accessories concomitant with his office, and were now, at the very last moment, tearing out each other's carefully coiffed hair over who was to hand him the glove and who place the embroidered scarf around his neck. Arthur unburdened all his dammed-up despair upon them, yelled at them so loudly and with such pointless violence that it must have been audible through the curtain and all the way into the hall. No one was used to hearing this man, normally so mild and reticent, using such tones, and the startled ladies very quickly reached an agreement.

Sally Steigrad put his hand on Arthur's shoulder and said, 'I'm excited too, but one must be able to maintain one's composure.'

The act of consecration began with an orchestral prelude for which Monsieur Fleur-Vallée had borrowed extensively from Richard Wagner. When the curtain opened at last, all the gymnasts, male and female, were standing to attention on the stage, with Sally and Arthur in the front row. The flag-bearer – chosen because of his imposing physique – stepped forward and allowed the representatives of the ladies' squad to hand him the insignias of his office. After Fräulein Jacobsohn had handed him the scarf, she kissed him on the cheek, at which point Arthur also realised why the two ladies had been arguing so violently about the task.

The flag-bearer, so charmingly fitted for his function, left the stage before stepping back onto it with the wrapped flag in his fist. He was followed by Janki Meijer, who, supporting himself on his walking stick with the silver lion's-head handle, slowly and solemnly limped to the lectern.

As flag sponsor he had prepared an address that included lots about masculinity and courage, and in which the gymnasts were compared with all kinds of heroes, from the Maccabees to the founders of Switzerland. Only his family noticed that Janki untypically avoided drawing the obvious connection with his own heroic feats in the Franco-Prussian War. Chanele listened to her husband with observant concern, and moved her lips mutely as if she were at a service. He had read his address out loud to her so often, in all its new versions, that she could speak along with it by heart.

Janki hadn't even got halfway through his speech when a murmur arose in a corner of the hall, one that couldn't be silenced even with shushing hisses from the other tables, but which instead gradually took hold of other parts of the hall, just as a glowing ember eats its way through dry wood before suddenly turning into wildfire.

Janki paused irritably. Chanele had warned him several times that his speech was far too long; it was probably better to skip a whole passage, perhaps the one in which he described Old Testament figures as prototypes of modern athletes, David with his sling as the first marksman and Samson as the model of all strongmen. Perhaps he should cut straight to the end, he thought, and get without further ado to the handover of the new flag to the association. If only one knew what was going on down there in the hall.

What was going on had nothing to do with Janki and his address. It was world history which, as is world history's wont, disturbed the flag consecration of the Jewish Gymnastics Association at the worst possible moment. In the streets outside special editions of the paper were being sold by shouting newsboys, and one of them had made its way into the big hall of the Volkshaus. Herr Knüsel, senior salesman with Schuhhaus Weill, was the bearer of bad news, because he felt obliged to tell his boss, who bought in all sorts of goods from all over the world, about what had happened straight away. The heir to the Austrian throne, Franz Ferdinand, had been shot in the Bosnian capital Sarajevo; the murderer was a nineteen-year-old schoolboy and his name was Princip. Whether he had acted alone or as part of a plot was not yet known with any certainty, but a telegram had arrived from Berlin saying that the signs of a Greater Serbian conspiracy had been piling up for some time, and it had even said in a special edition of the Vienna *Freie Presse*, that the Serbian ambassador had expressly warned the Archduke against travelling to Bosnia. One could only speculate about the consequences of the bloody deed, but – and in this conviction the people in the street were just as united as the people in the Volkshaus hall – they were bound to be terrible.

There were whispers and soon loud discussions at all the tables; it was only on the stage that no one yet knew where the sudden disturbance was coming from. Out of fear of finally losing his thread, Janki didn't dare to shorten his speech, instead rattling his text off with ever greater speed. The unveiling of the new flag, which was actually the absolute highlight of the evening, was acknowledged only by a few stalwarts with fleeting applause, and the heralded programme of artistic entertainment (songs performed by Frau Modes-Wolf and Jewish recitations by Herr Karl Leser) was cancelled completely. Not even the tombola draw could be carried out in an orderly fashion; Sally Steigrad was obliged to publish the winning numbers two weeks later in the *Israelitisches Wochenblatt*. He still tried at least to let them perform the pyramid, the traditional finale of any gymnastics party, but it proved completely impossible to prise even half of the participants away from the discussion groups that had formed all around the hall.

Neither was there any dancing. When the musicians of the orchestra packed their instruments away, Rachel burst into tears and had to be comforted by her twin sister.

Very slowly, page after page, Janki tore up his manuscript and said to Chanele, 'Never again, for as long as I live, will I deliver another speech.'

'That's fine,' she replied.

Joni Leibowitz edged his chair closer to Désirée's, stroked his sprouting moustache and said with vain courage, 'If there should be a war, of course I will have to fight. You'll see, my uniform really suits me.'

Désirée had allowed his compliments to wash over her all evening without reacting. Now she smiled at him, which he took as a hopeful sign. But she had only been thinking, 'If there's a war, Alfred will come home very soon.'

'You see,' Sally Steigrad said to Arthur and tried to look as if he had planned even this surprising outcome to the evening, 'this is why we need insurance. Because you never know what's going to happen.'

'A war would be a punishment from God,' said Pinchas.

'But is it good for the Jews?' asked Mimi.

In front of everybody, Zalman Kamionker put his arm around his wife Hinda and drew her to him. 'I feel sorry for Emperor Franz Joseph,' he said. 'He really has no luck with his children.'

51

The war broke out, and Alfred didn't come home.

On the day of Germany's ultimatum to France, François sent a telegram to Monsieur Charpentier. Alfred set off on his journey the following day, but the order had already been issued for general mobilisation. He was a French citizen, and when his train reached the border, he was taken out of his compartment and asked for his military leave orders. His train had set off from the Gare de l'Est before the official start of mobilisation, so he was not accused of desertion. Alfred was only brought back to Paris and brought before the recruitment board. He was, like almost all candidates in those days, found to be fit, and assigned to a training unit. By the time his family in Zurich found out, Alfred was already a recruit.

François, convinced that most problems can be solved with money, gave Monsieur Charpentier *plein pouvoir* to buy Alfred out, but in France patriotism had broken out along with the war, and the traditional little channel of corruption no longer worked.

Training wasn't all that bad, Alfred wrote to his family; so far in the general chaos they hadn't even found rifles for the new recruits, and exercises with broom-handles had an almost comical character. The French had as little a chance against the well-organised Germans, this was his firm conviction, as they had in 1870–71, and the war would be over long before he himself got to the front.

Janki travelled unannounced to Zurich to talk to François. When he didn't find him in his office, he looked for him all around the department store and in the end made a scene in front of him in the middle of the fabric department. He wasn't doing enough to solve the problem, he told him, not every soldier was as fortunate as he, Janki, had been in his own day, and if Alfred had to go to the front and died there, it was all François's fault. When François tried to calm him down – one doesn't discuss family problems in front of other people – Janki lost control and started hitting his son with his lion's-head stick. For the first time, François was glad that business hadn't been good since the outbreak of war, which meant that only a few customers were able to observe the embarrassing scene.

Meanwhile Chanele had gone to see her daughter-in-law Mina, and the two women were trying to give one another encouragement. But try as she might to conceal her own anxiety, Chanele could not suppress the thought that Mina had only ever been unlucky all her life. Why should it be any different with her son?

Mina, the only member of the family council to vote against Alfred's banishment, gave no outward sign of what was going on within. Only once, when she met Parson Widmer in town, did she spit on the ground in front of him, and then had to struggle to resist the urge to apologise to him. The misfortune had begun not with him, but with that plot of land for which François was prepared to do anything.

François, in the meantime, in his attempt to change the situation, had abandoned his lifelong resistance and decided to become Swiss. There were several communes which were known to like refurbishing their coffers with increased fees for – mostly Jewish – new citizens; he opted for Wülflingen near Winterthur, where they declared themselves willing to speed up the procedure for an acceptance fee of five thousand francs above the usual amount. As at his baptism, Alfred was involved in this too, without having been asked first. But at first the argument of his new citizenship did not persuade the French authorities to free him from military service.

Désirée did nothing but cry now, and Mimi dragged her to see Dr Wertheim. He diagnosed anaemia and general nerves and prescribed a strengthening diet. But one doesn't heal broken hearts with beef broth, even if it's made according to the recipe of Grandmother Golde.

Pinchas said Tehillim every morning and even, without making much fuss about it, had several personal fast days. There was much to be asked for during those days, because prayer had to be said for Ruben too.

Immediately after the events in Sarajevo, Zalman and Hinda had urged their son to come home straight away. He had written back to say that he only wanted to stay the few days until Siyum, the traditional feast that is always celebrated when the students of the yeshiva have finished studying a section of the Talmud. Then the war broke out, and all connections with Eastern Galicia were suddenly interrupted. At the Post Office they were told only that telegrams could unfortunately no longer be accepted for regions where battles were being fought.

Hinda did not moan or complain, but became very quiet, and did her work mechanically. Lea and Rachel had only ever known their mother to be cheerful, and found it hard to accept the change. During this time they were more hard-working and helpful than anyone had known them before. It was the only way they could show their concern for their brother.

With Pinchas's support Zalman set up a fund for refugees from Galicia, more and more of whom arrived in Zurich in the course of September. He asked each one of them who registered with him whether he had heard any-thing of the yeshiva in Kolomea, but the new arrivals were all too preoccupied with their own fates. The invading Russian troops, they said, treated the Ruthe-nian inhabitants with perfect correctness; the Galician Jews, on the other hand, were generally suspected of collaboration with the Austrians, which constantly gave the Cossacks new excuses for acts of violence and looting.

Even though Switzerland was neutral, even here the war changed life from the bottom up. It was shocking how quickly one got used to it.

Arthur, the most unmilitary member of the whole family, volunteered for the emergency medical services, but was not taken because of his weak eyes. Joni Leibowitz was in active service as an infantryman with Fusilier Company IV/59, where he quickly rose to the rank of corporal. As a quartermaster, Sally Steigrad finally had the adventures he had always yearned for.

Alfred reported from Paris that they had by now received their guns, but they still lacked ammunition, which is why, ludicrously, they were only being trained in bayonet fighting. The German victory at Tannenberg confirmed him in his conviction that the war would not last long, and he was already making plans for the time that came after. 'If they still want to part us,' he wrote poste restante to Désirée, 'I will win you back with my bayonet.'

On Erev Shabbos and on the eve of the feast days, all the Jewish refugees, whether they were religious or not, turned up for service at one of the two congregations. Because of the mitzvah, but also out of genuine pity, people tripped over themselves to invite them to dinner, and it even turned into a real competition over the most pitiful figures. On Erev Sukkot, Pinchas Pomeranz brought a whole family home, a couple with a grown-up daughter, all three of whom had to be kitted out from the various wardrobes before they could sit down at the table reasonably yontevdik. They had fled full pelt from the Russians, and spent the whole of Yom Kippur on a train, crammed tight into a cattle truck with many fellows in misery. 'Even the treyfest among them fasted,' the man said bitterly, when he climbed the stairs to the attic behind his host, 'because there was nothing to eat or drink.'

Pinchas had set up his tabernacle on the roof, where the washing was normally hung. Its board walls were decorated with faded pictures of famous rabbonim, and chains of wrinkled chestnuts and now colourless paper gar-lands crossed above the solemnly laid table. Where there are no children in the house, no one makes new decorations. The October evening was cool, but at least it wasn't raining, which was why, in accordance with the rules, they were able to open the solid roof to eat, and see the stars. Arthur too was invited into the sukkah every year, and Mimi complained to Pinchas – in French, as

424

one should when discretion is called for – that it would be very cramped in there with seven people. Basically, however, she was very proud to be able to demonstrate that they didn't need to economise in her household, and were entirely capable of entertaining even unexpected guests. The bean soup, so full of sausage and smoked meat that a spoon would have stood up in it, would have fed twenty people.

Quite contrary to his normal habits, Arthur was late and nearly missed the kiddush. He had been called out to an emergency at the last minute, he apologised, to tend to an elderly Galician who had, while escaping, received a serious wound in the foot that was now beginning to fester dangerously.

When he was introduced to the foreign guests – 'The Wasserstein family, Dr Arthur Meijer!' – something strange happened. The daughter of the family, a very reserved young woman who hadn't said a word all evening, suddenly burst into loud laughter. It was a reaction that had nothing to do with cheerfulness, a hysterical, breathless screaming or panting. As she did so she pointed her finger at Arthur and repeated over and over again: 'Arthur Meijer! Arthur Meijer! Arthur Meijer!' The laughter broke off as abruptly as it had begun, and turned just as swiftly into tears. She shook off all attempts by her mother to console her, but then allowed Désirée to take her in her arms and rock her like a baby.

'Please be moichel,' said Herr Wasserstein. He seemed to be just as discomfited as his daughter by the fact that Dr Arthur Meijer was sitting opposite him here in a Zurich sukkah. He shook his head again and again, and ran his fingers through his curly hair as if he were about to rip it out in bunches. 'This coincidence ...'

'You must know, Doctor,' his wife explained, 'you two were to be married.'

Chanele and Janki had never mentioned the encounter in Westerland, they had been very tight-lipped about their summer holiday, so it came as a complete surprise to discover that – at least in his parents' plans – he had once been to a certain extent engaged to Chaje Sore Wasserstein.

'But now of course she will never marry,' said Hersch Wasserstein.

Chaos knows no order, so the story was told in fragments and without a logical sequence. The listeners had to assemble much of it from hints, and complete certain things left unsaid. There were many such stories around this time, and the only special thing about this one was that it very tangentially touched the Meijer family.

The Wassersteins had been extremely surprised by Janki and Chanele's hasty departure. Their own stay on Sylt had come to an end without further events, but also without a shidduch. Back in Marjampol they had tried to resume contact with the Meijers, but no reply came from Baden. 'So, not every business deal ends with a handshake,' said Hersch Wasserstein. 'One learns that as a businessman.'

And he quickly added, as if his words might be thought presumptuous, 'Now I am of course no longer a businessman, but only a shnorrer. I must put on other people's clothes and be grateful for it.'

'We are grateful,' his wife said quickly. 'We have nebbech lost everything.'

The Russian troops had burned down the sawmill; there was wood enough for a magnificent blazing pyre. Hersch Wasserstein had tried to stop them from destroying his life's work, there had been an argument, and little Motti – 'A boy like that doesn't know how bad people can be!' – had run to help his father. He probably thought the war was like the parading children on the spa promenade, just a game, and they wouldn't let his father join in.

They impaled him on the bayonet, 'not even in anger', Malka said in a voice of wonder, as if her son would still be alive if only someone could explain that one circumstance to her. 'They weren't even furious.'

'Praised be the judge of truth,' murmured Pinchas.

'*Affreux*,' said Mimi. That too sounded like a prayer.

Chaje Sore had pressed her head to Désirée's dress, and was moving it up and down very slowly, as if to be stroked by the silk fabric.

The Cossacks – 'Only a little shock troop, but you don't need an army to make a family unhappy' – had then celebrated, which in their case meant: they had had a drink. What soldiers do when the vodka goes to their heads and their loins was well known, and Chaje Sore was a pretty girl.

The tabernacle had neither gas nor electricity. An old-fashioned paraffin lamp cast flickering shadows on the walls; the lips of the framed sages seemed to move, as if they were speaking kaddish for little Motti.

And a prayer that won't be found in any siddur for Chaje Sore Wasserstein, who had been too good for any man, and then good enough for twenty.

Later, when they were saying goodbye, Malka Wasserstein said something surprising to Arthur.

'If you had married her, she wouldn't have been there,' she said.

Arthur took off his glasses and rubbed the bridge of his nose. Two hours before, he hadn't known that there was such a person as Chaje Sore Wasserstein, and now he felt responsible for her fate.

All night he kept starting awake, as he had often started awake in his school-days and as a student before exams, and when he did go back to sleep he dreamed of questions he was being asked, for which he didn't know the answers.

The next morning he went to the prayer hall, right at the beginning, when only the most pious are there, to help form the minyan on time, and for hours read along word for word with all the blessings, pleadings and songs of praise, as if they might somewhere conceal a sentence that was meant for him and him alone.

The Sukkot service has a quite special character; the palm frond, the lulav, is waved in all four directions, and laid out on the lecterns; the essrogim, the ritual citrus fruits that have no name in any other language, spread their very special fragrance. But when Arthur tried to find an answer in the familiar words and gestures, there was none to be found. Only the haftarah, the word of the prophet, which follows the reading from the Torah, seemed to contain a reference to the events of the previous evening: 'The city shall be taken,' Zachariah threatened, 'the houses shall be rifled and the women defiled.' But even the prophet could not say what one was supposed to do if one felt guilty for all of that, when in fact one was not.

In the short break that always happens before the Torah rolls are lifted, Pinchas murmured to him, 'Désirée had another letter from Alfred. Yontif or no yontif, we opened it. He writes that at last they have ammunition. But he is sure that the war will be over long before new recruits have to go into battle.'

'Nothing seems certain to me any more,' Arthur whispered back.

Only when service was over did he notice that Hersch Wasserstein had been there as well, right at the back in the last row meant for strangers and beggers. He wore the suit that Pinchas had given him the day before, and now, in daylight, it was impossible to ignore the fact that the jacket was too tight and the trouser legs too long, the clothes of a shnorrer who has not yet learned his craft. Each time someone held out their hand to him to wish him a good yontif – as if he could ever have a good day again! – he hesitated for a moment before taking it. He was used to waving away the submissive cordialities of supplicants, and had to keep reminding himself that he himself was now the supplicant.

Arthur very slowly folded up his tallis, the fine one that Zalman had given him for his bar mitzvah, and just as he was putting the cloth back in its velvet case, he knew what he had to do. It was quite clear to him, beyond any doubt, and the fact that the matter would not have a happy conclusion made it all the more correct. 'I wasn't born to be happy,' he said to himself, and he felt as if that was the answer that he had sought in vain in all the prayers.

Most of the men had left already. Hersch Wasserstein was now standing all on his own by the door of the prayer hall. Arthur walked over to him, and it seemed to be a very long way. 'Herr Wasserstein,' he said, 'I would like to ask for your daughter's hand.'

His own voice sounded strange to him, but the idea of walking under the marriage baldaquin with Chaje Sore, whom he barely knew, made his eyes quite moist.

Hersch Wasserstein made an uneasy scraping movement with his foot, as if stubbing out a cigarette. Then he looked Arthur in the eye, and his gaze was not that of a shnorrer. 'It isn't decent to mock the afflicted,' he said.

He turned away and walked off, and nothing that Arthur said to him would make him come back.

'You're meshuga,' said Hinda, when Arthur told her about it.

The siblings were sitting in the Kamionkers' sukkah. The twins had taken a lot of trouble over decorating it; their father had had to bring home colourful scraps of fabric from work, and they had used them to create something almost like an oriental palace. That too was for Ruben.

'I meant it quite seriously,' Arthur assured her.

'I know. That's exactly the meshuganeh thing about it.'

'If I'd married her then ...'

'You didn't even know her.'

'But if ...'

It did Arthur good to argue in favour of his moral duties towards the Wassersteins, above all – even though he might not have admitted it to himself – because he knew that he would not win the debate. Hinda knew him too well.

'You aren't responsible for everything in this world,' she said. 'You are not the Lord God.' And then Hinda, confident, ever-cheerful Hinda, suddenly started crying, wailing, threw her arms around her brother's neck and whispered to him, 'But if you are the Lord God – please, please bring my Ruben home to me.'

Arthur clumsily patted her back, and had the feeling that he was consoling himself.

Meanwhile Zalman was sitting in the back room of Pinchas's shop, where the relief committee for Galician refugees had set up a makeshift office between sacks of lentils and barrels of pickled gherkins. Frau Okun, who had fled from Russia herself many years ago, acted as secretary, and the people coming to her for help seemed to like her brusque, matter-of-fact manner. Even too much empathy can be painful.

War pays no heed to feast days, so even today new refugees had arrived, who were supplied with absolute necessities and needed lodging somewhere for the first few nights. Zalman asked few questions: 'if someone's tongue is hanging from his throat, you don't need to ask him if he's thirsty.' But of course he asked each one of them if he could tell him anything about the fate of the yeshiva of Kolomea. The front had been a few days' journey away from the homes of these refugees, and today's new arrivals came from a quite different area. Only one old man with a strange half-beard – a joker in Russian uniform had burned off the other half – thought he had heard that the rabbi had left the city with all his students, but couldn't say where they had got to.

Zalman found lodging for all the refugees, told them where they could get something to eat and gave the sick and wounded the address of Arthur's surgery. Then he carefully, without chivvying, recorded the details of the new arrivals on file cards, put them in order and passed the box to Frau Okun.

'From tomorrow you will have to get by without me. I'm sure Pinchas will help you.'

'And you?'

'I'm going to Galicia,' said Zalman. 'I am a peaceful man, but this is about my son.'

52

He went to the barber's, even though it was still Yontif, sat down on the chair with the revolving seat, laid his hands on the arm rests, felt the rustling paper against the back of his neck, took a deep breath, smelled hair water and pomade and soap, blew the air spluttering back out like someone emerging from water, and was ready.

Herr Dallaporta, who had now been in Switzerland for twenty-five years, and whose first shop had been destroyed in the disturbances of 1896, was surprised to see him. 'Isn't it Sunday for the Jews today?' he asked, and Zalman replied. 'Sometimes you have to work even on Sunday.' They spoke in Zurich German, one of them with a Neapolitan, the other a Galician intonation. Neither man noticed the accent of the other.

'The side whiskers,' said Zalman. 'They will have to go.'

Herr Dallaporta was an aesthetic person, and had even decorated a wall of his drawing room with a painting of Vesuvius done by himself. Zalman's magnificent whiskers were a work of art, and one on which he himself had worked for many years, and destroying them struck him as blasphemy. 'Why?' he asked, and in a dramatic gesture that could as easily have had a Yiddish as an Italian accent, raised his hands to the heavens. 'Emperor Franz Joseph does not have finer ones.'

'That's exactly why. Only an Austrian would wear such whiskers. And for the foreseeable future it is better if I don't look like an Austrian.'

He had his moustache trimmed as he had worn it two decades before: bushy and not very tidy. When he came home with his new face, Hinda didn't recognise him at first, when in fact it was only the old, young Zalman coming back to light. Rachel declared her altered father to be dashing, her favourite word of the moment, and only Lea, who like her grandmother Chanele had a keen eye for what people were up to, said straight away, 'You're up to something.'

He told them about his plan, which wasn't yet a plan, but just an intention – 'But doing nothing at all would be the worst possible plan' – and they tried to dissuade him from it. He had been expecting that, and wouldn't be put off. 'You of all people must understand this,' he said to Hinda. 'Some things are non-negotiable.'

They went on debating with him when he was already packing his rucksack

– 'No, not a suitcase, I'm not going on holiday' – they went on talking at him as he wrapped his big scissors and his sewing kit in a cloth – 'You never know what you're going to need' – and when he went to the station without knowing where the trains even went, Pinchas and Arthur had turned up and were trying to persuade him that he was risking his life unnecessarily.

'Unnecessarily?' asked Zalman. 'My son is there.' And he pulled on his fingers until the joints cracked, as one brings a tool that one hasn't used for a long time back into operation.

There might, the man at the counter said, still be trains for Cracow. But he would rather sell Zalman a ticket to Vienna, a choice for which he had a reassuringly everyday explanation: 'If there is no connection, we can't refund the ticket. According to our terms and conditions, acts of war count as an act of God, and then you'd be throwing your money away.'

Zalman bought a ticket to Vienna, one-way. He almost said, 'If I don't come back, it would be throwing my money away.'

Pinchas hadn't really expected to be able to dissuade him from his decision, and now, murmuring a prayer, stuffed a huge piece of smoked meat into his rucksack. It would turn out to be a very precious gift.

'And where are you going to sleep on the way?' Arthur asked, as if nothing could be more important.

'I will build myself a tabernacle. That's very appropriate, since it's Sukkot.'

Hinda laughed with him, and it was the hardest thing she had ever had to do for her husband. She managed until his train had pulled away. Only then would she let herself be comforted by her daughters.

Later, when it was all a long time ago, Zalman's journey into the war became a legend, a heroic family epic that was told over and over again, and smoothed and embellished each time until it assumed the clarity and unbelievability of a saga. Even for his grandchildren, who knew him only as a grandfather who was always ready for childish pranks, his adventures were no more real than their favourite bedtime story about the huge fish on whose back the sailors cooked their dinner.

After his first report, Zalman himself spoke little about his experiences, and was much more silent about the matter than people were used to. When pressed, he always told the same anecdotes, none of which were really fit for proper society. There was the story of the Austrian soldiers who wanted to be sent home, so they swallowed soap, because it gave you diarrhoea that no field doctor could tell from the symptoms of cholera, and the one about the smokers who had no papers to roll their tobacco in, so fished the paper out of the latrine, 'this one's clean, this one isn't.' The latter became a catchphrase in the family, which was used both during the washing up and the sorting of the laundry. 'This one's clean, this one isn't.'

At the core of the legend there was a real event, and even without embellishment Zalman's experiences throughout those weeks were adventurous enough.

It began without particular difficulties: the connection from Vienna to Cracow still existed. In his compartment he was the only civilian among Austrian officers, and was therefore looked at with great suspicion. They were already having to transport the refugees in goods wagons in the opposite direction, there were so many of them, and here was someone voluntarily travelling into the thick of it? Lest he be mistaken for a spy, Zalman remembered his time in New York and started talking in an American accent. He claimed to be a correspondent for the *Herald*, and noted the names of all his passengers for a report he was writing about the heroic Austrian army. The prospect of international fame quickly made the officers forget their suspicion. War has a lot to do with vanity.

The Russians, they explained to him, as insulted as if they had broken the rules of a respectable game by gaining such an unpredicted advantage for themselves, the Russians had advanced on Galicia through the Pripyat Swamps, which according to all the strategic plans were impossible to cross, which meant that they must have been preparing for this conflict for years, which wasn't fair at all. From Lemberg in Northern Galicia to Czernowitz in Bukovina they had overrun a whole series of towns and quickly made their way westwards. But as a result – the officers said it behind their hands, as if the General Chief of Staff von Hötzendorf had confided it to them in person – all their supply routes were now far too long, and in fact, all the people in the compartment were convinced the Russians, even though they didn't know it, had won a Pyrrhic victory. Zalman was reminded of the trade union meetings at which, to keep one's spirits up, one always persuaded oneself that the strike was having an effect, and the fact that the opposition still refused to negotiate was only proof of their weakness.

He agreed with the officers on all points, which was why they considered him an expert in strategic matters, and even asked him how the fortress of Przemysl, trapped and surrounded by the Russians, might best be relieved.

They became such friends that in Cracow they organised a place for him in a medical train which was travelling to a place near Tarnow; the town itself had already been taken by the enemy. The train stopped close behind the front; rifle fire could be heard. The victory procession of the Russians seemed unstoppable, and the inhabitants of the villages in which the hospital tents had been erected were already hanging Russian Orthodox icons on their houses having heard that these were likely to make the Cossacks more lenient towards them: Jesus, Mary and St Nicholas. 'There were pictures like that on the Jewish houses too,' Zalman said later, 'and perhaps they helped. The Russians never got beyond Tarnow.'

He never spoke of how he had battled his way through the Austrian and then the Russian lines. He only said once to Arthur, 'I saw more wounded people there than you will ever experience in your practice, and believe me: if someone is clutching his own intestines, and begging you to shoot him to put an end to his pain, your only regret is that you don't have a gun.'

The only good road would have led eastwards via Rzeszow, Jaroslaw and Przemysl. But because the fortress there, the last Habsburg island, was still resisting and the battles were fierce, Zalman had to seek a route further south, where the landscape became mountainous and there was therefore little to conquer and little to gain. Here on the slopes of the Beskids no great armies had ever clashed, and no decision had ever been made concerning them. Only small units skirmished sporadically there, weary boxers still slugging away at each other even though neither side had a hope of landing the deciding blow.

The war, which was nothing here but a series of bloody assaults, took place among the population; potato cellars served as foxholes, and machine-gunners were hidden in the church towers. There were no clear borders now, large or small. Even the garden fences had disappeared, chopped up for firewood or to reinforce the muddy roads.

The war had swirled up the land just as Mimi liked to shuffle the cards: throwing the whole pack on the bedcovers, closing her eyes and rummaging blindly around in them.

Many families had been torn apart, and if they had been lucky enough to stay together, they didn't know where to go. Sometimes two groups would meet, each seeking safety in exactly the direction from which the other had just fled. So many refugees were wandering around that with sad mockery they were called 'the second army'. An individual man in torn and dirty clothes didn't attract attention here.

The region had always been poor, and the war had made it even poorer. Everything edible had been confiscated against worthless requisition vouchers – 'to be redeemed when Moshiach comes' – and the hungry soldiers were digging the last potatoes out of the ground with their bayonets. Anyone who had to retreat, and here, where there was no clear front, that now meant the Austrians and then the Russians again, first blew up all the supplies that they couldn't take with them, with a charge of picric acid.

Hunger abolishes laws, and every time Zalman wanted to cut off a piece of the smoked meat that Pinchas had given him at the last moment, he had to find a hiding place.

The land was full of beggars, old and new. 'They were easy to tell apart,' Zalman said. 'The practised ones are shameless and look you in the eye when they hold their hand out to you.'

Once, afterwards, he couldn't remember if it had been near Samok or near Sambor, an experienced shnorrer had attached himself to him for a whole day, an old man who had never been in a battle, but who nonetheless had a whole row of Russian medals for bravery rattling on his chest. In the pocket of his coat, just in case the fortunes of war should change, he had just as many Austrian medals at the ready. 'People want to be able to feel sorry for someone who's one of their own,' was his explanation. 'In my profession you owe your customers that.'

When Zalman reported on such encounters, everything sounded like a big adventure, but there were lots of things he never spoke about, and which one could only guess from little details, just as an archaeologist assembles a whole culture from a few shards. Thus, for example, he never mentioned a looted manor house, but there must have been one, because once he said, 'Piano wood burns best,' and another time, when he already had his own tailor's workshop and someone tried to sell him some strikingly green velvet, 'I once used a billiard-table covering like that to stitch lining in the coat of a freezing sergeant.'

The really bad things, and there must have been plenty of those, he kept to himself, or confided them only in Hinda. She alone knew why Zalman never touched a pear for as long as he lived – a dead man had lain under a pear tree, and the rotting fruits had mingled with the rotting body – or why he plunged himself with such commitment into his work for the relief committee. To the others he said only, 'The Jews will experience nothing worse this century than what has happened to them in Galicia,' and looked people in the eye as he asked them for a donation.

'And you never gave up hope of finding Ruben?' Hinda asked him.

'Hope costs nothing,' he replied. It was supposed to be a joke, but he didn't smile as he said it.

Even if only half of the stories the family would later tell each other had really happened, Zalman must have been through a lot, and been involved in a lot as well. He had set off from Zurich at Sukkot, and it was already November when he arrived at last, via Stryj and Stanislawow in Kolomea.

He had grown up there, and he no longer knew the city.

In front of the station, which lay on the outskirts, a coachman seemed to be waiting for arriving guests, but when Zalman came closer all that stood there was the skeleton of a droschke, just as the whole building was only the skeleton of a station. From here it was two kilometres into the city, and it was a strange feeling for him to have the wide street, where in his day pedestrians, carts and coaches had jostled for space, all to himself.

Kolomea, far in the East of Galicia, had been one of the first cities taken by the Russian troops, and because in the first flush of the new war they wanted to do particularly well, they had organised a real shooting competition with their guns, in which even the Greek Orthodox church had lost its tower. What remained was just a shapeless lump of stone that looked a bit like a stable, and which the Cossacks also used for that purpose in the first days of the occupation. A building in the classical style, which Zalman had never seen – it must have been built after he left – showed no sign of impact, but had been completely burned out.

One walked past it on a carpet of charred scraps of paper; he thought at first that it might have been a library, and only the Hebrew letters under his feet made him realise that this must be the new synagogue that Ruben had described with such admiration in one of his letters.

In Ring Square, the city's central market, there was no sign of the crammed stalls from which Hutsul peasants in bright costumes once sold poultry and vegetables; only a few starving city-dwellers had lined up spare household utensils in front of them, and waited hopelessly for takers. The windows of the shop buildings all around were boarded up, as if they could no longer bear the sight of their sick city. Most of the shops were shut, only the Righietti patisserie on Kosciuszko Street had bravely kept going. A sign on the door asked the honoured clientele for forgiveness, but 'for reasons beyond our control' they were unfortunately unable to serve cakes or coffee.

The people he met avoided his eye. Any stranger could be an enemy or, even more of a threat, someone looking for help. It was more sensible simply not to notice him.

There was no sign of Russian soldiers. The only ones were two sentries outside the Hotel Bellevue on Jagiellonska Street. They had probably set up their headquarters inside.

It wasn't far to the yeshiva, but Zalman first made his way to Jablonowka, the little alley in the Jewish quarter where his old friend lived, the one who had taken Ruben in. The whole area was filled with a smell of burned wood that had been rained on, and Zalman started running as if, after more than three weeks on the road, every minute suddenly counted.

The alley was undamaged, the one-storey wooden buildings still pressed up against one another, as if trying to keep each other's spirits up. But the street was silent, more silent than he had ever experienced it before, even on Yom Kippur, when everyone was in the synagogue.

The front doors weren't locked.

In his friend's house even the cupboards were open, they had been thoroughly and carefully emptied, the tableware and the linen had been cleared away, and not even chaos had been left behind. The books alone had been of interest to nobody.

Names were written in chalk on tables and chairs, Sawicki, Truchanowicz, Brzezina. Only later did Zalman discover the explanation: the looters, all respectable neighbours, had signed their booty so that when the corresponding space in their own house was liberated, they could calmly come and take it away. There was no particular hurry, as no one worried that the Jewish owners were ever coming back.

Ruben's suitcase lay on the bed in a little room on the first floor.

Empty.

Zalman sat down beside it and stroked the dark brown cardboard.

When he was standing in the deserted alley again, not knowing who to turn to, a voice suddenly called out his name. It was a thin, old, lisping voice that seemed to come out of nowhere, because he couldn't see a soul. 'Kamionker!' called the voice. 'Are you not Kamionker?'

In the open window of a house, he only saw it now, there stood an old woman who seemed familiar, but whom he couldn't quite place. She beckoned him over, and it was only when he was standing in front of her – in this house, too, the doors were unlocked and the cupboards had been completely emptied – that he remembered.

'Frau Heller?'

Back in the days when he had worked as a young boy in Simon Heller's tallis-weaving mill, she had been the boss, a woman you took your cap off to when she walked through the workshops, and who had always, Zalman could smell it still, pulled a fine veil of violet perfume behind her. Now an old woman stood in the cleared-out house, even though Frau Heller could not have been all that old. She no longer wore a sheitel, and her scalp, yellow as Torah parchment, shimmered through her tangled grey hair.

'Why aren't you in Ottynia with the rest, Kamionker?' she asked.

She hadn't lisped before.

The Hellers had never lived in Jablonowka, only ever in a stately manufacturer's house beside the mill. But she had probably grown up here, and had crept back into her parents' house after...

Zalman didn't ask her for her story. He had heard too many atrocities over the previous few weeks.

'Ottynia?'

'That's where they've all gone. To the Rebbe of Ottynia. He's a holy man, they said, and he will protect them.'

'Even the bochrim from the yeshiva?'

'In Ottynia. All in Ottynia.' She said it almost in a singsong voice, and smiled at him the way one smiles at stupid people who ask obvious questions. A rifle butt had knocked her teeth out, but it was still the old, detached smile with which she had walked past them when she was the boss, with her scent of violets. 'I haven't seen you at work for a long time, Kamionker,' she said. 'Have you been ill?'

In the kitchen, where there were no dishes in the cupboards, he left her his last piece of smoked meat. He had been saving it for an emergency, but now that he knew where Ruben was there could be no more emergencies.

Ottynia had been on his route, and he had avoided the town just as he avoided, where possible, all places where there might be soldiers. It was only a few kilometres away, back towards Stanislawow. He could be there that evening.

He passed the Yeshiva, another defencelessly open building.

A shell had struck the old Jewish cemetery, right in the middle of the graves. Its crater looked like the calyx of a flower, and the gravestones, toppled in all directions, like its petals.

53

The family had a better idea of the end of the story, because Ruben had been there and liked to talk about it, with the religious zeal of someone who has personally experienced a miracle. Because had it not been a miracle, a nes min hashamayim, that his father was suddenly standing in front of him in the rebbe's house. 'And,' he said, and however many times he told the story, he always failed to grasp it, 'at first I mistook him for a stranger, just as Joseph's brothers didn't recognise him when they stood before him in Egypt.' Ruben had become accustomed to speaking in Biblical similes, but his religious sense overall had become much more tolerant. The more certain someone is of his conviction, the less need he has to force it on others.

Zalman had had no difficulty finding the house of the Ottynia rebbe. It was the most magnificent building in the place, which didn't mean much, because Ottynia was a poor small town where the people, as the saying goes, could only have Shabbos if everyone borrowed something from his neighbour. Piety alone doesn't build palaces. But Rabbi Chajim Hager, a son of Rabbi Baruch of the famous Vizhnitz family, was a tsadik, a prince of the Torah, a scion of old scholarly nobility, so his Hassidim took care of him even if they had to go hungry themselves to make their contributions. Unlike almost all the other houses in the town, made only out of wood, the building in which he resided and held court for his devotees was made of stone. It had two further storeys above the ground floor, and the three-cornered gable that had been placed on it like a stage set, was adorned with a Star of David.

Most of the ground floor was taken up with the room for prayer and study – 'shul' in Yiddish, because a pious person is always also a student – and on feast days more than a hundred Hassidim could gather here and still had enough room to throw themselves on the floor in the Yom Kippur prayer.

Now almost five hundred people crowded into the building. If one needed the Rebbe's presence even in peace, as a child needs his father, how much more did one need him in time of war? Where else was one to seek shelter?

For many years the devotees of the Rebbe of Ottynia had come here on pilgrimages, to take advice and blessing from their spiritual leader. They prayed and sang with him, and when the got their bite from the shirayim, the leftovers from the Rebbe's table, it tasted as delicious to them as the Leviathan to the righteous in Paradise.

Now there was no more than a bowl of buckwheat groats a day for each of them, and people had stopped leaving shirayim long ago.

In Ottynia they had always liked to see the Hassidim arriving, because they brought in modest takings. Even the Zionists, who were so proud of their enlightened modernity and secretly mocked miracle rabbis, were happy to rent the pious pilgrims a bed or spanned their thin horses to take them to the station in Kolomea.

Now there was nothing more to be earned from them. The community's poor box had long been emptied, and the price of food was rising further every day: people were now asking a whole crown for a single loaf of bread. If it was meant for the trapped Jews, it could easily be twice as much; he who has no choice cannot bargain. The Russian district commander had declared the rabbi's house a place of detention, and all its residents prisoners. The Jews had destroyed a telephone line important for the war effort, was the official explanation, and that made them all saboteurs. Anyone who tried to leave the building and was caught received twenty-five lashes. Sometimes it was seventy-five, or just as many lashes as it took before the provost's arm got sore.

It was not forbidden to enter the house, but no one was permitted to leave. When Zalman knocked at the door, the sentry didn't stop him, but just laughed and said to his comrade, 'Look at this, now the calves are coming to the slaughter of their own free will.' The new arrival was assailed from all sides and asked about news from the outside world. If Zalman hadn't been so tired, he would happily have lifted the spirits of the inmates with a few hopeful lies. But first he had to look for Ruben.

He found him in a room in which six people could have lived and in which twenty of the Talmud students from Kolomea were staying. They slept in shifts, none longer than four hours, so that each of them could lie down once in the course of the day.

Ruben, his sidelocks longer than he would ever have worn them in Zurich, sat by the wall, emaciated and hollow-cheeked, his arms wrapped around his bent knees, had closed his eyes and was rocking his torso back and forth as if praying or weeping. Zalman had to climb over the sleeping bodies to reach him; one sought peace where one could find it, even if a pious person should not lie on the floor, because that is the place for the dead. He knelt beside his son and hugged him, and Ruben opened his eyes and didn't know who this strange man was, who smelled of smoke and country roads, and who had tears running down his unshaven cheeks. Then he recognised him and moved his mouth in silence, had forgotten how to speak, and when at last he found his voice again, his first words were from a verse of the scripture.

'Pletah gadolah,' stammered Ruben, words which mean 'great deliverance'.

'God sent me before you', Joseph said to his brothers, 'to preserve you a posterity on the earth, and to save your lives by a great deliverance.'

Years later, when Ruben was ordained a Rabbi and delivered his very first sermon, that was the text that he took as his theme.

'Let's go home now,' Zalman whispered. Ruben explained to him that they were locked in here and no one could leave the building, but his father just cracked the joints of his fingers and said, 'A way can always be found.'

Zalman's friend, the one whose house Ruben had lived at in Kolomea, had never arrived in Ottynia. Something must have happened to him, no one knew what. It was a time when people just got lost like a handkerchief or a keyring.

Zalman had come to Ottynia on the Friday, and in the evening he was standing beside Ruben in the prayer hall. They had really had to fight their way in, because even though the Ottynia rebbe was a gebentschter, one of the thirty-six righteous men, his devotees said, for whom God had not destroyed the world, his shul was not the Temple in Jerusalem which, legend relates, grew larger every year to make room for all the pilgrims. They stood shoulder to shoulder, pressed so tightly together that at the end of the Shemoneh Esrei no one could take the three steps back and the forward that are part of the prayer.

They stood in absolute darkness. They had run out of candles long ago. Above them, a red dot in the void, floated the eternal light.

Since the Baal Shem, the holiest of holies and wisest of the wise, was freed from the clutches of pirates, all Hassidim greet the Sabbath with the 107th Psalm, in which God is praised for delivering the prisoners and the lost, and letting the hungry sow their fields and plant their vines once more. 'And led them forth by the right way,' the voices sang around Zalman, 'that they might go to a city of habitation.' They sang it jubilantly in the darkness of their prayer hall, as if the prediction had already come to be.

Somewhere right at the front, at the eastern wall, was their rebbe, leading the prayer. The fact that he could not be seen, or heard through the confusion of voices, made him a mystical presence, so unreal and yet as real as the invisible Sabbath bride to whom they all turned as they entered.

They prayed and sang and would also, in their ecstasy, have danced if there had been room to dance.

Zalman had never been a pious person. He often said, with a mixture of mockery and resignation, 'I don't know if there's a God, I just know that we are his chosen people.'

Later, when he told Hinda about this Friday evening in shul in Ottynia, he said thoughtfully, 'Whether a God exists, I still don't know. But there's something there.'

'Lamp down, worries up,' they said in the Meijer family. There was no Shabbos lamp here that could be lowered over the table and lit, and had there been, there would have been no oil for it. And yet in the darkness of the prayer hall Zalman had the feeling of being able to let go at last, at least for a day.

The sude, the solemn Sabbath dinner, consisted of a piece of bread and a pinch of salt. Zalman took the olive-sized bite that means one has done one's duty, and left the rest to Ruben.

For a few hours they slept side by side on the floor. Zalman had put an arm around his son and inhaled the smell of his hair, as he had done when Ruben had climbed into his parents' bed as a terrified little boy because there was a storm outside his window.

A piece of oilcloth was found, which had once been a tablecloth – who needs tablecloths when he has nothing to eat? – and from it he made a long bag with two long straps at either end. He didn't explain anything, he just said to his son, 'If you want to say goodbye to someone, do it quickly, because we two are about to leave.'

In the rebbe's house, where all the rooms and corridors were full of people, rumours spread quickly, so everyone soon knew that there was a man there, a meschuggener or a gebentshter, who could tell, who said he could simply stroll pass the guards into freedom. Even though no messenger or formal invitation had come, the rumour also knew that the Rebbe wanted to see them both, the tailor Zalman and his son Ruben. Standing in front of the Rebbe and being able to ask him his advice and his blessing was a great honour, but also a formal occasion, at which the rules to be respected were just as strict as at a royal audience. One didn't present one's problems orally to the Rebbe, but wrote them on a piece of paper, the kvitel, which mustn't contain anything but the name of the supplicant, his place of origin, and the matter involved. A sage like the Rebbe of Ottynia needs no explanations, he just understands.

'Ruben ben Hinda and Zalman ben Scheindl,' they wrote, because in a kvitel you give the name of the mother and not the father, 'both from Zurich'. As the reason for his audience Ruben gave the first thing that had come into his head at the sight of his father: 'Pletah gadolah', great deliverance.

The Rebbe was the only one in this overcrowded house who still had a room of his own, even if it was no longer the big study room, just the little room to which he had sometimes retreated in the past to get half an hour's rest. The gabbai, the rebbe's steward, opened the door to them and let them in.

Rabbi Chaijim Hager sat behind a table full of books. The first thing that struck Zalman about him was his eyes, because they were so completely different: one wide open and penetrating, the other, with a hanging eyelid, half narrowed as if the Ottynian were seeing through his interlocutor with an admonitory gaze, and at the same time forgiving him for everything again. Only later did he discover that the Rebbe – 'But he still sees more than anyone else!' – was blind in one eye. Under his thick grey beard his lips were always somewhat pursed, as if for a kiss or to taste an unfamiliar morsel. He wore the black silk kaftan, but on his head he was not wearing, as he had done on the Sabbath, the shtraiml, the fur beret with thirteen dark brown sable tails, but a stiff black hat, a bowler, of the kind worn by a Galician schoolteacher, or market trader. His hat was pushed to the back of his neck, and the velvet cap was visible on his high, bald forehead.

The gabbai had closed the door behind him a long time before, but Rabbi Chaijim stared into the distance with his good eye, and didn't look at them.

The set the kvitel down in front of him, along with the obligatory coin that the Rebbe would pass on to the poor. A few minutes passed in silence. Only then did he pick up the piece of paper and hold it up to his good eye. 'Pletah gadolah,' he read, and spoken by the quiet, but powerful voice of the rebbe the words sounded like a promise. Of course he knew the Bible passage; he was said to know by heart not only the Tanakh with all its books, but also the whole Mishnah. He smiled at them, and when the Rebbe smiles no more bad things can happen to you. 'It was not you who sent me hither,' he continued the Bible quotation in Hebrew, 'but God.' And added in Yiddish, 'If someone is sent by God – how can he fail?' He raised his hand in blessing and sank back into his thoughts.

That was the whole audience that Zalman and Ruben Kamionker had with the great Rabbi Chaijim Hager of Ottynia. It was time to set off.

Behind the house, where in more peaceful times the vegetable garden had been, a latrine had been dug, enlarged twice and still too small, and there Zalman knelt down on the dirty boards and, holding his breath, fished out a handful of filth and then another and then another. He did it with his bare hands and filled the oilcloth bag with the repellent mass. He wiped his hands on his son's trousers – 'That too has a purpose,' he said – and then he set about the most difficult tailoring task of his life: he sewed up his bag full of shit, with coarse stitches and in great haste, because it cost him a great deal of effort not to vomit.

Ruben had to tie the bag around him and pull his trousers over to it. Because the stitch, quite deliberately, was not quite tight, he soon felt the strange excrement running slowly and disgustingly down his legs.

'That's good,' said Zalman.

He put his son over his shoulder, a hunter with a slain deer, walked back through the courtyard at the back and marched resolutely down the long corridor and past the shul, opened the front door, and when the guards blocked his way, bayonets at the ready, he said only one word.

'Cholera,' said Zalman.

In the Russian army, too, more soldiers had been killed by this insidious disease than by enemy bullets, and when the soldiers saw the shit running out of the young Jew's trousers, when they smelled the nauseating miasma and saw his sunken face and closed eyes, they took a step back and then another and let him pass.

'It must have been like that when Moses parted the Red Sea,' Ruben said later.

With his son over his shoulder, Zalman walked through the whole of Ottynia. It was only in the little forest, where in the spring you could pick tiny strawberries and in the autumn huge mushrooms, only when no one could see and hear them any more, that he put him back on the ground, took a few steps to the side and threw up. 'Try and clean yourself as best you can,' he said, and retched again.

When Ruben was clean – not really clean, he wouldn't be able to do that until he could finally take a bath in Czernowitz – when the oilcloth bag was buried under a pile of rotten leaves and there was no longer any sign of it, Zalman opened his now threadbare rucksack, took out his sewing kit and unrolled the scissors from the cloth. 'They will grow back, but a head doesn't grow back,' he said as he cut off his son's sidelocks. For what he planned it would not have been good to be seen as a Jew.

They took the way south-east, taking a wide arc around Kolomea, because Zalman wouldn't have been able to bear seeing his home town as he had found it three days before.

Their goal was the border with Bukovina, where the front was as well. The way there was easy to find: they only had to take the direction from which the refugees were coming.

They reached Sniatyn, where they were so close to the armies that they would have heard their guns, except that the Russians had run out of ammunition, and the Austrians were waiting for victory in the West before going back on the attack along with their German allies.

Compared to what Zalman had already been through, the way to the other side was a pleasant stroll. In this border area there had always been smuggling, and because people have to earn their money even in wartime, a farmer was found who showed them a secret path through the positions.

The Russians had also overrun Czernowitz, and had only just been driven from it, but there was already proper coffee in the coffee-houses again, and in the hotel they would fill you a tub of hot water for half a crown.

They bought trousers, jackets and warm coats from an outfitter, not elegant, but clean. The only item of clothing, in fact the only object Ruben had left Zurich with, and which he brought back home, was his arba kanfes with the tzitzits at the four corners.

The timetable had not yet come back into force, but once a day a train travelled to the capital, with a conductor who was as unfriendly as in the best days of peace.

In Vienna they ate at Schmeidel Kalisch's famous kosher restaurant. It was so good that Ruben had cramp afterwards. He was no longer used to rich food.

Zalman bought a copy of the *Freie Presse* from a newspaper seller at the station. In Galicia, it said, the Russian troops were not adhering to martial law, but it was only a matter of time before they were driven back to the Steppes from where they had come. Not least for that reason it was extremely regrettable, the author of the editorial wrote, that so many citizens of the Mosaic persuasion had fled irrationally from the country; one should, he wrote, be able to endure a certain amount of hardship in such difficult times. Zalman spread the newspaper out on the empty seat in front of him, put his feet on it and went to sleep.

When he woke up in the middle of the night Ruben needed to talk to him urgently, right now. He hadn't yet thanked his father and had been trying to find the right words for hours.

Zalman wouldn't hear of it. 'Just leave it be,' he said. 'I am a peaceful man, but when people get solemn on me I get furious.'

'It was a nes min hashamayim!'

'Then thank the Lord,' said Zalman and went back to sleep. That was the only exchange on the matter that ever passed between father and son.

When they had passed the border, Ruben spoke the prayer after a danger has passed.

He wanted to get out in St Gallen to send a telegram home. In Austria that had been forbidden for fear of espionage: secret information about force levels and troop deployments might be concealed behind apparently harmless words. But the walk to the telegram office would have taken too long, the train would have left without them, and they would have arrived in Zurich four hours later.

So no one collected them at the station, and in fact they were both glad of it. On the way to Rotwandstrasse they received hostile and disapproving glares, because they were wearing ill-fitting clothes, and it was obvious that they had just been on a long journey. There were already enough refugees in Switzerland, the glances said, where the war had caused enough hardship already.

But the streets were full of traffic and the shop windows full of goods.

The closer they came to home, the slower they walked. One can also be afraid of things that one has long yearned for.

When they were outside the door, Ruben kissed the mezuzah, the little capsule with the verses of the scripture that all Jewish families fix to the front door of their flat or apartment. Only then could Zalman ring.

It was Rachel who opened the door, and when she saw them both she screamed so loudly that Hinda thought she was being attacked and came running out of the kitchen with a frying-pan in her hand.

'You are even more dangerous than a Cossack, Frau Kamionker,' said Zalman.

Then no one said anything else for a very long time.

54

By the start of December 1914, Alfred's military training was declared complete. Admittedly, the time scheduled for it was not yet over, but the war was going badly, and the fatherland needed every man it could find.

He was assigned to Infantry Regiment 371, and he and the other young soldiers were inoculated against typhus, because the whole battalion was to be posted to Indochina. But plans had changed, and they were sent instead to Alsace, not far from the Swiss border, where the regiment was given the task of re-establishing the connection, interrupted by German troops, between Aspach-le-Haut and Aspach-le-Bas. Alfred was waiting with his comrades at the assembly point near Thann, for transport to the front, when a stray French shell exploded beside them.

He died instantly.

At induction the recruits had been asked for an address to which the news should be sent in the event of their heroic death. Alfred had written Désirée's name on the envelope. The practice of using these pre-addressed envelopes was later abandoned; they saved time, but it proved damaging to morale on the home front when families had to take the news of their son's death out of an envelope written in his own handwriting.

The letter was delivered to Morgartenstrasse by Frau Reutener, a notoriously nosy individual who stood in for the postman while he was on active service. She met Mimi on the stairs, and when she had fished the envelope from her bag she said, 'So, so, Frau Pomeranz, from France,' in the tone that one uses when one would like to have an answer from the other person, but is prevented by convention from asking the question. Mimi said 'merci', stressing the second syllable correctly in the French style, to distinguish it from the vulgar Zurich 'märsi', and disappeared into the flat without satisfying Frau Reutener's curiosity.

Since he had been called up, Alfred's communications had all arrived censored, as one could tell by the sloppy strips of paper with which the opened envelopes had been sealed again. No one had opened this letter. A Frenchman would have known immediately what that meant: it was a official letter, and in these days that could not bode well.

Mimi, for whom the war was far away, didn't know this rule and didn't worry.

She had acquired a certain skill in opening envelopes over the hot steam from the kettle, because even though she had announced quite clearly and distinctly from the start that she would keep a personal eye on her daughter's correspondence with the unloved Alfred, one couldn't do such things too conspicuously. Lately Désirée had been inclined to burst into tears at the drop of a hat in any case.

Mimi read the letter and at first didn't understand it, just stared at the letters and could find no meaning in them. 'Sur le champ de bataille,' it said. 'En défendant sa patrie.' 'Sans avoir souffert.' None of it made any sense.

When she could no longer resist comprehension, the crazy idea ran though her head, 'If I didn't understand French, Alfred would still be alive.'

She didn't faint, as they did in plays at the Municipal theatre, but considered quite calmly and objectively what needed to be done now. Only in the cold wind of the December morning did she realise that she had run out of the house without her coat and hat.

It was Wednesday, when there were never very many customers. Mimi knew that on such days her husband liked to leave the shop in charge of his daughter and Frau Okun, and sat down at his Gemara. Since Zalman had come back from Galicia, Pinchas had had more time for it; previously the Refugee Relief Association had occupied every free minute. He had had to organise accommodation and modest financial support for several dozen people.

A classroom of this kind is a purely masculine refuge. Mimi had only ever ventured into it before when it was used for an alternative purpose, such as the obligatory receptions at bar mitzvahs or engagements. Now she came charging in, without even noticing the disapproving glances of the other students.

She set the letter down in front of Pinchas, and her lower lip trembled like that of a little girl who has experienced something so terrible that she doesn't even have the courage to cry.

Pinchas looked at her, looked at the letter and didn't understand a word. Only now did it occur to her that he didn't speak French.

In a quavering voice she started translating, just as one renders the tanakh into German in cheder: a short fragment of sentence, followed immediately by its translation. 'J'ai la lourde charge – I have the sad duty – de vous announcer – to inform you – que le soldat Alfred Meijer...'

Le soldat Alfred Meijer.

Sur le champ de bataille.

Pinchas rubbed his forehead as he did when a difficult passage in the Talmud refused to yield up its meaning. Then he praised the judge of truth

447

and asked the only question that remained to be asked at that moment: 'Does Désirée know?'

Mimi shook her head. She yearned to be able to weep at last, but everything inside her was dried up.

That they did not go straight to Désirée was only partly down to cowardice; François's department store was really on the way. Regardless of how one felt about him in other respects: you must shake the hand of a father who has lost his only son, and say a few consoling words to him.

Mimi knew the little door in the laundry section. The lady with the severe hairdo who tried to stop her she simply pushed aside. Pinchas asked her with a gesture to forgive his wife's haste.

François was sitting at his desk with his hands over his face. He was thinking about business problems, but Pinchas and Mimi couldn't have known that, and thought it was grief.

He reacted brusquely to the disturbance. 'I know that Alfred has been writing your daughter love letters in secret. But it has happened behind my back. If I hadn't happened to see Mina at the counter in the post office...'

He hadn't heard.

Neither Mimi nor Pinchas could find the right words. Mimi just held the letter out to François, but he waved it away and refused to read it and repeated, 'I'm telling you: behind my back.'

When he finally understood, he said in bewilderment, 'But I bought him Swiss citizenship.'

And only then did he start screaming.

He shouted only one name, and it wasn't the name of his son.

'Mina!' François shouted.

Désirée read the letter standing behind the counter, as if it were a shopping list.

She read it without a break, the way one reads something that one knows already and only has to call to mind. '*J'ai la lourde charge. Sur le champ de bataille. Sans avoir souffert. Veuillez accepter, Mademoiselle, l'expression de ma profonde sympathie.*' Capitaine Waltefagule had never met Alfred, but he had still added the sentence: '*Il était beaucoup apprécié par ses camarades.*' There were instructions for the writing of such letters.

Désirée read twice and three times. Mimi wanted to take her in her arms, but her daughter stepped away from her. Then she folded the sheet up very slowly and put it back in the envelope, which bore her name in Alfred's handwriting, which she knew so well. She went to the drawer with the sweet bonbons that no one wanted to buy, opened the drawer, covered the letter with bonbons, really buried it underneath them, then took a handful of the little caster-sugar-covered balls, rosewater and almonds, and held them out to her parents.

'Would you like one?' she asked. 'They're very sweet.'

Only now did Mimi remember how to cry.

Mina, who had been an onlooker all her life, listened in silence as she was told of the death of her only child. She sat by her husband for seven days and held his hand. It was not a real shiva – how could a goy sit shiva? – but they were together and thinking of Alfred. When François was urgently needed in the shop, she stood in the doorway and straightened his tie. That was the last time he saw her.

When he came home in the evening, Mina had disappeared, she had just left, without saying goodbye, leaving only a note that said in her neat hand-writing, 'I'm going to my son.' Whether that meant that she was trying to go to France or something much worse no one could tell. Although her limping gait was a striking characteristic, Mina was never found. 'She could have drowned in Lake Zurich,' the police said, but there were no clues suggesting that either.

It was as if there had never been a Mina.

The worst thing was that life simply continued. It should have been like the kinematograph, when the film gets caught in the projector and stops, when the heat from the bulb eats its way into the picture, at first there's just a patch, then a hole that gets bigger and bigger, a brown-edged nothing into which everything that was on the screen only a moment before disappears, faces, heads, people, loving couples, when the pianist goes on playing at first before noticing that there is nothing more to accompany, when he lifts his hands from the keys, mid-tune, unfinished and with no closing chord, when everyone shouts for the projectionist and the light in the theatre comes on and everyone sits there, not having quite returned to the real world, thinking about how it would have continued.

If it had continued.

That was how it should have been. But the world didn't stop.

Désirée kept going to the shop, weighed pearl barley and wrapped salted herring in newspaper full of reports on the war, listened to the chit-chat of the customers and was considered particularly polite because she herself didn't want to speak. No one outside of the family knew about her secret love, so she didn't need to listen to any messages of condolence, which would have been nothing but empty words.

Once a customer asked if they sold those old fashioned bonbons, the ones that tasted of almonds and rosewater, and Désirée said, no, they didn't have those any more and they weren't being supplied either.

When François came back to his department store after the week of mourning, he didn't let anyone talk to him about his twofold loss. He plunged himself into his work, sat at his desk until late at night and now slept almost always in his office. 'He can't stand it at home any more,' his staff said, and felt their suspicions confirmed when François sold his villa in the university quarter, for a very bad price, because it was a time when there were no buyers for such objects.

But his feelings were not the reason for the sale. François, who everyone was convinced was a rich man, urgently needed money. Since the start of the war the turnover in his store had declined by almost half; people were buying only absolute necessities, and even that they were putting off for as long as possible. With the little money that the men sent home from the occupation of the borderlands, the store wasn't about to go from strength to strength.

That could all have been borne, they could have scaled down, shed staff, allowed the business to hibernate to some extent. But there was also the fact that François had got into serious debt buying the plot of land. According to his contract with Landolt's heirs the deposit would lapse if he failed to pay the agreed instalments on time, and when the Kantonalbank, with many words of regret – 'This is just how times are, Herr Meijer, you must have some understanding!' – terminated a credit, that was exactly what happened. François was not completely ruined, he kept his department store, and things improved eventually too, but the plot of land on Paradeplatz, the plot of land that had defined all his plans and considerations for so many years, that plot of land went to someone else.

All he was left with was a drawn plan on which a stone lion guarded the city coat of arms and impatient customers waited outside the door.

A plan that Mimi's heels had torn holes in.

For the last twenty years, the whole lifetime of his son Alfred, François had been working for nothing.

On 11 November 1918 the Armistice was signed in Compiègne. According to its conditions the Germans were to withdraw from Alsace-Loraine, and as soon as that had happened, François went to Pinchas and asked him for a big favour.

Pinchas hesitated at first. He sat over his books for a whole night and tried to find guidance for his decision. But there are requests that one cannot turn down, however much one might give never to have heard them.

The Buchet had stood jacked up in the garage of the department store all throughout the war. Now François got it going again. In Alsace most railway tracks were still destroyed; the automobile was the only way to get there.

François drove himself. He had fired his chauffeur Landolt long ago, with a surprisingly generous final payment. The car wasn't easy to steer, but François endured the pains in his arms as part of his penance.

During the long journey the two men said very little to one another. Although they were both thinking of the same thing, they were thinking about it in quite different ways.

In Mulhouse the after-effects of the war were still tangibly apparent, and they had to share a hotel room. When Pinchas put on his tefillin for morning prayer, François looked awkwardly aside, as one studiously ignores another person's nudity.

Without agreeing in advance, they both did without breakfast. As soon as it was light outside, they were already sitting in the car again.

For several weeks during the war the front line had passed precisely between Mulhouse and Thann, and the road on which they were driving had been fiercely fought over. One could still imagine that the narrow avenue must once have looked very picturesque, even though it was now lined with ragged, splintered trees. Some of them were already showing green shoots again.

Thann was an unprepossessing little provincial town, or rather it had once been an unprepossessing little provincial town. Then, with the clear-sightedness that the war always brings, the armies had recognised that its houses were not really houses at all, in fact, but cover for enemy soldiers, and had systematically shot them to pieces.

The big square in front of the church, or in front of what the gunners on both sides had left of the church, had once been the assembly point for newly arrived troops. Now the rubble of the demolished houses piled up there into good-sized mountains, shattered gables here, burnt wood there. For once it was not the residents but the stones of a town that had gathered there, as if to discuss how things would go from here.

An elderly gentleman with the armband of an auxiliary gendarme with a severe expression ensured that no one offloaded his rubble on the wrong mountain. Where chaos had long prevailed, rules and regulations could only be beneficial.

When François and Pinchas asked the way to their destination, at first he looked at them suspiciously. But then François's Swiss German accent convinced him that these were no Boches in front of him, and he kindly gave them information. So take the next left past the mairie – 'You can still read the sign, even though there's only a wall left of the building' – and then carry straight on, to the little stream with the improvised bridge of wooden planks. Not across the bridge, which would probably not have supported the weight of the car – 'A lovely automobile, by the way, a Buchet, am I right?' – but turn right and keep on the path along the water. 'Or even better: leave the car by the bridge and walk the rest. The wheels might sink into the mud, you see. A lot of people have been there recently.'

The path was lined with a blackthorn hedge. The little violet-blue sloes still hung from the branches. François couldn't stand the silence and said: 'They should have been picked after the first frost.'

He received no reply.

When they had reached their destination, François took off his hat. Pinchas shook his head, and he put it back on.

The cemetery wasn't fenced; it wasn't really a proper cemetery. They had just taken a field where once maize or rape had grown. Certainly not the best kind of ground; peasants are economical people, and corpses bring in no income.

Later they would set up a monument here, perhaps a martial sandstone poilu, watching alertly towards the East, his gun ready in his hand. Once a year they would lower a wreath at his feet, always with the same ribbon and the same speech. Then they would also carve all the names into an imposing plinth, arranged by year, and alphabetically within each year. Then it would be easier to find an Alfred Meijer.

Rubric 1914, between Marceau and Milleret.

But for now the dead had to be their own monument.

There, in the place where they began their search, lay the fallen of 1917. It was a long journey from the end to the beginning of the war, but François and Pinchas did not allow themselves a shortcut, but paced out the line of graves in the sequence in which they had been laid. Always one row to the left and a row to the right.

1917.

1916.

1915.

The closer they got to them, the more often they had to bend to decipher the names. In those few years the letters had faded, just as memory fades, in which someone is at first a hero, but then only a corpse, a name and then nothing at all.

On some graves there lay the remains of flowers. As they decayed, they emulated the fate of the men for whom they had been brought.

Then they found him. Meijer, Alfred. 1914.

François bent down to the grave, as clumsy as an old man. He ran his right hand through the dried leaves that the wind had formed into a mound. The actual mound of the grave had long since become one with the ground again.

He picked up a stone from the ground, not a pebble, as is customary in Jewish cemeteries, but a sharp-edged piece of rock, of the kind that repeatedly comes to the surface, however carefully ploughed it is. But there was no gravestone on which he could lay it as a sign of commemoration, so he just dropped the stone, which sank into the pile of rotten leaves.

François rose to his feet very slowly. His back would not fully straighten.

'Please, Pinchas,' he said.

'I don't know if it's right.'

'Is anything right in this world?' said François. And then, after a pause, 'It's what Mina would have wanted.'

And so it was that Pinchas Pomeranz spoke the Kaddish at a Christian grave, Yisgadal veyiskadash shmey raba.

The Kaddish for Alfred Meijer, who had been made a Christian, and a Swiss citizen, from which he had benefited not at all.

The Kaddish for a Jew with a cross on his grave.

1937

55

The tables had been cleared; only Chanele and Arthur were still sitting there. The nice woman with the hygienic white bonnet had wanted to take her tablecloth away, but Chanele had refused, quite violently, as she sometimes did, and the woman had nodded pleasantly and just wiped down the bluish-white oil-cloth with a sponge.

Bluish-white meaning milky food.

'It'll be breakfast in a minute,' said Chanele, even though she had just eaten her bread and butter and drunk her malt coffee. 'They will bring you a plate as well. Please join us.'

She was usually at her most alert shortly after getting up That was why Arthur liked going home early when he visited his mother in the old people's home in Lengnau. The last time she had asked him to go with her to the cemetery, and even though he knew that she had forgotten that wish long ago, he still felt obliged to fulfil it for her.

Janki had come from Alsace back then, so he wasn't from one of the two old Jewish communities. Still, he had insisted on being buried in the cemetery shared between Endingen and Lengnau, not in Baden, where he had lived for so long, and certainly not in Zurich, his last, unloved dwelling place. He and Chanele had explained the fact that they had moved there anyway by saying they wanted to be closer to the children, but it was probably more important that Janki's leg had got worse over the years, and he didn't trust small-town doctors. Now, at the University Hospital they couldn't help him either, even though they had tried to do so shortly before his death of necrosis.

All the old furniture, even the big mahogany table, had been sold long ago by then. Arthur had only asked for the Tantalus, in which the golden fluid was evaporating more and more. The old Shabbos lamp from Endingen, about which Mimi and Chanele had never been able to agree, now hung over Hinda and Zalman's dinner table in Rotwandstrasse.

Chanele hadn't given up her butter knife, and held it menacingly in her fist as if arming herself for an attack.

'Why didn't you bring the children?' she asked.

'I have no children, Mama.'

'You could have brought them.'

She had lost none of her persistence. Much else that had seemed exactly as inseparable a part of her had flaked away from her without really changing her, just as one can still discern the broad form in a weathered sandstone monument.

Physically, too, Chanele had become smaller. She had complained about this change, three and four times – just as she said everything three and four times, without being aware of the repetition – she had complained that the hem of her skirt dragged on the ground and she tripped over it, the fabric must have stretched, poor quality, she would complain to the supplier. François, who had become a good son now that Chanele was no longer aware of it, had finally had an exact copy of the old dress made in his tailor's workshop, cut slightly smaller, but no different in any other way, the same severe black, with the same old-fashioned lace trim around the collar. To make the new material familiar to her, he dabbed it himself with the expensive eau de cologne that Chanele had been given by Janki in Westerland that time, and which she had used even since his death. That way she could go on dressing as if she were going to work at the Modern Emporium and not just to breakfast at a table for six in the Jewish old people's home.

'Why didn't you bring the children?'

'I have no children, Mama.'

'You could have brought your wife.'

'I'm not married.'

Chanele smiled slyly; she had known that, of course, and had just wanted to test his memory. A little game to see if the boy was listening.

'Of course not. Shmul is the married one.'

As ever, it took Arthur a few moments to work out who his mother meant by that name. It was a long time since François had been called that.

'At least he always brings his wife.'

'Mina is dead, Mama.'

'He brings her,' Chanele insisted, and Arthur didn't contradict her any further. Perhaps, in her world, she was right.

'Hinda's married too.' You had to know Chanele very well to hear the timid request for confirmation in the apparent statements of the obvious that she made like this one. In her better moments, she knew that there was much that she no longer knew, but the attitude that she always preserved was part of the core of her being, and would probably be the very last to go. Only her eyebrows betrayed her: every time she worried away at some uncertainty, she raised them quizzically. Over the years the unbroken line had turned white, and in her wrinkled face, because Chanele still wore the same dark sheitel, it looked as artificial as the stuck-on cotton-wool eyebrows of the St Nicholases who had just paraded through Zurich.

'Yes,' Arthur confirmed. 'Hinda is married.'

'And she has children.'

'How many?' He couldn't help asking the trick question.

'Not as many as I would like,' said his mother. A triumphant smile darted over her face. She wasn't as easy to catch out as that.

'What's the eldest one called?'

'Tell them to bring me my breakfast.' In a gesture reminiscent of old Salomon Meijer — except that apart from her there was no one left who remembered him — she rubbed her hands together as if washing them without water, reached for her knife again and drummed impatiently on the oilcloth with the other. When Arthur asked her for a second time what her eldest grandson was called, she didn't listen.

Didn't want to listen.

In January, for Chanele's eighty-fifth birthday, they had all come to the old people's home in Lengnau. Ruben, the son of Zalman and Hinda, had been there too, although without his family. He had been worried that the German authorities, who were coming up with fresh kinds of anti-Semitic bullying every day, wouldn't let him enter the country again. A few years previously he had taken a post as rabbi in Halberstadt, a centre of Jewish Orthodoxy, where he held the office of deputy and, he hoped, future successor of the famous Dr Philipp Frankl at the Klaus Synagogue. His wife, who looked eternally youthful even under her sheitel, and who was only ever called Lieschen, even by her own children, was a Steinberg from Berlin; Ruben had met her when attending the rabbinical seminar there. They had four children, three boys and a girl, a fact upon which Zalman tended to comment by saying that his son had outdone him in this respect at least.

Ruben could only spend three days at home. A longer absence would have been construed as definitive emigration, and he wouldn't have been allowed back in the country. Germany was trying to get rid of its Jews, and using its bureaucracy to that end. They had told him over and over again not to stay in that dangerous country, and to come back to Switzerland with his family, but Ruben, who had even assumed German citizenship as a precondition of his office, and renounced his Swiss nationality, wanted on no account to leave his community in the lurch at this difficult time. 'They're bullying us, of course,' he said, ' but we Jews are used to that. It's not as if they're about to kill us.'

'Ruben!' said Chanele with sudden recognition. 'Ruben and Lea and Rachel. Three children.' Sometimes a window opened unexpectedly in her head and then, for a few minutes or, if you were lucky, half an hour, she was almost herself again. 'Why are we actually still sitting here?' she asked impatiently. 'Breakfast is long past. You're always dawdling.'

She threw the knife on the table and said, as strict as she had often had to be when she was Madame Meijer, 'When they clear away they always leave half of it there. I shall attend to it later. Not now. We should be going.'

It wasn't a memory that made her say that. A coat that seemed familiar to her lay ready on the back of the chair, and she had drawn her conclusion from that. Time and again she managed to bridge the gaps in her reality with such deductions. These little successes made her quite boisterous, so for once she dared to wander out quite far on the black ice of confusing facts.

'Are we going in the Buchet?' she asked.

'Not quite, Mama.'

Arthur didn't really need a car. His practice kept him busy, but most of his patients lived nearby, in a shabbosdik walking distance around the new synagogue in Freigutstrasse in Zurich Enge. There were so many of them crammed into the area that neighbours said, 'God must have sent them here for our sins.' So he didn't need a car for his patient visits, and he could have come to Lengnau on the coach. No, if he was honest, Arthur had bought the car out of pure pleasure, had convinced himself that one could afford to treat oneself every once in a while, if one worked all day and had no family.

As if a car could replace a family.

He had chosen a new Italian model, a tiny Fiat with room for only two people. There was a third seat only when the weather was fine; then you could roll back the window and the extra passenger in the back could sit more or less straight. The car had been painted bright red, and Arthur was insanely proud of its thirteen horsepower.

Chanele sat beside him, her hands folded girlishly in her lap in accordance with the eternal diminutive of her first name. It was how she would have sat in a carriage next to a strange coachman, taking inconspicuous care not to touch him. Before he set off, Arthur leaned over and kissed her on the cheek. The familiar, dear smell of her skin was overlaid with something that reminded him of the sweat-drenched sheets of fever patients.

'Ruben, Lea, Rachel. Ruben, Lea, Rachel.' Chanele sang the three rediscovered names over and over to herself, a descending triad.

'Lea is called Rosenthal now,' Arthur tried to help her. 'Do you remember her husband? Adolf?'

That was two decades ago now. It had even been before the end of the war, a few weeks before Lea's – and of course Rachel's – twentieth birthday. The whole family had been surprised that she, always the more reticent and, if one was going to be honest, also the less pretty of the two, came under the chuppah so much sooner than her lively twin sister. Dr Adolf Rosenthal, her husband, was a few years older than she, but today everyone who saw them together thought they were the same age. Perhaps that was down to the thick glasses that Lea now needed.

Adolf was a maths and geometry teacher at the Cantonal School, a job that suited him down to the ground. He loved precision, in his convictions as much as in his habits. Lunch, for example, had to start at exactly ten minutes past twelve, so that one could set one's cutlery down at precisely half past, to hear the radio news. Nuances were not his thing; as far as he was concerned there was a wrong and a right opinion about everything, and he was able to put forward the correct one in long monologues with irrefutable logic as long as one accepted his premises. So he was the only one in the family to have read *Mein Kampf* from the first page to the last and drawn hope from it. A system, he argued, that was constructed upon a pamphlet of so many inner contradictions, was simply unsustainable. When he lectured away, Lea just raised her eyebrows and at such moments looked like her grandmother Chanele.

They had a son called Hillel. According to his papers his name was Heinrich, but quite unlike his Uncle François, he only liked to be addressed by his Jewish name. He was an enthusiastic Zionist, and was already making plans for his aliya, which led to violent arguments with his very Swiss father. The worst blow for Adolf was that after secondary school Hillel refused to learn one of the usual professions of the community. 'In Eretz they don't need accountants or sales representatives,' he said. 'Eretz' means simply 'land', but for a Zionist there is no other land than this one. 'Farmers are what they need in Eretz,' said Hillel, and registered for the agricultural school in Strickhof, where as a child of the city and the first Jew in the school's history he was marvelled at like a calf with two heads.

'Ruben, Lea, Rachel. Ruben, Lea, Rachel.' Chanele's thoughts had got into a circular track; they chased after one another and couldn't keep up. Arthur knew that this could go on for hours. Sometimes she sang songs like that until she was hoarse. He braked sharply and then accelerated again straight away, so that the car gave a sudden jolt. The monotonous song broke off and Chanele said crossly, 'You should fire this fellow Landolt. His driving is very erratic.'

'What about Rachel? Does she visit you?'

'Of course. She always brings her children along. Not like you.'

Rachel had no children.

She was single, and the family was even more surprised by that than by Lea getting married so quickly. With her adventurous openness Rachel had attracted men from an early age, and soon fallen in love for the first time, and then a second, third and fourth time. Nothing had ever come of it. She had, Chanele had put it when she was still Chanele, fallen in love not with men, but with being in love, and once that first euphoria had passed she could not be satisfied with everyday happiness. Now she was nearly forty, an age that no woman likes to pass through unaccompanied, and she became irritable when Hillel called her 'Aunt Rachel'. Her vociferously demonstrated love of life – one wasn't living in the nineteenth century, after all, and didn't have to hide oneself away as a single woman – had lately assumed a shrill undertone. She worked in Zalman's clothes factory, a business that had effectively founded itself a few years previously, and as she liked to stress, she was completely indispensable there.

They had now reached the cemetery, a little way off the road on a wooded slope. Arthur wanted to help his mother up, but she turned her head away so as not to see the offered arm. 'I'm not an old woman,' the gesture said. 'A Madame Hanna Meijer does not need any help.'

A hint of snow still lay on the solid, frozen ground. Chanele poked search-ingly around among the graves, murmuring quietly to herself; it might have been a prayer, or just the attempt to conjure up a forgotten name. She walked unheedingly past the double grave of Salomon and Golde, which she had vis-ited so often. Arthur, who didn't want to move too far away from her, hardly had time to bend down and, as custom dictates, set a pebble down on the grave.

Chanele stopped among some strange graves and said in a tiny, helplessly confused voice, 'They aren't here any more. Someone has jumbled every-thing up.'

'Who are you looking for, Mama?'

'Mimi and Pinchas. I married her husband, but she was still my friend.'

Sometimes Chanele was very confused.

'Uncle Melnitz lay in bed with me...' She broke off abruptly, looked at her son with empty eyes and asked reproachfully, 'Why didn't you bring the children?'

Aunt Mimi and Uncle Pinchas had died of the same illness within for-ty-eight hours of each other. That was in the winter of 1918, when the wave of Spanish flu had luckily seemed to have ebbed away, and had then swept across Europe for a second time, and with twice the force. Arthur remembered that time as if it were a bad dream. He had really sacrificed himself for his patients, and had still been able to do nothing for many but close their eyes. Mimi had died first, and Arthur had thoughtfully had to lie to Pinchas, whom he liked very much, for another two days, and told him that she was on the way to recovery. Now they lay side by side in Steinkluppe cemetery, and if Arthur had known them at all, Pinchas was still incredibly happy that they were so close even after his death.

Désirée had taken over the grocery shop, and ran it even today. She was still unmarried. In her case, unlike Rachel's, this seemed quite natural.

Arthur took his mother by the hand. She allowed him to lead her like a little girl to the broad stone with 'Jean Meijer' carved into half of it, while the other half had waited more than fifteen years for Chanele. 'Here lies Papa.'

'His leg hurts,' said Chanele, and was quite happy when Arthur confirmed that yes, that was right, Janki had always had problems with his leg.

'That was from the war,' said Chanele.

'Yes, Mama, Papa was in the war.'

He put a pebble in her hand. She didn't set it down on the grave, but put it in her mouth, sucked on it for a while and spat it out again. 'Janki doesn't like the taste of it,' she said.

Arthur wanted to give her a hug, but she pulled away and looked at him searchingly. 'Where is my father?' she asked.

'You mean Uncle Salomon?'

'My father's name isn't Salomon.' She beckoned him over, as one does when one wants to confide a particularly secret secret in someone. 'His name is Menachem.'

There was no one in the family called Menachem.

'Menachem Bär.'

'Bär?'

'Yes,' said Chanele. 'Bär, Bär, Bär, Bär.'

'The journey must have taken its toll,' thought Arthur.

'And do you know what he's doing?' Chanele giggled, a little girl telling a rude joke that she doesn't really understand. 'He dies. He dies every day.'

'Let's go back to the home, Mama.'

Chanele shook his hand away. She felt more clear and alive than she had for ages, and she didn't want that to be cut short. 'Menachem Bär,' she said. 'It's a secret, but you're old enough to learn it. After all, my father is your... your...' She closed her eyes firmly, trying so hard to think the idea through to the end, but she couldn't work out how her father could be related to her son. 'His name is Menachem Bär,' she repeated at last, and was glad to be quite sure about one point, 'and my mother's name is Sarah. Menachem and Sarah. Menachem and Sarah.' She started singing again, one name in a high note, the other in a low one, and even stamped her foot on the hard ground as if she were about to start dancing.

He would have to get her back to the home soon.

'It's too cold for you here, Mama,' he said. She didn't hear him.

'You can tell your children,' said Chanele and patted his hand. 'You need to know where you come from. One of them always marched up and down with a rifle. But it wasn't a real rifle. Dr Hellstiedl says none of them are dangerous.'

Arthur took off his glasses and rubbed the bridge of his knows. He knew the doctors who looked after the inmates of the old people's home, and none of them was called Hellstiedl.

'There were poplars on either side,' said Chanele, 'and it was hot. It's easier if you count your footsteps. Forty-five. Forty-six. A million.'

'I'm sure lunch will be ready at the home.'

'One of them raked the leaves.' Chanele had started giggling again. 'But there were no leaves.'

He tried to lead his mother to the way out, but she resisted, as violently as before, when the waitress tried to take her table cloth away. 'We haven't been to his grave yet,' she said. 'He's celebrating Bris there. Dr Hellstiedl is invited too. They're going to have a party, and everyone will sing. Menachem and Sarah. Menachem and Sarah. Menachem and Sarah.'

At last, because there was no other way of calming her down, he led her to a strange grave, it must have been one of the first in the cemetery, because the stone was weathered and half sunk into the ground. Perhaps it was one of the ones rescued from the old Judenäule in the Rhine. The inscription had long been overgrown with moss, and could no longer be deciphered.

'Here, Mama. This is the grave of Menachem and Sarah.'

'You see.' Chanele had the triumphant expression of someone who has been proved right. 'You wanted to lie to me. They all want to lie to me, but I know.' She bent down to the ground, she did it all by herself, even though it was hard for her, picked up a pebble and set it down on the strange grave. 'If you touch him,' she said, 'his skin is like paper.'

Then she accepted his help, let him lead her back to the car and would probably have liked to be picked up and carried. Arthur wouldn't even have found that very difficult. There was not much left of his mother.

On the way back she sang both songs at the same time, 'Ruben, Lea, Rachel' and 'Menachem and Sarah'. Arthur could not have said what made him sadder, that she didn't recognise her grandchildren, or that she remembered a father she had never had.

Back at the old people's home he took off her coat and Chanele sat down, rubbing her hands against each other, at one of the empty tables. 'It will soon be breakfast,' she said. 'My treat. Why didn't you bring the children?'

56

It was an act of stupidity, of course it was, a loutish prank which one could not tolerate as headmaster, but it was also the kind of loutish prank that would be transformed within ten or twenty years into a heroic deed, something that you could tell and tell again at the old-boys' table, before clapping the boys who hadn't had the chance to see such things sympathetically on the shoulder and saying, 'Ah yes, that's the kind of thing we used to get up to in the good old Strickhof.'

So Headmaster Gerster struggled to maintain a severe expression and gave the pair a stern talking-to. They would be ruthlessly expelled from the school, both of them, if ever, just once, he heard the slightest thing. He would drive them both firmly into the ground. And besides: they should be ashamed of themselves, because the things that could have come of such a piece of coltish nonsense – what was he saying, coltish, a colt had far more intelligence than the two of them put together! – the things that could have happened hadn't even occurred to them. They probably both thought the Lord God had given them their heads to smoke cigars with rather than to think.

Böhni, standing to attention, a great lump of a young man, let the storm pass over him. He was wearing short trousers, as he did in almost all weathers, and had even rolled up the sleeves of his grey shirt. And the schoolroom wasn't heated, it was Sunday, and at agricultural college you don't have money to burn. Gerster had been sitting comfortably at home in the warm parlour, chatting to a visitor, when the phone had rung, just as his wife was serving up the plum tart.

The young hooligans!

Böhni's face had reddened slightly, Gerster noticed, but certainly not because he was ashamed, and not because of the cold either. He always looked like that. It made Headmaster Gerster, who liked to theorise about physiognomy and body language, think he was short-tempered.

That Rosenthal, on the other hand ... He couldn't work that boy out at all. The fact that he wanted to study agriculture, of all things, when no one else in his family had anything to do with it. There was only supposed to have been one cattle trader in the family, or at least that was what Rosenthal had told him. But his father was a scholar, and they usually sent their sons to the Gymnasium, and farming wasn't really in the blood of the Jews. He was a hard worker, you had to give him that, even though he had to learn a few things that the others had known from childhood. The way he'd picked up the scythe the first time, as if it was going to bite him! They had also laughed long and hard at him for that. He took their jibes in good part, and never even complained about the blisters on his fine city-boy hands. Headmaster Gerster liked students who gritted their teeth. Agriculture wasn't crocheting.

His stance was quite different from the other boy's as well. Arms folded and legs far apart, they way you stand when you want to say, 'No one knocks me over, just him try.' Not exactly challenging, he couldn't be accused of that, but he certainly was hard-headed. He was the kind of person who didn't put up with any nonsense, and that was how the unfortunate matter had come about.

'Idiots!' yelled Herr Gerster. 'Snot-nosed brats!' But his heart wasn't really in his lecture. What that Rosenthal had done was one hell of a thing.

It was this: even though they had their own mechanised testing station, they didn't set much store by modern technology at the Strickhof. Kudi Lampertz, the deputy head who also taught arable farming, even raged against the modern fad for tractors – 'As if a small farmer in Säuliamt could afford such an expensive thing!' – and insisted on his students continuing to learn to plough with a four-in-hand, even if it looked a little old-fashioned, particularly on the Strickhof farm where the city had grown so much that the agricultural college was now in the middle of residential buildings. They hadn't been able to resist buying a truck for ever, but one old tradition had survived: on Sunday, when there wasn't much traffic in town, they hitched up two horses and transported the milk-cans on the box-cart to the association dairy. The task was in great demand. A coach-man like that, with a coloured ribbon on his whip, cut a fine figure, and if you whistled at girls from the high box, hardly any of them turned away insulted.

Today the job had fallen to Walter Böhni and Hillel Rosenthal, Böhni because he had learned to drive a coach on his parents' farm, and Rosenthal because he wanted to practise. They put the more and less experienced students together for the sake of camaraderie, and also because the Canton never provided enough teaching posts.

So no one else had been there, but Gerster's knowledge of human nature allowed him to imagine how it might have happened. Of course Böhni had acted the expert, and set himself up as the man in charge, had given the new boy the lowly job of curry-combing the horses and chewed his head off when the stencil slipped and the checker-board pattern on its crop wasn't clearly visible. He would also have kindly assigned him the task of harnessing up, but then of course he would have taken the reins himself and played the big master-coachman, all the way across Schaffhauserplatz and the Kornhaus Bridge. On Langstrasse, Gerster didn't even need to ask, and Böhni wouldn't have admitted it either, he had doubtless crossed the Railway Bridge at a thundering gallop. That was expressly forbidden, but they all did it, and you can't be that strict with grown adults.

But then again...

'Riff-raff!' shouted Gerster. 'Damned day labourers!' 'Day labourers' was more or less the worst curse you could hurl at a farmer's son, and Böhni actually flinched. Rosenthal, the city-dweller, didn't bat an eyelid.

Then the following had happened outside the dairy: when the full milk churns had been offloaded and the empty ones loaded on – Böhni would generously have allowed his companion to perform that task too – and Rosenthal was to take the reins for the return journey, Böhni had probably needled him a bit too much, or rather prodded him with a pitchfork, because delicate weapons were not his style. What had been said, and whether it had concerned a lack of horse sense or something entirely different, neither Böhni nor Rosenthal wished to confess, and Herr Gerster was basically satisfied with that. Some things are better sorted out in private, with fists. It certainly had something to do with the fact that Rosenthal was a Jew, and that Böhni was wearing a grey shirt, not exactly like the ones worn by members of the fascist Fröntler movement, but the same colour, so at any rate Rosenthal felt obliged to demonstrate his skill as a driver, so he took the team back to the Strickhof not by the prescribed, direct route, but...

'Stupid oafs!' yelled Gerster, and even he realised that this last insult had sounded a bit feeble.

He had driven right into the centre of the city, that lunatic, which of course wasn't allowed at all. And Böhni had let him do it, had just let him run headlong into disaster, rather than assuming responsibility as the more experienced of the pair. Responsibility! But then that was a word that had probably been scrapped from their dictionary. That they had had more luck than intelligence and nothing really serious had happened was a matter beyond their control, which meant that they were both equally culpable, regardless of who was holding the reins in the end. Cling together, swing together.

Herr Gerster couldn't even think, he raged, about how it would have reflected on the school and on himself if things had gone badly, all the reports that people would have had to write, and the explanations. And, almost worst of all, the people who had been trying to move the Strickhof away from the city for such a long time, who wanted to win building land where there were now only fields and orchards, they would have had their arguments served up to them on a plate, there it was again, they had said, plain as your face, an agricultural business and a big city, the two things just don't go together.

He looked for a sufficiently violent insult, couldn't find one and instead brought the flat of his hand down on his desk, so that it echoed around the empty room like a cannon-shot. A headmaster's life was far from easy.

And at home they would be eating up all that delicious plum tart.

The lout had ridden around the back to the station and then crossed to the other side and into Bahnhofstrasse, which was wide enough for him to have negotiated if necessary, but then he had suddenly turned off to the left into Rennweg, and then into Fortunagasse, which was so narrow that even the King of England's personal coachman would have thought twice.

'Why did you go there, of all places?' roared Gerster, and Rosenthal spread his arms and said, 'No reason.'

That was, of course, a lie. Hillel hadn't taken that path by chance at all, but he wasn't going to let Gerstli – as the headmaster was secretly known – in on that one. In Fortunagasse was the 'Beth Hechalutz', a house in which two dozen young pioneers, the Chaluzim, were waiting for the opportunity to be able to travel on to Palestine. They were all refugees, Germans and Poles expelled from Germany; they lived there as a collective, exactly as it would be later in the kibbutz, they paid the bit of money that they had earned somewhere into a kitty, cooked in a communal kitchen and went on talking until far into the night about how they would build a Jewish state, and a socialist one at that. On Sunday, Hillel knew, they would all be at home, it was too cold to go for a walk and no one could afford to go to the café.

All of them – that is: even a certain Malka Sofer from Warsaw, who was already twenty-two and thus unattainable for a seventeen-year-old, but who had beautiful black curls and a very serious face on which Hillel would have loved to put a smile. But for that to happen, she would have had to notice him, and what better means could there be to that end than to drive past her in a coach, so to speak, with a team of horses and a coloured ribbon on his whip?

He had planned to stop on the Rennweg, where, a bit further on, even an unpractised driver could have turned his team without much difficulty. There was a big brass bell fixed to the box, the kind they have on ships; the police demanded a warning signal in traffic, and a horn really wouldn't have been right on a horse-drawn vehicle. He would ring the bell, he had worked out, and then everyone in the Beth Hechalutz would look out of the window, even Malka, he would wave nonchalantly with his whip and then later, when they met on their own – he was already working out plans about how he would organise this – they would have an ice-breaker, and once something has begun there is always the possibility that it might continue.

But when he looked into Fortunagasse, there was a group of men, ten or twenty, in such haste it was impossible to count them. From up there on the box you could look out on everything as if from a balcony, they were wearing their grey Fröntler shirts, and stood there in rank and file, looking almost military. They also had their flag with them, the white bars of the Swiss cross extended to the edge against the red background. They were standing outside the house of the Chaluzim and shouting something that Hillel couldn't, or wouldn't, at first understand. It was a very simple line, which they were shouting over and over again: 'Get back to Poland, damn your eyes!' One of them had a landsknecht field drum, and was striking out the beat on it. They were demonstrating against his people, and Böhni sat next to him and had a great grin on his face that seemed to say, 'You're in the shit not just because you took a forbidden detour, but just generally!'

Hillel hadn't thought, he hadn't thought at all, in that respect Gerstli was completely right, he had just tugged on the reins and shouted 'Giddy up!' and somehow done everything right, better than he had ever managed in the practice yard. The horses had turned into the Fortunagasse, had started galloping on the thoroughfare that was far too narrow for them, he had struck at them with his whip and rung the bell like the fire service in an emergency. The Fröntlers had scattered, into people's doorways and against the wall where it goes up to the Lindenhof. The flag-bearer dropped his bit of cloth, and how the drummer and his drum managed to get to safety Hillel couldn't quite say. But no one had been hurt, otherwise they wouldn't have been standing in front of the headmaster right now getting a telling off, they would have been told to pack their things together long ago.

'Even that would have been worth it,' thought Hillel.

He had had no time to look up, so he didn't know whether the Chaluzim had really been standing at the window, and whether Malka had been there. It had all happened far too quickly, he had just had time to hold on to the reins and hold back the horses. It had happened and nothing could be done about it, they were past the house, and in their wake the first of them were already shaking menacing fists. Only then did it occur to him that you can't keep going at the end of Fortunagasse, because there's just that steep path off to the left, the one with the steps that leads down to the Limmat. He had tugged like mad on the reins, had tried somehow to stop the horses, but the nags had long since developed a mind of their own and could no longer be controlled, at least not by him. And Böhni, who might have been able to do something, sat there petrified with fear, his eyes wide open and his mouth as well, as if he wanted to scream and couldn't remember how to do it.

Then, quite naturally, the horses had turned off to the left all by themselves, at a perfect, even gallop of the kind that you learn at coach-driving school, except that the pupils there would never have been allowed to take a bend so sharply, and certainly not at that speed. The cart leaned to the side, it balanced on only two wheels and would have tipped over had the passage not been so narrow that it scraped along a bay window on the ground floor and righted itself again. At the back, an empty milk churn fell from the cart, and then the wheels were already clattering down the steps, bumping so hard with each one that they were nearly thrown from the box.

Somehow the cart managed to come to a standstill, Hillel couldn't have said how. Perhaps Kudi Lampertz was right when he said, as he always did, 'Just let the horses get on with it, they're cleverer than you are.' All of a sudden it was completely still. Only the milk churn rolled very slowly from step to step behind them, clanking as if calling out, 'Wait for me, I'm coming!'

Only then had he done what he should have done long ago: applied the handbrake. He had climbed down from the box and tended to the horses. They were sweat-drenched and steaming and were foaming at the mouth, but they hadn't been hurt – Lampertz would have killed him! – none of them was limping, and eventually, when his heart had stopped thumping quite so hard, Hillel was able to drive on, right onto the Rudolf Brun Bridge, left onto the Limmatquai and then uphill to Schaffhauserplatz and back to the Strickhof.

There, alerted by telephone, Herr Gerster was already waiting for them, gave them an initial earful and then, as they were rubbing the horses dry, walked impatiently up and down, firmly resolved to give them the mother of all bollockings, which they would never forget as long as they lived.

'Sons of bitches blithering bloody idiots!' yelled the headmaster. 'Why did you drive down there?'

'No reason,' said Hillel.

That story would be told for a long time to come, thought Gerster. You would have to be a dashed good horseman to come out of a hussar's trick like that unharmed. He went on swearing a little longer, as his office decreed, but he was only doing it automatically now, and even looking at his watch.

The punishment he was giving them was a harmless one, just as thunder and lightning sometimes crashes like mad until you think the whole harvest is lost, and then there's only a little shower of rain. They were to sort out the milk-cart, straight away. The scratches would have to be painted over where it had scraped along the wall, and they would have to do that together, to learn that camaraderie was the name of the game here at the Strickhof – 'camara-derie, damn it all!' – and if anything, the slightest thing, reached his ears, he would tear their heads off with his own bare hands.

He said again, 'Sons of bitches bloody blithering stupid idiots!', left them standing there and went back to his plum tart.

When the door slammed shut behind Gerster, Böhni was still standing to attention. Hillel turned to him and said, 'Amod no'ach!' He grinned when Böhni looked at him uncomprehendingly. In the Hashomer Haza'ir, the Zionist youth association, they liked to put on military airs, and that was the command when you were allowed to stand at ease at mifkad, or muster.

'But you'll paint the box,' said Böhni.

'Why?'

'Because it's all your fault.'

'Camaraderie, Walter! Have you forgotten? Camaraderie is quite the thing at the Strickhof, damn it all!' Hillel was so drunk on all the excitement and its happy outcome that he was even copying Gerstli.

The cart was already outside on the gravel, and that was quite sensible. Mending scratches is delicate work, and done better by daylight.

In the shed there were two brushes and a tin of green paint.

Kudi Lampertz had arrived quite unexpectedly; the headmaster had probably alerted him by telephone. Now he behaved as if he were only briefly interrupting his Sunday stroll, and watched their work with his hands propped on his hips. 'The farmer works with his hands, not his mouth,' was one of his favourite sayings, so Böhni and Rosenthal only went on arguing very quietly.

'You're a prick,' whispered Böhni.

'You know all about pricks,' Hillel whispered back.

'What do you mean?'

'Looking at your shirt...'

'I can wear whatever I like.'

'You know why Fröntler shirts are such a dirty grey colour? Because character shows through.'

Böhni would have liked to floor him with a quicker answer, but none came to mind. 'They're going to beat the crap out of you,' he whispered instead.

First they'll have to find out who it was.'

'Somebody might tell them.'

'Are you going to be the snitch?'

Böhni didn't reply, just assumed a devious expression that was supposed to mean: Jews always thought they were the only clever ones, but other people were just as good at settling scores.

'Is that your plan?'

'And if it was?'

'I'd have to have a word with my uncle.'

'Eh?'

'He's a famous wrestler. In the Jewish gymnastics association. Have you never heard of Arthur Meijer? If he and his troop turn up, you'll be picking up your bones one at a time.'

'Never put anything past the Jews,' thought Böhni, that was what Rolf Henne always said in the Front. They might have some kind of secret fighting troop that you had to keep an eye out for. Why else would Rosenthal be grinning in spite of the threat of a good Swiss kicking? He couldn't have known that Hillel was only amusing himself with the idea of his peaceful, short-sighted uncle as a dangerous street-fighter.

Walter Böhni wasn't a bad person. Having grown up on a little farm near Flaach, in the middle of wine country, he had had to work hard even as a child, particularly in the spring, when the nobs in the city wanted their asparagus and people in the country had to break their backs to pick it. For him, agricultural college was a great chance to get on in life and amount to something, so he couldn't stand people like Rosenthal, who only ever did things on a whim and didn't really need to. He wanted to go to Palestine and farm there, he had said on the first day of school when they were all supposed to explain what they expected of the Strickhof. And everyone knew that there was nothing in Palestine but desert and bogs and nothing to farm at all.

Böhni's parents had always worked hard, they'd grafted, and often didn't know where they would get the next bit of meat to go with their potatoes. It wasn't fair, and Böhni, who was also a thinker in his way, had been grateful when someone had given him an explanation for it. The Jews were to blame, with their department stores and banks, whose sole purpose was to suck the common man dry and keep him in his place. He hadn't joined the National Front himself, you had to go to too many meetings and marches, but he read their paper regularly, and thought everything in it made perfect sense. Perhaps it wasn't such a bad thing if the comrades were kept informed about what the Jews were planning.

So he whispered, 'What sort of house is that, in fact, on Fortunagasse?'

'It's full of people who want exactly what your friends are demanding so noisily: to get out of Switzerland as quickly as possible.'

'To Poland?'

'Much further East.'

'So why did they even...?'

He fell silent, because Lampertz was coming closer. Normally Lampertz was more of a ramrod-straight marcher, but now he strolled over in an exaggeratedly relaxed manner, to stress that it was really, really just by chance that he had happened to drop in here at the Strickhof on his day off.

'Do you think the paint's all right like that, or does it need another coat?' asked Hillel.

'Two at least. No bodging here.' He stood beside them for a moment and then said, 'Did you actually drive down those steps with a team of horses?'

'I'm sorry, Herr Lampertz.'

'And rightly so. But I'd have to say: well done! I wouldn't have thought you capable of it. Not even you would have managed that one, Böhni.'

Zalman Kamionker had come to his clothes factory like the Virgin to the Child or, to use his own simile, like the patriarch Abraham to his son Isaac, at an age when such a change in his life was no longer to be expected. His work with the Relief Committee for refugees from Galicia had forced him to become a labour broker, which had at first, during the Great War, not been a very difficult job for an experienced negotiator. Active service and the border watch meant that there was a universal shortage of manpower, and anyone who was willing to put in a bit of elbow grease was welcome. Over time, the committee gradually started falling asleep. It only became active occasionally, when there was acute emergency, and took account of its meagre holdings once a year, a task that Frau Okun was more than capable of doing all on her own. Then, in the economic crisis of the early 1930s, unemployment started rising faster and faster, and the committee had to be reactivated. The crisis was a particularly serious blow to the Eastern Jews, whose origins could still clearly be heard and who, to be honest, were not held in particularly great esteem by Swiss Jews of long standing. These refugees, who had in fact become relatively well acclimatised in Switzerland, had suddenly reverted to being foreign scoundrels, who were overrunning the country and taking away the few remaining jobs. When people were fired, they were the first to go, and then who did they go to with their problems? To Zalman, of course, and he didn't send them away, even though Hinda observed tartly that his readiness to help others had also cost him his own parnassah. He approached all kinds of people for work, and because there was none to be found, he decided to create some.

As he had once done in his time in the Golden Medina, he did the rounds of the department stores and offered to supply the buyers with off-the-peg clothes, exactly according to their wishes and cheaper than any other suppliers. He just wanted to create a bit of employment at a time when people were already standing on street corners holding cardboard signs, hawking themselves around as a shmattes dealer would hawk an old pair of trousers. If someone had told him it would make him the balebos of his own company, he would have told them he was meshuga. Zalman Kamionker as a capitalist? You might as soon have had Joseph Goebbels as a minyan man.

The first order came from François, whose department store had run out of warm coats after a sudden cold spell in the spring. The order, François made a point of stressing, had nothing at all to do with charity, what would someone baptised be doing supporting Jewish refugees? He was a businessman, and in business neither Jewish charity nor Christian love of one's fellow man had any place. If the coats delivered were not the very best quality, Zalman was never to show his face there again, was that clear? But he did place the order.

That was how it began.

In the first year he employed people as the work came in, by the day or even by the hour. They each worked at home, practically operating the sewing machine with one foot and rocking the cradle with the other. As they were all sewing for dear life, the working day could sometimes last fourteen hours or even more. Zalman often felt like an exploiter, Zalman of all people, the trade unionist who had been foremost in fighting for a forty-eight hour week in the 1918 General Strike, and who had, of course, therefore promptly lost his job. At first they delivered only coats – Zalman was very well acquainted with those from his time in America – and they were later joined by dresses and dressing gowns, and soon the KK monogram appeared on every item of monogrammed clothing. KK was actually supposed to stand for Konfektion Kamionker – Konfektion meaning 'ready-made' – but the workers had their own understanding of the letters. For them KK meant, quite simply: Koschere Kleiderfabrik – kosher clothes factory.

Strangely enough, the final breakthrough came via the customs of a continent far away. A German refugee, the former owner of a fashion shop in Magdeburg, had by chance been given a visa to move to Kenya, where there was an apparently limitless need for cotton clothes of size 50 and up, with brightly coloured polka-dot fabrics most in demand. When, because of bureaucratic difficulties, the man was stuck in Zurich for a few weeks before travelling back to Kenya, Zalman's committee had supported him – it had stopped restricting its charity only to Galicians long ago – and out of gratitude he now remembered the kosher clothes factory. There were more and more repeat orders, which enabled KK to rent its own business properties in Wollishofen, and take on its first permanent staff.

At first Zalman didn't work for the company himself, or else did his work unpaid. Even though he regularly fought with his employers, he had always managed to find a job, and he wouldn't have thought of taking someone else's job away from him. But the more successful the business became, the harder it was to run it casually and just as an act of kindness, and eventually Zalman had had to come to terms with the fact that he was now the company director whether he liked it or not. To remain true to his principles in at least one respect, at first he wanted to pay himself no more than he paid one of his cutters, but then Hinda, who never normally got involved in his job, had made a terrible fuss. Did he really think he would get a better seat in Gan Eden, she demanded to know, if he was satisfied with seventy rappen an hour, and would he please explain to her how such starvation wages were to pay for the suits and the good shirts that his new role would demand of him. That was almost the worst thing for Zalman: he would now have to put on a tie every day, because he would be dealing with customers all the time. He was a peaceful man, but it made him furious every time.

The argument that convinced him in the end was the fact that Rachel was working in the factory as well. There was no possible reason why Zalman, who worked his back off for the company around the clock should not earn more than his daughter, who as office manager did nothing but sit on her tochus and order people around.

Meanwhile he had got quite used to being the Herr Direktor. The kosher clothes factory was a recognised business, they worked on *Deutschland* brand central bobbin sewing machines, and used electric irons with regulating switches. But what was much more important: they provided work for almost thirty people. The staff register included a 'directrice' for the designs, fourteen stitchers, six cutters, four ironers, three people in the office, an apprentice, a travelling salesman and their own model. Only two employees were not Jewish: the directrice, one Fräulein Bodmer, who visited all the fashion shows so that their designs very quickly followed current trends, and the mannequin, a tearful peroxide blonde called Blandine Flückiger, who set a great deal of store by her sensitive soul and had to be consoled almost every day over some slight or other.

Rachel, who ruled the office with an iron hand, regularly argued with her, just as she had argued with her two predecessors. She was not at all happy with the idea of a silly trollop of just twenty-four being sweet-talked by all the men just because she had a cute punim and was a size 38. And besides, Rachel was almost sure of it, there was something going on between Blandine and Joni Leibowitz, the travelling salesman. By now the KK's clientele stretched as far as St Gallen, Bern and Basle, and everywhere the buyers wanted to have the new designs presented on the living model. Joni Leibowitz and she often travelled alone together in the car, and everybody knew what models were like.

The deeper reason for her animosity lay in the fact that Rachel, so many years ago that it wasn't true, had herself once taken an interest in Joni Leibowitz. Back in the war, and before he drank himself a little petit-bourgeois belly, he had been a handsome man in his uniform, a stationery representative by profession; only later had he switched to the shmattes profession. In those days he had in fact danced attendance to Désirée, but because no one had had a sensible word out of her since Alfred's death, he slowly lost interest in her and her grocer's shop and started looking elsewhere. Rachel and he had gone dancing together a few times, and once – God knows, one had been young and stupid – she had let him kiss her, and he had immediately tried to put his hand under her blouse. Which she hadn't let him do, she hadn't been as young and stupid as that even when she was in nappies.

With each year that she herself remained single, Rachel found more and more fault in married and attractive women.

She herself had nothing more exciting to do than go to the office every day, which was why she claimed to do it entirely out of conviction. 'We live in the twentieth century; there's no room for fashion plates and old biddies.' She still had her flaming red hair, even though she had to touch it up discreetly with henna every month, and still wore the smartest dresses from the KK collection, 'not out of vanity, as a working woman such a thing would be completely alien to me, but because in the end I have to represent the company.' When visitors came into the shop, this representation assumed two completely different forms. She received buyers with a kind of tomboyish chumminess, and preceded each sentence with the unspoken introduction: 'Among us business people...' Towards job-seekers and other supplicants she was off-puttingly severe, although this was a bitter necessity. Zalman in his generosity was something of a pushover, and often she had had to say to him, 'If it was up to you, we'd employ every shnorrer who walked in off the street, and the company would be mechullah in a year.'

The man who was standing in front of her was just such a one. She didn't like his manner. He had studied her keenly for a moment, she sensed something like that, and now he was making an uninterested face as if it wasn't worth looking at her any more closely. Stood there as if rooted to the spot, hat in hand, and didn't move even when she kept him waiting and then took a phone call and then another. Not once did he so much as shift the weight of his body from one foot to the other. This was someone who had learned to wait, one of those patient people who are particularly annoying because you can't get rid of them again so easily.

'And you want...?' Rachel had to ask at last.

'Work.'

He said it as one delivers a military report, not one syllable too many or too few. He was a German, 'a Berliner', thought Rachel, who didn't know much about dialects, but for whom everything that sounded unpleasantly Teutonic came from Berlin. His voice was surprisingly loud. Usually if people wanted something they were rather timid. 'I'm sorry to bother you,' the tone of their voice meant, 'but if it isn't too much trouble, I have something to ask you for.'

He wasn't someone who asked. If he bothered someone, than he bothered them.

'Are you a tailor?' asked Rachel, although of course she knew he wasn't. You could see that. His suit was cut for a much fatter man, and really hung off him; an expert, if he had had to make do with cast-off clothes, would have made it much smaller, so that it fit.

'If a tailor is what you need, then I'm a tailor,' said the man.

'Can you sew?'

'I can learn.'

'Like that? From one day to the next?'

'If necessary, yes.'

'How hard do you imagine it is?'

'There are harder things.'

'Listen,' said Rachel, and because the man was so much bigger than she was and she didn't want to do the koved for him, to stand up, she bobbed up and down on her office chair. 'We don't take on untrained staff here.'

He laughed. No, he didn't laugh. He produced a noise that could have been a laugh if a laugh could be pickled, stored in the cellar and eventually, if there was nothing else in the house, taken back out again.

'Believe me, Fräulein,' he said. 'I can do anything anyone asks of me. I'm a skilled practitioner.'

Rachel didn't like being called 'Fräulein'. She always suspected concealed mockery behind the word, along the lines of: 'Soon be forty, and still no husband.'

The visitor was hard to guess. He could be fifty. Or less. Not that she was interested.

'What do you actually expect me to do for you?'

'You could ask my name,' said the man. 'I'm called Grün.'

'Grün and what else?'

'Grünberg, Grünfeld, Grünbaum. Pick one.'

'Excuse me?'

There was nothing unusual about him, apart from his oversized suit. No one would have thrown him out of a Jewish simcha; with a face like that he would have been mishpocha in any house. And there were crow's feet around his eyes, even if Rachel hadn't yet seen him smiling yet. Nothing unusual.

The craziest people always look the most normal, she had read somewhere.

'In fact, Herr Grün, I just wanted to know your first name.'

'Felix,' said the man. 'Isn't that a good joke?'

'What's so funny about it?'

'Felix means "happy".'

She couldn't make him out at all, and that alone made her dislike him. Either a person can sew or they can't; you don't just turn up hat in hand and get a job straight away.

'I'm sorry, Herr Grün, but...'

'You aren't sorry,' the man said without a hint of reproach. 'You even enjoy it. Not much, but you do. I'm familiar with this. Maybe I'd be exactly the same if I had power over other people.'

'Why power?'

'You have work, I need work.'

'You're not a tailor.'

'I can pretend to be one. Remarkably realistic. Like your hair.'

The cheek.

'What about my hair?'

'You should mix a little black coffee in with the paste, then the henna won't be so bright. I know that from a work colleague.'

'And what sort of work is that supposed to be? Know-all?' This man was making her simply furious.

'She was in the same field as me,' said Herr Grün. 'When I still had a job. Well, yes' – he sighed, and the sigh came from the cellar, from some pickling jar where his feelings were stored – 'well, yes, tailor isn't the worst thing in the world. If you like I can start straight away.'

'There's nothing here for you,' said Rachel, and noticed with some irritation that her voice had grown shrill.

'No, there is,' said Herr Grün. 'There's work here, and I need work. So I'll wait till someone gives me some.'

'I've told you...'

'You're not the boss here.' He didn't say even that unpleasantly. 'I've learned to recognise such things. You're put in command, but you can't really give orders.'

'How do you think you know that?' She couldn't choke back the question, even though one shouldn't really debate with such people.

'You make too much of an effort,' said Herr Grün.

Then he went and stood against the wall, without leaning against it, he didn't ask for a chair, he didn't ask when the boss would be there, he just stood there and waited. Each time someone came in he looked at him for a moment and always knew straight away that he wasn't yet the right one. Even when Joni

Leibowitz came back from a customer and complained loudly about the fact that the replacement buttons on a delivery of ladies' coats had not been sewn in, even though that was what he had expressly requested, and who had to listen to the buyers' complaints? He did! – even then Herr Grün only turned his head briefly and then sank back in on himself, a man who has done a lot of waiting, and for whom another few hours won't matter.

Zalman had an appointment at the bank. He didn't like going there, but he had no alternative; the more successful a company became, the more money it seemed to need. They had been extremely polite to him, and the clerk in charge had not only authorised credit for the purchase of a special button machine, but even congratulated him: he was doing everything quite correctly. Now, as long as the work force was cheap and the unions had no objections to make, one would have to start setting the markers; he would see how they started crawling out of their holes at the first sign of a recovery. In the interest of the company Zalman hadn't been able to contradict him, and that level of self-control alone, he thought, would have been worth a director's salary.

The man who had waited so long took a step forward when Zalman came in, like a soldier when the order to that effect has been given. 'You are the boss here,' she said.

'And who are you?'

'My name is Grün.'

'Papa, I told him we weren't taking on untrained workers, but he insisted on waiting for you anyway, Papa.' Rachel would have liked to weave a third 'Papa' into the sentence. She was more than happy for this Herr Grün to know that she was the managing director's daughter.

Zalman looked at the man. A refugee, of course, the world was full of refugees. The suit was good English fabric, so someone who had enjoyed better days. That counted against him, not because one should be ashamed of losing one's possessions, but because people who were once rich generally don't make good workers. You could teach the hands to do something, was his experience, but not the head. The suit, Zalman saw things like this at first sight, was made to measure, but for a much fatter man than Grün. So he must have been through some terrible things; that too wasn't a rare thing for a Jew coming from Germany.

'What's your profession?'

'Whatever is needed.'

'He isn't a tailor, Papa.'

'I haven't always been a refugee, either,' said Herr Grün. 'But I've learned it quickly.'

'You must understand,' said Zalman, and for the second time that day cursed the fact that he had to be the managing director here. 'You must understand: twenty people come here every week. If I wanted to employ them all...'

'Give me five minutes,' said Herr Grün.

A real company director would have left him standing. But you can't teach an old dog new tricks, and Zalman had long lived according to the principle that you should give everyone a hearing before you say no to him.

'All right, then, five minutes.'

The two men disappeared into the manager's room, which was only really a cupboard, separated from the office by thin plaster walls. The door closed behind them, and Rachel raised her eyes to the ceiling in ostentatious despair.

Joni Leibowitz had observed the scene and was now, a cigarette in the corner of his mouth, leaning on Rachel's desk. She didn't like the fact that he still took for granted a familiarity between them that had long ceased to exist.

'I bet you a bottle of wine that he'll take him on.'

'Never.'

'He'll never take him on, or you never bet?'

'Both.' She had asked him several times not to use the intimate form of address with her in the office.

Joni let the ash from his cigarette drop into the hollow of his hand, a habit that Rachel thought was impossible, and then clapped his hands clean over the waste paper basket. 'Would you like one?' he asked, and held out the open case. It was made of electrum, but he hoped people would assume it was silver.

'I don't smoke.'

'Then the stubs with the traces of lipstick that I keep finding in the packing room must come from someone else.'

He grinned at her. Joni was a person who liked digging out secrets because he enjoyed the power that they gave him over others.

Having fun with power? That strange Herr Grün had said exactly the same thing about her.

'Might I be allowed to carry on with my work?' she said severely.

'I don't want to stop you.' He let his cigarette butt fall into the waste paper basket – another of his typically reckless habits – and went outside. In the past, but that was now a very long time ago, Rachel had found his pointedly casual strolling gait actually quite attractive.

It took longer than five minutes, at least half an hour. Only then did the door of the manager's office open, and the two men came out.

'Herr Grün will start here tomorrow,' said Zalman. 'Somebody please show him how to operate a sewing machine.'

58

Arthur's surgery was closed every second Wednesday. His receptionist, the elderly Fräulein Salvisberg, turned all his patients away and he drove to Heiden to do a free consultation at the Jewish children's home, the Wartheim.

The journey to Appenzell would have been equally pleasant by train – Arthur had been particularly taken with the little cog railway that climbed the gentle slopes from Rorschach – but if the weather permitted he preferred to get into his little Fiat. What's the point of having a car of your own if you don't use it? However, it was almost embarrassing to him that he enjoyed this part of his voluntary work so much; his over-eager conscience was of the opinion that one could only take credit for a good deed if one had also suffered for it.

The fact that the Wartheim was forced to bring in a doctor from Zurich had to do with money, or rather with a lack of money. For the private children there were enough doctors in the village, and if they couldn't provide a diagnosis, a specialist was called in for them from St Gallen. A child was considered private if his parents paid the full costs, which only Swiss people could do, and not all of those. The 'official children' whose lodging was paid for by a state agency for reasons of poverty, had a claim to medical treatment, although local doctors prudently guarded against diagnosing any illnesses that would have required costly treatment. The problem was the 'women's association children', most of them wards of court who required support from the Union of Jewish Women's Associations because their parents had stopped sending money, either because they had none left, or because the constantly tightening exchange regulations made regular transfers impossible. The children weren't allowed to starve, of course not, but even though they were required to fill every school-free minute with menial work, and thus earned at least part of their keep, they were still a burden, and there was never enough money for unusual expenses such as visits to the doctor.

Arthur hadn't needed to be asked twice to take on the job. 'If I said no, I would feel as if I was playing truant from school,' he had said to Hinda, and his sister had replied, 'No, Arthur, what you're playing truant from is life.'

The journey was quick today, and in Heiden he even had time to call in at the Schützengarten for half an hour. His Zurich dialect sounded exotic in Appenzell, and when he ordered a coffee he was immediately marked down as an outsider. Here they drank beer at all times of day, or a nice glass of red wine.

Two pipe-smoking men were sitting at the regulars' table talking about politics. They were united in their noisy conviction that Hitler wouldn't survive for long in Germany. He had picked a fight with international Jewry, and that was always a mistake.

On the steep road that led from the village to the children's home Arthur drove too quickly and nearly missed the entrance.

Fräulein Württemberger, the director of the home, was already waiting for him. Her little office was furnished with two over-full shelves of books, like a study. 'I came to Switzerland with nothing but a box of books,' she liked to say, and did nothing to dispel the impression that she had voluntarily left much more valuable things behind in Germany to save her library. She was what Chanele would have called 'a late girl', in this case an academically late girl. She liked to slip into conversations the fact that she had sat at Heidegger's feet as a philosophy student, and although her great master had later become a member of the Nazi Party and rector of 'Führeruniversität Freiburg', she continued to defend him. 'Freiburg is the only university where books were never burned,' she said, continuing to defend him in the face of all objections, taking from her shelf, as her definitive proof, what was probably her most precious possession, a personally signed copy of the *Yearbook of Philosophy and Phenomonological Research* from 1927, with the first part of the famous treatise on Being and Time.

Fräulein Württemberger loved books significantly more than she did people, because people refused to fit into any rational system, instead rebelliously insisting on their own unclassifiable individuality. The fact that she had taken the job in the Wartheim at all she saw as a sacrifice of the kind that emigrants often have to make. In her introductory speech she had treated the well-meaning ladies from the Women's Association with such polysyllabic contempt that they saw her as an experienced pedagogical expert and employed her on the spot.

'I'd expected you earlier,' she said by way of greeting. With a disparaging expression, as if the ritual of a handshake were far too intimate, she held out her fingertips. 'Chewed nails,' thought Arthur, as he did every time. 'She wouldn't let the children get away with that.' Fräulein Württemberger withdrew her hand straight away, as one takes a fragile object from a clumsy child, and ran her hand in a nervous gesture over the severely tied bun on the back of her head. She was looking for unruly strands of hair like a prison warder for escaped prisoners.

'There are four today.' Fräulein Württemberger said it as reproachfully as if Arthur were personally responsible for this unfitting high state of illness among the children of the Women's Association. As always, she hadn't offered him a chair. Arthur doubted whether anyone had ever been allowed to sit in the precisely arranged visitor's armchair in front of her desk, just as he sometimes suspected that the glasses in Fräulein Württemberger's round spectacles were made of clear glass, and had the sole purpose of making the director of the children's home seem even more intellectual than she did already.

There was no separate consulting room in the home; even if there had been room for one, it wouldn't have been wasted on the Women's Association children. As long as the little patients were not bed-bound, they had to turn up in an orderly line – 'No talking!' – outside the ironing room on the second floor and wait for the doctor there. The big table, on which linen sheets and pillow-cases were usually laid, served as the examination couch, and if the children had to get undressed, their clothes ended up in a laundry basket. A whiff of soap-flakes hung in the air, and gave the place, otherwise so unsuited for consultations, a suggestion of antiseptic cleanliness.

'Consultation' was, however, a very euphemistic term for a process in which the children were not really consulted about anything at all. Fräulein Württemberger insisted on being present during every examination, and on answering Arthur's questions herself.

'He's so clumsy,' she complained about a little boy who had cut deep into the ball of his left thumb while peeling potatoes. 'I've shown him ten times how to hold a knife, but he simply refuses to understand it.'

The boy did not contradict her, and did not cry when the gaping wound was cleaned with iodine. Only when Arthur bent over to him as he stitched up the wound did he say timidly, 'I'm left-handed.'

'Is that why you cut yourself?'

'When I use my right hand I can't really...'

He got no further than that. 'There is one pretty little hand, and one ugly little hand,' Fräulein Württemberger cut in. Martin Heidegger himself could not have delivered the axiom with greater conviction. 'A pretty one and an ugly one. You must learn that, or you'll never come to anything in life.'

Arthur secretly winked at the little boy to say to him, 'You don't need to take things so seriously.' But the little boy didn't react to the gesture, he just said very politely, 'Thank you, Doctor,' and left the room.

Arthur knew the second patient already. She had – 'Because you always run, rather than walking like a sensible person!' – broken her arm a few weeks previously, and Köbeli, the janitor of the Wartheim, who was slightly mentally handicapped but a skilled craftsman, had sawed open the plaster on Arthur's telephoned instructions that morning. The fracture had healed without a hitch.

'I hope you kept the plaster as a souvenir?' asked Arthur. He remembered the other children immortalising themselves on it with signatures and little drawings.

'We place great value on hygiene,' Fräulein Württemberger, rather than the girl, replied. 'We have of course thrown it away.'

Next he was presented with a boy who had, in Arthur's opinion, nothing at all wrong with him. He had just recently started wetting the bed – 'At the age of eleven!' – and although Fräulein Württemberger had done her pedagogical best to prevent such a thing – she made him wash the soiled sheet with his own hands every day, and as it dried on the line, he had to stand next to it while the other children laughed at him – even though she had done everything, therefore, that one might reasonably have expected of her, he simply wouldn't stop. Fräulein Württemberger, who considered all psychology to be unscientific, insisted that the bad habit, regardless of fear or loneliness, must have a physiological reason, and repeated the formulation three times, as people do when they are proud to have understood a specialist term from a field alien to them. After a lengthy discussion, Arthur could do nothing more for the boy than prescribe him a weak sedative, even though he knew from his own experience that nightmares cannot be banished by sleeping pills.

'But there really is something wrong with the last one,' said Fräulein Württemberger, as if half-severed fingers and broken arms were not accidents, but merely annoying malfunctions. 'She's coughing blood.' And she added in a people-are-always-causing-me-problems voice, 'I was only told about it a few days ago.'

'How long has she been here?'

'Her three months are nearly up.'

The three months were the maximum negotiated with the Swiss immigration authorities for the residence of foreign children. *Gouverner, c'est prévoir*: the strict limit of a quarter of a year was to prevent welcome spa guests from eventually turning into unloved immigrants. On the other hand, Switzerland was still a tourist country, and in spite of all the upheavals in Europe long might it remain one, and from the economic standpoint the powers that be had no objection to German children getting red cheeks in the healthy air of Appenzell.

Except that in this particular case the red cheeks hadn't happened.

'She's coughing blood? All of a sudden? And you never noticed anything before?'

'I've had nothing but trouble with the child,' complained Fräulein Württemberger. 'She's a rover.'

'Has she run away?'

'Such things don't happen here. I take my caring duties very seriously.'

She checked that no strands had still escaped from her bun. 'It's much more unpleasant than that.' She lowered her voice and said almost in a whisper. 'I caught her in Köbeli's room.'

'I'm sorry?'

'In the room of a halfwit! In his bedroom!' She uttered the word as furiously as if the janitor had a whole suite of rooms at his disposal, apart from his cramped bedroom.

'I know Köbeli. He's harmless.'

'One can never be quite sure,' Fräulein Württemberger said darkly. 'Luckily he wasn't there at the time. Which doesn't alter the question: what would a twelve-year-old girl want in a strange man's room?'

'I'm sure there's a quite harmless reason for it.'

The director of the home would not be reassured so easily. 'She was in her nightshirt,' she said grimly. 'So practically naked. And one knows all the things that can happen at that age.' Fräulein Württemberger's expression was eloquent: there are aberrations that she could not discuss with a man, even if he was a doctor. 'And then this illness, on top of everything! When they were both supposed to go back next week.'

'Both of them?' Arthur repeated the surprising plural.

'She's here with her little brother. Irma and Moses Pollack from Kassel. Here are their certificates.'

Every child who came to the Wartheim from abroad had to show a medical certificate before crossing the border, attesting to his or her perfect health. That was also required at a higher level, because proud as one was of the health-giving properties of good Swiss air, one didn't want sick people coming into the country. A tourist country cannot afford plagues.

A Privatdozent, Dr Saul Merzbach (before his specialisation, 'consultant in gynaecology at the Red Cross Hospital, Kassel' the word 'former' had been added in ink) had confirmed that he had carried out a thorough examination, including nasal smear for diphtheria bacilli on the siblings Pollack, Irma (twelve years old) and Moses (nine years old), and found no signs of illness in either the physical or the mental spheres. That had been three months ago.

But now Irma was coughing blood.

'And her brother?'

'Completely healthy. Now he's clinging to his sister far too much. I've tried to separate the two of them. To encourage his independence. But there were scenes...'

Children can be so unreasonable.

'Then I'll take a look at Irma.'

Both children came in, hand in hand. Arthur would have guessed that the little girl was younger, perhaps ten, eleven at the most. She was small for her age, but had a rather adult face with big brown eyes and a slight squint. Her wandering gaze made her look as if she were constantly lost in thought and her attention were elsewhere. She didn't look ill.

Moses wasn't much smaller than his sister, but he looked up at her so trustingly, and she held his hand so protectively that one couldn't help thinking of a mother with her child.

'So you're Irma,' said Arthur. 'And you're little Moishi.'

'My name is Moses,' the boy corrected the diminutive. He had a very small voice, as if he had brought only part of himself from Germany and left the rest behind there. 'The name comes from Moses Mendelssohn.'

'And do you know who Moses Mendelssohn was?'

'Not exactly. A musician, I think. But my father said it's a name you can be proud of.'

'Your father is quite right. Do you write to him regularly?'

'We can't write to him,' said the girl. 'He's dead.'

Arthur wanted to bite off his tongue.

Fräulein Württemberger had no time for such useless chitchat. 'There's no need for any of this. Tell the doctor what's wrong with you.'

'I have no cough. It hurts, in here.' She put her hand to her chest. 'And sometimes there's blood.'

'Show the doctor!'

With her free hand, and without letting go of her brother, Irma reached into the pocket of her black-and-white checked apron, took out a crumpled handkerchief and held it out to Arthur. A big blood-stain had dried dark brown into the fabric.

'Sure enough,' said Arthur.

He held out the handkerchief to Fräulein Württemberger, but she stepped quickly back, startled and repelled.

'The doctor in Kassel should have noticed that,' she groused, and patrolled her bun once more for escaping tendrils. 'Such things don't just happen from one day to the next.'

'Sometimes they do.'

Fräulein Württemberger held out her index finger with the chewed fingernail to the little girl in an accusatory fashion and snapped, 'I hold you responsible! You should have told me this much sooner.' And in a no less reproachful voice to Arthur, 'What sort of illness is it? I hope it's nothing infectious?'

Arthur was a mild-mannered person, far too mild-mannered, as Hinda was always reminding him. But enough was enough. 'It may not have escaped even you,' he said sarcastically, 'that doctors sometimes examine their patients before making their diagnosis. And now please leave me alone with the child.'

'I insist that...'

'As you wish.' Arthur put the stethoscope that had already taken out back in its case and snapped the lock shut. 'Then I will finish my work now and inform the Women's Association that here in the Wartheim we may have a case of a highly infectious pulmonary disease.'

'But...'

'Establishing who bears responsibility for such an epidemic will no longer be my concern.'

Once her bastion of polysyllabic words and unquestioned articles of faith had been penetrated, Fräulein Württemberger had little left to throw into the battle. She practically tore Moses away from his sister and marched outside with him, pulling the boy behind her like a prisoner of war.

The door slammed shut. Irma was about to run after her brother, but then stayed put.

'If she isn't nice to him,' Arthur said consolingly, 'I will give her some medicine to make her have a sore tummy for three days.'

Perhaps little Irma didn't understand his joke. Arthur liked children, but he wasn't used to dealing with them very much. The little girl just looked at him with big eyes, or rather, she looked past him and asked, 'Shall I get undressed? So that you can examine me?'

'Yes, of course. Let's have a look at your chest.'

Most people, even children, turned away when they took off their clothes for an examination, hid for a few seconds the nakedness that she was about to present to the doctor. Irma didn't. On the contrary: she looked at him as concentratedly as if she wanted to find something out from him, or solve a riddle that involved him.

'You can't see from outside,' she said, as she folded her apron and laid it in a laundry basket. 'But when I cough it hurts quite badly.'

'Where exactly?'

'Everywhere,' came the voice from under the pullover that she was just pulling over her head.

'And how frequent are these attacks?'

'Sometimes every day and sometimes...It always comes as a surprise.'

She put her vest carefully in the basket as well, and stood in front of him wearing only a pair of white panties and grey hand-knitted socks.

This was not a sick child. Perhaps a little undernourished, with excessively prominent collar-bones, but otherwise...Her skin was rosy and by no means cyanotic.

But when she coughed she spat blood.

From the courtyard came the sound of children playing and the voice of Fräulein Württemberger demanding that they be quiet.

The girl was not tubercular, he would have bet his medical certificate on it. He examined her thoroughly, according to all the rules of the discipline, and found not the slightest symptom of any illness. In percussion the sound was sonorous, and in auscultation there was neither a rattle nor a buzz. He had her whisper 'sixty-six' strictly according to the textbook, something he had not done since training at the university hospital, and then say 'ninety-nine' in a deep voice. It all sounded exactly as it was supposed to sound. In the notes that he filled in for every Women's Association child, he used the abbreviation n.n.s.

No noticeable symptom.

But her handkerchief was full of blood.

He made her turn away from him and applied the stethoscope again, this time to her back.

'Please cough.'

She coughed violently and put her hand to her chest.

'Is there blood again?'

She held her hand in front of her mouth, spat into the palm and held it out to him. 'Not this time.' Then she rubbed her hand on her pants, pulled a face and added, 'But it hurts.'

'When you cough?'

'It hurts a lot.'

Where she had rubbed her hand dry there was something red on the seam of her pants. Not blood, as Arthur thought for a moment, but the red stitching of a laundry mark: 'I.P.' for Irma Pollack. They were keen on order here in the Wartheim.

Outside the children squealed with delight as they played. The ironing room smelled of soap flakes and damp.

'Can I get dressed again?' asked Irma.

'One moment. When blood comes when you cough – what colour is the blood?'

The two diverging eyes looked at him in surprise. 'Like blood. Red.'

'How exactly?'

'Just normal dark red. I don't know what you want to know.'

'I only want to know one thing from you, Irma,' said Arthur. He took off his glasses and rubbed the bridge of his nose. 'Just one little thing. Why are you lying to me?'

59

'But it *is* real blood,' she said.

She had tried everything, she had coughed for him and bowed her back as if the pain was unbearable, she had described how sometimes in the night she couldn't breathe at all, and had to open the window wide, and the other girls in the dormitory had complained about the draught, he could ask them, she had, as he went on merely shaking his head, resorted to childish defiance, stamped her foot and declared that she had a very special form of tuberculosis, a kind that you couldn't spot just with a bit of knocking and listening, she had, when none of that did any good, shaken out her encrusted handkerchief and held it up in front of his eyes, 'Blood, real blood, can't you see?' She had tried everything.

But she hadn't cried.

'You should get dressed again,' said Arthur. 'We don't want you catching a cold.'

At the end of an examination there is always that embarrassing moment when patients are no longer impersonal actors of their illness, but are once again themselves, and hence no longer just undressed, but naked. Irma too suddenly folded her thin arms over her little-girl chest and turned away. It was a sign of submission. She had done her best, but now she was admitting defeat.

Only when she had put on her vest again did she ask, 'How did you know?'

'It was the wrong sort of blood.'

'It was real blood,' she protested.

'Let me explain,' said Arthur, and at that moment, as so often, he wished he had experienced children of his own. 'If someone coughs blood, you see, and if that blood comes out of the lungs, as it does in tuberculosis, for example, it's always bright red. And slightly foamy. You have to imagine, as if someone had stirred in a little pinch of sherbet powder. But on your handkerchief…'

'It's real blood!' As if she just had to repeat it often enough to convince him.

'I realise that. Where did you get it?'

She looked cautiously around, even though they were alone in the ironing room and no one could see in through the window, and lifted the leg of her pants a little. On the inside of her thin thigh was a whole series of scars, one beside the other.

'Fräulein Württemberger always checks to see if we're clean,' Irma explained.

'But we have to keep our pants on, even under our night-shirts. That was why I cut myself there and then held the handkerchief to it.' A quick smile spread across her face. She was also a little girl whose attempt to trick the adult world had nearly worked.

'Where did you get the knife?' Arthur asked.

'I stole a razor blade from Köbeli's room.'

'I understand.'

'No,' said Irma. 'You don't understand at all.'

Then they were sitting side by side on the ironing board. For confessions, Arthur had learned in the past, it's good to sit side by side; you're close to the other person and don't have to look him in the eye.

It was a long story that she told him, and when he remembered it later he could still smell soap flakes and damp sheets and the smell of cleanly washed children's hair.

Irma's story began with all Jewish organisations in Germany being dissolved, which was why from one day to the next Irma's mother had no work and nowhere to live. No, in fact, it had actually started earlier than that.

With the accident.

'He slipped,' said Irma, 'he just slipped like that, he didn't even fall over, Mama says. She was there. He just stumbled, from the pavement into the street, and then there was this lorry coming along.'

She told of the death of her father without shedding a tear, she had probably decided once and for all not to cry, at least not here in Heiden, where she was responsible for her little brother and had to be strong.

It was five years since that accident now, she had been seven at the time and Moses only four. 'He doesn't remember anything about it, not really, but we tell him about his father, Mama and I, over and over again, and then it's as if he can remember it all himself.'

She always talked about 'his father' and 'my father', she never said 'Papa'. She had built a lot of walls for herself, to shelter behind and find her way along.

'Then Mama found a job, in the B'nai B'rith old people's home. Do you know what B'nai B'rith is?'

Yes, Arthur knew what B'nai B'rith was. He was even a member of that charitable organisation himself.

'We lived there too. Up in the attic. Before, it had been a room for the maids. With very crooked walls. Mama said, "The old flat's far too big for us, now that there's only the three of us." But I think she just couldn't pay the rent any more.'

'You must have been very sad.'

'Oh,' said Irma, 'in fact it was quite fun in the new place at first.'

She said it bravely, as she had probably often said it to console her mother. Clever children knew that high spirits are expected of them, and when they have to grow up prematurely they know that best of all.

'Then the Nazis closed the home, from one day to the next. They just sent the old people away. And some of them, Mama said, had paid a lot of money to be able to live there forever. Mama says there's nothing to be done about it. But it's all wrong. Do you understand that?'

You can't explain everything you understand to a child. The German authorities, not long ago, had banned the B'nai B'rith and confiscated all its property. Where the sick had once been tended or orphans raised, various Nazi organisations now resided. Strength through joy.

'No,' he said, 'I don't really understand it either.'

Irma nodded, she hadn't expected anything else, and went on telling her story. 'Then we moved in with Uncle Paul, but he's only got one room for the three of us, and we always have to be quiet and aren't allowed to disturb him. He has a nervous heart, and noise is very bad for that. So Mama said it would be good for me to go to Switzerland for three months. So that she can get on with looking for work and a new place to stay. I said a trip like that would be far too expensive, but Mama said we'd been invited and it wouldn't cost anything at all.'

Probably, Arthur thought, someone from the forbidden B'nai B'rith had written to the Augustin Keller Lodge, the sister lodge in Zurich, and asked for help. That lodge actually owned the Wartheim, it had been bought with donated money and placed at the disposal of the Women's Associations for free.

'And now we're to move back to Kassel, but...'

But...

She sat beside him, quite still. Only her feet played with each other as if they had nothing to do with the rest of her body.

But...

She made a decision and slipped down from the table. She went and stood in front of Arthur, her hands clasped behind her back. She had to throw back her head to look up at him.

'I want to ask you something,' she said. She looked him in the eyes and past him at the same time.

'Yes?'

'Dr Merzbach, who used to bring the children into the world at the hospital, and isn't allowed to do that any more, he told me that all doctors have to take a great oath not to give away people's secrets.'

'That's true,' said Arthur, eager to know what secret he was about to be told. 'It's called medical confidentiality.'

'Does it apply in Switzerland as well?'

'It applies all over the world. If a patient tells me something, I'm never, ever allowed to tell anyone else. Unless the patient lets me.'

'I won't let you, though,' said Irma and hopped triumphantly onto her tiptoes. 'I'm your patient and I won't let you.' She performed a proper war dance, so proud was she over her cunning. 'So you mustn't tell Fräulein Württemberger that I'm not sick.'

'I'll have to think about that,' said Arthur. 'But it's still your turn. Why are you so keen to suffer from something so serious?'

She had, it turned out, a very good reason.

'Mama wrote to say that she still hasn't found work, and that she's now looking for a job abroad.'

Irma, the twelve-year-old adult, had translated that correctly: her mother saw no future in Germany, and had decided to emigrate.

'And that it would make much more sense if Moses and I didn't have to travel back and then leave again straight away.'

You can't write to your children, 'Don't come home, you're not safe here.' You don't explain to them, 'My chances of a visa are better if you're already out of the country.' You write, 'It would make more sense for you not to make the journey twice,' and if a twelve-year-old is clever and listens when the grown-ups are talking about politics, she will understand what's meant. Particularly when she's promised her mother to take care of her little brother.

In the Wartheim, Mama had said, they were looked after well, and it would be best if they could stay there longer than the three months allowed by the rules. To get to Switzerland, Irma had needed a medical certificate. Why shouldn't there be another one that prevented her from travelling home? For example, if she was coughing blood and incapable of travelling?

So, now she had told him, but he wasn't allowed to say a word to Fräulein Württemberger. Because he was a doctor and Irma was his patient, and because he had sworn that oath that all doctors have to swear, and you're not allowed to break an oath.

Arthur let his glasses dangle back and forth by one leg, as he often did when he was trying to think. His eyes had grown moist. Probably from the smell of soap.

'What made you think of tuberculosis?' he asked at last.

'I read it in a book.'

'A book about medicine?'

'No,' said Irma, 'a novel.'

There was a library in the Wartheim, or at least a cupboard full of books, from which each child was allowed to borrow a book once a week. There were only a few children's books, *Nesthäkchen Flees the Nest*, and *The Turnach Children in Winter*, and they were hard to get hold of. When you were choosing them, as with all things in the Wartheim, there was a strict order: first came the private children, whose parents were, after all, paying a lot of money, then the official children, and last of all the Women's Association children who could pick through what was left. They were mostly adult books, battered volumes that had ended up in the Wartheim because charitable ladies had used a collection appeal to weed out their bookshelves. Irma had chosen the book because of its title: *Alone Among Strangers*. Perhaps, she had thought, it might be about a girl who can't go home because bad things are happening there. But as it turned out it was a romantic tear-jerker, a maid's novel, at the tragic end of which a spurned Juliet, estranged from her Romeo by a series of unfortunate misunderstandings, is coughing her way to the grave in a pulmonary sanatorium in Davos, until at the last moment her beloved turns up at her sick bed and inspires her to go on living. The endless protestations of love and outbreaks of emotion, all those adult complications, had only bored Irma, but the many descriptions of dark red stains on snow white handkerchiefs had given her an idea. In the novel everything had turned out well as soon as the heroine had started spitting blood.

Except that the author had neglected to specify that the blood had to be bright red. And mixed with sherbet powder.

The confession was over, and there was silence in the ironing room. There was only the sound of children squealing as they played outside, with no one telling them off.

'And now?' asked Arthur.

'Can't you just say that I really have tuberculosis?'

'You mean I should lie?'

When Irma thought, her forehead wrinkled. 'It wouldn't really be a lie, she said. 'They just wouldn't have noticed.'

'But then I would be a very bad doctor.'

Irma shrugged. It was a very grown-up gesture.

He hadn't locked the door, so Fräulein Württemberger could simply come storming in dragging little Moses behind her. She thrust the boy at Irma and stood in front of Arthur with her arms propped on her hips. For the last half hour she had been in her office, outside in the courtyard and again in the office, and all that time she had been collecting arguments, as she might have collected quotations and evidence for a seminar dissertation, she had assembled all the things she wanted to say to this stuck-up Dr Meijer, and now it all came bubbling out of her, like water from a saucepan when steam lifts the lid.

She wanted to know exactly what was going on her here, right now, on the spot. She had no intention, not the slightest intention did she have, of simply being sent away and fobbed off, after all, she was the director of the home, and bore the responsibility, almost twenty children more than usual and most of them from Germany, and they couldn't even pay for their expenses. And if an epidemic broke out now, who was going to take the blame? So what was going on?

Arthur was a man who was rather impressed by authorities and superiors, and if she had asked a little more politely, he would probably have told her the truth.

No, not even then. Even though he couldn't have said when exactly he made his decision, he had switched entirely to Irma's side.

'On one point I can reassure you, Fräulein Württemberger,' he said therefore. 'The girl is not infectious.'

Irma lowered her head, and put an arm around her brother, ready to draw him comfortingly to her.

'But she does have a serious, dangerous illness that requires a great deal of treatment.'

Irma raised her head again and looked at him. Big, brown, slightly squinting eyes. No one had ever looked at him so trustingly before.

'Attentive and loving care,' he repeated.

'She can get that in Kassel. She's going home next week.'

'No,' said Arthur. 'She isn't going. From a medical viewpoint I cannot allow that under any circumstances. The child is not capable of travelling. Far too dangerous.'

Once one has started lying, exaggeration isn't difficult.

'But the boy can't travel on his...'

'I couldn't allow that either. Given the girl's debilitated condition, such abrupt separation could lead to a shock.'

Now a stray tendril actually had escaped from the bun, and Fräulein Württemberger couldn't stuff it back into place.

'Of course,' said Arthur, 'of course I will issue the appropriate certificates, to be delivered to the relevant authorities.'

'But what's wrong with her?' Fräulein Württemberger asked the question so loudly that her voice broke, and she tried to conceal the fact behind a cough.

'It isn't so simple to explain to a non-professional. Let me put it this way:

I suspect a very rare and protracted pulmonary illness. Not infectious, as I say, but grave.'

Little Moses gripped his sister's hand tightly. 'Is Irma going to die?' he asked in his little voice.

'Of course not.' Arthur comfortingly ran his hand over the boy's short hair. 'She will get better. Because she'll be looked after very, very well here. Isn't that right, Fräulein Württemberger?'

'We are not a hospital. They need too many staff and—'

'I have no doubt,' said Arthur, 'that a woman of your famous diligence would find a solution even for this problem. A lot of care isn't needed. Just particularly rich food. The child seems a little undernourished to me.'

Everyone in the Wartheim got enough to eat, Fräulein Württemberger snapped agitatedly, she wouldn't hear such accusations, and in any case, who would cover the costs? But it was only a parting skirmish, and in her mind she was already formulating the letter in which she could complain to the Women's Association about this Dr Meijer. Oh, she would find the right words all right.

'And there is one other thing that I would urgently advise,' said Arthur. 'Give Irma a room of her own. Ideally with her brother. Because of the calming effect.'

Fräulein Württemberger hesitated and then decided at least to do of her own accord what she was in any case being forced to do. 'I have been thinking the very same thing myself,' she lied, and almost believed it herself. 'We will get you well again, won't we, little Irma?' And she left the room as proudly as if she had just emerged triumphant from a difficult philosophical debate.

Irma shook his hand quite formally as he left, even gave a little curtsey, as one learned to do in Germany, and pressed her little brother's head down in a proper bow. Arthur would have liked to hug her, had even spread his arms, and then lowered them again because it felt too officious. She looked at him as if she had guessed his thoughts, and said, 'You're a good doctor, Dr Meijer.' And she suddenly winked and laughed, the first time he had heard her laugh, lifted her brother, who was almost as big as she was, and ran from the room with him.

On the way back to Zurich Arthur picked up a hitch-hiker who was standing at the side of the road with his thumb in the air. He was an old man, dressed in black, and when he sat down in the passenger seat he filled the beautiful new car with the smell of unaired cellars.

'Bravo, Arthur,' said Uncle Melnitz. 'Now you're proud of yourself. You're slapping your own back and you think you're terrific, yes.'

The road down towards the lowlands, it seemed to Arthur, had more bends in it than usual.

'You've given a sick note to a girl who isn't really sick,' said Uncle Melnitz. 'And of course that makes you a hero. You've defeated National Socialism, and the Swiss immigration authorities as well, yes.'

'I can do no more than that,' said Arthur.

'Of course not. No one can.' Uncle Melnitz coughed and spat blood into a big white handkerchief. 'No one can ask more than that. Open their wallets when there's a collection. Pull a serious face at protest meetings. Perhaps even write a letter to the papers. Signed bravely with your own name. Bravo, Arthur, yes.'

The steering wheel was hard to move today, and Arthur couldn't take his eyes off the road for a moment.

'It's started like that every time,' said Uncle Melnitz. 'With everyone persuading themselves that there's nothing more they can do, and that things aren't going to get any worse. That it will stop of its own accord because it can't go on like that.'

Both sides of the street were lined with strangers, who had to be carefully avoided.

'But it does go on,' said Uncle Melnitz. 'It goes on like this every time.'

'We're living in the twentieth century.'

'Of course that's something else.' Uncle Melnitz laughed and coughed and spat. 'Something very, very different, yes. We live in the wonderful twentieth century. Not in the bad nineteenth or the wicked eighteenth or the terrible seventeenth.'

'It's not the same thing!'

The old man laughed so hard that little flecks of blood sprayed the windscreen. Bright red, foaming flecks of blood. Sherbet powder. 'The present is always different. And never has it been as different as in the oh-so-wonderful twentieth century. When there is electric light. And aeroplanes. And radio. And only good people. Such things can't happen again. Never, ever again, isn't that right, Arthur?'

'So what are we to do?'

'You can't ask me,' said Uncle Melnitz. 'I'm dead and buried.'

60

'There must be a special word for it,' thought Hillel. If you're definitely not really friends with someone, but you aren't really enemies with him either, because you're far too indifferent about him, if you still somehow belong together, in the eyes of the others and, whether you like it or not, in your own as well – what would you call such a person? Mate? No, that smacked of grey shirts and army boots. Comrade? Böhni would have bridled at that one, it would have meant the Comintern and orders from Moscow. And he certainly wasn't a chaver, as they said in Ivrit.

A colleague, well, fair enough, you could call it that. Although…You couldn't really say that they were detached from one another, that they just happened to sit side by side at their desks. They had experienced that adventure together, down the steps with the box-cart and a team of horses. Which had, incidentally, not fulfilled its most important aim, because Malka Sofer had not been impressed in the slightest. On the contrary: she had called Hillel childish, and wanted nothing to do with him.

But it had been an adventure.

At first Böhni had distanced himself from the affair, Rosenthal had been driving, not he, but when he realised that the wild ride was admired as a heroic feat at the Strickhof, when he told the story he soon moved from 'he' and 'that lunatic' to 'we': 'We gripped the reins, drove the horses on, took the bend.' Except of course he didn't mention that they had scattered a crowd of Fröntlers, either saying 'we' or 'that other fellow'.

Because one can't support such things, the teachers all pretended they hadn't heard a thing about the forbidden excursion, but they became accustomed, as if it were the most natural thing in the world, to bringing the two of them together on practical tasks, and putting them side by side in theoretical lessons. Which was more use to Böhni than it was to Hillel, because he was better able to copy from him.

The impulse behind this partnership – yes, that was perhaps a word that one could use, even it still wasn't quite the right one – to some extent the initial spark had come from Headmaster Gerster. That Sunday evening, over the pitiful remains of his plum flan, he had reached the conclusion that in spite of the hefty bollocking he had given them the two sinners had got off far too lightly, and he had come up with an additional punishment for them, which he announced to them the following day. They were to write an essay – 'Yes, both of you together, so that you learn that you can work through cooperation, and not opposition!' – which was to be delivered the following Monday, eight pages in their best handwriting. As a pedagogically instructive subject he had chosen, 'The meaning of a healthy farming class for our nation'.

Of course that was a red rag to a bull. Böhni wasn't much good at writing, but on the other hand he couldn't just let Rosenthal do it. Even if it would have been easy for him, given that Jews, as everyone knew, preferred to work with their heads rather than their hands. At any rate, he tried it on his own, and fiddled around with it until Wednesday, but only managed to get two pages together, and they didn't make sense at all. Then, when he asked Rosenthal, quite casually and in passing, how far he had got, Hillel just grinned and said he wasn't planning on making his life difficult if there was an easy way of doing things. He had found a brochure on this very subject, and they could just copy out its introduction, Gerstli would never notice. But he liked to leave such hard work to Böhni – after all, he was supposed to do something as well, because how had Gerster put it so well? They were to work through cooperation, not through opposition.

Böhni furiously refused, these were Jewish tricks, and he wouldn't have anything to do with them. But by Friday he hadn't got any further, and on Sunday he wanted he wanted to go to the international in the Hardturm, Germany versus Switzerland. So in the end – 'But you take responsibility!' – he had to accept the suggestion and set about copying. But the brochure, and this was one of Rosenthal's typical tricks, wasn't a nice Swiss pamphlet from the school library, as Böhni had expected, but a Zionist treatise with one of those Jewish candelabras on the title page. But the text, one had to admit, wasn't at all bad. The author wrote that a state can only remain healthy if its citizens farm the soil with their own hands, that the sciences still have their significance, but that only agriculture can strengthen a people's soul. In principle these were all thoughts to which Böhni could not have objected, but he wasn't happy with where they came from. Besides, when copying it out he had to be as careful as a hawk to see that he always wrote 'the Swiss' rather than 'the Jews', and 'the Confederacy' rather than the 'Yishuv'. Once he made a mistake and had to start a whole page over from the beginning.

Gerster didn't notice a thing. He was even very impressed by their observations, and praised them both for their genuinely patriotic way of thinking. Afterwards Böhni could never tell anyone how Rosenthal had bamboozled him. It was another secret between them, which bound them together somewhere between enmity and friendship.

There must be a special word for it.

It was also a part of their special relationship that they squabbled at every opportunity. When, for example, Germany had won the international one nil, the next day Rosenthal asked pointedly who Böhni had really been cheering for, the Swiss or his beloved Germans with the swastikas on their shirts. Böhni replied that he should stay out of it, football was a thing that his people knew absolutely nothing about. Whereupon Rosenthal actually claimed that a totally Jewish team, Hakoah Vienna, had won the Austrian championship a few years before. You could never tell whether he was taking the piss out of you or not.

In turn, Böhni felt superior in practical subjects, and where that superiority was not obvious, one could help it along a little with some little tricks. For example there was a method of making a cow so crazy (by sticking pepper up its arse) that it could barely be milked, and then when it knocked the pail over for the third time, you could say, 'Oh, yes, these city people, who think milk comes from the milkman.' At the next opportunity, Rosenthal swung the pitchfork so vigorously that Böhni got a load right in the face, whereupon Hillel apologised very politely, because as an inexperienced city boy he had mistaken a pitchfork for a flail.

As we have said: a very special relationship.

At home Hillel didn't say much about the Strickhof, but his parents worked out that he had more to do with one of his fellow pupils than the others, and Lea insisted that he invite him to dinner, quite informally, it didn't have to be a Friday evening with candle-lighting and Kiddush. Hillel wasn't keen on the suggestion, and kept putting off the invitation; such things weren't customary at his school, he said, and Böhni certainly wouldn't feel at ease at their house. But if Lea wanted something, she had a very calm way of insisting on it, and Hillel had no answer to the rhetorical question of whether he was ashamed of his family.

So in the end he invited Böhni. To his relief Böhni wasn't quite sure at first, and had a thousand excuses. But as is so often the case: precisely because Böhni responded like this, the matter suddenly became important for Hillel, he was even quite offended that Böhni should have baulked, he started over again every day, and in the end even ironically reassured him that he didn't need to be scared, the feast of Pesach was over, and it would be next year before they needed to slaughter a Christian boy to bake matzos out of his blood. Böhni refused to be accused of cowardice, and finally: a dinner isn't such a big deal, and it's soon over.

And so it happened.

Normally they cycled into town, but for some reason Böhni insisted that they take the twenty-two, even though a tram journey like that was just a waste of money, thirty rappen in each direction. When they met – 'Please be on time, Böhni! My father insists on it!' – at the Milchbuck tunnel, Hillel had to suppress a smile, because Böhni turned up in his dark blue Sunday suit, and had tied his tie so tightly that he had to stretch his neck even to be able to breathe. He had even brought flowers for Lea, a bunch of pink tulips. They were bred at the Strickhof for the weekly market on Bürkliplatz, and anything that came back unsold ended up on the compost heap. Böhni had wrapped the bouquet in an old edition of the Front, although at the last moment that struck him as unsuitable, so he quickly unwrapped it again outside the front door. He crumpled up the newspaper and stuffed it in his jacket pocket, where it went on rustling all evening.

Hillel's parents actually looked quite normal, not like Jews at all. His father had no sidelocks, and neither a hat nor a cap on his head. He didn't have a crooked nose either. Hillel's mother, with her thick glasses and the continuous line of her eyebrows reminded him of Fräulein Fritschi, with whom they had had to sing those pious songs in confirmation class.

The good blue suit had been a mistake; his hosts were dressed quite normally. Only Herr Rosenthal was wearing a smoking jacket that looked a little oriental, but peeping out from underneath it was the same kind of dotted bow tie that Herr Gerster liked to wear.

There was nothing unusual about the flat itself either, except that they had lots of books. But that could also have been because Herr Rosenthal was a teacher. The only striking thing was that beside every inside door there was an odd capsule with a Hebrew sign on it. Böhni knew what Hebrew looked like; in the caricatures in the Front the German letters were sometimes written with thin vertical lines and broad horizontal bars so that you knew straight away: Jews. Herr Rosenthal, who couldn't stop being a teacher even in his leisure time, noticed him glancing at the doorposts and went off on a complicated explanation of which Böhni understood only that there were Bible quotations in the capsules. He was reminded of the Lord's Prayer that hung in the kitchen at home in Flaach, with angels printed in four colours hovering around it. He wasn't happy with the parallel.

'Flowers? You really didn't need to,' said Lea, and to Hillel, 'So, this is your friend.' That was the moment when Hillel started to look for the word that best describes a non-friend and non-enemy.

The visit took place on the day after Shavuot, the Feast of Weeks. That was sensible, because it meant that Lea didn't have to cook anything extra; there was still enough left of the cheesecake that goes with the feast. She prepared it exactly according to the recipe of the legendary Grandmother Pomeranz from Endingen, and got even better results than Hinda.

Böhni also had to listen to a lecture on the subject of the Feast of Weeks. Hillel rolled his eyes at his father's mania for teaching, but his father refused to be put off by such reactions. As he often did at the Strickhof during theory classes, Böhni only listened with half an ear, but still grasped that Herr Rosenthal didn't know much about agriculture. He claimed, for example, that the first wheat of the year had been brought into the temple as a sacrifice on this day, and that was plainly nonsense: in May the wheat isn't nearly ready to be harvested. Although…Maybe down in Palestine it was different. He would have to ask Rosenthal afterwards.

Also left over from the Feast of Weeks was an opened bottle of wine on the dresser, also from Palestine, and Herr Rosenthal poured each of them a little glass. The wine was as sweet as syrup, and Böhni would have preferred a beer.

Hillel's mother wanted to hear something about his family and how he liked school, but he just gave taciturn answers, not out of shyness, but just because he wasn't used to people talking so much over dinner. Apart from that, the cheesecake was really particularly good.

As long as there was anything to eat on the table things went well, but eventually the plates were cleared away, Lea filled up everyone's tea again and they made conversation. In this household that meant: Hillel's father delivered a monologue, while everyone else got to make tiny interventions. Perhaps he had got used to that in school, where doubtless no one was allowed to interrupt his lectures on trigonometry or the calculation of probability, but in all likelihood chattiness was just his way. Sometimes, if he developed a thought too long-windedly, his wife nudged him under the table and reminded him with a look that they had a visitor. But that only made things worse, because then Herr Rosenthal would try to create the appearance of a conversation with questions. Böhni felt as if he was taking an exam. He soon started sweating, as if he had to tell Kudi Lampertz the correct proportion of phosphate and potassium in fertiliser for feed corn.

Before dinner, Herr Rosenthal had read the evening edition of the *Neue Zürcher Zeitung* – he did that every day and finished precisely to coincide with the meal – and now he was arguing about something called the Peel Commission that Böhni had never heard of. It had apparently delivered some kind of report that he didn't know about either. 'And this is a report about which,' said Herr Rosenthal, 'we might, to put it very cautiously, be very much in two minds.'

'I don't think Böhni's interested in this,' Hillel tried to rein in his father.

'Why not? He's an intelligent young man. So, what is your opinion on the subject?'

As he sometimes had to do in class, Böhni first tried to talk around the subject. So he said very carefully that he thought Herr Rosenthal was completely right, but then there were two sides to every question.

He wasn't getting away that easily, Herr Rosenthal insisted, he must surely be interested in politics. Böhni could confirm that at least with a good conscience, after all, he read the Front every day, even though a whole year's subscription cost eighteen francs, a lot of money for a small farmer's son from the wine-growing country.

That was what he thought, Herr Rosenthal nodded, he noticed it again and again, even in school, that young people today were much more interested in these things than they had been even a few years previously. But now Herr Böhni should not duck the question, but freely express his opinion. 'So, what is your view of the work of Lord Peel?'

'Of who?'

He was the leader of the commission, Frau Rosenthal helped him, that had now presented a plan for the division of the mandated territories.

Mandated territories. What was that again?

'Could we please talk about something else?' asked Hillel and glared furiously at his father.

Herr Rosenthal paid him as little attention as he would have an unruly pupil in class. He would be very interested, he went on, to know Herr Böhni's opinion about this planned division. It was always very instructive to learn how an unprejudiced and neutral observer saw a subject.

Hillel was no help at all to anyone. He had folded his hands behind his head, rocked his chair back and forth and looked up at the ceiling as if to say, 'I'm not even here.'

Böhni finally rescued himself with a method that always worked with Kudi Lampertz as well. The subject struck him as difficult, he said, really complicated, so he would be grateful if Herr Rosenthal could explain it to him very precisely once more, if that wasn't too much trouble.

It wasn't too much trouble for Herr Rosenthal at all. Quite the contrary, he nodded encouragingly to Böhni – if you don't ask, you won't learn – and launched into his next monologue.

In Palestine, he explained, an uprising by the Arab population against the Jewish settlers had been under way for a year. There had been repeated shootings and attacks, and also many people killed, as he was sure Herr Böhni must be aware. Now the British Government, which had been administrating

Palestine since the end of the Great War, as everybody knew – 'Aha!' thought Böhni – had finally set up a commission that was to make proposals for bringing peace to the region. And this commission had now put forward a proposal for a division of the territory, with a very small Jewish state in the North West and a corridor from Jaffa to Jerusalem, which was to remain under British control. According to this plan the whole of the rest would go to Transjordan, which brought it under the sway of King Abdullah.

'What's your opinion, Herr Böhni? Should one accept such a plan?'

Böhni would have liked to give him the right answer, just to stop having all these questions fired at him. But he didn't know what Herr Rosenthal wanted to hear. So he said very carefully that at first glance that all sounded very reasonable.

That was an unfortunate move. It was extremely unreasonable, Herr Rosenthal thundered, as could be proven with reference to a thousand historical examples. Founding a state in such a small territory was pure suicide, above all when that small territory was itself divided by a foreign corridor, and one could only hope that the World Congress in the Stadttheater...

Where the Stadttheater suddenly came into it Böhni had no idea, and his confusion was visible.

'The World Zionist Congress,' Lea explained helpfully, 'is meeting in Zurich this year, and at the Stadttheater.'

Böhni nodded, even though he didn't really know what Zionist meant. The word had cropped up in the brochure that he had copied out for his punishment essay, and in the Front the pro-Jewish Basler Nationalzeitung was always mocked as a 'Zional Zeitung'. But that probably wasn't the same thing.

'... that the World Congress will reject this suggestion once and for all.'

'Rubbish,' said Hillel, and was suddenly no longer indifferent, but to Böhni's surprise absolutely furious. 'What you're saying is complete nonsense.'

'Hillel!' his mother said, trying to calm him down, but father and son had argued too often about this subject, and so they could start up again right in the middle of an old quarrel, with a flying start, as they called it in the six-day race.

What his father was coming out with was total nonsense, Hillel said. Of course they had to found the state, even if was only a few square metres.

And excuse me, what good would that do, Herr Rosenthal inquired quite tartly.

It was only if one finally took a first step that other steps could eventually follow, said Hillel, and brought his fist down on the table, making the tea glasses dance. If you wanted to wait for the British or the League of Nations or a good fairy to agree to a Greater Israel one day, then one could equally well decide to spend another two thousand years in exile. What good had it done, spending all those centuries praying every day for the chance to return? None at all! Now that a practical chance seemed to present itself, they had to grasp it, and not make unrealisable demands and be left empty-handed in the end.

That was a short-sighted view, his father contradicted, that was practically fanatical. A state of one's own was by no means the most important thing, and exaggerated nationalism had never led to anything good.

So, said Hillel, that was exaggerated nationalism, and could his father perhaps explain where all the refugees from Germany were supposed to go, if not to their own state?

It was regrettable that so many people were being driven out of Germany, said Herr Rosenthal, but in both the literal and the figurative sense no state could be made with them, because they did not come from conviction, but only from Germany. Besides, the refugees were a passing phenomenon, Hitler wouldn't stay in power for ever, and by the time such a state was founded in Palestine, National Socialism would have faded from the scene. It wouldn't keep going for long.

Actually Böhni would have liked to contradict him on that point, but he didn't get the chance to speak, and it was better that way.

Luckily, said Hillel, the reasonable Zionists would definitely be in the majority at the World Congress, and not reject the Peel Plan without further ado.

It was very questionable, said Herr Rosenthal, whether there could even be such a thing as a reasonable Zionist.

Whereupon Hillel pushed back his chair and rose to his feet. 'Come on, Böhni, we're going!'

'Let's talk about something else,' Lea tried to mediate. 'What sort of things are you interested in, Herr Böhni?'

'He wants to get back to his room on time,' said Hillel. 'That's the only thing he's interested in.' According to the rules of the Strickhof, farmers in training had to spend the night in the school, which was only sensible when you had to be back up at five o'clock in the morning for milking. No exceptions were made even for rare city pupils like Hillel.

'There's a bit of cheesecake left over,' said Lea. 'Shall I wrap it up for you?'

'Sure,' said Hillel sarcastically. 'Böhni still has a page of his favourite paper in his pocket. That would be the ideal wrapping for a piece of kosher cake.'

The hasty departure was a bit like a flight, and on the tram back to the Irchel – the twenty-two to the Milchbuck had stopped running by this time of night – Hillel was in a bad mood, and not saying a word.

'I would never dare contradict my father like that,' Böhni said, trying to start up another conversation after they got out.

'I hope your father doesn't talk as much rubbish as mine.'

'To be honest: I didn't quite understand what it was actually about.'

'You can't understand, either, with all that Fröntler crap you fill your head up with.'

If he hadn't been so annoyed with his father, Hillel wouldn't have yelled at Böhni like that. And if Böhni hadn't felt so ill at ease all evening he wouldn't have reacted so sensitively and given Rosenthal a shove. Either way, regardless of who started it, on the way from the tram stop to Strickhof they fought for the first time. It felt really good venting their tempers like that, they rolled on the ground almost with pleasure, in spite of Böhni's good blue suit, and it actually felt good as they beat each other's noses bloody.

Their pleasure wasn't visible to the naked eye, however. If someone had walked past he would have thought the two young men were trying to kill each other.

When it was over, and neither of them had won, they had come strangely closer to one another. It didn't make them friends, certainly not, but neither did it make them enemies. They were not mates, and not chaverim, but something different, for which there must be a special word.

61

Arthur wasn't one of those bachelors who knew how to operate a stove. When he came back to his little flat after work he heedlessly stuffed something into his mouth, a bit of chocolate or a few slices of salami, whatever came to hand. So when Désirée paid him a visit she always brought along something she had cooked herself. As she heated it up in his kitchen, Arthur cleared up or arranged his papers and magazines into manageable piles. He laid the little table with the fine Sarreguemines crockery from the Baden flat. He had inherited a whole cupboard of it, enough for the big family he would never had.

With melancholy self-irony they called these evenings they spent together the 'lonely hearts' ball', because they had both come to terms with the idea of spending their lives alone. Since Alfred's death Désirée had seen herself as a widow, and even though her grief for him had settled into a scar, any interest in another man would have felt like infidelity. Arthur had slipped into being alone as a drinker slips into alcohol: with no conscious decision, but also with no prospect for change. When they sat there together, both alone, their conversation was almost like that of an old married couple, they repeated the same phrases over and over again and felt quite at home in them. When Arthur had emptied his plate, for example, he always said, 'A family of one's own would be nice.' And Désirée replied, 'When it comes to that, let's swap flats.'

She didn't really mean it, because she had now spent forty years living in the same place, she had grown up in the flat on Morgartenstrasse and had, in spite of the fact that it had far too many rooms, taken it over quite naturally after Pinchas and Mimi's death and never changed anything in it. She often didn't step into Pinchas's office, its desk still covered with unread papers, for weeks at a time, she only had disagreements with the cleaning lady and hence kept coming up with plans for a change. They remained plans, because there was something that always held her back: just as a jar of formaldehyde captures a scientific specimen for all time, the flat preserved for her the young girl she had once been, the smitten teenager with her bedside table full of bonbons that smelled of almonds and rosewater.

After dinner, and this too had become a tradition, they both sat together in the sitting room, where the bronzed oak-leaf wreath from Arthur's Gymnastics Society days still hung on the wall, and the tantalus, unopened since the previous century, still stood among the books on the shelf. Only a bachelor could have kept the leather armchairs, rubbed dull with use, for so many years; they were unsightly, yet as comfortable as a pair of worn-out slippers. 'They're a good match for me,' thought Arthur.

It was part of their shared ritual that Arthur took a cigar from the box that a grateful patient gave him every year as mishloach manot at Purim, turned it around between his fingers, without really knowing what one was actually supposed to look out for in that exploratory rustling sound, and then lit it, puffing the while. It usually went out soon afterwards, and ended up forgotten in the ashtray; Arthur didn't particularly like cigars, but would have felt ungrateful if he hadn't used the present at all.

Désirée drank port, 'an old maid's drink', as she called it. She emphasised her old-maid status with her hairstyle: parted in the middle, the way she had worn it as a young girl. Except that her hair was thinner now, and showing its first grey strands.

Today too everything could have been as it always was. But their conversation, which usually revolved around pleasantly trivial matters, kept drifting inexorably towards the same point, where it was tugged by the overwhelming current of facts into the same unchanging whirlwind. Beyond the border, just a few kilometres from Zurich, the world had been thrown out of joint, the pub politicians had left the regulars' table for the government benches, and published their thuggish slogans as legal documents.

In his letters Ruben gave an account of the fresh torments that were constantly being introduced, all with the same goal in mind: to drive as many Jews as possible out of Germany. His Halberstadt congregation had shrunk almost by half in the previous four years, often with an apparently minor detail providing the final impulse to emigration. For example the 'Stürmer box', a display case carved in the old German style with the latest edition of Streicher's hate sheet; it had been put up right by the entrance to the Klaus Synagogue, so that the faithful had to push their way past the caricatures of girl-defiling Jewish doctors and blood-sucking Jewish bankers on their way to service. For others it was a simple question in their children's maths lesson that was the final straw. In a letter, Ruben had quoted the example from a school textbook: 'Some intellectual professions in Berlin were dominated by Jews during the Weimar Republic. So among theatre people the Jewish proportion was eighty per cent, among lawyers sixty per cent, among doctors forty per cent, among university teachers in the Philosophy faculty twenty-five per cent. Show these figures in a graph!' A committee member in the congregation, a soldier from the Great War with German nationalist leanings, who had sworn not to be driven from his fatherland under any circumstances, had emigrated overnight, after a polite voice had explained to him, when he had tried to send a telegram by telephone, that Jewish names could no longer be spelled out on the phone, it was incompatible with the racial pride of German postal officials.

'A whole country has gone mad,' Arthur said. 'We can thank God that we live in Switzerland.'

'Can we really do that?' Désirée ran her fingernail thoughtfully along the rim of her glass. 'Maybe the mad people haven't yet floated to the surface here.'

Again, it wasn't the first time they had had this conversation either, and on this subject too they both argued like an old married couple, each one knowing the views of the other so well that they react to certain words even before they are uttered. Désirée knew better than Arthur himself that he couldn't imagine the world as anything other than reasonable, with laws which, while they might sometimes have been abused, were still correct in their fundamental traits. For a person like him there simply had to be reliable rules, because otherwise one lost one's bearings. Arthur, for his part, knew Désirée's fundamental scepticism about anything that proclaimed its rationality and objectivity too noisily. Behind that lay her firm conviction that unreason and blind emotion always lay behind such things. She had inherited that attitude from her father. As long as he lived, Pinchas had never got over the fact that the very first people's initiative in Switzerland had been to forbid shechita, that a new law had immediately been used to create a new injustice. 'An individual can make judgements,' was the lesson he had learned from that. 'The mass know only prejudices.' And as if to prove this thesis, what had been one of the first rulings made by Hitler's government? A prohibition on shechita. 'We're being forced into vegetarianism,' Ruben had written in one of his letters.

'Are we really supposed to wait until the same thing happens here? It might be more intelligent to start packing before it's too late.'

'To emigrate where?'

Désirée spread her arms, a gesture that took in the whole world, then lowered them again so that the world one could flee into dissolved and fell into a thousand pieces. 'Anywhere,' she said.

'That would be cowardice.'

Désirée nodded. 'And we aren't brave enough to be cowardly.'

She didn't have to explain what she meant by that. If Alfred had been brave enough at the outbreak of the war simply to run away, to desert, to go into hiding – perhaps he would still have been alive now.

Perhaps everything would have been different.

'Don't let these Fröntlers scare you. They'll never get a majority here.'

'Maybe. But sometimes I'm not sure if this is really still our country.'

In her shop Désirée always got to hear everything that happened. She learned of the children who had been shouted at in the street, 'Jewboy, Jewboy, your time is nearly through, boy!' although the worst thing wasn't the mocking verse, but the fact that no one was bothered about it, she heard about the German refugee who was congratulated in a shop, because his Jewishness wasn't visible, on the way his country was finally cleaning up and putting things in order, the story of the lawyer who argued in court that the slogan 'Perish the Jews!' on the wall of the Bern synagogue had nothing to do with anti-Semitism, but was an expression of political opinion protected by the constitution, and who was able to back it up with reference to a judgement by the Swiss Federal Court.

'And have you heard what happened in François's department store?'

No, Arthur hadn't heard.

Someone had taken a dislike to the trademark with which François had decorated each of his shop windows for years. This someone, whom the police could not identify, had taken offence at the horizontal and vertical name M-E-I-E-R and corrected it back to its original form, carefully adding the missing J, window by window, back in with oil paint.

Meijer without a yud had become Meier with a yud again.

'Nothing but rascally pranks,' said Arthur. And he didn't believe the reassuring words himself.

'Possible. Except that we are living in a time when the rascals are in charge.'

'Not in Switzerland.'

'Are you sure?' asked Désirée.

To Arthur's luck, at precisely that moment the phone rang, and kept him from having to admit that he was very far from sure.

He had expected one of his patients, and was surprised to hear Rachel's voice. 'You've got to come to the factory straight away,' she said with the over-distinct articulation of someone struggling to control their panic.

'There's been a murder.'

Désirée insisted on coming.

The Fiat's headlights crept along the dark façades of the houses like curious fingers. Every time they took in a late passer-by, it was as if they had caught him, a whole city full of twilight figures, all on their way to do something forbidden. Arthur was nervous, he kept forgetting to double-declutch, making the gears clash so that one might have thought the car was resisting the journey it was being asked to take so late at night.

'Do you know if the police are there?' Désirée asked.

'I don't think so. Something must have happened that they don't want to make a great song and dance about.'

'I still can't imagine it. A murder in Zalman's factory?' Désirée spoke the unfamiliar word as if wearing gloves, the way one picks up things that seem strange very carefully.

'Rachel said: there's been a murder.'

'Does she know the difference?'

Even though it wasn't really appropriate, or perhaps precisely because it wasn't appropriate, Arthur couldn't help laughing at the question, out of nerves, of course, but also because Désirée had caught Rachel Kamionker's character so precisely. 'Does she know the difference?' The years when men had swarmed around Rachel, and received even her most casual remark with applause, were long gone, but even today her behaviour was defined by her certainty, which had come into being back then, that people would always agree with what she said even if she didn't give it much thought.

When they charged into the factory, Arthur clutching his medical case, there was a cordon of people waiting for them, a whole row of employees with concerned expressions, who all wanted to show them the way to the big sewing room, and hoped to use the opportunity to get a glimpse of the dramatic events from which they had been excluded.

Just as Arthur was about to reach for the door handle, it sprang open, and a young woman in a state of complete distress dashed towards them. She was very pretty, Arthur could see that straight away, and he felt guilty for noticing that first and only then the big bloodstain on her dress. She clutched his sleeve and stammered, 'Thank God, Doctor! You've got to save him! Otherwise he's going to die on me, he's going to die!' She wouldn't let go, and Désirée actually had to tear her away from him. Only now did he see that the young woman's hands were smeared with blood, and the inappropriate thought darted through his head: would the stains ever come out of his coat?

The sewing room glowed in an unnaturally white, bright light. It must have been those new-fangled neon lamps that Zalman had talked about with such pride. In two neat rows, like the desks in a classroom, stood the sewing machines. At the front a figure lay motionless on the floor. Around it, Zalman, Rachel and a man that Arthur didn't know. None of them looked up when Arthur came in.

Someone had tried to cover up the body they were guarding, and even though they would have had all kinds of other materials to choose from here, had reached for a gently shimmering white fabric, too impractical for a sheet and too valuable for a shroud. Around the man's head the fabric was covered with blood, but he still seemed to be breathing and...

It wasn't just a man.

It was Joni Leibowitz.

His Joni.

Arthur knelt down next to him, he knelt next to Joni as he had once, a thousand years ago, knelt beside that body, in a gym on that occasion, he could still smell the moment, sweat and dust, he knelt next to him, and in that face, puffy now, he sought the familiar features, in the stale cigarette smoke the scent he had often inhaled, so similar to his own, he knelt on the floor and for a long moment he had forgotten everything a doctor has to be able to do, he just waited helplessly for Joni to open his eyes, waited for the private smile that wasn't given to everybody, waited for a visit from the past, to say, 'Oh please, Doctor, when can I have another appointment with you?'

But the only voice was that of the woman who went on wailing outside the door. 'He's dying on me,' she howled, 'he's dying on me, no one can save him.'

Then the moment was over, it had really been just a moment, he was a doctor again, as he had been a hundred times in emergencies, and his hands did everything that needed to be done all by themselves. The bones of the skull, whose lines he knew so well, were undamaged, there was just a laceration, a tear in the skin that could be stitched up without much difficulty. Of course Joni had lost a lot of blood, but a head like that bleeds easily, and it doesn't necessarily mean it's anything dramatic. It would have been smarter to bandage the wound rather than just covering it up, but perhaps no one had dared to do that, or else the hysterical woman hadn't let them. She must have rested his head in her lap, hence the blood on her dress, she must have stroked him, which was both senseless and unhygienic.

Arthur envied her that.

At last Joni opened his eyes. He didn't seem to recognise Arthur, which might have been because of the injury, looked at him as if he were a stranger, without a smile, private or public. Ran his tongue over his lips as if to check that his mouth was still there and working, and then said with quiet fury, 'I'm going to sue that meshuganeh.'

Outside the woman screamed, 'He's dying on me!' Joni tried to turn his head, pulled a painful face and whispered, 'Please could someone get that Blandine to shut up?'

He should really have been taken to hospital for observation, he had had a bump on the head and been unconscious. Concussion couldn't be ruled out, in such cases it could lead to complications, to vestibular disorders or even worse. But Zalman was concerned about the good reputation of the company, and Joni's condition seemed to be improving from one minute to the next. So the decision was made that he would be taken to Arthur's surgery to have the wound stitched, but Arthur's car was too small for that – not for nothing was the car called Topolino, the little mouse – and a taxi had to be called from Welti-Furrer, the removals firm. Until it arrived, a bed was organised for Joni in the cutters' room, and the woman who was so concerned about him, Blandine Flückiger – the house model, Arthur learned – was given the task of putting damp, cool cloths on his forehead.

What had happened? Zalman wanted to tell him, but Rachel wouldn't let her father get a word in. After all, she had been there when it happened, she said, while Zalman had been sitting in his office and was therefore unable to provide any reliable information.

Today the company had received another hasty commission, one of those impatient orders that landed at the Kamionker Clothes Company because it was well known that they needed the work and would sometimes work through one night or two. Zalman didn't like that overtime, but what was one to do? As things stood, the customers had the upper hand.

So they didn't stop work as usual at half past six, gave the apprentice, who had to go to the post office with the daily parcels anyway, the task of buying bread and cheese for everyone and prepared for a long night. At about nine o'clock they took a break and ate something. On these occasions there was always an atmosphere a bit like a picnic outing, they were all tired and excited at the same time, they walked around a little to stretch their legs and talked about everything imaginable.

The table with the makeshift supply centre was set up right by the entrance, and most people gathered there. Only a few preferred to take their sandwiches to their work stations. One of these was the man who had been standing beside Zalman all this time, and whom Arthur had never met before. His name was Grün, and he was new.

Herr Grün, even Rachel had to admit, had learned how to sew very quickly. Admittedly he couldn't yet be used for complicated work, but he could make a straight seam without any difficulties, and with the necessary speed.

But he was still a meshuganeh.

He had been sitting at a sewing machine – 'He always sits apart from the rest!' – and was the only one, or almost the only one, in the sewing room when Joni Leibowitz and the model came in, perhaps because they hoped they wouldn't be disturbed there. Rachel left no doubt about what purpose that lack of disturbance might have been supposed to serve.

She herself had just happened to be standing in the doorway.

'Just happened?' asked Zalman, and Rachel replied with unexpected vehemence that she had not the slightest interest either in Herr Leibowitz or in

Fräulein Flückiger, and if anyone thought she had been spying on the two of them, then he would also need to explain why she should have been doing such a thing.

No matter. At any rate, she had been standing in the doorway and could confirm that Joni and Blandine had been chatting quite peacefully, about politics, of course, what else were people talking about these days, until Herr Grün had suddenly risen to his feet. Not leapt to his feet, as if he had been furious or agitated, no, he had risen quite calmly, he had taken the heavy iron that always stood ready in the sewing room because certain pieces always need to be pre-ironed before they can be sewn, so he had picked up the iron and hit Joni so hard on the head with it that he collapsed straight away. And then? Then he had put the iron carefully back in its holder, had gone back to his seat as if nothing had happened, had sat down again and gone on eating his bread.

Joni had lain there, one might have thought he was dead, everything was covered in blood, and Blandine had screamed her head off until everyone was suddenly standing in here, the whole workforce, it was Bedlam, or the Burghölzli. Only Rachel had kept her seichel and phoned Arthur straight away.

During this account Herr Grün stood there in the three-piece suit that was far too big for him and inappropriate for a factory stitcher, and when everyone looked at him quizzically, he just nodded and said, 'You observed that very well, Fräulein Kamionker. That's exactly how it was.'

'So why?' asked Zalman.

'The iron was the only thing to hand.'

'What did Leibowitz do to you?'

Herr Grün shrugged and held his hands in front of him, fingers spread, a very Jewish gesture that means more or less, 'What is a person to do? A man plans his way, but God guides his steps.' Then he turned to Zalman and said, 'Of course you're going to fire me now.'

'First of all I want to know what on earth got into you.'

'That is a point in your favour,' said Herr Grün quite matter-of-factly. 'But how am I to explain it to you? Let's put it this way: I didn't like what Herr Leibowitz said to the young lady.'

'What?' Zalman was a peaceful man, but now he was raising his voice.

'He was prancing around in front of the girl. He wants to get her into bed, and he hasn't managed it yet.'

'How do you know that?' Rachel cut in.

'You can see,' said Herr Grün. 'And you can hardly blame him either, she's a pretty girl. And it's none of my business.'

'And still you...?'

Herr Grün talked calmly on, as if they weren't all standing impatiently around him

'He was trying to impress her with his chochme, he wanted to show her what a clever person he is, and how much he knows about the world of politics. They talked about what was happening in Germany, and he declared that nothing like that would ever happen to him personally. He always got on famously with all non-Jews, even if they sympathised with the Front or thought Hitler was a great statesman. Because he was adaptable, unlike lots of other people, because he didn't attract attention and he wasn't stand-offish.

'Lots of Jews, he told her, still didn't understand that, and if someone was bullied or put in the camps, it was always partly his own fault. "His own fault," he said. So I picked up the iron and hit him over the head with it.'

Zalman walked over to him and rested a hand on his shoulder. 'I would be grateful, Herr Grün,' he said, 'if next time you settled for an object that wasn't quite so hard.'

'Next time?' asked Rachel, furiously.

'I can't sack him for that,' said Zalman.

62

'Just ask him!'

Always the same answer, however much Rachel might have urged her father. 'Ask him! If he wants to tell you, he'll tell you.' And Hinda, who must have been let in on the secret, was no help either.

Of course there was an official version. There was always an official version.

It had been an accident, they had told everyone in the shop, an unfortunate slip, a stumble, whatever. Admittedly no one was really convinced by that, but what Blandine Flückiger was going around saying was even less credible. Herr Grün had quite deliberately picked up the iron, she claimed in all seriousness, and simply lashed out with it. 'Impossible,' people said. She was known to play the tormented victim, and to over-dramatise her not particularly interesting life.

If someone doesn't know the truth, he creates one for himself, so in the kosher clothes factory they agreed that it must have been a story of jealousy. Two men, no longer in the first flush of youth, fighting tooth and nail over a peroxide Jean Harlow – it was a good story, so it was the one that people chose to believe.

Neither of them wanted to say anything about what happened, and their persistent silence was generally seen as a confirmation of the legend. That night Zalman had gone with Joni Leibowitz to Arthur's surgery, and used the opportunity to press him to be silent – Rachel didn't know what arguments he had used. Just two days later Joni had turned up for work again, with a fat bandage around his head, on which his hat sat two sizes too small. He batted away the jokes of the buyers with the same, unchanging joke: 'Ok, I fell on my head – but that doesn't mean you can push my prices down!'

Herr Grün got on with his work for a few more days as if nothing had happened; he had just become even more taciturn, he said 'Good morning' and 'Goodbye' and otherwise didn't talk to anybody. Every time Blandine Flückiger saw him, she took cover behind someone with a shrill cry, to which Herr Grün responded with a smile, or with a facial expression that must once have been a smile.

'Ask him!' was all that Rachel heard each time she tried to find out, but of course she wouldn't have dreamt of asking Herr Grün. How could she have?

But then, a few days later, he was no longer sitting at his sewing machine, and his landlady, Frau Posmanik, informed them that he had a high fever, and there was no way of telling when he might recover. So it fell to Rachel to look after him. If you're responsible for the staff in a company and you fill the pay packets, you have a certain duty of care.

'And you can use the opportunity to ask a few questions,' mocked Zalman.

Rachel had not, as she replied in a dignified voice, even thought of such a thing. She was just doing her duty. So in the evening she dutifully took the money for a fortifying bottle of tonic wine from petty cash and set off.

The Posmaniks lived on Molkenstrasse, right behind the barracks' parade ground, in one of those cheaply built rental blocks that look derelict while they're still new. Five people crammed themselves into three small rooms, and they'd had to rent out one of those. Herr Posmanik spent his days looking for work, which in practice meant that he boosted himself for the task with his first beer in the morning, and consoled himself for his lack of success with the last schnapps in the evening. His wife kept the family afloat by taking little scraps of brocade, which she begged from Zalman, among others, embroidering them with gold thread and then selling these coasters from door to door among the Jewish houses. Her products were neither useful nor really decorative, but people felt sorry for this sickly woman – 'Her skin is like blue milk,' Hinda had once said – and always bought something from her. In Zurich you almost had the impression that a Jewish flat without a brocade coaster was just as incomplete as one without a mezuzah on the door post.

The sound of children shouting could be heard from the top-floor flat. At first Rachel knocked politely, but in the end she had to hammer on the door with her fist to be heard at all. The shouting died down, she heard whispering and then at last the door opened, at least as far as the security chain on the door permitted. A little boy, stark naked, eyed her suspiciously through the chink. 'We're not buying anything,' he said, a phrase that he had probably often heard his mother say on similar occasions, and thought was a correct form of greeting.

'I'm Frau Kamionker,' said Rachel in her best aunty voice. 'I've come to visit.'

'There's no one at home,' said the little boy, and was about to shut the door again. Rachel was just able to wedge her foot in it.

'Your lodger is at home. Herr Grün.'

When he heard the name, the little boy beamed. 'He's such a funny man,' he said. And then, suddenly serious, 'But now he's sick.'

A funny man? 'Funny' wasn't really a word that seemed to apply to Herr Grün.

'Shall I tell you a poem?' asked the little boy.

'What?'

'A poem. Uncle Grün taught me it.'

'Won't you let me in first?'

'No, first the poem,' he said, as seriously as if in polite circles such a recitation was one of the most natural preliminaries to visit.

'Off you go, then.'

The naked boy in the crack of the door took a deep breath and recited in one breath: 'My parrot won't eat carrots, he thinks they're rather grim, he's the loveliest of parrots, but carrots aren't for him.'

'That's a song,' said Rachel.

'Only if you sing it,' the little boy replied and went on, 'He's wild about cough sweets and biscuits, and celery keeps him trim, he's been known to try an oyster, but carrots aren't for him. Do you know what cough sweets are?'

'They're sweet things that you eat when you have a cold.'

'Have you got any for him?' asked the little boy. 'I think Uncle Grün has a cold.'

'Does he teach you lots of poems like that?'

'He knows at least a million,' said the little boy. 'Or even more.'

'How lovely.' Rachel was feeling more and more ridiculous standing outside the half-closed door to the flat. 'But will you please open up for me now?'

The boy thought for a minute, even raised his hand as if to say, 'Don't bother me when I'm thinking,' and then nodded. 'All right, then.'

To open up, he first had to close the door again and then, to judge by the rattle and clatter on the other side, he had trouble unhooking the chain. But then it was done; Rachel was finally able to make her visit. When she stepped inside the flat, two even smaller children looked at her curiously.

'I'd like to have a parrot as well,' said the boy, and walked straight ahead of her, stark naked as he was. 'If he doesn't want the carrots, I'll eat them myself.'

Herr Grün's room was tiny. A bed, a wardrobe, a chair. There was no room for a table; the window sill had to serve as a substitute.

'Herr Grün?'

No reply. Just a strange sound, like someone drumming nervously on a glass with their fingernails.

The room smelled of illness. You didn't need to be a doctor to recognise that.

It wasn't fingernails. It was teeth. Clattering teeth.

He was in bed. The day was warm, almost summery, but Herr Grün's teeth were chattering. He had laid a coat over the thin blue bedcover and crept under both, had drawn up his legs like a baby, his arms wrapped protectively around his body, and still he was shivering.

'Herr Grün!'

When he heard his name he tried to sit up, tried to say something, but didn't have the strength. The breath whistled out of his throat. Deep inside him a door was open, a window was broken. He moved his lips and couldn't put the syllables together. He tried again and again and again.

Rachel bent down to him. He smelled unpleasant, as sick people do.

A number. He was trying to force out a number.

'Four thousand eight hundred and ninety-two,' whispered Herr Grün.

A thread of saliva ran from his mouth. Even though Rachel was repelled by it, she wiped it away with a corner of the sheet.

A shabby, worn, pauper's sheet. Far too thin for a sick man.

When she asked the naked little boy about a telephone, he looked at her as if she'd asked him for something unheard-of, something from a fairy-tale, a lump of gold or a parrot.

'No one in the building has a telephone,' he said.

'And where does your mother go when she needs to call somebody?'

'Who would I want to call?' Frau Posmanik had come home, from a journey, one might have thought, because she was holding a big suitcase in her hand, covered with faded souvenir stickers from expensive hotels, St Moritz, Carlsbad, Nice. Someone had given her the old thing out of pity, and since then she had been carting her collection of useless brocade coasters around the city in it.

'What an honour, Frau Kamionker,' she said. Anyone who depends on the sympathy of others to earn a living develops fine antennae, so she knew that Rachel didn't like being addressed as Fräulein. 'I had no idea – Aaron, put your trousers on immediately! – no idea that you were going to come and visit...'

'My trousers are wet,' wailed the little boy.

'You'll have to forgive me, Frau Kamionker. I had to wash them, and they're the only ones he's got.'

'That doesn't matter. I'm here for Herr Grün.'

'He really can't come to work,' said Frau Posmanik, and forgot to set down her suitcase, she was so eager to stand up for her lodger. 'He tried to get up, but he just couldn't.' Because of her life's experience, she could only imagine that Rachel had come on a punitive mission.

'The man is seriously ill!'

'Why didn't you bring cough sweets?' the little boy asked and immediately started reciting again, 'He's wild about cough sweets and biscuits...'

'Sha!'

'Herr Grün needs a doctor.'

'I've done what I could,' Frau Posmanik defended herself. 'I made him some tea but he wouldn't drink it, and I can't spend all day...'

'Is there a telephone anywhere around here?'

'Only at the Kreuel in Kanonengasse. It's a pub. But you're better off not going there. It's not a place for...'

'For our people,' she had wanted to say, but then she choked the words back. It would have struck her as presumptuous to put herself on the same level as the daughter of Herr Kamionker the factory owner. Although the people in the Kreuel wouldn't have distinguished between them, and would have treated them both with equal rudeness. 'It's the Frontists' pub.'

'Kreuel,' Rachel repeated. 'Good. Perhaps in the meantime you can find something to wrap him up in.' And was already out the door, with a competent efficiency unfamiliar in this household.

Frau Posmanik was already holding her suitcase, with all the stuck-on memories that weren't hers.

When Rachel came home at last that night, back to the safety of her own flat, she stood in front of the mirror for a long time.

She just couldn't get it. There was nothing unusual about her. She looked like a thousand other Zurich women. All right, not all of them had such flaming red hair, but it couldn't be that.

And yet they had known straight away. Had smelled it. Hunting dogs, picking up a scent.

She turned to one side and tried to appraise her profile from the corner of her eye. There was nothing remarkable about it. Nothing that would make you think straight away, of course, a Jew. There was nothing.

She didn't wear a sheitel, even as a married woman she wouldn't have worn one, and she would never have put on one of those old-fashioned high-necked dresses by which you could recognise the Orthodox women, above all the ones from the East, at first glance. She dressed fashionably, always from the latest collection, she owed the company that, and her lipstick was the colour of the season.

And yet...

She was already lighting her fourth cigarette, and still couldn't calm down.

She had gone to the pub, Kanonengasse was just around the corner from the Posmaniks, three steps led from the street up to the front door, the door had been open, it was a mild evening, she had pushed aside the curtain, a piece of fabric, heavy and saturated with cigar-smoke, she had gone in, a woman like a thousand others in a perfectly ordinary pub, no one had paid her any attention, not at first, she had gone up to the counter, the landlord no different from other landlords, his shirt-sleeves rolled up and fastened with a rubber band, she had asked him for the telephone, and he had pointed the way with his thumb, without taking the Brissago out of his mouth, not very polite, but that was nothing special, it was just his way.

The phone was fixed to the wall, opposite the corridor to the toilets, she had dialled Arthur's number, other numbers and names were scribbled in pencil on the wallpaper, and an there was an enamel sign for Wädenswiler beer, even though they served Hürlimann here. She hadn't had to wait long. Arthur answered immediately, with his mouth full, he was just eating, she told him what she had to say, he promised to come, it only took a minute, two at the most, but when she hung up and turned round again, all the people were sitting at the table with their heads raised, they'd picked up a scent, they looked at her, almost pleased, as one might look at an unexpected gift, one of them got up and was about to walk towards her, another held her back, she felt it more than she saw it, and then there was the landlord who didn't want her to pay for her call, 'you can keep your dirty Jewish money,' the Brissago still in his mouth. Ash fell into a half-poured beer glass, she saw it as if there was nothing else to see.

And then another one got up, and another one, no one was holding the men back now. Faces that frightened her, and then she had run away, had stumbled down the three steps and almost fallen into the street. Behind her they had laughed, a jeering, barking laugh, and if she had broken her neck they'd have been really happy.

How had they known? Rachel couldn't work it out

They might have listened to her conversation, but she didn't talk any differently from anyone else from Zurich, and she didn't have a crooked nose.

She didn't give anyone a reason, a cause, she didn't stand out.

And even if she had stood out...That still gave them no right. If someone walked through the city in peasant costume, he stood out. If someone was big or small or had a hunchback. That couldn't be a reason.

'If you stand out, it's your own fault,' Joni Leibowitz had said, and Herr Grün had taken an iron and hit him on the head with it.

Herr Grün, with his teeth chattering under the blanket.

Luckily it wasn't pneumonia, Arthur had said, not quite. With peace and attention and good food everything would be cured. Herr Grün had had an injection, and already his breathing was calmer now, and he didn't try to get up again. He slept, or at least he was anaesthetised.

Arthur had written out a prescription for a medicine that was to be collected from the chemist's, and had pressed the money for it into Frau Posmanik's hand. He had done it secretly, almost awkwardly, not because he was embarrassed about his generosity, but because he didn't want her husband to see it, when he would probably have converted the few francs into alcohol. The little boy – who was dressed now – asked him for cough sweets, and Arthur actually did conjure something sweet for him and his two siblings out of his case.

Later, when he drove Rachel home in his little Fiat, he asked her, 'Did he ever say anything about being in a re-education camp?'

Re-education camp. Some also said: concentration camp.

'He never says anything. What gives you that idea?'

'His back is covered with scars. From beatings, I would say.'

Of course.

Four thousand eight hundred and ninety-two.

What importance does one's own name have if one has been given a number in one of those camps? 'Grünbaum, Grünfeld – just choose something.'

His suit was made for a fat man, and that fat man had been Herr Grün himself. Before he …

Of course.

Joni had claimed that it was your own fault if you ended up in a camp, and he had torn into him.

Of course.

But why didn't he say so?

In one of his letters Ruben had written, 'The ones who come back don't talk about it.'

Just like Herr Grün.

Only he must have told Zalman about it, after he had waited for him for so long, he must have told him everything he'd been through, and then Zalman had decided to help him. Even though Herr Grün couldn't sew. He was a learned man. Someone who had had to learn to deal with everything.

Rachel had only been verbally abused, that was all. And even that could have been avoided if she'd listened to Frau Posmanik's warning. But why shouldn't she go wherever she wanted to go? This was Switzerland, not Germany.

'With the difference you can make Shabbos,' said Uncle Melnitz. He was standing behind her, looking at himself over her shoulder in the mirror. 'When they come marching in with their boots on, then you just say, "Gentlemen, this is Switzerland." And then they'll say, "Oops, sorry, we didn't know that." And they'll march back out again. One, two, one, two, yes.'

He looked at himself in profile and let his nose grow until in the mirror it looked like the caricatures in the Stürmer display case outside Ruben's synagogue. 'Everything's very different in Switzerland,' he said. 'Yes. They don't

522

even notice if someone's a Jew. It doesn't even strike them. Not if you dye your hair and put on clothes from the latest collection. They don't notice it, do they, Rachel?'

'That was an exception. They were Frontists.'

'There's always an exception,' said Uncle Melnitz, standing closer behind her. 'They're always good citizens. Orderly people. Pillars of society. Until they get the opportunity not to be. It's like that everywhere in the world, yes. Except for here in Switzerland, of course. Except in the good old Confederacy. They love us here.' He let his face swell until it turned into the fat, sated face of an exploiter. 'In Switzerland they have no prejudices.'

'Of course here too...'

'Of course,' repeated Uncle Melnitz. 'We don't want to ask too much. When they help us wherever they can. When they have opened their borders to all refugees. When a red carpet is rolled out at every border crossing, whenever someone comes and needs a new homeland. Of course. Everything's different in Switzerland, you're quite right, Rachel, my child.' And he made a wart sprout from his nose and a hunch from his back.

'You have to understand that too. There are so many emigrants.'

'Correct. And it would be undemocratic to let one into the country and not the other. Much better for them all to stay out. Dear God, make my excuse a good one.'

63

Dear Frau Pollack,

My name is Dr. Arthur Meijer. I am a general practitioner here in Zurich, and I also sometimes treat the children in the Wartheim in Heiden. I am a member of the B'nai B'rith, for which you yourself have also worked, and it was they who asked me to take on this task.

I am writing to you because I have just had a copy of the letter in which the director of the Wartheim informs you of the state of your daughter Irma's health. I fear she may have alarmed you unnecessarily. Fräulein Württemberger is not especially gifted when it comes to dealing with other people. (But then who is?)

Please don't worry, and forget everything that Fräulein Württemberger has written to you. Irma is perfectly healthy.

For the first time in my thirty-year practice as a doctor (it's only when one writes it down that one realises how old one has grown) I deliberately made a wrong diagnosis, and am, strangely, even proud of it. If I have correctly understood Irma (she is a girl who can express herself far better than one would expect at that age), it is very important for you and your children that they remain in Switzerland for the time being. The situation in Germany must be very difficult, probably far more difficult than we can imagine here in safe Switzerland. My nephew Ruben lives in Halberstadt, and what he reports in his letters often leaves me unable to sleep.

I sometimes think that the world has been sick since the Great War, and even today no one has found a prescription for healing it again. Perhaps there is none.

But always expecting the worst doesn't help either.

I hope that with my 'misdiagnosis' I have acted in line with your wishes, and that I have been able to help you (I should have written 'help you a little bit', because a little bit is all it can be.) If I can do anything else for you, please let me know.

With very best regards

Dr Arthur Meijer

Brandschenkestrasse 34

PS: Reading it through, it occurs to me that this letter is full of parentheses. My sister Hinda would say: your writing is as chaotic as your thought.

Dear Dr. Meijer!

Many thanks for your kind letter. You must be a very nice person.

Luckily your well-meant concern was unnecessary. I have never been concerned about the state of my daughter's health. Even before Fräulein Württemberger contacted me, Irma had told me everything in a letter. She even crept secretly into the village to bring it to the post office unnoticed. I have the impression that she's really enjoying the whole conspiracy. She was a diva even as a very little girl.

So by the time Frl. W.'s letter reached me, I already knew everything. This woman who runs the home really seems to know very little about psychology.

By the way: Irma also expresses herself much better than her twelve years would suggest. In other circumstances I would be proud of it, but as it is I worry. It isn't good when children have to grow up in a time that makes them grow up too quickly.

Irma writes to me that you are a Goliath, and from her that is a great compliment.

I have to explain that to you. She doesn't mean the Biblical Goliath, who had no chance against David's sling, but the hero of the bedtime stories that I have told my children for many years. (And which Moses still likes to hear.)

You must have infected me: now I too am starting to write in brackets, even though it was dinned into us in school that that's the sign of a badly organised mind. (Apologies.)

In these stories, without which my children would never go to sleep, the family got into terrible difficulties of some sort in each new episode. If they climbed a mountain, it would turn out to be a volcano and erupt. If they were travelling on a ship, they would find themselves in a tornado. And so on. The disaster could not be bad enough, because at the very last moment Goliath would always appear and put everything right again. For example if they were about to be run over, he would suddenly be standing there and stop the car. Effortlessly, just with one hand. And smile as he did it. A hero, in fact.

You see: you have made a big impression on Irma.

I had to tell my children the episode with the car over and over again. Perhaps Irma has told you that my husband lost his life in a traffic accident.

I am very grateful for the fact that my children are allowed to stay in Switzerland for now. It is a great relief to me. Ideally they would never have to come back to Germany at all. It's no longer our country. In Moses' class they are now practising reading from a picture book: 'Trust not the fox who roams the heath, nor Jews who all lie through their teeth,' it is called, and the verses in it are so terrible that one can hardly imagine. There, for example, beside a real Stürmer picture, it says, 'This is the Jew, it's plain to see; the greatest rogue in Germany!'

I don't want my son to learn such things by heart. And possibly recite them in front of the whole class. His teacher was a Party member early on.

The worst thing is that the author of this book is supposed to be just seventeen or eighteen years old. Such a young mind is quickly poisoned.

No, this is no longer my Germany.

I have decided to go to Berlin for a few days, and approach the various embassies. There must be a visa somewhere, regardless of which country it is for! Even though that is very difficult at the moment, particularly for someone who has no money. They say that you can sometimes spend two days waiting in the queue outside the British Embassy, before you can even fill in the application form to emigrate to Palestine.

I would most like to go to America. Do you know anyone there who could issue me with an affidavit?

Forgive me for asking you for something yet again. It isn't my way.

One becomes so helpless.

Irma writes to tell me that she now has a room of her own with Moses in the Wartheim. Did you organise that too? Then you really are a Goliath.

Once again: I am really grateful to you. It's good to know that there is some-one who cares.

With best regards.

Rosa Pollack

Zurich, 1 June 1937

Dear Frau Pollack,

I am certainly not a Goliath. Heroes are not short-sighted, and they don't run out of breath if they have to go up a flight of stairs to see a patient. (Although: do we know whether heroes aren't sometimes exhausted too? I've never met one I could have asked.)

(And we live in times in which such a Goliath would have a lot to do.)

Sadly I don't know anyone in America. My brother-in-law once lived there for some years, and he also promised me to inquire whether one of his old acquaintances might be able to do something for you. But he isn't giving me any great hopes. His time in New York was a long time ago, and he says that when it comes to asking favours of people they tend to have very short memories. (I'm afraid he may be right.)

I do have a good contact in Kenya who might be able to make something possible. But who wants to go there?

I also asked my brother, who does a lot of work with French companies. He says Paris is overflowing with German emigrants at the moment, and if you can't speak the language perfectly you haven't a chance of making a living. If I understood you correctly, however, that wouldn't be an absolute necessity for you.

Have you actually ever thought of trying Switzerland?

With best wishes

Dr Arthur Meijer

PS: I will be going to Heiden again next week.

'Until the end of October,' Fräulein Württemberger said proudly. The tone of her voice made it clear: Irma and Moses had her and no one else to thank for this period of grace. She was one of those people who can constantly rewrite the world and their own role in it.

'No further extension of the present exemption may be granted,' she read from the decision by the immigration authorities, 'and this office can process no corresponding application hereto.' The official German of the letter skipped as nimbly from her tongue as if it were an essay by her beloved Professor Heidegger. She snapped the file shut and put it back in its place on the shelf, precise to the millimetre. 'So, until the end of October, and then…' Her right hand came down on the desk like a guillotine blade.

'And then?' asked Arthur.

Fräulein Württemberger didn't reply.

'How is Irma?'

She looked at him irritably.

'Better,' she said at last.

'So the medication I sent her is working?'

Glucose. In a jar with an impressively complicated Latin name on the label.

'We ensure that she takes it punctually.' Fräulein Württemberger took the credit even for this success. And added, with the quiet joy that comes from rubbing the nose of someone one doesn't like in a mistake they've made, 'But she's still having these attacks, which would make you think she was about to die at any moment.'

'Really?'

'Proper spasms. Then she rolls around on the bed and screams.'

Arthur took off his glasses and rubbed his nose. The gesture also allowed him to conceal a smile.

'Is she still coughing blood?' he asked with his serious medical face.

'Sometimes. I've made an observation.' A nervous hand went in search of escaping strands of hair. 'I don't know if it's important.' The modest doubt was only an empty phrase. Of course Fräulein Württemberger's observations were always important.

'Yes?'

'Once I was standing next to her when she spat blood. It smelled quite sweet. Like sherbet powder. Tell me, Doctor, is that normal?'

'Yes,' said Dr Arthur Meijer. 'In this special case it is entirely normal.'

He found the pair in the adjacent building normally reserved for children's camps during the summer months, but was now constantly occupied because of the extraordinary circumstances. Irma was making the beds in the big dormitory: the Women's Association children who were no longer being paid for were used as labour wherever possible. His patient was wearing a grey work smock that was far too big for her, in which she looked like a little nurse. Moses assisted her, or at least tried to make himself useful. To make sure he stayed eager, Irma had come up with a special task for him: whenever a bed was made, he was to hit the pillow with the edge of his hand and ensure the perfect dimple.

And each time she praised him.

Arthur could have stood in the doorway and watched them for ever. He liked going to the cinema, and whenever a plot ended happily after a lot of setbacks, he shed a few pleasant tears in the dark from time to time. That was exactly what happened to him now: he was watching a strange harmony, and would have liked to be a part of it.

At last he cleared his throat. Irma – she seemed used to it – reached into the pocket of her apron, took out a handkerchief and held it to her mouth. Only then did she turn round. When she recognised him, she dropped the handkerchief and came running over to him. 'Dr Goliath!' she cried excitedly. 'That means I can stop coughing.'

Moses came over as well, more timid than his sister, shook hands very formally with Arthur, bowed and asked, 'Will Irma be well now?'

'Not quite today. But we'll get there, won't we, Irma?'

'Yes,' said Irma and looked at him trustingly with her squinting eyes. 'We'll get there.'

In the grounds there was a small hill which could be all kinds of things in the games of the children at the home, the crow's nest of a pirate ship, the tip of a jungle tree, the cockpit of a zeppelin, in which one could fly round the world and even all the way home. Today the hill was the parapet of a knightly castle, and Moses, a broken branch over his shoulder as a pike, was guarding the only entrance with a serious expression on his face.

Arthur checked that the little boy couldn't hear them, and then said, 'You're exaggerating your illness.'

'The witch has fallen for it.' Impolite, but not a bad description.

'You mixed sherbet powder with the blood.'

'No, I didn't,' said Irma. One of her eyes looked at him innocently, while the other seemed to be looking for something in the distance beside his face.

'So?'

'It wasn't blood!' Irma giggled, as only a little girl who has managed to trick the adult world can giggle. 'I promised you I would stop cutting myself. It was just red sherbet powder. If you put a spoonful in your mouth and then let the bubbles pour out...'

She was so triumphant that she couldn't go on talking, and started to laugh. Arthur was infected by it too. The idea of the hygienic Fräulein Württemberger disgustedly sniffing a handkerchief and making the medical discovery that Irma's bloody sputum smelled of sherbet powder was just too absurd.

'Strawberry flavour!' Irma managed to gasp between two fits of laughter. Arthur had never heard a funnier phrase. It was a while before he could speak again.

'She asked me if that sweet smell was normal with this illness.'

'And what did you say?'

'Yes, Fräulein Württemberger, with this very rare illness it is entirely normal.'

This time they laughed so loudly that Irma's eyes actually crossed. Moses came running excitedly up the hill because he thought his sister was having a coughing fit.

'The doctor tickled me when he was examining me,' Irma lied, and then asked with her severest knightly expression. 'What do you have to report, squire Moses? No hostile dragons on the way?'

'All dragons repelled,' reported the squire and marched, proud of his own importance, back to his sentry post.

'You're very fond of your brother, aren't you?'

'That's normal.'

'Of course,' said Arthur, and was almost a bit envious of being this age when such normalities were not called into doubt.

And then, on this imaginary parapet, there took place what must have been the strangest lesson ever given in the Wartheim. Dr Arthur Meijer, experienced general practitioner by profession, showed a twelve-year-old girl how to pretend to be ill.

'In future we'll leave out the spasms and all that play-acting,' he began his lecture.

'Oh,' said Irma, disappointed.

'We don't want Fräulein Württemberger flying into a panic and calling a doctor from the village.'

It was hard for Irma to forego her dramatic scenes, but she was prepared to do so for her Dr Goliath.

'If anyone asks you how you are, you always say, "I'm fine."'

'Why?'

'But you say it in a very weak voice. And when you go out, you hold onto the doorpost as if you were dizzy.'

Irma's face was full of admiration at such cunning.

'Every time you're in the bathroom, hold your hands under ice-cold water for one minute.'

Never in his whole life had Arthur had such an attentive listener.

'And then make sure someone holds your hand, and shake a little.'

Even Fräulein Württemberger, in a one-to-one class with Martin Heidegger, could not have listened with greater devotion.

'And soap. If you rub some in your eyes, they will turn red and produce tears.'

'But that will sting!"'

'Only if you can stand it, of course.'

'I can stand anything,' Irma said proudly.

'Can you also *swallow* soap?'

'Then I'd feel sick.'

'Good.'

Irma looked at him admiringly for a moment. Then she blinked at him, shook as if she already had soap in her mouth and asked anxiously, 'Does it make you very sick?'

'Quite sick,' said Arthur. 'Soldiers used to do it so that they didn't have to go into battle. It can even give you a fever.'

'Fever?' she smiled dreamily as if he had promised her a particularly lovely present. 'Then I'll do that.'

When they came down from the hill, Irma was holding his hand.

'No dragons or hostile armies,' Moses reported.

'Very good, squire Moses,' said Arthur, and saluted, although in all likelihood that wasn't the custom among knights in armour.

After his consultation with the Women's Association children – a scald from kitchen duty, a sprained ankle from sport – when he was back in his topolino and driving down into the valley, he sang quietly to himself.

Dear Frau Pollack,

Yesterday I was in Heiden again, and spent a most enjoyable hour with Irma. Interesting, by the way: every time she laughs, her squint gets worse. Have you ever noticed that? (Stupid question. Of course you have. You're her mother.)

Together we practised making yourself convincingly ill without exaggerating too much. At first Irma was very disappointed, I think. She likes drama. What did you call her? A diva. If it was up to her, she would be miming the closing scene from *La Bohème* once a day. At least. Do you like the opera? (Forgive me, that was another stupid question, I'm sure you have other things on your mind.)

Moses has grave concerns about his sister, and I couldn't really take them away from him, even though I did my best to reassure him. Irma and I have never dared to let him in on our conspiracy. We fear he might blab sooner or later. (The scribble on the last word is because I used a Swiss phrase that you mightn't have understood. Sometimes I think that if all the words in all the countries meant the same thing there would be no more wars.)

Moses did a drawing for me. It's on the wall in front of me as I write this letter. The picture shows your family, with a very big father who has put his arms around the others and is protecting them. It must be very hard when such protection suddenly is no longer there. But somehow in these times it is almost reassuring that it was a traffic accident, and hence something impersonal.

Please write and tell me how your plans are progressing.

Kindest regards

Dr Arthur Meijer

PS: (I don't think I've ever written a letter without a PS.) I hope you won't misunderstand me if I refer to the chance nature of a traffic accident as something reassuring. I have here a patient whose back is covered with scars, and imagine that he will never be able to forget the faces of the people (people?) who did that to him.

64

At the Strickhof the pupils slept in rooms of six, and they were expected to make their beds with military precision, the sheets smoothed flat and the woollen blankets given an edge as if with a ruler. The shoes had to stand as if on parade, laces tied in a bow, under the bed – only the smart shoes, of course, there was a wire shelf near the front door for the dirty work boots in which one had tramped around in the fields or the stables. Kudi Lampertz, who was also in charge of the rooms, had been a corporal in military service, and held the view that it was only order in one's belongings that led to order in one's head.

The only untidy thing that he was unable to do anything about was the locker doors. It was an old tradition in the Strickhof that everyone was allowed to pin up whatever he liked on his own locker door, however odd or tasteless it might be. Even caricatures of the teachers had to be tolerated there, and even much worse things than that. Once Lampertz complained to the headmaster about the photograph of a blonde with a shamelessly revealing cleavage – he never went to the cinema, so he didn't recognise Mae West – and Gerster replied with one of his strange jokes: 'Let him have the picture. It's probably his mother.'

The iconoclastic controversy in which Hillel and Böhni now became embroiled, and which finally led to the fateful bet, was not about film stars, but about idols of a quite different kind. Böhni started it, by hanging on his locker door – just to annoy Rosenthal, in fact – a picture of the far-right leader Dr Rolf Henne, standing at the microphone at a National Front meeting, his left thumb hooked in his belt and his right hand sticking into the air; it could have been seen as a rhetorical pose, or as a Hitler salute. Hillel countered with a photograph of Chaim Weizmann, the president of the World Zionist organisation, he too photographed delivering an address, but without any big gestures, his hands resting on the lectern, an academic delivering a lecture. Böhni looked at the face, the bald head and the little beard and asked, 'Who's that meant to be? Lenin?'

Next he brought in a poster that he'd kept at home in Flaach for almost four years, because he had thought it was funny even as a boy. Under the promise 'We're clearing up!' an iron broom was sweeping away three kinds of undesirables: fat cats with top hats on their heads and fat cigars in their mouths, Communists with the hammer and sickle on their hats and Jews with hooked noses.

Hillel said nothing about it, but just put up a new photograph: a shomer on the plain of Chule, peering alertly out across the landscape, blond and tanned. The gun over his shoulder and the resolute, manly features, the eyes narrowed into the sun clearly signalled, 'We Zionists won't put up with anything, and are prepared to defend ourselves.' The photograph was generally appreciated in the six-man room, and Kudi Lampertz said he hadn't thought Hillel was interested in cowboys.

To escalate matters, Böhni actually wanted to get hold of a photograph of Hitler, but then he started feeling uneasy, so instead he merely jibed at the shomer. Far away in Palestine, perhaps the Jews had balls and knew how to use a gun, he said, but here in Switzerland he'd never seen one at the shooting club. He wasn't casting aspersions at anybody, people weren't all the same, some had timidity in the blood, and were startled by the slightest bang.

Whereupon Hillel – he was eighteen by now, and you can't let such accusations go unpunished – naturally had to declare that he was willing to take up Böhni's bravery challenge any day, whether on a trip in the box-cart or wherever he liked. And thus the bet was sealed after lights-out in front of witnesses, which went as follows: Böhni was to determine a test of courage, but lest he come up with something impossible, he himself must be willing to submit to it. The loser, it was solemnly decreed, must make himself available to the victor as his personal servant for a whole week, and obey all his orders, make his bed, clean his shoes, indeed, if he called for it, even butter his breakfast bread. Böhni, already sure of his victory, described how he was going to go stomping specially through slurry every time his shoes were due to be polished.

The others in the room, who saw the whole thing as a great joke, expected Böhni to choose something that would be much easier for him, the farmer's son, than for city-boy Rosenthal. It would, most of them assumed, have something to do with Napoleon, the Strickhof's prize-winning bull. This particular creature was a cunning and malevolent great hunk of a thing, which could barely be tamed even with a nose ring, and Böhni was one of the few who was able to cope with him to any extent at all.

But the challenge that Böhni finally made was quite different, and apart from Rosenthal himself the witnesses to the bet at first didn't understand what it was actually about. Böhni explained that the most horrible and scary thing that he himself had had to do recently had been a perfectly ordinary visit, he wouldn't say where to quite yet. They'd tried to bore him to death, and that, he could assure his listeners, was a particularly painful way of being killed. Hillel had to put up with the mockery, because any kind of denial would only have made him look ridiculous. So, Böhni went on, he had decided that as a test of his courage Rosenthal should also go with him on a visit. Yes, just a visit, they didn't have to look so surprised. Where they were going to go, however, he would only say once Rosenthal had accepted the invitation. Of course he could refuse, but then he would have lost the bet, and his week as a servant would begin immediately. He, Böhni, thought that cleaning the toilet would be a nice first task, ideally with his bare hands, so that at least they got something out of it. So, what was it to be, yes or no?

What option did Hillel have but to say yes?

That was very brave of him, Böhni grinned. He had in fact decided to go the Bauschänzli on Saturday evening, the National Front meeting, that was a kind of visit, and Rosenthal could go with him if he dared. He could imagine that they would have a special warm welcome there for a Hillel Rosenthal.

'You're a sly bastard,' said Hillel.

'And you always thought cunning was your speciality? You're going to pull out, of course.'

'What makes you think that?' asked Hillel, proud that his voice didn't tremble. 'Of course I'm going to come.'

He said nothing about any of this at home. His mother would only have tried to persuade him out of the whole thing, and his father would have thought he could forbid him from going. But some things you just have to go through with, when you're eighteen and it's a matter of honour. Even at the Hashomer Hatza'ir, where they met on Shabbos afternoon, he didn't say a word about it. They wouldn't have let him go on his own, and there would have been a big fight before they even got to the front door.

He went quite deliberately in his work gear. As Grandmother Chanele would have said: where does it say in the Shulchan Orech that you have to put on a tie for reshoim? And in any case, his work gear includes heavy boots, and if it came to the crunch those might come in useful.

They had agreed to meet at seven, a time when it was still light in the summer. Even so, the Fröntlers had already set up burning torches in front of the pub, which flickered away unnoticed in the daylight. A Bavarian band in lederhosen blared out tunes for people to sway back and forth to; but the music had nothing to do with the event in the hall, it was to entertain drinkers in the beer garden. Children played tag on the gravel paths between the rows of tables. The men had hung their jackets over the backs of the chairs and pushed back their hats, there was a general hubbub, and they were already waving for the waiter while they washed down their bratwurst or pig's knuckle with the last dregs of their beer. The women laughed too loudly and fed the ducks in the Limmat with bits of bread. The smoke from countless cigarettes and cigars mixed in the air with the black, oily fug from the torches.

The atmosphere was peaceful, as if on a big family's excursion into the country. And yet Hillel was about to set off on an adventure even bolder than his race down the steps on the box-cart.

He had deliberately arrived a few minutes early, and spent a while strolling around between the tables, like someone who has already got a seat but just wants to stretch his legs for a few minutes. He noticed a few policemen who were sitting at a table by the entrance to the pub. They had taken off their helmets, and were trying to look as if they had just come from police headquarters after a hard day's work, to enjoy a quiet beer in privacy by the river. But their glasses were still full, even though – as one could tell from the dried-on foam – they had been served some time ago, and they studied everyone who walked past them with an interest that was far from private. Hillel didn't know whether he should feel threatened or protected by their presence.

No sign of Böhni. But the Fraumünster clock was striking seven, and Hillel had decided to be exactly on time. A minute's lateness would have been construed as cowardice.

Coming from outside, one first entered a narrow entrance hall, and after the late sunlight on the terrace he had first to stop for a moment to let his eyes get used to the gloom. He was almost rammed into by a waiter coming out of the kitchen with a fully laden tray. The man murmured a curse, but only very quietly, and looked anxiously over his shoulder. Hillel followed his gaze, and only then did he spot the two stout lads guarding the entrance to the hall. They were part of the Harst, the fighting troops of the National Front. You could tell by their grey shirts, their black ties and red armbands with the party emblem, the long-legged Swiss flag with the spiked club – the 'Morgenstern' – in the middle.

'Morgenstern is a Jewish name,' Hillel found himself thinking, and agitated though he was, he nearly burst out laughing. There were two brothers by that name in the Hashomer Hata'ir.

He walked towards the entrance, and the two bouncers stopped him. They didn't actually stand in his way or hold out a hand, but the way they just looked at him with their arms folded clearly said: no stranger was going to get past them.

Was Aunt Rachel right after all? Could they really tell you were Jewish just by looking at you?

But probably they stopped anyone they didn't know.

'Is this where the meeting's being held?' asked Hillel, and tried to peer into the hall. Böhni must be waiting for him somewhere.

No reply.

'A friend invited me. His name's Böhni. Walter Böhni. We're at agricultural college together.'

'Aha, a man of the farming class,' said the other of the two bouncers, and appreciatively pondered Hillel's working gear. 'We can use someone like you. Name?'

Hillel was prepared for this one. 'Rösli,' he said, and almost stood slightly to attention. 'Heinrich Rösli.'

'Admitted,' said the bouncer, and for a moment Hillel thought he meant he had just admitted that his name was Rösli. It was only when the other Harst man gave the appropriate nod of the head that he walked quickly – but not too quickly, that would have attracted attention! – past the two men.

Böhni had been standing just behind the door, and had listened to the conversation. 'Rösli,' he repeated. 'I see, I see.'

That was the crucial moment. What was Böhni capable of? He only had to tell one of these Harst men – and there were plenty of them in the hall – what this fellow Rösli's name was, and all hell would break loose.

But he just nodded appreciatively. 'You've got a neck. Have to give you that…' He nearly said 'Rosenthal', which was what he always called him, but he quickly swallowed the name. 'I'll have to give you that, Heinrich. How did you choose the first name?'

'That's what it says in my papers.'

'Not Hillel?'

This really wasn't the place to explain the difference between an official and a Jewish first name. So Hillel quickly distracted him and said, 'There aren't very many people,' and Böhni actually forgot his question and eagerly explained that the leader Dr Henne would not be talking until half past seven, and since the weather was nice many people were bound still to be sitting outside, and would only come in at the last moment.

The hall wasn't very big, and at half past seven it was still barely half full. There was nothing remarkable about the appearance of the audience, except that almost all of them wore grey shirts. It seemed to be customary here to keep your hat on during the meeting.

Without talking about it for long, Böhni and Hillel went and found seats far at the back.

The Hast bouncers had lined up by the stage at the front, they were also standing at the sides and by the door at the back, their resolute faces turned towards the audience as if they were guarding a room full of prisoners. They all wore the same shirts, ties and armbands, only their trousers were different. They probably weren't part of the uniform.

When the speakers came in through the side door, the Harst leader ordered: 'Stand to attention!' whereupon they all adopted far more rigid postures, stuck their right arms aloft and roared 'Harus!' Then someone performed a roll on a landsknecht drum, and Hillel wondered whether he might have been one of the people in Fortunagasse.

He was glad when the speeches began. If Böhni had planned to reveal him as a Jew, he had missed the most suitable opportunity.

The leader seemed – like Propaganda Minister Goebbels in Germany – to place great value on his doctorate. The man who introduced him only ever referred to him as 'Dr Rolf Henne', and Henne himself peppered his speech with phrases like 'as a scholar of the law I can tell you'. The first thing that struck Hillel about him was his Schaffhausen accent, which always sounds slightly ludicrous to someone from Zurich. There was nothing obviously threatening about the man as a whole. He spoke hurriedly, was proud of his own arguments, couldn't wait to put them forward and in this reminded Hillel of his own father. When Henne became combative, and that always happened all of a sudden, as if the moments were written down in the manuscript of his address, and he only noticed the instruction at the very last minute, he clenched his hand into a fist and struck the lectern two or three times, but very carefully, like someone who isn't entirely at ease with physical force.

The subject of the meeting was department stores and the threat they represented to Swiss craftspeople. Henne only ever called them Jew shops. They were the root of all economic evil, he declared, because with their tempting sale offers they drove the small shopkeeper into a price competition that he would never be able to win. Their big turnover also meant that the market was excessively saturated, which would lead to a drop in manufacturing and thus unemployment, plummeting tax revenue and general ruin. His argument rambled on: thus for example he explained in detail and with an expression of extreme rage that the bristles of brushes bought at a one-price store were shorter and less firmly ensconced than in specialist shops, or that all metal goods were manufactured from lighter materials than had previously been the case.

This obsession with detail made his address not more credible, but less. Only someone unsure of his own case needs to make such an effort to prove his own theses.

At first Hillel had planned to pay very close attention, but there was something soporific about Henne's style. Even the other members of the audience, who had responded to his harangue with occasional words of agreement, seemed to feel much the same. Even Böhni, sitting next to him, seemed to have glazed over.

'And that's your idol?' Hillel whispered to him.

'Henne's right in what he says,' Böhni whispered back. 'But he is a lawyer, and they always make things complicated.'

One of the Harst men saw their two heads stretching towards each other, and took a menacing step towards them. Chatting was not tolerated at this meeting.

The speaker noticed that the hall was slipping away from him and only woke up when he started talking about the Jews. So he concentrated more and more on that subject and explained that it wasn't just the department stores that were controlled by Jewish cultural Bolshevism, but also half the press – one need only think of the Galician *Volksrecht* and the Basel '*Zionalzeitung*' – and obviously the dark red city council. They were all in it together, and that was why a flyer against department stores and one-price stores published by the National Front had been forbidden and confiscated. That provoked fury, the listeners woke up again, and Henne's closing sentence, 'One cannot improve Jews, one can only get rid of them,' was received with shouts of 'Quite right!' and much applause.

So far everything had gone well for Hillel, and in fact he had already won the bet. The longer Böhni sat next to him without announcing him as the arch-enemy who had crept in secretly, the safer he felt. One had to acknowledge that. Böhni played fair.

But then things went wrong.

The people were already getting up and starting to talk to each other, while an official reminded them from the lectern to turn up at the following weekend's propaganda march. Then suddenly two of their fellow pupils made their way across the hall to Hillel and Böhni. They had witnessed the bet in the dormitory, and now come to observe its outcome on the spot.

'Well, Böhni,' thundered one of them from a distance, 'we'll be watching you brushing shoes from tomorrow.'

'And cleaning the shithouse,' laughed the other.

'Shh!' said Böhni.

'Didn't think Rosenthal had it in him, did you?'

'Shh!'

'But respect where it's due,' said the first boy, as loudly as if he was summoning the cattle in the meadow. He slapped Hillel appreciatively on the shoulder. 'That's quite some achievement, coming here as a Jew.'

And that was it. The people had been bored all evening, and now at last they had the opportunity to do politics the way they liked to, with their fists. Particularly the men from the Harst, for whom a meeting without a brawl was an evening wasted, really came to life.

Böhni saw a circle of people coming towards them, grabbed Hillel by the hand and cried, 'Come on, let's get out of here!'

They made it to the door, and that was their great good fortune, because the anteroom was too narrow for a proper free-for-all. Their two fellow pupils fought with them, because even if they didn't particularly like Rosenthal, he was in their class, and when it came to fighting the principle was, 'One for all and all for one.'

The Fröntlers came at them from all sides. Hillel didn't even have time to wonder why Böhni was suddenly standing shoulder to shoulder with him and defending him. They found each other very disagreeable, after all, and friends, no, they certainly weren't friends.

It wasn't a long scrap. The policemen who were getting mightily bored outside on the terrace in front of their beer glasses, from which they still weren't allowed to drink, were relieved when they were finally able to grab their truncheons and let rip. If nothing at all happened, there were no laurels to be earned on Front patrol. They came thundering into the anteroom and discharged their duties.

Soon the two sides had been driven apart, and the landlord's damages claim had been recorded.

Of the participants in the scuffle, only two people had not stopped in time and were arrested. One had a bloody nose and the other was starting to get a black eye.

'Name?'

'Böhni, Walter.'

'And you?'

'Rosenthal, Hillel.'

'Hillel? How do you spell that?'

'His name's actually Heinrich,' said Böhni.

'My name is Hillel. It's a good Jewish first name.'

'A Jew? Great,' said the constable.

'How do you mean?'

'It means we've got one of each. Our commander's been saying for ages, "That's the only way we can make an example, so that there's peace in this city at long last."'

'But we weren't fighting with each other.' It isn't easy to argue when you have to press a bloody handkerchief to your sore nose at the same time.

'Then you can tell that to the judge,' said the policeman. 'Except it won't interest him. Who against whom – it's completely irrelevant. Paragraph 133. Disturbance of the peace. You're liable for prosecution just by being there.'

'But that's not fair!'

'You should have thought of that before,' said the policeman. 'Take them away!'

He was in a hurry. Once you've finished the day's work, no one can stop you having a beer.

65

Herr Grün's illness dragged on. The fever had subsided, certainly, and his lungs sounded quite normal again, but he just couldn't get back on his feet. Arthur said he had noticed such things in other patients, but most of them had been much older people. Rachel would have to imagine it as something like a flood, where someone would cling on to something with the last of their strength and keep themselves above water. If he lost his strength and let go, it would be hard for him to grab hold of anything else.

That might certainly be the case, Rachel said, although she would have preferred the doctor to have given her an effective remedy rather than fine words. But be that as it may, she was a busy woman and didn't have time to play the Samaritan all the time. She was responsible for fifteen members of staff, and you hadn't time to hold hands with each individual.

On the other hand...

When Herr Grün lay in bed under his bedcover like that – a new bedcover, of course, with real down, she'd made sure of that – when he just lay there like that, above all when he had just woken up and hadn't yet had time to put the old grumpy mask back on, he had a quite different face. His smile, if he had such a thing, he still kept in the basement, but to remain with the image, the door was already open a crack.

And besides...

No, that wasn't it. The fact that Frau Posmanik always greeted her as submissively as if the next person after a daughter of Herr Kamionker the factory director would be the Prophet Elijah, followed by the moshiach in person, had nothing whatever to do with it. She didn't care for flattery. Not she. A professional woman has no time for such shmontses. And Frau Posmanik had only been after leftover swatches of brocade. No, that was certainly not why she went all the way to Molkenstrasse.

But...

She was interested in Herr Grün, she didn't dispute that. She really knew her way around people, Oh yes, she had had her experiences, and they hadn't always been the most pleasant, but she didn't understand this man. There were a number of things about him that just didn't fit together, a suit that he'd begged from various different places, trousers here, jacket there.

If she wanted to make conversation with him, as one should when visiting a patient, he wouldn't open his mouth, you had to drag the words out of him one by one. But then when little Aaron came into the room — he visited the lodgers several times a day, in spite of Rachel's strict reminder that Herr Grün had to get better and needed peace and quiet — when he knocked at the door, twice slowly and three times quickly, nobody knew what that was supposed to mean, the patient sat up on his pillows, even though that had taken a lot out of him at first, and started entertaining the boy. Yes, entertaining him. You might have thought the bed was a stage and Aaron had bought a ticket. Herr Grün had all kinds of silly poems and song lyrics that no sane person would ever have learned by heart. Aaron couldn't understand most of it, he was far too young, but he listened to it all with a beaming face and sometimes actually squealed with pleasure. Then his younger siblings poked their heads into the room and wanted to join in the fun. But Aaron sent them out with a severe expression. 'Uncle Grün has to get better, and needs peace and quiet.'

Even the oranges that Rachel brought, Herr Grün shared with the boy. And they cost a fortune, now that it was summer, and Rachel had had to pay for them out of her own purse when there wasn't enough in petty cash at the shop. Not that she would have said as much to Herr Grün, heaven knows what he would have thought.

But he could have said thank you.

'Do you actually have to be a child to be treated decently by you?' she once asked, whereupon Herr Grün nodded very seriously and replied, 'It would be an advantage.'

No, Rachel really didn't have time to make patient visits every day, certainly not if it wasn't appreciated. Luckily there were other people for this kind of thing, people who weren't as tired as she was in the evening, who could shut their grocery shop at seven on the dot, and who had never heard of last minute commissions and overtime. Generally speaking, when a person is always alone and has no real family, it's practically a mitzvah to do find something sensible for him to do.

Désirée took on the task without asking too many questions. She didn't just attend to the patient, but looked after the Posmanik family as well. On her visits she always brought a box of groceries and wouldn't even let anyone thank her for it. She was happy if anyone would take it off her hands, she claimed, in her field it was hard to judge precisely how much she needed, and if you'd bought too much then it was better for it to be eaten than to go off. She found a job for Herr Posmanik in the warehouse of a pasta factory, and even made sure that his wife dropped by every week and collected his pay packet in person.

'She's an angel,' said Frau Posmanik to Rachel, who replied, 'Well, if she has time on her hands.'

When she paid her visits Désirée didn't just sit by Herr Grün's bed and wait for him to chat to her; she preferred to make herself useful. One day, when she was cleaning the window so that the bit of sunlight that wandered into the courtyard at the back could also find its way into the room, he suddenly said, 'You were very fond of him.'

'Of whom?'

'The person you lost.'

'How do...?'

'It's obvious,' said Herr Grün.

Désirée rubbed away at a piece of putty that was stuck to the glass and just wouldn't go away. 'Yes,' she said. 'I was very fond of him.'

It was so quiet in the room that the drill sergeant could be heard issuing orders in the parade ground.

'I once had someone like that,' Herr Grün said after a pause. 'My best friend. His name was Blau. Not really, of course. That would have been too much of a coincidence. But it looked good on the posters.'

Désirée didn't turn around and went on cleaning. In the years of her solitude she had become just as good a listener as Mina had once been.

'His real name was Schlesinger,' the voice behind her said. 'Siegfried Schlesinger. But because everyone called me Grün, we had the idea that he should be Blau. Grün and Blau. That was our act.'

Herr Grün – whose name wasn't Grünberg, Grünfeld or Grünbaum, but really Grün – had appeared in cabaret, never in the really big Berlin venues like the Chat Noir or the Kadeko, but always in Friday theatres, so-called because the artistes received their wages once a week and not every morning after the performance as they were in the small clubs. His speciality had been the double act, with his partner Schlesinger, who called himself Blau because it looked better on the posters.

Grün and Blau.

'We even made a record,' said Herr Grün, 'and sold it at the interval. We were always on before the interval, never in the second part like the famous acts. No one would have stayed there and ordered another round of sekt. Although we were good. You'll laugh,' said Herr Grün, 'but people once laughed at me.'

'Guten Tag, Herr Grün.'

'Guten Tag, Herr Blau.'

That was how their act always began, it had been a real trademark. Sometimes they came on in coats and hats and were passersby in the street, sometimes they were holding cups and were customers in a café, but the first sentences were always the same, and eventually the time came when the audience laughed even after their greeting, sometimes even applauded, even though no one had said anything funny. That was popularity.

'Guten Tag, Herr Grün.'

'Guten Tag, Herr Blau.'

He imitated both voices, exaggerated the rumbling bass of his own and the shrill descant of his partner's.

'You shouldn't strain yourself,' said Désirée.

'No, I should. It does me good.'

Blue was small and thin, a straight line in the landscape, and Herr Grün had been fat in those days. Yes, really. 'I filled my suit well, and never skimped on the butter sauce. It was a professional belly, my most important prop.'

Grün had been the authority figure, the man who knew everything and could explain everything. Blau was the nebbish who didn't understand a thing and only ever asked stupid questions. 'When in fact it was exactly the other way round. Schlesinger sat in the wardrobe reading books, while I romped with the twirlies. The chorus girls,' he added by way of explanation.

'I'd translated that for myself.' Désirée was now sitting on the chair beside the bed, but was still holding the cleaning rag, as if to say, 'Just for a moment.'

'Hello, Herr Blau.'

When Herr Grün imitated himself, he spoke 'jargon', the linguistic bastard that the Germans mistake for Yiddish. That had been their role: two cliché Jews who make the simplest things unnecessarily complicated and thus come to surprising conclusions.

'We weren't the only ones in Berlin with that shtick. Other people had noticed that all you had to do was get up on stage and say "mishpocha" and people would start laughing. But we were the best.'

Herr Grün closed his eyes as if talking for such an unusually long time had exhausted him, but he was only trying to block out a painful image. 'They're still laughing,' he said. 'But it isn't funny any more.'

The dialogue about the apples, that had been their biggest hit, in the years before 1933. They talked about the red ones, which always thought they were ripe at last, and hadn't noticed that they were already starting to turn brown. About the brown ones, which you had to get rid of quickly because otherwise they infected all the other ones. And then, when Hitler was Reich Chancellor, they'd invented the punchline about the Reich apple that everyone had to bite into, but you couldn't eat it, it was so disgusting.

'When people stopped laughing at it, we should have got out straight away,' said Herr Grün. 'But we were actors. So we thought it was our fault.'

And then...

They were interrupted. Little Aaron knocked at the door, twice slowly, three times quickly, as Herr Grün had taught him. They were secret agents, Herr Grün and he, and they need signals like that.

'Not now,' said Désirée, but Herr Grün smiled – he actually smiled, suddenly he remembered how it was done – and said, 'Let him.'

'Do you know a new poem, Uncle Grün?'

'I know a million billion poems,' said Herr Grün.

'But today I've got something much better for you. A magic spell, it goes like this: "Owa, Tanah, Siam."'

The little boy waited and then, when nothing came next, looked at his idol as disappointedly as if Herr Grün had promised him a wonderful sweet and then held out nothing but empty silver paper. 'And?'

'It's a magic spell. You have to say it five times in a row, as quickly as you can, and then you'll see.'

Aaron looked slightly dubious, but Herr Grün had never disappointed him, so he started practising talking really quickly. 'Owa Tanah Siam, Owa Tanah Siam...' When he worked out what a wonderfully rude sentence lay hidden behind it, he beamed as radiantly as if it were his birthday.

'But whatever you do, don't try the trick out on your brother and sister!'

'Of course not,' said Aaron, and ran out to try it on his brother and sister straight away. And all the other children in the house.

'Now we've got some peace,' said Herr Grün, and sat up straight in his bed for the first time in ages.

'You're very different from what one might expect.'

Herr Grün shook his head. 'No, Fräulein Pomeranz,' he said. 'I've just learned not to let everyone see past my face.'

He didn't want to chat, that much was clear, he wanted to tell a story. About how it had been, and how it had stopped.

At first everything seemed to be going on as before. They mightn't have belonged to the Reich Culture Chamber, but they were allowed to go on performing. In cabaret people didn't seem to take it all too seriously. They were used to Nazis disrupting the performance with catcalls. It was part of their job, and was no worse than the drunks who thought, after the second bottle of wine, that they were funnier than the people on stage. After Hitler came to power it wasn't very different. Perhaps you were less direct in your phrasing, perhaps you were a bit more discreet with your barbs, but people listened much more precisely and reacted to nuances. 'A dictatorship does wonders for your sense of hearing,' said Herr Grün.

And then, in 1934, two men were waiting for them after the show. They were standing quite patiently by the stage door. As if they wanted an autograph. 'In those days they didn't yet have the leather coats they wear now, each of them just had an armband, and they still looked slightly uncertain, two comedians who aren't sure about the lines in their new sketch. They hadn't rehearsed it yet. One of them hit me in the face, but his heart wasn't in it. I've learned to tell the difference in the meantime. Amateurs.'

And then...

But Herr Grün had overtaxed himself, a convalescent who wants to cross the whole city the first time he goes for a walk, and doesn't yet have the strength for it. 'I need to sleep a bit now,' he said.

Perhaps Désirée was just imagining it, but when she looked quickly in on him before she left she thought his face had a bit more colour than usual.

She told Rachel about it, and Rachel was strangely insulted. 'Sorry if people don't trust me. I don't force myself on anyone. I'm a busy woman.'

But she was firmly resolved never to visit Herr Grün again.

And then there was this delivery of autumn models of the Ober department store, and old Frau Ober was always so fussy, and carped about every individual thread, so it was better for Rachel to go and clear the air. In the end no one in the company was as good at dealing with people as she was. The Ober wasn't far from the barracks, and from the barracks it was only a few steps to Molkenstrasse, so could Rachel please be so kind and drop the bag of leftover brocade off with Frau Posmanik, because she'd set it aside for her anyway. If she called in to see Herr Grün at the same time, it was the most natural thing in the world, after all, you have to know when you can expect your workers to be back on their feet.

Herr Grün wasn't in his bed, as he should have been if he'd been signed off sick. 'He isn't here,' said Aaron through the crack in the door. It was really infuriating how often Frau Posmanik left her children alone. It was only after a number of questions that the little boy condescended to reveal to Rachel that Herr Grün hadn't gone out or anything, but that he was on the roof.

The impertinence of it.

You had to fish for a hook with a pole and lower a ladder. You had to find the way through a dusty attic, and afterwards you had cobwebs in your hair, the lengths you have to go to sometimes. And then after you'd bent through far too low a door, you were standing on a metal roof where you were constantly tripping over a seam, really not the right place for a businesswoman who's put on almost her very best shoes for a conversation with an important customer.

At first she didn't see Herr Grün at all. Someone had put washing out to dry on the roof, the unsightly intimacies of a big family. She had to duck under clothes lines hung with underpants and vests, and then at last discovered, in a niche between two chimneys, a wicker chair with someone sitting in it, someone of whom only a pair of slippers and an adventurously colourful dressing gown could be seen. The rest of the man was hidden by an open newspaper.

'Herr Grün?'

He didn't lower the newspaper straight away. As if he wanted to finish an article before he was prepared to notice her. But then he was exquisitely polite, which Rachel found merely aggravating.

'Fräulein Kamionker! What a pleasant surprise! Unfortunately I can't offer you a chair. There's only one, and it's not worthy of you.' He briefly raised his backside to show her that the wicker chair was completely worn out, and should long since have been sent to the blind people's workshop on Stauffacher for repair.

Désirée had been right: Herr Grün had changed. Whether it was for the better – Rachel wasn't so sure. Previously he had been taciturn and hardheaded, now he seemed talkative, but she could have sworn he was no less stubborn.

'I thought you were ill.'

'Convalescent. Dr Meijer says the sun will do me good. Except I can't climb down all the steps to the street and then back up again quite yet. So I'd rather come up on the roof.' He had rolled up his newspaper, and was now using it to point, like a tour guide, at the panorama of surrounding houses. 'The view is glorious.'

'Nothing special.' All that could be seen were parapets, chimneys and washing lines. A poor area of town isn't the sort of place to find historic buildings.

'Exactly,' said Herr Grün. 'Nothing special. That's the wonderful thing about this country: that it doesn't want to be anything special. You can't imagine how much I envy you that ordinariness.'

Rachel wasn't sure whether that was a compliment or a veiled criticism, so she changed the subject. 'I hear interesting things about you.'

'I envy you that too,' said Herr Grün.

'I'm sorry?'

'Your curiosity.'

'I am not curious!'

'Yes you are,' said Herr Grün. 'Believe me. I've had to learn to assess people correctly.'

'You flatter yourself!' Rachel took a furious step back, and came into unpleasant contact with a wet sheet. 'If you think that even for a minute I would...'

'Curiosity is a fortunate quality in a person. If someone is curious, he also hopes that something good might happen. I'm not curious about anything any more.'

'Nothing at all?'

'You see,' said Herr Grün, 'back in the cabaret...Did Fräulein Pomeranz also...? Stupid of me. Of course she did. You'll have got everything out of her.'

'I have absolutely no...'

But Herr Grün had started telling stories again, and heard no objections. Arthur had said that a blockage of words is like an abscess; once it's pierced everything comes pouring out, and only then can the cure be lasting.

'Back in the cabaret,' said Herr Grün, 'Blau was always the popular one, not me. I got the punchlines and he just supplied the prompts. You know why that was? Because he asked the questions and I gave the answers. If you ask questions you're curious, and if you're curious you're likeable.'

If Rachel had been even slightly interested in Herr Grün, that could have been the link for some teasing banter. But as it was, she just folded her arms and tried to find a rather more relaxed position on the smooth metal of the roof. Her shoes were elegant, but they were also uncomfortable.

'What happened to your Herr Blau?' she asked.

'Blau is dead. His name was Siegfried Schlesinger. Siegfried, of all things. I always teased him about his cufflinks. He had had his monogram engraved on them, and I said, "It's outrageous, making me work with the SS." It was a good punchline at the time.

'Then we ended up in the camp. That was a scene we hadn't performed before. Grün and Blau at the races, we'd done that one. Grün and Blau at the zoo. And so on. But now: Grün and Blau in the camp. A lousy sketch.

'You know what bad comedians do when their punchlines don't work? They slap each other. Kick each other in the backside. So that the audience have something to laugh at. Slapstick. The stick you slap someone with. Beatings always go down well, it's an old stage rule. It's a hit, a smash.

'Blau got the biggest laugh of his life when they broke his nose. Had them rolling in the aisles. And then they tore into him again. *Da capo*.

'Yes, Blau is dead.' His voice was quiet now. 'And Grün should be too. He just missed his prompt.'

His feelings were stowed away in jars, sealed and screwed tight. But now one of the jars had opened. The jar in which Herr Grün kept his tears.

66

Dear Dr Meijer!

I have had to read your last letter over and over again. In it you have written something that moved me very much. It would really be a great comfort for me if my husband's death had been something impersonal.

But the car that drove him over didn't come along by chance, and my husband didn't stumble into its bonnet by accident. That's just what I've told the children, to make it easier for them.

It was one of those open trucks that they used to drive around the streets in to kick up a row and intimidate people. Twenty men in the back, always ready to leap on somebody and beat him up.

My husband was a lawyer and had brought some cases against them. He even won a few. In 1932 such things were still sometimes possible.

It was on Königsstrasse here in Kassel, right in the centre of town, just in front of the town hall. My husband and I were walking side by side along the pavement, arm in arm. They drove by and recognised him. The driver wrenched the wheel around, I could see his face as he did it. His face open wide as if he were sitting on a roller coaster, in delighted panic or panicking delight. The car swung over and rode up onto the pavement, the uniformed men in the back all bounced up in rhythm, and then it was there, so close that I could smell the petrol, hot metal and the rubber of the tyres.

I can still smell it.

My husband let go of my arm. It all happened so quickly, but I'm sure he did it on purpose so that I wouldn't be dragged along. Attentive until the final thought. And then there was that blow, not even particularly loud, just like a big suitcase falling off a luggage trolley. Then the truck hopped again, back into the street.

At first it looked as if nothing bad had happened. My husband was lying on his back, eyes open. There was no sign of an injury.

Until the blood started spreading beneath his head.

So much blood.

I told the children a different version. They couldn't have borne it otherwise.

We filed an action against the perpetrators, we were still as naïve as that in those days, but by the time the case came to court it was 1933 and they were in power. I was advised to withdraw the accusation, but my husband wouldn't have wanted that. The result was that he was given a fine. He was. Posthumously. For damage to property. Because a brownshirt truck got a dent in its mudguard.

I paid the bill for the repairs. With interest.

You're right: it would have been easier if it had really been an accident.

That's all five years ago now, but since the court case I've never told anyone about it in such detail. The memory hurts, but I realise: it's also good to share it with someone.

I trust you because I don't know you. No, that sounds wrong. I meant: although I don't know you.

I've since been to Berlin. Nothing about my situation has changed, except that I'm now on some waiting lists. I haven't been to the Swiss Embassy. Everyone tells me there's no point.

A shame Goliath doesn't really exist.

With warm regards

Yours

Rosa Pollack

Zurich, 2 July 1937

Dear Frau Pollack,

I would dearly love to say something consoling to you, but I don't know how. It's so terrible, what people do to each other.

Arthur Meijer

Zurich, 3 July 1937

Dear Frau Pollack

Don't think ill of me for sending you such a stupid letter yesterday. I found no words, and still needed to say something to you straight away.

In the letters that my nephew Ruben writes from Halberstadt, there has been much talk of bullying, of a thousand perfidious little pinpricks, but he's never said anything about spontaneous violence. From his reports I had the sense that lots of terrible things are happening in Germany, but that for each fresh outrage a law or a bill had first to be passed. Until now I couldn't have imagined anything like what has happened to you. (That may be naiveté, or simply just cowardice.)

(It was probably cowardice. I'm not a brave person.)

Of course it's impossible for you to be exposed to such things for even a day longer.

I have thought all night, and would like to make you a suggestion, which I ask you not to interpret as charity. It would help me too. Really.

I do have a receptionist at my surgery, but my Fräulein Salvisberg is an elderly lady, who finds the work too much, and could use some relief. (At least one can put it that way without insulting the dear soul too much.)

Irma told me that you have worked as a geriatric nurse, and a step from there to the waiting room of a general practitioner is not a very great one. If it would be convenient – empty words. After everything I know about your situation, it will be more than convenient. So, to rephrase – If you will permit me, I will contact the immigration authorities here to see about the prospects of a work permit. It shouldn't actually be all that difficult.

To this end it would be useful if you could assemble your personal details on a piece of paper for me, age, place of birth and all those things. The authorities are doubtless going to want all those things.

With warmest greetings

Your Arthur Meijer

PS: I wonder whether Irma hasn't known the truth for ages, and only goes on talking about an accident because she thinks she owes you that. I would not put such consideration beyond her.

PERSONAL DETAILS

Name: Pollack, née Bernstein

First name: Rosa Recha (my father was a big fan of Lessing.)

Date of birth: 30 September 1900 (I would seem to have been conceived during the night of the turn of the century.)

Place of birth: Melsungen, District of Melsungen, Hessen (perhaps you have seen a picture of the beautiful half-timbered houses there? My father had a little weaving mill there.)

Professional training: primary school teacher (but I never practised the profession, because I met my husband while I was doing the course and married him straight after my exams. Pointlessly wasted fees.)

Current occupation: unemployed

Religion: (three guesses.)

(So, is that enough parenthetical observations for your liking?)

Kassel, 10.7.37

Dear Goliath!

The personal details that I enclose sound remarkably silly. Your letter has left me light-headed with hope.

Of course I can imagine nothing better than to help in your surgery. Or in any other way. Do you need a cook? My children say I bake the best cakes in the world. Oh, it would be so lovely if this really worked! The situation here gets more dreadful by the day.

The impression that you will have gained from your nephew's letters is not incorrect. Most of the things being done to us are entirely legal. It is only the laws themselves that are criminal. As if highway robbers were to wear collars and ties and keep strictly to shop opening hours.

An example: they don't simply take people's houses away. They just pass a bill according to which each house-owner is obliged to become a member of a house-owner's association. Sounds harmless enough, doesn't it? But the association doesn't accept Jews, so the houses sadly, sadly, have to be sold. At a price determined by the purchaser.

And that is happening everywhere.

I myself have worked in an old people's home run by the B'nai B'rith. The association was compulsorily dissolved and its assets confiscated. So far so orderly. First you invent a clause, and then you enforce it.

Before they pulled all the bedclothes out of the cupboards and took them away, I had to produce an exact list of them, sheet for sheet, pillow case for pillow case. They even waited until the dirty laundry had been washed, ironed and sorted again. To make sure that nothing was missing. Only then did they come and take it all away. They paid me my wages for that one day. Minus social insurance contributions, as prescribed by the regulations. All according to the book.

When the old people had long since been thrown out of their rooms, a Party member sat in our director's office for weeks going through the accounts. B'nai B'rith members who were behind with their contributions were sent a reminder and had to pay the difference. Your view of things is quite correct: we are an orderly country, where stealing is only ever done against receipt.

I will be so happy when I no longer have to live here.

By the way: I naturally assumed that you and your family are Swiss. If that is the case – what is your nephew doing in this accursed Germany?

A work permit for Switzerland would be wonderful. If it works out, I will only ever call you Goliath for as long as you live.

With warmest, warmest greetings

Your

Rosa Pollack

'How do you imagine this?'

Herr Bisang pulled a face as if he had toothache. He had set his pocket watch down on the desk in front of him and now straightened the chain, aligning it so that it was precisely parallel with the dark brown cardboard portfolio containing Arthur's application.

'Really, Dr Meijer, how do you imagine this?'

The official had the pursed lips of a man who has an unpleasant taste in his mouth, but whom propriety forbids to spit.

'Stomach problems,' Arthur thought automatically.

'Just as this Zionist Congress is being held in Zurich. With delegates from all over the world. I have talked to my colleagues in Basel, who have experience of such things. They all say we should brace ourselves. You have no idea how much work we have to do already.' With a reproachfully exhausted gesture he pointed to a shelf full of lever-arch files. 'Entry permits. Special authorisations. Applications, applications, applications.'

'I don't quite see the connection.'

'But Doctor Meijer!' Herr Bisang pressed both thumbs to his temples and pulled a face again. 'You are an intelligent person. One can tell just by looking at you. No, no, don't contradict me. I have an eye for these things. You have to be able to read people in a post such as mine. You understand what I mean.'

'To be quite honest: no. I'm asking you for a work permit for a receptionist, and you...'

'Stop there,' said Herr Bisang and raised his hand like a traffic policeman. 'Let's not muddle things up. You have made an application; I have received an application to process. It has nothing at all to do with a personal request. If it were up to me...'

'Yes?'

'But it isn't up to me,' said Herr Bisang. 'We have our instructions. Rules. Guidelines.'

'Frau Pollack would really be the ideal receptionist for me.'

'Ah, you see, Doctor Meijer...' Herr Bisang seem to have reached a favourite topic of his. 'What is ideal? It would be ideal if I could retire tomorrow on a full pension. But authorities are not there for the ideal, but for the doable. And this work permit is not doable.'

'My I ask you the reason?'

Herr Bisang coughed and brought a hand to his throat as if to check that some new illness wasn't on its way.

'Application for entry with a view to accepting a workplace can only be authorised if in the professional sector in question it can be demonstrated that there is an inadequate supply of local applicants.' The sentence sounded as if it had been learned by heart, as indeed it probably had been.

'In this special case...'

'There are only special cases.' Herr Bisang laid his fingertips together as carefully as if it were a difficult trick. 'Particularly among you Jews.'

'Excuse me?'

'Please don't misunderstand me, Dr Meijer. I have no prejudices. I do not know such things. For me there are only facts. Figures. Statistics. And it is an indisputable fact that the number of applications from German citizens of the Mosaic faith has risen very sharply over the past few years.'

Arthur had planned to remain very calm, but now he noticed something welling up in him that would not be held back, just as nausea often needs release at the most unsuitable moment.

'It is also an indisputable fact,' he said sarcastically, 'that something else has risen sharply over the past few years. Namely the persecution of the Jews in Germany.'

'Doubtless, doubtless.' Herr Bisang nodded as if Arthur had just agreed with him. 'That is also presented as a reason in many of these applications. Rightly, I assume. But...' He was not yet content with the alignment of his watch chain, which required all his concentration.

'But what?'

'It cannot be the task of a Swiss authority to solve German problems.'

'These are human beings!'

'Yes,' said Herr Bisang and nodded again. 'There you come precisely to the point, dear Doctor Meijer. You see, that is the first and the hardest thing that one must learn in such an office. Almost everyone who places an application here is right. As a human being. As a single person. As an individual. And yet we must turn down most of these applications. Because we must think of the whole.'

'These are empty words! Anti-Semitism in Germany is a reality!'

'Precisely because it is a reality.' Herr Bisang had discovered a sensitive spot on his neck, and was touching it very carefully with his fingers. 'Precisely because we see every day the terrible effects such a reprehensible philosophy can have. Persecutions. Bullying. Loutish behaviour in broad daylight. As if it were the Middle Ages.'

'That's precisely why...'

'That's precisely why, my dear Dr Meijer, we can't let the same thing happen in Switzerland. Nip it in the bud! If I reflect that there has been a Frontist representative for Zurich on the national council for two years – that is an alarm signal!'

'And we defeat the Front by closing the borders?' Arthur was really furious now, and it was an emotion that he only allowed himself very rarely.

'I didn't say that. But neither can we open the gates wide. We must precisely regulate immigration, with a dropper, as one might say. You as a doctor should understand that.'

'I'm probably too stupid,' said Arthur. 'But I'm sure you'll explain it to me.'

'Only too happily. Although...' Herr Bisang pulled his pocket watch over, looked at the time and shook his head resignedly. 'Ah well, time is marching on. Where were we?'

'You were trying to explain to me why I should be in favour of the rejection of my own request.' Arthur's voice trembled with the effort of not simply yelling in response to the official's dusty calm.

'Of course, of course. There is that rule in medicine: any substance applied in the correct dosage can be curative. Or at least not damaging. Is that not the case? But if one introduces an overdose of anything to the organism...'

'An overdose of what?'

'A state, my dear Doctor Meijer, is also a kind of organism. In which all the parts must work together. Each one in its place, and each in its God-given quantity. As long as nothing changes, the whole remains healthy. But if that equilibrium is disturbed... In our neighbouring country we can see what that can lead to. Irritations. Reactions. Convulsions.' The medical vocabulary seemed to remind him of something. He took a silver pillbox from a desk drawer and reached into it with pointed fingers.

'Do you mean...?'

'I was only trying to give you an example. From your own sphere. Our country is still healthy. Largely healthy. We have fortunately been spared the illness of anti-Semitism. Largely spared. But if there were suddenly a Jew standing on every street corner, a foreign Jew to boot – for how long would Switzerland remain immune? And once such an infection has taken root...' Herr Bisang nodded significantly, he knew his way around infections, that was supposed to mean, and put a small pink pill in his mouth by way of precaution. 'It must be in the greatest interest of the Swiss Jews to avoid anything that might encourage anti-Semitism in this country.'

'Do I understand you correctly, Herr Bisang? You are refusing Frau Pollack's accusation because one Jew more might encourage anti-Semitism in Switzerland?' Now Arthur was really raising his voice.

'My dear Doctor Meijer! How can you accuse me of saying any such thing? I don't mean the individual. Not the single person. Not the human being, as you so rightly said a moment ago. But as an official I am obliged to see the larger contexts. To think beyond the day. In your interest too.'

He pushed aside the folder containing the application, as if everything was sorted out and finished, and rose to his feet. 'If there's anything else I can do for you...It's always a pleasure to talk to an intelligent person.'

Zurich, 1 August 1937

Dear Frau Pollack,

I would so have loved to be able to report a positive result, so I have repeatedly postponed writing this letter.

But everything turns out to be much more difficult than I had expected. I fear I have failed.

Outside in the street a brass band is passing. Today is the Swiss national holiday, and many fine speeches will be delivered. Has it always been the case that there is barely a connection between words and deeds? Or has it only struck me so clearly in recent times? (Do brass bands play so loudly because so many hypocrisies need drowning out?)

I have been informed, very kindly and correctly, that a work permit is absolutely out of the question. If at all, such a paper is issued only for positions for which no Swiss applicants can be found. (Which actually means none at all.)

At the moment I am at a loss about what to do next. One would really have to be a Goliath and shake these officials until their polite smile falls from their faces. They actually expect one to be grateful on top of everything.

I do not want to raise false hopes, but I have firmly undertaken not to give up on this matter. We still have a small amount of time before Irma and Moses finally have to leave the country.

They are both well. I shamelessly pretended to Fräulein Württemberger that the striking improvement in my patient's health was entirely down to her good care and supervision, and if she continued to perform her services so efficiently, a complete recovery might be possible. (I have often observed that people who despise other human beings are particularly susceptible to flattery.)

I assume that the weather in Kassel is as lovely as it is here. If circumstances were different, I would write: enjoy these fine days!

With kind regards

Arthur Meijer

PS: I have firmly resolved to write a letter without a PS today.

67

Every month François paid the chief nurse at the old people's home, one Frau Olchev, a few francs to devote special care to Chanele, and to alert him immediately, in the middle of the night if necessary, if anything was wrong with his mother. This morning she had rung him at about half past three. Frau Meijer was breathing with difficulty, and saying confused things, apparently in French. She, Frau Olchev, had not understood everything, but she was sure that it had something to do with a drummer and some ravens, perhaps Herr Meijer knew what it meant. She didn't want to frighten him, heaven forbid, but on the other hand if something was wrong and she hadn't told him in time, she would blame herself, particularly when Herr Meijer had always been so generous towards her. In her experience, on more than one occasion, such confused states often preceded death, the understanding fled before the soul. She had, as she was sure Herr Meijer would have intended, called the doctor, and perhaps it was something quite harmless, but if the worst came to the worst, she didn't want to have to blame herself…

And so on. Frau Olchev, and perhaps this had something to do with her profession, was chatty even at this early hour.

François called his brother and sister – they had agreed that he would do this some months previously – and got the car out of the garage. For a few years he had been driving a French product again, a Citroen 11 CV that his business partner in Paris had bought for him under particularly favourable conditions. On other days he could wax as lyrical about the model's advantages – front wheel drive! Steel monocoque chassis! – as his father once had about an exotic wood dining table, but today no one in the car uttered a word as they drove to Lengnau in the summer dawn. François spoke only once, to say, 'How empty the roads are at this time of day.'

Hinda and Arthur sat side by side in the back and held hands.

They arrived at the old people's home just before six, and all three ran up the steps, as if every second counted. When they charged into their mother's room – the best room in the house, François had seen to that – the doctor had already come from the village and gone again. He had given Chanele an injection; she was sleeping now, and would not wake up for the next few hours. She lay there with a thumb in her mouth, a little girl who had dressed up as an old woman and gone to sleep after her game. Her breathing was quite calm and peaceful.

It had been a false alarm.

Frau Olchev, feeling guilty about all the excitement that she had caused, and at the same time proud of the importance granted her by the event, was even chattier than usual, and construed the meaningless phrases uttered by the doctor she had summoned as statements of profound significance. He hadn't been able to find anything really alarming, she said, reporting his diagnosis, but given the patient's great age and her weakened general condition, one must always expect dramatic changes, so it had only been correct – Frau Olchev repeated the words with red underlining – it had been absolutely correct to call him straight away, because once they started fantasising it was always an alarm signal. She, Frau Olchev, hoped very much that she had acted as Herr Meijer would have wished, she knew how concerned he was about his mother – as indeed were the other ladies and gentlemen – and he would certainly have taken it amiss of her if she had neglected to make the phone-call out of concern for his sleep, and then, God forbid, the worst might have come to the worst.

She used the phrase 'if the worst comes to the worst' and its variants as a universally applicable specialist term. Arthur could easily imagine her recording deaths at the home in the incident book in the same terms: 'Frau So-and-so at such-and-such a time: the worst came to the worst.'

Basically, he thought, it was the most honest opinion that one could express.

After the excitement of the nocturnal alarm, the sudden relief also had an aftertaste of disappointment, as if someone had at the very last moment removed an obstacle at which they were already running. In fact they could have driven back to Zurich straight away, but they agreed, quickly and silently, that they would, since they were here, visit Chanele again later, once she had woken up. There was nowhere in the old people's home where they could have waited in any great comfort; the cleaning women had just arrived, and were putting the dining room and the common rooms under water. So they got back into the Citroen and drove into Lengnau, since they were all ready for a small breakfast or at least a cup of coffee.

But that wish turned out not to be easily fulfilled. The pubs – here in the country there were no cafés – were all still closed, so at last they found themselves in the deserted garden of Die Sonne, where a table with two benches stood beneath a massive chestnut tree. All around the foundations for other seating opportunities were fastened to the ground, smaller stones for the benches, larger ones for the tables, but because the requisite boards were missing it looked as if the siblings had sat down in the middle of a neatly arranged graveyard.

The three of them didn't find themselves sitting together like that very often any more. The days when they had really been close were now long gone; they weren't children any more, and with every new grey hair one grows further apart from one's brothers and sisters. They turn into strangers, or perhaps it only seems that way because strangers become more familiar. Either way, a special kind of awkwardness had arisen between them, as often happens when private feelings have been made public, when one is ill at ease with mutually agreed silence, and prefers to create a safe feeling of detachment by batting a few commonplaces back and forth.

'We should actually be grateful to Frau Olchev,' said Hinda. 'She's brought about another family reunion.'

The first at which we've sat around an empty table.

'That's true,' said Arthur. 'We'll probably have to wait a long time for a coffee, at such an unchristian hour — Oh, forgive me, François.' His brother and sister looked at him in surprise. He was the only one to have noticed any allusions in his words.

The benches had no backs, so they weren't sitting very comfortably.

Arthur started talking about the vote in the religious community, at which they had just decided by 236 six votes to 178 to remove the harmonium from the synagogue, again, but he couldn't even pretend to himself that he was interested.

The silence between them grew louder.

As a distraction, Hinda opened her handbag, took out an envelope and rubbed away at the digestive traces that a bird had left on the table.

François saw the Hitler stamp and asked, 'News from Ruben?'

Hinda nodded. Grateful for a topic of conversation, she reported that a letter had arrived at Rotwandstrasse only yesterday, and it had been so strange that neither she nor Zalman had really been able to make head or tail of it. The letter itself was at home, but she could recite it almost by heart. Previously, Ruben had kept reporting new irritations and instances of bullying, his letters, Hinda said, could have been bound into a Black Book, and now all of a sudden here he was writing that they shouldn't worry about him, and please to lend no credence to the horrific propaganda that was sadly being disseminated even in the Swiss newspapers. Germany was a country in which law and order prevailed, he wrote, where nothing was ever done to anyone unless he had broken the law. A new Reich was coming into being, so exemplary that it almost corresponded to that ideal state described by the scholar Rabbah bar bar Chana in the Talmud, and he, Ruben, was grateful that he had been allowed to make a modest contribution to that construction in his own town of Halberstadt.

'Do you understand that?' asked Hinda. 'He can't really mean it.'

François ran both index fingers from his upper lip and across his cheeks, his old gesture when he felt superior to others. 'Do I really have to explain that to you as a goy? Have you forgotten the stories Uncle Pinchas always told us? About the campfire on the back of a fish, or about the crocodile as big as a town with sixty houses? Those were all stories told by Rabbah bar bar Chana.'

'So?'

'They're all lies. Tall stories.'

'You mean...?'

'They've probably started censoring letters going abroad. So he's writing the opposite of what he means, and mentions Rabbah bar bar Chana so that we know how to read it. They may even have threatened him. From what one hears, in Germany you can end up in a re-education camp for less than a letter.'

Hinda, entirely accustomed to the orderly conditions in Switzerland, had never even thought of such a thing, but now that François said it, she was sure he was right. The most terrible rumours were going around about those education camps and the things that happened in them. No one knew exactly, but it was assumed to be terrible. And now her son Ruben...? She took a shocked, deep breath, as someone falling from a bridge gasps for water just before the water closes over him.

Arthur was shocked as well, but in his case the emotion had little to do with Ruben. He was thinking about all the letters Rosa Pollack had written to him from Kassel. If she found herself in difficulties, if she was arrested or even locked up, it would be his fault.

His alone.

Because he had failed in everything that he had tried to do for her.

'Anyway, I don't understand why Ruben didn't come back to Switzerland long ago,' said François.

'He doesn't want to.'

'Meshuga,' said François, and the word sounded strange from his lips.

'It's because of his community. But now,' Hinda said resolutely, 'now he has to think about his children. I'll write to him today and tell him to come.'

'And if he doesn't?'

'Then Zalman will have to go and get him.'

'I should go and fetch someone too,' thought Arthur. 'But they wouldn't let her over the border.' He took off his glasses and rubbed the bridge of his nose.

'I'm sorry to have kept you waiting.'

A waiter came out of the pub. His apron reached to the ground; you couldn't see his feet moving, so that he seemed to float. On a tray he balanced everything that belongs to a lavish breakfast: a steaming jug, fresh rolls, eggs, cheese, jam. He set the tray on the table, where it sank like a stone into dark water, without leaving a trace. Then he shoved up alongside François on the bench, carefully straightening his apron as a well-bred lady might straighten the hem of her skirt. 'You don't mind if I join you for a moment?'

'You're dead!' said François. 'When will you finally admit it?'

'When I no longer need to be alive.'

Uncle Melnitz looked cheerful, almost exuberant. Even the smell that emanated from him had changed, as dust changes its smell when it rains. 'It's starting up again,' he said, and rubbed his hands as if before an interesting job or a good meal. 'I can feel it in all my bones: it's starting up again, yes.'

'I don't want to hear about it,' said Hinda.

'Of course not, my lovely, of course not.' Uncle Melnitz's arm was suddenly so long that he was able to pat Hinda's cheek across the table. 'Just you keep your hands over your ears. Shut your eyes. Then nothing will happen to your son. If you can't see it, it doesn't happen.'

'What do you want from us?' asked Arthur, even though he knew exactly what Uncle Melnitz wanted.

'I want to tell you a story,' said the old man. They had never seen him so full of life. 'I'm sure you want to know where I got my name.'

They didn't want to know. Actually they didn't want to know anything about him at all. But when Uncle Melnitz wanted to tell a story, he did so.

'Sixteen hundred and forty-eight,' he said. He let the syllables melt away on his tongue. 'A wonderful year. The Thirty Years' War was coming to an end, and there was peace all across Europe. Although not for the Jews. Perhaps because we calculate time differently. For us it wasn't 1648, it was 5408. 5409. Terrible years.'

'We don't want to hear your old stories,' said François. He tried to stand up, but Uncle Melnitz pressed him effortlessly back down onto his seat. The more often he died, the stronger he became.

'You'll like this story,' he said. 'You most of all, Shmul. There are Jews in it who have themselves baptised.'

Uncle Melnitz hadn't been so young for ages.

'It was in the Ukraine,' he said, 'which wasn't yet called the Ukraine. Countries change their names. They also change their friends. Only their enemies always stay the same. We always stay the same, yes.

'The story I want to tell you is about Bohdan Khmelnitsky. Do you know the name? Of course you do. For our sins God punished us Jews with a good memory. If someone has done something particularly bad to us, we say, "May his name be erased." And then we remember it for all eternity.' Uncle Melnitz laughed. He threw his laughter onto the table, a hand full of sharp-edged pebbles.

'Bohdan Khmelnitsky, yes. He wanted to wage a war with his Cossacks against the Polish magnates who ruled the Ukraine, and because it was such a long way to Poland he first took it out on the Jews. It's an old game. The crusaders played it in their day too. Jerusalem was so far away, and the Jews were so close at hand. Khmelnitsky never got to Warsaw. He only got as far as Pereiaslav. Pyriatyn. Lokhvytsya.'

'You're dead,' said Hinda. 'You don't exist any more.'

'Good!' said Uncle Melnitz, and drew out the vowel as if he were praising a child. 'Goooood! You've worked it out. None of them exist any more. They're all dead. In Pohrebyshche. In Zhivotov. In Nemyriv. In Tulchyn. In Polonne.'

'I don't even know where those places are!' Arthur heard himself shouting, even though he hadn't shouted at all.

'Of course you don't,' said Uncle Melnitz. 'That's why I'm telling you about them. So that you remember when it starts up again there. In Sasov. In Ostroh. In Kostyantyniv. In Bar.'

Hinda threw her hands over her face, as she had done when Zalman's train set off from the station for Galicia and disappeared among the winding tracks. 'Please, please, please...'

'Pleading doesn't help,' said Melnitz, and threw the next handful of pebbles on the table. 'It never helped. Not in Kremenetz. Not in Chernigov. Not in Starodub. Not in Narol.'

'Please...'

'Not in Tomaszow. Not in Sczebreczin. Not in Hrubieszow. Not in Bilgoraj. Not in Homiel.'

'That no longer has anything to do with us.'

'Of course not,' replied Uncle Melnitz. 'Nothing at all. It's all such a long time ago. People today are so much more intelligent than they were in those days. Do you know what the idiots in the Ukraine called their times? The birth pangs of the Messiah. Because they thought Salvation would have to come after so much suffering. But the birth was a long time coming. It must have been a phantom pregnancy.' He gave a bleating laugh and, without standing up – ei! ei! ei! – did a little dance.

'They were funny people, Bohdan Khmelnitsky and his haidamaks. People with imagination. When they tied a belt around a woman's neck and dragged her behind their horses by it, they called it: giving her a red ribbon. Isn't that ingenious? When they cut someone's throat they called it: playing shechita.

Come on, that's a good one! When they cut open a pregnant woman's belly and sewed in a living cat...'

'That was then,' said Hinda quickly.

'In the Dark Ages,' said Arthur.

'They don't have things like that any more,' said François.

'I'm sure you're right. I'm a stupid old man, and besides, I'm dead. Today none of those things would be possible. The animal protection society would intervene and protect the cat.'

The gravel rattled on the table and sprayed away in all directions.

'Even in those days they weren't always so imaginative,' said Uncle Melnitz. 'At least they were only doing their duty. What would become of the world if people didn't carry out orders as they were given? In Homiel, for example, there were no acts of cruelty. Everything went its orderly way, yes. There was a wooden synagogue there, but they didn't drive the Jews into it to barricade the doors and set it on fire. Even though synagogues burn so well. Because of all the books.

'No, Khmelnitsky's Cossacks were too sensible for that. A synagogue is a building, and you can always use buildings again. As a stable. As a granary.

'If it had been possible to take them all away, the Jews themselves could have been sold. The Turks paid per head and claimed their investments back as ransom from the communities in Italy and Holland. But the Cossacks had no carts to hand.

'They weren't cruel people, but they had their orders. When they sat around their fires in the evening, they sang beautiful songs, with dark, soughing basses, but they had their orders. When they drank vodka, they became sentimental and melancholy, and the tears ran into their beards. But they had their orders.

'They had the whole village line up. In rank and file. The men, the women, the old, the young. The children too. They had to take off their clothes, because they could be used again. If you want to win a war, you can't waste a thing.

'The old rabbi stood there, his skin as thin and grey as if it had been made of yellowing tomes. The young girl for whose hand two men were fighting; she secretly loved a third, who was now standing there too, quite close to her and yet too far away for her to take his hand. Two men who had scrambled all their lives for honours and dignities. Now each would have yielded to the other, but they were no longer asked. The village idiot stood there, the one who had always laughed when carrying water and chopping wood, and who was now afraid, because everyone had such serious faces and he didn't know if it was his fault. The beautiful woman stood next to the ugly one; for the first time they were naked, and could have compared one another. But there was no longer any difference between them; they were dead, even though they were still alive. The fat man stood next to the thin, the rich next to the poor, the one with all the plans next to the hopeless one, and between even them there was no longer any difference.

'The Cossacks did their work as they had been instructed to, without cruelty or ill will. They had a row step forward, their sabres struck, the next row stepped forward, the one behind that and so on and so on. Last of all they killed old Bathsheba, who had lost five children and therefore become a midwife. She had brought every other person in the village into the world, and now she had to watch as they were driven from it again.

'That was how it was in Homiel, during the birth pangs of the Messiah, yes. Nothing of the kind could happen today. We're living in the twentieth century, and no one uses sabres any more.'

The air was warm, and even though it hadn't yet struck seven, you could already tell that it was going to be a hot day. The birds were waking up in the chestnut tree above their heads, and the stones around them were not gravestones, but the bases for benches and tables, so that you could sit down, order a beer and enjoy your day.

'You're not asking me,' said Melnitz. 'I haven't even told you how I got my name.'

They didn't ask, and he told them anyway.

'The prettiest girls,' said Melnitz. 'The Cossacks didn't kill them. They dragged them inside the church and had them baptised, they made them their wives and impregnated them with their children.

'When the horror had passed – it always passes, and it is always too late – when Khmelnitsky was defeated and everyone despised him, even those who had admired him – especially those who had admired him, that's always how it is – when they wrote the special prayers in which Khmelnitsky would be remembered for all time – may his name be erased! – they called a great va'ad in Lublin, a synod of all the scholars who had survived the bad times. Only a few came, and they had a lot to discuss and to decide. It isn't easy to recreate a normal, everyday life, when for a few years nothing was everyday or normal.

'And now,' said Melnitz, 'now I have something that will make you laugh. They also made a decision because of all the women who had been baptised, or who had given birth to Cossack children even without baptism. It was decided that they were to be brought back into the community of Israel. Every soul was needed, because many had not remained alive during those years, when the rest of Europe was enjoying its new-found peace. They were to belong to the community again, it was decided, they and their children.

'What they didn't decide, and what happened anyway: these children, whose fathers were unknown, were given a nickname. They were called Khmelnitskys. Because they owed their existence to the wicked enemy.

'Perhaps,' said Uncle Melnitz, and bleated his gravelly laugh, 'perhaps we Jews only continue to exist because we have so many enemies. They ensure that we don't forget who we are, yes.

'Khmelnitsky is my name,' he said. 'Melnitz. A name that cannot be erased.'

When they got back to the old people's home, Chanele was awake again and even recognised them. At least she smiled and said, 'Nice of you to come.' With Frau Olchev's help she had put on her black dress with the white edging and sat very straight in her armchair.

'Why didn't you bring your children, Arthur?' she asked.

68

They missed everything. The solemnities, the debates, the brawling. Simply everything.

The Zionist Congress was taking place, for once and at last in his own city, and Hillel wasn't there. Chaim Weizmann, whose picture he had hung on his locker, walked each day to the meetings in the Stadttheater, and Hillel didn't get to see him. The scholar Nachum Goldman had travelled in specially from Honduras, where he had lived in exile since being expatriated from Germany, and Hillel couldn't ask him for an autograph. David Ben-Gurion was there, the union leader, and many others whose names one only ever read in the newspapers. They were all there, all of them. But not Hillel, even though he had been chosen to go on guard duty for Shomer Hatzair, even though he could have stood outside the front of the theatre in his blue shirt, his arms propped on his hips and his alert gaze staring into the distance, like one of the guards of the Hula Valley in a photograph.

Böhni fared no better. Not that he would have been interested in the Congress, of course not, but something was going on in the street. Demonstrations were being organised and flyers distributed against the invasion of straggly beards, against these foreign-looking figures who tried to haggle over the price of the ticket in the tram and didn't even know that you were supposed to leave a tip in the café. They acted as if the city belonged to them, they were pushy and noisy, and they couldn't even speak proper German. No wonder there were arguments, but Böhni wasn't there, he could only read the appeals in the Front not to let Zurich become Zurisalem, or Bahnhofstrasse Zionsallee.

And the worst thing was: they had to put up with each other, twenty-three hours a day, or even twenty-four if you added an hour's yard exercise. They stayed together there as well, and stood apart from the others, because the others were all real criminals, and they had a healthy respect for them.

The judge had given them short shrift: brawling under Article 133, three hundred franc fine for each of them, or thirty days detention, that's that. An example had to be set, he had roared, in Switzerland they didn't pursue political arguments with street fights and skirmishes, and if anyone couldn't see that then they needed to be taught a lesson until they did. He didn't care who had started it, who had provoked whom, and the law wisely didn't care either. 'Anyone involved in a brawl...' was all it said, neither of the accused had disputed their involvement, and political convictions were not mitigating circumstances. The legislator, and in the end that was the people, didn't care in the least whether they were reds, blacks, browns or as far as he was concerned grass-greens or lemon-yellows, these fellows who tore into each other with their fists, brawling was forbidden either way, and involvement was punished by prison or a fine.

Böhni, Walter, and Rosenthal, Heinrich: three hundred francs, pay up or do your time, next case, please.

Three hundred francs was a fortune for an agricultural student. Böhni didn't even have to think about asking his parents, in Flaach they'd never seen as much money as that all at once, and even if they'd had it, it certainly wasn't going to a son who brought shame on their heads, for a lad with previous convictions at whom everyone in the village was already pointing a finger. Böhni's parents hadn't been in the courtroom, at harvest time they had, God knew, better things to be getting on with, when they were in any case missing a few hands they had firmly expected to be working for them, now that the Strickhof was on holiday.

Hillel's father had sat there throughout, with such a wounded expression on his face that one might have thought the whole punch-up had taken place solely to defy him. He had always been opposed to Hillel's Zionism, and now one could see where it led when an adolescent burrowed his way into an ideology and didn't listen to his father or, which in Adolf Rosenthal's opinion amounted to the same thing, to reason. Bad company and fighting. A Jewish boy thumping people in public – it only caused rish'es. Hillel knew that his father, if he had asked him subserviently enough, would have would have been able to drum up the three hundred francs one way or another, with interest in the form of contrition and obedience. But he didn't even think of paying such a price. He would rather be locked up. And Adolf Rosenthal remained stubborn as well, however much Lea might complain. No help without an admission of guilt. If you won't listen, you go to jail.

'Not a bad daily wage,' Hillel said to Böhni while they were still in the court-room. 'Ten francs a day, seven times a week. Some workers don't earn half that.'

What he hadn't reckoned with, and neither had Böhni, was that the governor of the local prison was a person with a sense of humour, and had thus come up with the idea of locking the two of them up together in a cell. 'Then you will have plenty of time for your philosophical discussions,' he said. 'And If you want to beat the living daylights out of each other, that's up to you. But no bloodstains on the blankets.'

Twenty-three hours a day. Twenty-four with yard exercise. In a cell, for which a room in the Strickhof was a luxury hotel in comparison.

There was one stool. One of them always had to lie on his mattress or sit on the edge of the bunk, either on top, where your feet dangled into the void, or on the bottom, where you had to bend your back. Right at the start, when he still refused to grasp that they were real prisoners, Hillel had asked for a second stool. The guard said only that his Majesty should be so kind as to go and sit on the throne, meaning the toilet bowl. And he laughed at his own joke as if he had made it for the first time.

They weren't assigned to work. It wasn't worth training them for four weeks. But they were given prison clothes, a brown suit not much different from the ones they wore to work in the Strickhof stables.

The worst thing was the boredom. They were woken at half past five, to which they were accustomed from school, there was breakfast at six, the daily ration of bread, a glob of jam and coffee so thin that even when the metal cup was full one could still make out the Zurich crest stamped on the bottom. The cleanliness of the cell was checked at eight, and having been drilled by Kudi Lampertz they never had any problems with that.

And then: nothing else.

Apart from yard exercise, nothing at all, for the whole day.

Books were only allowed from the second month. At first only one news-paper each, which meant that their only intellectual stimulation was the *Front* and the *Volksrecht*. At first each refused to read the other's newspaper, and they just made jokes about it: it was nice of Böhni to have fresh toilet paper sent in every day, or: Rosenthal wasn't to forget to wash his hands after reading, the *Volksrecht* was so red that the colour was bound to come off.

But soon the boredom was stronger than their convictions. Böhni in par-ticular was bad at being locked in, he was a person who had to be on the move, and he could drive Hillel round the bend by marching back and forth, the few paces from one wall to the other, or doing sit-ups on the floor out of a surplus of energy. You had to distract yourself somehow, and so it was that Hillel studied the *Front* from cover to cover for the first time in his life, from the leading article entitled 'Oy veh!' to the advertisements, in which the Kreuel restaurant at 33 Kanonengasse recommended itself to its kind customers with Hürlimann beer.

Böhni read the *Volksrecht*, where in the reports from Spain he failed to recog-nise the civil war as he understood it, and in all seriousness believed at first that there was two wars going on down there, the just struggle of a nation under the yoke of Communism against its oppressors, and the terror bombing of squadrons of foreign planes against Basque towns. Even where the politics of the city was concerned, the *Volksrecht* seemed to inhabit a different world from his own; here they supported the red majority on the council, even though everyone knew that the comrades were hand in glove with international Jewry and...

'You're a dickhead,' said Hillel.

'No one can dispute that the Jews...'

'Give me an example.'

'There are hundreds!'

'Give me one!'

'Erm...' said Böhni.

'Aha!' said Hillel.

But then Böhni did come up with an irrefutable argument.'The department stores,' he said. 'They're finishing off the small businesses. Epa, for example. Or Jelmoli.'

'They're Italians.'

'If you fall for their names! Meier, for example, with his department store, his name isn't even Meier. He writes his name up on all the shop windows and it isn't even his name. But we've...they've carried out a few improvements on that. Did you know he's a Jew?'

Hillel thought of his baptised Uncle François and nodded.'Yes, I knew that.'

'There you have it!' said Böhni.

And so it went on all day. Neither of them convinced the other, no one could have expected that, but the hours passed.

Not that they talked about politics all the time. Their most frequent subject was the Strickhof, and how headmaster Gerster would react to their sentence. There was something in the school regulations about 'blameless students'. It could be interpreted in various different ways, but that they were now blameful — was there even such a word — there could be no doubt, and if Gerstli went stubborn on them, they would be flying out of the school in a high arc.

A disaster.

Böhni, normally a fellow of few words, couldn't stop telling Hillel about the grave consequences that such an expulsion would have for him personally. He would have to creep home like someone who had wanted to make something better of himself and had failed in his task; the rich farmers' sons would laugh at him and the girls in the village wouldn't so much as look at him. And his parents...Böhni knew very well what his time at school meant for them: two years with one pair of hands too few on the farm, and no money to take on a labourer.

Hillel also thought out loud about how his parents would react. His father would point out that he had been right – 'What business did you have at an agricultural college? That's goyim naches,' he had always said – and Adolf Rosenthal wasn't the kind of person who would ever forget such a defeat. He would rub Hillel's nose in the story at every opportunity, and Hillel wouldn't have a single argument to silence him. But worst of all – except he didn't tell Böhni this – Hillel was worried about what Malka Sofer would say. And he had only ever talked to her properly on one occasion. Then she had described him as childish over his adventure with the box-cart, but had still acknowledged that he was going to an agricultural college so that he could later be a useful member of society in a Jewish state. If he was expelled now…

Later it turned out that this worry at least had been superfluous. Malka had received her permit for Palestine and had left without saying goodbye.

'Maybe we should write Gerstli a letter,' Hillel said thoughtfully.

Böhni shook his head, with his mouth full. They were sitting over lunch, Böhni, whose turn it was today, on the stool, and Hillel cross-legged on the lower bunk. It was beef roulade, tough as saddle straps, with overcooked Brussels sprouts swimming in a sweetish sauce. Hillel had let Böhni have his roulade – he couldn't get used to treyfene food, was his excuse – and ate only the bread, of which they were given half a loaf per day.

Böhni choked down a mouthful so big that his Adam's apple practically burst out of his throat, and said. 'You're crazy, Rosenthal. What would you say to him?'

'That school is important to us, blah blah, that we love it, that the trial has been a salutary lesson, that in future we will be model students. All the things my father likes to hear.'

'What does your father have to do with it?'

'Teachers are all the same.'

Böhni wasn't happy about the idea. Like many people who aren't good with words, he had far too high an opinion of all things written. 'That's why you believe in the Front,' mocked Hillel. Böhni was in favour of doing nothing at all, just drawing in his head and hoping the whole business would come to nothing, at least as far as the school was concerned. After all, there had only been a small item in the papers, with no names. And besides, by the time they had sat out the three hundred francs, the summer holidays would be coming to an end; so they wouldn't miss a single day of lessons. And Gerstli might have gone away or been otherwise engaged and wouldn't hear a thing about the whole affair. No, the letter was a very bad idea.

They didn't agree, but the argument about Hillel's suggestion still filled the whole afternoon, and in fine weather, when you had to look out through the barred windows to where the sun was shining, the afternoons were always particularly long.

The next day Böhni was called to the visiting room. There was a man waiting for him there.

'My father?' he asked, quite startled, and involuntarily reached for his throat as if there were a noose there that someone was about to pull tight.

'I don't think so,' said the warder. Today this was a cosy, elderly officer who had seen everything in his long years of service, and who set a great deal of store by his knowledge of human beings. 'An accountant or a teacher, I would say. He's wearing a funny polka dot bow tie.' He looked at the docket that had to be filled out at every prison visit. 'Gerster's his name.'

Headmaster Gerster.

Böhni trotted behind the warder as if going to his own execution.

For the first time in more than two weeks Hillel was alone in the cell. He had the stool and the beds and the toilet all to himself, and yet it still seemed to him that the room had grown smaller, that it had shrunk like the skin over a wound when it slowly scars over.

What did Gerster want from Böhni? Why was he visiting only him?

He tried to convince himself that he wasn't interested, he flicked through the Front and didn't understand a word of what he read there. 'A Jew as theatre director makes it impossible for Swiss artists to be discovered; a Jew as university teacher influences young academics against the necessary renewal of our nation.'

What sort of renewal?

Gerstli was basically not a grumpy person, but he had said clearly and distinctly that if even the smallest thing should occur...Expulsion, no ifs or buts. Finished, once and for all.

Why was he only visiting Böhni?

There was only a corner left of the daily ration of bread. Hillel pulled a piece out of the sticky middle and shaped it into a grey ball between the palms of his hands. He drew a mouth and two eyes in it with his fingernails. Then he flattened the head with his fist.

How long had Böhni been gone? You couldn't take a watch with you into the cell, you had to hand it in with your other belongings.

Why had Gerster even come?

And why was he only visiting Böhni?

If he was thrown out of school...

'Away with the bad apples,' it said in the Front. 'We don't want the plague to spread.'

When the keys rattled outside again, Hillel was lying on the top bunk, reading. 'A Jew in the editing room suppresses any view with which he is unhappy. A Jew as film distributor seeks only immoral films for his cinemas.' He didn't lower the paper when Böhni came in.

'Come on, Rosenthal,' said the warder's voice. 'Get up, come with me. A visitor for you.'

'He wants to talk to you too,' said Böhni.

'What about?'

'He asked me who it was who started all this nonsense. The instigator will be thrown out, in the case of the other he will put mercy before justice.'

'So? What did you tell him?'

'The truth,' said Böhni, without looking at him.

The old warden unlocked the cell door from outside and kept the keys in his hand. They rattled with each step that he took, like bells on a harness.

The corridor smelled of cheap scouring powder.

The visiting room wasn't much bigger than their cell. A table, a chair for the visitor, a stool for the prisoner.

Headmaster Gerster stood by the window and looked through the bars at the courtyard.

'Ten minutes,' said the warder.

Ten minutes? Böhni had been away for much longer than that.

Or had it only seemed that way?

'Grüezi, Herr Gerster.'

The headmaster turned towards him very slowly, looked at him as a doctor might look at a seriously ill patient who is beyond help, and then said, more in sorrow than in anger, 'Why do you do such things?'

'I'm sorry, Herr Gerster.'

'Everyone's sorry in retrospect. It's not enough. You have a head on your shoulders, Rosenthal! What on earth were you doing at a Front meeting?'

'I know, it was idiotic.'

'"Idiotic," he says.' Herr Gerster didn't even raise his voice, and that scared Hillel. After the box-cart journey, when Gerstli had given them a proper earful, he had felt better. 'Behaves like the most unreasonable ragamuffin in the whole world and then says: "idiotic". Is it true that it was about a bet?'

Hillel nodded.

'Give a decent answer when I ask you a question! Was it about a bet?'

'Yes, Herr Gerster.'

'And who started this bet?'

'He'll be expelled, won't he?'

572

Gerster didn't reply. He just stood there, his arms behind his back, and clapped the back of his hand impatiently into his palm.

'Who?'

'Böhni will be finished if you throw him out,' said Hillel.

'That doesn't answer my question.'

'They'll finish him off in his village.'

Back of hand against palm.

'His whole life will fall apart.'

'I want to know who is to blame.'

On the wall there was a sign: 'The passing over of objects is strictly forbidden.'

'Who?'

A wooden hatch, like the one between kitchen and dining room at home, but higher up. Probably you could keep an eye on the visits from there.

'I'm waiting.'

The sweetish taste of lunch rose up in Hillel's throat. He swallowed.

Back of hand against palm.

'Me,' said Hillel. 'I'm to blame for this.'

Gerster turned away as if he hadn't heard him, and walked back over to the barred window as if he were about to deliver a speech to the courtyard.

'Did you agree that in advance?'

'I don't know what you mean, Herr Gerster.'

'That each of you was to shoulder the blame?'

Even the visiting room smelled of cleaning fluids, but less sharply. They probably used a better product here.

'Did Böhni say...?'

Gerster turned back towards him. If Hillel hadn't known it wasn't possible, he could have sworn that his headmaster was smiling.

'Then I will have a great deal of difficulty discovering the true culprit. Tell Böhni, "In dubio pro reo." He doesn't understand Latin, but you can translate it for him.'

When the warder had left and closed the cell door, Hillel said, 'You tried to save my skin, didn't you, Böhni?'

Böhni was busy scratching a stick figure into the wall with the handle of his spoon, and couldn't look up.

'Do you know what, Rosenthal?' he said. 'You're off your head.'

'But you're a dick,' said Hillel.

'At least I'm not a Jewish one.'

'Gerster says I'm to tell you, "In dubio pro reo."'

'What does that mean?'

'That I have to put up with your stupid face for another whole year of school.'

'And I have to put up with yours,' said Böhni. 'That's much worse.'

69

When Herr Grün had returned to health he went to the kosher clothes factory
to quit his job.

He thanked Zalman, whom he had told, on the first day, about what had
happened in the camp, and who had understood that you have to help such
people.

'If you need anything else...' said Zalman.

'I don't need anything else.'

Herr Grün shook Rachel's hand and said, 'Without you I would never have
got better.'

'Nonsense,' said Rachel.

'I'm still wondering whether I should be grateful to you for that.'

He was always saying things like that.

'Would you rather have died?'

'It might have been better,' said Herr Grün, 'but now this is how things are.'

'Where are you going to work from now on?'

'I'll send you free tickets,' said Herr Grün. 'You and Fräulein Pomeranz.'

He kept his word.

In the foyer of the Corso Theatre Rachel handed in her coat at the cloakroom
and noticed very quickly that she had chosen too elegant a dress. Admittedly
this was the premiere, but in a revue theatre like the one managed by Wladimir Rosenbaum, the word meant nothing more than all the 'Sensationals!',
'Uniques!' or 'You'll Weep With Laughters!' that he splashed so liberally over
his posters. There was a premiere here every few weeks, and Rachel was the
only one wearing a proper evening ensemble for the occasion, in the bold,
modern colour combination that Fräulein Bodmer, the directrice, had seen at
Patou in Paris: skirt and jacket of red duvetine, green satin neckline. Still: the
women looked at her enviously, and the men looked at her the way one likes
men to look at one, so that one may assume an expression that suggests one
hasn't noticed their gaze at all.

She got there early and had to wait for Désirée. The people, it seemed to
her, came to the Corso with stubbornly cheerful faces, they had decided to
spend money on an enjoyable evening, and the investment was to pay itself
back from the very start. The women laughed shrilly and held their fingertips,
with their red lacquered nails, in front of their mouths; as they walked, the

men bounced at the knee with an excess of vigour, and when they could be persuaded to buy cigarettes or a cuddly toy from the trays of the salesgirls with the page costumes, they tried to look as if they had planned the purchase from the outset.

At last Désirée arrived, right at the agreed time but much too late for Rachel's impatience. Her hair was parted severely in the middle as always, and she was wearing a very simple brown dress with floral embroidery around the collar and the hem, 'a young girl's dress,' Rachel thought, 'and she isn't – me neshuma – a young girl any more'. But she had to admit that Désirée, with her slender figure, could still carry off such a thing.

The usherettes were also dressed as pages, with a tight bodice that thrust out their bosoms, and flesh-coloured tights on their long legs. The peroxide blonde who showed Rachel and Désirée to their seats could have been a sister of Blandine Flückiger: a dress size of thirty-eight and a smile for every man in a ten-metre radius.

They were sitting in the expensive part of the theatre, where the seats were upholstered, and with a tiny table in front of each pair. There were also tables that sat four and six, and there the laughter and conversations were particularly noisy. Rachel saw only bottles standing on the tables and wondered whether it was also possible to order wine by the glass here. But then the waiter – a real water, not a fake page – was already bringing an ice bucket with a bottle of champagne to their table. 'A little gift from Herr Grün,' he said. 'With best wishes for an enjoyable evening.' He popped the cork and poured two glasses so precisely that the crown of foam rose over the edge and then settled back down without a single drop being wasted.

They clinked glasses – 'To Herr Grün!' – and then Rachel said, 'In for a penny,' waved over one of the page-girls with her tray and bought a programme. One franc fifty, completely meshuga. A stitcher would have had to sit at the sewing machine for a whole hour for that.

Herr Grün's name was nowhere to be seen in the programme. They didn't have time to wonder which of the many other names he might be hiding behind, because the orchestra was already rising from the pit on a hydraulic lift. Twelve men in glittery jackets, three saxophones, and on drums a Negro with a broad, white grin. The bandleader had no baton, but instead used his clarinet to tell the musicians when to come in.

'A little different from Fleur-Vallée.' Rachel had wanted to whisper that to Désirée, but had had to repeat the words at the top of her voice to drown out the orchestra and the conversations going on all around them. They both laughed. In their youth no Jewish occasion was imaginable without the old conductor with the powdered nose. Every time you had to beg and plead with him to play something, and every time he just happened to have brought his violin along.

The orchestra sank back down again, the red curtain rustled open and ten girls swung their legs. They were dressed as sailors, because the title of the revue was *Journey Round the World*. In their final pose they turned their backs to the audience, bent low and smiled at the audience with red painted lips from between their spread legs. Fastened to their lace panties were letters spelling the words BON VOYAGE! The effect received hearty applause.

Every act on the programme was assigned to a different country, which could sometimes only be achieved with some clever bits of stage management. Thus Miss Mabel, with her trained poodles, had to represent the whole of Africa, to which end she appeared in a white tropical suit and a sola topee, and the poor creatures had crêpe paper lions' manes tied around their heads. For the apache dance (Paris), a French accordion wailed from the pit, and during the plate-spinning (China), the orchestra did its very best to imitate the sounds of the Far East. The knife-thrower and his fearless partner wore wild west costumes; but Rachel and Désirée were sitting near enough to the stage to hear the partner cursing in a pronounced central Swiss dialect every time a knife landed too close. The girls danced the Spanish flamenco and the Russian kazachok; both countries seemed to be very thrifty with their material when it came to making the national costume.

By the interval Herr Grün still hadn't appeared on the stage.

'He probably won't be on until the second half,' said Désirée. 'He told me once that that's when the big acts come on.'

'Really?' said Rachel. 'He told you that?' She flicked through the programme and then said, 'This must be him. Here: "Herbert Horowitz, the famous comedian from Berlin."'

'Horowitz?'

'He must have come up with a new pseudonym or himself. These variety people often do that.'

The gesture with which she waved over the waiter was appropriate in its elegance for the expensive seats. She asked for the champagne to be topped up, and when Désirée held her hand defensively over her own glass, she said, 'It's a shame to let something so expensive go to waste.'

In the second part of the revue the Great Karnak, a magician with a turban and a Viennese accent, locked his assistant in a box and pierced her with swords. Miss Mabel made another appearance, this time without her poodles, and sang a saucy chanson with the refrain, 'That's just the way of the world.'

Three muscle men painted gold and bronze stretched themselves into poses that contradicted all the laws of gravity. The half-naked women belly-danced as Arabs, and twitched their backsides to the Black Bottom. Then at last the time came. Director Wladimir Rosenbaum, who had guided the audience through the programme in the best-cut tailcoat that Rachel had ever seen, introduced Herbert Horowitz, 'the darling of the Berlin audience and star of the Comics' Cabaret!'

Horowitz wasn't Herr Grün.

He was a short, fat, scruffy little man in an ill-fitting dinner jacket. His speciality was suggestive stories, delivered in a fake Jewish accent, each story being announced with the words, 'A few more bits from Horowitz!' His appearance was received with resounding laughter, especially at those tables where they had had emptied more than one bottle in the course of the evening. He told the story of the man who calls for help because his mother-in-law wants to throw herself out of the window and can't open it all by herself, and the joke about the Jewish salesman who orders a burnt schnitzel and over-cooked potatoes in the restaurant because he wants to eat as he does at home.

It was terrible.

But it was popular.

When the girls had shrieked and lifted their skirts through the closing can-can, there was enthusiastic final applause. Director Rosenbaum, who bowed in the middle of his ensemble under a hail of confetti, was visibly pleased.

'But what's happened to Herr Grün?' Rachel wondered. 'If he wasn't even on the bill, where did he get the free tickets from?'

Désirée shrugged.

Herr Grün had told them just to stay in their seats after the performance and he would come and get them from their table, but he was keeping them waiting for a long time.

'Such a rude man!' Rachel complained.

'You're interested in him, aren't you?'

'Not at all,' said Rachel. 'What makes you think such a thing?'

The audience had gone, and the hall, so festive just a moment before, quickly returned to the everyday. The elegant pages were now only women with sore feet; the permanent smiles had slipped from their faces, and the seductive twitter vanished from their voices. The waiters were all flat footed, and walked down the rows of seats in their shirtsleeves, collecting empty bottles and glasses.

The curtain was open again, but the stage was now just a big empty space without any magic at all. Two stage hands were sweeping up confetti.

At last Herr Grün arrived, from the wings, across the stage, and hurriedly down the few steps into the auditorium. He was wearing his old three-piece suit. Was it actually the only one he had? His coat was over his arm, and he was holding his hat in his hand.

'I'm sorry,' he said. 'There was a problem with Wurmser's cape.'

'Who is Wurmser?'

'The Great Karnak. He got stuck on a nail behind the stage.'

'Why am I interested in your magician?' Two decades before, Rachel's feigned rudeness would have seemed like a tease. Now she was often just rude. 'And why am I interested in his cape?'

'It's part of my job,' said Herr Grün. 'I am the chief dresser here in the theatre. It's a bit closer to home than the Kamionker clothes factory.'

'Cloakroom attendant?'

'There are worse jobs. I learned sewing from you.'

'Congratulations on your new post,' said Désirée. 'But if you won't take my question amiss, Herr Grün – wouldn't you rather be on the stage?'

'Of course,' he said. 'And I'd like to be a millionaire. Or the King of England.'

'But you're at least ten times better than that Horowitz chap.'

'Horowitz!' Herr Grün laughed. 'In Zurich he's the sensation of Berlin. In Berlin nobody's ever heard of him.'

'And you...?'

'Come,' Herr Grün interrupted. 'We must collect your coats.'

The weary girls in the page costumes, the waiters, the old lady in the cloakroom – they were all very polite to Herr Grün, as people treat an abdicated noble with exaggerated correctness precisely when he insists on remaining incognito.

Rachel asked her question again in the street. 'If you're so much better than this Horowitz fellow, and more famous too, why don't they engage you?'

'Of course Wladimir has offered to do just that.' He called the theatre director by his first name, but without sounding smarmy. 'But I can't take to the stage. Never again.'

'Because you don't have a partner any more?'

'On the contrary,' said Herr Grün. 'Because I will always have my partner.'

He insisted on offering them another glass of wine. 'I have much to be grateful to you for.'

'I'm already quite tiddly,' Rachel objected.

'And it suits you very well.'

It was the first time she had heard anything like a compliment from him. They walked along side by side, Herr Grün in the middle, Rachel and

Désirée on either side of him, taking an arm each. Twenty years before, Rachel had often strolled through the city at night like that, with an admirer on each side and her whole life ahead of her.

Herr Grün took them to the White Cross, a pub to which 'one' did not go, because the only people who did were those who didn't distinguish between drinking and getting drunk. The two women came along without demur; Rachel because she didn't want to appear like a fuddy-duddy, and Désirée because she didn't know about the pub's bad reputation.

It wasn't far from the theatre to Rössligasse. Herr Grün opened the door, and they were standing in front of a wall of noise, smoke and clinking glasses.

The pub was cramped, and there wasn't a single empty seat to be seen. But they seemed to know Herr Grün, and freed a table for him. One guest stood up voluntarily, protectively clutching his beer glass to his chest with both hands, a second who had fallen asleep over his glass was lifted away and sat back down next to two others on a bench, where he immediately put his head on the table and went on sleeping.

The landlady herself wiped down the table with a cloth, or distributed the puddles of beer and wine more evenly. 'The usual?' she said to Herr Grün, and when he nodded, 'And the ladies?' Her tone made it clear that they weren't equipped for ladies here. Never before had Rachel felt so out of place in her elegant dress.

'Half a litre of white wine.' Herr Grün didn't specify the variety. Such refinements were not called for in the White Cross.

He looked around, as if to make sure that everything was in its place, and said, 'I like coming here. A place for people who want to forget. That suits me.'

Rachel wrinkled her nose. It was a facial expression that she had got used to in the days when she was much in demand. It had been cute back then. 'It isn't very elegant here.'

Herr Grün pushed a few bits of cigarette ash together into a little pile with a beer mat. 'Depends what you compare it to,' he said.

The landlady brought the carafe of wine. She set a big glass of clear liquid don in front of Herr Grün.

'Schnapps?' said Désirée, without reproach.

'Water,' said Herr Grün. 'I like to allow myself something good.'

Rachel studied her own glass suspiciously and wiped the rim with her handkerchief. Herr Grün smiled.

'Why are you looking at me like that?' she asked.

'You know something, Fräulein Kamionker? You shouldn't mix coffee with your henna. Once you've got used to it, the colour really suits you.'

She didn't understand this man.

A few tables away a drunk stood up, reached unsteadily for the back of his chair and dragged it – as a support or as a weapon – over to the three. A tall, thickset man with a puffy face, an athlete who had let himself go, or a worker who drank too much. He placed the chair next to their table, sat down and leaned over to Rachel.

'Princess,' said the man. 'You're a princess.'

You could hear the alcohol in his voice.

'I'm the king,' said the drunk man. 'Princess and king. Do you notice anything?'

'Please leave us alone.' Later Rachel would claim she had remained quite calm.

'Come home with me,' said the man. 'I'll show you my sceptre.' He laughed, and when no one at the table joined in, he repeated more loudly, 'My sceptre. You understand? Sceptre!'

'That'll do.' Herr Grün said it quite calmly, but the man's head spun around as if someone had cracked a whip.

'You can't say that to me.'

'You want to check?' asked Herr Grün. His voice hadn't got any louder, but all conversations fell silent in the White Cross, and someone shook the sleeping man at the next table awake to say to him, 'You can't miss this!'

The drunk man looked at Herr Grün.

Herr Grün tilted his head slightly to one side, not menacingly, just asking amicably.

How would you like it?

The drunk man started laughing, not very convincingly, and said, 'We're jolly people here. Jolly people. You can take a joke, can't you?' And then, to Herr Grün and not at all to Rachel, 'Excuse me. I'm sorry. It wasn't meant in a nasty way.' He got off, dragged his chair back to his table, sat down with his back to them and didn't turn round again.

All around them the conversations struck up again, but no longer quite as loudly as before.

'Thank you,' said Rachel.

'You're welcome,' said Herr Grün.

Désirée ran her fingernail along the rim of her wine glass. 'He's stronger than you,' she said without looking at Herr Grün. 'He could have beaten you up.'

'Beatings aren't a matter of strength. It depends how far you're prepared to go.'

'How far would you go for me?' The alarm was over, and Rachel's voice was flirty again.

'No one hits me any more,' said Herr Grün. 'Not any more.' He took a deep draught from his water glass. 'I'm skilled.'

'What does that actually mean?'

'You live here in Switzerland,' he said 'you can't understand. On an island you don't know what it means to drown. I had to learn to swim. If you didn't do that…'

He raised both hands above his head and let them fall back down on the table.

'You're talking about your friend Blau,' said Désirée quietly. It wasn't a question.

'His name was Schlesinger. Siegfried Schlesinger. Studied German. Knew the Merseburg Charms off by heart, and when he was in a good mood he liked to recite poems in Middle High German. "Du bist beslozzen in minem herzen. Verlorn ist daz slüzzelin, du muost immer drinne sin." Beslozzen in minem herzen. Locked in my heart,' Herr Grün repeated and drank his water as if it was schnapps.

'He would have liked to be a teacher, but for some reason they wouldn't have him. They wanted to have him as Herr Blau.'

Guten Tag, Herr Blau.

Guten Tag, Herr Grün.

'Brought a different book to the dressing room every day. If reading books made you fat we'd have had to swap roles.' Herr Grün laughed, and again it was that pickled laugh from the basement.

'He had a funny face. Sticking-out ears. That was his good fortune on stage and his misfortune in the camp. He stood out, and if you stand out you haven't a chance.'

He waved to the landlady, as impatient as a drinker whose alcohol has run out. She brought him his next glass of water and he drank greedily.

'Not a chance,' he said. 'If you hit someone with a stick, it sounds different from when you use a whip. Did you know that? With a glove it's different from when you use your bare hand. Some people didn't even punch. They preferred to kick. They made you stand bolt upright and then rammed their knee into your privates. Everyone has his own style. Like comics on the stage. There were also double-acts. Just as Grün and Blau were double-acts. One punched, the other kicked. If you have the right partner you understand each other implicitly.

'You can't understand that, here in Switzerland. In the auditorium you don't really understand what's happening on stage.

'Beslozzen in minem herzen,' said Herr Grün. 'Verlorn ist daz slüzzelin. Lost is the key.'

'Herr Blau...' Désirée began to frame a question.

'His name was Schlesinger.'

'Herr Schlesinger – did he die in the camp?'

'No,' said Herr Grün. 'It was much worse. They let us go.'

70

He stood up so suddenly and violently that his chair fell over, just left it lying there and said into the sudden silence in the pub, 'We're going.' He threw a handful of coins on the table – he carried his money loose in his pocket, something that people usually do only when the small change doesn't matter – spoke into the gap between Rachel and Désirée as if someone invisible were sitting there, or as if he couldn't look them in the face, and repeated impatiently, 'Let's go.' Didn't help them into their coats, did hold the door out for them, but not like a gentleman, more like a bouncer, and outside in the alleyway he made so quickly for the Limmat Quai and Münster Bridge that they practically had to run after him.

Then, in the middle of the bridge, he suddenly stopped, had a very old, sad face and said, 'I'm sorry. You think you'll get used to it, but…You don't. You just don't…'

'You don't have to talk about it if you don't want to.'

'No,' said Herr Grün. 'I do. Otherwise it will never get better.'

All three together, yet apart, they walked from the Münsterhof to the St Peterhofstatt, and then up a narrow, dark path to the Lindenhof, sat down on one of the benches where lovers usually sit, or drunks, looked out over the Limmat and down at the meat market, the dark façades of the guild-houses, the empty windows of the museum society, and waited for Herr Grün to find the words he needed for his healing.

The night was warm. The moon lit the square as the cold neon light lit the sewing room in Zalman's factory. On a fountain a woman stood in full armour and guarded the unthreatened city. Everything was still. Only sometimes did a heavy beetle buzz over their heads as if on its way to deliver an important message or drop a bomb somewhere.

'They set us free in the summer of 1936,' Herr Grün said at last. 'Because of the Olympic Games.'

The weeks of the Summer Olympics, he said, were an exceptional time in Germany. The dictatorship took a holiday, outwardly at least. The tourists wanted to see a Berlin that was open to the world, so the order was issued by the Propaganda Ministry to present them with a Berlin that was open to the world. The way one might take the backdrop of a long-forgotten play out of the props room. Iron the mothballed costumes. Have the music played one last time.

'They'd always known a lot about show business,' said Herr Grün with the reluctant acknowledgement that one grants to the professionalism of an unloved branch of something. Yes, their actual speciality might have been mass marches and rallies, but a good director can stage anything that the management puts on the bill. Olympic tolerance is an easy exercise in that respect. Particularly when you have enough extras at your disposal. A whole country full of extras. You just have to be careful that no embarrassing details disturb the beautiful picture as a whole.

So on the Ku'damm the 'Jews unwelcome' stickers on the shop doors were suddenly no longer desirable. The glass Stürmer cases around the Olympic stadium stopped showing hate-filled caricatures, and instead displayed pictures of defiant-looking athletes. And at the Wannsee beach baths they took down the signs saying that 'bathing is forbidden for Jews and those with skin conditions.' Berlin smartened itself up. Put a white waistcoat over its brown shirt.

It was just for a few weeks, after all.

They took away the seals and padlocks from the doors of the long-closed cabarets and gay bars. The international guests wanted to enjoy themselves, they expected the wicked pleasures of the big city, and their expectations were to be fulfilled. The performers were at hand, in fact. They were all sitting in the camps. You just had to take their striped suits off them and put their old costumes back on. It was still all there. The feather boas for the transvestites and the tailcoats for the masters of ceremonies.

It was only for a few weeks.

'We were to tread the boards again,' said Herr Grün. '"If you're not willing to join in, you stay in the camp," they said. Which amounted to, "Would you rather live, or would you rather be beaten to death?" We had a free choice.

'We even got our names back. On loan. Suddenly I was Felix Grün again, rather than prisoner 4892. That was my number in the camp.'

'I know,' said Rachel quietly.

'We were to play the old sketches. Including the dialogue about the apples. Particularly that one.'

The text was placed on the table in front of them. Someone had sat at one of the shows and written it down. Word for word. They were to play it again exactly like that. With the punchline about the browns that had to be got rid of and the joke about the Reich that's not for eating, it's for throwing up. 'And if you can think of anything especially pointed about us,' said the man in the brown uniform, 'don't hold back. We're not like that. We've got a sense of humour.'

'And after the Games?' one of them dared to ask.

'We'll see.'

If you cast a person's feet in a concrete block and throw him in the water – does he drown?

We'll see.

It was just for a few weeks.

'We had got the same dressing-room.' Herr Grün said it as if nothing had ever given him such grounds for amazement. The same dressing-room. The same stage. The same sketches. 'Only my suit didn't fit any more. You don't stay fat in a concentration camp.'

In the stalls the sport tourists from all over the world ordered expensive wines, had the punchlines translated for them and were amazed to find such freedom of thought in a Germany that had been decried as a dictatorship. Evidence once again that you couldn't believe everything you read in the papers.

Guten Tag, Herr Grün.

Guten Tag, Herr Blau.

All as it had been.

Not quite everything. For the first time in the career, Grün and Blau were on after the interval. The big names weren't there any more. One had emigrated to Holland. One to America. One had been run over by a tipper in a quarry.

There was no applause to greet them when they came on stage, either. They had been forgotten. 'A year in the camps does nothing for your popularity,' said Herr Grün, and there was not a trace of irony in his voice.

Much had changed behind the scenes as well. Between their performances Schlesinger no longer read clever books, and Grün no longer romped with the twirlies. They sat in their dressing-room, looked at their own strange faces in the mirror, and every now and again one of them asked, 'What do you think?'

'It isn't true,' said Herr Grün, 'that you think more quickly when it's a matter of life and death. On the contrary. Thoughts get bogged down like car wheels in the sand. Wheels in the sand.'

He fell silent and looked out into the peaceful Zurich night, without seeing it.

On the Limmat Quay a light came on in a bathroom. A shadow moved behind the frosted glass. Only when the window was dark again did Herr Grün go on talking.

'We put on our performances, two every evening. But it was as if we weren't really standing on the stage. As if we were just pushing ourselves back and forth, like big puppets. I don't know if you can understand that.'

'I understand it very well,' said Désirée.

At two in the morning, when the audience had gone, they met up with their colleagues. They sat in the cold smoke of an empty auditorium and asked the same questions over and over. They called themselves 'the temporary ones'. No one knew who had invented the expression, but everyone used it. And had thus already given himself his answer.

They were only there temporarily, all of the ones who had been released from the camps because the Olympic guests needed entertainment. The gigolos who had once again swapped their clogs for patent leather shoes: temporary. The masculine women with their monocles and starched shirt-fronts: temporary. The cabaret artistes with the funny lyrics and sad eyes: temporary.

The dead on leave.

It was all just for a few weeks. After the Games they would be rounded up again.

Should one try to escape before then? That was the question.

And how best to do it? That was the problem.

There were a few optimists among them, and Schlesinger was one of those. 'We have an agreement with them,' he said. 'We've fulfilled our part. We appear again, and in return they leave us in peace afterwards. Of course they will close our venues again. I'm not naïve. In future we'll have to do something else. Anything. Cart bricks about on a building site. If need be. But they won't lock us up again. What good would it do them? We aren't dangerous to them any more.'

Grün couldn't persuade him otherwise. There's always someone who thinks you can strike a deal with the devil.

For three weeks they appeared on stage. For three weeks people laughed.

Guten Tag, Herr Grün.

Guten Tag, Herr Blau.

And then, on the very last day, when Siegfried Schlesinger still refused to abandon his blind hope, clinging to it like a child to a favourite cat that had been run over by a car – no, it isn't true, it isn't dead, I'm just not going to believe it! – on the very last day Herr Grün didn't come on stage.

'I'm a skilled practitioner,' he said into the silence of the night. 'I knew what was on the cards. I went to Vienna, where I had friends, I just took the night train. It wasn't even difficult. I had fake papers, and the border guards were dozy. Once I was there, I found out that they'd all ended up back in the camp. All rounded up again.'

'They ordered Schlesinger to tell them where I was. He didn't know, but they tried to beat it out of him anyway. This time they didn't just break his nose.'

A beetle flew over their heads, rumbling like a plane.

'Yes,' said Herr Grün, 'they let us go. That was the worst thing they did to us.'

All of a sudden he stood up and walked to the edge of the hill, which after a low wall falls down to the Limmat. He spread his arms, it looked in the moonlight as if he was about to pray or argue or fly away, and then Herr Grün whispered something. 'Du bist beslozzen in minem herzen,' whispered Herr Grün. 'Verlorn ist daz slüzzelin, du muost immer drinne sin.' The key is lost, you are there for ever. It sounded almost like Swiss German.

Then he came back to the two women, stopped in front of them, impatient again, and quickly finished the story, the way you sometimes rush to the end of a bedtime story when you can't wait to clap the book shut at last and turn out the light. 'Then I crossed the Swiss border on foot. Wladimir Rosenbaum got hold of a work permit for me. He knows an official who likes to meet up with ballerinas. Shall we go?'

Their footsteps rang out in the sleeping city. And there was no conversation for them to drown out.

First they brought Rachel home, and then Herr Grün insisted on walking Désirée to Morgartenstrasse as well. Outside the door – she had already opened it – he stopped and took off his hat.

'I've been doing some thinking,' said Herr Grün. 'Even though one can't actually say that. You don't do thoughts. They do themselves. They eat their way through your head like worms through wood.'

'And where have your woodworms crept to?' Perhaps Désirée was smiling, but it was impossible to tell in the darkness.

'You have lost someone you were very fond of,' said Herr Grün. 'That is obvious. You've been alone since then. That is obvious too. And I...'

'No,' she said.

'We go well together.'

'No, Herr Grün.' She had expected his question and formulated the answer long ago. 'We are too similar. Two left shoes, bent in the same direction. But two left shoes don't make a pair.'

'I'm not that much older than you.'

Now Désirée really was smiling, you could tell even without any light. 'And you aren't that much older than Rachel either,' she said.

'Fräulein Kamionker?'

'Yes,' said Désirée. 'You need someone you can argue with.'

Her lips ran softly over his without really touching them, and then the door had closed behind her and the key turned in the lock.

Herr Grün didn't bring Rachel flowers, and she didn't put a picture of him on her desk. Still: the relationship between them was noticed, and there was much talk in the kosher clothes factory. Not just because Rachel was the boss's daughter, although of course that made the story even more interesting, but because Joni Leibowitz opened a book on the subject. You put a franc on a particular date, and the one closest to the day the engagement was officially announced won the whole pot. So, for example, early dates were much sought-after because it was said that Rachel and Herr Grün had been seen together at the cinema, *You Are My Happiness* with Beniamino Gigli and Isa Miranda, and even during the big aria they hadn't looked at the screen once, so preoccupied were they with each other. Then again it was said that the couple had been seen arguing loudly over a coffee in the Old India on Bahnhofplatz, which meant the whole thing was over. Joni revealed this with hand-rubbing satisfaction, because as banker he had reserved nil for himself, which meant: if no shidduch had happened within six months, the whole pot went to him. So sure was he of his win that he had already spent, as an advance, some of the stakes he was supposed to be administrating. 'Rachel will never marry,' that was his firm conviction, because she had after all, nearly twenty years before, fended off his advances, and that could mean only that the woman was frigid.

Both the rumours were incidentally true, and false. Herr Grün really hadn't heard anything of Beniamino Gigli, not, however, because he had been using the darkness of the cinema to canoodle, but because he had fallen asleep during the first act. And that in turn had to do with politics. The Frontists had decided that the scantily clad dancers in Wladimir Rosenbaum's revues were undermining public morals in a typically Jewish way, and to prevent graffiti and broken windows a round-the-clock guard had been mounted around the Corso. After a sleepless night even the most musical of love stories can't keep you awake.

The argument in the Old India had actually happened as well, but anyone who had bet for that reason on a failure of the relationship was backing the wrong horse by miles. Rachel and Herr Grün enjoyed arguing with one another, as two jazz musicians enjoy improvising variations on a given tune together. And Rachel had to admit that Herr Grün was by far her superior in verbal combat, or rather: she would have had to admit it if the admission of any kind of weakness had not been so alien to her nature.

Her Grün complimented her, and she insulted him for it. Or else she insulted him and he complimented her about it. Désirée had been right: they needed one another.

At first they didn't see each other very often. By day Rachel sat in the office, and in the evening Herr Grün was in the Corso. Then they gradually stole more and more time for each other. He still had his room with the Posmanik family, but he no longer slept there every night. 'He has so much to do that he spends the night in the theatre,' Frau Posmanik explained to little Aaron.

No one in the kosher clothes factory knew anything about the event that would have influenced the betting more than any other. For Rosh Hashanah, the New Year festival, Herr Grün had been invited to Zalman and Hinda's for an official lunch. Désirée, Arthur and the Rosenthals were also coming to Rotwandstrasse; on such days the family should be together. Such an invitation, one would think, is not a special occasion among adults, but in the run-up Rachel was as touchy as a teenager who is about to present her boyfriend to the family for the first time. Even so, Herr Grün refused to put on anything but the suit he always wore. Still: he put on the new bow tie she had bought for him, and even brought flowers, even though that isn't really appropriate for Rosh Hashanah.

Hinda had, as always at family occasions, taken a great deal of trouble cooking, and was disappointed that her guest ate so little. Until he explained to her that someone who has had to go hungry for a long time has only two options: give in to the unstinting desire to eat yourself to death, or else to keep strict control of yourself, not only when eating, and to keep a tight rein on your emotions. 'It isn't a wonderful life,' said Herr Grün, 'but being alive at all is more than I was allowed to expect.'

Of course the conversation turned to the situation in Germany. Adolf Rosenthal, who never turned down the opportunity to deliver a lecture, wanted to explain his favourite thesis over soup, namely that National Socialism would be destroyed by its internal contradictions, but Herr Grün just looked at him, from the side and without uttering a word of disagreement, which made the mathematician, who could not otherwise be interrupted, stutter and quickly change the subject.

It was exactly the way the drunk in the White Cross had reacted to Herr Grün's calm voice, Rachel thought proudly. Hillel too was full of admiration for the man from Germany and said smarmily, 'I've been in jail as well.'

'No,' said Herr Grün, 'you were on holiday.'

It wasn't really a comfortable meal; they weren't living in comfortable times. They had, as is customary, begun the meal by dipping a piece of apple in honey, but no one thought it would be a sweet year because of that.

When the talk turned to Ruben, Herr Grün said, 'Get him out of there. If you have anyone at all important to you in that country, get them out!'

Arthur took off his glasses and rubbed the bridge of his nose.

'He doesn't want to leave his congregation,' said Hinda. Herr Grün reacted with so impatient a gesture that he knocked over the yontevdik salt cellar. 'Go and fetch him back,' he said to Zalman. 'Rachel tells me you've fetched him back once before. From Galicia.'

Whereupon of course all the old stories had to be told, about the soldiers who ate soap in order to be signed off sick, and about the smokers looking for cigarette papers in the latrine, 'this one's clean, this one isn't.' Even though today was New Year and not Seder evening: stories about old deliverances are always welcome.

Zalman asked Herr Grün to say the blessing, but he refused, on the grounds that he didn't see himself in the position of ever acting again in his life. No one asked him what exactly he meant. Afterwards he cleared his throat right from the very bottom; he had probably got used to doing that backstage, so that his voice was clear from the first sentence of his act.

Guten Tag, Herr Blau.

'There's also this, Herr Kamionker,' he said. 'You gave me work, and I am grateful to you for that.'

Zalman, who had never been good with gratitude, gestured dismissively, as if waving away the smoke of his cigar.

'It has caused you nothing but problems,' said Herr Grün. 'First of all I nearly killed that fellow Leibowitz...'

'What?' No one had told Adolf Rosenthal the story.

'...and now I'm taking your best worker away.'

'Does that mean...?' asked Hinda.

'He asked me.' Quite out of character, Rachel was a little embarrassed. 'And I said yes. But it was Felix's idea.'

'Felix', she said, not 'Herr Grün'.

'How lovely!' Hinda hugged her daughter, and Lea beamed at her twin sister and cried, 'Mazel tov!'

Rachel blushed, not as a young bride might be expected to – a bride is always young, even if she's approaching forty – but like someone who has been the victim of an awkward misunderstanding. 'No, it's not...You've got it wrong...Felix has just...'

'Wladimir Rosenbaum wants someone for the artistic manager's office,' said Herr Grün. 'I suggested Rachel.'

'Ah.' Lea had to polish her thick glasses out of sheer disappointment. 'And I thought...'

'The things you think!'

'So we'll have more time for each other,' Herr Grün explained. 'When you're working in the same place.'

'What did you think, Lea?' asked Adolf Rosenthal, who had no ear for undertones. He got no answer.

The pause was long and awkward. It was so quiet in the room that everyone could hear the faint singing note when Désirée ran her fingertip along the rim of her glass. She let the sound fade away and then said quietly, 'One left and one right shoe. Why not, in fact?'

She didn't look at Herr Grün as she said it, but he first raised his head and then shook it, quite violently, like someone trying to wake up. Then Herr Grün shrugged and spread his arms. It was an exaggerated gesture, the kind one might make on stage to be seen from the very back row. 'You're right: why not, in fact?' he repeated. 'What do you say, Rachel? I'll get used to it. I'm a skilled practitioner.'

The glasses of mazel tov bronfen had already been poured when Rachel was still explaining to Herr Grün that that was really no way to propose to somebody.

71

The three of them bullied him without making much noise about it, with a chummy cosiness that had a lot to do with their South German dialect. It had been a mistake to keep the confirmation from the Jewish congregation in his passport, of all places; one of them unfolded it, read the few sentences and then held the piece of paper out to the others, smiling expectantly, a child that has found a new toy under the tree, and is already imagining all the things that can be done with it.

The train stopped in open countryside, far from any station. There was nothing there but a shack, with a flagpole looming over it. As polite as hotel porters they asked him to get out, and please to take his little suitcase with him too, no, his papers were in order, as a Swiss citizen, that was quite correct, he didn't need a visa, but there were a few checks to go through, nothing personal, just a few technical things relating to customs and hygiene. Yes, they understood that he was in a hurry, and really, they were sorry that the train had now left without him, but they also had their duty to do, just as the train driver did, and they wouldn't advise him to try and deter them from doing their duty in the correct manner, that was a punishable offence, and if they had to file a complaint against him it would take even longer.

'Meijer?' they asked, 'So, so, Meijer?' and held his passport up to the light, and what had his original name been, Meierwitz or Meierssohn or Meier-Rosen-Blumen-Lilienfeld?

They left him his underpants, just peeked into them briefly, one after the other, and smiled. Then he was allowed to watch as they rummaged through his belongings for contraband. They did it thoroughly, and with a certain care. When they cut off the heels of his shoes because, you never knew, diamonds might be hidden in them, they put the severed pieces back, each tidily next to its shoe, 'so that they don't get confused.'

They ignored the rings. He had, so as not to lose them, fastened them to his key-ring, and they probably thought they were worthless pendants.

He hadn't packed much, he planned, they planned, to travel back the next day, so the officials found nothing that might have been described as contraband. But then, when he was starting to think he had passed the test, they moved on to the anti-epidemic examination. In Germany they were in the process of freeing themselves from vermin, and one had to be alert to ensure that no new ones were smuggled in. They cut open the seams of his jacket with a razor blade, but found neither lice nor fleas inside, and the new tie that he had packed for the ceremony they dipped in the inkwell, for disinfection, they said.

Then, very suddenly, their examination was over, there was probably a break in their timetable, or else the game had gone stale. He was allowed to get dressed, slip into his heel-less shoes and pack his belongings again. They even gave him a piece of twine to tie up his suitcase; they had only been doing their duty when they pulled out the bottom, to ensure that it wasn't double.

The next train left in three hours, they informed him considerately, thirty-four minutes past two exactly, and no, they couldn't let him get in here, this was purely an official stop, and use by private individuals was not permitted. But he was welcome to walk back to the border station, it was only a few kilometres, just keep following the rails, he was bound to get there in time, although walking without heels was a bit of an effort. They waved as he left, and one of the border guards who had proved particularly humorous during the procedure, called after him, 'Goodbye, Charlie!' – 'He shuffles like Charlie Chaplin,' he explained to the others, but they weren't cinema-goers and didn't join in.

Breathless and drenched in sweat Arthur caught the next train. The rage that he wasn't allowed to vent on anybody stuck in his throat, a lump that couldn't be swallowed or spat out. On any other day and on any other journey he would have turned around, immediately, he would have gone back to Zurich and hidden himself away in his flat.

But it wasn't just any day or any journey.

The second-class carriages were all full; in the end he found a seat in a compartment full of travelling salesmen, who bunched up reluctantly for him. With his broken shoes and the twine around his suitcase he probably looked like a tramp. As he sat down, he pushed his jacket together behind him so that they didn't see the ragged seam.

The same three guards checked him this time again, but they left him in peace and wished him a pleasant journey. They had probably decided they had had enough fun with him for one day.

He had set off from Zurich early in the morning, because he had wanted to have enough time in Kassel to freshen up in a hotel room. Now he would get there at the very last minute. If indeed he had enough time.

No, they weren't late, the conductor reassured him. He didn't know what it was like in Switzerland, but here in Germany the trains were punctual.

You had to admit, said an artificial honey salesman, that many things had improved. In his field at any rate, agreed a representative in leather goods, boots in particular were selling like mad. Of course one couldn't agree with everything, a third began, there were things that actually shouldn't have been happening. But the others didn't want to talk politics, they preferred to get on with their card game.

Photographs hung over the seats in the compartment: festively decorated buildings with half-timbered facades and mountain-tops reflected in romantic lakes. 'Germans, go on holiday in Germany!' it said underneath. In one picture a girl in peasant costume carried a bunch of flowers in her arm and smiled shyly from under her beribboned bonnet.

'I don't even know what she looks like,' thought Arthur.

He should have asked her, of course, he should have asked for some photographs, but at first he hadn't even thought about it, and now there was censorship, and you didn't know who read the letters. Everything had to look perfectly natural, as if it had all been discussed and agreed. There should be nothing to suggest that the marriage was about anything other than a Swiss passport.

So he hadn't even formally proposed, in his letter he had acted as if everything was long since resolved between them. Without advance notice he had written to her to say that he, for his part, had the necessary papers for the marriage contract, and very much hoped that she would soon have them as well. He had also received confirmation: for the wife of a Swiss citizen, immigration was not a problem.

Irma and Moses sent their greetings and were already looking forward to showing her Switzerland. 'Particularly the city of Zurich,' he had added in brackets.

She had replied just as matter-of-factly, in a curt letter without surprises or objections. She just reminded him – she actually wrote 'remind' – please under no circumstances to forget to bring his certificate of non-Aryan descent, otherwise they would assume at the register office that he, being Swiss, was of German or congeneric blood, and then marriage to a Jewess would not be permitted.

So he had asked the Israeli Religion Society to confirm his membership, and stupidly kept the officially accredited paper in his passport, in which his religious affiliation was not recorded. If only he had simply put it in his pocket...'Meijer' had a good Swiss ring about it, and they would probably have left him in peace.

François or even Hinda would have warned him against such recklessness, but he hadn't told his siblings anything about his journey, his wedding trip. They would just have advised him against it. François would have listed, point by point, all the reasons why the business should not go ahead, never under any circumstances, and Hinda would have shaken her head and said, 'Really, Arthur, one can overdo the idealism.'

For the second time in his life he had asked for a woman's hand, and again it was a woman he didn't know at all.

Any more than he had, that time before, known Chaje Sore Wasserstein. At least he had seen her, that evening in the tabernacle. And had immediately felt obliged...

He didn't even know what she looked like.

Perhaps she was ugly. Not that it would have mattered, of course not, but if you were going to be sitting opposite one another at the table every day, if you even had to sleep in the same...

He had asked Dr Strauss, the lawyer, it didn't concern him personally, he had said, it was one of his patients, but he would be interested, purely out of curiosity, what the conventions were in such a situation. The authorities examined everything, said Dr Strauss, dropped in after a year or two and checked whether the marriage actually existed. They rang your doorbell without warning, and had them show you the bathroom, whether there were really two toothbrushes in the tooth-mugs. They looked at the bedroom.

The bedroom.

Arthur couldn't imagine that side of things.

He didn't even know what colour her hair was.

Perhaps he would stand outside the register office and not recognise her. Nor she him.

He had once heard about a woman, in a very Orthodox community, who had been brought together with her husband by a shadchen, and when her veil was lifted under the chuppah for the first time, she found him so ugly that she'd thrown up.

But people said it had been a happy marriage anyway.

Would she expect him to kiss her?

He was fifty-seven, and was worried that he would look awkward.

Ridiculous.

Fifty-seven.

Twenty years' difference.

You can overdo idealism.

But Irma would smile at him with her squinting eyes. And Moses would give all the cushions in the flat a perfect dimple with the edge of his hand.

He would have to buy a few cushions. Throw out the old leather armchairs and get a sofa. So that they could sit together in the evening like a real family.

At the weekend they would go to the zoo. Once a year to the Sechseläuten parade. They'd go on holiday.

Germans, go on holiday in Germany! Germans, go on holiday in Germany!

Why was that slogan rattling through his head, to the rhythm of the wheels?

Why was he suddenly alone in the compartment?

He must have gone to sleep, he didn't know for how short or how long a time.

Outside the windows a happy landscape passed by as if in a propaganda film.

Germans, go on holiday in Germany!

In the fields, farmers were bringing in the last harvest under a cloudless sky. In the towns contented citizens went about their business. People waited with patient expressions at railway crossings.

Everything was so normal.

Normal?

Arthur was on his way to marry a complete stranger.

Perhaps he wouldn't get there in time. Perhaps it would be impossible to get another appointment. Perhaps everything would already have been cancelled by the time he got there. What time was it anyway?

Eventually he would have to get a wrist-watch. Having to flip up a lid every time you wanted to tell the time was far too laborious. Nobody nowadays carried a watch on a heavy chain in their waistcoat pocket. He would have to change, become more mobile. Now that he had all these new obligations.

But perhaps he had missed everything anyway. Without being able to do anything about it. He had boarded the right train, the earliest one there was, but they'd taken him off that one, and the next one wasn't until three hours later. What if the town hall wasn't right next to the station?

No, said the conductor, long-distance trains stopped in Kassel-Wilhelmshöhe. To get into town he would have to change for the local train to the station or take a taxi if he was in a great hurry.

Was he in a great hurry?

When he was a little boy looking at the panopticon, he couldn't wait to have all the mysteries revealed to him. 'A youth there was, who, burning with a thirst for knowledge, to Egyptian Sais came.' And the first time he had seen Joni ...

What was it he had said by way of farewell? 'A family would be the best thing even for you. You'd be a wonderful father.'

Meanwhile, whenever they approached a larger town, the train slowed down, almost to a standstill, and Arthur didn't know if he should be pleased. But in the next station they set off precisely on time. As was only proper in a country that set such store by order.

The railway track now ran through a forest, and on either side the trees were lined up in order, presenting themselves in rank and file for the woodcutters.

Through villages that looked as if they'd been built from construction kits. The same village over and over again.

Past a barracks that looked like a factory, and lots of factories that looked like barracks.

And then, much too late, much too soon, the train stopped.

Only a single taxi was waiting outside the ornate station, and at first it didn't want to take him. Broken suitcases don't inspire confidence, and neither do shoes without heels. It was only the banknotes in his wallet that made the driver friendlier. Arthur paid in advance, and was probably short-changed. That didn't matter any more either.

He couldn't have said what he had expected, but irritatingly the town they were driving through struck him as all too ordinary. There shouldn't, it seemed to him, have been such a thing as everyday life here. But there was nothing particularly striking. People, cars, shops. Like everywhere. It could have been Zurich. If it hadn't been for all the flags with the crooked cross.

When Arthur told him he was in a hurry, the driver seemed delighted. He pushed back his cap and honked all the other cars out of the way.

'You're Swiss?' he asked.

'Yes.'

'Another one of ours,' said the driver, and nodded like someone who has secret information. 'Just like Austria. You'll see.'

In the course of the journey he became more and more talkative, treated Arthur as a rich uncle treats a poor relative, and with proprietorial pride explained to him the sights that they were passing, the regional museum and the Torwache.

Then they were turning into Königstrasse.

The same street where Rosa Pollack's husband had been run over.

'Here's the town hall,' said the driver. 'Do you want to visit the mayor?'

And laughed and waved to Arthur, who stood forlornly on the pavement with his twined suitcase, once again as he drove off.

The big clock over the entrance – flanked by two stone lions, that too could have been in Zurich – showed him that he had arrived on time. Ten minutes early, in fact. Now he only had to find the right room.

Was there a porter with whom he could leave his suitcase?

And then a woman came out of the town hall door, a fat, agitated woman clutching a little bunch of flowers, looked searchingly around and then hurried towards Arthur. The closer she came the more slowly she walked, more and more hesitant, looked at him as one looks at a present one can tell one doesn't like even from a distance, but about which one must pretend to be delighted, out of pure politeness.

Looked at his suitcase, the broken shoes, the jacket with its lining hanging out. He should have kept his coat on and not carried it over his arm.

'Arthur Meijer?' she asked. Plainly she hoped she was mistaken. 'Are you Arthur Meijer?'

She was so ugly.

A bloated woman who had tried to powder a better colour on her face. A brightly coloured dress that bulged all over her body. The swollen, discoloured scar of an inexpert vaccination on her left upper arm.

'Yes,' said Arthur, 'I'm...' He had first to put down his suitcase, that tied-up, unsightly relic of a suitcase, on the ground in order to doff his hat. 'Doctor Arthur Meijer,' he introduced himself, and involuntarily bowed slightly as he had seen little Moses do.

She shook her head in disbelief.

Hairs on her upper lip. Short, prickly hairs. Something he'd always found unbearable in a woman.

'You're not as I imagined,' she said.

'Nor you...' but he had committed himself now, he had given his word without anyone asking him for it, he hadn't given anyone the chance to talk him out of it, so it was only right that he should choke back the words on his lips right now. Instead he said, 'Those people pulled my shoes apart.'

In her amazement she stuck out her tongue, which gave her face a babyishly stupid expression.

'The border guards,' he tried to explain. 'They took me off the train and...'

'We've got to hurry.' She breathed out deeply, as one does before unpleasant or unavoidable decisions, and then, before he could do it himself, picked up his suitcase. Even though it wasn't a very hot day, she had patches of sweat under her arms.

In silence, and without even checking that he was following her, she stamped her way up the stairs in front of him. 'Legs like fat Christine,' he thought. It was only when they got to the third floor that she stopped by a door, not even breathing heavily, as one might have expected given her weight, and told him, 'In fact the smart wedding room is downstairs, all carved oak, but it's only for Aryan marriages.'

'Yes,' he said resignedly, 'then we'll just have to get on with it,' and was about to give her his arm. She looked at him, as she had been looking at him all the time, with disbelief and disappointment, and stepped aside. 'Let's hope it's the right thing,' she said. 'Give me your coat and your hat. It's better if your hands are free. And hurry up! Rosa's already waiting in there.'

72

The next morning they were at the station before sunrise. If there had been an earlier train, they would have taken it. Arthur was in a hurry to get back to Switzerland, and Rosa couldn't wait not to be in Germany any more.

They were sitting opposite one another and they were married.

They had set off while it was still dark. Now it was gradually brightening outside, but neither of them felt like looking out of the window.

In this compartment too there was a picture frame above each seat, but the frames were empty. The photographs had probably shown something undesirable, and they'd had no time to replace them.

There was much to talk about, but they sat mutely facing one another, only every now and again saying inconsequential things as one might to a stranger. 'No, I don't mind not facing the front,' or 'It looks like it might rain.'

He asked none of the questions that really interested him, because they didn't know where to start. 'It's like that first term,' thought Arthur, 'when I took the big anatomy atlas home and didn't dare to open it for two days. I was too scared of having to memorise it all.'

Reality ran after the train and couldn't catch up with it.

They sat opposite one another.

Her face, he could find no other terms to describe it, was precise, with clear, distinct lines, as if drawn by a draftsman who doesn't hesitate when he sets down his strokes. A confident nose and a resolute chin. Hair shorter than was fashionable in Switzerland, almost a boyish cut. Her earlobes had once been pierced and were growing closed again. Perhaps she had had to sell her earrings.

'You're looking at me as if you want to learn me off by heart,' said Rosa.

But he hadn't even got that far. He was only just starting to spell her out.

She wasn't beautiful, no one would have said that of her at first glance, but then not every woman is a woman for the first glance. It was easy to imagine looking at her anew, over and over again, across a table.

Or from bed to bed.

No, he couldn't imagine that.

'It'll be all right,' she said, having read his thoughts. 'We managed that thing yesterday.'

And she suddenly burst out laughing.

'Like my sister,' he thought. 'When Hinda was still a girl, she would suddenly explode with laughter for no good reason.'

Rosa had a very young laugh. And she was the mother of two children,
with a fate and with memories that must have hurt.

A young laugh.

'Sorry,' she said. 'But the fact that you actually mistook my friend Trude for
the bride...Admit it, you like her more than me! Admit it: you're sorry that
you had to take me instead of her.'

It had been a strange wedding. Even standing outside that town hall, in a
suit like a homeless man standing in worn-out shoes at the door of strange
houses, begging for a bowl of soup. That was probably what he had looked
like. Or when they had been supposed to swap the rings and he couldn't get
them off his key-ring. Tugged away at them and apologised at the same time.
Until she took the keys and liberated the rings.

Deft hands.

How the register had tried to give them a copy of *Mein Kampf*, as was the
regulation for all newlyweds, had automatically started saying the words and
then broken off mid-sentence because it wasn't an Aryan wedding and the
regulation didn't apply. Many other regulations, but not that one. How he
had then very hastily had them sign the wedding certificate, first the groom,
Dr Arthur Meijer, then the bride, Rosa Recha Meijer, née Bernstein, widowed
name Pollack, and then the witnesses, Trude Speyer and Dr Saul Merzbach. Rosa
had been at teacher training college with Trude; Dr Merzbach had brought her
children into the world and, now that he was no longer allowed to work at
the hospital, he was her family doctor. Arthur remembered the name; he had
read it at the bottom of the health certificate that Irma and Moses had needed
to travel to Heiden.

Then, at Merzbach's house, they had celebrated. Four people eating sandwiches and drinking Sekt. Could you call it celebrating? One bottle of Sekt, and
yet Arthur had managed to get slightly light-headed, well, all the excitement,
and he hadn't eaten a thing all day.

After his dismissal from the hospital Dr Merzbach had had to set up a
surgery at home; no one would rent him anything. The familiar smell of carbolic soap and cleanliness made Arthur careless, and of course the alcohol and
the excitement. When Trude discovered a gramophone in the next room and
insisted that the bride and groom dance together, right now, a little mitzvah
tantz, he didn't even try to get out of it. Then of course he had tripped and
nearly tumbled over with Rosa. Whereupon Dr Merzbach wanted to give him
a pair of his shoes, with heels. No, no, he could happily take them, sooner or

later most things would have to be given away in any case. He had made some inquiries: doctors were needed in South America.

But then the shoes hadn't fit.

Trude, who was good at such things, repaired the seam of his jacket.

Their suitcases had stood side by side the whole time, the picture had lodged in Arthur's mind, his own, broken and tied together, and her two with the light patches where she had scratched off the stickers, the last remains of beautiful experiences that she didn't want to be reminded of any more. Two suitcases, she took no more than that from her old life. She had taken her luggage to Dr Merzbach's that afternoon. She didn't want to go back to the little room in the house of her uncle with the heart condition.

They spent the night at Dr Merzbach's too, the few hours until they had to leave again. Rosa slept on the sofa and Arthur in an armchair. They kept their clothes on, and he preferred it that way.

He couldn't imagine it.

Rosa had asked that no one accompany them to the station, but Trude had come along anyway, and cried a little. Outside it was already starting to rain. Just individual droplets at first, so that you could follow the trace of each single drip on the glass, and then more and more until the landscape blurred as if behind frosted glass.

'In one of your letters,' she said quietly, 'you wrote to say that I should enjoy the good days. Do you think they're starting now?'

'I'll do my best.'

She shook her head. 'These Goliaths! They even want to be responsible for the weather.'

When she laughed, she squinted very slightly, not like Irma, but still noticeably. He was pleased by the observation. Precious things belong to one much more when one knows their hidden little flaws.

He had been mistaken: she was a beautiful woman after all.

While he...

Would she expect caresses from him? Or even put up with them? Arthur felt guilty again.

At the wedding he had kissed her, of course, but it had had nothing to do with the two of them, it had just been a formality. 'Sit down, give me your papers, kiss the bride!' A ritual. When his patients got undressed in front of him, they weren't really naked either, but had just brought their bodies to him as one takes a watch that has stopped working to the watchmaker.

But she wasn't a patient. She was...

A slender waist under the flower-patterned dress.

She was now his wife.

Rosa Meijer.

'Rosa Recha Meijer.'

He must have said the name out loud, because she nodded and repeated it a few times, like someone who wants to commit to memory a word in a new language.

Rosa Recha Meijer.

'Will you be able to get used to it?'

She took his hand and very slowly ran her finger along the outline of his. She held her head tilted, and a strand of hair fell into her face.

'You have good hands,' she said at last, and even though she might not have answered his question, he was still pleased.

At the next station two noisy women pushed their way into their compartment, talking about their husbands and their neighbours and paid no heed to the couple by the window.

'They're all equally annoying,' said one, and the other agreed and confirmed that that was how it was, but you had to take them as they came, there were no others.

Anyone who was under illusions about people had only themselves to blame, said the first, and the other one nodded and said, they weren't as stupid as that any more, by no means.

Then they took thick sausage sandwiches out of their baskets, and choked their irritation with humanity down with them.

Rosa and Arthur looked at each other, and Rosa squinted very slightly. Nothing connects two people more than being able to laugh at the same things.

There were no problems at the Swiss border. The border guard looked at their marriage certificate, studied the date, paused, then put his hand to his cap and said, 'Many congratulations.'

They changed in Basel, and soon they were sitting in the train bound for home. 'Home,' repeated Rosa, and that too was a new word.

'What sort of flat do you have?'

'Too small for four people,' he said, too hastily. 'But perhaps Désirée will swap with us.' Now, of course he had to explain to her who Désirée was, and why she was called Déchirée, what had happened with Alfred and why his brother François was a goy. He grew talkative without noticing.

'I think I'm going to get on with Désirée,' said Rosa.

Then they were already pulling in to Baden, where there was also much to tell, they passed through Dietikon and Schlieren, the train slowed down, it wasn't even afternoon, and they were in Zurich.

They got out, he carried her big suitcases and she his small one. Suddenly he stopped and said, 'We should take them to the left luggage office.'

'Why not home?'

'We could take a detour via Rorschach.' And in response to the question in her face, 'That's where you catch the train to Heiden.'

When she was happy, her face was much less precise.

In Heiden she ran down the gravel path to the children's home, in completely inappropriate shoes, tripped in the rut of a cartwheel and fell over. When she struggled back to her feet, unkempt and laughing, the heel of her shoe had broken off.

'We're a match,' said Arthur.

She had torn her stockings and scraped one of her knees. 'You marry a doctor,' she said, 'and when you need him, he just ties a hanky around your leg.'

Fräulein Württemberger wasn't pleased to see them. She was trying, with hourly, daily, weekly timetables, to drive from the Wartheim the chaos that lurks everywhere there are people and above all children, and now here was this Dr Meijer, turning up on a day that wasn't even scheduled for the examination of the Women's Association children, he just stood in her office and had even brought his wife with him, when everyone said he was a confirmed bachelor. A woman with torn stockings and broken shoes. Like a tramp. And then, as if it were the most natural thing in the world, he wanted her to call Irma and Moses, right there and then, when they were on kitchen duty, and if they were four hands short in the kitchen her whole plan would fall apart, and dinner would never be on the tables on time. And they had already had enough of a fuss with all the special treatment that Irma needed because of her illness.

'She isn't ill any more,' said Arthur.

I see, said Fräulein Württemberger and searched for escapees from her bun, I see, she had recently sometimes had the impression that the girl was significantly better, but on the other hand...

'She is quite well again.'

How he claimed to know that without even having seen the child.

'Under your good care it could hardly be otherwise,' said Arthur.

And then such scenes as there were – in Fräulein Württemberger's personal office! – scenes were played out, with shouting and hugs and kisses and tears, scenes that simply had no room in a children's home run on scientific principles. And this Dr Meijer, who was somehow to blame for it all, she would find out what sort of a game he was playing, this Dr Meijer stood there with his arms folded and looked as if he'd won a prize. And let the children kiss him too, even the girl, a grown man. Uncouth it was, yes, that was the word: uncouth.

And then, when the children's things were to be packed away, right now, because they were going to take them away, just take them away, just like that without further ado, when any references to rules and duties were simply swept away, Fräulein Württemberger gave in surprisingly quickly. She just insisted that Dr Meijer confirm in writing that he had now assumed full and complete responsibility for the two children. You had to cover your back, whatever happened. Whatever might have been behind this matter, she was glad she no longer had anything to do with it. Yes, she was glad. Good riddance to bad rubbish, as they say.

She even sent Köbeli and his handcart with them to the station, just to be sure that they were really leaving.

On the train the children fought about who was going to be allowed to sit on Rosa's lap. She decided, with the Wisdom of Solomon, that they should switch at each stop; whoever's turn it wasn't had to sit on Arthur's lap instead. When Irma pressed up against him for the first time and put her thin arms around his neck, he had to take off his glasses and rub the bridge of his nose. His eyes were inflamed after the long journey, he explained.

Since her mother had been there, Irma seemed to have got younger. It was probably because she was able to shed her responsibilities.

'I did that,' she whispered in Arthur's ear. 'Because I was so good at being sick.'

When they changed in Rorschach Arthur bought four bags of sherbet powder at the kiosk, strawberry flavour, of course, and Irma showed them both how to spit blood. Moses was frightened of the game at first, until Arthur explained to him that sherbet powder was the best medicine there was. Then he joined in enthusiastically and slobbered it all over his pullover with great delight.

An elderly gentleman irritably folded his paper and complained to Arthur about his children making so much noise in the train compartment, where they were not, after all, alone. 'And we're not even his children,' said Moses.

When they arrived at last it was already evening. They had to take a taxi, so many suitcases had come with them from Kassel and Heiden. Moses wanted to know why Arthur's suitcase had such a big hole in it, and Rosa said, 'So that the fresh air can get at his things.'

There weren't enough beds in the flat. Arthur was a bachelor with no practical sense, and hadn't thought of such things. But they put mattresses on the floor and dug out some blankets. Arthur retreated to his bedroom and Rosa and the children slept side by side on the floor, as if they were at a holiday camp. It was probably the best solution; Irma and Moses wouldn't have let go of their mother in any case.

To be able to have breakfast the following day, they first had to go shopping together. Irma was very proud that she was able to explain Swiss money to her mother.

Arthur put the good Sarreguemines plates on the table and they all ate whatever came to hand, bread and honey and peaches and chocolate. Because they had forgotten to get cocoa when they were out shopping, the children had a little bit of coffee poured into their milk and felt very grown-up.

At that breakfast Arthur discovered a little foible of his wife's: every time she took a bite she licked the corner of her mouth clean with the tip of her tongue. He stared at her with such fascination that she asked him, 'What are you learning by heart this time?'

Afterwards the children explored the flat. Moses discovered the drawing that he had made for Arthur, and was very proud of it. Then he wanted to count the books on the shelf, but there were too many. 'Are they all full of stories?' he asked. His sister explained to him from the superiority of her twelve years that Arthur was a doctor, so he only had books that you could learn things from.

'You can learn things from novels as well,' said Arthur and winked at her. Irma would have liked to perform her trick again, but there was no sherbet powder left.

The children found the bronze-covered oak-leaf wreath particularly interesting. When Arthur announced that he had won it as a wrestler, Irma squinted at him dubiously, but it seemed quite straightforward to Moses that a Goliath should win every battle.

They also tried in vain to liberate the bottle locked in the Tantalus, in which a darkened residue of the golden fluid still sloshed back and forth. Irma refused to believe that no one had managed to drink a drop of it in nearly a hundred years. 'I'd just have broken the lock,' she said.

'And what if the stuff didn't taste nice?'

'I wouldn't care,' said Irma. 'At least I'd know.'

Arthur had decided not really to be there that day, and not to call anybody. Tomorrow or the day after it would still be soon enough to inform his family about all the surprising changes in his life. By tomorrow or the day after, he had tried to persuade himself, he could certainly have found the correct form for that communication.

But then there was a ring at the flat doorbell, and when he opened up, Hinda was standing there and handed him a big bouquet.

'Where's your wife?' she asked.

He must have looked stupid, with his startled facial expression, because she said very pityingly, 'Arthur!' just as she had, as the older sister, always said

'Arthur!' when her little brother didn't understand the world. 'When someone from Zurich gets married, here or elsewhere, the banns are posted at the city hall for four weeks. Didn't you think about that?'

No, he hadn't thought about that.

'The whole community's talking about it. Zalman says, "If he wants to make a secret of it, then let him have his secret." But now that it's happened ... I'm just too curious. Where is she?'

They knew everything.

They knew nothing at all, because there hadn't been anything about the two children in the banns.

'Otherwise I'd have brought presents for them!' Hinda was very disappointed.

'That doesn't matter,' said Irma. 'We'll take them later, too.' Then they all talked at the same time, couldn't find any words and therefore used a lot, had to look at each other and hug and look again, and Arthur for once didn't stand aside, but was right in the middle, awkwardly proud and proudly awkward.

'You're a lucky chap,' Hinda whispered in his ear. 'Where did you actually meet her?'

'At the register office, of course,' said Arthur. 'Where else does one meet one's wife?'

73

Chanele's death was as orderly as her life.

Even in her confusion, at the home she never forgot to lay out the things she needed for the next day; she had always done it, so that the following morning you could get dressed and go to the shop without wasting any time. But she didn't get up, she just lay there and was no longer in a hurry. Her body displayed no unpleasant outward signs of death, as if she had given practical thought to that as well, and wanted to make the chevra's work easier. Only her thin white hair lay tangled on the pillow, a disorderly sight that she would have not have allowed anyone to see during her lifetime. The dark sheitel by which she was known waited on its stand and was no longer needed.

The white line of the eyebrows ran through her face, a sum that's been added up and is over and done with.

In an old people's home dying is nothing unusual, no more than a final hurdle that everyone has to take. You expect it and are prepared for it. Routine. Most of the fuss is usually caused by the choice of who is next in line for the room, particularly this room, given that Chanele had had the best one in the whole house, the one with the view of the street from where you could see visitors arriving from a long way off, even if you didn't recognise them any more.

On the telephone to François, Frau Olchev said what she always said to the bereaved: the worst had now really come to the worst, but she had seen to it that everything that needed to be done had been done, and all the preparations made. Herr Meijer could rely on her completely, she said, and needn't worry about a thing. Even though she knew it couldn't really be a comfort for him, of course not, it might do him good to hear that his mother – such a lovely person! – had gone to sleep quite peacefully, you might say, if he would allow her the image, that she had slipped through the gates of heaven without having to wait outside for long.

And as she said, everything had been organised. She, Frau Olchev, had just assumed that Herr Meijer would be happy if she ordered the chevra, so that everything would be done according to the old tradition, although he himself might...

And so on, and so on, even after François had long since stopped listening.

The funeral was held two days later. Canton regulations meant that it couldn't be performed the same day, as Jewish customs would have dictated, but things went very quickly even so. No circulars had been sent out, but a surprising number of mourners still turned up. Such news spread even without mail. But only a few people were able to come from Zurich, because of course Chanele was buried next to Janki, in the old cemetery of the Aargau Jews, and it took at least half a day to get there and then travel back afterwards. Even though they would have liked to pay koved to the family in person, one can't necessarily travel all the highways and byways to do so.

The kosher clothes factory had sent a delegation, and Sally Steigrad was there, who went to all his customers' funerals. Wicked tongues said you could tell the extent of the life insurance from his facial expression by the graveside. In this case there was an additional, to some extent official reason for his presence: he had in the meantime become honorary chairman of the Jewish Gymnastics Association, and Janki had been flag sponsor after his big donation, and so Chanele effectively the co-sponsor.

Not many people came from Endingen, which was closest; since it had been possible to live anywhere, the old Jewish communities had shrunk. On the other hand, a whole busload arrived from Baden, mostly old women who wanted to take a look at the descendants of the Shmatte-Meijers. With a lot of significant nodding, they confirmed to each other how good the service had been in the Modern Emporium in Chanele's day, much better than it was now the wealthy Schneggs were in charge, but then the Schneggs didn't feel the need to encourage their employees to be polite.

They generally kept their distance from Frau Olchev and the other representatives of the old people's home. Their presence was too potent a reminder that new rooms were always becoming available in Lengnau.

Very surprisingly, at the last minute, Siegfried Kahn arrived, Mina's brother, whom Aunt Mimi had wanted to match up with Hinda many, many years previously. He stayed apart from the rest and didn't say hello to anyone, to demonstrate that he was here only to pay his respects to Chanele, and not to the rest of the family. During the short ceremony he turned his owlish head, now grey, quite malevolently towards the place where François stood with his brother and sister. 'A goy has no business at a Jewish funeral,' his eyes said. 'Whether he is the son or not.' Still, François had been sensitive enough not to have a tear made in his jacket as a sign of mourning, as Arthur had done. That wouldn't have been at all appropriate. François wore a black coat with a beaver-fur collar, and in the opinion of the old people from Baden he looked particularly un-Jewish.

The only family members missing were the ones from Halberstadt. It was possible that Ruben didn't yet know anything about his grandmother's death:

for some reason the telephone call they had booked immediately had still not come through. They had now sent him a telegram, but so far he hadn't replied.

They were all really mourning, which isn't necessarily the case at funerals, for Chanele, although not for the Chanele of the last few years. With her death, she had become once again in all their minds what she had once been.

If one is unused to crying, it can easily tear one's face apart. Hinda was born to laugh and didn't know how to deal with tears. She wore her pain like a disguise, as if she had bought it quickly without spending very long choosing it, as she had done with the hat with the little black veil.

Zalman listened to the rabbi's hesped with a critical expression. Sometimes, when the speaker got unnecessarily lost in commonplaces – 'Eyshes chayil, loving wife, exemplary mother' – without being aware of it, he shook his head disapprovingly and seemed to be preparing the arguments for a contradiction. He had always been particularly close to his mother-in-law; Chanele had been his ally from that first evening, when – 'If it's not negotiable!' – she had forced him to make a formal proposal to Hinda.

Lea, who was standing beside her father, went on tugging nervously at her coat or straightening her hat. Something didn't seem to be quite right, because the people, particularly the ones from Baden, were staring at her and whispering. She could even feel the glances on her back, like the touch of tiny fingers. She should have taken more care with her clothes: the old people of Baden, most of whom had previously known the Kamionker twins by name at best, now agreed how much Lea, with her eyebrows that met in the middle, looked like her grandmother, may her memory be blessed. You had to imagine her without the glasses – Chanele had never worn them, even when she was very old – but then it was, God preserve her, the spit, the very same punim.

Lea's husband would have liked to give the whisperers a good telling-off, as he would have done at school. But Adolf Rosenthal had no say here. If you've only married into a family, at levayas you're inevitably a marginal figure, a role that didn't suit him at all. He stood stiffly among the others, almost insulted, and had to confirm his authority by digging his son in the ribs a number of times to make him stand up straight.

Hillel was wearing his old Shabbos suit, and didn't feel at all comfortable in it. During his time at the Strickhof he had developed new muscles, so that the fabric bulged all over him. He felt as if with this disguise people were trying to force him back into a role that he had outgrown once and for all. He felt like Böhni in it. Still, he had successfully resisted the peaked cap that his father had tried to force on him, and instead insisted on the little embroidered kippah that identified him as a Zionist.

Rachel wore a dark grey suit from the winter collection of the Kamionker Clothes Factory. Her hat was too elegant for a funeral, but should one really wear an ugly one only so one didn't put people's noses out of joint? Her clothes were, however, subject to fewer comments than her red hair: it was generally agreed that this colour was entirely unsuitable for a sad occasion. At the same time her hairdo wasn't a sheitel that could be donned or doffed as the situation required.

She had brought along her fiancé, an artiste or a circus man, one heard. ('A fiancé? At her age?' – 'Well, of course a nice fat dowry takes years off a bride. Zalman Kamionker's clothes factory is supposed to be booming.') During the whole ceremony Herr Grün stood there as motionlessly as he had stood by Rachel's desk on his very first day: someone who had learned to wait as other people learn a profession.

Every time Arthur visited his mother in the old people's home, she had asked him, 'Why didn't you bring your children?' Today, the day of her funeral, he was finally able to fulfil her wish.

His new family set a lot of tongues wagging. The filing cabinet in which public opinion organises its objects has its drawers, and his had always been quite clearly and emphatically marked 'bachelor'. Even though he was a doctor and from a good family, all attempts to make a shidduch for him had long since been abandoned, and here he was all of a sudden turning up with this wife from Germany. As if the mothers hereabouts didn't have beautiful daughters too. And besides, she was too young for him, far too young. Such things seldom turned out well, there were plenty of examples of that. Admittedly she looked quite nice, not at all dolled up, and yet it remained to be seen how she would fit in here. The children seemed to be well brought up, only the girl was cross-eyed and the little boy was anxious. In fact, Moses held tightly on to Arthur's hand all the time; according to local custom only the men here went right up to the grave, and he was so keen to be a man.

The only one about whom no objections were raised was Désirée. Funerals suited her, and she suited funerals.

Eventually what had to be said had been said, the prayers and the eulogies. Nothing makes a person a tsadik as quickly as the fact of his death.

They set off for the last mitzvah that could be done for Chanele. The leaves had been falling from the trees for days, and under their carpet it was hard to tell where the paths ended and the graves began. Arthur tried to think of the reliable, protecting, ever-busy mother that he had known, not of the white, shrouded body that lay there in a wooden box with clay shards over its eyes, a bag of soil from the Holy Land as a pillow.

They drilled holes into the coffin, François had whispered to him at Uncle Salomon's funeral, so that the worms could get at the corpse more quickly.

Someone – it later turned out to have been the over-eager Frau Olchev – had seen to it that the double gravestone was cleaned and freed of moss. The free half now looked indecently empty, as if people had been waiting impatiently for it to be filled out correctly like a blank form.

Janki and Chanele.

Jean Meijer and Hanna Meijer.

No maiden name, as would normally have been the case for a wife. Chanele had never known her parents.

Even though weeping constricted his throat like a tie knotted too tightly, Arthur spoke the kaddish for his mother in a firm voice. As before, at his bar mitzvah, he didn't make a single mistake from the first word to the last.

Chanele could be proud of him.

One after the other they threw a handful of earth on the coffin, but they didn't even succeed in hiding its lid. The official gravediggers with their shovels waited in the background and tried out of politeness to look as if they were especially affected by this particular death.

The bereaved passed through the lines of mourners and let the murmur of the mandatory words float over them. 'May God console you among the mourners of Zion and Jerusalem.' It did them good for a moment, but it wasn't real consolation, just as a brief shower on a hot day isn't really cooling.

Then it was over, and they were all able to get into their cars again and drive back to Zurich. Why should they hold the shiva in Lengnau, which their mother had only ever visited during all those years? They would sit down together with Zalman and Hinda, under the Shabbos lamp that Chanele had polished so often as a young girl in Endingen.

How long ago was it now? Uncle Salomon was only a memory now, and Aunt Golde not even that.

'François and I are the last Meijers,' thought Arthur. 'There will be no more after us.'

Arthur's little topolino had been just right for his new family. Irma and Moses were firmly convinced that the back seat, far too small for adults, had always been meant for them.

He had to concentrate on the road, and therefore couldn't look across at Rosa. But precisely that gave him the courage to ask the question that had preoccupied him since he had received the news of his mother's death. Many things were easier to say if you didn't have to look other people in the eye as you did so. That had always been his experience.

'Could you imagine…' he began.

'Yes?'

'Could you imagine Irma and Moses…I mean, now that we're…It wouldn't have to be straight away. Could you imagine that?'

Later, when it had long been plain that they belonged together, he often said to her, 'The fact that you understood me then, when I was stammering around – at that moment I knew our marriage wasn't simply one of convenience.'

'Yes,' said Rosa, 'I agree that the children should take your name. The Meijer line must continue.'

Even though it had not been directly discussed or decided, Zalman's flat on Rotwandstrasse had become the place where the family met when there was something to celebrate or mourn. The last occasion had been the engagement between Rachel and Herr Grün, but the same room had also held the seder at which drunken Alfred had stumbled back into the family, and at the same table they had made the fateful decision to separate the lovers and send Alfred to Paris and thus in the end to his death.

When they arrived, Uncle Melnitz was already waiting impatiently for them. He was dressed in black as always, and yet in some inexplicable way he looked less old-fashioned than usual. Sometimes a style from days long gone imperceptibly becomes fashionable again, so that you can't tell whether the old times have come back, or whether the new ones were always there.

As soon as each of them came in he shoved the low mourning stool towards them, an over-eager maître d' already praising the specialities of the house before his guests have even taken their coats off. 'Sit down, sit down,' he said. 'It's time to start mourning.'

They tried not to notice him, they didn't want be defined by him and stayed where they were.

Uncle Melnitz made a particularly low waiterly bow in front of François and even hummed the tune of the 133rd psalm for him: 'Hine ma tov u ma nayim…' – 'Behold how good and pleasant it is for brethren to dwell together in unity.'

'Now sit down, sit down!'

They had all agreed that François had to be present at that shiva. He had decided not to be a Jew any more, but he still belonged to the family. To spare him any embarrassment, they had even cancelled the daily minyan that is normally part of the mandatory prayer times at shivas.

'Ruben can say the prayers,' Hinda had said, but they hadn't been able to get hold of him yet. Immediately after the funeral they tried again, and the helpful woman from the telephone exchange even asked her colleagues in Halberstadt specially. No, the number was correct, they said, and that was how it was listed in the directory, but it was coming up as temporarily disconnected.

Temporarily disconnected.

Herr Grün made his most expressionless face and said that didn't sound good.

Rachel nudged her fiancé in the ribs. 'What a prophet of doom you can be, Felix!' She was the only one who used his first name. Everyone else called him 'Herr Grün', even if they were on familiar terms with him.

Ruben was temporarily disconnected.

It was a phrase, the lady from the exchange had said, that she had never heard before. It wasn't internationally customary either.

Herr Grün nodded gloomily. In Germany at the moment lots of things were customary that were unknown in other countries.

'Wrong,' said Uncle Melnitz. 'It's known everywhere. It's also customary everywhere. Because it's been the custom everywhere. It sometimes falls out of fashion, for a century or two. But then it comes back in, and then they enjoy themselves again, yes.'

They didn't have to listen to him, because he was dead, after all. Dead and many times buried. No one had to listen to him.

'Now sit down! Sit down!'

No one had to start the shiva just because he urged them to.

Ruben was disconnected.

What could that mean?

Adolf Rosenthal tried to explain that the telephone network in Germany was particularly efficient, he had been reading an article about it in the *Neue Zürcher Zeitung* only the day before.

'Oh, shut up!' Lea interrupted him. She had never spoken to her husband like that before.

They were all much more keen to hear Rosa's opinion. She had, after all, just arrived from Germany and must know what was going on there. What could that mean, 'Temporarily disconnected?'

Rosa didn't want to scare anyone, far from it, but since the Nazis had been in power there it was never a good sign if something was suddenly different from the norm.

'It's no different from the norm,' said Uncle Melnitz. 'It's exactly as it always is, yes.' He rubbed his hands, not like someone who is cold, but like someone who has been proved right. 'It's as it always is,' he repeated, 'Because it has always been like that. We just forget it sometimes. So sit down, sit down!'

His smell had changed too, as the smell of a cellar changes when you clear it out to make way for new things.

But he was dead and buried, he no longer existed, once and for all he had ceased to exist.

He could not exist any more.

At shivas you don't close the door.

Anyone who wants to bring condolences to the mourners doesn't ring the bell, he just steps in and joins them.

But now someone did ring. Twice.

'Ruben's getting back to us!' cried Hinda and ran outside. It was just the reply from the post office, saying that it had not been possible for her message, addressed to Ruben Kamionker, 16 Lichtwerstrasse, Halberstadt, to be delivered as normal.

Not known at this address.

Which was of course nonsense. Complete nonsense. Ruben lived there, had lived there since taking the job at the Klaus, lived there with his wife Lieschen and their four children.

Three boys and a girl.

He lived there. Something must have happened.

'So sit down, sit down!' urged Uncle Melnitz. 'And let's start mourning at last.'

Epilogue

74

Every time he died, he came back.

His shoes were coated with dust, as if from a long and strenuous journey, but he walked weightlessly, light-footed, a dancer who hears the music even before the instruments have been tuned. He came in on tiptoe like someone who doesn't want to disturb, and drew the door closed behind him as carefully as someone who has decided to stay for a long time. He still kept his eyes closed, not like a sleeping man, but like someone who has enough pictures inside him. He didn't have to see the way to find his seat. His chair was waiting. They had expected him even when they thought he was never coming back.

When they still hoped.

He sat down and was there again.

Had always been there.

Every time he died, he came back.

He inhaled the new air, searchingly at first, like something strange and forgotten that you first have to remember, then greedily, in quick, impatient gulps. His lung rattled, a long unused machine. He said 'Ah!' as if after the first cooling draught of water on a hot day, opened his eyes, looked round and recognised them all. Had never forgotten them. They avoided his gaze, and he noticed it and smiled. 'This is my shiva,' this smile said. 'They're mourning for me here. My own shiva, from which no one will drive me. I am Uncle Melnitz, who got his name from Khmelnitsky.'

Uncle Melnitz.

He cleared his throat and coughed, blew black stains into a handkerchief the side of a map, big enough for a list of all the countries in which he had experienced death. A white flag like that waved by someone surrendering.

He smelled of damp, of must, of memories. He brought alive the scent of distant lands, just as Janki's first shop had held the scent of cardamom and nutmeg. But he brought no spices to them; he came from cold countries and carried with him only smells that choked the throat.

When one of them edged away he didn't edge after them, he just sat where he was and waved after the departing one. He was already waiting for him at the next place, he had made himself comfortable at a table or in his favourite armchair under the lamp. Or else he lay in his bed, in a long white shirt that wasn't a nightshirt.

He sat opposite them when they read their newspaper at the breakfast table, and when they gave a start as they read and said, 'We didn't know that' – they said it every day and every day they gave a start again – when they didn't finish reading and set the paper aside and didn't want to know anything more about everything because they couldn't bear the knowledge, then he patted their hands comfortingly and said, 'You should have asked me. You should just have asked me.'

They hadn't asked him because they were afraid of his answers.

He had never been away and now he was everywhere.

He sat on all the benches along the lake shore, he stared into the sun with his eyes wide open, for days, and yet his skin stayed pale as if he had never emerged from the shadow of his hiding place. He ran after all the prams, he bent his back low again and again to peer in and every time he was disappointed. He begged for bread at every door, only to let it go hard and say, 'My teeth have been knocked out.' Where someone laughed loudly, he stood in the room and put his finger to his lips, a bony finger with which he could also drum on the table, making it sound like the precise rattle of a firing squad. From all the family trees he drew names at random, kept them in big baskets, unripe fruits from which he distilled a brandy that no one could drink without their eyes watering. He sat in all the libraries and scribbled notes in the margins of the books. He wrote with red ink, dipped the old-fashioned quill in his own veins and became paler and paler. If a couple kissed, he stood behind them, if they made love, he lay down with them, whispered in their ears tender words that didn't belong to them, he knew a different story for each couple and another and another, and in none of them did they live happily ever after. He gave the children names, and every time he knew how to name a thousand other children who had had exactly the same name, and who had also fared badly. He scraped the putty from the windows so that the panes came loose and the wind whistled into the room. He ate the window putty, stuffed it greedily into his mouth and chewed it toothlessly. He had a crudely carved flute in his pocket, and he took it out, played infinitely sad tunes and demanded that everyone hum along. He told of far-away countries in which it had been cold, oh so cold. Walked close behind people and wrapped his bony arms around them to show them how one had tried in vain to warm oneself there. He sat at all the tables; his plate was empty, however much was ladled into it. He stuck the fork through his hand, and he scratched notches into the spoon, a new one every day. He smiled from all the mirrors, pale and patient, let his face seep into that of his beholder like an ineradicable colour, infected him with an incurable illness, became an inseparable part of him. Soon no one knew which part was him and which part was them.

Every time he died, he came back.

He belonged to the family.

He belonged to all families.

When they talked about Ruben – and when didn't they speak about him? – he repeated the name like a spell, 'Ruben, Ruben, Ruben'. Hinda and Zalman had grown old, older than their years, and still lived entirely on what once had been. They sat under the Shabbos lamp that no one lit now, because it couldn't make their worries vanish, they sat there looking at the same photographs over and over again until he took them out of their hands and fanned them out on the games table like playing cards. He listed the tricks as they had been played, for twelve whole years. One game after another, and they hadn't won a single one. He could tell them where Ruben had been collected and where he had been taken to, on what day and at which hour, where he had been first and where he had ended up after that, which way they had gone and on which transport. He told them where he had been seen and where he had eventually not been seen, told them what had happened to him before his trail had disappeared amid millions of other trails that Uncle Melnitz all knew as well, and whose stories he could all tell on long dark days and on long wakeful nights. He spoke calmly and without haste, like one who knows: I will never run out of stories.

So many stories.

He knew how to talk about Ruben's wife, who had been a Sternberg from Berlin, and who everyone had only ever called Lieschen. Those two names were all that was left of her, Lieschen and Sternberg, everything else had been carried away by a cold wind, grey dust and flakes of ash. 'Where it blows, the flowers grow better,' he said. They couldn't really remember their daughter-in-law, they had only ever visited her or been visited by her, and you don't get to know people that way. Not the way you would like to know somebody. They couldn't even have named her hair colour, the photographs were black and white, black and ivory, black and brown. Each time they took the album out, her face was less familiar to them. There was only one detail that they never forgot, the one small, unusual thing that everyone has left over if he's lucky, the detail which is like a nail that you can hang things on, a picture or a memory. They'd called her Lieschen, a child's name, even when she was long grown up, only ever Lieschen. Even her own children had got used to it; you remembered that even if you remembered nothing else about her. It had been four children, three boys and a girl; there was one photograph in which they would never grow older. Uncle Melnitz was the only one who could tell them apart, who still knew their names. The only one who had played with them, and now he wanted to teach the game to everyone else, you count down and clap your hands and sing, 'Ei! Ei! Ei!'

Every time he died, he came back.

He was a stranger here in Zurich, and yet he was at home, just as he was at home in every place to which he had been exiled. At Sechsläuten he marched with the parade, in a costume that was older than everyone else's, and stamped out the beat of the brass band music with dusty shoes. The bouquets thrown to the others dried in his hands, and he greeted and laughed and waved and was the guest of honour. In the Knabenschiessen shooting competition he stood in front of the targets and unbuttoned his red frock coat, waved to the riflemen not to keep him waiting. And he also liked to pick up the black wand and point it at the hits, on the chest, on the belly, on the forehead. At Schulsilvester, the tumultuous last day of school before the Christmas holidays, he went from house to house at dawn and roused the people from their beds with lots of noise. 'They often came at this time of day,' he said.

When Adolf Rosenthal walked past the Cantonal school – he was retired now, and had had to give up his authority along with the key to the staff room – when he just happened to walk past it, as he just happened to do every day, when he then looked up to his old classroom, where no one had been allowed to interrupt him, Uncle Melnitz was standing at the window, waving at him and calling, 'You're late! My class has already started.'

They had a lot to learn from him, and this time they had to listen to him.

He had been right.

As he was right every time.

Came back and reported.

Telling stories made him vivid. He had brought new stories with him, lots of new stories, each one so fatally vivid that the others paled in comparison. In the modern age everything gets bigger and better and more efficient. Six million new stories, a fat book from which you could read for a generation without repeating yourself a single time. Stories that could not be believed, certainly not here in Switzerland, where they had lived all those years on an island, on dry land in the middle of a deluge. Stories that wouldn't go into people's heads, not here, where supplies had never run out. Here you had lit your fire to cook and not noticed that you were doing it on the back of a huge fish that only had to roll over once in the water or beat its fins and you would be crushed and suffocated and drowned straight away. They hadn't known it, here in Switzerland. They were finding it out now, and would have been happier if they never had.

He told and told and told his tales and had been buried so often that it almost bored him to think of it.

These were no heroic tales that he had brought. Not the kind that one knew in this country.

Hillel, for example, had stood at the border, for five whole years. He had defended his fatherland with his rifle in his hand and would one day defend another fatherland. No one had yet found the knife to cut it from the map. Hillel had been a hero in active service, or had at least been granted permission by the state to remember heroism, to hang it on the wall in a frame: a dark green soldier staring into the distance, as unbowed and alert as a shomer in a different picture. Uncle Melnitz liked to stand before it, twist his head to study the signature of General Guisan, and say to Hillel, 'Don't forget to keep your rifle clean.'

Melnitz loved Switzerland. Even those who fear war like to play with tin soldiers. He loved this country, in which you could complain of hunger when chocolate was in short supply. It was interesting to visit Noah's Ark after its thousand-year voyage.

In the watch shops on Bahnhofstrasse he made the hands stop. 'Nothing changes here,' he said. 'Why would time need to change?' On Bürkliplatz he walked from market stall to market stall and asked the farmers for rotten fruit and potato peelings. 'I've got used to it,' he said. 'Why should I lose the habit?' In François's department store he stood in all the window displays, always behind the company emblem that decorated every pane, stood in such a way that the sun cast the shadow of the company insignia on his chest, where the circle in which the letters MEIER intersected sat over his heart like the bull's-eye of a target. 'Doesn't it suit me?' he asked.

Meijer with or without a yud.

He kept François company in his office, pushed the photographs of Mina and Alfred aside and sat down on the desk. With a small, modest gesture that was supposed to mean, 'Don't be distracted!' Watched François as he checked accounts and added up columns of numbers, only nodded appreciatively from time to time and said, 'A fine result. You've really achieved something.'

He loved the ringing of the tills and the cold solemnity of the strong rooms. He scratched secret signs into the gold bars, knew their origins and made them recognisable. When the shutters rattled down over the riches at night, he let himself be locked in, studied the neat columns of figures in the books and couldn't stop laughing.

In the darkness he often went walking arm in arm with Herr Grün. They got on very well. They silently recited old texts – 'Guten Tag, Herr Grün!', 'Guten

Tag, Herr Blau!' – or marched in uniform boots down the narrow alleys of the old town and startled the people with the songs in their heads.

He lived in the cemeteries, in the Steinkluppe, in the Binz, in the Friesenberg, and scratched the numbers of the years into the stones with his fingernails. 'It was yesterday,' he said, 'Yesterday, yesterday, yesterday.'

Every time he died, he came back.

At every funeral he spoke the kaddish, and at every wedding he crushed the glass, at every bris he held the child on his lap and at every bar mitzvah he was the first to fill the cup. 'L'chaim!' he cried, 'To life!' Where three spoke the table prayer, he was the fourth, where ten met for the minyan he was there as the eleventh. When they danced with the Torah roll, once a year, he was the first dancer and the last, and when fasting was done, he rubbed his belly and said, 'You call that going hungry? That's nothing.'

Every time he died, he came back.

He also visited Désirée, in her shop, where people met to get hold of kosher butter, kosher biscuits and kosher gossip. He brought her bonbons, old-fashioned bonbons that smelled of almonds and rosewater, they played games with them on the counter, and the winner was allowed to stop remembering for a whole night.

He knew all the secrets and revealed them even to those who didn't want to know.

He looked in on Arthur and Rosa, who had become a happily married couple without having been a real one. They now lived on Morgartenstrasse, in the big flat that had once belonged to Mimi and Pinchas and after that to Désirée, and when they sat in the evening as married couples do, Uncle Melnitz sat between them, put one arm around Arthur and one around Rosa and became a part of it.

The children weren't children any more, certainly not Irma, who turned the heads of all the young men in the community with her distinctive squint, but Uncle Melnitz still knelt by their beds and whispered fairy-tales to them all night, stories in which bad things happened until everyone called for Goliath. But Goliath didn't come. Then, when they woke up screaming, he moved on, bolstering himself with a deep swig from the locked crystal bottle in the Tantalus. He could drink from it without opening it; he had learned so much in his life.

Every time he died, he came back.

He didn't come alone. This time he had brought reinforcements. One on his own can't tell so many stories.

The whole city was full of them.

The whole country.

The whole world.

They live in attics, in ocean-crossing chests that had missed setting off in time. They hid in the cellars, under piles of rags that had once been festive costumes. They met in every corner. They sat in the empty Gotthard mail coach outside the National Museum, they travelled without horses to the end of the world. In the station they chalked numbers on the freight wagons. In the junk shop on Neugasse they looked for objects that had once belonged to them, and didn't want them when they found them. At Sprüngli they scraped cream cakes from tin plates. On the terrace of the meat market they lined up as if on parade; only sometimes one of them jumped into the Limmat and was allowed to drown.

They were everywhere.

They sat in all the trees, a swarm of black birds, playing chess with each other. Melnitz had carved the pieces out of bones; he could name the origins of every beaten peasant, his country and his family. He knew everything and wouldn't let anyone forget it.

'Enjoy your lives,' he said. 'You've been lucky, here in Switzerland.'

Every time he died, he came back.

Acknowledgements

For their help with research I wish to thank the historian Ursulina Wyss and the helpful ladies in the ICZ Library. My wonderful daughter Tamar Lewinsky corrected the Hebrew and Yiddish expressions and wrote the glossary.

The translator wishes to thank Pro Helvetia and the Max Geilinger Foundation for their generous award in funding the translation, and the staff at Looren Translation House, as well as John Stevens, Nina-Anne Kaye and the Guggenheim family of Zurich for their help and hospitality.

Glossary

Most Yiddish expressions come from the Hebrew. The pronunciation varies according to the origins of the speaker.

adir hu	'mighty is He', start of a song from the Pesach Haggadah
aliya	'ascent'. Immigration to Palestine/Israel
almemor	platform for reading from the Torah
amod no'ach!	at ease! (military language)
arba kanfes	'four corners'; undershirt with tassels
Ashkenazi	refers to the rites, customs, texts and Hebrew pronunciation of western, central and eastern European Jews
badchen	a wedding entertainer
balebos	master of the house, owner
bar mitzvah	'son of the commandment'; ceremony of maturity for boys reaching their 13th year
beheimes	livestock, cow
bekovedik	respectable
bentch	bless; say the mealtime prayer
bentch gomel	give thanks after a danger survived
berches m.	plaited Sabbath bread, usually covered with poppy-seed
bishge	serving girl, maid
B´nai B´rith	'Sons of the Covenant', name of an international Jewish charitable organisation
bocher pl. **bochrim**	Talmud student, pupil
boruch Hashem	God be praised
Bovo Basro	'the last gate'; name of a Talmudic tractate
Bris, bris milah	circumcision
bronfen	spirits
bundel	stuffed cow's stomach
Chai	life; in numerology: eighteen

chaluz pl. chaluzim	pioneer
Chanukah	eight-day festival commemorating the reconsecration of the Temple after the Maccabean revolt
Charoset	mixture of apples, nuts, wine and cinnamon. One of the symbolic meals eaten at Pesach
chassene	wedding
chaver pl. chaverim	colleague, friend, comrade
chazer-treyf	'pig-treyf', a strong way of describing things impure according to the dietary rules
cheder	'room', Jewish school in which only religious subjects are taught
chevra	society, association
chevra kadisha	a burial society
chochem	a wise man, an intelligent person (also ironic)
chochme pl. chochmes	wisdom, cleverness (also ironically)
Chol HaMoed	half-holidays between the first and last two days of Pesach and the feast of tabernacles, on which the prohibition on work is largely suspended
chossen m.	bridegroom
chumash	Pentateuch, the
chuppah	wedding baldaquin; wedding
droosh	sermon
Echod mi yodea	'Who knows one', the beginning of a counting song from the Pesach Haggadah (q.v.)
eretz	literally 'country'; Palestine/Israel
Erev Shabbos	the eve of Shabbos
esrog pl. esrogim	citrus fruit used in the ritual of the feast of tabernacles
eyshes chayil	a 'woman of valour' 'virtuous woman'; the beginning of a prayer spoken by the husband on Friday evening
gabbai	community chairman; secretary of a Hassidic rabbi
galekh	Catholic priest
Gan Eden	Garden of Eden, paradise
ganev	thief
gematria	numerology
Gemore	a term for the Talmud

get	letter of divorce, divorce
getzines-lecker	someone who sucks up to the wealthy
goy pl. goyim	non-Jew (adj.) non-Jewish
goyim naches	'the pleasures of non-Jews', unjewish things
Hachnossas Kallo	a charitable association to fund brides without dowries
haftarah, haftoroh	a Bible reading presented after the weekly selection on the Sabbath and feast days
Haggadah	collection of prayers and songs for seder (q.v.) evening
halevei!	if only!
Hallel	term applied to Psalms 113–118 in liturgical use
HaMotzi	the prayer for the breaking of the bread, spoken before meals
hanoe	delight, pleasure
Hashomer Hatza'ir	'the youth guard', a socialist-Zionist youth organisation
Hassid pl. Hassidim	'pious', devotee of Hassidism
Hatikva	'Hope', Zionist and later Israeli national anthem
Havdole	'separation'; ceremony at the end of the Sabbath
heimish	home-like, friendly
Hershele Ostropoler	legendary prankster
hesped m.	funeral oration
holekrash	naming ceremony for girls, no longer practised
Ivrit	Modern Hebrew
Kaddish	prayer for the dead
kaf, shin, resh	Hebrew letters
kalleh	bride
kauhen, pl. kauhanim	priest, descendant of Aaron
Kiddush	sanctification; blessing spoken over the wine on the Sabbath and on feast days
klafte	'bitch', derogatory term for a woman
klezmer m.	musician
Kol Nidre, Kol Nidrei	'all vows'; prayer said on the eve of the Day of Atonement
koved	honour
krechzen	to moan, complain

kugel	traditional baked dish of pasta or potatoes for the Sabbath
kvitel	note; petition to a rabbi
l'chaim	'to life', cheers!
lekoved	in honour of
levaya	funeral
Levi	a Levite; a member of the tribe of Levi
lulav	palm frond used in the ritual of tabernacles
maasseh	a story
matzo	unleavened bread eaten on Pesach
mazel tov!	good luck!
mechullah	broke
medina	state, country (**golden medina**, America)
me neshuma!	by my soul!
menucha	peace
meshuga, meshugena	mad, a madman
meshugas	madness
metsiya	a bargain
mezuzah	capsule of Bible verses fixed to the house door post
mifkad	muster (military language)
mikvah	ritual bath
Mincha	midday prayer
minhag	religious practice, accepted tradition
minyan	quorum of ten men required for prayer
minyan man	extra member of the congregation paid to complete the minyan
mishloach manot	gifts traditionally given at Purim (q.v.)
mishpocha	family
Misrach	East; the direction of prayer
mitzvah pl. **mitzvot/ mitzves**	commandment; good deed; honorary post in synagogue
Mitzvah tantz	traditional dance with the bride/bridegroom after the wedding
mohel	person who performs ritual circumcisions
moichel: be moichel	forgive
Moshiach	Messiah, redeemer

moyreh	fear
mussar	moral instruction
nafka	prostitute, whore
narrishkeit	stupidity, foolishness
nebbish!	(exclamation) alas!
Nebbish (noun) diminutive nebbishle	a pathetic creature; a simpleton
nedinye	dowry
nes min hashamayim	a miracle from heaven
nigun pl. nigunim	melody
oberbalmeragges	an important person
Omeyn	Amen
parnooseh	earnings, income
payes	sidelocks
Pesach	the feast of Passover
pilpul	textual analysis of the Talmud; casuistry
pitum	stem of the esrog (q.v.)
punim	face
Purim	the feast of Purim, commemorating the deliverance of the Jews in Persia
rachmones	pity
rav pl. Rabbonim	rabbi
Rashi	11th-century Talmudic commentator
Reb	polite form of address for respected Jews; sir
rebbe	rabbi
reshoim	anti-Semites, heretics or unbelievers
Riboyne shel Oylem	Lord of the world, God
reyvech	profit
rish'es	anti-Semitism, anti-Jewish behaviour
Rosh Hashanah	Jewish feast of New Year
ruddel	gossip
sargenes	shroud
Schippe Malke	the queen of spades; a woman in her best clothes
Schippe Siebele	the seven of spades; an inferior person
Schulchan Orech	'the laid table', a collection of religious rules for every day

Seder	'order'; domestic religious service on the eve of Pesach, at which the Haggadah (q.v.) is read
seder plate	dish on which the traditional symbolic meals of the seder are served
sefer	religious book
seichel	intelligence, common sense
Sephardim	the Jews originally from Spain
seudah	a meal, especially a festive one
Shabbes	the Sabbath
shabbosdik	pertaining to the Sabbath
Shacharit	morning prayer
shadchen pl. shadchonim	marriage broker
shammes	synagogue servant
shassgener	drunkard
Shavuot	the Feast of Weeks, celebrating the giving of the Torah to the Jewish people on Mount Sinai
Shechinah	the divine presence
shechita	ritual slaughter
sheitel	the wig worn by married women
Shema, beni!	'Hear, my son!'; exclamation of surprise
Shema Yisrael Adonai Eloheinu	'Hear, O Israel, the Lord is our God...'; beginning of the most important Jewish prayer
Shemoneh Esrei	the eighteen blessings,
shidduch	arranged marriage
shirayim	the leftovers from the rabbi's table, revered by the Hassidim as having healing powers
Shir Hama'a lot	'song of ascents', sung before the mealtime prayer
shiur	a lesson
shiva pl. shivas	the traditional week-long period of mourning
shlachmones	see mishloach manot
shlattenschammes	gofer, skivvy
shmatten past participle geshmat	to baptise (of a Jew)
shmattes	fabrics; rags
shmontses	unimportant, worthless things
shnoder	to donate

shnorrer	a beggar
shochet	ritual slaughterer
shockel	to rock rhythmically while praying
shofar	ram's horn blown on Rosh Hashana and Yom Kippur (q.v.)
shomer	watchman
shtiebel	small (Hassidic) room for communal prayer
shtraiml	Hassidic fur hat
shul	synagogue
siddur	prayer book
sidra	weekly reading from the Torah
simcha	celebration
Simchas Torah	celebration at the end of the annual cycle of Torah readings
siyum	celebration at the end of a unit of Torah study
sude	solemn Sabbath dinner
sukkah	tabernacle
Sukkot	feast of tabernacles
tallis	prayer shawl
Talmid chochem	Talmud scholar
Talmud-Torah Association	association for the religious education of laypeople
Tata	father
Techías Hameisim	resurrection of the dead
tefillin	phylacteries, black boxes worn on the head and affixed with straps
tehillim	psalms
tekiyoh	a blast on the shofar (q.v.)
Tenach	the Old Testament
tochus	bottom, backside
treyf	forbidden by dietary laws
tsadik	a pious, holy man
tseylem	cross, crucifix
tsibeles	a speciality made from chopped onions
tsuris	sorrow
tzdoke	charity donation

va'ad	a council meeting, synod; committee
viduy	the confession of sins
Voch	the days of the week apart from the Sabbath
voyleh Juden	respected Jews
women's shul	the part of the synagogue reserved for women
yahrzeit candle	candle lit on the anniversary of the death of a deceased relative
yeshiva	Talmudic college
yis'chadesh	'May it renew', word of congratulation used for a new item of clothing
Yisgadal veyiskadash shmey raba	'Magnified and sanctified be his great name', the opening words of the Kaddish (q.v.)
yishuv	'settlement'; term applied to the Jewish population in Palestine
Yom Kippur	Day of Atonement
Yontev	feast, celebration
yontevdik	festive
Yossel Pendrik	derisory name for Christ on the cross